WILD CARDS

WILD CARDS

Edited by

George R. R. Martin

www.georgerrmartin.com
www.orionbooks.co.uk

Copyright © 1986 by George R. R. Martin

Expanded edition © 2010 by George R. R. Martin and the Wild Cards Trust

The right of George R. R. Martin to be identified
as the editor of this work has been asserted by him
in accordance with the Copyright, Designs and Patents Act 1988.

First published in Great Britain in 2012
by Gollancz
an imprint of the Orion Publishing Group
Orion House, 5 Upper St Martin's Lane, London WC2H 9EA
An Hachette UK Company

This edition published in Great Britain in 2012 by Gollancz

5 7 9 10 8 6 4

A CIP catalogue record for this book
is available from the British Library

ISBN 978 0 575 13411 9

Typeset by Deltatype Ltd, Birkenhead, Merseyside

Printed in Great Britain by
CPI Group (UK) Ltd, Croydon, CR0 4YY

The Orion Publishing Group's policy is to use papers that are
natural, renewable and recyclable products and made from wood
grown in sustainable forests. The logging and manufacturing
processes are expected to conform to the environmental
regulations of the country of origin.

For Ken Keller, who grew from
the same four-colour roots as me.

Editor's Note

WILD CARDS I

PROLOGUE

From Wild Times:
An Oral History of the Postwar Years

by Studs Terkel (Pantheon, 1979).

HERBERT L. CRANSTON

Years later, when I saw Michael Rennie come out of that flying saucer in *The Day the Earth Stood Still*, I leaned over to the wife and said, 'Now that's the way an alien emissary ought to look.' I've always suspected that it was Tachyons arrival that gave them the idea for that picture, but you know how Hollywood changes things around. I was there, so I know how it really was. For starts, he came down in White Sands, not in Washington. He didn't have a robot, and we didn't shoot him. Considering what happened, maybe we should have, eh?

His ship, well, it certainly wasn't a flying saucer, and it didn't look a damn thing like our captured V-2s or even the moon rockets on Werner's drawing boards. It violated every known law of aerodynamics and Einstein's special relativity too.

He came down at night, his ship all covered with lights, the prettiest thing I ever saw. It set down plunk in the middle of the proving range, without rockets, propellers, rotors, or any visible means of propulsion whatsoever. The outer skin looked like it was coral or some kind of porous rock, covered with whorls and spurs, like something you'd find in a limestone cavern or spot while deep-sea diving.

I was in the first jeep to reach it. By the time we got there, Tach was already outside. Michael Rennie, now, he looked right in that silvery blue spacesuit of his, but Tachyon looked like

5

a cross between one of the Three Musketeers and some kind of circus performer. I don't mind telling you, all of us were pretty scared driving out, the rocketry boys and eggheads just as much as the GIs. I remembered that Mercury Theater broadcast back in '39, when Orson Welles fooled everybody into thinking that the Martians were invading New Jersey, and I couldn't help thinking maybe this time it was happening for real. But once the spotlights hit him, standing there in front of his ship, we all relaxed. He just wasn't scary.

He was short, maybe five three, five four, and to tell the truth, he looked more scared than us. He was wearing these green tights with the boots built right into them, and this orangy shirt with lace sissy ruffles at the wrists and collar, and some kind of silvery brocade vest, real tight. His coat was a lemon-yellow number, with a green cloak snapping around in the wind behind him and catching about his ankles. On top of his head he had this wide-brimmed hat, with a long red feather sticking out of it, except when I got closer, I saw it was really some weird spiky quill. His hair covered his shoulders; at first glance, I thought he was a girl. It was a peculiar sort of hair too, red and shiny, like thin copper wire.

I didn't know what to make of him, but I remember one of our Germans saying that he looked like a Frenchman.

No sooner had we arrived than he came slogging right over to the jeep, bold as you please, trudging through the sand with a big bag stuck up under one arm. He started telling us his name, and he was still telling it to us while four other jeeps pulled up. He spoke better English than most of our Germans, despite having this weird accent, but it was hard to be sure at first when he spent ten minutes telling us his name.

I was the first human being to speak to him. That's God's truth, I don't care what anybody else tells you, it was me. I got out of the jeep and stuck out my hand and said, 'Welcome to America.' I started to introduce myself, but he interrupted me before I could get the words out.

'Herb Cranston of Cape May, New Jersey,' he said. 'A rocket scientist. Excellent. I am a scientist myself.'

He didn't look like any scientist I'd ever known, but I made allowances, since he came from outer space. I was more concerned about how he'd known my name. I asked him.

He waved his ruffles in the air, impatient. 'I read your mind. That's unimportant. Time is short, Cranston. Their ship broke up.' I thought he looked more than a little sick when he said that; sad, you know, hurting, but scared too. And tired, very tired. Then he started talking about this globe. That was the globe with the wild card virus, of course, everyone knows that now, but back then I didn't know what the hell he was going on about. It was lost, he said, he needed to get it back, and he hoped for all our sakes it was still intact. He wanted to talk to our top leaders. He must have read their names in my mind, because he named Werner, and Einstein, and the President, except he called him 'this President Harry S Truman of yours.' Then he climbed right into the back of the jeep and sat down. 'Take me to them,' he said. 'At once.'

PROFESSOR LYLE CRAWFORD KENT

In a certain sense, it was I who coined his name. His real name, of course, his alien patronymic, was impossibly long. Several of us tried to shorten it, I recall, using this or that piece of it during our conferences, but evidently this was some sort of breach of etiquette on his home world, Takis. He continually corrected us, rather arrogantly I might say, like an elderly pedant lecturing a pack of schoolboys. Well, we needed to call him something. The title came first. We might have called him 'Your Majesty' or some such, since he claimed to be a prince, but Americans are not comfortable with that sort of bowing and scraping. He also said he was a physician, although not in our sense of the word, and it must be admitted that he did seem to know a good deal of genetics and biochemistry, which seemed to be his area of expertise. Most of our team held advanced degrees, and we addressed each other accordingly, and so it was only natural that we fell to calling him 'Doctor' as well.

The rocket scientists were obsessed with our visitor's ship, particularly with the theory of his faster-than-light propulsion system. Unfortunately, our Takisian friend had burned out his ship's interstellar drive in his haste to arrive here before those relatives of his, and in any case he adamantly refused to let any of us, civilian or military, inspect the inside of his craft. Werner and his Germans were reduced to questioning the alien about the drive, rather compulsively I thought. As I understood it, theoretical physics and the technology of space travel were not disciplines in which our visitor was especially expert, so the answers he gave them were not very clear, but we did grasp that the drive made use of a hitherto-unknown particle that traveled faster than light.

The alien had a term for the particle, as unpronounceable as his name. Well, I had a certain grounding in classical Greek, like all educated men, and a flair for nomenclature if I do say so myself. I was the one who devised the coinage 'tachyon.' Somehow the GIs got things confused, and began referring to our visitor as 'that tachyon fellow.' The phrase caught on, and from there it was only a short step to Doctor Tachyon, the name by which he became generally known in the press.

COLONEL EDWARD REID, U.S. ARMY INTELLIGENCE (RET.)

You want me to say it, right? Every damned reporter I've ever talked to wants me to say it. All right, here it is. We made a mistake. And we paid for it too. Do you know that afterwards they came within a hair of court-martialing all of us, the whole interrogation team? That's a fact.

The hell of it is, I don't know how we could have been expected to do things any differently than we did. I was in charge of his interrogation. I ought to know.

What did we really know about him? Nothing except what he told us himself. The eggheads were treating him like Baby Jesus, but military men have to be a little more cautious. If you want to understand, you have to put yourself in our shoes and remember how it was back then. His story was utterly preposterous, and he couldn't prove a single damned thing.

Okay, he landed in this funny-looking rocket plane, except it didn't have rockets. That was impressive. Maybe that plane of his *did* come from outer space, like he said. But maybe it didn't. Maybe it was one of those secret projects the Nazis had been working on, left over from the war. They'd had jets at the end, you know, and those V-2s, and they were even working on the atomic bomb. Maybe it was Russian. I don't know. If Tachyon had only let us examine his ship, our boys would have been able to figure out where it came from, I'm sure. But he wouldn't let anyone inside the damned thing, which struck me as more than a little suspicious. What was he trying to hide?

He said he came from the planet Takis. Well, I never heard of no goddamned planet Takis. Mars, Venus, Jupiter, sure. Even Mongo and Barsoom. But Takis? I called up a dozen top astronomers all around the country, even one guy over in England. Where's the planet Takis? I asked them. There is no planet Takis, they told me.

He was supposed to be an alien, right? We examined him. A complete physical, X rays, a battery of psychological tests, the works. He tested human. Every which way we turned him, he came up human. No extra organs, no green blood, five fingers, five toes, two balls, and one cock. The fucker was no different from you and me. He spoke English, for crissakes. But get this – he also spoke *German*. And Russian and French and a few other languages I've forgotten. I made wire recordings of a couple of my sessions with him, and played them for a linguist, who said the accent was Central European.

And the headshrinkers, whoa, you should have heard their reports. Classic paranoid, they said. Megalomania, they said. Schizo, they said. All kinds of stuff. I mean, look, this guy claimed to be a prince from outer space with magic fucking powers who'd come here all alone to save our whole damned planet. Does that sound sane to you?

And let me say something about those damned magic powers of his. I'll admit it, that was the thing that bothered me the most. I mean, not only could Tachyon tell you what you were thinking, he could look at you funny and make you jump up on your desk and drop your pants, whether you wanted to or not. I spent hours with him every day, and he convinced *me*. The thing was, my reports didn't convince the brass back east. Some kind of trick, they thought, he was hypnotizing us, he was reading our body posture, using psychology to make us think he read minds. They were going to send out a stage hypnotist to figure out how he did it, but the shit hit the fan before they got around to it.

He didn't ask much. All he wanted was a meeting with the President so he could mobilize the entire American military to search for some crashed rocket ship. Tachyon would be in command, of course, no one else was qualified. Our top scientists could be his assistants. He wanted radar and jets and submarines and bloodhounds and weird machines nobody had ever heard of. You name it, he wanted it. And he did not want to have to consult with anybody, either. This guy dressed like a fag hairdresser, if you want the truth, but the way he gave orders you would've thought he had three stars at least.

And why? Oh, yeah, his story, that sure was great. On this planet Takis, he said, a couple dozen big families ran the whole show, like royalty, except they all had magic powers, and they lorded it over everybody else who didn't have magic powers. These families spent most of their time feuding like the Hatfields and McCoys. His particular bunch had a secret weapon they'd been working on for a couple of centuries. A tailored artificial virus designed to interact with the genetic makeup of the host organism, he said. He'd been part of the research team.

Well, I was humoring him. What did this germ do? I asked him. Now get this – it did *everything*.

What it was *supposed* to do, according to Tachyon, was goose up these mind powers of theirs, maybe even give them some new powers, evolve 'em almost into gods, which would sure as hell give his kin the edge over the others. But it didn't always do that. Sometimes, yeah. Most often it killed the test subjects. He went on and on about how deadly this stuff was, and managed to give me the creeps. What were the symptoms? I asked. We knew about germ weapons back in '46; just in case he was telling the truth, I wanted us to know what to look for.

He couldn't tell me the symptoms. There were all kinds of symptoms. Everybody had different symptoms, every single person. You ever hear of a germ worked like that? Not me.

Then Tachyon said that sometimes it turned people into freaks instead of killing them. What kind of freaks? I asked. All kinds, he said. I admitted that it sounded pretty nasty, and asked him why his folks hadn't used this stuff on the other families. Because sometimes the virus worked, he said; it remade its victims, gave them powers. What kinds of powers? All kinds of powers, naturally.

So they had this stuff. They didn't want to use it on their enemies, and maybe give them powers. They didn't want to use it on themselves, and kill off half the family.

They weren't about to forget about it. They decided to test it on us. Why us? Because we were genetically identical to Takisians, he said, the only such race they knew of, and the bug was designed to work on the Takisian genotype. So why were we so lucky? Some of his people thought it was parallel evolution, others believed that Earth was a lost Takisian colony – he didn't know and didn't care.

He did care about the experiment. Thought it was 'ignoble.' He protested, he said, but they ignored him. The ship left. And Tachyon decided to stop them all by himself. He came after them in a smaller ship, burned out his damned tachyon drive getting here ahead of them. When he intercepted them, they told him to fuck off, even though he was family, and they had some kind of space battle. His ship was damaged, theirs was crippled, and they crashed. Somewhere back east, he said. He lost them, on account of the damage to his ship. So he landed at White Sands, where he thought he could get help.

I got down the whole story on my wire recorder. Afterwards, Army Intelligence contacted all sorts of experts: biochemists and doctors and germ-warfare guys, you name it. An alien virus, we told them, symptoms completely random and unpredictable. Impossible, they said. Utterly absurd. One of them gave me a whole lecture about how Earth germs could never affect Martians like in that H. G. Wells book, and Martian germs couldn't affect us, either. Everybody agreed that this random-symptom bit was a laugh. So what were we supposed to do? We all cracked jokes about the Martian flu and spaceman's fever. Somebody, I don't know who, called it the wild card virus in a report, and the rest of us picked up on the name, but nobody believed it for a second.

It was a bad situation, and Tachyon just made it worse when he tried to escape. He almost pulled it off, but like my old man always told me, 'almost' only counts in horseshoes and grenades. The Pentagon had sent out their own man to question him, a bird colonel named Wayne, and Tachyon finally got fed up, I guess. He took control of Colonel Wayne, and together they just marched out of the building. Whenever they were challenged, Wayne snapped off the orders to let them pass, and rank does have its privileges. The cover story was that Wayne had orders to escort Tachyon back to Washington. They commandeered a jeep and got all the way back to the spaceship, but by then one of the sentries had checked with me, and my men were waiting for them, with direct orders to ignore anything Colonel Wayne might say. We took him back into custody and kept him there, under heavy guard. For all his magic powers, there wasn't much he could do about it. He could make one person do what he wanted, maybe three or four if he tried real hard, but not all of us, and by then we were wise to his tricks.

Maybe it was a bonehead maneuver, but his escape attempt did get him the date with Einstein he'd been badgering us for. The Pentagon kept telling us he was the world's geatest hypnotist, but I wasn't buying that anymore, and you should have heard what Colonel Wayne thought of the theory. The eggheads were getting agitated too. Anyway, together, Wayne and I managed to wrangle authorization to fly the prisoner to Princeton. I figured a talk with Einstein couldn't do any harm, and might do some good. His ship was impounded, and we'd gotten all we were going to get from the man himself. Einstein was supposed to be the world's greatest brain, maybe he could figure the guy out, right?

There are still those who say that the military is to blame for everything that happened, but it's just not true. It's easy to be wise in hindsight, but I was there, and I'll maintain to my dying day that the steps we took were reasonable and prudent.

The thing that really burns me is when they talk about how we did nothing to track down that damned globe with the wild card spores. Maybe we made a mistake, yeah, but we weren't stupid, we were covering our asses. Every damned military installation in the country got a directive to be on the lookout for a crashed spaceship that looked something like a seashell with running lights. Is it my fucking fault that none of them took it seriously?

Give me credit for one thing, at least. When all hell broke loose, I had Tachyon jetting back toward New York within two hours. I was in the seat behind him. The redheaded wimp cried half the fucking way across the country. Me, I prayed for Jetboy.

THIRTY MINUTES OVER BROADWAY!

JETBOY'S LAST ADVENTURE!

by Howard Waldrop

Bonham's Flying Service of Shantak, New Jersey, was socked in. The small searchlight on the tower barely pushed away the darkness of the swirling fog.

There was the sound of car tires on the wet pavement in front of Hangar 23. A car door opened, a moment later it closed. Footsteps came to the Employees Only door. It opened. Scoop Swanson came in, carrying his Kodak Autograph Mark II and a bag of flashbulbs and film.

Lincoln Traynor raised up from the engine of the surplus P-40 he was overhauling for an airline pilot who had got it at a voice-bid auction for $293. Judging from the shape of the engine, it must have been flown by the Flying Tigers in 1940. A ball game was on the workbench radio. Linc turned it down.

''Lo, Linc,' said Scoop.

''Lo.'

'No word yet?'

'Don't expect any. The telegram he sent yesterday said he'd be in tonight. Good enough for me.'

Scoop lit a Camel with a Three Torches box match from the workbench. He blew smoke toward the Absolutely No Smoking sign at the back of the hangar. 'Hey, what's this?' He walked to the rear. Still in their packing cases were two long red wing extensions and two 300-gallon teardrop underwing tanks. 'When these get here?'

'Air Corps shipped them yesterday from San Francisco. Another telegram came for him today. You might as well read it, you're doing the story.' Line handed him the War Department orders.

TO: Jetboy (Tomlin, Robert NMI)
HOR: Bonham's Flying Service
Hangar 23,
Shantak, New Jersey

1. Effective this date 1200Z hours 12 Aug '46, you are no longer on active duty, United States Army Air Force.
2. Your aircraft (model-experimental) (ser. no. JB-1) is hereby decommissioned from active status, United States Army Air Force, and reassigned you as private aircraft. No further materiel support from USAAF or War Department will be forthcoming.
3. Records, commendations, and awards forwarded under separate cover.
4. Our records show Tomlin, Robert NMI, has not obtained pilot's license. Please contact CAB for courses and certification.
5. Clear skies and tailwinds,

> For
> Arnold, H.H.
> CofS, USAAF

ref. Executive Order #2, 08 Dec '41

'What's this about him having no pilot's license?' asked the newspaperman. 'I went through the morgue on him – his file's a foot thick. Hell, he must have flown faster and farther, shot down more planes than anyone – five hundred planes, fifty ships! He did it without a pilot's license?'

Linc wiped grease from his mustache. 'Yep. That was the most plane-crazy kid you ever saw. Back in '39, he couldn't have been more than twelve, he heard there was a job out here. He showed up at four A.M. – lammed out of the orphanage to do it. They came out to get him. But of course Professor Silverberg had hired him, squared it with them.'

'Silverberg's the one the Nazis bumped off? The guy who made the jet?'

'Yep. Years ahead of everybody, but weird. I put together the plane for him, Bobby and I built it by hand. But Silverberg made the jets – damnedest engines you ever saw. The Nazis and Italians, and Whittle over in England, had started theirs. But the Germans found out something was happening here.'

'How'd the kid learn to fly?'

'He always knew, I think,' said Lincoln. 'One day he's in here helping me bend metal. The next, him and the professor are flying around at four hundred miles per. In the dark, with those early engines.'

'How'd they keep it a secret?'

'They didn't, very well. The spies came for Silverberg – wanted him *and* the plane. Bobby was out with it. I think he and the prof knew something was up. Silverberg put up such a fight the Nazis killed him. Then, there was the diplomatic stink. In those days the JB-1 only had six .30 cals on it – where the professor got them I don't know. But the kid took care of the car full of spies with it, and that speedboat on the Hudson full of embassy people. All on diplomatic visas.

'Just a sec,' Linc stopped himself. 'End of a doubleheader in Cleveland. On the Blue Network.' He turned up the metal Philco radio that sat above the toolrack.

'*Sanders to Papenfuss to Volstad, a double play. That does it. So the Sox drop two to Cleveland. We'll be right—*' Linc turned it off. 'There goes five bucks,' he said. 'Where was I?'

'The Krauts killed Silverberg, and Jetboy got even. He went to Canada, right?'

'Joined the RCAF, unofficially. Fought in the Battle of Britain, went to China against the Japs with the Tigers, was back in Britain for Pearl Harbor.'

'And Roosevelt commissioned him?'

'Sort of. You know, funny thing about his whole career. He fights the *whole* war, longer than any other American – late '39 to '45 – then right at the end, he gets lost in the Pacific, missing. We all think he's dead for a year. Then they find him on that desert island last month, and now he's coming home.' There was a high, thin whine like a prop plane in a dive. It came from the foggy skies outside. Scoop put out his third Camel. 'How can he land in this soup?'

'He's got an all-weather radar set – got it off a German night fighter back in '43. He could land that plane in a circus tent at midnight.'

They went to the door. Two landing lights pierced the rolling mist. They lowered to the far end of the runway, turned, and came back on the taxi strip.

The red fuselage glowed in the gray-shrouded lights of the airstrip. The twin-engine high-wing plane turned toward them and rolled to a stop.

Linc Traynor put a set of double chocks under each of the two rear tricycle landing gears. Half the glass nose of the plane levered up and pulled back. The plane had four 20mm cannon snouts in the wing roots between the engines, and a 75mm gunport below and to the left of the cockpit rim.

It had a high thin rudder, and the rear elevators were shaped like the tail of a brook trout. Under each of the elevators was the muzzle of a rear-firing machine gun. The only markings on the plane were four nonstandard USAAF stars in a black roundel, and the serial number JB-1 on the top right and bottom left wings and beneath the rudder.

The radar antennae on the nose looked like something to roast weenies on.

A boy dressed in red pants, white shirt, and a blue helmet and goggles stepped out of the cockpit and onto the dropladder on the left side.

He was nineteen, maybe twenty. He took off his helmet and goggles. He had curly mousy brown hair, hazel eyes, and was short and chunky.

'Linc,' he said. He hugged the pudgy man to him, patted his back for a full minute. Scoop snapped off a shot.

'Great to have you back, Bobby,' said Linc.

'Nobody's called me that in years,' he said. 'It sounds real good to hear it again.'

'This is Scoop Swanson,' said Linc. 'He's gonna make you famous all over again.'

'I'd rather be asleep.' He shook the reporter's hand. 'Any place around here we can get some ham and eggs?'

The launch pulled up to the dock in the fog. Out in the harbor a ship finished cleaning its bilges and was turning to steam back southward.

There were three men on the mooring: Fred and Ed and Filmore. One man stepped out of the launch with a suitcase in his hands. Filmore leaned down and gave the guy at the wheel of the motorboat a Lincoln and two Jacksons. Then he helped the guy with the suitcase.

'Welcome home, Dr. Tod.'

'It's good to be back, Filmore.' Tod was dressed in a baggy suit, and had on an overcoat even though it was August. He wore his hat pulled low over his face, and from it a glint of metal was reflected in the pale lights from a warehouse.

'This is Fred and this is Ed,' said Filmore. 'They're here just for the night.'

''Lo,' said Fred.

''Lo,' said Ed.

They walked back to the car, a '46 Merc that looked like a submarine. They climbed in, Fred and Ed watching the foggy alleys to each side. Then Fred got behind the wheel, and Ed rode shotgun. With a sawed-off ten-gauge.

'Nobody's expecting me. Nobody cares,' said Dr. Tod. 'Everybody who had something against me is either dead or went respectable during the war and made a mint. I'm an old man and I'm tired. I'm going out in the country and raise bees and play the horses and the market.'

'Not planning anything, boss?'

'Not a thing.'

He turned his head as they passed a streetlight. Half his face was gone, a smooth plate reaching from jaw to hatline, nostril to left ear.

'I can't shoot anymore, for one thing. My depth perception isn't what it used to be.'

'I shouldn't wonder,' said Filmore. 'We heard something happened to you in '43.'

'Was in a somewhat-profitable operation out of Egypt while the Afrika Korps was falling apart. Taking people in and out for a fee in a nominally neutral air fleet. Just a sideline. Then ran into that hotshot flier.'

'Who?'

'Kid with the jet plane, before the Germans had them.'

'Tell you the truth, boss, I didn't keep up with the war much. I take a long view on merely territorial conflicts.'

'As I should have,' said Dr. Tod. 'We were flying out of Tunisia. Some important people were with us that trip. The pilot screamed. There was a tremendous explosion. Next thing, I came to, it was the next morning, and me and one other person are in a life raft in the middle of the Mediterranean. My face hurt. I lifted up. Something fell into the bottom of the raft. It was my left eyeball. It was looking up at me. I knew I was in trouble.'

'You said it was a kid with a jet plane?' asked Ed.

'Yes. We found out later they'd broken our code, and he'd flown six hundred miles to intercept us.'

'You want to get even?' asked Filmore.

'No. That was so long ago I hardly remember that side of my face. It just taught me to be a little more cautious. I wrote it off as character building.'

'So no plans, huh?'

'Not a single one,' said Dr. Tod.

'That'll be nice for a change,' said Filmore. They watched the lights of the city go by.

♠

He knocked on the door, uncomfortable in his new brown suit and vest.

'Come on in, it's open,' said a woman's voice. Then it was muffled. 'I'll be ready in just a minute.'

Jetboy opened the oak hall door and stepped into the room, past the glass-brick room divider.

A beautiful woman stood in the middle of the room, a dress halfway over her arms and head. She wore a camisole, garter belt, and silk hose. She was pulling the dress down with one of her hands.

Jetboy turned his head away, blushing and taken aback. 'Oh,' said the woman. 'Oh! I – who?'

'It's me, Belinda,' he said. 'Robert.'

'Robert?'

'Bobby, Bobby Tomlin.'

She stared at him a moment, her hands clasped over her front though she was fully dressed.

'Oh, Bobby,' she said, and came to him and hugged him and gave him a big kiss right on the mouth.

It was what he had waited six years for.

'Bobby. It's great to see you. I – I was expecting someone else. Some – girlfriends. How did you find me?'

'Well, it wasn't easy.'

She stepped back from him. 'Let me look at you.'

He looked at her. The last time he had seen her she was fourteen, a tomboy, still at the orphanage. She had been a thin kid with mousy blond hair. Once, when she was eleven, she'd almost punched his lights out. She was a year older than he. Then he had gone away, to work at the airfield, then to fight with the Brits against Hitler. He had written her when he could all during the war, after America entered it. She had left the orphanage and been put in a foster home. In '44 one of his letters had come back from there marked 'Moved – No Forwarding Address.' Then he had been lost all during the last year.

'You've changed, too,' he said.

'So have you.'

'Uh.'

'I followed the newspapers all during the war. I tried to write you but I don't guess the letters ever caught up with you. Then they said you were missing at sea, and I sort of gave up.'

'Well, I was, but they found me. Now I'm back. How have you been?'

'Real good, once I ran away from the foster home,' she said. A look of pain came across her face. 'You don't know how glad I was to get away from there. Oh, Bobby,' she said. 'Oh, I wish things was different!' She started to cry a little.

'Hey,' he said, holding her by the shoulders. 'Sit down. I've got something for you.'

'A present?'

'Yep.' He handed her a grimy, oil-stained paper parcel. 'I carried these with me the last two years of the war. They were in the plane with me on the island. Sorry I didn't have time to rewrap them.'

She tore the English butcher paper. Inside were copies of *The House at Pooh Corner* and *The Tale of the Fierce Bad Rabbit*.

'Oh,' said Belinda. 'Thank you.'

He remembered her dressed in the orphanage coveralls, just in, dusty and tired from a baseball game, lying on the reading-room floor with a Pooh book open before her.

'The Pooh book's signed by the real Christopher Robin,' he said. 'I found out he was an RAF officer at one of the bases in England. He said he usually didn't do this sort of thing, that he was just another airman. I told him I wouldn't tell anyone. I'd searched high and low to find a copy, and he knew that, though.

'This other one's got more of a story behind it. I was coming back near dusk, escorting some crippled B-17s. I looked up and saw two German night fighters coming in, probably setting up patrol, trying to catch some Lancasters before they went out over the Channel.

'To make a long story short, I shot down both of them; they packed in near a small village. But I had run out of fuel and had to set down. Saw a pretty flat sheep pasture with a lake at the far end of it, and went in.

'When I climbed out of the cockpit, I saw a lady and a sheepdog standing at the edge of the field. She had a shotgun. When she got close enough to see the engines and the decals, she said, "Good shooting! Won't you come in for a bite of supper and to use the telephone to call Fighter Command?"

'We could see the two ME-110s burning in the distance.

'"You're the very famous Jetboy." she said, "We have followed your exploits in the Sawrey paper. I'm Mrs. Heelis." She held out her hand.

'I shook it. "Mrs. William Heelis? And this is Sawrey?"

'"Yes," she said.

'"You're Beatrix Potter!" I said.

'"I suppose I am," she said.

'Belinda, she was this stout old lady in a raggedy sweater and a plain old dress. But when she smiled, I swear, all of England lit up!'

Belinda opened the book. On the flyleaf was written

To Jetboy's American Friend,
Belinda,
from
Mrs. William Heelis
('Beatrix Potter')
12 April 1943

Jetboy drank the coffee Belinda made for him. 'Where are your friends?' he asked.

'Well, he – they should have been here by now. I was thinking of going down the hall to the phone and trying to call them. I can change, and we can sit around and talk about old times. I really can call.'

'No,' said Jetboy 'Tell you what. I'll call you later on in the week; we can get together some night when you're not busy. That would be fun.'

'Sure would.'

Jetboy got up to go.

'Thank you for the books, Bobby. They mean a lot to me, they really do.'

'It's real good to see you again, Bee.'

'Nobody's called me that since the orphanage. Call me real soon, will you?'

'Sure will.' He leaned down and kissed her again.

He walked to the stairs. As he was going down, a guy in a modi-fied zoot suit – pegged pants, long coat, watch chain, bow tie the size of a coat hanger, hair slicked back, reeking of Brylcreem and Old Spice – went up the stairs two at a time, whistling 'It Ain't the Meat, It's the Motion.'

Jetboy heard him knocking at Belinda's door. Outside, it had begun to rain.

'Great. Just like in a movie,' said Jetboy.

◆

The next night was quiet as a graveyard.

Then dogs all over the Pine Barrens started to bark. Cats screamed. Birds flew in panic from thousands of trees, circled, swooping this way and that in the dark night.

Static washed over every radio in the northeastern United States. New television sets flared out, volume doubling. People gathered around nine-inch Dumonts jumped back at the sudden noise and light, dazzled in their own living rooms and bars and sidewalks outside appliance stores all over the East Coast.

To those out in that hot August night it was even more spec-tacular. A thin line of light, high up, moved, brightened, still falling. Then it expanded, upping in brilliance, changed into a blue-green bolide, seemed to stop, then flew to a hundred falling sparks that slowly faded on the dark starlit sky.

Some people said they saw another, smaller light a few minutes later. It seemed to hover, then sped off to the west, growing dim-mer as it flew. The newspapers had been full of stories of the 'ghost rockets' in Sweden all that summer. It was the silly season.

A few calls to the weather bureau or Army Air Force bases got the answer that it was probably a stray from the Delta Aquarid meteor shower.

Out in the Pine Barrens, somebody knew differently, though he wasn't in the mood to communicate it to anyone.

Jetboy, dressed in a loose pair of pants, a shirt, and a brown aviator's jacket, walked in through the doors of the Blackwell Printing Company. There was a bright red-and-blue sign above the door: Home of the Cosh Comics Company.

He stopped at the receptionist's desk.

'Robert Tomlin to see Mr. Farrell.'

The secretary, a thin blond job in glasses with swept-up rims that made it look like a bat was camping on her face, stared at him. 'Mr. Farrell passed on in the winter of 1945. Were you in the service or something?'

'Something.'

'Would you like to speak to Mr. Lowboy? He has Mr. Farrell's job now.'

'Whoever's in charge of *Jetboy Comics*.'

The whole place began shaking as printing presses cranked up in the back of the building. On the walls of the office were garish comic-book covers, promising things only *they* could deliver.

'Robert Tomlin,' said the secretary to the intercom.

'*Scratch squawk* never heard of him *squich*.'

'What was this about?' asked the secretary.

'Tell him Jetboy wants to see him.'

'Oh,' she said, looking at him. 'I'm sorry. I didn't recognize you.'

'Nobody ever does.'

Lowboy looked like a gnome with all the blood sucked out. He was as pale as Harry Langdon must have been, like a weed grown under a burlap bag.

'Jetboy!' He held out a hand like a bunch of grub worms. 'We all thought you'd died until we saw the papers last week. You're a real national hero, you know?'

'I don't feel like one.'

'What can I do for you? Not that I'm not pleased to finally meet you. But you must be a busy man.'

'Well, first, I found out none of the licensing and royalty checks had been deposited in my account since I was reported Missing and Presumed Dead last summer.'

'What, really? The legal department must have put it in escrow or something until somebody came forward with a claim. I'll get them right on it.'

'Well, I'd like the check now, before I leave,' said Jetboy.

'Huh? I don't know if they can do that. That sounds awfully abrupt.'

Jetboy stared at him.

'Okay, okay, let me call Accounting.' He yelled into the telephone.

'Oh,' said Jetboy. 'A friend's been collecting my copies. I checked the statement of ownership and circulation for the last two years. I know *Jetboy Comics* have been selling five hundred thousand copies an issue lately.'

Lowboy yelled into the phone some more. He put it down. 'It'll take 'em a little while. Anything else?'

'I don't like what's happening to the funny book,' said Jetboy.

'What's not to like? It's selling a half a million copies a month!'

'For one thing, the plane's getting to look more and more like a bullet. And the artists have swept back the wings, for Christ's sakes!'

'This is the Atomic Age, kid. Boys nowadays don't like a plane that looks like a red leg of lamb with coat hangers sticking out the front.'

'Well, it's always looked like that. And another thing: Why's the damned plane blue in the last three issues?'

'Not me! I think red's fine. But Mr. Blackwell sent down a memo, said no more red except for blood. He's a big Legionnaire.'

'Tell him the plane has to look right, and be the right color.

25

Also, the combat reports were forwarded. When Farrell was sitting at your desk, the comic was about flying and combat, and cleaning up spy rings – real stuff. And there were never more than two ten-page Jetboy stories an issue.'

'When Farrell was at this desk, the book was only selling a quarter-million copies a month,' said Lowboy.

Robert stared at him again.

'I know the war's over, and everybody wants a new house and eye-bulging excitement,' said Jetboy. 'But look what I find in the last eighteen months ...

'I never fought anyone like The Undertaker, anyplace called The Mountain of Doom. And come on! The Red Skeleton? Mr. Maggot? Professor Blooteaux? What is this with all the skulls and tentacles? I mean, evil twins named Sturm and Drang Hohenzollern? The Arthropod Ape, a gorilla with six sets of elbows? Where do you get all this stuff?'

'It's not me, it's the writers. They're a crazy bunch, always taking Benzedrine and stuff. Besides, it's what the kids want!'

'What about the flying features, and the articles on real aviation heroes? I thought my contract called for at least two features an issue on real events and people?'

'We'll have to look at it again. But I can tell you, kids don't want that kind of stuff anymore. They want monsters, spaceships, stuff that'll make 'em wet the bed. You remember? You were a kid once yourself!'

Jetboy picked up a pencil from the desk. 'I was thirteen when the war started, fifteen when they bombed Pearl Harbor. I've been in combat for six years. Sometimes I don't think I was ever a kid.'

Lowboy was quiet a moment.

'Tell you what you need to do,' he said. 'You need to write up all the stuff you don't like about the book and send it to us. I'll have the legal department go over it, and we'll try to do something, work things out. Of course, we print three issues ahead, so it'll be Thanksgiving before the new stuff shows up. Or later.'

Jetboy sighed. 'I understand.'

'I sure do want you happy, 'cause *Jetboy*'s my favorite comic.

No, I really mean that. The others are just a job. My god, what a job: deadlines, working with drunks and worse, riding herd over printers – you can just imagine! But I like the work on *Jetboy*. It's special.'

'Well, I'm glad.'

'Sure, sure.' Lowboy drummed his fingers on the desk. 'Wonder what's taking them so long?''

'Probably getting out the other set of ledgers,' said Jetboy.

'Hey, no! We're square here!' Lowboy came to his feet.

'Just kidding.'

'Oh. Say, the paper said you were, what, marooned on a desert island or something? Pretty tough?'

'Well, lonely. I got tired of catching and eating fish. Mostly it was boring, and I missed everything. I don't mean missed, I mean missed out. I was there from April twenty-ninth of '45 until last month.

'There were times when I thought I'd go nuts. I couldn't believe it one morning when I looked up, and there was the USS *Reluctant* anchored less than a mile offshore. I fired off a flare, and they picked me up. It's taken a month to get someplace to repair the plane, rest up, get home. I'm glad to be back.'

'I can imagine. Hey, lots of dangerous animals on the island? I mean, lions and tigers and stuff?'

Jetboy laughed. 'It was less than a mile wide, and a mile and a quarter long. There were birds and rats and some lizards.'

'Lizards? Big lizards? Poisonous?'

'No. Small. I must have eaten half of them before I left. Got pretty good with a slingshot made out of an oxygen hose.'

'Huh! I bet you did!'

The door opened, and a tall guy with an ink-smudged shirt came in.

'That him?' asked Lowboy.

'I only seen him once, but it looks like him,' said the man.

'Good enough for me!' said Lowboy.

'Not for me,' said the accountant. 'Show me some ID and sign this release.'

Jetboy sighed and did. He looked at the amount on the check. It had far too few digits in front of the decimal. He folded it up and put it in his pocket.

'I'll leave my address for the next check with your secretary. And I'll send a letter with the objections this week.'

'Do that. It's been a real pleasure meeting you. Let's hope we have a long and prosperous business together.'

'Thanks, I guess,' said Jetboy. He and the accountant left. Lowboy sat back down in his swivel chair. He put his hands behind his head and stared at the bookcase across the room.

Then he rocketed forward, jerked up the phone, and dialed nine to get out. He called up the chief writer for *Jetboy* Comics.

A muzzy, hung-over voice answered on the twelfth ring.

'Clean the shit out of your head, this is Lowboy. Picture this: fifty-two-page special, single-story issue. Ready? *Jetboy on Dinosaur Island!* Got that? I see lots of cavemen, a broad, a what-you-call-it-king rex. What? Yeah, yeah, a tyrannosaur. Maybe a buncha hold-out Jap soldiers. You know. Yeah, maybe even samurai. When? Blown off course in A.D. 1100? Christ. Whatever. You know exactly what we need.

'What's this? Tuesday. You got till five P.M. Thursday, okay? Quit bitchin'. It's a hundred and a half fast bucksl See you then.'

He hung up. Then he called up an artist and told him what he wanted for the cover.

Ed and Fred were coming back from a delivery in the Pine Barrens.

They were driving an eight-yard dump truck. In the back until a few minutes ago had been six cubic yards of new-set concrete. Eight hours before, it had been five and a half yards of water, sand, gravel, and cement and a secret ingredient.

The secret ingredient had broken three of the Five Unbreakable Rules for carrying on a tax-free, unincorporated business in the state.

He had been taken by other businessmen to a wholesale

construction equipment center, and been shown how a cement mixer works, up close and personal.

Not that Ed and Fred had anything to do with that. They'd been called an hour ago and been asked if they could drive a dump truck through the woods for a couple of grand.

It was dark out in the woods, not too many miles from the city. It didn't look like they were within a hundred miles of a town over five-hundred population.

The headlights picked out ditches where everything from old airplanes to sulfuric-acid bottles lay in clogged heaps. Some of the dumpings were fresh. Smoke and fire played about a few. Others glowed without combustion. A pool of metal bubbled and popped as they ground by.

Then they were back into the deep pines again, jouncing from rut to rut.

'Hey!' yelled Ed. 'Stop!'

Fred threw on the brakes, killing the engine. 'Goddamn!' he said. 'What the hell's the matter with you?'

'Back there! I swear I saw a guy pushing a neon cat's-eye marble the size of Cleveland!'

'I'm sure as hell not going back,' said Fred.

'Nah! Come on! You don't see stuff like that every day.'

'Shit, Ed! Someday you're gonna get us both killed!'

◆

It wasn't a marble. They didn't need their flashlights to tell it wasn't a magnetic mine. It was a rounded canister that glowed on its own, with swirling colors on it. It hid the man pushing it.

'It looks like a rolled-up neon armadillo,' said Fred, who'd been out west.

The man behind the thing blinked at them, unable to see past their flashlights. He was tattered and dirty, with a tobacco-stained beard and wild, steel-wool hair.

They stepped closer.

'It's mine!' he said to them, stepping in front of the thing, holding his arms out across it.

'Easy, old-timer,' said Ed. 'What you got?'

'My ticket to easy street. You from the Air Corps?'

'Hell, no. Let's look at this.'

The man picked up a rock. 'Stay back! I found it where I found the plane crash. The Air Corps'll pay plenty to get this atomic bomb back!'

'That doesn't look like any atomic bomb I've ever seen,' said Fred. 'Look at the writing on the side. It ain't even English.'

'Course it's not! It must be a secret weapon. That's why they dressed it up so weird.'

'Who?'

'I told you more'n I meant to. Get outta my way.'

Fred looked at the old geezer. 'You've piqued my interest,' he said. 'Tell me more.'

'Outta my way, boy! I killed a man over a can of lye hominy once!'

Fred reached in his jacket. He came out with a pistol with a muzzle that looked like a drainpipe.

'It crashed last night,' said the old man, eyes wild. 'Woke me up. Lit up the whole sky. I looked for it all day today, figured the woods would be crawlin' with Air Corps people and state troopers, but nobody came.

'Found it just before dark tonight. Tore all hell up, it did. Knocked the wings completely off the thing when it crashed. All these weird-dressed people all scattered around. Women too.' He lowered his head a minute, shame on his face. 'Anyway, they was all dead. Must have been a jet plane, didn't find no propellers or nothing. And this here atomic bomb was just lying there in the wreck. I figured the Air Corps would pay real good to get it back. Friend of mine found a weather balloon once and they gave him a dollar and a quarter. I figure this is about a million times as important as that!'

Fred laughed. 'A buck twenty-five, huh? I'll give you ten dollars for it.'

'I can get a million!'

Fred pulled the hammer back on the revolver. 'Fifty,' said the old man.

'Twenty.'

'It ain't fair. But I'll take it.'

'What are you going to do with that?' asked Ed.

'Take it to Doctor Tod,' said Fred. 'He'll know what to do with it. He's the scientific type.'

'What if it is an A-bomb?'

'Well, I don't think A-bombs have spray nozzles on them. And the old man was right. The woods would have been crawling with Air Force people if they'd lost an atomic bomb. Hell, only five of them have ever been exploded. They can't have more than a dozen, and you better believe they know where every one of them is, all the time.'

'Well, it ain't a mine,' said Ed. 'What do you think it is?'

'I don't care. If it's worth money, Doctor Tod'll split with us. He's a square guy.'

'For a crook,' said Ed.

They laughed and laughed, and the thing rattled around in the back of the dump truck.

The MPs brought the red-haired man into his office and introduced them.

'Please have a seat, Doctor,' said A. E. He lit his pipe.

The man seemed ill at ease, as he should have been after two days of questioning by Army Intelligence.

'They have told me what happened at White Sands, and that you won't talk to anyone but me,' said A. E. 'I understand they used sodium pentathol on you, and that it had no effect?'

'It made me drunk,' said the man, whose hair in this light seemed orange and yellow.

'But you didn't talk?'

'I said things, but not what they wanted to hear.'

'Very unusual.'

'Blood chemistry.'

A. E. sighed. He looked out the window of the Princeton office. 'Very well, then. I will listen to your story. I am not saying I will believe it, but I will listen.'

'All right,' said the man, taking a deep breath. 'Here goes. '

He began to talk, slowly at first, forming his words carefully, gaining confidence as he spoke. As he began to talk faster, his accent crept back in, one A. E. could not place, something like a Fiji Islander who had learned English from a Swede. A. E. refilled his pipe twice, then left it unlit after filling it the third time. He sat slightly forward, occasionally nodding, his gray hair an aureole in the afternoon light.

The man finished.

A. E. remembered his pipe, found a match, lit it. He put his hands behind his head. There was a small hole in his sweater near the left elbow.

'They'll never believe any of that,' he said.

'I don't care, as long as they do something!' said the man. 'As long as I get it back.'

A. E. looked at him. 'If they did believe you, the implications of all this would overshadow the reason you're here. The fact that you are *here*, if you follow my meaning.'

'Well, what can we do? If my ship were still operable, I'd be looking myself. I did the next best thing – landed somewhere that would be sure to attract attention, asked to speak to you. Perhaps other scientists, research institutes ...'

A. E. laughed. 'Forgive me. You don't realize how things are done here. We will need the military. We will *have* the military and the government whether we want them or not, so we might as well have them on the best possible terms, ours, from the first. The problem is that we have to think of something that is *plausible* to them, yet will still mobilize them in the search.

'I'll talk to the Army people about you, then make some calls to friends of mine. We have just finished a large global war, and many things had a way of escaping notice, or being lost in the shuffle. Perhaps we can work something from there.

'The only thing is, we had better do all this from a phone booth. The MPs will be along, so I will have to talk quietly. Tell me,' he said, picking up his hat from the corner of a cluttered bookcase, 'do you like ice cream?'

'Lactose and sugar solids congealed in a mixture kept just below the freezing point?' asked the man.

'I assure you,' said A. E., 'it is better than it sounds, and quite refreshing.' Arm in arm, they went out the office door.

Jetboy patted the scarred side of his plane. He stood in Hangar 23. Linc came out of his office, wiping his hands on a greasy rag.

'Hey, how'd it go?' he asked.

'Great. They want the book of memoirs. Going to be their big Spring book, if I get it in on time, or so they say.'

'You still bound and determined to sell the plane?' asked the mechanic. 'Sure hate to see her go.'

'Well, that part of my life's over. I feel like if I never fly again, even as an airline passenger, it'll be too soon.'

'What do you want me to do?'

Jetboy looked at the plane.

'Tell you what. Put on the high-altitude wing extensions and the drop tanks. It looks bigger and shinier that way. Somebody from a museum will probably buy it, is what I figure – I'm offering it to museums first. If that doesn't work, I'll take out ads in the papers. We'll take the guns out later, if some private citizen buys it. Check everything to see it's tight. Shouldn't have shaken much on the hop from San Fran, and they did a pretty good overhaul at Hickam Field. Whatever you think it needs.'

'Sure thing.'

'I'll call you tomorrow, unless something can't wait.'

HISTORICAL AIRCRAFT FOR SALE: Jetboy's twin-engine jet. 2 x 1200 lb thrust engines, speed 600 mph at 25,000 ft, range 650 miles, 1000w drop tanks (tanks and wing exts. inc.) length 31 ft, w s 33 ft (49 w exts.) Reasonable offers accepted. Must see to appreciate. On view at Hangar 23, Bonham's Flying Service, Shantak, New Jersey.

Jetboy stood in front of the bookstore window, looking at the pyramids of new titles there. You could tell paper rationing was off. Next year, his book would be one of them. Not just a comic book, but the story of his part in the war. He hoped it would be good enough so that it wouldn't be lost in the clutter.

Seems like, in the words of someone, every goddamn barber and shoeshine boy who was drafted had written a book about how he won the war.

There were six books of war memoirs in one window, by everyone from a lieutenant colonel to a major general (maybe those PFC barbers didn't write that many books?).

Maybe they wrote some of the two dozen war novels that covered another window of the display.

There were two books near the door, piles of them in a window by themselves, runaway best-sellers, that weren't war novels or memoirs. One was called *The Grass-Hopper Lies Heavy* by someone named Abendsen (Hawthorne Abendsen, obviously a pen name). The other was a thick book called *Growing Flowers by Candlelight in Hotel Rooms* by someone so self-effacing she called herself 'Mrs. Charles Fine Adams.' It must be a book of unreadable poems that the public, in its craziness, had taken up. There was no accounting for taste.

Jetboy put his hands in the pockets of his leather jacket and walked to the nearest movie show.

♦

Tod watched the smoke rising from the lab and waited for the phone to ring. People ran back and forth to the building a half-mile away.

There had been nothing for two weeks. Thorkeld, the scientist he'd hired to run the tests, had reported each day. The stuff didn't work on monkeys, dogs, rats, lizards, snakes, frogs, insects, or even on fish in suspension in water. Dr. Thorkeld was beginning to think Tod's men had paid twenty dollars for an inert gas in a fancy container.

A few moments ago there had been an explosion. Now he waited.

The phone rang.

'Tod – oh, god, this is Jones at the lab, it's—' Static washed over the line. 'Oh, sweet Jesus! Thorkeld's – they're all—' There was thumping near the phone receiver on the other end. 'Oh, my …'

'Calm down,' said Tod. 'Is everyone outside the lab safe?'

'Yeah, yeah. The … *oooh*.' The sound of vomiting came over the phone.

Tod waited.

'Sorry, Dr. Tod. The lab's still sealed off: The fire's – it's a small one on the grass outside. Somebody dropped a butt.'

'Tell me what happened.'

'I was outside for a smoke. Somebody in there must have messed up, dropped something. I – I don't know. It's – they're most of them dead, I think. I hope. I don't know. Something's – wait, wait. There's someone still moving in the office, I can see from here, there's—'

There was a click of someone picking up a receiver. The volume on the line dropped.

'Tog, Tog,' said a voice, an approximation of a voice.

'Who's there?'

'Torgk—'

'Thorkeld?'

'Guh. Hep. Hep. Guh.'

There was a sound like a sack full of squids being dumped on a corrugated roof. 'Hep.' Then came the sound of jelly being emptied into a cluttered desk drawer.

There was a gunshot, and the receiver bounced off the desk.

'He – he shot – it – himself,' said Jones.

'I'll be right out,' said Tod.

After the cleanup, Tod stood in his office again. It had not been pretty. The canister was still intact. Whatever the accident had been had been with a sample. The other animals were okay. It was only the people. Three were dead outright. One, Thorkeld, had killed himself. Two others he and Jones had *had* to kill. A seventh person was missing, but had not come out any of the doors or windows.

Tod sat down in his chair and thought a long, long time. Then he reached over and pushed the button on his desk.

'Yeah, Doctor?' asked Filmore, stepping into the room with a batch of telegrams and brokerage orders under his arm.

Dr. Tod opened the desk safe and began counting out bills. 'Filmore. I'd like you to get down to Port Elizabeth, North Carolina, and buy me up five type Blimp balloons. Tell them I'm a car salesman. Arrange for one million cubic feet of helium to be delivered to the south Pennsy warehouse. Break out the hardware and give me a complete list of what we have – anything we need, we can get surplus. Get ahold of Captain Mack, see if he still has that cargo ship. We'll need new passports. Get me Cholley Sacks; I'll need a contact in Switzerland. I'll need a pilot with a lighter-than-air license. Some diving suits and oxygen. Shot ballast, couple of tons. A bombsight. Nautical charts. And bring me a cup of coffee.'

'Fred has a lighter-than-air pilot's license,' said Filmore.

'Those two never cease to amaze me,' said Dr. Tod.

'I thought we'd pulled our last caper, boss.'

'Filmore,' he said, and looked at the man he'd been friends with for twenty years, 'Filmore, some capers you *have* to pull, whether you want to or not.'

'Dewey was an Admiral at Manila Bay,
Dewey was a candidate just the other day
Dewey were her eyes when she said I do;
Do we love each other? I should say we do!'

The kids in the courtyard of the apartment jumped rope. They'd started the second they got home from school.

At first it bothered Jetboy. He got up from the typewriter and

36

went to the window. Instead of yelling, he watched. The writing wasn't going well, anyway. What had seemed like just the facts when he'd told them to the G-2 boys during the war looked like bragging on paper, once the words were down:

Three planes, two ME-109s and a TA-152, came out of the clouds at the crippled B-24. It had suffered heavy flak damage. Two props were feathered and the top turret was missing.

One of the 109s went into a shallow dive, probably going into a snap roll to fire up at the underside of the bomber.

I ease my plane in a long turn and fired a deflection shot while about 700 yards away and closing. I saw three hits, then the 109 disintegrated.

The TA-152 had seen me and dived to intercept. As the 109 blew up, I throttled back and hit my air brakes. The 152 flashed by less than 50 yards away. I saw the surprised look on the pilot's face. I fired one burst as he flashed by with my 20mms. Everything from his canopy back flew apart in a shower.

I pulled up. The last 109 was behind the Liberator. He was firing with his machine guns and cannon. He'd taken out the tail gunner, and the belly turret couldn't get enough elevation. The bomber pilot was wigwagging the tail so the waist gunners could get a shot, but only the left waist gun was working.

I was more than a mile away, but had turned above and to the right. I put the nose down and fired one round with the 75mm just before the gunsight flashed across the 109.

The whole middle of the fighter disappeared – I could see France through it. The only image I have is that I was looking down on top of an open umbrella and somebody folded it suddenly. The fighter looked like Christmas-tree tinsel as it fell.

Then the few gunners left on the B-24 opened up on me, not recognizing my plane. I flashed my IFF code, but their receiver must have have been out.

There were two German parachutes far below. The pilots of the first two fighters must have gotten out. I went back to my base.

When they ran maintenance, they found one of my 75mm

*rounds missing, and only twelve 20mm shells. I'd shot down three
enemy planes.*

*I later learned the B-24 had crashed in the Channel and there
were no survivors.*

Who needs this stuff? Jetboy thought. The war's over. Does anybody really want to read *The Jet-Propelled Boy* when it's published?
Does anybody except morons even want to read *Jetboy Comics*
anymore?

I don't even think *I'm* needed. What can I do now? Fight crime?
I can see strafing getaway cars full of bank robbers. That would be
a *real* fair fight. Barnstorming? That went out with Hoover, and
besides, I don't want to fly again. This year more people will fly on
airliners on vacation than have been in the air all together in the
last forty-three years, mail pilots, cropdusters, and wars included.

What can I do? Break up a trust? Prosecute wartime profiteers?
There's a real dead-end job for you. Punish mean old men who
are robbing the state blind running orphanages and starving and
beating the kids? You don't need me for that, you need Spanky and
Alfalfa and Buckwheat.

'A tisket, a tasket,
Hitler's in a casket.
Eenie-meenie-Mussolini,
Six feet underground!'

said the kids outside, now doing double-dutch, two ropes going
opposite directions. Kids have too much energy, he thought. They
hot-peppered a while, then slowed again.

'Down in the dungeon, twelve feet deep,
Where old Hitler lies asleep.
German boys, they tickle his feet,
Down in the dungeon, twelve feet deep!'

Jetboy turned away from the window. Maybe what I need is to go to the movies again.

Since his meeting with Belinda, he'd done nothing much but read, write, and go see movies. Before coming home, the last two movies he'd seen, in a crowded post auditorium in France in late '44, had been a cheesy double bill. *That Nazty Nuisance,* a United Artists film made in '43, with Bobby Watson as Hitler, and one of Jetboy's favorite character actors, Frank Faylen, had been the better of the two. The other was a PRC hunk of junk, *Jive Junction,* starring Dickie Moore, about a bunch of hepcats jitterbugging at the malt shop.

The first thing he'd done after getting his money and finding an apartment, was to find the nearest movie theater, where he'd seen *Murder, He Says* about a house full of hillbilly weird people, with Fred McMurray and Marjorie Main, and an actor named Porter Hall playing identical twin-brother murderers named Bert and Mert. 'Which one's which?' asks McMurray, and Marjorie Main picked up an axe handle and hit one of them in the middle of the back, where he collapsed from the waist up in a distorted caricature of humanity, but stayed on his feet. 'That there's Mert,' says Main, throwing the axe handle on the woodpile. 'He's got a trick back.' There was radium and homicide galore, and Jetboy thought it was the funniest movie he had ever seen.

Since then he'd gone to the movies every day, sometimes going to three theaters and seeing from six to eight movies a day. He was adjusting to civilian life, like most soldiers and sailors had, by seeing films.

He had seen *Lost Weekend* with Ray Milland, and Frank Faylen again, this time as a male nurse in a psycho ward; *A Tree Grows in Brooklyn; The Thin Man Goes Home,* with William Powell at his alcoholic best; *Bring on the Girls; It's in the Bag* with Fred Allen; *Incendiary Blonde; The Story of G.I. Joe* (Jetboy had been the subject of one of Pyle's columns back in '43); a horror film called *Isle of the Dead* with Boris Karloff; a new kind of Italian movie called *Open City* at an art house; and *The Postman Always Rings Twice.*

And there were other films, Monogram and PRC and Republic

westerns and crime movies, pictures he'd seen in twenty-four-hour nabes, but had forgotten about ten minutes after leaving the theaters. By the lack of star names and the 4-F look of the leading men, they'd been the bottom halves of double bills made during the war, all clocking in at exactly fifty-nine minutes running time.

Jetboy sighed. So many movies, so much of everything he'd missed during the war. He'd even missed V-E and V-J Days, stuck on that island, before he and his plane had been found by the crew of the USS *Reluctant*. The way the guys on the *Reluctant* talked, you'd have thought they missed most of the war and the movies, too.

He was looking forward to a lot of films this fall, and to seeing them when they came out, the way everybody else did, the way he'd used to do at the orphanage.

Jetboy sat back down at the typewriter. *If I don't work, I'll never get this book done. I'll go to the movies tonight.*

He began to type up all the exciting things he'd done on July 12, 1944.

In the courtyard, women were calling kids in for supper as their fathers came home from work. A couple of kids were still jumping rope out there, their voices thin in the afternoon air:

> *'Hitler, Hitler looks like this,*
> *Mussolini bows like this,*
> *Sonja Henie skates like this,*
> *And Betty Grable misses like this!'*

The Haberdasher in the White House was having a pissass of a day.

It had started with a phone call a little after 6 A.M. – the Nervous Nellies over at the State Department had some new hot rumors from Turkey. The Soviets were moving all their men around on that nation's edges.

'Well,' the Plain-speaking Man from Missouri said, 'call me when they cross the goddamn border and not until.'

Now this.

Independence's First Citizen watched the door close. The last thing he saw was Einstein's heel disappearing. It needed half-soling.

He sat back in his chair, lifted his thick glasses off his nose, rubbed vigorously. Then the President put his fingers together in a steeple, his elbows resting on his desk. He looked at the small model plow on the front of his desk (it had replaced the model of the M-1 Garand that had sat there from the day he took office until V-J Day). There were three books on the right corner of the desk – a Bible, a thumbed thesaurus, and a pictorial history of the United States. There were three buttons on his desk for calling various secretaries, but he never used them.

Now that peace has come, I'm fighting to keep ten wars from breaking out in twenty places, there's strikes looming in every industry and that's a damn shame, people are hollering for more cars and refrigerators, and they're as tired as I am of war and war's alarm.

And I have to kick the hornet's nest again, get everybody out looking for a damn germ bomb that might go off and infect the whole U. S. and kill half the people or more.

We'd have been better off still fighting with sticks and rocks.

The sooner I get my ass back to 219 North Delaware in Independence, the better off me and this whole damn country will be.

Unless that son of a bitch Dewey wants to run for President again. Like Lincoln said, I'd rather swallow a deer-antler rocking chair than let that bastard be President.

That's the only thing that'll keep me here when I've finished out Mr. Roosevelt's term.

Sooner I get this snipe hunt under way, the faster we can put World War Number Two behind us.

He picked up the phone.

'Get me the Chiefs of Staff,' he said.

'Major Truman speaking.'

'Major, this is the other Truman, your boss. Put General Ostrander on the horn, will you?'

While he was waiting he looked out past the window fan (he hated air-conditioning) into the trees. The sky was the kind of blue that quickly turns to brass in the summer.

He looked at the clock on the wall: 10:23 A.M., eastern daylight time. What a day. What a year. What a century.

'General Ostrander here, sir.'

'General, we just had another bale of hay dropped on us ...'

A couple of weeks later, the note came:

> Deposit 20 Million Dollars account # 43Z21, Credite Suisse, Berne, by 2300Z 14 Sept or lose a major city. You know of this weapon; your people have been searching for it. I have it; I will use half of it on the first city. The price goes to 30 Million Dollars to keep me from using it a second time. You have my word it will not be used if the first payment is made and instructions will be sent on where the weapon can be recovered.

The Plain-speaking Man from Missouri picked up the phone.

'Kick everything up to the top notch,' he said. 'Call the cabinet, get the joint Chiefs together. And Ostrander ...'

'Yessir?'

'Better get ahold of that kid flier, what's his name ...?'

'You mean Jetboy, sir? He's not on active duty anymore.'

'The hell he's not. He is now!'

'Yessir.'

It was 2:24 P.M. on the Tuesday of September 15, 1946, when the thing first showed up on the radar screens.

At 2:31 it was still moving slowly toward the city at an altitude of nearly sixty thousand feet.

At 2:41 they blew the first of the air-raid sirens, which had not been used in New York City since April of 1945 in a blackout drill.

By 2:48 there was panic.

Someone in the CD office hit the wrong set of switches. The power went off everywhere except hospitals and police and fire stations. Subways stopped. Things shut down, and traffic lights quit working. Half the emergency equipment, which hadn't been checked since the end of the war, failed to come up.

The streets were jammed with people. Cops rushed out to try to direct traffic. Some of the policemen panicked when they were issued gas masks. Telephones jammed. Fistfights broke out at intersections, people were trampled at subway exits and on the stairs of skyscrapers.

The bridges clogged up.

Conflicting orders came down. Get the people into bomb shelters. No, no, evacuate the island. Two cops on the same corner yelled conflicting orders at the crowds. Mostly people just stood around and looked.

Their attention was soon drawn to something in the south-eastern sky. It was small and shiny.

Flak began to bloom ineffectually two miles below it. On and on it came.

When the guns over in Jersey began to fire, the panic really started.

It was 3 P.M.

♦

'It's really quite simple,' said Dr. Tod. He looked down toward Manhattan, which lay before him like a treasure trove. He turned to Filmore and held up a long cylindrical device that looked like the offspring of a pipe bomb and a combination lock. 'Should anything happen to me, simply insert this fuse in the holder in the explosives' – he indicated the taped-over portion with the opening in the canister covered with the Sanskrit-like lettering – 'twist it to the number five hundred, then pull this lever.' He indicated the bomb-bay door latch. 'It'll fall of its own weight, and I was wrong about the bombsights. Pinpoint accuracy is not our goal.'

He looked at Filmore through the grill of his diving helmet. They all wore diving suits with hoses leading back to a central oxygen supply.

'Make sure, of course, everyone's suited with their helmet on. Your blood would boil in this thin air. And these suits only have to

43

hold pressure for the few seconds the bomb door's open.'

'I don't expect no trouble, boss.'

'Neither do I. After we bomb New York City, we go out to our rendezvous with the ship, rip the ballast, set down, and head for Europe. They'll be only too glad to pay us the money then. They have no way of knowing we'll be using the whole germ weapon. Seven million or so dead should quite convince them we mean business.'

'Look at that,' said Ed, from the co-pilot's seat. 'Way down there. Flak!'

'What's our altitude?' asked Dr. Tod.

'Right on fifty-eight thousand feet,' said Fred. 'Target?'

Ed sighted, checked a map. 'Sixteen miles straight ahead. You sure called those wind currents just right, Doctor Tod.'

They had sent him to an airfield outside Washington, D.C., to wait. That way he would be within range of most of the major East Coast cities.

He had spent part of the day reading, part asleep, and the rest of it talking over the war with some of the other pilots. Most of them, though, were too new to have fought in any but the closing days of the war.

Most of them were jet pilots, like him, who had done their training in P-59 Airacomets or P-80 Shooting Stars. A few of those in the ready room belonged to a P-51 prop-job squadron. There was a bit of tension between the blowtorch jockeys and the piston eaters.

All of them were a new breed, though. Already there was talk Truman was going to make the Army Air Force into a separate branch, just the Air Force, within the next year. Jetboy felt, at nineteen, that time had passed him by.

'They're working on something,' said one of the pilots, 'that'll go through the sonic wall. Bell's behind it.'

'A friend of mine out at Muroc says wait till they get the Flying Wing in operation. They're already working on an alljet version of it. A bomber that can go thirteen thousand miles at five hundred per, carries a crew of thirteen, bunk beds for seven, can stay up for a day and a half!' said another.

'Anybody know anything about this alert?' asked a very young, nervous guy with second-looie bars. 'The Russians up to something?'

'I heard we were going to Greece,' said someone. 'Ouzo for me, gallons of it.'

'More like Czech potato-peel vodka. We'll be lucky if we see Christmas.'

Jetboy realized he missed ready-room banter more than he had thought.

The intercom hissed on and a klaxon began to wail. Jetboy looked at his watch. It was 2:25 P.M.

He realized he missed something 'more than Air Corps badinage. That was flying. Now it all came back to him. When he had flown down to Washington the night before it had been just a routine hop.

Now was different. It was like wartime again. He had a vector. He had a target. He had a mission.

He also had on an experimental Navy T-2 pressure suit. It was a girdle manufacturer's dream, all rubber and laces, pressure bottles, and a real space helmet, like out of Planet Comics, over his head. They had fitted him for it the night before, when they saw his high-altitude wings and drop tanks on the plane.

'We'd better tailor this down for you,' the flight sergeant had said.

'I've got a pressurized cabin,' said Jetboy.

'Well, in case they need you, and in case something goes wrong, then.'

The suit was still too tight, and it wasn't pressurized yet. The arms were built for a gorilla, and the chest for a chimpanzee. 'You'll appreciate the extra room if that thing ever inflates in an emergency,' said the sergeant.

'You're the boss,' said Jetboy.

They'd even painted the torso white and the legs red to match his outfit. His blue helmet and goggles showed through the clear plastic bubble.

As he climbed with the rest of the squadron, he was glad now that he had the thing. His mission was to accompany the flight of P-80s in, and to engage only if needed. He had never exactly been a team player.

The sky ahead was blue as the background curtain in Bronzino's *Venus, Cupid, Folly and Time,* with a two-fifths cloud to the north. The sun stood over his left shoulder. The squadron angled up. He wigwagged the wings. They spread out in a staggered box and cleared their guns.

Chunder chunder chunder chunder went his 20mm cannons.

Tracers arced out ahead from the six .50 cals on each P-80. They left the prop planes far behind and pointed their noses toward Manhattan.

They looked like a bunch of angry bees circling under a hawk.

The sky was filled with jets and prop fighters climbing like the wall clouds of a hurricane.

Above was a lumpy object that hung and moved slowly on toward the city. Where the eye of the hurricane would be was a torrent of flak, thicker than Jetboy had ever seen over Europe or Japan.

It was bursting far too low, only at the level of the highest fighters.

Fighter Control called them. 'Clark Gable Command to all squadrons. Target at five five zero ... repeat, five five zero angels. Moving ENE at two five knots. Flak unable to reach.'

'Call it off,' said the squadron leader. 'We'll try to fly high enough for deflection shooting. Squadron Hodiak, follow me.' Jetboy looked up into the high blue above. The object continued its slow track.

'What's it got?' he asked Clark Gable Command.

'Command to Jetboy. Some type of bomb is what we've been

told. It has to be a lighter-than-air craft of at least five hundred thousand cubic feet to reach that altitude. Over.'

'I'm beginning a climb. If the other planes can't reach it, call them off, too.'

There was silence on the radio, then, 'Roger.'

As the P-80s glinted like silver crucifixes above him, he eased the nose up.

'Come on, baby,' he said. 'Let's do some flying.'

◆

The Shooting Stars began to fall away, sideslipping in the thin air. Jetboy could hear only the sound of his own pressure-breathing in his ears, and the high thin whine of his engines. 'Come on, girl,' he said. 'You can make it!'

The thing above him had resolved itself into a bastard aircraft: made of half a dozen blimps, with a gondola below it. The gondola looked as if it had once been a PT boat shell. That was all he could see. Beyond it, the air was purple and cold. Next stop, outer space.

The last of the P-80s slid sideways on the blue stairs of the sky. A few had made desultory firing runs, some snap-rolling as fighters used to do underneath bombers in the war. They fired as they nosed up. All their tracers fell away under the balloons. One of the P-80s fought for control, dropping two miles before leveling out.

Jetboy's plane protested, whining. It was hard to control. He eased the nose up again, had to fight it.

'Get everybody out of the way,' he said to Clark Gable Command.

'Here's where we give you some fighting room,' he said to his plane. He blew the drop tanks. They fell away like bombs behind him. He pushed his cannon button. *Chunder chunder chunder chunder* they went. Then again and again.

His tracers arced toward the target, then they too fell away. He fired four more bursts until his cannon ran dry. Then he cleaned out the twin fifties in the tail, but it didn't take long for all one hundred rounds to be spent.

He nosed over and went into a shallow dive, like a salmon sounding to throw a hook, gaining speed. A minute into the run he nosed up, putting the JB-1 into a long circling climb. 'Feels better, huh?' he asked.

The engines bit into the air. The plane, relieved of the weight, lurched up and ahead.

Below him was Manhattan with its seven million people. They must be watching down there, knowing these might be the last things they ever saw. Maybe this is what living in the Atomic Age would be like, always be looking up and thinking, *is this it?*

Jetboy reached down with one of his boots and slammed a lever over. A 75mm cannon shell slid into the breech. He put his hand on the autoload bar, and pulled back a little more on the control wheel.

The red jet cut the air like a razor.

He was closer now, closer than the others had gotten, and still not close enough. He only had five rounds to do the job. The jet climbed, beginning to stagger in the thin air, as if it were some red animal clawing its way up a long blue tapestry that slipped a little each time the animal lurched.

He pointed the nose up. Everything seemed frozen, waiting.

A long thin line of machine-gun tracers reached out from the gondola for him like a lover.

He began to fire his cannon.

FROM THE STATEMENT OF PATROLMAN
FRANCIS V ('FRANCIS THE TALKING COP') O'HOOEY,
SEPT. 15, 1946, 6:45 P.M.

We was watching from the street over at Sixth Avenue, trying to get people from shoving each other in a panic. Then they calmed down as they was watching the dogfights and stuff up above.

Some birdwatcher had this pair of binocs, so I confiscated 'em. I watched pretty much the whole thing. Them jets wasn't having no luck, and the antiaircraft from over in the Bowery wasn't doing no good either. I still say the Army oughta be sued 'cause them Air Defense guys got so panicky they forgot to set the timers on them shells and I heard that some of them came down in the Bronx and blew up a whole block of apartments.

Anyway, this red plane, that is, Jetboy's plane, was climbing up and he fired all his bullets, I thought, without doing any damage to the balloon thing.

I was out on the street, and this fire truck pulls up with its sirens on, and the whole precinct and auxiliaries were on it, and the lieutenant was yelling for me to climb on, we'd been assigned to the west side to take care of a traffic smash-up and a riot.

So I jump on the truck, and I try to keep my eyes on what's happening up in the skies.

The riot was pretty much over. The air-raid sirens was still wailing, but everybody was just standing around gawking at what was happening up there.

The lieutenant yells to at least get the people in the buildings. I pushed a few in some doors, then I took another gander in the field glasses.

I'll be damned if Jetboy hasn't shot up some of the balloons (I hear he used his howitzer on 'em) and the thing looks bigger – it's dropping some. But he's out of ammo and not as high as the thing is and he starts circlin'.

I forgot to say, all the time this blimp thing is got so many machine guns going it looks like a Fourth of July sparkler, and Jetboy's plane's taking these hits all the time.

Then he just takes his plane around and comes right back and crashes right into the what-you-call-it-the gondola, that's it, on the blimps. They just sort of merged together. He must have been going awful slow by then, like stalling, and the plane just sort of mashed into the side of the thing.

And the blimp deal looked like it was coming down a little, not a lot, just some. Then the lieutenant took the glasses away from me, and I shaded my eyes and watched as best I could.

There was this flare of light. I thought the whole thing had blown up at first, and I ducked up under a car. But when I looked up the blimps was still there.

'Look out! Get inside!' yelled the lieutenant. Everybody had another panic then, and was jumping under cars and around stuff and through windows. It looked like a regular Three Stooges for a minute or two.

A few minutes later, it rained red airplane parts all over the streets, and a bunch on the Hudson Terminal ...

There was steam and fire all around. The cockpit cracked like an egg, and the wings folded up like a fan. Jetboy jerked as the capstans in the pressure suit inflated. He was curved into a circle, and must have looked like a frightened tomcat.

The gondola walls had parted like a curtain where the fighter's wings crumpled into it. A wave of frost formed over the shattered cockpit as oxygen blew out of the gondola.

Jetboy tore his hoses loose. His bailout bottle had five minutes of air in it. He grappled with the nose of the plane, like fighting against iron bands on his arms and legs. All you were supposed to be able to do in these suits was eject and pull the D-ring on your parachute.

The plane lurched like a freight elevator with a broken cable. Jetboy grabbed a radar antenna with one gloved hand, felt it snap away from the broken nose of the plane. He grabbed another.

The city was twelve miles below him, the buildings making the island look like a faraway porcupine. The left engine of his plane, crumpled and spewing fuel, tore loose and flew under the gondola. He watched it grow smaller.

The air was purple as a plum – the skin of the blimps bright as fire in the sunlight, and the sides of the gondola bent and torn like cheap cardboard.

The whole thing shuddered like a whale.

Somebody flew by over Jetboy's head through the hole in the metal, trailing hoses like the arms of an octopus. Debris followed through the air in the explosive decompression.

The jet sagged.

Jetboy thrust his hand into the torn side of the gondola, found a strut.

He felt his parachute harness catch on the radar array. The plane twisted. He felt its weight.

He jerked his harness snap. His parachute packs were ripped away from him, tearing at his back and crotch.

His plane bent in the middle like a snake with a broken back, then dropped away, the wings coming up and touching above the shattered cockpit as if it were a dove trying to beat its pinions. Then it twisted sideways, falling to pieces.

Below it was the dot of the man who had fallen out of the gondola, spinning like a yard sprinkler toward the bright city below.

Jetboy saw the plane fall away beneath his feet. He hung in space twelve miles up by one hand.

He gripped his right wrist with his left hand, chinned himself up until he got a foot through the side, then punched his way in.

There were two people left inside. One was at the controls, the other stood in the center behind a large round thing. He was pushing a cylinder into a slot in it. There was a shattered machine-gun turret on one side of the gondola.

Jetboy reached for the service .38 strapped across his chest. It was agony reaching for it, agony trying to run toward the guy with the fuse.

They wore diving suits. The suits were inflated. They looked like ten or twelve beach balls stuffed into suits of long underwear. They were moving as slowly as he was.

Jetboy's hands closed in a claw over the handle of the .38. He jerked it from its holster.

It flew out of his hand, bounced off the ceiling, and went out through the hole he had come in.

The guy at the controls got off one shot at him. He dived toward the other man, the one with the fuse.

His hand clamped on the diving-suited wrist of the other just as the man pushed the cylindrical fuse into the side of the round canister. Jetboy saw that the whole device sat on a hinged doorplate.

The man had only half a face – Jetboy saw smooth metal on one side through the grid-plated diving helmet.

The man twisted the fuse with both hands.

Through the torn ceiling of the pilot-house, Jetboy saw another blimp begin to deflate. There was a falling sensation. They were dropping toward the city.

Jetboy gripped the fuse with both hands. Their helmets clanged together as the ship lurched.

The guy at the controls was putting on a parachute harness and heading toward the rent in the wall.

Another shudder threw Jetboy and the man with the fuse together. The guy reached for the door lever behind him as best he could in the bulky suit.

Jetboy grabbed his hands and pulled him back.

They slammed together, draped over the canister, their hands entangled on each other's suits and the fuse to the bomb. The man tried again to reach the lever. Jetboy pulled him away. The canister rolled like a giant beach ball as the gondola listed.

He looked directly into the eye of the man in the diving suit. The man used his feet to push the canister back over the bomb door. His hand went for the lever again.

Jetboy gave the fuse a half-twist the other way.

The man in the diving suit reached behind him. He came up with a .45 automatic. He jerked a heavy gloved hand away from the fuse, worked the slide. Jetboy saw the muzzle swing at him.

'Die, Jetboy! Die!' said the man. He pulled the trigger four times.

STATEMENT OF PATROLMAN FRANCIS V O'HOOEY,
SEPT. 15, 1946, 6:45 P.M. (CONTINUED).

So when the pieces of metal quit falling, we all ran out and looked up.

I saw the white dot below the blimp thing. I grabbed the binocs away from the lieutenant.

Sure enough, it was a parachute. I hoped it was.

Jetboy had bailed out when his plane crashed into the thing.

I don't know much about such stuff, but I do know that you don't open a parachute that high up or you get in serious trouble.

Then, while I was watching, the blimps and stuff all blew up, all at once. Like they was there, then there was this explosion, and there was only smoke and stuff way up in the air.

The people all around started cheering. The kid had done it

– he'd blown the thing up before it could drop the A-bomb on Manhattan Island.

Then the lieutenant said to get in the truck, we'd try to get the kid.

We jumped in and tried to figure out where he was gonna land. Everywhere we passed, people was standing in the middle of the car wrecks and fires and stuff, looking up and cheering the parachute.

I noticed the big smudge in the air after the explosion, when we'd been driving around for ten minutes. Them other jets that had been with Jetboy was back, flying all around trough the air, and some Mustangs and Thunderjugs, too. It was like a regular air show up there. Somehow we got out near the Bridge before anybody else did. Good thing, because when we got to the water, we saw this guy pile right in about twenty feet from shore. Went down like a rock. He was wearing this diving-suit thing, and we swam out and I grabbed part of the parachute and a fireman grabbed some of the hoses and we hauled him out onto shore.

Well, it wasn't Jetboy, it was the one we got the make on as Edward 'Smooth Eddy' Shiloh, a real small-time operator.

And he was in bad shape, too. We got a wrench off the fire truck and popped his helmet, and he was purple as a turnip in there. It had taken him twenty-seven minutes to get to the ground. He'd passed out of course with not enough air up there, and he was so frostbit I heard they had to take off one of his feet and all but the thumb on the left hand.

But he'd jumped out of the thing before it blew. We looked back up, hoping to see Jetboy's chute or something, but there wasn't one, just that misty big smudge up there, and all those planes zoomin' round.

Thirty Minutes Over Broadway!

We took Shiloh to the hospital. That's my report.

STATEMENT OF EDWARD 'SMOOTH EDDY' SHILOH,
SEPT. 16, 1946 (EXCERPT).

... all five shells into a couple of the gasbags. Then he crashed the plane right into us. The walls blew. Fred and Filmore were thrown out without their parachutes.

When the pressure dropped, I felt like I couldn't move, the suit got so tight. I tried to get my parachute. I see that Doctor Tod has the fuse and is making it to the bomb thing.

I felt the airplane fall off the side of the gondola. Next thing I know, Jetboy's standing right in front of the hole his plane made.

I pull out my roscoe when I see he's packing heat. But he dropped his gat and he heads toward Tod.

'Stop him, stop him!' Tod's yelling over the suit radio. I get one clean shot, but I miss, then he's on top of Tod and the bomb, and right then I decide my job's been over about five minutes and I'm not getting paid any overtime.'

So I head out, and all this gnashing and screaming's coming across the radio, and they're grappling around. Then Tod yells and pulls out his .45 and I swear he put four shots in Jetboy from closer than I am to you. Then they fall back together, and I jumped out the hole in the side.

Only I was stupid, and I pulled my ripcord too soon, and my chute don't open right and got all twisted, and I started passing out. Just before I did, the whole thing blew up above me.

Next thing I know, I wake up here, and I got one shoe too many, know what I mean? …

… what did they say? Well, most of it was garbled. Let's see. Tod says 'Stop him, stop him,' and I shot. Then I lammed for the hole. They were yelling. I could only hear Jetboy when their helmets slammed together, through Tod's suit radio. They must have crashed together a lot, 'cause I heard both of them breathing hard.

Then Tod got to the gun and shot Jetboy four times and said 'Die, Jetboy! Die!' and I jumped and they must have fought a second, and I heard Jetboy say:

'I can't die yet. I haven't seen *The Jolson Story*.'

It was eight years to the day after Thomas Wolfe died, but it was his kind of day. Across the whole of America and the northern hemisphere, it was one of those days when summer gives up its hold, when the weather comes from the poles and Canada again, rather than the Gulf and the Pacific.

They eventually built a monument to Jetboy – 'the kid that couldn't die yet.' A battle-scarred veteran of nineteen had stopped a madman from blowing up Manhattan. After calmer heads prevailed, they realized that. But it took a while to remember that. And to get around to going back to college, or buying that new refrigerator. It took a long time for anybody to remember what anything was like before September 15, 1946.

When people in New York City looked up and saw Jetboy blowing up the attacking aircraft, they thought their troubles were over.

They were as wrong as snakes on an eight-lane highway.

> – Daniel Deck
> *Godot Is My Co-Pilot:*
> *A Life of Jetboy*
> Lippincott, 1963

From high up in the sky the fine mist began to curve downward.

Part of it stretched itself out in the winds, as it went through the jet stream, toward the east.

Beneath those currents, the mist re-formed and hung like virga, settling slowly to the city below, streamers forming and re-forming, breaking like scud near a storm.

Wherever it came down, it made a sound like gentle autumn rain.

THE SLEEPER

by Roger Zelazny

I. THE LONG WALK HOME

He was fourteen years old when sleep became his enemy, a dark and terrible thing he learned to fear as others feared death. It was not, however, a matter of neurosis in any of its more mysterious forms. A neurosis generally possesses irrational elements, while his fear proceeded from a specific cause and followed a course as logical as a geometrical theorem.

Not that there was no irrationality in his life. Quite the contrary. But this was a result, not the cause, of his condition. At least, this is what he told himself later.

Simply put, sleep was his bane, his nemesis. It was his hell on an installment plan.

Croyd Crenson had completed eight grades of school and didn't make it through the ninth. This was not because of any fault of his own. While not at the top of his class he was not at the bottom either. He was an average kid of average build, freckly-faced, with blue eyes and straight brown hair. He had liked to play war games with his friends until the real war ended; then they played cops and robbers more and more often. When it was war he had waited – not too patiently – for his chance to be the ace fighter pilot, Jetboy; after the war, in cops and robbers, he was usually a robber.

He'd started ninth grade, but like many others he never got through the first month: September 1946 ...

'What are you looking at?'

He remembered Miss Marston's question but not her expression, because he didn't turn away from the spectacle. It was not uncommon for kids in his class to glance out the window with increasing frequency once three o'clock came within believable distance. It *was* uncommon for them not to turn away quickly, though, when addressed, feigning a final bout of attention while awaiting the dismissal bell.

Instead, he had replied, 'The blimps.'

In that three other boys and two girls who also had a good line of sight were looking in the same direction, Miss Marston – her own curiosity aroused – crossed to the window. She halted there and stared.

They were quite high – five or six of them, it seemed – tiny things at the end of an alleyway of cloud, moving as if linked together. And there was an airplane in the vicinity, making a rapid pass at them. Black-and-white memories of flashing newsreels, still fresh, came to mind. It actually looked as if the plane were attacking the silver minnows.

Miss Marston watched for several moments, then turned away.

'All right, class,' she began. 'It's only—'

Then the sirens sounded. Involuntarily, Miss Marston felt her shoulders rise and tighten.

'Air raid!' called a girl named Charlotte in the first row.

'Is not,' said Jimmy Walker, teeth braces flashing. 'They don't have them anymore. The war's over.'

'I know what they sound like,' Charlotte said. 'Every time there was a blackout—'

'But there's no more war,' Bobby Tremson stated.

'That will be enough, class,' Miss Marston said. 'Perhaps they're testing them.'

But she looked back out the window and saw a small flash of fire in the sky before a reef of cloud blocked her view of the aerial conflict.

'Stay in your seats,' she said then, as several students had risen and were moving toward the window. 'I'm going to check in the office and see whether there's a drill that hadn't been announced. I'll be right back. You may talk if you do it quietly.'

She departed, banging the door behind her. Croyd continued to stare at the cloud screen, waiting for it to part again.

'It's Jetboy,' he said to Bobby Tremson, across the aisle.

'Aw, c'mon,' Bobby said. 'What would he be doing up there? The war's over.'

'It's a jet plane. I've seen it in newsreels, and that's how it goes. And he's got the best one.'

'You're just making that up,' Liza called from the rear of the room.

Croyd shrugged.

'There's somebody bad up there, and he's fighting them,' he said. 'I saw the fire. There's shooting.'

The sirens continued to wail. From the street outside came the sound of screeching brakes, followed by the brief hoot of an auto horn and the dull thud of collision.

'Accident!' Bobby called, and everyone was getting up and moving to the window.

Croyd rose then, not wanting his view blocked; and because he was near he found a good spot. He did not look at the accident, however, but continued to stare upward.

'Caved in his trunk,' Joe Sarzanno said.

'What?' a girl asked.

Croyd heard the distant booming sounds now. The plane was no longer in sight.

'What's the noise?' Bobby asked.

'Anti-aircraft fire,' Croyd said.

'You're nuts!'

'They're trying to shoot the things down, whatever they are.'

'Yeah. Sure. Just like in the movies.'

The clouds began to close again. But as they did, Croyd thought that he glimpsed the jet once more, sweeping in on a collision course with the blimps. His view was blocked then, before he could be sure.

'Damn!' he said. 'Get 'em, Jetboy!'

Bobby laughed and Croyd shoved him, hard.

'Hey! Watch who you're pushing!'

Croyd turned toward him, but Bobby did not seem to want to pursue the matter. He was looking out of the window again, pointing.

'Why are all those people running?'

'I don't know.'

'Is it the accident?'

'Naw.'

'Look! There's another!'

A blue Studebaker had swung rapidly about the corner, swerved to miss the two stopped vehicles, and clipped an oncoming Ford. Both cars were turned at an angle. Other vehicles braked and halted to avoid colliding with them. Several horns began to sound. The muffled noises of anti-aircraft fire continued within the wail of sirens. People were rushing along the streets now, not even pausing to regard the accidents.

'Do you think the war started again?' Charlotte asked.

'I don't know,' Leo said.

The sound of a police siren was suddenly mixed with the other noises.

'Jeez!' Bobby said. 'Here comes another!'

Before he finished speaking a Pontiac had run into the rear of one of the stopped vehicles. Three pairs of drivers confronted each other on foot; one couple angrily, the others simply talking and occasionally pointing upward. Shortly, they all departed and hurried off along the street.

'This is no drill,' Joe said.

'I know,' Croyd answered, staring at the area where a cloud had grown pink from the brightness it masked. 'I think it's something real bad.'

He moved back from the window.

'I'm going home now,' he said.

'You'll get in trouble,' Charlotte told him.

He glanced at the clock.

'I'll bet the bell rings before she gets back,' he answered. 'If you don't go now I don't think they'll let you go with whatever that is going on – and I want to go home.'

He turned away and crossed to the door.

'I'm going, too,' Joe said.

'You'll both get in trouble.'

They passed along the hallway. As they neared the front door an adult voice, masculine, called out from up the hall, 'You two! Come back here!'

Croyd ran, shouldered open the big green door, and kept going. Joe was only a step behind him as he descended the steps. The street was full of stopped cars now, for as far as he could see in either direction. There were people on the tops of buildings and people at every window, most of them looking upward.

He rushed to the sidewalk and turned right. His home was six blocks to the south, in an anomalous group of row houses in the eighties. Joe's route took him half that way, then off to the east.

Before they reached the corner they were halted as a stream of people flowed from the side street to the right, cutting into their line of pedestrian traffic, some turning north and trying to push through, others heading south. The boys heard cursing and the sound of a fistfight from up ahead.

Joe reached out and tugged at a man's sleeve. The man jerked his arm away, then looked down.

'What's happening?' Joe shouted.

'Some kind of bomb,' the man answered. 'Jetboy tried to stop the guys who had it. I think they were all blown up. The thing might go off any minute. Maybe atomic.'

'Where'd it fall?' Croyd yelled.

The man gestured to the northwest.

'That way.'

Then the man was gone, having seen an opening and pushed his way through.

'Croyd, we can get past on the street if we go over the hood of that car,' Joe said.

Croyd nodded and followed the other boy across the still-warm hood of a gray Dodge. The driver swore at them, but his door was blocked by the press of bodies and the door on the passenger side could only open a few inches before hitting the fender of a taxi. They made their way around the cab and passed through the intersection at its middle, traversing two more cars on the way.

Pedestrian traffic eased near to the center of the next block, and it looked as if there was a large open area ahead. They sprinted toward it, then halted abruptly.

A man lay upon the pavement. He was having convulsions. His head and hands had swollen enormously, and they were dark red, almost purple in color. Just as they caught sight of him, blood began to rush from his nose and mouth; it trickled from his ears, it oozed from his eyes and about his fingernails.

'Holy Mary!' Joe said, crossing himself as he drew back. 'What's he got?'

'I don't know,' Croyd answered. 'Let's not get too close. Let's go over some more cars.'

It took them ten minutes to reach the next corner. Somewhere along the way they noticed that the guns had been silent for a long time, though the air-raid sirens, police sirens, and auto horns maintained a steady din.

'I smell smoke,' Croyd said.

'Me, too. If something's burning no fire truck's going to get to it.'

'Whole damn town could burn down.'

'Maybe it's not all like this.'

'Bet it is.'

They pushed ahead, were caught in a press of bodies and swept about the corner.

'We're not going this way!' Croyd yelled.

But it did not matter, as the mass of people about them was halted seconds later.

'Think we can crawl through to the street and go over cars again?' Joe asked.

'Might as well try.'

They made it. Only this time, as they worked their way back toward the corner it was slower, as others were taking the same route. Croyd saw a reptilian face through a windshield then, and scaly hands clutching at a steering wheel that had been torn loose from its column as the driver slowly slumped to the side. Looking away, he saw a rising tower of smoke from beyond buildings to the northeast.

When they reached the corner there was no place to descend. People stood packed and swaying. There were occasional screams. He wanted to cry, but he knew it would do no good. He clenched his teeth and shuddered.

'What're we going to do?' he called to Joe.

'If we're stuck here overnight we can bust the window on an empty car and sleep in it, I guess.'

'I want to go home!'

'Me, too. Let's try and keep going as far as we can.'

They inched their way down the street for the better part of an hour, but only made another block. Drivers howled and pounded on windows as they climbed over the roofs of their cars. Other cars were empty. A few others contained things they did not like to look at. Sidewalk traffic looked dangerous now. It was fast and loud, with brief fights, numerous screams, and a number of fallen bodies which had been pushed into doorways or off the curb into the street. There had been a few seconds' hesitation and silence when the sirens had stopped. Then came the sound of someone speaking over a bullhorn. But it was too far away. The words were not distinguishable, except for 'bridges.' The panic resumed.

He saw a woman fall from a building across the street and up ahead, and he looked away before she hit. The smell of smoke was still in the air, but there were yet no signs of fire in the vicinity. Ahead, he saw the crowd halt and draw back as a person – man or woman, he could not tell – burst into flames in its midst. He slid to the road between two cars and waited till his friend came up.

'Joe, I'm scared shitless,' he said. 'Maybe we should just crawl under a car and wait till it's all over.'

'I've been thinking of that,' the other boy replied. 'But what if part of that burning building falls on a car and it catches fire?'

'What of it?'

'If it gets to the gas tank and it blows up they'll all go, this close together, like a string of firecrackers.'

'Jesus!'

'We've got to keep going. You can come to my place if it seems easier.'

Croyd saw a man perform a series of dancelike movements, tearing at his clothing. Then he began to change shape. Someone back up the road started howling. There came sounds of breaking glass.

During the next half-hour the sidewalk traffic thinned to what might, under other circumstances, be called normal. The people seemed either to have achieved their destinations or to have advanced their congestion to some other part of town. Those who passed now picked their way among corpses. Faces had vanished from behind windows. No one was in sight atop the buildings. The sounds of auto horns had diminished to sporadic outbursts. The boys stood on a corner. They had covered three blocks and crossed the street since they had left school.

'I turn here,' Joe said. 'You want to come with me or you going ahead?'

Croyd looked down the street.

'It looks better now. I think I can make it okay,' he said.

'I'll see you.'

'Okay.'

Joe hurried off to the left. Croyd watched him for a moment, then moved ahead. Far up the street, a man raced from a doorway screaming. He seemed to grow larger and his movements more erratic as he moved to the center of the street. Then he exploded. Croyd pressed his back against the brick wall to his left and stared, heart pounding, but there was no new disturbance. He heard the bullhorn again, from somewhere to the west, and this time its words were more clear: '... The bridges are closed to both auto and foot traffic. Do not attempt to use the bridges. Return to your homes. The bridges are closed ...'

He moved ahead again. A single siren wailed somewhere to the east. A low-flying airplane passed overhead. There was a crumpled body in a doorway to his left; he looked away and quickened his pace. He saw smoke across the street, and he looked for the flames and saw then that it rose from the body of a woman seated on a doorstep, her head in her hands. She seemed to shrink as he watched, then fell to her left with a rattling sound. He clenched his fists and kept going.

An Army truck rolled from the side street at the corner ahead of him. He ran to it. A helmeted face turned toward him from the passenger side.

'Why are you out, son?' the man asked.

'I'm going home,' he answered.

'Where's that?'

He pointed ahead.

'Two blocks,' he said.

'Go straight home,' the man told him.

'What's happening?'

'We're under martial law. Everybody's got to get indoors. Good idea to keep your windows closed, too.'

'Why?'

'It seems that was some kind of germ bomb that went off. Nobody knows for sure.'

'Was it Jetboy that …?'

'Jetboy's dead. He tried to stop them.'

Croyd's eyes were suddenly brimming.

'Go straight home.'

The truck crossed the street and continued on to the west. Croyd ran across and slowed when he reached the sidewalk. He began to shake. He was suddenly aware of the pain in his knees, where he had scraped them in crawling over vehicles. He wiped his eyes. He felt terribly cold. He halted near the middle of the block and yawned several times. Tired. He was incredibly tired. He began moving. His feet felt heavier than he ever remembered. He halted again beneath a tree. There came a moaning from overhead.

When he looked up he realized that it was not a tree. It was tall and brown, rooted and spindly, but there was an enormously elongated human face near its top and it was from there that the moaning came. As he moved away one of the limbs plucked at his shoulder, but it was a weak thing and a few more steps bore him out of its reach. He whimpered. The corner seemed miles away, and then there was another block ...

He had long yawning spells now, and the remade world had lost its ability to surprise him. So what if a man flew through the skies unaided? Or if a human-faced puddle lay in the gutter to his right? More bodies ... An overturned car ... A pile of ashes ... Hanging telephone lines ...

He trudged on to the corner. He leaned against the lamppost, then slowly slid down and sat with his back to it.

He wanted to close his eyes. But that was silly. He lived right over there. Just a bit more and he could sleep in his own bed.

He caught hold of the lamppost and dragged himself to his feet. One more crossing ...

He made it onto his block, his vision swimming. Just a little farther. He could see the door ...

He heard the sliding, grating sound of a window opening, heard his name called from overhead. He looked up. It was Ellen, the neighbors' little girl, looking down at him.

'I'm sorry your daddy's dead,' she called.

He wanted to cry but he couldn't. The yawning took all of his strength. He leaned upon his door and rang the bell. The pocket with his key in it seemed so far away ...

When his brother Carl opened the door, he fell at his feet and found that he could not rise.

'I'm so tired,' he told him, and he closed his eyes.

II. THE KILLER AT THE HEART OF THE DREAM

Croyd's childhood vanished while he slept, that first Wild Card Day. Nearly four weeks passed before he awoke, and he was changed, as was the world about him. It was not just that he was a half-foot taller, stronger than he had thought anyone could be, and covered with fine red hair. He quickly discovered, also, as he regarded himself in the bathroom mirror, that the hair possessed peculiar properties. Repelled by its appearance, he wished that it were not red. Immediately, it began to fade until it was pale blond in color, and he felt a not-unpleasant tingling over the entire surface of his body.

Intrigued, he wished for it to turn green and it did. Again, the tingling, this time more like a wave of vibration sweeping over him. He willed himself black and he blackened. Then pale once more. Only this time he did not halt at light blond. Paler, paler; chalky, albino. Paler still ... What was the limit? He began to fade from sight. He could see the tiled wall behind him now, through his faint outline in the mirror. Paler ...

Gone.

He raised his hands before his face and saw nothing. He picked up his damp washcloth and held it to his chest. It, too, became transparent, was gone, though he still felt its wet presence.

He returned himself to pale blond. It seemed the most socially acceptable. Then he squeezed into what had been his loosest jeans and put on a green flannel shirt that he could not button all the way. The pants only reached to his shins now. Silently, he padded down the stairs on bare feet and made his way to the kitchen. He was ravenous. The hall clock told him that it was close to three. He had looked in on his mother, his brother, and his sister, but had not disturbed their slumber.

There was a half-loaf of bread in the breadbox and he tore it apart, stuffing great chunks into his mouth, barely chewing before he swallowed. He bit his finger at one point, which slowed him only slightly. He found a piece of meat and a wedge of cheese in the refrigerator and he ate them. He also drank a quart of milk. There were two apples on the countertop and he ate them as he searched the cupboards. A box of crackers. He munched them as he continued his search. Six cookies. He gulped them. A half-jar of peanut butter. He ate it with a spoon.

Nothing. He could find nothing more, and he was still terribly hungry.

Then the enormity of his feast struck him. There was no more food in the house. He remembered the mad afternoon of his return from school. What if there were a food shortage? What if they were back on rationing? He had just eaten everyone's food.

He had to get more, for the others as well as for himself. He went to the front room and looked out the window. The street was deserted. He wondered about the martial law he had heard of on the way home from school – how long ago? How long had he slept, anyway? He'd a feeling it had been a long while.

He unlocked the door and felt the coolness of the night. One of the unbroken streetlights shone through the bare branches of a nearby tree. There had still been a few leaves on the roadside trees on the afternoon of the troubles. He removed the spare key from the table in the hall, stepped outside, and locked the door behind him. The steps, which he knew must be cold, did not feel particularly chill on his bare feet.

He halted then, retreated into shadow. It was frightening, not knowing what was out there.

He raised his hands and held them up to the streetlight.

'Pale, pale, pale ...'

They faded until the light shone through them. They continued to fade. His body tingled.

When they were gone, he lowered his eyes. Nothing of him seemed to remain but the tingle.

Then he hurried up the street, a feeling of enormous energy within him. The odd, treelike being was gone from the next block. The streets were clear for traffic now, though there was considerable debris in the gutters and almost every parked vehicle he saw had sustained some damage. It seemed that every building he passed had at least one window blocked with cardboard or wood. Several roadside trees were now splintered stumps, and the metal signpost at the next corner was bent far to one side. He hurried, surprised at the rapidity of his progress, and when he reached his school he saw that it remained intact, save for a few missing panes of glass. He passed on.

Three grocery stores he came to were boarded up and displayed

CLOSED UNTIL FURTHER NOTICE signs. He broke into the third one. The boards offered very little resistance when he pushed against them. He located a light switch and threw it. Seconds later, he flipped it off. The place was a shambles. It had been thoroughly looted.

He proceeded uptown, passing the shells of several burned-out buildings. He heard voices – one gruff, one high and fluting – from within one of these. Moments later, there came a flash of white light and a scream. Simultaneous with this, a portion of a brick wall collapsed, spilling across the sidewalk at his back. He saw no reason to investigate. It also seemed on occasion that he heard voices from beneath sewer gratings.

He wandered for miles that night, not becoming aware until he was nearing Times Square that he was being followed. At first he thought that it was simply a large dog moving in the same direction he was headed. But when it drew nearer and he noted the human lines to its features, he halted and faced it. It sat down at a distance of about ten feet and regarded him.

'You're one, too,' it growled.

'You can see me?'

'No. Smell.'

'What do you want?'

'Food.'

'Me, too.'

'I'll show you where. For a cut.'

'Okay. Show me.'

It led him to a roped-off area where Army trucks were parked. Croyd counted ten of them. Uniformed figures stood or rested among them.

'What's going on?' Croyd asked.

'Talk later. Food packages in the four trucks to the left.'

It was no problem to pass the perimeter, enter the rear of a vehicle, gather an armload of packages, and withdraw in the other direction. He and the dog-man retreated to a doorway two blocks away. Croyd phased back to visibility and they proceeded to gorge themselves.

Afterward, his new acquaintance – who wished to be called Bentley – told him of the events during the weeks following Jetboy's death, while Croyd had slept. Croyd learned of the rush to Jersey, of the rioting, of the martial law, of the Takisians, and of the ten thousand deaths their virus had caused. And he heard of the transformed survivors – the lucky ones and the unlucky ones.

'You're a lucky one,' Bentley concluded.

'I don't feel lucky,' Croyd said.

'At least you stayed human.'

'So, have you been to see that Doctor Tachyon yet?'

'No. He's been so damn busy. I will, though.'

'I should, too.'

'Maybe.'

'What do you mean, "maybe"?'

'Why should you want to change? You got it made. You can have whatever you want.'

'You mean stealing?'

'Times are tough. You get by however you can.'

'Maybe so.'

'I can put you on to some clothes that will fit you.'

'Where?'

'Just around the corner.'

'Okay.'

It was not difficult for Croyd to break into the rear of the clothing store to which Bentley led him. He faded again after that and returned for another load of food parcels. Bentley padded beside him as he headed home.

'Mind if I keep you company?'

'No.'

'I want to see where you live. I can put you on to lots of good things.'

'Yeah?'

'I'd like a friend who can keep me fed. Think we can work something out?'

'Yes.'

♦

69

In the days that followed, Croyd became his family's provider. His older brother and sister did not ask whence he acquired the food or, finally, the money he obtained with seeming facility during his nightly absences. Neither did his mother, distracted in her grief over his father's death, think to inquire. Bentley – who slept somewhere in the neighborhood – became his guide and mentor in these enterprises, as well as his confidant in other matters.

'Maybe I should see that doctor you mentioned,' Croyd said, lowering the case of canned goods he had removed from a warehouse and perching himself upon it.

'Tachyon?' Bentley asked, stretching himself in an undoglike fashion.

'Yeah.'

'What's wrong?'

'I can't sleep. It's been five days since I woke up this way, and I haven't slept at all since then.'

'So? What's wrong with that? More time to do what you want.'

'But I'm finally starting to get tired and I still can't sleep.'

'It'll catch up with you in time. Not worth bothering Tachyon over. Anyway, if he tries to cure you your chances are only like one in three or four.'

'How do you know that?'

'I went to see him.'

'Oh?'

Croyd ate an apple. Then, 'You going to try it?' he asked.

'If I can get up the nerve,' Bentley answered. 'Who wants to spend his life as a dog? And not a very good dog, at that. By the way, when we go past a pet shop I want you to break in and get me a flea collar.'

'Sure. I wonder ... If I do go to sleep, will I sleep a long time like before?'

Bentley tried to shrug, gave up.

'Who knows?'

'Who'll take care of my family? Who'll take care of you?'

'I see the point. If you stop coming out nights, I guess I wait awhile and then go and try the cure. For your family, you'd better pick up a bunch of money. Things will loosen up again, and money always talks.'

'You're right.'

'You're damn strong. Think you could tear open a safe?'

'Maybe. I don't know.'

'We'll try one on the way home, too. I know a good place.'

'Okay.'

'... And some flea powder.'

It was getting on toward morning, as he sat reading and eating, that he began to yawn uncontrollably. When he rose there was a certain heaviness to his limbs that had not been present earlier. He climbed the stairs and entered Carl's room. He shook his brother by the shoulder until he awoke.

'Whassamatter, Croyd?' he asked.

'I'm sleepy.'

'So go to bed.'

'It's been a long time. Maybe I'll sleep a long time again, too.'

'Oh.'

'So here's some money, to take care of everybody in case that's what happens.'

He opened the top drawer of Carl's dresser and stuffed a huge wad of bills in under the socks.

'Uh, Croyd ... Where'd you get all that money?'

'None of your business. Go back to sleep.'

He made it to his room, undressed, and crawled into bed. He felt very cold.

When he awoke there was frost on the windowpanes. When he looked outside he saw that there was snow on the ground beneath a leaden sky. His hand on the sill was wide and swarthy, the fingers short and thick.

Examining himself in the bathroom, he discovered that he was about five and a half feet tall, powerfully built, with dark hair and eyes, and that he possessed hard scarlike ridges on the front of his legs, the outside of his arms, across his shoulders, down his back, and up his neck. It took him another fifteen minutes to learn that he could raise the temperature of his hand to the point where the towel he was holding caught fire. It was only a few more minutes before he discovered that he could generate heat all over, until his entire body glowed – though he felt badly about the footprint that had burned into the linoleum, and the hole his other foot made in the throw rug.

This time, there was plenty of food in the kitchen, and he ate steadily for over an hour before his hunger pangs were eased. He'd put on sweatpants and a sweatshirt, reflecting on the variety of clothing he would have to keep about if he were going to change in form each time that he slept.

There was no pressure on him this time to forage for food. The enormous number of deaths that had occurred following the release of the virus had resulted in a surplus in local warehouses, and the stores were open again with distribution routines back to normal.

His mother was spending most of her time in church, and Carl and Claudia were back in school, which had reopened recently. Croyd knew that he would not be returning to school himself. The money supply was still good, but on reflecting that he had slept nine days longer this time than he had on the previous occasion he felt it would be a good idea to have some extra cash on hand. He wondered whether he could heat a hand sufficiently to burn through the metal door of a safe. He had had a very hard time tearing open that one – had almost given up, actually – and Bentley had assured him that it was a 'tin can.' He went outside and practiced on a piece of galvanized pipe.

He tried to plan the job carefully, but his judgment was bad. He had to open eight safes that week before he obtained much in the way of money. Most of them just held papers. He knew that he set off alarms also, and this made him nervous; he hoped that his fingerprints changed too when he slept. He worked as quickly as he could and wished that Bentley were back. The dog-man would have known what to do, he felt. He had hinted on several occasions that his normal occupation had involved something somewhat less than legal.

The days passed more quickly than he would have wished. He purchased a large, all-purpose wardrobe. Nights, he walked the city, observing the signs of damage that still remained and the progress of repair work. He caught up on the news, of the city, the world. It was not hard to believe in a man from outer space when the results of his virus were all about him. He asked a bullet-domed man with webbed fingers where he might find Dr. Tachyon. The man gave him an address and a phone number. He kept them in his wallet and did not call or visit. What if the doctor examined him, told him there was no problem, and cured him? Nobody else in the family was able to make a living at this point.

The day came when his appetite peaked again, which he felt might mean that his body was getting ready for another change. This time, he observed his feelings more carefully, for future reference. It took him the rest of that day and night and part of the next day before the chills came and the waves of drowsiness began. He left a note saying good night to the others, for they were out when the feeling began to overwhelm him. And this time he locked his bedroom door, for he had learned that they had observed him regularly as he slept, had even brought in a doctor at one point – a woman who had prudently recommended that they simply let him sleep, once she learned his case history. She had also suggested that he see Dr. Tachyon when he awoke, but his mother had misplaced the paper on which she had written this. Mrs. Crenson's mind seemed to wander often these days.

He had the dream again – and this time he realized that it was *again* – and this was the first time that he remembered it: The apprehension was reminiscent of his feelings on the day of his last return home from school. He was walking down what seemed an empty twilit street. Something stirred behind him and he turned and looked back. People were emerging from doorways, windows, automobiles, manholes, and all of them were staring at him, moving toward him. He continued on his way and there came something like a collective sigh at his back. When he looked again they were all hurrying after him in a menacing fashion, expressions of hatred on their faces. He began to run, with a certainty that they intended his destruction. They pursued him ...

When he awoke he was hideous, and he had no special powers. He was hairless, snouted, and covered with gray-green scales; his fingers were elongated and possessed of extra joints, his eyes yellow and slitted; he developed pains in his thighs and lower back if he stood upright for too long. It was far easier to go about his room on all fours. When he exclaimed aloud over his condition there was a pronounced sibilance to his speech.

It was early evening, and he heard voices from downstairs. He opened the door and called out, and Claudia and Carl both hurried to his room. He opened the door the barest crack and remained behind it.

'Croyd! Are you all right?' Carl asked.

'Yes and no,' he hissed. 'I'll be okay. Right now I'm starving. Bring me food. Lots of it.'

'What's the matter?' Claudia asked. 'Why won't you come out?'

'Later! Talk later. Food now!'

He refused to leave his room or to let his family see him. They brought him food, magazines, newspapers. He listened to the radio and paced, quadrupedally. This time, sleep was something to be courted rather than feared. He lay back on the bed, hoping it would come soon. But it was denied him for the better part of a week.

The next time he woke he found himself slightly over six feet tall, dark-haired, slim, and not unpleasantly featured. He was as strong as he had been on earlier occasions, but after a while he concluded that he possessed no special powers – until he slipped on the stair in his rush to the kitchen and saved himself by levitating.

Later, he noticed a note in Claudia's handwriting, tacked to his door. It gave a phone number and told him he could reach Bentley there. He put it in his wallet. He'd another call to make first.

Dr. Tachyon looked up at him and smiled faintly.

'It could be worse,' he said.

Croyd was almost amused at the judgment.

'How?' he asked.

'Well, you could have drawn a joker.'

'Just what did I draw, sir?'

'Yours is one of the most interesting cases I've seen so far. In all of the others it's simply run its course and either killed the person or changed him – for better or worse. With you— Well, the nearest analogy is an earth disease called malaria. The virus you harbor seems to reinfect you periodically.'

'I drew a joker once …'

'Yes, and it could happen again. But unlike anyone else to whom it's happened, all you have to do is wait. You can sleep it off.'

'I don't ever want to be a monster again. Is there some way you could change just that much of it?'

'I'm afraid not. It's part of your total syndrome. I can only go after the whole thing.'

'And the odds against a cure are three or four to one?'

'Who told you that?'

'A joker named Bentley. He looked sort of like a dog.'

'Bentley was one of my successes. He's back to normal now. Just left here fairly recently, in fact.'

'Really! It's good to know that someone made it.'

Tachyon looked away.

'Yes,' he answered, a moment later.

'Tell me something.'

'What?'

'If I only change when I sleep, then I could put off a change by staying awake – right?'

'I see what you mean. Yes, a stimulant would put it off a bit. If you feel it coming on while you're out somewhere, the caffeine in a couple of cups of coffee would probably hold it off long enough for you to get back home.'

'Isn't there something stronger? Something that would put it off for a longer time?'

'Yes, there are powerful stimulants – amphetamines, for example. But they can be dangerous if you take too many or take them for too long.'

'In what ways are they dangerous?'

'Nervousness, irritability, combativeness. Later on, a toxic psychosis, with delusions, hallucinations, paranoia.'

'Crazy?'

'Yes.'

'Well, you could just stop them if it gets near that point, couldn't you?'

'I don't believe it's that easy.'

'I'd hate to be a monster again, or— You didn't say it, but isn't it possible that I could just die during one of the comas?'

'There is that possibility. It's a nasty virus. But you've come through several attacks now, which leads me to believe that your body knows what it is doing. I wouldn't worry myself unduly on that ...'

'It's the joker part that really bothers me.'

'That is a possibility you simply have to live with.'

'All right. Thank you, Doctor.'

'I wish you would come to Mount Sinai the next time you feel it coming on. I'd really like to observe the process in you.'

'I'd rather not.'

Tachyon nodded.

'Or right away after you awaken ... ?'

'Maybe,' Croyd said, and he shook his hand. 'By the way, Doctor ... How do you spell "amphetamine"?'

Croyd stopped by the Sarzannos' apartment later, for he had not seen Joe since that day in September when they had made their way home from school together, the exigencies of making a living had limited his spare time since then.

Mrs. Sarzanno opened the door a crack and stared at him. After he had identified himself and tried to explain his changed appearance, she still refused to open the door farther.

'My Joe, he is changed, too,' she said.

'Uh, how is he changed?' he asked.

'Changed. That's all. Changed. Go away.'

She closed the door.

He knocked again, but there was no response.

Croyd went away then and ate three steaks, because there was nothing else he could do.

Croyd studied Bentley – a small foxy-featured man with dark hair and shifty eyes – feeling that his earlier transformation had actually been in keeping with his general demeanor. Bentley returned the compliment for several seconds, then said, 'That's really you, Croyd?'

'Yep.'

'Come on in. Sit down. Have a beer. We've got a lot to talk about.'

He stepped aside, and Croyd entered the brightly furnished apartment.

'I got cured and I'm back in business. Business is lousy,' Bentley said, after they had seated themselves. 'What's your story?'

Croyd told him, of the changes and powers he'd experienced and of his talk with Tachyon. The one thing he never told him was his age, since all of his transformations bore the appearance of adulthood. He feared that Bentley might not trust him in the same fashion as he had if he knew otherwise.

'You went about those other jobs wrong,' the small man said, lighting a cigarette and coughing. 'Hit or miss is never good. You want a little planning, and it should be tailored to whatever your special talent is, each time around. Now, you say that this time you can fly?'

'Yes.'

'Okay. There are lots of places high up in skyscrapers that people think are pretty secure. This is the time we hit those. You know, you've got the best setup of anyone there is. Even if someone sees you, it don't matter. You're going to look different next time around ...'

'And you'll get me the amphetamines?'

'All you want. You come back here tomorrow – same time, same station. Maybe I'll have a job worked out for us. And I'll have your pills for you.'

'Thanks, Bentley.'

'It's the least I can do. If we stick together we'll both get rich.'

Bentley did plan a good job, and three days later Croyd brought home more money than he had ever held before. He took most of it to Carl, who had been handling the family's finances.

'Let's take a walk,' Carl said, securing the money behind a row of books and glancing significantly toward the living room where their mother sat with Claudia.

Croyd nodded.

'Sure.'

'You seem a lot older these days,' said Carl – who would be eighteen in a few months – as soon as they were on the street.

'I feel a lot older.'

'I don't know where you keep getting the money ...'

'Better you don't.'

'Okay. I can't complain, since I'm living off it, too. But I wanted you to know about Mom. She's getting worse. Seeing Dad torn apart that way ... She's been slipping ever since. You missed the worst of it so far, the last time you were asleep. Three different nights she just got up and went outside in her nightgown – barefoot yet, in February, for crissake! – and she wandered around like she was looking for Dad. Fortunately, someone we knew spotted her each time and brought her back. She kept asking her – Mrs. Brandt – if she'd seen him. Anyhow, what I'm trying to say is she's getting worse. I've already talked to a couple of doctors. They think she should be in a rest home for a while. Claudia and I think so, too. We can't watch her all the time, and she might get hurt. Claudia's sixteen now. The two of us can run things while she's away. But it's going to be expensive.'

'I can get more money,' Croyd said.

When he finally got hold of Bentley the following day and told him that they had to do another job soon, the small man seemed pleased, for Croyd had not been eager for a quick follow-up to the last one.

'Give me a day or so to line something up and work out the details,' Bentley said. 'I'll get back to you.'

'Right.'

The next day Croyd's appetite began to mount, and he found himself yawning occasionally. So he took one of the pills.

It worked well. Better than well, actually. It was a fine feeling that came over him. He could not recall the last time he'd felt quite that good. Everything seemed as if it were going right for a change. And all of his movements felt particularly fluid and graceful. He seemed more alert, more aware than usual, also. And, most importantly, he was not sleepy.

It was not until nighttime, after everyone else had retired, that these feelings began to wear off. He took another pill. When it began to work he felt so fine that he went outside and levitated high above the city, drifting in the cold March night between the bright constellations of the city and those far above, feeling as if he possessed a secret key to the inner meaning of it all. Briefly, he thought of Jetboy's battle in the sky, and he flew over the remains of the Hudson Terminal which had burned when pieces of Jetboy's plane fell upon it. He had read of a plan to build a monument to him there. Was this how it felt when he fell?

He descended to swoop among buildings – sometimes resting atop one, leaping, falling, saving himself at the last moment. On one such occasion, he beheld two men watching him from a doorway. For some reason that he did not understand, this irritated him. He returned home then and began cleaning the house. He stacked old newspapers and magazines and tied them into bundles, he emptied wastebaskets, he swept and mopped, he washed all of the dishes in the sink. He flew four loads of trash out over the East River and dropped them in, trash collections still not being quite regular. He dusted everything, and dawn found him polishing the silverware. Later, he washed all of the windows.

It was quite sudden that he found himself weak and shaking. He realized what it was and he took another pill and set a pot of coffee to percolating. The minutes passed. It was hard to remain seated, to be comfortable in any position. He did not like the tingling in his hands. He washed them several times, but it would not go away. Finally, he took another pill. He watched the clock and listened to the sounds of the coffeepot. Just as the coffee became ready the tingling and the shaking began to subside. He felt much better. While he was drinking his coffee he thought again of the two men in the doorway. Had they been laughing at him? He felt a quick rush of anger, though he had not really seen their faces, known their expressions. Watching him! If they'd had more time they might have thrown a rock ...

He shook his head. That was silly. They were just two guys. Suddenly, he wanted to run outside and walk all over the city, or perhaps fly again. But he might miss Bentley's call if he did. He began pacing. He tried to read but was unable to focus his attention as well as usual. Finally, he phoned Bentley.

'Have you come up with anything yet?' he asked.

'Not yet, Croyd. What's the rush?'

'I'm starting to get sleepy. You know what I mean?'

'Uh – yeah. You take any of that shit yet?'

'Uh-huh. I had to.'

'Okay. Look, go as light on it as possible. I'm working on a couple angles now. I'll try to have something lined up by tomorrow. If it's no go then, you stop taking the stuff and go to bed. We can do it next time. Got me?'

'I want to do it this time, Bentley.'

'I'll talk to you tomorrow. You take it easy now.'

He went out and walked. It was a cloudy day, with patches of snow and ice upon the ground. He realized suddenly that he had not eaten since the day before. That had to be bad, when he considered what had become his normal appetite. It must be the pills' doing, he concluded. He sought a diner, determined to force himself to eat something. As he walked, it occurred to him that he did not care to sit down in a crowd of people and eat. The thought of having all of them around him was unsettling. No, he would get a carryout order ...

As he headed toward a diner he was halted by a voice from a doorway. He turned so quickly that the man who had addressed him raised an arm and drew back.

'Don't ...' the man protested.

Croyd took a step back.

'Sorry,' he mumbled.

The man had on a brown coat, its collar turned all the way up. He wore a hat, its brim drawn about as low as it would go and still permit vision. He kept his head inclined forward. Nevertheless, Croyd discerned a hooked beak, glittering eyes, an unnaturally shiny complexion.

'Would you do me a favor, sir?' the man asked in a clipped, piping voice.

'What do you want?'

'Food.'

Automatically, Croyd reached for his pocket.

'No. I got money. You don't understand. I can't go in that place and get served, looking like I do. I'll pay you to go in and get me a couple hamburgers, bring them out.'

'I was going in anyway.'

Later, Croyd sat with the man on a bench, eating. He was fascinated by – jokers. Because he knew he was partly one himself. He began wondering where he would eat if he ever woke up in bad shape and there was nobody home.

'I don't usually come this far uptown anymore,' the other told him. 'But I had an errand.'

'Where do you guys usually hang out?'

'There's a number of us down on the Bowery. Nobody bothers

81

us there. There's places you get served and nobody cares what you look like. Nobody gives a damn.'

'You mean people might – attack you?'

The man uttered a brief, shrill laugh.

'People ain't real nice, kid. Not when you really get to know 'em.'

'I'll walk you back,' Croyd said.

'You might be taking a chance.'

'That's okay.'

It was down in the forties that three men on a bench stared at them as they passed. Croyd had just taken two more pills a few blocks back. (Was it only a few blocks back?) He hadn't wanted the jitters again while talking with his new friend John – at least, that's what he'd said to call him – so he'd taken two more to ease him over the next hump, in case one was due soon, and he knew right away when he saw the two men that they were planning something bad for him and John, and the muscles in his shoulders tightened and he rolled his hands into fists within his pockets.

'*Cock-a-doodle-doo,*' said one of the men, and Croyd started to turn, but John put his hand on his arm and said, 'Come on.'

They walked on. The men rose and fell into step behind them.

'*Kirkiriki,*' said one of the men.

'*Squak, squak,*' said another.

Shortly, a cigarette butt sailed over Croyd's head and landed in front of him.

'Hey, freak lover!'

A hand fell upon his shoulder.

He reached up, took hold of the hand, and squeezed. Bones made little popping noises within it as the man began to scream. The screaming stopped abruptly when Croyd released the hand and slapped the man across the face, knocking him into the street. The next man threw a punch at his face and Croyd knocked the arm aside with a flick of his hand that spun the man full-face toward him. He reached out then with his left hand, caught hold of both the other's lapels, bunching them, twisting them, and raised the man two feet into the air. He slammed him back against the brick wall near which they stood and released him. The man slumped to the ground and did not move.

The final man had drawn a knife and was swearing at him through clenched teeth. Croyd waited until he was almost upon him, and then levitated four feet and kicked him in the face. The man went over backward onto the sidewalk. Croyd drifted into position above him then and dropped, landing upon his midsection. He kicked the fallen knife into the gutter, turned away, and walked on with John.

'You're an ace,' the smaller man said after a while.

'Not always,' Croyd replied. 'Sometimes I'm a joker. I change every time I sleep.'

'You didn't have to be that rough on them.'

'Right. I could have been a lot rougher. If it's really going to be like this we should take care of each other.'

'Yeah. Thanks.'

'Listen, I want you to show me the places on the Bowery where you say nobody bothers us. I may have to go there someday.'

'Sure. I'll do that.'

'Croyd Crenson. C-r-e-n-s-o-n. Remember it, okay? If you see me again I'll look different, that's why.'

'I'll remember.'

John took him to several dives and pointed out places where some of them stayed. He introduced him to six jokers they encountered, all of them savagely deformed. Remembering his lizard phase, Croyd shook appendages with all of them and asked if there was anything they needed. But they shook their heads and stared. He knew that his appearance was against him.

'Good evening,' he said, and he flew away.

His fear that the uninfected survivors were watching him, waiting to jump him, grew as he flew up along the course of the East River. Even now, someone with a rifle with telescopic sights might be taking aim ...

He moved faster. On one level, he knew that his fear was

ridiculous. But he felt it too strongly to put it aside. He landed on the corner, ran to his front door, and let himself in. He hurried upstairs and locked himself in his bedroom.

He stared at the bed. He wanted to stretch out on it. But what if he slept? It would be all over. The world would end for him. He turned on the radio and began to pace. It was going to be a long night ...

When Bentley called the next day and said that he had a hot one but that it was a little risky, Croyd said he didn't care. He would have to carry explosives – which meant he would have to learn to use them between now and then – because this safe would be too tough even for his enhanced strength. Also, there was the possibility of an armed guard ...

He didn't mean to kill the guard, but the man had frightened him when he came in with a drawn gun that way. And he must have miscalculated on the fuse, because the thing blew before it should have, which is how the piece of flying metal took off the first two fingers of his left hand. But he wrapped the hand in his handkerchief and got the money and got out.

He seemed to remember Bentley's saying, 'For crissake, kid! Go home and sleep it off!' right after they split the take. He levitated then and headed in the proper direction, but he had to descend and break into a bakery where he ate three loaves of bread before he could continue, his mind reeling. There were more pills in his pocket, but the thought of them tied his stomach into a knot.

He slid open his bedroom window, which he had left unlatched, and crawled inside. He staggered up the hall to Carl's room and dumped the sack of money onto his sleeping form. Shaking then, he returned to his own room and locked the door. He switched on the radio. He wanted to wash his injured hand in the bathroom, but it just seemed too far away. He collapsed onto the bed and did not rise.

He was walking down what seemed an empty twilit street. Some-thing stirred behind him and he turned and looked back. People were emerging from doorways, windows, automobiles, manholes, and all of them were staring at him, moving toward him. He continued on his way and there came something like a collective sigh at his back. When he looked again they were all hurrying after him, expressions of hatred on their faces. He turned upon them, seized hold of the nearest man and strangled him. The others halted, drew back. He crushed another man's head. The crowd turned, began to flee. He pursued ...

III. DAY OF THE GARGOYLE

Croyd awoke in June, to discover that his mother was in a sana-torium, his brother had graduated high school, his sister was engaged, and he had the power to modulate his voice in such a fashion as to shatter or disrupt virtually anything once he had determined the proper frequency by a kind of resonant feedback that he lacked the vocabulary to explain. Also, he was tall, thin, dark-haired, sallow, and had regrown his missing fingers.

Foreseeing the day when he would be alone, he spoke with Bentley once again, to line up one big job for this waking period, and to get it over with quickly, before the weariness overcame him. He had resolved not to take the pills again, as he had thought back over the nightmare quality of his final days the last time around.

This time he paid even more attention to the planning and he asked better questions as Bentley chain-smoked his way through a series of details. The loss of both his parents and his sister's impending marriage had led him to reflect upon the imperma-nence of human relationships, with the realization that Bentley might not always be around.

He was able to disrupt the alarm system and damage the door to the bank's vault sufficiently to gain entrance, though he had not counted on shattering all of the windows in a three-block area while seeking the proper frequencies. Still, he was able to make good his escape with a large quantity of cash. This time he rented a safe-deposit box in a bank across town, where he left the larger portion of his share. He had been somewhat bothered by the fact that his brother was driving a new car.

He rented rooms in the Village, Midtown, Morningside Heights, the Upper East Side, and on the Bowery, paying all of the rents for a year in advance. He wore the keys on a chain around his neck, along with the one for his safe-deposit box. He wanted places he could reach quickly no matter where he was when the sleep came for him. Two of the apartments were furnished; the other four he equipped with mattresses and radios. He was in a hurry and could take care of amenities later. He had awakened with an awareness of several events that had transpired during his most recent sleep, and he could only attribute it to an unconscious apprehension of news broadcasts from the radio he had left playing this last time. He resolved to continue the practice.

It took him three days to locate, rent, and equip his new retreats. In that his place on the Bowery was his last one, he looked up John, identified himself, and had dinner with him. The stories he heard then of a gang of joker-bashers depressed him, and when the hunger and the chill and the drowsiness came upon him that evening he took a pill so as to stay awake and patrol the area. Just one or two, he decided, would hardly matter.

The bashers did not show up that night, but Croyd was depressed by the possibility that he might awaken as a joker the next time around. So he took two more pills with his breakfast to put things off a bit, and he decided to furnish his local quarters in the fit of energy that followed. That evening he took three more for a last night on the town, and the song he sang as he walked along Forty-second Street, shattering windows building by building, caused dogs to howl for several miles around and awakened two jokers and an ace equipped with UHF hearing. Bat-ears Brannigan – who expired two weeks later beneath a falling statue thrown by Muscles Vincenzi the day he was gunned down by the NYPD – sought him out to pound on him in payment for his headache and wound up buying him several drinks and requesting a soft UHF version of 'Galway Bay.'

The following afternoon on Broadway, Croyd responded to a taxi driver's curse by running his vehicle through a series of vibrations until it fell apart. Then, while he was about it, he turned the force upon all of those others who had proven themselves enemies by blowing their horns. It was only when the ensuing traffic snarl reminded him of the one outside his school on that first Wild Card Day that he turned and fled.

He awoke in early August in his Morningside Heights apartment, recalling slowly how he had gotten there and promising himself he would not take any more pills this time. When he looked at the tumors on his twisted arm he knew that the promise would not be hard to keep. This time he wanted to return to sleep as quickly as possible. Looking out the window, he was grateful that it was night, since it was a long way to the Bowery.

On a Wednesday in mid-September he woke to find himself dark blond, of medium height, build, and complexion, and possessed of no visible marks of his wild card syndrome. He ran himself through a variety of simple tests that experience had taught him were likely to reveal his hidden ability. Nothing in the way of a special power came to light.

Puzzled, he dressed himself in the best-fitting clothing he had on hand and went out for his usual breakfast. He picked up several newspapers along the way and read them while he devoured plate after plate of scrambled eggs, waffles, pancakes. It had been a chill morning when he'd entered the street. When he left the diner it was near to ten o'clock and balmy.

He rode the subways to midtown, where he entered the first decent-looking clothing store he saw and completely refitted himself. He bought a pair of hot dogs from a street vendor and ate them as he walked to the subway station.

He got off in the seventies, walked to the nearest delicatessen, and ate two corned beef sandwiches with potato pancakes. Was he stalling? he asked himself then. He knew that he could sit here all day and eat. He could feel the process of digestion going on like a blast furnace in his midsection.

He rose, paid, and departed. He would walk the rest of the way. How many months had it been? he wondered, scratching his forehead. It was time to check in with Carl and Claudia. Time to see how Mom was doing. To see whether anybody needed any money.

When Croyd came to his front door he halted, key in his hand. He returned the key to his pocket and knocked. Moments later, Carl opened the door.

'Yes?' he said.

'It's me. Croyd.'

'Croyd! Jeez! Come in! I didn't recognize you. How long's it been?'

'Pretty long.'

Croyd entered.

'How is everybody?' he asked.

'Mom's still the same. But you know they told us not to get our hopes up.'

'Yeah. Need any money for her?'

'Not till next month. But a couple of grand would come in handy then.'

Croyd passed him an envelope.

'I'd probably just confuse her if I went to see her, looking this different.'

Carl shook his head.

'She'd be confused even if you looked the same as you did, Croyd.'

'Oh.'

'Want something to eat?'

'Yeah. Sure.'

His brother led him to the kitchen.

'Lots of roast beef here. Makes a good sandwich.'

'Great. How's business?'

'Oh, I'm getting established now. It's better than it was at first.'

'Good. And Claudia?'

'It's good you turned up when you did. She didn't know where to send the invitation.'

'What invitation?'

'She's getting married Saturday.'

'That guy from Jersey?'

'Yeah. Sam. The one she was engaged to. He manages a family business. Makes pretty good money.'

'Where'll the wedding be?'

'In Ridgewood. You come with me for it. I'm driving over.'

'Okay. I wonder what kind of present they'd like?'

'They've got this list. I'll find it.'

'Good.'

Croyd went out that afternoon and bought a Dumont television set with a sixteen-inch screen, paid cash, and arranged for its delivery to Ridgewood. He visited with Bentley then, but declined a somewhat-risky-sounding job because of his apparent lack of special talent this time around. Actually, it was a good excuse. He didn't really want to work anyway, to take a chance on getting screwed up – physically or with the law – this close to the wedding.

He had dinner with Bentley in an Italian restaurant, and they sat for several hours afterward over a bottle of Chianti, talking shop and looking ahead as Bentley tried to explain to him the value of long-range solvency and getting respectable one day – a thing he'd never quite managed himself.

He walked most of the night after that, to practice studying buildings for their weak points, to think about his changed family. Sometime after midnight, as he was passing up Central Park West, a strong itching sensation began on his chest and spread about his entire body. After a minute, he had to halt and scratch himself violently. Allergies were becoming very fashionable about this time, and he wondered whether his new incarnation had brought him a sensitivity to something in the park.

He turned west at the first opportunity and left the area as quickly as possible. After about ten minutes the itching waned. Within a half-hour it had vanished completely. His hands and face felt as if they were chapped, however.

At about four in the morning he stopped in an all-night diner off Times Square, where he ate slowly and steadily and read a copy of *Time* magazine which someone had left in a booth. It's medical section contained an article on suicide among jokers, which depressed him considerably. The quotations it contained reminded him of things he had heard said by many people with whom he was acquainted, causing him to wonder whether any of them were among the interviewees. He understood the feelings too well, though he could not share them fully, knowing that no matter what he drew he would always be dealt a new wild card the next time around – and that more often than not it was an ace.

All of his joints creaked when he rose, and he felt a sharp pain between his shoulder blades. His feet felt swollen, also.

He returned home before daybreak, feeling feverish. In the bathroom, he soaked a washcloth to hold against his forehead. He noted in the mirror that his face seemed swollen. He sat in the easy chair in his bedroom until he heard Carl and Claudia moving about. When he rose to join them for breakfast his limbs felt leaden, and his joints creaked again as he descended the stairway.

Claudia, slim and blond, embraced him when he entered the kitchen. Then she studied his new face.

'You look tired, Croyd,' she said.

'Don't say that,' he responded. 'I can't get tired this soon. It's two days till your wedding, and I'm going to make it.'

'You can rest without sleeping, though, can't you?'

He nodded.

'Then, take it easy. I know it must be hard … Come on, let's eat.'

As they were sipping their coffee, Carl asked, 'You want to come into the office with me, see the setup I've got now?'

'Another time,' Croyd answered. 'I've got some errands.'

'Sure. Maybe tomorrow.'

'Maybe so.'

Carl left shortly after that. Claudia refilled Croyd's cup.

'We hardly see you anymore,' she said.

'Yeah. Well, you know how it is. I sleep – sometimes months. When I wake up I'm not always real pretty. Other times, I have to hustle to pay the bills.'

'We've appreciated it,' she said. 'It's hard to understand. You're the baby, but you look like a grown man. You act like one. You didn't get your full share of being a kid.'

He smiled.

'So what are you – an old lady? Here you are just seventeen, and you're getting married.'

She smiled back.

'He's a nice guy, Croyd. I know we're going to be happy.'

'Good. I hope so. Listen, if you ever want to reach me I'm going to give you the name of a place where you can leave a message. I can't always be prompt, though.'

'I understand. What is it that you do, anyway?'

'I've been in and out of a lot of different businesses. Right now I'm between jobs. I'm taking it easy this time, for your wedding. What's he like, anyhow?'

'Oh, very respectable and proper. Went to Princeton. Was a captain in the Army.'

'Europe? The Pacific?'

'Washington.'

'Oh. Well-connected.'

She nodded.

'Old family,' she said.

'Well ... Good,' he said. 'You know I wish you happiness.'

She rose and embraced him again.

'I've missed you,' she said.

'Me, too.'

'I've got errands to run, too, now. I'll see you later.'

'Yes.'

'You take it easy today.'

When she left he stretched his arms as far as they would go, trying to relieve the ache in his shoulders. His shirt tore down the back as he did this. He looked in the hall mirror. His shoulders were wider today than they had been yesterday. In fact, his entire body looked wider, huskier. He returned to his room and stripped. Most of his torso was covered with a red rash. Just looking at it made him want to scratch, but he restrained himself. Instead, he filled the bathtub and soaked in it for a long while. The water level had lowered itself visibly by the time he got out. When he studied himself in the bathroom mirror he seemed even larger. Could he have absorbed some of the water through his skin? At any rate, the inflammation seemed to have vanished, though his skin was still rough in those areas where it had been prominent.

He dressed himself in clothing he had left from an earlier time when he had been larger. Then he went out and rode the subways to the clothing store he had visited the previous day. There, he re-outfitted himself completely and rode back, feeling vaguely nauseous as the car jounced and swayed. He noted that his hands looked dry and rough. When he rubbed them, flakes of dead skin fell off like dandruff.

After he left the subway he walked on until he came to the Sarzannos' apartment building. The woman who opened the door was not Joe's mother, Rose, however.

'What do you want?' she asked.

'I'm looking for Joe Sarzanno,' he said.

'Nobody here by that name. Must be someone who moved out before we moved in.'

'So you wouldn't know where they went?'

'No. Ask the manager. Maybe he knows.'

She closed the door.

He tried the manager's apartment, but there was no answer. So he made his way home, feeling heavy and bloated. The second time that he yawned he was abruptly fearful. It seemed too soon to be going back to sleep. This transformation was more puzzling than usual.

He put a fresh pot of coffee on the stove and paced while he waited for it to percolate. While there was no certainty that he would awaken with a special power on each occasion, the one thing that had been constant was change. He thought back over all of the changes he had undergone since he had been infected. This was the only one where he had seemed neither joker nor ace, but normal. Still ...

When the coffee was ready, he sat down with a cup and became aware that he had been scratching his right thigh, half-consciously. He rubbed his hands together and more dry skin flaked off. He considered his increased girth. He thought of all the little twinges and creaks, of the fatigue. It was obvious that he was *not* completely normal this time, but as to what his abnormality actually constituted, he was uncertain. Could Dr. Tachyon help him? He wondered. Or at least give him some idea as to what was going on?

He called the number that he had committed to memory. A woman with a cheerful voice told him that Tachyon was out but would be back that afternoon. She took Croyd's name, seemed to recognize it, and told him to come in at three.

He finished the pot of coffee; the itching had increased steadily all over his body as he sat drinking the final cup. He went upstairs and ran the water in the bathtub again. While the tub was filling he undressed and studied his body. All of his skin now had the dry, flaky appearance of his hands. Wherever he brushed himself a small flurry occurred.

He soaked for a long while. The warmth and the wetness felt good. After a time he leaned back and closed his eyes. Very good ...

He sat up with a start. He had begun dozing. He had almost drifted off to sleep just then. He seized the washcloth and began rubbing himself vigorously, not only to remove all of the detritus. When he had finished he toweled himself briskly as the tub drained, then rushed to his room. He located the pills at the back of a clothing drawer and took two of them. Whatever games his body was playing, sleep was very much his enemy now.

He returned to the bathroom, cleaned the tub, dressed. It would feel good to stretch out on his bed for a time. To rest, as Claudia had suggested. But he knew that he couldn't.

Tachyon took a blood sample and fed it to his machine. On his first attempt, the needle had only gone in a short distance and stopped. The third needle, backed with considerable force, penetrated a subdermal layer of resistance and the blood was drawn.

While awaiting the machine's findings, Tachyon conducted a gross examination.

'Were your incisors that long when you awoke?' he asked, peering into Croyd's mouth.

'They looked normal when I brushed them,' Croyd replied. 'Have they grown?'

'Take a look.'

Tachyon held up a small mirror. Croyd stared. The teeth were an inch long, and sharp looking.

'That's a new development,' he stated. 'I don't know when it happened.'

Tachyon moved Croyd's left arm up behind his back in a gentle hammerlock, then pushed his fingers beneath the protruding scapula. Croyd screamed.

'That bad, is it?' Tachyon asked.

'My God!' Croyd said. 'What is it? Is something broken back there?'

The doctor shook his head. He examined some of the skin flakes under a microscope. He studied Croyd's feet next.

'Were they this wide when you woke up?' he asked.

'No. What the hell is happening, Doc?'

'Let's wait another minute or so for my machine to finish with your blood. You've been here three or four times in the past ...'

'Yes,' Croyd said.

'Fortunately, you came in once right after you woke up. Another time, you were in about six hours after you awoke. On the former occasion you possessed a high level of a very peculiar hormone which I thought at the time might be associated with the change process itself. The other time – six hours after awakening – you still had traces of the hormone, but at a very low level. Those were the only two times it was evident.'

'So?'

94

'The main test in which I am interested right now is a check for its presence in your blood. Ah! I believe we have something now.'

A series of strange symbols flashed upon the screen of the small unit.

'Yes. Yes, indeed,' he said, studying them. 'You have a high level of the substance in your blood – higher even than it was right after awakening. Hm. You've been taking amphetamines again, too.'

'I had to. I was starting to get sleepy, and I've got to make it to Saturday. Tell me in plain words what this damn hormone means.'

'It means that the process of change is still going on within you. For some reason you awoke before it was completed. There seems to be a regular cycle of it, but this time it was interrupted.'

'Why?'

Tachyon shrugged, a movement he seemed to have learned since the last time Croyd had seen him.

'Any of a whole constellation of possible biochemical events triggered by the change itself. I think you probably received some brain stimulation as a side effect of another change that was in progress at the time you were aroused. Whatever that particular change was, it is completed – but the rest of the process isn't. So your body is now trying to put you back to sleep until it finishes its business.'

'In other words, I woke up too soon?'

'Yes.'

'What should I do?'

'Stop taking the drugs immediately. Sleep. Let it run its course.'

'I can't. I have to stay awake for two more days – a day and a half will do, actually.'

'I suspect your body will fight this, and as I said once before, it seems to know what it's doing. I think you would be taking a chance to keep yourself awake much longer.'

'What kind of chance? Do you mean it might kill me – or will it just make me uncomfortable?'

'Croyd, I simply do not know. Your condition is unique. Each change takes a different course. The only thing we can trust is whatever accommodation your body has made to the virus – whatever it is within you that brings you through each bout safely. If you try to stay awake by unnatural means now, this is the very thing that you will be fighting.'

'I've put off sleep lots of times with amphetamines.'

'Yes, but those times you were merely postponing the onset of the process. It doesn't normally begin until your brain chemistry registers a sleep state. But now it is already under way, and the presence of the hormone indicates its continuance. I don't know what will happen. You may turn an ace phase into a joker phase. You may lapse into a really lengthy coma. I simply have no way of telling.'

Croyd reached for his shirt.

'I'll let you know how it all turns out,' he said.

Croyd did not feel like walking as much as he usually did. He rode the subway again. His nausea returned and this time brought with it a headache. And his shoulders were still hurting badly. He visited the drugstore near his subway stop and bought a bottle of aspirins.

He stopped by the apartment building where the Sarzannos had formerly resided, before he headed home. This time the manager was in. He was unable to help him, however, for Joe's family had left no forwarding address when they departed. Croyd glanced in the mirror beside the man's door as he left, and he was shocked at the puffiness of his eyes, at the deep circles beneath them. They were beginning to ache now, he noted.

He returned home. He had promised to take Claudia and Carl to a good restaurant for dinner, and he wanted to be in the best shape he could for the occasion. He returned to the bathroom and stripped again. He was huge, bloated-looking. He realized then that with all of his other symptoms, he had forgotten to tell Tachyon that he had not relieved himself at all since awakening. His body must be finding some use for everything that he ate or drank. He stepped on the scale, but it only went up to three hundred and he was over that. He took three aspirins and hoped that they would work soon. He scratched his arm and a long strip of flesh came away, painlessly and without bleeding. He scratched more gently in other areas and the flaking continued. He took a shower and brushed his fangs. He combed his hair and big patches of it came out. He stopped combing. For a moment he wanted to cry, but he was distracted by a yawning jag. He went to his room and took two more amphetamines. Then he recalled having heard somewhere that body mass had to be taken into account in calculating doses of medication. So he took another one, just to be safe.

Croyd found a dark restaurant and he slipped the waiter something to put them in a booth toward the rear, out of sight of most of the other diners.

'Croyd, you're really looking – unwell,' Claudia had said when she'd returned earlier.

'I know,' he replied. 'I went to see my doctor this afternoon.'

'What did he say?'

'I'm going to need a lot of sleep, starting right after the wedding.'

'Croyd, if you want to skip it, I'll understand. Your health comes first.'

'I don't want to skip it. I'll be okay.'

How could he say it to her when he did not fully understand it himself? Say that it was more than his favorite relative's wedding? – that the occasion represented the final rending of his home and that it was unlikely he would ever have another? Say that this was the end of a phase of his existence and the beginning of a big unknown?

Instead, he ate. His appetite was undiminished and the food was particularly good. Carl watched with the fascination of a voyeur, long after he had finished his own meal, as Croyd put away two more chateaubriands-for-two, pausing only to call for extra baskets of rolls.

When they finally rose Croyd's joints were creaking again.

He sat on his bed later that evening, aching. The aspirins weren't helping. He had removed his clothing because all of his garments were feeling tight again. Whenever he scratched himself now, his skin did more than flake. Big pieces of it came away, but they were dry and pale with no signs of blood. No wonder I look pasty-faced, he decided. At the bottom of one particularly large rent in his chest he saw something gray and hard. He could not figure what it was, but its presence frightened him.

Finally, despite the hour, he phoned Bentley. He had to talk to someone who knew his condition. And Bentley usually gave good advice.

After many rings Bentley answered, and Croyd told him his story.

'You know what I think, kid?' Bentley said at last. 'You ought to do what the doctor said. Sleep it off.'

'I can't. Not yet. I just need a little over a day. Then I'll be all right. I can keep awake that long, but I hurt so damn much and my appearance—'

'Okay, okay. Here's what we'll do. You come by about ten in the morning. I can't do anything for you now. But I'll talk to a man I know first thing, and we'll get you a really strong painkiller. And I want to have a look at you. Maybe there's some way of playing down your appearance a bit.'

'Okay. Thanks, Bentley. I appreciate it.'

'It's all right. I understand. It was no fun being a dog either. G'night.'

''Night.'

Two hours later, Croyd was stricken with severe cramps followed by diarrhea; also, his bladder felt as if it were bursting. This continued through the night. When he weighed himself at three-thirty he was down to 276. By six o'clock he weighed 242 pounds. He gurgled constantly. Its only benefit, he reflected, was that it kept his mind off the itching and the aches in his shoulders and joints. Also, it was sufficient to keep him awake without additional amphetamines.

By eight o'clock he weighed 216 and he realized – when Carl called him – that he had finally lost his appetite. Strangely, his girth had not decreased at all. His general body structure was unaltered from the previous day, though he was pale now to the point of albinism – and this, combined with his prominent teeth, gave him the look of a fat vampire.

At nine o'clock he called Bentley because he was still gurgling and running to the john. He explained that he had the shits and couldn't come for the medicine. Bentley said that he'd bring it by himself as soon as the man dropped it off. Carl and Claudia had already left for the day. Croyd had avoided them this morning, claiming an upset stomach. He now weighed 198.

It was near eleven o'clock when Bentley came by. Croyd had lost another twenty pounds by then and had scratched off a large flap of skin from his lower abdomen. The area of exposed tissue beneath it was gray and scaly.

'My God!' Bentley said when he saw him.

'Yeah.'

'You've got big bald patches.'

'Right.'

'I'll get you a hairpiece. Also, I'll talk to a lady I know. She's a beautician. We'll get you some kind of cream to rub in. Give you some normal color. I think you'd better wear dark glasses, too, when you go to the wedding. Tell 'em you got drops in your eyes. You're getting hunchbacked, too. When'd that happen?'

'I didn't even notice. I've been – occupied.'

Bentley patted the lump between his shoulders and Croyd screamed.

'Sorry. Maybe you'd better take a pill right away.'

'Yeah.'

'You're going to need to wear a big overcoat, too. What size do you take?'

'I don't know – now.'

'That's okay. I know someone's got a warehouse full. We'll send you a dozen.'

'I've got to run, Bentley. I'm gurgling again.'

'Yeah. Take your medicine and try to rest.'

By two o'clock, Croyd weighed 155. The painkiller had worked fine, and he was without aches for the first time in a long while. Unfortunately, it had also made him sleepy and he had had to take amphetamines again. On the plus side, this combination gave him his first good feeling since the whole business had started, even though he knew it was fake.

When the load of coats was delivered at three-thirty he was down to 132 pounds and felt very light on his feet. Somewhere deep within him his blood seemed to be singing. He found a coat that fit him perfectly and took it back to his room, leaving the others on the sofa. The beautician – a tall, lacquered blonde who chewed gum – came by at four o'clock. She combed out most of his hair, shaved the rest, and fitted him with a hairpiece. She made up his face then, instructing him in the use of the cosmetics as she went along. She also advised him to keep his mouth closed as much as possible to hide his fangs. He was pleased with the results and gave her a hundred dollars. She observed then that there were other services she might perform for him, but he was gurgling again and had to bid her a good afternoon.

By six o'clock his guts began to ease up on him. He was down to 116 by then and still feeling very good. The itching had finally stopped also, though he had scratched more skin from his thorax, forearms, and thighs.

When Carl came in, he yelled upstairs, 'What the hell are all these coats doing here?'

'It's a long story,' Croyd answered. 'You can have them if you want.'

'Hey, they're cashmere!'

'Yeah.'

'This one's my size.'

'So take it.'

'How you feeling?'

'Better, thanks.'

That evening he felt his strength returning, and he took one of his long walks. He raised the front end of a parked car high into the air to test it. Yes, he seemed to be recovering now. With the hair and the makeup he looked like a garden-variety fat man, so long as he kept his mouth closed. If only he'd had a little more time he'd have sought a dentist to do something about the fangs. He did not eat anything that night or in the morning. He did feel a peculiar pressure on the sides of his head, but he took another pill and it did not turn to pain.

♠

Before he and Carl left for Ridgewood, Croyd had indulged in another soak. More of his skin had come away, but that was all right. His clothes would cover his patchwork body. His face, at least, had remained intact. He applied his makeup carefully and adjusted the hairpiece. When he was fully dressed and had put on a pair of sunglasses, he thought that he looked fully presentable. And the overcoat did minimize the bulging of his back somewhat.

The morning was brisk and overcast. His intestinal problem seemed ended. He took another pill as a prophylactic, not knowing whether there was really any remaining pain to be masked. This necessitated another amphetamine. But that was all right. He felt fine, if a bit nervous.

As they were passing through the tunnel he found himself rubbing his hands. To his dismay, a large flap of skin came loose on the back of his left hand. But even that was all right. He had remembered to bring gloves.

He did not know whether it was the pressure in the tunnel, but his head was beginning to throb again. It was not a painful sensation, merely a vicinity of heavy pressure in his ears and temples. His upper back also throbbed, and there was a movement within it. He bit his lip and a piece of it came loose. He cursed.

'What's the matter?' his brother asked.

'Nothing.'

At least it wasn't bleeding.

'If you're still sick, I can take you back. Hate to have you get ill at the wedding. Especially with a stodgy bunch like Sam's gang.'

'I'll be okay.'

He felt light. He felt the pressure at many points within his body. The sense of strength from the drug overlaid his genuine strength. Everything seemed to be flowing perfectly. He hummed a tune and tapped his fingers on his knee.

'... coats must be worth quite a bit,' Carl was saying. 'They're all new.'

'Sell 'em somewhere and keep the money,' he heard himself saying.

'They hot?'

'Probably.'

'You in the rackets, Croyd?'

'No, but I know people.'

'I'll keep quiet.'

'Good.'

'You sort of look the part, though, you know? With that black coat and the glasses ...'

Croyd did not answer him. He was listening to his body, which was telling him that something was coming free in his back. He rubbed his shoulders against the back of the seat. This made him feel better.

When he was introduced to Sam's parents, William and Marcia Kendall – a rugged-looking gray-haired man gone slightly to fat, and a well-preserved blond woman – Croyd remembered to smile without opening his mouth and to make his few comments through barely moving lips. They seemed to study him carefully, and he felt certain they would have had more to say, save that there were others waiting to be greeted.

'I want to talk to you at the reception,' were William's final words.

Croyd sighed as he moved away. He'd passed. He had no intention of attending the reception. He'd be in a taxi heading back to Manhattan as soon as the service ended, be sleeping in a matter of hours. Sam and Claudia would probably be in the Bahamas before he awoke.

He saw his cousin Michael from Newark and almost approached him. The hell with it. He'd have to explain his appearance then and it wasn't worth it. He entered the church and was shown to a pew in the front, to the right. Carl would be giving Claudia away. At least he had awakened too late to be impressed as an usher himself. There was that much to be said for his timing.

As he sat waiting for the ceremony to begin he regarded the altar decorations, the stained-glass windows at either hand, the arrangements of flowers. Other people entered and were seated. He realized that he was sweating. He glanced about. He was the only one wearing an overcoat. He wondered whether the others would think that strange. He wondered whether the perspiration was causing his makeup to run. He unbuttoned his coat, let it hang open.

The sweating continued, and his feet began to hurt. Finally, he leaned forward and loosened the shoelaces. As he did, he heard his shirt tear across his back. Something also seemed to have loosened even further in the vicinity of his shoulders. Another flap of skin, he supposed. When he straightened he felt a sharp pain. He could not lean all the way back in the pew. His hump seemed to have grown, and any pressure on it was painful. So he assumed a position partway forward, bowed slightly as if in prayer. The organist began playing. More people entered and were seated. An usher conducted an elderly couple past his row and gave him a strange look as he went by.

Soon everyone was seated, and Croyd continued to sweat. It ran down his sides and his legs, was absorbed by his clothing which became blotchy, then drenched. He decided that it might be a bit cooler if he slipped his arms out of the coat's sleeves and just let it hang about his shoulders. This was a mistake, for as he struggled to free his arms he heard his garments tear in several more places. His left shoe burst suddenly, and his toes protruded grayly from its sides. A number of people glanced his way as these sounds occurred. He was grateful that he was incapable of blushing.

He did not know whether it was the heat or something psychological that set off the itching again. Not that it mattered. It was a real itch, whatever had brought it on. He had painkillers and amphetamines in his pocket, but nothing for skin irritation. He clasped his hands tightly, not to pray but to keep from scratching – though he threw in a prayer too, since the circumstances seemed about as appropriate as they came. It didn't work.

Through perspiration-beaded lashes he saw the priest enter. He wondered why the man was staring at him so. It was as if he did not approve of non-Episcopalians sweating in his church. Croyd clenched his teeth. If only he still had the power to make himself invisible, he mused. He'd fade for a few minutes, scratch like mad, then phase back and sit quietly.

By dint of sheer will he was able to hold himself steady through Mendelssohn's 'March.' He was unable to focus on what the priest was saying after that, but he was now certain that he was not going to be able to remain seated through the entire ceremony. He wondered what would happen if he left right then. Would Claudia be embarrassed? On the other hand, if he stayed, he was certain that she would be. He must look ill enough to justify it. Still, would it become one of those incidents that people would talk about for years afterward? ('Her brother walked out ...') Perhaps he could stay a little longer.

There was movement on his back. He felt his coat stirring. He heard female gasps from behind him. Now he was afraid to move, but—

The itching became overpowering. He unclasped his hands to scratch, but in a final act of resistance he seized hold of the back of the pew before him. To his horror, there came a loud cracking noise as the wood splintered within his grip.

There followed a long moment of silence.

The priest was staring at him. Claudia and Sam had both turned to stare at him, where he sat clutching a six-foot length of broken pew-back and knowing that he couldn't even smile or his fangs would show.

He dropped the wood and clasped himself with both arms. There were exclamations from behind as his coat slipped away. With his full strength he dug his fingers into his sides and scratched cross-body.

He heard his clothes tear and felt his skin rip all the way up to the top of his head. He saw the hairpiece fall away to his right. He threw down the clothing and the skin and scratched again, hard. He heard a scream from the rear and he knew that he would never forget the look on Claudia's face as she began to cry. But he could no longer stop. Not until his great batlike wings were unfurled, the high, pointed vanes of his ears freed, and the last remnants of clothing and flesh removed from his dark, scaled frame.

The priest began speaking again, something that sounded like an exorcism. There came shrieks and the sounds of rapid footfalls. He knew that he couldn't exit through the door where everyone else was headed, so he leapt into the air, circled several times to get a feeling of his new limbs, then covered his eyes with his left forearm and crashed out through the stained-glass window to his right.

As he beat his way back toward Manhattan he felt that it would be a long time before he saw the in-laws again. He hoped that Carl wouldn't be getting married for a while. He wondered then whether he'd ever meet the right girl himself . . .

Catching an updraft he soared, the breezes sobbing about him. The church looked like a disturbed anthill when he glanced back. He flew on.

WITNESS

by Walter Jon Williams

When Jetboy died I was watching a matinee of *The Jolson Story*. I wanted to see Larry Parks's performance, which everyone said was so remarkable. I studied it carefully and made mental notes. Young actors do things like that.

The picture ended, but I was feeling comfortable and had no plans for the next few hours, and I wanted to see Larry Parks again. I watched the movie a second time. Halfway through, I fell asleep, and when I woke the titles were scrolling up. I was alone in the theater.

When I stepped into the lobby the usherettes were gone and the doors were locked. They'd run for it and forgotten to tell the projectionist. I let myself out into a bright, pleasant autumn afternoon and saw that Second Avenue was empty.

Second Avenue is never empty.

The newsstands were closed. The few cars I could see were parked. The theater marquee had been turned off. I could hear angry auto horns some distance off, and over it the rumble of high-powered airplane engines. There was a bad smell from somewhere.

New York had the eerie feeling that towns sometimes got during an air raid, deserted and waiting and nervous. I'd been in air raids during the war, usually on the receiving end, and I didn't like the feeling at all. I began walking for my apartment, just a block and a half away.

In the first hundred feet I saw what had been making the bad smell. It came from a reddish-pink puddle that looked like several gallons of oddly colored ice cream melting on the sidewalk and oozing down the gutter.

I looked closer. There were a few bones inside the puddle. A human jawbone, part of a tibia, an eye socket. They were dissolving into a light pink froth.

There were clothes beneath the puddle. An usherette's uniform. Her flashlight had rolled into the gutter and the metal parts of it were dissolving along with her bones.

My stomach turned over as adrenaline slammed into my system. I started to run.

By the time I got to my apartment I figured there had to be some kind of emergency going on, and I turned on the radio to get information. While I was waiting for the Philco to warm up I went to check the canned food in the cupboard – a couple cans of Campbell's was all I could find. My hands were shaking so much I knocked one of the cans out of the cupboard, and it rolled off the sideboard behind the icebox. I pushed against the side of the icebox to get at the can, and suddenly it seemed like there was a shift in the light and the icebox flew halfway across the room and damn near went through the wall. The pan I had underneath to catch the ice-melt slopped over onto the floor.

I got the can of soup. My hands were still trembling. I moved the icebox back, and it was light as a feather. The light kept doing weird shifts. I could pick up the box with one hand.

The radio warmed finally and I learned about the virus. People who felt sick were to report to emergency tent hospitals set up by the National Guard all over the city. There was one in Washington Square Park, near where I was living.

I didn't feel sick, but on the other hand I could juggle the icebox, which was not exactly normal behavior. I walked to Washington Square Park. There were casualties everywhere – some were just lying in the street. I couldn't look at a lot of it. It was worse than anything I'd seen in the war. I knew that as long as I was healthy and mobile the doctors would put me low on the list for treatment, and it would be days before I'd get any help, so I walked up to someone in charge, told him I used to be in the Army, and asked what I could do to help. I figured if I started to die I'd at least be near the hospital.

The doctors asked me to help set up a kitchen. People were screaming and dying and changing before the doctors' eyes, and the medics couldn't do anything about it. Feeding the casualties was all they could think to do.

I went to a National Guard deuce-and-a-half and started picking up crates of food. Each weighed about fifty pounds, and I stacked six of them on top of each other and carried them off the truck in one arm. My perception of the light kept changing in odd ways. I emptied the truck in about two minutes. Another truck had gotten bogged down in mud when it tried to cross the park, so I picked up the whole truck and carried it to where it was supposed to be, and then I unloaded it and asked the doctors if they needed me for anything else.

I had this strange glow around me. People told me that when I did one of my stunts I glowed, that a bright golden aura surrounded my body. My looking at the world through my own radiance made the light appear to change.

I didn't think much about it. The scene around me was overwhelming, and it went on for days. People were drawing the black queen or the joker, turning into monsters, dying, transforming. Martial law had slammed down on the city – it was just like wartime. After the first riots on the bridges there were no disturbances. The city had lived with blackouts and curfews and patrols for four years, and the people just slipped back into wartime patterns. The rumors were insane – a Martian attack, accidental release of poison gas, bacteria released by Nazis or by Stalin. To top it all off, several thousand people swore they saw Jetboy's ghost flying, without his plane, over the streets of Manhattan. I went on working at the hospital, moving heavy loads. That's where I met Tachyon.

He came by to deliver some experimental serum he was hoping might be able to relieve some symptoms, and at first I thought, Oh, Christ, here's some fruitbar got past the guards with a potion his Aunt Nelly gave him. He was a weedy guy with long metallic red hair past his shoulders, and I knew it couldn't be a natural color. He dressed as if he got his clothes from a Salvation Army in the theater district, wearing a bright orange jacket like a bandleader might wear, a red Harvard sweater, a Robin Hood hat with a feather, plus-fours with argyle socks, and two-tone shoes that would have looked out of place on a pimp. He was moving from bed to bed with a tray full of hypos, observing each patient and sticking the needles in people's arms. I put down the X-ray machine I was carrying and ran to stop him before he could do any harm.

And then I noticed that the people following him included a three-star general, the National Guard bird colonel who ran the hospital, and Mr. Archibald Holmes, who was one of F.D.R.'s old crowd at Agriculture, and who I recognized right away. He'd been in charge of a big relief agency in Europe following the war, but Truman had sent him to New York as soon as the plague hit. I sidled up behind one of the nurses and asked her what was going on.

'That's a new kind of treatment,' she said. 'That Doctor Tack-something brought it.'

'It's *his* treatment?' I asked.

'Yeah.' She looked at him with a frown. 'He's from another planet.'

I looked at the plus-fours and Robin Hood hat. 'No kidding,' I said.

'No. Really. He is.'

Closer up, you could see the dark circles under his weird purple eyes, the strain that showed on his face. He'd been pushing himself hard since the catastrophe, like all the doctors here – like everyone except me. I felt full of energy in spite of only getting a few hours' sleep each night.

The bird colonel from the National Guard looked at me. 'Here's another case,' he said. 'This is Jack Braun.'

Tachyon looked up at me. 'Your symptoms?' he asked. He had a deep voice, a vaguely mid-European accent.

'I'm strong. I can pick up trucks. I glow gold when I do it.'

He seemed excited. 'A biological force field. Interesting. I'd like to examine you later. After the' – an expression of distaste crossed his face – 'present crisis is over.'

'Sure, Doc. Whatever you like.'

He moved on to the next bed. Mr. Holmes, the relief man, didn't follow. He just stayed and watched me, fiddling with his cigarette holder.

I stuck my thumbs in my belt and tried to look useful. 'Can I help you with something, Mr. Holmes?' I asked.

He seemed mildly surprised. 'You know my name?' he said.

'I remember you coming to Fayette, North Dakota, back in '33,' I said. 'Just after the New Deal came in. You were at Agriculture then.'

'A long time ago. What are you doing in New York, Mr. Braun?'

'I was an actor till the theaters shut down.'

'Ah.' He nodded. 'We'll have the theaters running again soon. Dr. Tachyon tells us the virus isn't contagious.'

'That'll ease some minds.'

He glanced at the entrance to the tent. 'Let's go outside and have a smoke.'

'Suits me.' After I followed him out I dusted off my hands and accepted a custom-blended cigarette from his silver case. He lit our cigarettes and looked at me over the match.

'After the emergency's over, I'd like to run some more tests with you,' he said. 'Just see what it is that you can do.'

I shrugged. 'Sure, Mr. Holmes,' I said. 'Any particular reason?'

'Maybe I can give you a job,' he said. 'On the world stage.'

Something passed between me and the sun. I looked up, and a cold finger touched my neck.

The ghost of Jetboy was flying black against the sky, his white pilot's scarf fluttering in the wind.

I'd grown up in North Dakota. I was born in 1924, into hard times. There was trouble with the banks, trouble with the farm surpluses that were keeping prices down. When the Depression hit, things went from bad to worse. Grain prices were so low that some farmers literally had to pay people to haul the stuff away. Farm auctions were held almost every week at the courthouse – farms worth fifty thousand dollars were selling for a few hundred. Half Main Street was boarded up.

Those were the days of the Farm Holidays, the farmers withholding grain to make the prices rise. I'd get up in the middle of the night to bring coffee and food to my father and cousins, who were patrolling the roads to make sure nobody sold grain behind their backs. If someone came by with grain, they'd seize the truck and dump it; if a cattle truck came by, they'd shoot the cattle and toss them on the roadside to rot. Some of the local bigwigs who were making a fortune buying underpriced wheat sent the American Legion to break the farm strike, carrying axe handles and wearing their little hats – and the whole district rose, gave the legionnaires the beating of their lives, and sent them scampering back to the city.

Suddenly a bunch of conservative German farmers were talking and acting like radicals. F.D.R. was the first Democrat my family ever voted for.

I was eleven years old when I first saw Archibald Holmes. He was working as a troubleshooter for Mr. Henry Wallace in the Department of Agriculture, and he came to Fayette to consult with the farmers about something or other – price control or production control, probably, or conservation, the New Deal agenda that kept our farm off the auction block. He gave a little speech on the courthouse steps on his arrival, and for some reason I didn't forget it.

He was an impressive man even then. Well-dressed, gray-haired even though he wasn't yet forty, smoked a cigarette in a holder like F.D.R. He had a Tidewater way of talking, which sounded strange to my ear, as if there was something slightly vulgar about pronouncing one's R's. Soon after his visit, things started getting better.

Years later, after I got to know him well, he was always Mr. Holmes. I never could see myself calling him by his first name.

Maybe I can trace my wanderlust to Mr. Holmes's visit. I felt there had to be something outside Fayette, something outside the North Dakota way of looking at things. The way my family saw it, I was going to get my own farm, marry a local girl, produce lots of kids, and spend my Sundays listening to the parson talk about Hell and my weekdays working in the fields for the benefit of the bank.

I resented the notion that this was all there was. I knew, perhaps only by instinct, that there was another kind of existence out there, and I wanted to get my share of it.

I grew up tall and broad-shouldered and blond, with big hands that were comfortable around a football and what my publicity agent later called 'rugged good looks.' I played football and played it well, dozed through school, and during the long dark winters I played in community theater and pageants. There was quite a circuit for amateur theater in both English and German, and I did both. I played mainly Victorian melodramas and historical spectaculars, and I got good notices, too.

Girls liked me. I was good-looking and a regular guy and they all thought I'd be just the farmer for them. I was careful never to have anyone special. I carried rubbers in my watch pocket and tried to keep at least three or four girls in the air at once. I wasn't falling into the trap that all my elders seemed to have planned for me.

We all grew up patriotic. It was a natural thing in that part of the world: there is a strong love of country that comes with punishing climates. It wasn't anything to make a fuss over, patriotism was just there, part of everything else.

The local football team did well, and I began to see a way out of North Dakota. At the end of my senior season, I was offered a scholarship to the University of Minnesota.

I never made it. Instead, the day after graduation in May of 1942, I marched to the recruiter and volunteered for the infantry.

No big deal. Every boy in my class marched with me.

I ended up with the 5th Division in Italy, and had an awful infantryman's war. It rained all the time, there was never proper shelter, every move we made was in full view of invisible Germans sitting on the next hill with Zeiss binoculars glued to their eyes, to be followed inevitably by that horrific zooming sound of an 88 coming down ... I was scared all the time, and I was a hero some of the time, but most of the time I was hiding with my mouth in the dirt while the shells came whizzing down, and after a few months of it I knew I wasn't coming back in one piece, and chances were I wasn't coming back at all. There were no tours, like in Vietnam; a rifleman just stayed on the line until the war was over, or until he died, or until he was so shot up he couldn't go back. I accepted these facts and went on with what I had to do. I got promoted to master sergeant and eventually got a Bronze Star and three Purple Hearts, but medals and promotions never meant as much to me as where the next pair of dry socks was coming from.

One of my buddies was a man named Martin Kozokowski, whose father was a minor theatrical producer in New York. One evening we were sharing a bottle of awful red wine and a cigarette – smoking was something else the Army taught me – and I mentioned my acting career back in North Dakota, and in a gush of inebriated goodwill he said, 'Hell, come to New York after the war, and me and my dad will put you on the stage.' It was a pointless fantasy, since at that point none of us really thought we were coming back, but it stuck, and we talked about it afterward, and by and by, as some dreams have a way of doing, it came true.

After V-E Day I went to New York and Kozokowski the elder got me a few parts while I worked an assortment of part-time jobs, all of which were easy compared to farming and the war. Theater circles were full of intense, intellectual girls who didn't wear lipstick – not wearing lipstick was supposed to be sort of daring – and they would take you home with them if you listened to them talk about Anouilh or Pirandello or their psychoanalysis, and the best thing about them was that they didn't want to get married and make little farmers. Peacetime reflexes began to come back. North Dakota started to fade away, and after a while I began to wonder if maybe the war didn't have its consolations after all.

An illusion, of course. Because some nights I'd still wake up with the 88s whistling in my ears, terror squirming in my guts, the old wound in my calf throbbing, and I'd remember lying on my back in a shellhole with mud creeping down my neck, waiting for the morphine to hit while I looked up into the sky to see a flight of silver Thunderbolts with the sun gleaming off their stubby wings, the planes hopping the mountains with more ease than I could hop out of a jeep. And I'd remember what it was like to lie there furious with jealousy that the fighter jocks were in their untroubled sky while I bled into my field dressing and waited for morphine and plasma, and I'd think, If I ever catch one of those bastards on the ground, I'm going to make him pay for this …

When Mr. Holmes started his tests he proved exactly how strong I was, which was stronger than anyone had ever seen, or even imagined. Provided I was braced well enough, I could lift up to forty tons. Machine-gun slugs would flatten themselves on my chest. Armor-piercing 20mm cannon shells would knock me down with their transferred energy, but I'd jump back up undamaged.

They were scared to try anything bigger than a 20mm on their tests. So was I. If I were hit with a *real* cannon, instead of just a big machine gun, I'd probably be oatmeal.

I had my limits. After a few hours of it I'd begin to get tired. I would weaken. Bullets began to hurt. I'd have to go off and rest.

Tachyon had guessed right when he talked about a biological force field. When I was in action it surrounded me like a golden halo. I didn't exactly control it – if someone shot a bullet into my back by surprise, the force field would turn on all by itself. When I started to get tired the glow would begin to fade.

I never got tired enough for it to fade entirely, not when I wanted it on. I was scared of what would happen then, and I always took care to make sure I got my rest when I needed it.

When the test results came in, Mr. Holmes called me in to his apartment on Park Avenue South. It was a big place, the entire fifth floor, but a lot of the rooms had that unused smell to them. His wife had died of pancreatic cancer back in '40, and since then he'd given up most of his social life. His daughter was off at school.

Mr. Holmes gave me a drink and a cigarette and asked me what I thought about fascism, and what I thought I could do about it. I remembered all those stiff-necked SS officers and Luftwaffe para-troops and considered what I could do about them now that I was the strongest thing on the planet.

'I imagine that now I'd make a pretty good soldier,' I said.

He gave me a thin smile. 'Would you *like* to be a soldier again, Mr. Braun?'

I saw right away what he was driving at. There was an emergency going on. Evil lived in the world. It was possible I could do something about it. And here was a man who had sat at the right hand of Franklin Delano Roosevelt, who in turn sat at the right hand of God, as far as I was concerned, and he was *asking* me to do something about it.

Of *course* I volunteered. It probably took me all of three seconds.

Mr. Holmes shook my hand. Then he asked me another question. 'How do you feel about working with a colored man?'

I shrugged.

He smiled. 'Good,' he said. 'In that case, I'll have to introduce you to Jetboy's ghost.'

I must have stared. His smile broadened. 'Actually, his name is Earl Sanderson. He's quite a fellow.'

Oddly enough, I knew the name. 'The Sanderson who used to play ball for Rutgers? Hell of an athlete.'

Mr. Holmes seemed startled. Maybe he didn't follow sports.

'Oh,' he said. 'I think you'll find he's a little more than that.'

Earl Sanderson, Jr., was born into a life far different from mine, in Harlem, New York City. He was eleven years older than I, and maybe I never caught up to him.

Earl, Sr., was a railway car porter, a smart man, self-educated, an admirer of Fredrick Douglass and Du Bois. He was a charter member of the Niagara Movement – which became the NAACP – and later of the Brotherhood of Sleeping Car Porters. A tough, smart man, thoroughly at home in the combustive Harlem of the time.

Earl, Jr., was a brilliant youth, and his father urged him not to waste it. In high school he was outstanding as a scholar and athlete, and when he followed Paul Robeson's footsteps to Rutgers in 1930 he had his choice of scholarships.

Two years into college, he joined the Communist party. When I knew him later, he made it sound like the only reasonable choice.

'The Depression was only getting worse,' he told me. 'The cops were shooting union organizers all over the country, and white people were finding out what it was like to be as poor as the colored. All we got out of Russia at the time were pictures of factories working at full capacity, and here in the States the factories were closed and the workers were starving. I thought it was only a matter of time before the revolution. The CP were the only people working for the unions who were also working for equality. They had a slogan, "Black and white, unite and fight", and that sounded right to me. They didn't give a damn about the color bar – they'd look you in the eye and call you "comrade." Which was more than I ever got from anyone else.'

He had all the good reasons in the world for joining the CP in 1931. Later all those good reasons would rise up and wreck us all.

I'm not sure why Earl Sanderson married Lillian, but I understand well enough why Lillian chased Earl for all those years. 'Jack,' she told me, 'he just *glowed*.'

Lillian Abbott met Earl when he was a junior in high school. After that first meeting, she spent every spare minute with him. Bought his newspapers, paid his way into the theaters with her pocket change, attended radical meetings. Cheered him at sporting events. She joined the CP a month after he did. And a few weeks after he left Rutgers, summa cum laude, she married him.

'I didn't give Earl any choice,' she said. 'The only way he'd ever get me to be quiet about it was to marry me.'

Neither of them knew what they were getting into, of course. Earl was wrapped up in issues that were larger than himself, in the revolution he thought was coming, and maybe he thought Lillian deserved a little happiness in this time of bitterness. It didn't cost him anything to say yes.

It cost Lillian just about everything.

Two months after his marriage Earl was on a boat to the Soviet

Union, to study at Lenin University for a year, learning to be a proper agent of the Comintern. Lillian stayed at home, working in her mother's shop, attending party meetings that seemed a little lackluster without Earl. Learning, without any great enthusiasm for the task, how to be a revolutionary's wife.

After a year in Russia, Earl went to Columbia for his law degree. Lillian supported him until he graduated and went to work as counsel for A. Philip Randolph and the Brotherhood of Sleeping Car Porters, one of the most radical unions in America. Earl, Sr., must have been proud.

As the Depression eased, Earl's commitment to the CP waned – maybe the revolution wasn't coming, after all. The GM strike was solved in favor of the CIO when Earl was learning to be a revolutionary in Russia. The Brotherhood won its recognition from the Pullman Company in 1938, and Randolph finally started drawing a salary – he'd worked all those years for free. The union and Randolph were taking up a lot of Earl's time, and his attendance at party meetings began to slide.

When the Nazi-Soviet pact was signed, Earl resigned from the CP in anger. Accommodation with the fascists was not his style.

Earl told me that after Pearl Harbor, the Depression ended for white people when the hiring at defense plants started, but few blacks were given jobs. Randolph and his people finally had enough. Randolph threatened a railway strike – right in the middle of wartime – that was to be combined with a march on Washington. F.D.R. sent his troubleshooter, Archibald Holmes, to work out a settlement. It resulted in Executive Order 8802, in which government contractors were forbidden to discriminate on account of race. It was one of the landmark pieces of legislation in the history of civil rights, and one of the greatest successes in Earl's career. Earl always spoke of it as one of his proudest accomplishments.

The week after Order 8802, Earl's draft classification was changed to 1–A. His work with the rail union wasn't going to protect him. The government was taking its revenge.

Earl decided to volunteer for the Air Corps. He'd always wanted to fly.

Earl was old for a pilot, but he was still an athlete and his conditioning got him past the physical. His record was labeled PAF, meaning Premature Anti-Fascist, which was the official designation for anyone who was unreliable enough not to like Hitler prior to 1941.

He was assigned to the 332nd Fighter Group, an all-black unit. The screening process for the black fliers was so severe that the unit ended up full of professors, ministers, doctors, lawyers – and all these bright people demonstrated first-rate pilots' reflexes as well. Because none of the air groups overseas wanted black pilots, the group remained at Tuskegee for months and months of training. Eventually they received three times as much training as the average group, and when they were finally moved, to bases in Italy, the group known as 'the Lonely Eagles' exploded over the European Theater.

They flew their Thunderbolts over Germany and the Balkan countries, including the toughest targets. They flew over fifteen thousand sorties and, during that time, *not a single escorted bomber* was lost to the Luftwaffe. After word got out, bomber groups began asking specifically for the 332nd to escort their planes.

One of their top fliers was Earl Sanderson, who ended the war with fifty-three 'unconfirmed' kills. The kills were unconfirmed because records were not kept for the black squadrons – the military was afraid the black pilots might get larger totals than the whites. Their fear was justified – that number put Earl above every American pilot but Jetboy, who was another powerful exception to a lot of rules.

On the day Jetboy died, Earl had come home from work with what he thought was a bad case of the flu, and the next day he woke up a black ace.

He could fly, apparently by an act of will, up to five hundred miles per hour. Tachyon called it 'projection telekinesis.'

Earl was pretty tough, too, though not as tough as I was – like me, bullets bounced off him. But cannon rounds could hurt him, and I know he dreaded the possibility of midair collision with a plane.

And he could project a wall of force in front of him, a kind of traveling shock wave that could sweep anything out of his path. Men, vehicles, walls. A sound like a clap of thunder and they'd be thrown a hundred feet.

Earl spent a couple weeks testing his talents before letting the world know about them, flying over the city in his pilot's helmet, black leather flying jacket, and boots. When he finally let people know, Mr. Holmes was one of the first to call.

I met Earl the day after I'd signed on with Mr. Holmes. By then I'd moved into one of Mr. Holmes's spare rooms and had been given a key to the apartment. I was moving up in the world.

I recognized him right away. 'Earl Sanderson,' I said, before Mr. Holmes could introduce us. I shook his hand. 'I remember reading about you when you played for Rutgers.'

Earl took that in stride. 'You have a good memory,' he said.

We sat down, and Mr. Holmes explained formally what he wanted with us, and with others he hoped to recruit later. Earl felt strongly about the term 'ace,' meaning someone with useful abilities, as opposed to 'joker,' meaning someone who was badly disfigured by the virus – Earl felt the terms imposed a class system on those who got the wild card, and didn't want to set us at the top of some kind of social pyramid. Mr. Holmes officially named our team the Exotics for Democracy. We were to become visible symbols of American postwar ideals, to lend credit to the American attempt to rebuild Europe and Asia, to continue the fight against fascism and intolerance.

The Unites States was going to create a postwar Golden Age, and was going to share it with the rest of the world. We were going to be its symbol.

It sounded great. I wanted in.

With Earl the decision came a little harder. Holmes had talked to him before and had asked him to make the same kind of deal that Branch Rickey later asked of Jackie Robinson: Earl had to stay out of domestic politics. He had to announce that he'd broken with

Stalin and Marxism, that he was committed to peaceful change. He was asked to keep his temper under control, to absorb the inevitable anger, racism, and condescension, and to do it without retaliation.

Earl told me later how he struggled with himself. He knew his powers by then, and he knew he could change things simply by being present where important things were going on. Southern cops wouldn't be able to smash up integration meetings if someone present could flatten whole companies of state troopers. Strike-breakers would go flying before his wave of force. If he decided to integrate somebody's restaurant, the entire Marine Corps couldn't throw him out – not without destroying the building, anyway.

But Mr. Holmes had pointed out that if he used his powers in that way, it wouldn't be Earl Sanderson who would pay the penalty. If Earl Sanderson were seen reacting violently to provocation, innocent blacks would be strung from oak limbs throughout the country.

Earl gave Mr. Holmes the assurance he wanted. Starting the very next day, the two of us went on to make a lot of history.

The EFD was never a part of the U.S. government. Mr. Holmes consulted with the State Department, but he paid Earl and me out of his own pocket and I lived in his apartment.

The first thing was to deal with Perón. He'd gotten himself elected President of Argentina in a rigged election, and was in the process of turning himself into a South American version of Mussolini and Argentina into a refuge for fascists and war crimi-nals. The Exotics for Democracy flew south to see what we could do about it.

Looking back on things, I'm amazed at our assumptions. We were bent on overthrowing the constitutional government of a large foreign nation, and we didn't think anything about it … Even Earl went along without a second thought. We'd just spent years fighting fascists in Europe, and we didn't see anything remarkably different in moving south and smashing them up there.

When we left, we had another man with us. David Harstein just seemed to talk himself aboard the plane. Here he was, a Jewish chess hustler from Brooklyn, one of those fast-talking curly-haired young guys that you saw all over New York selling flood insurance or used auto tires or custom suits made of some new miracle fiber that was just as good as cashmere, and suddenly he was a member of EFD and calling a lot of the shots. You couldn't help but like him. You couldn't help but agree with him.

He was an exotic, all right. He exuded pheromones that made you feel friendly with him and with the world, that created an atmosphere of bonhomie and suggestibility. He could talk an Albanian Stalinist into standing on his head and singing 'The Star-Spangled Banner' – at least, as long as he and his pheromones were in the room. Afterward, when our Albanian Stalinist returned to his senses, he'd promptly denounce himself and have himself shot.

We decided to keep David's powers a secret. We spread a story that he was some kind of sneaky superman, like The Shadow on radio, and that he was our scout. Actually he'd just get into conferences with people and make them agree with us. It worked pretty well.

Perón hadn't consolidated his power yet, having only been in office four months. It took us two weeks to organize the coup that got rid of him. Harstein and Mr. Holmes would go into meetings with army officers, and before they were done the colonels would be swearing to have Perón's head on a plate, and even after they began to think better of things, their sense of honor wouldn't let them back down on their promises.

On the morning before the coup, I found out some of my limitations. I'd read the comics when I was in the Army, and I'd seen how, when the bad guys were trying to speed away in their cars, Superman would jump in front of the car, and the car would bounce off him.

I tried that in Argentina. There was a Perónist major who had to be kept from getting to his command post, and I jumped in front of his Mercedes and got knocked two hundred feet into a statue of Juan P. himself.

The problem was, I wasn't heavier than the car. When things collide, it's the object with the least momentum that gives way, and weight is a component of momentum. It doesn't matter how *strong* the lighter object is.

I got smarter after that. I knocked the statue of Perón off its perch and threw it at the car. That took care of things.

There are a few other things about the ace business that you can't learn from reading comic books. I remember comic aces grabbing the barrels of tank guns and turning them into pretzels.

It is in fact possible to do that, but you have to have the leverage to do it. You've got to plant your feet on something solid in order to have something to push against. It was far easier for me to dive under the tank and knock it off its treads. Then I'd run around to the other side and put my arms around the gun barrel, with my shoulder under the barrel, and then yank down. I'd use my shoulder as the fulcrum of a lever and bend the barrel around myself.

That's what I'd do if I was in a hurry. If I had time, I'd punch my way through the bottom of the tank and rip it apart from the inside.

But I digress. Back to Perón.

There were a couple critical things that had to be done. Some loyal Perónists couldn't be gotten to, and one of them was the head of an armored battalion quartered in a walled compound on the outskirts of Buenos Aires. On the night of the coup, I picked up one of the tanks and dropped it on its side in front of the gate, and then I just braced my shoulder against it and held it in place while the other tanks battered themselves into junk trying to move it.

Earl immobilized Perón's air force. He just flew behind the planes on the runway and tore off the stabilizers.

Democracy was victorious. Perón and his blond hooker took off for Portugal.

I gave myself a few hours off. While triumphant middle-class mobs poured into the street to celebrate, I was in a hotel room with the daughter of the French ambassador. Listening to the chanting mob through the window, the taste of champagne and Nicolette on my tongue, I concluded this was better than flying.

Our image got fashioned in that campaign. I was wearing old Army fatigues most of the time, and that's the view of me most people remember. Earl was wearing tan Air Force officer's fatigues with the insignia taken off, boots, helmet, goggles, scarf, and his old leather flying jacket with the 332nd patch on the shoulder. When he wasn't flying he'd take the helmet off and put on an old black beret he kept in his hip pocket. Often, when we were asked to make personal appearances, Earl and I were asked to dress in our fatigues so everyone would know us. The public never seemed to realize that most of the time we wore suits and ties, just like everyone else.

When Earl and I were together, it was often in a combat situation, and for that reason we became best friends ... people in combat become close very quickly. I talked about my life, my war, about women. He was a little more guarded – maybe he wasn't sure how I'd take hearing his exploits with white girls – but eventually, one night when we were in northern Italy looking for Bormann, I heard all about Orlena Goldoni.

'I used to have to paint her stockings on in the morning,' Earl said. 'I'd have to make up her legs, so it would look like she had silk stockings. And I'd have to paint the seam down the back in eyeliner.' He smiled. 'That was a paint job I always enjoyed doing.'

'Why didn't you just give her some stockings?' I asked. They were easy enough to come by. GIs wrote to their friends and relatives in the States to send them.

'I gave her lots of pairs,' Earl shrugged, 'but Lena'd give 'em away to the comrades.'

Earl hadn't kept a picture of Lena, not where Lillian could find it, but I saw her in the pictures later, when she was billed as Europe's answer to Veronica Lake. Tousled blond hair, broad shoulders, a husky voice. Lake's screen persona was cool, but Goldoni's was hot. The silk stockings were real in the pictures, but so were the legs under them, and the picture celebrated Lena's legs as often as the director thought he could get away with it. I remember thinking how much fun Earl must have had painting her.

She was a cabaret singer in Naples when they met, in one of the few clubs where black soldiers were allowed. She was eighteen and a black marketeer and a former courier for the Italian Communists. Earl took one look at her and threw caution to the winds. It was maybe the one time in his entire life that he indulged himself. He started taking chances. Slipping off the field at night, dodging MP patrols to be with her, sneaking back early in the morning and being on the flight line ready to take off for Bucharest or Ploeşti ...

'We knew it wasn't forever,' Earl said. 'We knew the war would end sooner or later.' There was a kind of distance in his eyes, the memory of a hurt, and I could see how much leaving Lena had cost him. 'We were grownups about it.' A long sigh. 'So we said goodbye. I got discharged and went back to work for the union. And we haven't seen each other since.' He shook his head. 'Now she's in the pictures. I haven't seen any of them.'

The next day, we got Bormann. I held him by his monk's cowl and shook him till his teeth rattled. We turned him over to the representative of the Allied War Crimes Tribunal and gave ourselves a few days' leave.

Earl seemed more nervous than I'd ever seen him. He kept disappearing to make phone calls. The press always followed us around, and Earl jumped every time a camera bulb went off. The first night, he disappeared from our hotel room, and I didn't see him for three days.

Usually I was the one exhibiting this kind of behavior, always sneaking off to spend some time with a woman. Earl's doing it caught me by surprise.

He'd spent the weekend with Lena, in a little hotel north of Rome. I saw their pictures together in the Italian papers on Monday morning – somehow the press found out about it. I wondered whether Lillian had heard, what she was thinking. Earl showed up, scowling, around noon on Monday, just in time for his flight to India: He was going to Calcutta to see Gandhi. Earl wound up stepping between the Mahatma and the bullets that some fanatic fired at him on the steps of the temple – and all of a sudden the papers were full of India, with what had just happened in Italy forgotten. I don't know how Earl explained it to Lillian.

Whatever it was he said, I suppose Lillian believed him. She always did.

Glory years, these. With the fascist escape route to South America cut, the Nazis were forced to stay in Europe where it was easier to find them. After Earl and I dug Bormann out of his monastery, we plucked Mengele from a farm attic in Bavaria and we got so close to Eichmann in Austria that he panicked and ran out into the arms of a Soviet patrol, and the Russians shot him out of hand. David Harstein walked into the Escorial on a diplomatic passport and talked Franco into making a live radio address in which he resigned and called for elections, and then David stayed with him on the plane all the way to Switzerland. Portugal called for elections right afterward, and Perón had to find a new home in Nanking, where he became a military adviser to the generalissimo. Nazis were bailing out of Iberia by the dozen, and the Nazi hunters caught a lot of them.

I was making a lot of money. Mr. Holmes wasn't paying me much in the way of wages, but I got a lot for making the Chesterfield endorsement and for selling my story to *Life*, and I had a lot of paid speaking engagements – Mr. Holmes hired me a speechwriter. My half of the Park Avenue apartment was free, and I never had to pay for a meal if I didn't want to. I got large sums for articles that were written over my name, things like 'Why I Believe in Tolerance' and 'What America Means to Me,' and 'Why We Need the U.N.' Hollywood scouts were making incredible offers for long-term contracts, but I wasn't interested just yet. I was seeing the world.

So many girls were visiting me in my room that the tenants' association talked about installing a revolving door.

The papers started calling Earl 'the Black Eagle,' from the 332nd's nickname, 'the Lonely Eagles.' He didn't like the name much. David Harstein, by those few who knew of his talent, was 'the Envoy.' I was 'Golden Boy,' of course. I didn't mind.

EFD got another member in Blythe Stanhope van Renssaeler, who the papers started calling 'Brain Trust.' She was a petite, proper upper-crust Boston lady, high-strung as a thoroughbred, married to a scumbag New York congressman by whom she'd had three kids. She had the kind of beauty that took a while for you to notice, and then you wondered why you hadn't seen it before. I don't think she ever knew how lovely she really was.

She could absorb minds. Memories, abilities, everything.

Blythe was older than me by about ten years, but that didn't bother me, and before long I started flirting with her. I had plenty of other female companionship, and everyone knew that, so if she knew anything about me at all – and maybe she didn't, because my mind wasn't important enough to absorb – she didn't take me seriously.

Eventually her awful husband, Henry, threw her out, and she came by our apartment to look for a place to stay. Mr. Holmes was gone, and I was feeling no pain after a few shots of his twenty-year-old brandy, and I offered her a bed to stay in – mine, in fact. She blew up at me, which I deserved, and stormed out.

Hell, I hadn't intended her to take the offer as a permanent one. She should have known better.

So, for that matter, should I. Back in '47, most people would rather marry than burn. I was an exception. And Blythe was too high-strung to fool with – she was on the edge of nervous collapse half the time, with all the knowledge in her head, and one thing she didn't need was a Dakota farm boy pawing at her on the night her marriage ended.

Soon Blythe and Tachyon were together. It didn't do my self-esteem any good to be turned down for a being from another planet, but I'd gotten to know Tachyon fairly well, and I'd decided he was okay in spite of his liking for brocade and satin. If he made Blythe happy, that was fine with me. I figured he had to have something right with him to persuade a blue-stocking like Blythe to actually live in sin.

The term 'ace' caught on just after Blythe joined the EFD, so suddenly we were the Four Aces. Mr. Holmes was Democracy's Ace in the Hole, or the Fifth Ace. We were good guys, and everyone knew it.

It was amazing, the amount of adulation we received. The public simply wouldn't *allow* us to do anything wrong. Even die-hard bigots referred to Earl Sanderson as 'our colored flyboy.' When he spoke out on segregation, or Mr. Holmes on populism, people listened.

Earl was consciously manipulating his image, I think. He was smart, and he knew how the machinery of the press worked. The promise he'd given with such struggle to Mr. Holmes was fully justified by events. He was consciously molding himself into a black hero, an untarnished figure of aspiration. Athlete, scholar, union leader, war hero, faithful husband, ace. He was the first black man on the cover of *Time*, the first on *Life*. He had replaced Robeson as the foremost black ideal, as Robeson wryly acknowledged when he said, 'I can't fly, but then Earl Sanderson can't sing.'

Robeson was wrong, by the way.

Earl was flying higher than he ever had. He hadn't realized what happens to idols when people find out about their feet of clay.

The Four Aces' failures came the next year, in '48. When the Communists were on the verge of taking over in Czechoslovakia we flew to Germany in a big rush, and then the whole thing was called off. Someone at the State Department had decided the situation was too complicated for us to fix, and he'd asked Mr. Holmes not to intervene. I heard a rumor later that the government had been recruiting some ace talents of their own for covert work, and that they'd been sent in and made a bungle of it. I don't know if that's true or not.

Then, two months after the Czechoslovakian fiasco, we were sent into China to save a billion-odd people for democracy.

It was not apparent at the time, but our side had already lost. On paper, things seemed retrievable – the generalissimo's Kuomintang still held all the major cities, their armies were well equipped, compared to Mao and his forces, and it was well known that the generalissimo was a genius. If he weren't, why had Mr. Luce made him *Time*'s Man of the Year twice?

On the other hand, the Communists were marching south at a steady rate of twenty-three point five miles per day, rain or shine, summer or winter, redistributing land as they went. Nothing could stop them – certainly not the generalissimo.

By the time we were called in, the generalissimo had resigned – he did that from time to time, just to prove to everyone that he was indispensable. So the Four Aces met with the new KMT president, a man named Chen who was always looking over his shoulder lest he be replaced once the Great Man decided to make another dramatic entrance to save the country.

The U.S. position, by then, was prepared to concede north China and Manchuria, which the KMT had already lost barring the big cities. The idea was to save the south for the generalissimo by partitioning the country. The Kuomintang would get a chance to establish itself in the south while they organized for an eventual reconquest, and the Communists would get the northern cities without having to fight for them.

We were all there, the Four Aces and Holmes – Blythe was included as a scientific adviser and ended up giving little speeches about sanitation, irrigation, and inoculation. Mao was there, and Zhou Enlai, and President Chen. The generalissimo was off in Canton sulking in his tent, and the People's Liberation Army was laying siege to Mukden in Manchuria and otherwise marching steadily south, twenty-three point five miles per day, under Lin Biao.

Earl and I didn't have much to do. We were observers, and mostly what we observed were the delegates. The KMT people were astonishingly polite, they dressed well, they had uniformed servants who scuttled about on their errands. Their interaction with one another looked like a minuet.

The PLA people looked like soldiers. They were smart, proud, military in the way that real soldiers are military, without all the white-glove prissy formality of the KMT. The PLA had been to war, and they weren't used to losing. I could tell that at a glance.

It was a shock. All I knew about China was what I'd read in Pearl Buck. That, and the certified genius of the generalissimo.

'*These* guys are fighting *those* guys?' I asked Earl.

'*Those* guys' – Earl was indicating the KMT crowd – 'aren't fighting anyone. They're ducking for cover and running away. That's part of the problem.'

'I don't like the looks of this,' I said.

Earl seemed a little sad. 'I don't, either,' he said. He spat. 'The KMT officials have been stealing land from the peasants. The Communists are giving the land back, and that means they've got popular support. But once they've won the war they'll take it back, just like Stalin did.'

Earl knew his history. Me, I just read the papers.

Over a period of two weeks Mr. Holmes worked out a basis for negotiation, and then David Harstein came into the room and soon Chen and Mao were grinning at each other like old school buddies at a reunion, and in a marathon negotiating session China was formally partitioned. The KMT and the PLA were ordered to be friends and lay down their arms.

It all fell apart within days. The generalissimo, who had no doubt been told of our perfidy by ex-Colonel Perón, denounced the agreement and returned to save China. Lin Biao never stopped marching south. And after a series of colossal battles, the certified genius of the generalissimo ended up on an island guarded by the U.S. fleet – along with Juan Perón and his blond hooker, who had to move again.

Mr. Holmes told me that when he flew back across the Pacific with the partition in his pocket, while the agreement unraveled behind him and the cheering crowds in Hong Kong and Manila and Oahu and San Francisco grew ever smaller, he kept remembering Neville Chamberlain and his little piece of paper, and how Chamberlain's 'peace in Europe' turned into conflagration, and Chamberlain into history's dupe, the sad example of a man who meant well but who had too much hope, and trusted too much in men more experienced in treachery than he.

Mr. Holmes was no different. He didn't realize that while he'd gone on living and working for the same ideals, for democracy and liberalism and fairness and integration, the world was changing around him, and that because he didn't change with the world the world was going to hammer him into the dust.

At this point the public were still inclined to forgive us, but they remembered that we'd disappointed them. Their enthusiasm was a little lessened.

And maybe the time for the Four Aces had passed. The big war criminals had been caught, fascism was on the run, and we had discovered our limitations in Czechoslovakia and China.

When Stalin blockaded Berlin, Earl and I flew in. I was in my combat fatigues again, Earl in his leather jacket. He flew patrols over the Russian wire, and the Army gave me a jeep and a driver to play with. Eventually Stalin backed down.

But our activities were shifting toward the personal. Blythe was going off to scientific conferences all over the world, and spent most of the rest of her time with Tachyon. Earl was marching in civil rights demonstrations and speaking all over the country. Mr. Holmes and David Harstein went to work, in that election year, for the candidacy of Henry Wallace.

I spoke alongside Earl at Urban League meetings, and to help out Mr. Holmes I said a few nice things for Mr. Wallace, and I got paid a lot of money for driving the latest-model Chrysler and for talking about Americanism.

After the election I went to Hollywood to work for Louis Mayer. The money was more incredible than anything I'd ever dreamed, and I was getting bored with kicking around Mr. Holmes's apartment. I left most of my stuff in the apartment, figuring it wouldn't be long before I'd be back.

I was pulling down ten thousand per week, and I'd acquired an agent and an accountant and a secretary to answer the phone and someone to handle my publicity; all I had to do at this point was take acting and dance lessons. I didn't actually have to work yet, because they were having script problems with my picture. They'd never had to write a screenplay around a blond superman before.

The script they eventually came up with was based loosely on our adventures in Argentina, and it was called *Golden Boy*. They paid Clifford Odets a lot of money to use that title, and considering what happened to Odets and me later, that linking had a certain irony.

When they gave the script to me, I didn't care for it. I was the hero, which was just fine with me. They actually called me 'John Brown.' But the Harstein character had been turned into a minister's son from Montana, and the Archibald Holmes character, instead of being a politician from Virginia, had become an FBI agent. The worst part was the Earl Sanderson character – he'd become a cipher, a black flunky who was only in a few scenes, and then only to take orders from John Brown and reply with a crisp, 'Yes, sir,' and a salute. I called up the studio to talk about this.

'We can't put him in too many scenes,' I was told. 'Otherwise we can't cut him out for the Southern version.'

I asked my executive producer what he was talking about.

'If we release a picture in the South, we can't have colored people in it, or the exhibitors won't show it. We write the scenes so that we can release a Southern version by cutting out all the scenes with niggers.'

I was astonished. I never knew they did things like that. 'Look,' I said. 'I've made speeches in front of the NAACP and Urban League. I was in *Newsweek* with Mary McLeod Bethune. I can't be seen to be a party to this.'

The voice coming over the phone turned nasty. 'Look at your contract, Mr. Braun. You don't have script approval.'

'I don't want to approve the script. I just want a script that recognizes certain facts about my life. If I do this script, my credibility will be gone. You're fucking with my *image*, here!'

After that it turned unpleasant. I made certain threats and the executive producer made certain threats. I got a call from my accountant telling me what would happen if the ten grand per week stopped coming, and my agent told me I had no legal right to object to any of this.

Finally I called Earl and told him what was going on. '*What* did you say they were paying you?' he asked.

I told him again.

'Look,' he said. 'What you do in Hollywood is your business. But you're new there, and you're an unknown commodity to them. You want to stand up for the right, that's good. But if you walk, you won't do me or the Urban League any good. Stay in the business and get some clout, then use it. And if you feel guilty, the NAACP can always use some of that ten grand per week.'

So there it was. My agent patched up an understanding with the studio to the effect that I was to be consulted on script changes. I succeeded in getting the FBI dropped from the script, leaving the Holmes character without any set governmental affiliation, and I tried to make the Sanderson character a little more interesting.

I watched the rushes, and they were good. I liked my acting – it was relaxed, anyway, and I even got to step in front of a speeding Mercedes and watch it bounce off my chest. It was done with special effects.

The picture went into the can, and I went from a three-martini lunch into the wrap party without stopping to sober up. Three days later I woke up in Tijuana with a splitting headache and a suspicion that I'd just done something foolish. The pretty little blonde sharing the pillow told me what it was. We'd just got married. When she was in the bath I had to look at the marriage license to find out her name was Kim Wolfe. She was a minor starlet from Georgia who'd been scuffling around Hollywood for six years.

After some aspirin and a few belts of tequila, marriage didn't seem like a half-bad idea. Maybe it was time, with my new career and all, that I settled down.

I bought Ronald Colman's old pseudo-English country house on Summit Drive in Beverly Hills, and I moved in with Kim, and our two secretaries, Kim's hairdresser, our two chauffeurs, our two live-in maids ... suddenly I had all these people on salary, and I wasn't quite sure where they came from.

The next picture was *The Rickenbacker Story*. Victor Fleming was going to direct, with Fredric March as Pershing and June Allyson as the nurse I was supposed to fall in love with. Dewey Martin, of all people, was to play Richthofen, whose Teutonic breast I was going to shoot full of American lead – never mind that the real Richthofen was shot down by someone else. The picture was going to be filmed in Ireland, with an enormous budget and hundreds of extras. I insisted on learning how to fly, so I could do some of the stunts myself. I called Earl long-distance about that.

'Hey,' I said. 'I finally learned how to fly.'

'Some farm boys,' he said, 'just take a while.'

'Victor Fleming's gonna make me an ace.'

'Jack.' His voice was amused. 'You're *already* an ace.'

Which stopped me up short, because somehow in all the activity I'd forgotten that it wasn't MGM who made me a star. 'You've got a point, there,' I said.

'You should come to New York a little more often,' Earl said. 'Figure out what's happening in the real world.'

'Yeah. I'll do that. We'll talk about flying.'

'We'll do that.'

I stopped by New York for three days on my way to Ireland. Kim wasn't with me – she'd gotten work, thanks to me, and had been loaned to Warner Brothers for a picture. She was very Southern anyway, and the one time she'd been with Earl she'd been very uncomfortable, and so I didn't mind she wasn't there.

I was in Ireland for seven months – the weather was so bad the shooting took forever. I met Kim in London twice, for a week each time, but the rest of the time I was on my own. I was faithful, after my fashion, which meant that I didn't sleep with any one girl more than twice in a row. I became a good enough pilot so that the stunt pilots actually complimented me a few times.

When I got back to California, I spent two weeks at Palm Springs with Kim. *Golden Boy* was going to premiere in two months. On my last day at the Springs, I'd just climbed out of the swimming pool when a congressional aide, sweating in a suit and tie, walked up to me and handed me a pink slip.

It was subpoena. I was to appear before the House Committee on Un-American Activities bright and early on Tuesday. The very next day.

♦

I was more annoyed than anything. I figured they obviously had the wrong Jack Braun. I called up Metro and talked to someone in the legal department. He surprised me by saying, 'Oh, we thought you'd get the subpoena sometime soon.'

'Wait a minute. How'd you know?'

There was a second's uncomfortable silence. 'Our policy is to cooperate with the FBI. Look, we'll have one of our attorneys meet you in Washington. Just tell the committee what you know and you can be back in California next week.'

'Hey,' I said. 'What's the FBI got to do with it? And why didn't you tell me this was coming? And what the hell does the committee think I know, anyway?'

'Something about China,' the man said. 'That was what the investigators were asking us about, anyway.'

I slammed the phone down and called Mr. Holmes. He and Earl and David had gotten their subpoenas earlier in the day and had been trying to reach me ever since, but couldn't get ahold of me in Palm Springs.

'They're going to try to break the Aces, farm boy,' Earl said. 'You'd better get the first flight east. We've got to talk.'

I made arrangements, and then Kim walked in, dressed in her tennis whites, just back from her lesson. She looked better in sweat than any woman I'd ever known.

'What's wrong?' she said. I just pointed at the pink slip.

Kim's reaction was fast, and it surprised me. 'Don't do what the Ten did,' she said quickly. 'They consulted with each other and took a hard-line defense, and none of them have worked since.' She reached for the phone. 'Let me call the studio. We've got to get you a lawyer.'

I watched her as she picked up the phone and began to dial. A chill hand touched the back of my neck.

'I wish I knew what was going on,' I said.

But I knew. I knew even then, and my knowledge had a precision and a clarity that was terrifying. All I could think about was how I wished I couldn't see the choices quite so clearly.

♥

To me, the Fear had come late. HUAC first went after Hollywood in '47, with the Hollywood Ten. Supposedly the committee was investigating Communist infiltration of the film industry – a ridiculous notion on the face of it, since no Communists were going to get any propaganda in the pictures without the express knowledge and permission of people like Mr. Mayer and the Brothers Warner. The Ten were all current or former Communists, and they and their lawyers agreed on a defense based on the First Amendment rights of free speech and association.

The committee rode over them like a herd of buffalo over a bed of daisies. The Ten were given contempt-of-Congress citations for their refusal to cooperate, and after their appeals ran out years later, they ended up in prison.

The Ten had figured the First Amendment would protect them, that the contempt citations would be thrown out of court within a few weeks at the most. Instead the appeals went on for years, and the Ten went to the slammer, and during that time none of them could find a job.

The blacklist came into existence. My old friends, the American Legion, who had learned somewhat more subtle tactics since going after the Holiday Association with axe handles, published a list of known or suspected Communists so that no one employer had any excuse for hiring anyone on the list. If he hired someone, he became suspect himself, and his name could be added to the list.

None of those called before HUAC had ever committed a crime, as defined by law, nor were they ever accused of crimes. They were not being investigated for criminal activity, but for associations. HUAC had no constitutional mandate to investigate these people, the blacklist was illegal, the evidence introduced at the committee sessions was largely hearsay and inadmissible in a court of law ... none of it mattered. It happened anyway.

HUAC had been silent for a while, partly because their chairman, Parnell, had gotten tossed into the slammer for padding his payroll, partly because the Hollywood Ten appeals were still going through the court. But they'd gotten hungry for all that great publicity they'd gotten when they went after Hollywood, and the public had been whipped into a frenzy with the Rosenberg trials and the Alger Hiss case, so they concluded that the time was right for another splashy investigation.

HUAC's new chairman, John S. Wood of Georgia, decided to go after the biggest game on the planet.

Us.

My MGM attorney met me at the Washington airport. 'I'd advise you not to talk with Mr. Holmes or Mr. Sanderson,' he said.

'Don't be ridiculous.'

'They're going to try to get you to take a First or Fifth Amendment defense,' the lawyer said. 'The First Amendment defense won't work – it's been turned down on every appeal. The Fifth is a defense against self-incrimination, and unless you've actually done something illegal, you can't use it unless you want to *appear* guilty.'

'And you won't work, Jack,' Kim said. 'Metro won't even release your pictures. The American Legion would picket them all over the country.'

'How do I know that I'll work if I talk?' I said. 'All you have to do to get on the blacklist is be *called*, for crissake.'

'I've been authorized to tell you from Mr. Mayer,' the lawyer said, 'that you will remain in his employ if you cooperate with the committee.'

I shook my head. 'I'm talking with Mr. Holmes tonight.' I grinned at them. 'We're the Aces, for heaven's sake. If we can't beat some hick congressman from Georgia, we don't *deserve* to work.'

So I met Mr. Holmes, Earl, and David at the Statler. Kim said I was being unreasonable and stayed away.

There was a disagreement right from the start. Earl said that the committee had no right to call us in the first place, and that we should simply refuse to cooperate. Mr. Holmes said that we couldn't just concede the fight then and there, that we should defend ourselves in front of the committee – that we had nothing to hide. Earl told him that a kangaroo court was no place to conduct a reasoned defense. David just wanted to give his pheromones a crack at the committee. 'The hell with it,' I said. 'I'll take the First. Free speech and association is something every American understands.'

Which I didn't believe for a second, by the way. I just felt that I had to say something optimistic.

I wasn't called that first day – I loitered with David and Earl in the lobby, pacing and gnawing my knuckles, while Mr. Holmes and his attorney played Canute and tried to keep the acid, evil tide from eating the flesh from their bones. David kept trying to talk his way past the guards, but he didn't have any luck – the guards outside were willing to let him come in, but the ones inside the committee room weren't exposed to his pheromones and kept shutting him out.

The media were allowed in, of course. HUAC liked to parade its virtue before the newsreel cameras, and the newsreels gave the circus full play.

I didn't know what was going on inside until Mr. Holmes came out. He walked like a man who had a stroke, one foot carefully in front of the other. He was gray. His hands trembled, and he leaned on the arm of his attorney. He looked as if he'd aged twenty years in just a few hours. Earl and David ran up to him, but all I could do was stare in terror as the others helped him down the corridor.

The Fear had me by the neck.

Earl and Blythe put Mr. Holmes in his car, and then Earl waited for my MGM limousine to drive up, and he got into the back with us. Kim looked pouty, squeezed into the corner so he wouldn't touch her, and refused even to say hello.

'Well, I was right,' he said. 'We shouldn't have cooperated with those bastards at all.'

I was still stunned from what I'd seen in the corridor. 'I can't figure out why the hell they're doing this.'

He fixed me with an amused glance. 'Farm boys,' he said, a resigned comment on the universe, and then shook his head. 'You've got to hit them over the head with a shovel to get them to pay attention.'

Kim sniffed. Earl didn't give any indication he'd heard.

'They're power-hungry, farm boy,' he said. 'And they've been kept out of power by Roosevelt and Truman for a lot of years. They're going to get it back, and they're drumming up this hysteria to do it. Look at the Four Aces and what do you see? A Negro Communist, a Jewish liberal, an F.D.R. liberal, a woman living in sin. Add Tachyon and you've got an alien who's subverting not just the country but our chromosomes. There are probably others as powerful that nobody knows about. And they've all got unearthly powers, so who knows what they're up to? And they're not controlled by the government, they're following some kind of liberal political agenda, so that threatens the power base of most of the people on the committee right there.

'The way I figure it, the government has their own ace talents by now, people we haven't heard of. That means we can be done without – we're too independent and we're politically unsound. China and Czechoslovakia and the names of the other aces – that's an excuse. The point is that if they can break us right in public, they prove they can break anybody. It'll be a reign of terror that will last a generation. Not anyone, not even the President, will be immune.'

I shook my head. I had heard the words, but my brain wouldn't accept them. 'What can we do about it?' I asked.

Earl's gaze held my eyes. 'Not a damn thing, farm boy.'

I turned away.

My MGM attorney played a recording of the Holmes hearing for me that night. Mr. Holmes and his attorney, an old Virginia family friend named Cranmer, were used to the ways of Washington and the ways of law. They expected an orderly proceeding, the gentlemen of the committee asking polite questions of the gentlemen witnesses.

The plan had no relation to reality. The committee barely let Mr. Holmes talk – instead they screamed at him, rants full of vicious innuendo and hearsay, and he was never allowed to reply.

I was given a copy of the transcript. Part of it reads like this:

MR. RANKIN: When I look at this disgusting New Deal man who sits before the committee, with his smarty-pants manners and Bond Street clothes and his effete cigarette holder, everything that is American and Christian in me revolts at the sight. The New Deal man! That damned New Deal permeates him like a cancer, and I want to scream, 'You're everything that's wrong with America. Get out and go back to Red China where you belong, you New Deal socialist! In China they'll welcome you and your treachery.'

CHAIRMAN: The honorable member's time has expired.

MR. RANKIN: Thank you, Mr. Chairman.

CHAIRMAN: Mr. Nixon?

MR. NIXON: What were the names of those people in the State Department who you consulted with prior to your journey to China?

WITNESS: May I remind the committee that those with whom I dealt were American public servants acting in good faith ...

MR. NIXON: The committee is not interested in their records. Just their names.

The transcript goes on and on, eighty pages of it altogether. Mr. Holmes had, it appeared, stabbed the generalissimo in the back and lost China to the Reds. He was accused of being soft on communism, just like that parlor-pink Henry Wallace, who he supported for the presidency. John Rankin of Mississippi – probably the weirdest voice on the committee – accused Mr. Holmes of being part of the Jewish-Red conspiracy that had crucified Our Savior. Richard Nixon of California kept asking after names – he wanted to know the people Mr. Holmes consulted with in the State Department so that he could do to them what he'd already done to Alger Hiss. Mr. Holmes didn't give any names and pleaded the First Amendment. That's when the committee really rose to its feet in righteous indignation: they mauled him for hours, and the next day they sent down an indictment for contempt of Congress. Mr.

Holmes was on his way to the penitentiary.

He was going to prison, and he hadn't committed a single crime.

'Jesus Christ. I've got to talk to Earl and David.'

'I've already advised you against that, Mr. Braun.'

'The hell with that. We've got to make plans.'

'Listen to him, honey.'

'The hell with that.' The sound of a bottle clinking against a glass. 'There's got to be a way out of this.'

When I got to Mr. Holmes's suite, he'd been given a sedative and put to bed. Earl told me that Blythe and Tachyon had gotten their subpoenas and would arrive the next day. We couldn't understand why. Blythe never had any part in the political decisions, and Tachyon hadn't had anything to do with China or American politics at all.

David was called the next morning. He was grinning as he went in. He was going to get even for all of us.

> MR. RANKIN: I would like to assure the Jewish gentleman from New York that he will encounter no bias on account of his race. Any man who believes in the fundamental principles of Christianity and lives up to them, whether he is Catholic or Protestant, has my respect and confidence.
>
> WITNESS: May I say to the committee that I object to the characterization of 'Jewish gentleman.'
>
> MR. RANKIN: Do you object to being called a Jew or being called a gentleman? What are you kicking about?

After that rocky start, David's pheromones began to infiltrate the room, and though he didn't quite have the committee dancing in a circle and singing 'Hava Nagila,' he did have them genially agreeing to cancel the subpoenas, call off the hearings, draft a resolution praising the Aces as patriots, send a letter to Mr. Holmes apologizing for their conduct, revoke the contempt of Congress citations for the Hollywood Ten, and in general make fools out of themselves for several hours, right in front of the newsreel cameras. John Rankin called David 'America's little Hebe friend,' high praise from him. David waltzed out, we saw that ear-to-ear grin, and we pounded him on the back and headed back to the Statler for a celebration.

We had opened the third bottle of champagne when the hotel dick opened the door and congressional aides delivered a new round of subpoenas. We turned on the radio and heard Chairman John Wood give a live address about how David had used 'mind control of the type practiced in the Pavlov Institute in Communist Russia,' and that this deadly form of attack would be investigated in full.

I sat down on the bed and stared at the bubbles rising in my champagne glass.

The Fear had come again.

Blythe went in the next morning. Her hands were trembling. David was turned away by hall guards wearing gas masks.

There were trucks with chemical-warfare symbols out front. I found out later that if we tried to fight our way out, they were going to use phosgene on us.

They were constructing a glass booth in the hearing room. David would testify in isolation, through a microphone. The control of the mike was in John Wood's hands.

Apparently HUAC were as shaken as we, because their questioning was a little disjointed. They asked her about China, and since she'd gone in a scientific capacity she didn't have any answers for them about the political decisions. Then they asked her about the nature of her power, how exactly she absorbed minds and what she did with them. It was all fairly polite. Henry van Renssaeler was still a congressman, after all, and professional courtesy dictated they not suggest his wife ran his mind for him.

They sent Blythe out and called in Tachyon. He was dressed in a peach-colored coat and Hessian boots with tassels. He'd been ignoring his attorney's advice all along – he went in with the attitude of an aristocrat whose reluctant duty was to correct the misapprehensions of the mob.

He outsmarted himself completely, and the committee ripped him to shreds. They nailed him for being an illegal alien, then stomped over him for being responsible for releasing the wild card virus, and to top it all off they demanded the names of the aces he'd treated, just in case some of them happened to be evil infiltrators influencing the minds of America at the behest of Uncle Joe Stalin. Tachyon refused.

They deported him.

♦

Harstein went in the next day, accompanied by a file of Marines dressed for chemical warfare. Once they had him in the glass booth they tore into him just as they had Mr. Holmes. John Wood held the button on the mike and would never let him talk, not even to answer when Rankin called him a slimy kike, right there in public. When he finally got his chance to speak, David denounced the committee as a bunch of Nazis. That sounded to Mr. Wood like contempt of Congress.

By the end of the hearing, David was going to prison, too.

Congress adjourned for the weekend. Earl and I were going before the committee on Monday next.

We sat in Mr. Holmes's suite Friday night and listened to the radio, and it was all bad. The American Legion was organizing demonstrations in support of the committee all around the country. There were rounds of subpoenas going out to people over the country who were known to have ace abilities – no deformed jokers got called, because they'd look bad on camera. My agent had left a message telling me that Chrysler wanted their car back, and that the Chesterfield people had called and were worried.

I drank a bottle of scotch. Blythe and Tachyon were in hiding somewhere. David and Mr. Holmes were zombies, sitting in the corner, their eyes sunken, turned inward to their own personal agony. None of us had anything to say, except Earl. 'I'll take the First Amendment, and damn them all,' he said. 'If they put me in prison, I'll fly to Switzerland.'

I gazed into my drink. 'I can't fly, Earl,' I said.

'Sure you can, farm boy,' he said. 'You told me yourself.'

'*I can't fly, dammit!* Leave me alone.'

I couldn't stand it anymore, and took another bottle with me and went to bed. Kim wanted to talk and I just turned my back and pretended to be asleep.

'Yes, Mr. Mayer.'

'Jack? This is terrible, Jack, just terrible.'

'Yes, it is. These bastards, Mr. Mayer. They're going to wreck us.'

'Just do what the lawyer says, Jack. You'll be fine. Do the brave thing.'

'Brave?' Laughter. '*Brave?*'

'It's the right thing, Jack. You're a hero. They can't touch you. Just tell them what you know, and America will love you for it.'

'You want me to be a rat.'

'Jack, Jack. Don't use those kind of words. It's a patriotic thing I want you to do. The right thing. I want you to be a hero. And I want you to know there's always a place at Metro for a hero.'

'How many people are gonna buy tickets to see a rat, Mr. Mayer? How many?'

'Give the phone to the lawyer, Jack. I want to talk to him. You be a good boy and do what he says.'

'The hell I will.'

'Jack. What can I do with you? Let me talk to the lawyer.'

Earl was floating outside my window. Raindrops sparkled on the goggles perched atop his flying helmet. Kim glared at him and left the room. I got out of bed and went to the window and opened it.

He flew in, dropped his boots onto the carpet, and lit a smoke.

'You don't look so good, Jack.'

'I have a hangover, Earl.'

He pulled a folded *Washington Star* out of his pocket. 'I have something here that'll sober you up. Have you seen the paper?'

'No. I haven't seen a damn thing.'

He opened it. The headline read: STALIN ANNOUNCES SUPPORT FOR ACES.

I sat on the bed and reached for the bottle. 'Jesus.'

Earl threw the paper down. 'He wants us to go down. We kept him out of Berlin, for god's sake. He has no reason to love us. He's persecuting his own wild card talents over there.'

'The bastard, the bastard.' I closed my eyes. Colors throbbed on the backs of my lids. 'Got a butt?' I asked. He gave me one, and a light from his wartime Zippo. I leaned back in bed and rubbed the bristles on my chin.

'The way I see it,' Earl said, 'we're going to have ten bad years. Maybe we'll even have to leave the country.' He shook his head. 'And then we'll be heroes again. It'll take at least that long.'

'You sure know how to cheer a guy up.'

He laughed. The cigarette tasted vile. I washed the taste away with scotch.

The smile left Earl's face, and he shook his head. 'It's the people that are going to be called after us – those are the ones I'm sorry for. There's going to be a witch hunt in this country for years to come.' He shook his head. 'The NAACP is paying for my lawyer. I just might give him back. I don't want any organization associated with me. It'll just make it harder for them later.'

'Mayer's been on the phone.'

'Mayer.' He grimaced. 'If only those guys who run the studios had stood up when the Ten went before the committee. If they'd shown some guts none of this would ever have happened.' He gave me a look. 'You'd better get a new lawyer. Unless you take the Fifth.' He frowned. 'The Fifth is quicker. They just ask you your name, you say you won't answer, then it's over.'

'What difference does the lawyer make, then?'

'You've got a point there.' He gave me a ragged grin. 'It really *isn't* going to make any difference, is it? Whatever we say or do. The committee will do what they want, either way.'

'Yeah. It's over.'

His grin turned, as he looked at me, to a soft smile. For a moment, I saw the glow that Lillian had said surrounded him. Here he was, on the verge of losing everything he'd worked for, about to be used as a weapon that would cudgel the civil rights movement and anti-fascism and anti-imperialism and labor and everything else that mattered to him, knowing that his name would be anathema, that anyone he'd ever associated with would soon be facing the same treatment ... and he'd accepted it all somehow, saddened of course, but still solid within himself. The Fear hadn't even come close to touching him. He wasn't afraid of the committee, of disgrace, of the loss of his position and standing. He didn't regret an instant of his life, a moment's dedication to his beliefs.

'It's over?' he said. There was a fire in his eyes. 'Hell, Jack,' he laughed, 'it's not over. One committee hearing ain't the war. We're aces. They can't take that away. Right?'

'Yeah. I guess.'

'I better leave you to fix your hangover.' He went to the window. 'Time for my morning constitutional, anyway.'

'See you later.'

He gave me the thumbs-up sign as he threw a leg over the sill. 'Take care, farm boy.'

'You too.'

I got out of bed to close the window just as the drizzle turned to downpour. I looked outside into the street. People were running for cover.

♦

'Earl *really was a Communist*, Jack. He belonged to the party for years, he went to Moscow to study. Listen, darling' – imploring now – '*you can't help him*. He's going to get crucified no matter what you do.'

'I can show him he ain't alone on the cross.'

'Swell. Just swell. I'm married to a martyr. Just tell me, how are you helping your friends by taking the Fifth? Holmes isn't coming back to public life. David's hustled himself right into prison. Tachyon's being deported. And Earl's doomed, sure as anything. You can't even carry their cross for them.'

'Now who's being sarcastic?'

Screaming now. '*Will you put down that bottle and listen to me?* This is something your country wants you to do! It's the right thing!'

I couldn't stand it anymore, so I went for a walk in the cold February afternoon. I hadn't eaten all day and I had a bottle of whiskey in me, and the traffic kept hissing past as I walked, the rain drizzling in my face, soaking through my light California jacket, and I didn't notice any of it. I just thought of those faces, Wood and Rankin and Francis Case, the faces and the hateful eyes and the parade of constant insinuations, and then I started running for the Capitol. I was going to find the committee and smash them, bang heads together, make them run gabbling in fear. I'd brought democracy to Argentina, for crissake, and I could bring it to Washington the same way.

The Capitol windows were dark. Cold rain gleamed on the marble. No one was there. I prowled around looking for an open door, and then finally I bashed through a side entrance and headed straight for the committee room. I yanked the door open and stepped inside.

It was empty, of course. I don't know why I was so surprised. There were only a few spotlights on. David's glass booth gleamed in the soft light like a piece of fine crystal. Camera and radio equipment sat in its place. The chairman's gavel glowed with brass and polish. Somehow, as I stood like an imbecile in the hushed silence of the room, the anger went out of me.

I sat down in one of the chairs and tried to remember what I was doing here. It was clear the Four Aces were doomed. We were bound by the law and by decency, and the committee was not. The only way we could fight them was to break the law, to rise up in their smug faces and smash the committee room to bits, laughing as the congressmen dived for cover beneath their desks. And if we did that we'd become what we fought, an extralegal force for terror and violence. We'd become what the committee claimed we were. And that would only make things worse.

The Aces were going down, and nothing could stop it.

As I came down the Capitol steps, I felt perfectly sober. No matter how much I'd had to drink, the booze couldn't stop me from knowing what I knew, from seeing the situation in all its appalling, overwhelming clarity.

I knew, I'd known all along, and I couldn't pretend that I didn't.

I walked into the lobby next morning with Kim on one side and the lawyer on the other. Earl was in the lobby, with Lillian standing there clutching her purse.

I couldn't look at them. I walked past them, and the Marines in their gas masks opened the door, and I walked into the hearing room and announced my intention to testify before the committee as a friendly witness.

Later, the committee developed a procedure for friendly witnesses. There would be a closed session first, just the witness and the committee, a sort of dress rehearsal so that everyone would know what they were going to talk about and what information was going to be developed, so things would go smoothly in public session. That procedure hadn't been developed when I testified, so everything went a little roughly.

I sweated under the spotlights, so terrified I could barely speak – all I could see were those nine sets of evil little eyes staring at me from across the room, and all I could hear were their voices, booming at me from the loudspeakers like the voice of God.

Wood started off, asking me the opening questions: who I was, where I lived, what I did for a living. Then he started going into my associations, starting with Earl. His time ran out and he turned me over to Kearney.

'Are you aware that Mr. Sanderson was once a member of the Communist party?'

I didn't even hear the question. Kearney had to repeat it.

'Huh? Oh. He told me, yes.'

'Do you know if he is currently a member?'

'I believe he split with the party after the Nazi-Soviet thing.'

'In 1939.'

'If that's what, when, the Nazi-Soviet thing happened. '39. I guess.' I'd forgotten every piece of stagecraft I'd never known. I was fumbling with my tie, mumbling into the mike, sweating. Trying not to look into those nine sets of eyes.

'Are you aware of any Communist affiliations maintained by Mr. Sanderson subsequent to the Nazi-Soviet pact?'

'No.'

Then it came. 'He has mentioned to you no names belonging to Communist or Communist-affiliated groups?'

I said the first thing that came into my head. Not even thinking.

'There was some girl, I think, in Italy. That he knew during the war. I think her name was Lena Goldoni. She's an actress now.'

Those sets of eyes didn't even blink. But I could see little smiles on their faces. And I could see the reporters out of the corner of my eye, bending suddenly over their notepads.

'Could you spell the name, please?'

So there was the spike in Earl's coffin. Whatever could have been said about Earl up to then, it would have at least revealed himself true to his principles. The betrayal of Lillian implied other betrayals, perhaps of his country. I'd destroyed him with just a few words, and at the time I didn't even know what it was I was doing.

I babbled on. In a sweat to get it over, I said anything that came into my head. I talked about loving America, and about how I just said those nice things about Henry Wallace to please Mr. Holmes, and I'm sure it was a foolish thing to have done. I didn't want to change the Southern way of life, the Southern way of life was a fine way of life. I saw *Gone With the Wind* twice, a great picture. Mrs.

Bethune was just a friend of Earl's I got photographed with. Velde took over the questioning.

'Are you aware of the names of any so-called aces who may be living in this country today?'

'No. None, I mean, besides those who have already been given subpoenas by the committee.'

'Do you know if Earl Sanderson knows any such names?'

'No.'

'He has not confided to you in any way?'

I took a drink of water. How many times could they repeat this? 'If he knows the names of any aces, he has not mentioned them in my presence.'

'Do you know if Mr. Harstein knows of any such names?'

On and on. 'No.'

'Do you believe that Doctor Tachyon knows any such names?'

They'd already dealt with this. I was just confirming what they knew. 'He's treated many people afflicted by the virus. I assume he knows their names. But he has never mentioned any names to me.'

'Does Mrs. van Renssaeler know the existence of any other aces?'

I started to shake my head, then a thought hit me, and I stammered out, 'No. Not in herself, no.'

Velde plodded on. 'Does Mr. Holmes—' he started, and then Nixon sensed something here, in the way I'd just answered the question, and he asked Velde's permission to interrupt. Nixon was the smart one, no doubt. His eager, young chipmunk face looked at me intently over his microphone.

'May I request the witness to clarify that statement?'

I was horrified. I took another drink of water and tried to think of a way out of this. I couldn't. I asked Nixon to repeat the question. He did. My answer came out before he finished.

'Mrs. van Renssaeler has absorbed the mind of Dr. Tachyon. She would know any names that he would know.'

The strange thing was, they hadn't figured it out about Blythe and Tachyon up till then. They had to have the big jock from Dakota come in and put the pieces together for them.

I should have just taken a gun and shot her. It would have been quicker.

Chairman Wood thanked me at the end of my testimony. When the chairman of HUAC said thank you, it meant you were okay as far as they were concerned, and other people could associate with you without fear of being branded a pariah. It meant you could have a job in the United States of America.

I walked out of the hearing room with my lawyer on one side and Kim on the other. I didn't meet the eyes of my friends. Within an hour I was on a plane back to California.

The house on Summit was full of congratulatory bouquets from friends I'd made in the picture business. There were telegrams from all over the country about how brave I'd been, about what a patriot I was. The American Legion was strongly represented.

Back in Washington, Earl was taking the Fifth.

♥

They didn't just listen to the Fifth and then let him go. They asked him one insinuating question after another, and made him take the Fifth to each. Are you a Communist? Earl answered with the Fifth. Are you an agent of the Soviet government? The Fifth. Do you associate with Soviet spies? The Fifth. Do you know Lena Goldoni? The Fifth. Was Lena Goldoni your mistress? The Fifth. Was Lena Goldoni a Soviet agent? The Fifth.

Lillian was seated in a chair right behind. Sitting mute, clutching her bag, as Lena's name came up again and again.

And finally Earl had had enough. He leaned forward, his face taut with anger.

'I have better things to do than incriminate myself in front of a bunch of fascists!' he barked, and they promptly ruled he'd waived the Fifth by speaking out, and they asked him the questions all over again. When, trembling with rage, he announced that he'd simply paraphrased the Fifth and would continue to refuse any answer, they cited him for contempt.

He was going to join Mr. Holmes and David in prison.

People from the NAACP met with him that night. They told him to disassociate himself from the civil rights movement. He'd set the cause back fifty years. He was to stay clear in the future.

The idol had fallen. He'd molded his image into that of a superman, a hero without flaw, and once I'd mentioned Lena the populace suddenly realized that Earl Sanderson was human. They blamed him for it, for their own naïveté in believing in him and for their own sudden loss of faith, and in olden times they might have stoned him or hanged him from the nearest apple tree, but in the end what they did was worse.

They let him live.

Earl knew he was finished, was a walking dead man, that he'd given them a weapon that was used to crush him and everything he believed in, that had destroyed the heroic image he'd so carefully crafted, that he'd crushed the hopes of everyone who'd believed in him ... He carried the knowledge with him to his dying day, and it paralyzed him. He was still young, but he was crippled, and he never flew as high again, or as far.

The next day HUAC called Blythe. I don't even want to think about what happened then.

Golden Boy opened two months after the hearings. I sat next to Kim at the premiere, and from the moment the film began I realized it had gone terribly wrong.

The Earl Sanderson character was gone, just sliced out of the film. The Archibald Holmes character wasn't FBI, but he wasn't independent either, he belonged to that new organization, the CIA. Someone had shot a lot of new footage. The fascist regime in South America had been changed to a Communist regime in Eastern Europe, all run by olive-skinned men with Spanish accents. Every time one of the characters said 'Nazi,' it was dubbed in 'Commie,' and the dubbing was loud and bad and unconvincing.

I wandered in a daze through the reception afterward. Everyone kept telling me what a great actor I was, what a great picture it was.

The film poster said *Jack Braun – A Hero America Can Trust!* I wanted to vomit.

I left early and went to bed.

I went on collecting ten grand per week while the picture bombed at the box office. I was told the Rickenbacker picture was going to be a big hit, but right now they were having script problems with my next picture. The first two screenwriters had been called up before the committee and ended up on the blacklist because they wouldn't name names. It made me want to weep.

After the Hollywood Ten appeals ran out, the next actor they called was Larry Parks, the man I'd been watching when the virus hit New York. He named names, but he didn't name them willingly enough, and his career was over.

I couldn't seem to get away from the thing. Some people wouldn't talk to me at parties. Sometimes I'd overhear bits of conversation. 'Judas Ace.' 'Golden Rat.' 'Friendly Witness,' said like it was a name, or title.

I bought a Jaguar to make myself feel better.

In the meantime, the North Koreans charged across the 38th Parallel and the U.S. forces were getting crunched at Taejŏn. I wasn't doing anything other than taking acting lessons a couple times each week.

I called Washington direct. They gave me a lieutenant colonel's rank and flew me out on a special plane.

Metro thought it was a great publicity stunt.

I was given a special helicopter, one of those early Bells, with a pilot from the swamps of Louisiana who exhibited a decided death wish. There was a cartoon of me on the side panels, with one knee up and one arm up high, like I was Superman flying.

I'd get taken behind North Korean lines and then I'd kick ass. It was very simple.

I'd demolish entire tank columns. Any artillery that got spotted by our side were turned into pretzels. I made four North Korean generals prisoner and rescued General Dean from the Koreans that had captured him. I pushed entire supply convoys off the sides of mountains. I was grim and determined and angry, and I was saving American lives, and I was very good at it.

There is a picture of me that got on the cover of *Life*. It shows me with this tight Clint Eastwood smile, holding a T-34 over my head. There is a very surprised North Korean in the turret. I'm glowing like a meteor. The picture was titled *Superstar of Pusan*, 'superstar' being a new word back then.

I was very proud of what I was doing.

Back in the States, *Rickenbacker* was a hit. Not as big a hit as everyone expected, but it was spectacular and it made quite a bit of money. Audiences seemed to be a bit ambivalent in their reactions to the star. Even with me on the cover of *Life*, there were some people who couldn't quite see me as a hero.

Metro re-released *Golden Boy*. It flopped again.

I didn't much care. I was holding the Pusan Perimeter. I was right there with the GIs, under fire half the time, sleeping in a tent, eating out of cans and looking like someone out of a Bill Mauldin cartoon. I think it was fairly unique behavior for a light colonel. The other officers hated it, but General Dean supported me – at one point he was shooting at tanks with a bazooka himself – and I was a hit with the soldiers.

They flew me to Wake Island so that Truman could give me the Medal of Honor, and MacArthur flew out on the same plane. He seemed preoccupied the whole time, didn't waste any time in conversation with me. He looked incredibly old, on his last legs. I don't think he liked me.

A week later, we broke out of Pusan and MacArthur landed X Corps at Inchon. The North Koreans ran for it.

Five days later, I was back in California. The Army told me, quite curtly, that my services were no longer necessary. I'm fairly certain it was MacArthur's doing. He wanted to be the superstar of Korea, and he didn't want to share any of the honors. And there were probably other aces – nice, quiet, anonymous aces – working for the U.S. by then.

I didn't want to leave. For a while, particularly after MacArthur got crushed by the Chinese, I kept phoning Washington with new ideas about how to be useful. I could raid the airfields in Manchuria that were giving us such trouble. Or I could be the point man for a breakthrough. The authorities were very polite, but it was clear they didn't want me.

I did hear from the CIA, though. After Dien Bien Phu, they wanted to send me into Indochina to get rid of Bao Dai. The plan seemed half-assed – they had no idea who or what they wanted to put in Bao Dai's place, for one thing; they just expected 'native anticommunist liberal forces' to rise and take command – and the guy in charge of the operation kept using Madison Avenue jargon to disguise the fact he knew nothing about Vietnam or any of the people he was supposed to be dealing with.

I turned them down. After that, my sole involvement with the federal government was to pay my taxes every April.

While I was in Korea, the Hollywood Ten appeals ran out. David and Mr. Holmes went to prison. David served three years. Mr. Holmes served only six months and then was released on account of his health. Everyone knows what happened to Blythe.

Earl flew to Europe and appeared in Switzerland, where he renounced his U.S. citizenship and became a citizen of the world. A month later, he was living with Orlena Goldoni in her Paris apartment. She'd become a big star by then. I suppose he decided that since there was no point in concealing their relationship anymore, he'd flaunt it.

Lillian stayed in New York. Maybe Earl sent her money. I don't know.

Perón came back to Argentina in the mid-1950s, along with his peroxide chippie. The Fear moving south.

I made pictures, but somehow none of them was the success that was expected. Metro kept muttering about my image problem.

People couldn't believe I was a hero. I couldn't believe it either, and it affected my acting. In *Rickenbacker*, I'd had conviction. After that, nothing.

Kim had her career going by now. I didn't see her much. Eventually her detective got a picture of me in bed with the girl dermatologist who came over to apply her makeup every morning, and Kim got the house on Summit Drive, with the maids and gardener and chauffeurs and most of my money, and I ended up in a small beach house in Malibu with the Jaguar in the garage. Sometimes my parties would last weeks.

There were two marriages after that, and the longest lasted only eight months. They cost me the rest of the money I'd made. Metro let me go, and I worked for Warner. The pictures got worse and worse. I made the same western about six times over.

Eventually I bit the bullet. My picture career had died years ago and I was broke. I went to NBC with an idea for a television series.

Tarzan of the Apes ran for four years. I was executive producer, and on the screen I played second banana to a chimp. I was the first and only blond Tarzan. I had a lot of points and the series set me up for life.

After that I did what every ex-Hollywood actor does. I went into real estate. I sold actors' homes in California for a while, and then I put a company together and started building apartments and shopping centers. I always used other people's money – I wasn't taking a chance on going broke again. I put up shopping centers in half the small towns in the Midwest.

I made a fortune. Even after I didn't need the money any more, I kept at it. I didn't have much else to do.

When Nixon got elected I felt ill. I couldn't understand how people could believe that man.

After Mr. Holmes got out of prison he went to work as editor of the *New Republic*. He died in 1955, lung cancer. His daughter inherited the family money. I suppose my clothes were still in his closets.

Two weeks after Earl flew the country, Paul Robeson and W.E.B. Du Bois joined the CPUSA, receiving their party cards in a public ceremony in Herald Square. They announced they were joining the protest of Earl's treatment before HUAC.

HUAC called a lot of blacks into their committee room. Even Jackie Robinson was summoned and appeared as a friendly witness. Unlike the white witnesses, the blacks were never asked to name names. HUAC didn't want to create any more black martyrs. Instead the witnesses were asked to denounce the views of Sanderson, Robeson, and Du Bois. Most of them obliged.

Through the 1950s and most of the 1960s, it was difficult to get a grasp on what Earl was doing. He lived quietly with Lena Goldoni in Paris and Rome. She was a big star, active politically, but Earl wasn't seen much.

He wasn't hiding, I think. Just keeping out of sight. There's a difference.

There were rumors, though. That he was seen in Africa during various wars for independence. That he fought in Algeria against the French and the Secret Army. When asked, Earl refused to confirm or deny his activities. He was courted by left-wing individuals and causes, but rarely committed himself publicly. I think, like me, he didn't want to be used again. But I also think he was afraid that he'd do damage to a cause by associating himself with it.

Eventually the reign of terror ended, just as Earl said it would. While I was swinging on jungle vines as Tarzan, John and Robert Kennedy killed the blacklist by marching past an American Legion picket line to see *Spartacus*, a film written by one of the Hollywood Ten.

Aces began coming out of hiding, entering public life. But now they wore masks and used made-up names, just like the comics I'd read in the war and thought were so silly. It wasn't silly now. They were taking no chances. The Fear might one day return.

Books were written about us. I declined all interviews. Sometimes the question came up in public, and I'd just turn cold and say, 'I decline to talk about that at this time.' My own Fifth Amendment.

In the 1960s, when the civil rights movement began to heat up in this country, Earl came to Toronto and perched on the border. He met with black leaders and journalists, talked only about civil rights.

But Earl was, by that time, irrelevant. The new generation of black leaders invoked his memory and quoted his speeches, and the Panthers copied his leather jacket, boots, and beret, but the fact of his continuing existence, as a human being rather than a symbol, was a bit disturbing. The movement would have preferred a dead martyr, whose image could have been used for any purpose, rather than a live, passionate man who said his own opinions loud and clear.

Maybe he sensed this when he was asked to come south. The immigration people would probably have allowed it. But he hesitated too long, and then Nixon was President. Earl wouldn't enter a country run by a former member of HUAC.

By the 1970s, Earl settled permanently into Lena's apartment in Paris. Panther exiles like Cleaver tried to make common cause with him and failed.

Lena died in 1975 in a train crash. She left Earl her money.

He'd give interviews from time to time. I tracked them down and read them. According to one interviewer, one of the conditions of the interview was that he wouldn't be asked about me. Maybe he wanted certain memories to die a natural death. I wanted to thank him for that.

There's a story, a legend almost, spread by those who marched on Selma in '65 during the voting rights crusade … that when the cops charged in with their tear gas, clubs, and dogs, and the marchers began to fall before the wave of white troopers, some of the marchers swore that they looked skyward and saw a man flying there, a straight black figure in a flying jacket and helmet, but that the man just hovered there and then was gone, unable to act, unable to decide whether the use of his powers would have aided his cause or worked against it. The magic hadn't come back, not even at such a pivotal moment, and after that there was nothing in his life but the chair in the cafe, the pipe, the paper, and the cerebral hemorrhage that finally took him into whatever it is that waits in the sky.

Every so often, I begin to wonder if it's over, if people have really forgotten. But aces are a part of life now, a part of the background, and the whole world is raised on ace mythology, on the story of the Four Aces and their betrayer. Everyone knows the Judas Ace, and what he looks like.

During one of my periods of optimism I found myself in New York on business. I went to Aces High, the restaurant in the Empire State Building where the new breed of ace hangs out. I was met at the door by Hiram, the ace who used to call himself Fatman until word of his real identity got out, and I could tell right away that he recognized me and that I was making a big mistake.

He was polite enough, I'll give him that, but his smile cost him a certain amount of effort. He seated me in a dark corner, where people wouldn't see me. I ordered a drink and the salmon steak.

When the plate came, the steak was surrounded with a neat circle of dimes. I counted them. Thirty pieces of silver.

I got up and left. I could feel Hiram's eyes on me the whole time. I never came back.

I couldn't blame him at all.

When I was making *Tarzan*, people were calling me well-preserved. After, when I was selling real estate and building developments, everyone told me how much the job must be agreeing with me. I looked so young.

If I look in the mirror now, I see the same young guy who was scuffling the New York streets going to auditions. Time hasn't added a line, hasn't changed me physically in any way. I'm fifty-five now, and I look twenty-two. Maybe I won't ever grow old.

I still feel like a rat. But I only did what my country told me.

Maybe I'll be the Judas Ace forever.

Sometimes I wonder about becoming an ace again, putting on a mask and costume so that no one will recognize me. Call myself Muscle Man or Beach Boy or Blond Giant or something. Go out and save the world, or at least a little piece of it.

But then I think, No. I had my time, and it's gone. And when I had the chance, I couldn't even save my own integrity. Or Earl. Or anybody.

I should have kept the dimes. I earned them, after all.

DEGRADATION RITES

by Melinda M. Snodgrass

A page of newsprint blew across the withered grass of the postage-stamp-sized park in Neuilly, and came to rest against the base of a bronze statue of Admiral D'Estaing. It flapped fitfully, like an exhausted animal pausing for breath; then the icy December wind caught it once more, and sent it skittering on its way.

The man who slumped on an iron bench in the center of the park eyed the approaching paper with the air of a person facing a monumental decision. Then, with the exaggerated care of the longtime drunk, he reached out with his foot and captured it.

As he bent down for the tattered scrap, a stream of red wine from the bottle nestled between his thighs poured down his leg. A string of curses, comprised of several different European languages, and punctuated every now and then by an odd, singsong word, poured from his lips. Capping the bottle, he mopped at the spreading stain with a large purple handkerchief, and collected the paper, the Paris edition of the *Herald Tribune*, and began to read. His pale lilac eyes flicked from column to column as he devoured the words.

> *J. Robert Oppenheimer has been charged with having Communist sympathies and with possible treason. Sources close to the Atomic Energy Commission confirm that steps are being taken to rescind his security clearance, and to remove him from the chairmanship of the commission.*

Convulsively, the man crumpled the paper, leaned against the back of the bench, and closed his eyes.

'Damn them, God damn them all,' he whispered in English.

As if in answer his stomach let out a loud rumble. He frowned peevishly, and took a long pull at the cheap red wine. It flowed sourly over his tongue, and exploded with burning warmth in his empty stomach. The rumblings subsided, and he sighed.

A voluminous overcoat of pale peach adorned with enormous brass buttons and several shoulder capes was thrown over his shoulders like a cloak. Beneath this he wore a sky-blue jacket, and tight blue pants which were tucked into worn, knee-high leather boots. The vest was of darker blue than either coat or pants, embroidered with fanciful designs in gold and silver thread. All of the clothing was stained and wrinkled, and there were patches on his white silk shirt. A violin and bow lay next to him on the bench, and the instrument's case (pointedly open) was on the ground at his feet. A battered suitcase was shoved beneath the bench, and a red leather shoulder bag embossed in gold leaf with a frond, two moons and a star, and a slender scalpel arranged in graceful harmony in the center lay next to it.

The wind returned, rattling the branches of the trees and ruffling his tangled, shoulder-length curls. The hair and brows were a metallic red, and the stubble which shadowed his cheeks and chin was the same unusual shade. The page of newsprint fluttered beneath his hand, and he opened his eyes and regarded it. Curiosity won out over outrage, and with a snap he shook open the paper, and resumed.

BRAIN TRUST DIES

Blythe van Renssaeler, aka Brain Trust, died yesterday at the Wittier Sanatorium. A member of the infamous Four Aces, she was committed to the Wittier Sanatorium by her husband, Henry van Renssaeler, shortly after her appearance before the House Committee on Un-American Activities ...

The print blurred as tears filled his eyes. Slowly the moisture gathered until one tear spilled over and ran swiftly down the bridge of his long, narrow nose. It hung ludicrously on the tip, but he made no move to brush it away. He was frozen, held in an awful stasis that had nothing to do with pain. That would come later; all he felt now was a great emptiness.

I should have known, should have sensed, he thought. He laid the paper on his knee, and gently stroked the article with one slender forefinger the way a man would caress the cheek of his lover. He noticed in a rather abstract way that there was more, facts about China, about Archibald, about the Four Aces, and the virus.

And all of it wrong! he thought savagely, and his hand tightened spasmodically on the page.

He quickly straightened the paper, and resumed his stroking. He wondered if her passing had been easy. If they had removed her from that grimy cubicle, and taken her to the hospital ...

The room stank of sweat and fear, and feces, and the sickly sweet odor of putrefaction, and over all floated the pungent scent of antiseptic. Much of the sweat and the fear was being generated by three young residents who huddled like lost sheep in the center of the ward. Against the south wall a screen shielded a bed from the rest of the patients, but it could not block the inhuman grunting sounds that emerged from behind this flimsy barrier.

Nearby, a middle-aged woman bent over her breviary reading the vespers service. A mother-of-pearl rosary hung from her thin fingers, and periodically drops of blood pattered on the pages. Each time it happened, her lips moved in quick prayer, and she would wipe away the gore. If her constant bleeding had been limited to a true stigmata she might have been canonized, but she bled from every available orifice. Blood ran from her ears, matting her hair and staining the shoulders of her gown, from mouth, nose, eyes, rectum ... everywhere. A worn-out doctor had dubbed her Sister Mary Hemorrhage in the lounge one night, and the result-ant hilarity could only be excused on grounds of mind-numbing exhaustion. Every health-care professional in the Manhattan area had been on almost constant call since Wild Card Day, September 15, 1946, and five months of unremitting work was taking its toll.

Next was a once-handsome black man who floated in a saline bath. Two days ago he had started to shed again, and now only remnants of skin remained. His muscles gleamed raw and infected, and Tachyon had ordered he be treated like a burn victim. He had survived one such molting. It was questionable if he would survive another.

Tachyon was leading a grim procession of physicians toward the screen.

'Are you going to join us, gentlemen?' he called in his soft, deep voice, overlaid with a lilting, musical accent that was rather reminiscent of central Europe or Scandinavia. The residents shuffled reluctantly forward.

An impassive nurse pulled back the screen, revealing an emaciated old man. His eyes gazed desperately up at the doctors, and horrible muffled sounds emerged from his lips.

'An interesting case, this,' said Mandel, lifting the file. 'For some bizarre reason the virus is causing every cavity in this man's body to grow closed. Within a few days his lungs will be unable to pull air, nor will there be room for the proper functioning of his heart ...'

'So why not end it?' Tachyon took the man's hand, noting the assenting squeeze that answered his words.

'What are you suggesting?' Mandel lowered his voice to an urgent hiss.

Tachyon enunciated each word clearly. 'Nothing can be done. Would it not be kinder to spare him this lingering death?'

'I don't know what passes for medicine on your world – or maybe I do, judging from this Hell-born virus you created – but on this world we do not murder our patients.'

Tach felt the hinges of his jaw tighten in anger. 'You'll put a dog or cat down mercifully, but you deny your people the only drug known to truly alleviate pain, and you force people into agonizing death. Oh ... be damned to you!'

He threw back his white coat, revealing a gorgeous outfit of dull gold brocade, and seated himself on the edge of the bed. The man reached desperately up, and Tachyon gripped his hands. It was an easy matter to enter his mind.

Die, let me die, came the thought tinged with the flavor of pain and fear, and yet there was a calm certainty in the man's request.

I cannot. They will not permit it, but I can give you dreams. He moved swiftly, blocking the pain and the reasoning centers of the man's mind. In his own mind he visualized it as a literal wall built of glowing silver-white blocks of power. He gave a boost to the man's pleasure centers, allowing him to drift away in dreams of his own concocting. What he had built was temporary, it would last only a few days, but that would be long enough – before then this joker would have died.

He rose, and looked down at the man's peaceful face.

'What did you do?' demanded Mandel.

He raked the other doctor with an imperious glance. 'Just a bit more Hell-born Takisian magic.'

With a lordly nod to the residents, he left the ward. Out in the hall, beds lined the walls, and an orderly was picking his way carefully down the passage. Shirley Dashette beckoned to him from the nurses' station. They had spent several pleasant evenings together exploring the differences and similarities between Takisian and human lovemaking, but tonight he could manage no more than a smile, and the lack of a physical response alarmed him. Maybe it was time to take a rest. 'Yes?'

'Doctor Bonners would like to consult with you. The patient's in shock, and occasionally lapses into hysterics, but there's nothing physically wrong with her, and he thought—'

'That she might be one of mine.' *Oh God, don't let her be another joker*, he groaned inwardly. *I don't think I can face another monstrosity.* 'Where is she?'

'Room 223.'

He could feel exhaustion shivering along his muscles and licking at the nerves. And close on the heels of the exhaustion came despair and self-pity. With a muttered curse he drove his fist into the top of the desk, and Shirley drew back.

'Tach? Are you all right?' Her hand was cool against his cheek.

'Yes. Of course.' He forced his shoulders back and a spring into his step, and headed off down the hall.

Bonners was huddled with another doctor when Tachyon pushed open the door. Bonners frowned, but seemed more than willing to allow him to take charge when the woman in the bed let out a piercing scream and arched against the restraints. Tach leaped to her side, laid a gentle hand on her forehead, and joined with her mind.

OH GOD! The election, would Riley come through? God knows he'd paid enough for it. He'd buy a victory, but he was damned if he'd buy a landslide ... Mama, I'm frightened ... The bite of a winter morning, and the hiss of a skate blade cutting across the ice ... A hand, gripping hers ... wrong hand. Where was Henry? To leave her now ... how many more hours ... he should be here ... Another contraction coming. NO. She couldn't hear it. Mama ... Henry ... PAIN!

He reeled back, and came up panting against the dresser.

'Good Lord, Doctor Tachyon, are you all right?' Bonners's hand was on his arm.

'No ... yes ... by the Ideal.' He pulled himself carefully upright. His body still ached in sympathetic memory of the woman's first anguished labor. But where in the hell had that second personality come from, that cold, hard-edged *man?*

Shaking off Bonners's hand, he returned to the woman and seated himself on the edge of the bed. More cautious this time, he ran swiftly through some calming and strengthening exercises, and struck out with his full psi powers. Her fragile mental defenses fell before the onslaught, and before she could sweep him up in her mental maelstrom he gripped her mind.

Like a blossom, delicate velvet trembling in a breeze with just a hint ...

He forced himself out of the almost-sensual enjoyment of the mental sharing, and back to the task at hand. Now fully in command, he quickly sifted through her head. What he found added a new wrinkle to the saga of the wild card.

In the early days of the virus they had seen mostly death. Close to twenty thousand of them in the Manhattan area. Ten thousand due to the effects of the virus, another ten due to the rioting, looting, and the National Guard. Then there were the jokers: hideous monsters created from a union of the virus and their own mental constructs. And finally there were the aces. He had seen about thirty of them. Fascinating people with exotic powers – the living proof that the experiment was a success. They had created, despite the terrible toll, super-beings. And now here was a new one with a power unique among the other aces.

He withdrew, leaving only a single tendril of control like reins in the hands of an accomplished horseman. 'Yes, you were quite correct, Doctor, she's one of mine.'

Bonners waggled his hands in a gesture of absolute and total confusion. 'But how ... I mean, don't you usually ... do tests?' he finished lamely.

Tach relaxed, and grinned at his colleague's confusion. 'I just did. And it's the most remarkable thing; this woman has somehow managed to absorb all of her husband's knowledge and memories.' His smile died as a new thought intruded. 'I suppose we really ought to send someone to their home to see if poor old Henry is a mindless hulk shambling around the bedroom. For all we know she may have sucked him dry. Mentally speaking, of course.'

Bonners looked decidedly queasy, and went. The other doctor left with him.

Tachyon dismissed them, and the fate of Henry van Renssaeler, from his thoughts, and concentrated on the woman on the bed. Her mind and psyche were fissured like rotten ice, and some very quick repair work would have to be done lest the personality shatter under the stress and she descend into madness. Later he would try for a more permanent construct, but it would be patchwork at best. His father would be perfect for this, the repair of broken minds being his gift. But since he was far away on Takis, she would have to depend on Tach's lesser abilities.

'There, my dear,' he murmured as he began to work at the knotted sheets that kept her tied to the bed. 'Let's make you a bit more comfortable, and then I'll begin teaching you some mental disciplines to keep you from going totally crazy.'

He reentered the full mindlink. Her mind fluttered beneath his, confused, unable to understand the magnitude of the change that had come over her.

I'm mad ... it couldn't have happened ... gone mad.

No, the virus ...

He's really there ... can't bear it.

Then don't. See, here and here, reroute and place him deep below.

NO! Take him out, away!

Not possible; control the only answer.

The ward sprang into life like a point of incandescent fire, and drew its intricate cage about 'Henry.'

There was a sense of wonder and peace, but he knew they were only halfway there. The ward stood because of his power, not because of any real understanding on her part; if she were to keep her sanity she would have to learn to create it herself. He withdrew. The rigidity had passed out of her body, and her breathing had become more regular. Tach returned to the task of freeing her, whistling a lilting dance tune through his teeth.

For the first time since being summoned to the room he was at leisure to look, really look, at his patient. Her mind had already delighted him, and her body set his pulse to hammering. Shoulder-length sable hair cascaded across the pillow onto the woman's breast, a perfect counterpoint to the champagne-colored satin of her thin nightgown and the alabaster quality of her skin. Long, sooty lashes fluttered on her cheeks, then lifted, revealing eyes of a profound midnight blue.

She regarded him thoughtfully for a few seconds, then asked, 'I know you, or do I? I don't know your face, but ... I ... feel you.' Her eyes closed again, as if the confusion was too much for her.

Stroking the hair off her forehead, he replied, 'I'm Doctor Tachyon, and yes, you do know me. We've shared mind.'

'Mind ... *mind*. I touched Henry's mind, but it was awful, awful!' She jerked upright, and sat quivering like some small frightened animal. 'He's done such terrible, dishonorable things, I had no idea, and I thought he was—' She bit off the flow of words, and grasped for his arm. 'I have to live with him now. Never be free of him. People should be more careful when they choose … it's better, I think, not to know what's behind their eyes.' Her eyes closed briefly, and her brow furrowed. Suddenly the lashes were lifted, and her nails bit deep into his bicep. 'I liked your mind,' she announced.

'Thank you. I believe I can say with some accuracy that I have an extraordinary mind. Far and away the best you're ever likely to meet.'

She chuckled, a deep, husky sound strangely at odds with her delicate looks. He laughed with her, pleased to see the color returning to her cheeks.

'*Only* one I'm likely to meet. Do people find you vain?' she continued in a more conversational tone, and she settled back against the pillows.

'No, not vain. Arrogant, sometimes overbearing, but never vain. You see, my face won't carry it.'

'Oh, I don't know.' She reached up, and drew her fingers softly down his cheek. 'I think it's a nice face.' He pulled prudently back although it cost him to do so. She looked hurt, and shrank in upon herself.

'Blythe, I've sent someone to check on your husband.' She turned her face away, nuzzling her cheek into the pillow. 'I know you feel sullied by what you've learned of him, but we have to make certain he's all right.' He rose from the bed, and her hands reached out for him. He caught them, and chafed the slender fingers between his.

'I can't go back to him, I can't!'

'You can make those kind of decisions in the morning,' he said soothingly. 'Right now I want you to get some sleep.'

'You saved my sanity.'

'It was my pleasure.' He gave her his best bow, and pressed the soft skin of her inner wrist to his lips. It was unconscionable behavior, but he felt pleased by his self-control.

'Please come back tomorrow.'

'I'll bring you breakfast in bed, and personally spoon-feed you the disgusting mess that passes for hot cereal in this establishment. You can tell me more about my wonderful mind and nice face.'

'Only if you promise to reciprocate.'

'You have nothing to fear on that score.'

They floated in a silvery white sea held by the lightest of mental touches. It was warm and maternal and sensual all at the same time, and he was dimly aware of his body responding to the first true sharing he had experienced in months. He forced his attention back to the session. The ward hung between them like a peripatetic firefly.

Again.

Can't. Hard.

Necessary. Now again.

The firefly resumed its erratic course, tracing out the complex lines and whorls of a mentatic ward. There was a bulge of darkness, like a tide of stinking mud, and the ward shattered. Tachyon snapped back to his body just in time to catch Blythe as she pitched face first toward the concrete of the rooftop terrace.

His mind was aching with strain. 'You *must* hold him.'

'I can't. He hates me, and wants to destroy me.' Sobs punctuated the words.

'We'll try again.'

'No!'

He gripped her, one arm about her shoulders, the other holding her slender hands. 'I'll be with you. I won't let him hurt you.'

She sucked in a breath, and gave a sharp nod. 'Okay, I'm ready.'

They began again. This time he stayed in closer link. Suddenly he became aware of a whirlpool of power sucking at his mind, his identity, drawing him ever deeper into her. There was a feeling of rape, of violation, of loss. He broke contact, and went staggering across the roof. When he returned to a sense of his surroundings he found himself in intimate embrace with a small willow tree drooping sadly out of a concrete planter, and Blythe was sobbing miserably into her hands.

She looked absurdly young and vulnerable in her Dior coat of black wool and fur collar. The severity of the color heightened the pallor of her skin, and the tight high-standing collar made her look like a lost Russian princess. His feeling of violation dwindled in the face of her obvious distress.

'I'm sorry, so sorry. I didn't mean to. I just wanted to be closer to you.'

'Never mind.' He dropped a few pecking kisses onto her cheek. 'We're both tired. We'll try again tomorrow.'

And so they did; working day after day until by the end of the week she had solid control over her unwelcome mental passenger. Henry van Renssaeler had yet to put in a physical appearance at the hospital; instead, a discreet black maid had brought Blythe her clothes. It suited Tachyon just as well. He was pleased that the man had come through his experience unharmed, but close contact with Representative van Renssaeler's mind had brought little enjoyment, and in truth he was jealous of the man. He had a right to Blythe, mind, body, and soul, and Tachyon craved that position. He would have made her his *genamiri* with all honor and love, and kept her safe and protected, but such dreams were fruitless. She belonged to another man.

One evening he came late to her room to find her in bed reading. In his arms he carried thirty long-stemmed pink roses, and while she laughed and protested he began to cover her with the fragrant blossoms. Once the flower coverlet was complete he stretched out beside her.

'You devil! If you poke me with thorns ...'

'I pulled them all off.'

'You're crazy. How long did that take?'

'Hours.'

'And didn't you have anything better to do with your time?'

He rolled over, wrapping his arms around her. 'I didn't stint my patients, I promise. I did it at weird o'clock this morning.' He nuzzled her ear, and when she didn't push him away he switched to her mouth. His lips played over hers, tasting the sweetness and the promise, and excitement coursed through him when her arms tightened about his neck. 'Will you make love with me?' he whispered against her mouth.

'Is that how you ask all the girls?'

'No,' he cried, stung by the laughter in her voice. He sat up, and brushed petals from his coat of dull rose.

She stripped petals from several roses. 'You have quite a reputation. According to Doctor Bonners you've slept with every nurse on this floor.'

'Bonners is an old busybody, and besides, some of them aren't pretty enough.'

'Then you admit it.' She used the denuded stem as a pointer.

'I admit I like to sleep with girls, but with you it would be different.'

She lay back, a hand over her eyes. 'Oh, spare me, Lord, I've heard these words before.'

'Where?' he asked, suddenly curious, for he sensed she wasn't talking about Henry.

'On the Riviera, when I was much younger and a good deal more foolish.'

He cuddled in close. 'Oh, tell me.'

A rose slapped him on the nose. 'No, you tell me about seduction on Takis.'

'I prefer to do my flirting while dancing.'

'Why dancing?'

'Because it's vastly romantic.'

The covers were flung aside, and she began shrugging into an amber peignoir. 'Show me,' she commanded, opening her arms.

He slipped his arm around her waist, and took her right hand in his left. 'I'll teach you Temptation. It's a very pretty waltz.'

'Does it live up to its name?'

'Let's try it, and you tell me.'

He alternated between humming in his light baritone and calling out instructions as they walked through the intricacies of the dance.

'My! Are all your dances so complicated?'

'Yes, it shows off what clever, graceful fellows we are.'

'Let's do it again, and this time just hum. I think I've got the basic steps, and you can just shove me when I get off.'

'I will *guide* you as befits a man with his lady.'

He was turning her under one arm, gazing down into her laughing blue eyes, when an outraged 'hrrmph' broke the moment. Blythe gasped, and seemed to realize what a scandalous picture she presented; her feet bare, unbound hair rippling across her shoulders, her filmy lace peignoir revealing far too much of her decolletage. She scurried back to bed, and pulled the covers up to her chin.

'Archibald,' she squeaked.

'Mr. Holmes,' said Tachyon, recovering himself and holding out his hand.

The Virginian ignored it, and stared at the alien from beneath knotted brows. The man had been assigned by President Truman to coordinate the relief efforts in Manhattan, and they had shared podium space during several frantic press conferences in the weeks immediately following the catastrophe. He looked a lot less friendly now.

He stepped to the bed and dropped a fatherly kiss on the top of Blythe's head. 'I've been out of town, and returned to find you've been ill. Nothing serious, I hope?'

'No.' She laughed. It was a little too high and a little too tight. 'I've become an *ace*. Isn't that remarkable?'

'An ace! What are your abilities—' He broke off abruptly, and stared at Tachyon. 'If you'll excuse us, I'd like to speak with my goddaughter alone.'

'Of course. Blythe, I'll see you in the morning.'

When he returned, seven hours later, she was gone.

Checked out, the desk said; an old friend of the family, Archibald Holmes, had picked her up about an hour before. For a moment he considered stopping by her penthouse, but decided it could only lead to trouble. She was Henry van Renssaeler's wife, and nothing could change that. He tried to tell himself it didn't matter, and returned to his pursuit of a young nurse up in the maternity ward.

He tried to put Blythe from his mind, but at the oddest moments he would find himself recalling the brush of her fingers across his cheek, the deep blue of her eyes, the scent of her perfume, and most of all, her mind. That memory of beauty and gentleness haunted him, for here among the psi-blind he felt very isolated. One simply didn't join in telepathic communication with everyone one met, and hers had been his first *real* contact since his arrival on earth. He sighed and wished he could see her again.

He had rented an apartment in a converted brownstone near Central Park. It was a sultry Sunday afternoon in August 1947, and he was wandering around the single room in a silk shirt and boxer shorts. Every window stood open in the hope of catching a breeze, his tea-kettle was whistling shrilly on the stove, and Verdi's *La Traviata* blared from the phonograph. The extreme decibel level was dictated by his neighbor one floor down who was addicted to Bing Crosby albums, and who had been listening over and over again to 'Moonlight Becomes You.' Tachyon wished Jerry had met his current girlfriend in sunlight on Coney Island; his musical selections seemed dictated by the times and places where he met his inamoratas.

The alien had just picked up a gardenia and was debating how best to place it in the glass flower bowl when there was a knock.

'Okay, Jerry,' he bellowed, lunging to the door. 'I'll turn it down, but only if you agree to bury Bing. Why don't we have a truce and try something nonvocal? Glenn Miller or somebody. Just don't make me listen to that harelip anymore.'

He yanked open the door, and felt his jaw drop. 'I think it would be a good idea if you did turn it down,' said Blythe van Renssaeler.

He stared at her for several seconds, then reached down and gave the tail of his shirt a discreet tug. She smiled, and he noticed that she had dimples. How had he missed that before? He had thought her face was indelibly printed on his mind. She waved a hand in front of his face.

'Hello, remember me?' She tried to keep her tone light, but there was a fearful intensity about her.

'Of ... of course. Come in.'

She didn't move. 'I've got a suitcase.'

'So I see.'

'I've been thrown out.'

'You can still come in ... suitcase and all.'

'I don't want you to feel ... well, trapped.'

He tucked the gardenia behind her ear, removed the case from her hand, and pulled her in. The flounces of her pale, peach-colored silk dress brushed against his legs, pulling the hair upright at the electric contact. Women's fashion was a pet hobby with Tachyon, and he noticed that the dress was a Dior original, the ankle-length skirt held out by a number of chiffon petticoats. He realized he could probably span her waist with his hands. The bodice was supported by two thin straps, leaving most of her back bare. He liked the way her shoulder blades moved beneath the white skin. There was an answering movement from within his jockey shorts.

Embarrassed, he darted for the closet. 'Let me put on some pants. Water's ready for tea, and turn down that record.'

'Do you take milk or lemon in your tea?'

'Neither. I take it over ice. I'm about to die.' He padded across the room, tucking in the shirt.

'It's a lovely day.'

'It's a lovely *hot* day. My planet is a good deal cooler than yours.'

Her eyes flickered away, and she plucked at a wisp of hair. 'I know you're an alien, but it seems strange to talk about it.'

'Then we won't.' He busied himself with the tea while studying her surreptitiously from the corner of one eye. 'You seem very composed for a woman who's just been thrown out,' he finally remarked.

'I had my hoo in the back of a taxi.' She smiled sadly. 'Poor man, he thought he had a real nut on his hands. Especially since—' She cut off abruptly, using the acceptance of the cup as a way to avoid his searching gaze.

'Not complaining, mind you, but why did you ... er ...'

'Come to you?' She drifted across the room and turned down the phonograph. 'This is a very sad part.'

He forced his attention back to the music and realized it was the farewell scene between Violetta and Alfredo. 'Uh … yes, it is.'

She spun to face him and her eyes were haunted. 'I came to you because Earl is too absorbed with his causes and marches and strikes and actions, and David, poor boy, would have been terrified at the thought of acquiring a hysterical older woman. Archibald would have urged me to patch things up and stay with Henry – fortunately, he wasn't home when I went by, but Jack was and he wanted me … well, far too badly.'

He shook his head like a stallion bedeviled by gnats. 'Blythe, who are these people?'

'How can you be so ill-informed,' she teased, and struck a dramatic pose – so dramatic that it made a mockery of the words. '*We* are the Four Aces.' Suddenly she began to shake, sending tea sloshing over the rim of the cup.

Tach crossed to her, took the cup, and held her against his chest. Her tears formed a warm, wet patch on his shirt, and he reached out for her mind, but she seemed to sense his intent, and pushed him violently away.

'No, don't, not until I explain what I've done. Otherwise you're likely to get a terrific shock.' He waited while she removed an embroidered handkerchief from her purse, gave her nose a resolute blow, and patted at her eyes. When she again raised her head she was calm, and he admired her dignity and control. 'You must think me a typical scatter-brained female. Well, I won't bore you anymore. I'll start at the beginning and be quite logical.'

'You left without saying good-bye,' he broke in.

'Archibald thought it best, and when he's being fatherly and commanding, I've never been able to say no to him.' Her mouth worked. 'Not about anything. When he learned what I could do, he told me that I had a great gift. That I could preserve priceless knowledge. He urged me to join his group.'

He snapped his fingers. 'Earl Sanderson, and Jack Braun.'

'That's right.'

He bounded up and paced the room. 'They were involved in something down in Argentina, and in capturing Mengele and Eichmann, but *four*?'

'David Harstein, otherwise known as the Envoy—'

'I know him, I treated him only a few … never mind, go on.'

'And me.' She smiled with a little girl's embarrassment. 'Brain Trust.'

He sank back down on the couch, and stared at her. 'What has he … what have *you* done.'

'Used my talent the way Archibald advised. Want to know anything about relativity, rocket technology, nuclear physics, biochemistry?'

'He's been sending you around the country absorbing minds,' he said. Then he exploded. 'Who in the hell do you have in your head?'

She joined him on the sofa. 'Einstein, Salk, Von Braun, Oppenheimer, Teller, and Henry of course, but I'd like to forget about that.' She smiled. 'And that's the crux of the problem. Henry didn't take kindly to a wife with several Nobel prizewinners in her head, much less a wife who knew where all his skeletons were buried, so this morning he threw me out. I wouldn't mind so much if it weren't for the children. I don't know what he's going to tell them about their mother, and – oh damn,' she whispered, banging her fists on her knees. 'I will *not* start crying again.

'Anyway, I was trying to think of what to do. I had just wrestled free from Jack, and was bawling in the back of a taxi, when I thought of you.' Suddenly Tachyon became aware that she was speaking German. He bit down hard, forcing his tongue against the roof of his mouth to hold back nausea. 'It's silly, but in some ways I feel closer to you than I do to anyone else in the world; which is strange when you consider that you're not even from this world.'

Her smile was half siren, half Mona Lisa, but there was no answering physical and emotional response. He was too sickened and angry. 'Sometimes I don't understand you people at all! Have you no conception of the dangers inherent in this virus?'

'No, how can I?' she interrupted. 'Henry took us out of the city within hours of the crisis, and we didn't return until he thought the danger was past.' She was back to English again.

'Well, he was wrong, wasn't he!'

'Yes, but that's not my fault!'

'I'm not saying it is!'

'Then what are you so angry about?'

'Holmes,' he ejected. 'You called him fatherly, but if he had had any affection for you at all, he would not have encouraged you in this mad course.'

'What is so mad about it? I'm young, many of these men are old. I'm preserving priceless knowledge.'

'At the risk of your own sanity.'

'You taught me—'

'You're a human! You're not trained to handle the stress of high-level mentatics. The techniques I taught you in the hospital to keep your personality separate from your husband's were inadequate, nowhere near strong enough.'

'Then teach me what I need to know. Or cure me.'

The challenge brought him up short. 'I can't ... at least not yet. The virus is hellishly complex, working out a counter strain to nullify ...' He shrugged. 'To trump the wild card, if you will, may take me years. I'm one man working alone.'

'Then I'll go back to Jack.' She picked up the case, and lurched toward the door. It was an oddly compelling mixture of dignity and farce as the heavy bag pulled her off balance. 'And if I should go mad, perhaps Archibald will find me a good psychiatrist. After all, I am one of the Four Aces.'

'Wait ... you can't just go.'

'Then you'll teach me?'

He dug thumb and middle finger into the corners of his eyes, and gave the bridge of his nose a hard squeeze. 'I'll try.' The case hit the floor, and she slowly approached him. He warded her off with his free hand. 'One last thing. I'm not a saint, nor one of your human monks.' He gestured toward the curtained alcove that held his bed. 'Someday I'll want you.'

'So what's wrong with now?' She pushed aside the restraining hand, and molded her body to his. It was not a particularly lush body. In fact, it could have been described as meager, but any fault he might have found vanished as her hands cupped his face and pulled his lips down to meet hers.

'A lovely day.' Tachyon sighed with satisfaction, scrubbed at his face with his hand, and stripped off his socks and underwear.

Blythe smiled at him from the bathroom mirror where she stood creaming her face. 'Any earth male who heard you say that would decide you were certifiably insane. A day spent in the company of an eight-year-old, a five-year-old, and a three-year-old is not held to be a high treat by most men.'

'Your men are stupid.' He stared off into space, for a moment remembering the feel of sticky hands in his pockets as a bevy of tiny cousins searched for the treats he carried there, the press of a soft, plump baby cheek against his when he went away promising most faithfully to *come again soon and play*.

He pushed back the past, and found her intently regarding him. 'Homesick?'

'Thinking.'

'Homesick.'

'Children are a joy and a delight,' he said hurriedly before she could reopen their ongoing argument. Picking up a brush, he pulled it through his long hair. 'In fact, I've often wondered if yours aren't changlings or if you cuckolded old Henry from the beginning.'

Six months ago, when Blythe had been thrown from the house, van Renssaeler had instructed the servants to refuse entrance to his estranged wife, thus barring her from her children. Tach had quickly remedied that situation. Every week, when they knew the representative was away from home, they went to the penthouse apartment, Tachyon mind-controlled the servants, and they'd spend several hours playing with Henry Jr., Brandon, and Fleur. He'd then instruct the nurse and housekeeper to forget the visit. It gave him great satisfaction to thumb his nose at the hated Henry, though for real vengeance the man should have been aware of their challenge to his authority.

Tossing the brush aside, he gathered up the evening paper and crawled into bed. On the front page was a picture of Earl receiving a medal for having saved Gandhi. Jack and Holmes stood in the background, the older man looking smug, while Jack looked ill at ease. 'Here's a picture from the banquet tonight,' he added. 'But I still don't see why all the fuss. It was only an attempt.'

'We don't share your callous attitude toward assassination.' Her voice was muffled by the folds of her flannel nightgown as she pulled it over her head.

'I know, and it still seems strange.' He rolled over on his side propped up on one elbow. 'Do you know that until I came to earth I had never gone *anywhere* without bodyguards?'

The old bed squeaked a bit as she settled in. 'That's terrible.'

'We're accustomed to it. Assassination is a way of life among my class. It's how the families jockey for position. By the time I was twenty I had lost fourteen members of my immediate family to assassination.'

'How immediate is immediate?'

'My mother ... I think. I was only four when she was found at the bottom of the stairs near the women's quarters. I've always suspected my Aunt Sabina was behind it, but there was no proof.'

'Poor little boy.' Her hand cupped his cheek. 'Do you remember her at all?'

'Just flashes. The rustle of silk and lace and the smell of her perfume mostly. And her hair, like a golden cloud.'

She rolled over and snuggled close, her buttocks pressing into his groin. 'What else is so different between Takis and earth?' It was an obvious attempt to change the subject, and he was grateful to her. Talking about the family he had abandoned always made him sad and homesick.

'Women, for one thing.'

'Are we better or worse?'

'Just different. You wander about free after you reach childbearing age. We would never allow that. A successful attack against a pregnant woman could wipe out years of careful planning.'

'I think that's horrible too.'

'We also don't equate sex with sin. A sin to us is casual reproduction which could upset the plan. But pleasure, now, that's another matter. For example, we take attractive young men and women from the lower class – the non-psi people – and train them to service the men and women of the great households.'

'Don't you ever see the women of your own class?'

'Of course. Until age thirty we grow up together, train and study together. It's only when a woman reaches childbearing years that she is secluded to keep her safe. And we still get together for family functions: balls, hunts, picnics, but all within the walls of the estate.'

'How long are the little boys left with their mothers in the women's quarters?'

'All children are left until they're thirteen.'

'Do they ever see each other again?'

'Of course, they're our *mothers*!'

'Don't be defensive. It's just very alien to me.'

'So to speak,' he said, snagging the gown and running his hand up her leg.

'So you have sex toys,' she mused while his hands explored her body, and she fondled his stiffening penis. 'Sounds like a nice idea.'

'Want to be my sex toy?'

'I thought I already was.'

◆

It was a chill that brought him awake. He sat up to find Blythe gone, and the covers trailing across the floor. He became aware of voices from beyond the beaded curtain. The wind was gusting about the building, setting up a keening howl as it sought out the cracks and crevices in the windows. The hair on the back of his neck was rising, but it had nothing to do with the cold. It was those deep guttural voices from behind the curtain, reminding him of children's boogy stories of unquiet ancestor ghosts possessing the living bodies of direct descendants. He shivered, and thrust through the beads. They fell tinkling behind him, and he saw

Blythe standing in the center of the room carrying on a spirited argument with herself.

'I tell you, Oppie, we must develop—'

'No! We've been over this before, our first priority is the device. We can't be sidetracked with this hydrogen bomb right now.'

For a long moment Tachyon stood frozen with horror. Such things had happened before, when she was tired or under stress, but never to such an extent. He knew he had to find her quickly if she was not to be lost, and he forced himself to move. In two strides he was at her side, gripping her close, reaching for her mind. And he almost retreated in terror, for inside was a nightmarish whirlpool of conflicting personalities, all battling for supremacy while Blythe spun helplessly in the center. He plunged toward her only to be blocked by Henry. Furiously Tachyon thrust him aside, and gathered her within the protective ward of his mind. The other six personalities orbited around them, fighting the ward. Blythe's strength combined with his, and they banished Teller to his compartment, and Oppenheimer to his; Einstein retreated mumbling while Salk just seemed bemused.

Blythe slumped against him, and the sudden weight was too much for his exhausted body. His knees gave way, and he sat down hard on the wood floor, Blythe cradled in his lap. Out in the street he could hear the milkman making his deliveries, and he realized it had taken hours to restore her balance.

'God damn you, Archibald,' he muttered, but it seemed inadequate, as inadequate as his ability to help.

'You don't want to do that,' murmured David Harstein. Tach's hand froze. 'The knight would be better.' The Takisian nodded, and quickly moved the chess piece. His jaw dropped as he contemplated the move.

'You cheat! Why, you miserable cheat!'

Harstein spread his hands in a helpless, placating gesture. 'It was just a suggestion.' The young man's tone was soft and aggrieved, but his dark brown eyes were alight with amusement.

Tachyon grunted, and wriggled back until he could lean against the sofa. 'I find it rather alarming that a person of your position would stoop to using your gifts in such a despicable manner. You should be setting an example for the other aces.'

David grinned, and reached for his drink. 'That's the public face. Surely with my creator I can fall back into my lazy, bohemian ways.'

'Don't.'

There was a moment of strained silence while Tach stared inward at pictures he would rather forget, and David with elaborate concentration gave the pocket pegboard chess set an infinitesimal shift to the left.

'I'm sorry.'

'It's all right.' He gave the younger man a soothing smile. 'Let's go on with the game.'

David nodded, and bent his wiry dark head over the board. Tach took a sip of his Irish coffee, and allowed the warmth to fill his mouth before swallowing. He was ashamed of his overreaction to the teasing remark. After all, the boy had meant no harm.

He had met David in the hospital in early 1947. On the Wild Card Day, Harstein had been playing chess at a sidewalk cafe. No symptoms had manifested themselves then, but months later he had been brought writhing and convulsing into the hospital. Tach had feared that this intense, handsome man would be yet another faceless victim, but against all expectations he had recovered. They had tested: David's body exuded powerful pheromones, pheromones that made him hard to resist on any level. He was recruited by Archibald Holmes, dubbed the Envoy by a fascinated press, and proceeded to use his awesome charisma to settle strikes, negotiate treaties, and mediate with world leaders.

Of the other male Aces he was Tachyon's favorite, and under David's tutelage he had learned to play chess. It was a testimonial both to his own growing abilities and to David's teaching skills that he had resorted to his powers in an effort to keep the game from Tach. The alien smiled, and decided to repay the other man for his interference.

He carefully sent out a probe, slipped beneath David's defenses, and watched as that fine mind weighed and evaluated possible moves. The decision was reached, but before Harstein could act upon it Tach gave a sharp twist, erasing the decision, and substituting another in its place.

'Check.'

David stared down at the board, then flipped it onto the floor with a howl while Tach climbed onto the couch, buried his head in a pillow, and laughed.

'Talk about *me* cheating. I can't control my power, but *you*! Reach into a man's head and ...'

A key scraped in the lock, and Blythe called out, 'Children, children, what are you battling about now?'

'He cheats,' the two men called in chorus, pointing at one another.

Tach gathered her into his arms. 'You're freezing. Let me fix you some tea. How was the conference?'

'Not bad.' She removed her fur hat, and shook snow from the silver-tipped ends. 'With Werner down with the croup they were grateful to have my input.' She leaned forward, and pressed a soft kiss on David's darkly shadowed cheek. 'Hello, dear, how was Russia?'

'Bleak.' He began collecting the scattered chessmen. 'You know, it doesn't seem fair.'

'What?' Tossing her coat onto the sofa, she pulled off her muddy boots, and curled up against the pillows with her feet tucked snugly beneath the silver fox fur.

'Earl gets to snatch Bormann out of Italy and save Gandhi from a Hindu fanatic, and you get to sit in a sleazy motel and attend a rocketry conference.'

'They also serve who only sit and talk. As you should well know. Besides, you've gotten your fair share of the glory. What about Argentina?'

'That was more than a year ago, and all I did was talk to the Perónists while Earl and Jack intimidated the jackboots in the street. Now, who do you think the press noticed? Us? Not likely.

You've got to have *flash* to get noticed in this business.'

'And just what is this business?' interjected Tachyon, pressing a mug of steaming tea into Blythe's hands.

David hunched forward, his head thrusting out from his stooped shoulders like an inquisitive bird. 'Salvaging something out of the disaster. Using these gifts to improve the human condition.'

'That's how it starts, but will it end there? My experience with super-races – being a member of one myself – is that we take what we want, and the devil take anyone else. When a tiny minority of people on Takis began to develop mental powers, they quickly began interbreeding to make certain no one else would get a chance at the powers. It gave us a planet to rule, and we're only eight percent of the population.'

'We'll be different.' Harstein's wry laugh made a mockery of the statement.

'I hope so. But I'm more comforted by the knowledge that there are only a few dozen of you aces, and that Archibald hasn't welded all of you into this great force for Democracy.' His thin lips twisted a bit on the final words.

Blythe reached out, and pushed his bangs off his forehead. 'You disapprove?'

'I worry.'

'Why?'

'I think you and David should be grateful that you're out of the public eye. The rage of the have-nots against the haves is never pretty, and your race has a tradition of suspicion and hostility toward the stranger. You aces are surpassing strange. What is it one of your holy books says? Suffer not the witch?'

'But we're just people,' Blythe objected.

'No, you're not ... not anymore, and the others won't forget it. I know of thirty-seven of you, there may be more, and you're un-detectable – not like the jokers. National hysteria is a particularly virulent and fast-growing weed. People are seeing Communists everywhere, and it probably wouldn't take much to transfer that distrust to some other terrifying minority – like an unseen, secret, awesomely powered group of people.'

'I think you're overreacting.'

'Am I? Take these HUAC hearings.' He gestured toward a pile of newspapers. 'And two days ago a federal jury indicted Alger Hiss for perjury. These are not the actions of a sane and stable nation. And this during your month of joy and rebirth.'

'No, that's Easter. This is the first birth.' David's weak joke sank into the heavy silence that washed through the room, broken only by the hiss of wind-driven snow against the windows.

Harstein sighed and stretched. 'What a gloomy bunch we are. What say we get some dinner, and find a concert? Satchmo is playing uptown.'

Tach shook his head. 'I have to go back to the hospital.'

'Now?' wailed Blythe.

'My darling, I must.'

'Then I'll go with you.'

'No, that's silly. Let David take you to dinner.'

'No.' Her lips had tightened into a mulish line. 'If you won't let me help, I can at least keep you company.'

He sighed and rolled his eyes as she pulled on her boots.

'Stubborn lady,' David remarked from beneath the coffee table, where he was scrabbling after the scattered chess pieces. 'We've all discovered that it does no good to argue with her.'

'You should try *living* with her.'

The delicate pillbox hat warped beneath the sudden tightening of her fingers. 'Believe me, we can solve that problem.'

'Don't start,' Tach said warningly.

'And don't take that disapproving-father tone with me! I'm not a child, nor one of your secluded Takisian ladies.'

'If you were, you'd behave better; and as for being a child, you're certainly acting like one – and a spoiled one at that. We've had this discussion before, and I'm *not* going to do what you want.'

'We have *not* had a discussion. You have constantly closed me off, changed the subject, refused to discuss the matter—'

'I'm due at the hospital.' He started for the door.

'You see?' she shot at the uncomfortable Harstein. 'Has he cut me off, or has he cut me off?'

The young man shrugged, and crammed the chess set into the pocket of his shapeless corduroy jacket. For once, he seemed at a loss for words.

'David, kindly take my *genamiri* to dinner, and try to return her to me in a somewhat better frame of mind.'

Blythe cast Harstein a pleading look, while Tachyon stared with regal disdain at the far wall.

'Hey, folks. I think you ought to take a nice romantic walk in the snow, talk things over, have a late supper, make love and quit bickering. Whatever it is, it can't be that big of a problem.'

'You're right,' murmured Blythe, the rigidity passing from her body under the relaxing wash of pheromones.

David placed a hand in Tach's back, and urged him out the door. Lifting Blythe's hand, he placed it firmly in Tachyon's, and made a vague gesture of benediction over their heads. 'Now go, my children, and sin no more.' He followed them down the stairs and into the streets, then bolted for the subway before the pacifying effects of his power could wear off.

'Now do you see why I don't want you working with me?'

The moon had managed to slip beneath the skirt of the clouds, and the pale silver light streaming across the snow made the city look almost clean. They stood on the edge of Central Park, breath mingling in soft white puffs as she stared seriously up into his face.

'I see that you're trying to protect and shelter me, but I don't think it's necessary. And after watching you tonight ...' She hesitated, searching for a way to soften her next words. 'I think I can deal with it better than you can. You care for your patients, Tach, but their deformities and insanities ... well, they disgust you too.'

He flinched. 'Blythe, I'm so ashamed. Do you think they know, can they sense?'

'No, no, love.' Her hand stroked his hair, soothing him as she would one of her young children. 'I see it only because I'm so close to you. They see only the compassion.'

'The Ideal knows I've tried to suppress it, but I've never seen such horrors.' He jerked away from her comforting arms, and paced the sidewalk. 'We don't tolerate deformity. Among the great houses such creatures are destroyed.' There was a faint noise, and he turned back to face her. One gloved hand was pressed to her mouth, and her eyes were wide, glittering pits in the glow from a nearby streetlight. 'And now you know I'm a monster.'

'I think your culture is monstrous. Every child is precious no matter what its disabilities.'

'So my sister thought, and our monstrous culture destroyed her too.'

'Tell me.'

He began drawing random patterns on a snow-covered park bench. 'She was the eldest, some thirty years my senior, but we were very close. She was married outside the house during one of those rare family truces. Her first child was defective and put down, and Jadlan never recovered. She killed herself several months later.' His hand swept across the bench, obliterating the drawings. Blythe lifted his hand, and chafed the chilled fingers between her gloved hands. 'It started me thinking about the whole structure of my society. Then came the decision to field-test the virus on earth, and that was the end. I couldn't sit by any longer.'

'Your sister must have been special, different, like you.'

'My cousin says it's the Sennari line that we carry. It's a throw-back recessive that – according to him, anyway – should never have been permitted to continue. But I'm losing you with all this talk of pedigree, and your teeth are rattling in your head. Let's get home and get you warm.'

'No, not until we settle this.' He didn't pretend not to understand. 'I can help you, and I insist that you let me share this with you. Give me your mind.'

'No, that would be eight personalities. It's too many.'

'Let me be the judge of that. I'm managing just fine with seven.'

He made a rude noise, and she stiffened with outrage. 'Like you managed in February when I found Teller and Oppenheimer battling over the hydrogen bomb, while you stood like a zombie in the center of the room?'

'This will be different. You're beloved to me, your mind will not harm me. And beyond the work … when I have your memories and knowledge you won't be lonely anymore.'

'I haven't been lonely, not since you came.'

'Liar. I've seen the way you gaze off into the distance, and the sad music you pull out of that violin when you think I'm not listening. Let me be there to provide you with a small part of home.' She placed a hand across his mouth. 'Don't argue.'

So he didn't, and he allowed himself to be convinced. More out of love for her than any real acceptance of her arguments. And late that night, as her legs tightened about his waist, and her nails raked down his sweat-slick back, and he came in violent release, she reached out, and sucked in his mind as well.

There was a terrible, gut-wrenching moment of *violation, theft, loss*, then it was over, and from the mirror of her mind came back two images. The beloved, lady-soft, gentle touch that was Blythe, and a frighteningly familiar and equally beloved image that was *him*.

'Damn them all!' Tachyon raged the length of the small antechamber, spun, and fixed Prescott Quinn with an outthrust forefinger. 'It is outrageous, unconscionable, to summon us in this manner. How dare they – and by what right do they – pull us from our home, and send us haring off to Washington on two hours' – *two hours*' – notice?'

Quinn sucked noisily on the stem of his pipe. 'By the right of law and custom. They're members of Congress, and this committee is empowered to call and examine witnesses.' He was a burly old man with an impressive gut that stretched his watch chain, complete with Phi Beta Kappa key, across the severe black of his waistcoat.

'Then call us in to witness – though God knows to what – and have an end to this. We came tumbling down here last night only to be told the hearing had been postponed, and now they keep us cooling our heels for *three* hours.'

Quinn grunted, and rubbed at his bushy white eyebrows. 'If you think this is much of a wait, young man, you've a lot to learn about the federal government.'

'Tach, sit down, have some coffee,' murmured Blythe, looking pale but composed in a black knit dress, veiled hat, and gloves.

David Harstein came mooching into the antechamber, and the two Marine guards at the chamber door stiffened and eyed him warily. 'Thank God, a touch of sanity in the midst of madness and nightmares.'

'Oh, David, darling.' Blythe's hands clutched feverishly at his shoulders. 'Are you all right? Was it terrible yesterday?'

'No, it was great ... all except being continually referred to as the "Jewish gentleman from New York" by that Nazi Rankin. They questioned me about China: I told them we had done everything possible to negotiate a settlement between Mao and Chiang. They of course concurred. I then suggested that they disband these hearings, and they agreed amid much joy and applause, and—'

'And then you left the room,' interrupted Tach.

'Yes.' His dark head drooped and he contemplated his clasped hands. 'They're constructing a glass booth now, and I'll be recalled. Damn them anyway!'

A supercilious page entered and called for Mrs. Blythe van Renssaeler. She started, her purse falling to the floor. Tach recovered it, and pressed his cheek against hers.

'Peace, beloved. You're more than a match for them alone, much less with all the rest of you along. And don't forget, *I'm* with you.' She smiled faintly. Quinn took her arm, and escorted her into the hearing room. Tachyon had a brief glimpse of backs, cameras, and a jumble of tables all washed in a fierce white light from the television spots. Then the door closed with a dull thud.

'Game?' asked David.

'Sure, why not.'

'I'm not imposing? Would you rather prepare your testimony?'

'What testimony? I don't know anything about China.'

'When did they get you?' His deft hands flew, setting up the board.

'Yesterday afternoon about one.'

'It's all such a crock,' the Envoy said with a marked lack of diplomacy, and viciously jammed in a pawn at Queen's pawn four.

They were still at the game when Blythe and Quinn returned. The board went flying with the alien's precipitous leap, but David didn't remonstrate with him. Blythe was as pale as death, and shaking.

'What did they do?' demanded Tach, the words harsh in his throat. She didn't answer, merely shivered within the circle of his arms like a wounded animal.

'Doctor Tachyon, this is going a bit beyond China. We must talk.'

'A moment.' He bent to her, and pressed his lips against her temple. He could feel the pulse beating there. Quickly he slipped beneath her defense, and sent a calming tide flowing through her mind. With a final shudder she relaxed, and loosened her grip on the lapel of his pale peach coat. 'Sit with David, love. I have to talk to Mr. Quinn.' He knew he was talking down to her, but stress could warp the fragile structure she had constructed to keep her divergent personalities separated, and what he had found in that brief incursion had been an eroding edifice.

The lawyer drew him aside. 'China was the excuse, Doctor. The issue now is this virus. I think this committee has gotten the idea that the aces are a subversive force, and they may reflect the mood in the country at large.'

'Doctor Tachyon,' called the page. Quinn waved him back with an abrupt slash.

'Absurd!'

'Nonetheless, I now understand why you're here. My advice to you is to take the Fifth.'

'Which means?'

'You refuse to answer all and any questions. That includes your name. Such a response has been construed as a waiver of the Fifth.'

Tach drew himself up to his full, unimpressive height. 'I do not fear these men, Mr. Quinn, nor will I sit and condemn myself by silence. We will stop this foolishness now!'

The room was an obstacle course of lights, chairs, tables, people, and the snaking cables. Once he caught his heel, stumbled, pulling himself up with a muttered curse. For an instant the room faded, and he saw the parqueted, chandelier-lit expanse of the Ilkazam ballroom and heard the titters of family and friends as he had stood lost in the midst of the intricacies of Princes Baffled. Because of his error the dance had come to a grinding, stumbling halt, and over the music he could hear his cousin Zabb's nasal voice describing in ruthless detail precisely which step he had missed. Hot blood rushed to his cheeks, and brought a line of sweat to his upper lip. Removing a handkerchief he dabbed at the moisture, then noticed that his discomfort was not entirely due to his memories; because of the television lights the room was broiling.

As he settled himself on the hard, straight-backed wooden chair, Tach noted the skeletal frame of the glass box that was being built to house David. It seemed somehow ominous, like a half-finished scaffold, and he quickly switched his gaze to the nine men who dared to sit in judgment on him and his *genamiri*. They were remarkable only for their expressions of grim portentousness. Otherwise they were merely a collection of middle-aged to elderly men dressed in ill-fitting dark suits. An expression of regal disdain settled over his features, and he lounged back in the chair, his very relaxation making a mockery of their power.

'Wish you had heeded me on the matter of your dress,' murmured Quinn as he opened his briefcase.

'You told me to dress well. I did.'

Quinn eyed the swallow-tailed coat and pants of pale peach, the vest embroidered in shades of green and gold, and the high soft boots with their gold tassels. 'Black would have been better.'

'I'm not a common laborer.'

'Would you state your name for the committee,' said Chairman Wood, without looking up from his papers.

He leaned in to the microphone. 'I am known on your world as Doctor Tachyon.'

'Your full and real name.'

'You're quite certain you want that?'

'Would I ask it otherwise?' Wood grunted testily.

'As you wish.' Smiling faintly, the alien launched into a recitation of his complete pedigree. 'Tisianne brant Ts'ara sek Halima sek Ragnar sek Omian. So ends my mother's line, Omian being a relative newcomer to the Ilkazam clan having married in from the Zaghloul. My maternal grandfather was Taj brant Parada sek Amurath sek Ledaa sek Shahriar sek Naxina. His sire was Bakonur brant Sennari—'

'Thank you,' Wood said hurriedly. He glanced down the table at his colleagues. 'Perhaps for the purposes of this hearing we can make do with his nom de plume?'

'De guerre,' he corrected sweetly, and enjoyed Wood's flush of irritation.

There followed several pointless and meandering questions about where he lived and worked; then John Rankin of Mississippi leaned in. 'Now as I understand it, Doctor Tachyon, you are not a citizen of the United States of America.'

Tach shot Quinn an incredulous glance. There were titters from the assembled journalists, and Rankin glared.

'No, sir.'

'Then you are an alien.' Satisfaction laced the words.

'Undeniably,' he drawled. Leaning nonchalantly back in the chair, he began to play with the folds of his cravat.

Case of South Dakota stepped in. 'And did you or did you not enter this country illegally?'

'There didn't seem to be an immigration center at White Sands, on the other hand I didn't ask, being concerned with more pressing matters at the time.'

'But you have at no time during the intervening years applied for American citizenship?'

The chair scraped back and Tach was on his feet. 'The Ideal grant me patience. This is absurd. I have no desire to become a citizen of your country. Your world I find compelling, and even if my ship were capable of hyperspatial travel I would remain because I have patients who need me. What I do not have is either the time or the inclination to bark and caper for the amusement of this ignorant tribunal. Please, carry on with your little games, but leave me to my work—'

Quinn pulled him bodily down into the chair, and laid a hand over the mike. 'Just keep it up, and you'll be surveying this world from behind the walls of a federal penitentiary,' he hissed. 'Accept it now! These men have power over you and the means to exercise it. Now apologize, and let's see what we can salvage from this mess.'

He did so, but with poor grace, and the questioning continued. It was Nixon of California who brought them to the heart of the matter.

'As I understand it, Doctor, it was your family who developed this virus that has cost so many people their lives. Is that correct?'

'Yes.'

'I beg your pardon?'

He cleared his throat, and said more audibly this time, 'Yes.'

'And so you came—'

'To try and prevent its release.'

'And what corroboration do you have for this claim, Tachyon?' granted Rankin.

'My ship's logs detailing my exchange with the crew of the other ship.'

'And can you obtain these logs?' Nixon again.

'They're on my ship.'

An aide skittered up onto the platform, and there was a hurried conference. 'Reports indicate that your ship has resisted all efforts to enter.'

'It was so ordered.'

'Will you arrange to open it, and allow the Air Force to remove the logs?'

'No.' They regarded each other for a long moment. 'Will you return my ship, and then I'll bring you the logs?'

'No.'

He fell back once more in the chair and shrugged. 'Well, they wouldn't have done you much good anyway; we weren't speaking English.'

'And what about these other aliens? Can we question them?' Rankin's mouth twisted as if he were regarding something peculiarly unpleasant and slimy.

WILD CARDS

'I'm afraid they're all dead.' His voice dropped as he again struggled with the guilt the memories still brought. 'I misjudged their determination. They fought the grappler beam, and broke up in the atmosphere.'

'Very convenient. So convenient that I wonder if it wasn't planned that way?'

'It was Jetboy's failure that released the virus.'

'Do not sully the name of that great American hero with your slanderous lies!' Rankin shouted, winding up into his full Southern-preacher mode. 'I submit to this committee and to the nation that you have remained on this world to study the effects of your evil experiment. That those other aliens were acting as kamikazes ready to die so that you might appear a hero, and live among us accepted and revered, but that in fact you are an alien subversive seekin' to undermine this great nation by the use of these dangerous wild elements—'

'No!' He was on his feet, hands braced on the table, leaning in on his inquisitors. 'No one regrets the events of '46 more than I. Yes, I failed ... failed to stop the ship, failed to locate the globe, failed to convince the authorities of the danger, failed to help Jetboy, and I must live with that failure for the rest of my life! All I can do is offer myself ... my talents, my experience working with this virus, to undo what I have created – I'm sorry ... sorry.' He broke off, choked, and sipped gratefully at the water offered by Quinn.

The heat was like a tangible thing, coiling about his body, stealing the breath from his lungs, and leaving him light-headed. He willed himself not to faint, and pulling the handkerchief from his pocket he wiped at his eyes, and knew he had made another mistake. Males in this culture were trained to suppress emotion. He had just violated another of their taboos. He dropped heavily back into the chair.

'If you are indeed repentant, Doctor Tachyon, then demonstrate it to this committee. What I require from you is a complete list of all the so-called "aces" you have ever treated or heard about. Names ... addresses if possible, and—'

'No.'

'You would be assistin' your country.'

'It's not my country, and I won't help you in your witch-hunts.'

'You are in this country illegally, Doctor. Could be that it's in the best interests of this nation if you were deported. So I'd think over your answer very carefully if I were you.'

'It requires no further thought ... I will not betray my patients.'

'Then the committee has no further questions of this witness.'

◆

At the front doors of the Capitol they walked full into a pale, sharp-featured man.

A tiny sound escaped Blythe, and she clutched at Tach's arm.

'Afternoon, Henry,' grunted Quinn, and the alien realized that this was the husband of the woman who had shared his bed and his life for two and a half years.

He seemed familiar. Tach had been contending with this persona every time he joined with Blythe in telepathic or physical union. Granted, Henry had been relegated to an unused corner of her mind like discarded lumber in a dusty attic, but the mind was there, and it wasn't a very nice mind.

'Blythe.'

'Henry.'

He raked Tachyon with a cold glance. 'If you would excuse us, I'd like to talk to my wife.'

'No, please, don't leave me.' Her fingers plucked at his coat, and he carefully freed them before she could utterly ruin the crease, and clasped her hand warmly in his.

'I think not.'

The congressman gripped his shoulder, and shoved. It was an error in judgment. Small he might be, but Tachyon had studied with one of the finest personal-defense masters on Takis, and his response was almost more reflexive than conscious. He didn't bother with martial arts subtlety, just brought his knee up, nailing van Renssaeler in the nuts, and as the other man folded, his fist took him in the face. The congressman hit the ground like he'd been poleaxed, and Tach sucked at his knuckles.

Blythe's blue eyes were unfocused, staring wildly down at her husband, and Quinn was frowning like a white-haired Zeus. Several people came running to assist the fallen politician, and Quinn, recovering himself quickly, herded them down the steps.

'That was a pretty dirty blow,' he rumbled as he waved down a passing taxi. 'It's not very sporting to kick a man in the balls.'

'I'm not interested in sporting. You fight to win, and failing that you die.'

'Mighty strange world you come from if that's the code you're taught.' He grunted again. 'And, as if you don't have troubles enough, I can guarantee that Henry will sue for assault and battery.'

'Consider yourself retained, Prescott,' Blythe said, raising her head from Tach's shoulder. She was wedged tightly between the two men in the taxi, and Tach could feel the faint shivering that was still running through her body.

'Might be you should consider filing for divorce. Can't imagine why you didn't before now.'

'The children. I knew I'd never see them if I divorced Henry.'

'Well, think about it.'

'Where are we going?'

'The Mayflower. Nice hotel, you'll like it.'

'I want to go to the station. We're going home.'

'Wouldn't advise that. My gut is telling me this isn't over yet, and my belly is an infallible indicator.'

'We've given our testimony.'

'But Jack and Earl are still to come, Harstein has to testify again, and there might be something that would require you to be recalled. Let's just stick until the final hurrah. It'll save you a trip back if I'm right.'

Tach grudgingly agreed, sinking back against the cushions to watch the city go by.

By Sunday night he was heartily sick of Washington, D.C., heartily sick of the Mayflower, and heartily sick of Quinn's doom and gloom prophecies. Blythe had tried to maintain the fantasy that they were having a lovely little vacation, and had dragged him about the city to gaze at marble buildings and meaningless statuary, but her dream world was shattered late Friday, when David was held to be in contempt of Congress and the case remanded to a grand jury.

The boy had huddled in their suite alternating between wild confidence that no indictment would be issued and fear that he would be convicted and imprisoned. The latter seemed the most likely, for he had been horribly abusive to the committee during that final day of testimony, even going so far as to compare them to Hitler's ruling elite. The climate was not forgiving. Tachyon had been driven nearly to distraction trying to suppress David's more vengeful plans against the committee, and trying to soothe Blythe, who seemed to have completely lost English as a first language, and spoke almost exclusively in German.

His efforts were not aided by the fact that they were under virtual siege in the room; surrounded and badgered by swarming reporters who were undeterred even after Blythe emptied a pot of hot coffee over one who had tried to enter while posing as room service. Only Quinn was permitted within their fortress, and he was so uniformly pessimistic that Tach was ready to pitch him out a window.

Now, as dawn was tinting the eastern sky, Tach lay listening to the even beating of Blythe's heart and the soft whisper of her breathing as she lay snuggled against his side. Their lovemaking had been long and frenzied, as if she feared to lose contact with him. It had also been disturbing, for he had found a large amount of leak between the various personalities. He had tried to make her concentrate on a new construct, but she had been too emotionally fragmented to make it work. Only rest and a respite from the stress would restore the balance, and Tach vowed that committee or no committee they were leaving Washington that day.

A furious hammering on the door of their suite brought him plunging out of the bed at one that afternoon. Befuddled, he didn't even think of his dressing gown, but instead wrapped the bedspread about his waist and blundered to the door. It was Quinn, and the look on his face drove the last vestige of sleep from his mind.

'What? What's happened?'

'The worst. Braun's ruined you all.'

'Huh?'

'Friendly witness. He's thrown you all to the wolves to save himself.' Tach sank into a chair. 'That's not all, they're recalling Blythe.'

'When? Why?'

'Tomorrow, right after Earl. Jack very generously volunteered the information that in addition to Von Braun and Einstein and all the rest of the eggheads, she also has *your* thoughts and memories. They want the names of those other aces, and if they can't get them from you, they'll get them from her.'

'She'll refuse.'

'She could go to jail.'

'No … they wouldn't … not a woman.'

The attorney just shook his head.

'*Do* something. You're the lawyer. I refused first, let them send me to jail.'

'There is another option.'

'What?'

'Give them what they want.'

'No, that is not an option. *You* must keep her out of that hearing room.'

The old man gusted a sigh, and scratched furiously at his head until his hair stood out from his head like the quills on an outraged porcupine. 'Okay, I'll see what I can do.'

It hadn't been enough, and on Tuesday morning they were back at the Capitol. Earl had marched in, taken the Fifth, and marched back out with an expression of utter contempt and disdain. He had expected nothing from the white man's government, and it hadn't disappointed him. Now it was Blythe's turn. At the door, two young Marine guards had tried to hold him back. He knew he was being unfair, lashing out at the wrong people, but their attempt to separate him from Blythe shattered his control, and he had brutally mind-controlled them both. He had ordered them to sleep, and they were snoring by the time they hit the floor. That display of his power had a strong effect on several observers, and they quickly found a seat for him in the back of the room among the press corps. He had tried to remonstrate, wanting to be with Blythe, but this time it was Quinn who demurred.

'No, you sitting up there with her would be like a red flag to a bull. I'll take care of her.'

'It's not just the legal thing. Her mind ... it's very fragile right now.' He jerked his head toward Rankin. 'Don't let them hammer at her.'

'I'll try.'

'My darling.' Her shoulders felt thin and bony beneath his hands, and when she raised her face to his, her eyes were like two darkened bruises in her white face. 'Remember, their freedom and safety is riding on you. Please don't say anything.'

'Don't worry, I won't,' she said with a flash of her old spirit. 'They're my patients too.'

He watched her walk away, a hand resting lightly on Quinn's arm, and terror seized him. He wanted to rush after her, and hold her one more time. He wondered if the feeling was his errant precognition kicking in, or just a disordered mind?

'Now, Mrs. van Renssaeler, let's get the chronology set in all our minds, shall we?' said Rankin.

'All right.'

'Now, when did you first discover you had this power?'

'February 1947.'

'And when did you walk out on your husband, Congressman Henry van Renssaeler?' He hit the word Congressman hard, glancing quickly to the left and right to see how his colleagues took it.

'I didn't, he threw me out.'

'And was that maybe because he had found out you were fooling around with another man, a man who isn't even human?'

'No!' cried Blythe.

'Objection!' shouted Quinn in the same breath. 'This is not a divorce proceeding—'

'You have no grounds upon which to object, Mr. Quinn, and may I remind you that this committee has sometimes found it necessary to investigate the backgrounds of attorneys. One has to wonder why you fellows would choose to represent enemies of this nation.'

'Because it is a tenet of Anglo-American law that a defendant have someone to shield him from the awesome might of the federal government—'

'Thank you, Mr. Quinn, but I don't think we need instruction in jurisprudence,' broke in Representative Wood. 'You may continue, Mr. Rankin.'

'I thank you, sir. We'll leave that for the moment. Now, when did you become one of the so-called Four Aces?'

'I think it was in March.'

'Of '47?'

'Yes. Archibald had shown me how I could use my power to preserve priceless knowledge, and had contacted several of the scientists. They agreed, and I—'

'Began to suck out their minds.'

'It isn't like that.'

'Don't you find it sort of disgustin', almost vampirelike, the way you eat a man's knowledge and abilities? It's a cheat, too. You weren't born with a great mind, nor did you study and work to gain your position. You just steal others'.'

'They were willing. I would never do it without permission.'

'And had Congressman van Renssaeler given you his permission?'

Tachyon could hear the tears thickening her voice. 'That was different. I didn't understand ... I couldn't control.' She dropped her face into her gloved hands.

'So let's move on. We're up to the time when you abandoned your husband and children.' He added in a more conversational tone, obviously for the benefit of the other committee members, 'I also find it incredible that a woman would leave her natural role, and strut herself in this fashion. Well, that's neither here nor there—'

'I didn't abandon them,' Blythe interrupted.

He brushed aside her remark. 'Semantics. Now, when was that?'

Blythe slumped hopelessly back in her chair. 'August the twenty-third, 1947.'

'And where have you been living since August twenty-third, 1947?' She sat silently. 'Come, come, Mrs. van Renssaeler. You have consented to answer questions before this committee. You can't withdraw that consent now.'

'At one seventeen Central Park West.'

'And whose apartment is that?'

'Doctor Tachyon's,' she whispered. There was a stir at this from the press corps, for they had kept a very low profile. Only the other three Aces and Archibald had known of their living arrangement.

'So, after violating your husband and stealing his mind you then walk out, and live in sin with an inhuman from another planet who created the virus that gave you this power. There's somethin' fairly convenient in all this.' He leaned forward over the desk, and bellowed down at her. 'Now you listen, madam, and you better answer because you stand in a great deal of danger. Did you take this Tachyon's mind and memories?'

'Y–yes.'

'And have you worked with him?'

'Yes.' Her replies were scarcely audible.

'And do you acknowledge that Archibald Holmes formed the Four Aces as a subversive element designed to undermine loyal allies of the United States?'

Blythe had swung around in the chair, her hands gripping the top rung with a desperate intensity, her eyes darting vaguely about the crowded room. Her face seemed to be writhing, trying to rearrange itself into different visages, and there was an almost psychic white noise coming off her mind. It drilled into Tachyon's head, and his shields snapped into place.

'Are you listening, Mrs. van Renssaeler? Because you better be. I'm beginnin' to think you and your bloodsucking power are a danger to this country. Maybe it's better you do go to jail before you take your ill-gotten knowledge and sell it to the enemies of this country.'

Blythe was shaking so hard that it seemed unlikely she could remain upright in the chair, and tears were streaming down her face. Tach came to his feet, and began pushing through the mob that separated them. 'No, no, please ... don't. Leave me alone.' She wrapped her arms protectively about her body, and rocked back and forth.

'Then give me those names!'

'All right ... all right.' Rankin sank back from the microphone, his pen tapping out a satisfied little rhythm on the pad before him. 'There's Croyd ...'

For Tachyon, time seemed to distend, stretch, almost stand still. Several rows of people still separated him from Blythe, and in that eon-long moment he made his decision. His mind lanced out, pinning her like a butterfly. Her voice choked off, and she emitted a funny little *acking* noise. For him it was akin to holding a snowflake, or some particularly delicate form of glass sculpture. Under his grip he felt the entire structure of her mind fragment, and *Blythe* went spinning away and down into some dark and fearsome cavern of the soul. Freed, the other seven ran rampant. Giggling, lecturing, posturing, ranting, they seemed to race along her central nervous system, setting her body to twitching like a maddened puppet. Words exploded from her: formulae, lectures in German, ongoing arguments between Teller and Oppenheimer, campaign speeches, and Takisian all jumbled in a swirling broth.

The instant he felt her mind give way he released her, but it was too late. Chairs and people were shoved ruthlessly aside as he fought his way to her side and gathered her in his arms. The chamber was in complete disorder with Wood hammering away with his gavel, reporters shouting and jostling, and over all Blythe's manic monologue. He seized her, reached out again with the coercive power of his mind, and carried her down into oblivion. She slumped in his arms, and an eerie silence fell over the chamber.

'I take it the committee has no further questions of this witness?' The words came grating out, and his hatred beat from him like a tangible force. The nine men shifted uncomfortably, then Nixon murmured in a voice that was scarcely audible.

'No, no more questions.'

Hours later he sat at the apartment rocking her in his lap, and crooning as he would have to one of his tiny cousins back home on Takis. His brain felt battered by his struggle to recall her to sanity; none of his efforts had shown the smallest success. He felt young and helpless; he wanted to drum his heels on the rug, and howl like a four-year-old. Images of his father rose up to taunt him; big, solid, and powerful, he had both the training and the natural talent to deal with such mental illness. But he was hundreds of light-years away, and had no idea where his errant son and heir had gotten to.

There was a pre-emptory knock on the door. Shifting his limp, unresisting burden into his left arm, he staggered to the door, and took a step back as his burning eyes focused on the two policemen and the bundled figure behind them. Henry van Renssaeler lifted his bruised face and stared at Tachyon.

'I have here a commitment order for my wife. Kindly hand her over.'

'No ... no, you don't understand. Only I can help her. I don't have the construct yet, but I'll get it. It'll just take a little work.'

The burly officers stepped forward, and gently but inexorably pried her from his encircling arms. He stumbled after them as they headed down the stairs, Blythe lolling in one of the policeman's arms. Van Renssaeler had made no move to touch her.

'Only a little time.' He was crying. 'Please, just give me a little time.'

He slumped down, clinging to the bottom banister post as the outer door fell shut behind them.

He had seen her only once after her commitment. The appeal of his deportation order was grinding through the courts, and seeing the end coming, he had driven to the private sanatorium in upstate New York.

They wouldn't let him in the room. He could have overridden that decision with mind control, but ever since that hideous day he had been unable to use his power. So he had peered through a small window in the heavy door, looking at a woman he no longer knew. Her hair hung in matted witchlocks about her twisted face as she prowled the tiny room lecturing to an unseen audience. Her voice was low and rasping; obviously her vocal cords were being damaged by her constant attempts to maintain a male tone.

Unable to stop himself, he had reached out telepathically, but the chaos of her mind sent him reeling back. Worse had been the infinitesimal flicker of Blythe crying for help from some deep and hidden source. So intense was his guilt that he spent several minutes in the bathroom vomiting, as if that could somehow cleanse his soul.

Five weeks later he had been put aboard a ship sailing for Liverpool.

◆

'*Le pauvre.*' A large matronly woman with two small girls at her side stood looking down at the slumped figure on the bench. She rummaged through her purse, and withdrew a coin. It fell with a dull clink into the violin case. Gathering her children to her she moved on, and Tachyon retrieved the coin with two grimy fingers. It wasn't much, but it would buy another bottle of wine, and another night of forgetfulness.

Rising, he packed away the instrument, gathered up his medical bag, and thrust the folded page of newsprint into his shirt. Later, during the night, it would shield him from the cold. He took a few weaving steps, then stumbled to a swaying halt. Juggling the two cases in one hand, he extracted the page, and took a final look at the headline. The cold east wind was back, tugging urgently at the paper. He released it, and it went skirring away. He walked on, not pausing to look back to where it hung, flapping forlornly, against the iron legs of the bench. Cold it might be, but he would trust to the wine to insulate him.

INTERLUDE ONE

From 'Red Aces, Black Years,'
by Elizabeth H. Crofton,
New Republic, May 1977.

From the moment in 1950 when he declared in his famous Wheeling, West Virginia, speech that 'I have here in my hand a list of fifty-seven wild cards known to be living and working secretly in the United States today,' there was little doubt that Senator Joseph R. McCarthy had replaced the faceless members of HUAC as the leader of the anti-wild-card hysteria that swept across the nation in the early 50s.

Certainly, HUAC could claim credit for discrediting and destroying Archibald Holmes's Exotics for Democracy, the 'Four Aces' of the halcyon postwar years and the most visible living symbols of the havoc the wild card virus had wrought upon the nation (to be sure, there were ten jokers for every ace, but like blacks, homosexuals, and freaks, the jokers were invisible men throughout this period, steadfastly ignored by a society that would have preferred they not exist). When the Four Aces fell, many felt the circus had ended. They were wrong. It was just beginning, and Joe McCarthy was its ringmaster.

The hunt for 'Red Aces' that McCarthy instigated and fronted produced no single, spectacular victory to rival HUAC's, but ultimately McCarthy's work affected many more people, and proved lasting where HUAC's triumph had been ephemeral. The Senate Committee on Ace Resources and Endeavors (SCARE) was birthed in 1952 as the forum for McCarthy's ace-hunts, but ultimately became a permanent part of the Senate's committee structure. In time SCARE, like HUAC, would become a mere ghost of its former self, and decades later, under the chairmanship of men like Hubert Humphrey, Joseph Montoya, and Gregg Hartmann, it would evolve into an entirely different sort of legislative animal, but McCarthy's SCARE was everything its acronym implied. Between 1952 and 1956, more than two hundred men and women were served with subpoenas by SCARE, often on no more substantial grounds than reports by anonymous informants that they had on some occasion displayed wild card powers.

It was a true modern witch-hunt, and like their spiritual ancestors at Salem, those hauled before Tail-Gunner Joe for the non-crime of being an ace had a hard time proving their innocence. How do you prove that you *can't* fly? None of SCARE's victims ever answered that question satisfactorily. And the blacklist was always waiting for those whose testimony was considered unsatisfactory.

The most tragic fates were suffered by those who actually *were* wild card victims, and admitted their ace powers openly before the committee. Of those cases, none was more poignant than that of Timothy Wiggins, or 'Mr. Rainbow,' as he was billed when performing. 'If I'm an ace, I'd hate to see a deuce,' Wiggins told McCarthy when summoned in 1953, and from that moment onward 'deuce' entered the language as the term for an ace whose wild card powers are trivial or useless. Such was certainly the case with Wiggins, a plump, nearsighted, forty-eight-year-old entertainer whose wild card power, the ability to change the color of his skin, had propelled him to the dizzy heights of second billing in the smaller Catskill resort hotels, where his act consisted of strumming a ukulele and singing wobbly falsetto versions of songs like 'Red, Red Robin,' 'Yellow Rose of Texas,' and 'Wild Card Blues,' accompanying each rendition with appropriate color changes. Ace or deuce, Mr. Rainbow received no mercy from McCarthy or SCARE. Blacklisted and unable to secure bookings, Wiggins hanged himself in his daughter's Bronx apartment less than fourteen months after his testimony.

Other victims saw their lives blighted and destroyed in only slightly less dramatic ways: they lost jobs and careers to the blacklist, lost friends and spouses, inevitably lost custody of their children in the all-too-frequent divorces. At least twenty-two aces were uncovered during SCARE's investigatory heyday (McCarthy himself often claimed credit for having 'exposed' twice that many, but included in his totals numerous cases where the accused's 'powers' were established only by hearsay and circumstantial evidence, without a shred of actual documentation), including such dangerous criminals as a Queens housewife who levitated when asleep, a longshoreman who could plunge his hand into a bathtub and bring the water to a boil in just under seven minutes, an amphibious Philadelphia schoolteacher (she kept her gills concealed beneath her clothing, until the day she unwisely gave herself away by saving a drowning child), and even a potbellied Italian greengrocer who displayed an astonishing ability to grow hair at will.

Shuffling through so many wild cards, SCARE inevitably turned up some genuine aces among the deuces, including Lawrence Hague, the telepathic stockbroker whose confession triggered a panic on Wall Street, and the so-called 'panther woman' of Weehawken whose metamorphosis before the newsreel cameras horrified theatergoers from coast to coast. Even that paled beside the case of the mystery man apprehended while looting New York's diamond center, his pockets bulging with gemstones and amphetamines. This unknown ace displayed reflexes four times as fast as those of a normal man, as well as astonishing strength and a seeming immunity to handgun fire. After flinging a police car the length of the block and hospitalizing a dozen policemen, he was finally subdued with tear gas. SCARE immediately issued a subpoena, but the unidentified man lapsed into a deep, comalike sleep before he could take the stand. To McCarthy's disgust, the man could not be roused – until the day, eight months later, when his specially reinforced maximum-security cell was suddenly and mysteriously found empty. A startled trusty swore that he had seen the man walk through the wall, but the description he gave did not match that of the vanished prisoner.

McCarthy's most lasting achievement, if it may be termed an achievement, came with the passage of the so-called 'Wild Card Acts.' The Exotic Powers Control Act, enacted in 1954, was the first. It required any person exhibiting wild card powers to register immediately with the federal government; failure to register was punishable by prison terms of up to ten years. This was followed by the Special Conscription Act, granting the Selective Service Bureau the power to induct registered aces into government service for indefinite terms of service. Rumors persist that a number of aces, complying with the new laws, were indeed inducted into (variously) the Army, the FBI, and the Secret Service during the late fifties, but if true the agencies employing their services kept the names, powers, and very existence of these operatives a closely held secret.

In fact, only two men were ever openly drafted under the Special Conscription Act during the entire twenty-two years that the statute remained on the books: Lawrence Hague, who vanished into government service after the stock manipulation charges against him were dropped, and an even more celebrated ace whose case made headlines all over the nation. David 'Envoy' Harstein, the charismatic negotiator of the Four Aces, was slapped with an induction notice less than a year after his release from prison, where HUAC had confined him for contempt of Congress. Harstein never reported for conscription. Instead he vanished totally from public life in early 1955, and even the FBI's nationwide manhunt failed to turn up any trace of the man whom McCarthy himself dubbed 'the most dangerous pink in America.'

The Wild Card Acts were McCarthy's greatest triumph, but ironically enough their passage sowed the seed of his undoing. When those widely publicized statutes were finally signed into law, the mood of the nation seemed to change. Over and over again McCarthy had told the public that the laws were needed to deal with hidden aces undermining the nation. Well, the nation now replied, the laws are passed, the problem is solved, and we've had enough of all this.

The next year, McCarthy introduced the Alien Disease

Containment Bill, which would have mandated compulsory steril-
ization for all wild card victims, jokers as well as aces. That was too
much for even his staunchest supporters. The bill went down to
crashing defeat in both House and Senate. In an effort to recoup
and recapture the headlines, McCarthy launched an ill-advised
SCARE investigation of the Army, determined to ferret out the
'aces in the hole' that rumor insisted had been secretly recruited
years before the Special Conscription Act. But public opinion
swung dramatically against him during the Army-McCarthy hearings, which culminated in his censure by the Senate.

In early 1955, many had thought McCarthy might be strong
enough to wrest the 1956 Republican presidential nomination
from Eisenhower, but by the time of the 1956 election, the political
climate had changed so markedly that he was hardly a factor.

On April 28, 1957, he was admitted to the Naval Medical Center
at Bethesda, Maryland, a broken man who talked incessantly about
those who he felt had betrayed him. In his last days, he insisted
that his fall was all Harstein's fault, that the Envoy was out there
somewhere, crisscrossing the country, poisoning the people against
McCarthy with sinister alien mind control.

Joe McCarthy died on May 2, and the nation shrugged. Yet his
legacy survived him: SCARE, the Wild Card Acts, an atmosphere
of fear. If Harstein was out there, he did not come forward to gloat.
Like many other aces of his time, he remained in hiding.

CAPTAIN CATHODE
AND THE SECRET ACE

by Michael Cassutt

INT. STRATO-JET – BRIDGE – DAY

The engines RUMBLE as the Wolf Joker puts the Strato-jet into a SCREAMING TURN. Cathode's hands are bound. We can hear POUNDING on the hatch.

Marty (V.O.)

Captain! We're running out of air!

At the controls, the Wolf Joker turns and sneers.

Wolf Joker

Your choice, Captain. Surrender the codes, or all three of your friends breathe their last!

Cathode

You'll die, too, Joker!

Wolf Joker

I'll aim the Strato-jet at the mountain and bail out.

Cathode

I knew it. Jokers are cowards at heart.

Wolf Joker

Insults, Cathode. Pointless … and ill-aimed.

The Wolf Joker rips off his face. It's a mask, of course. Under it … the smug, mustached face of ROWAN MERCADO, Cathode's Takisian nemesis.

Cathode

Mercado! I should have known.

Karl von Kampen closed the script and turned it facedown on his desk. It was early on a Monday morning, August 1956. The temperature outside the Republic Studio offices of *Captain Cathode* – close by the Santa Monica Mountains in the San Fernando Valley – was already approaching ninety, and would easily top a hundred. A rattling air conditioner promised more cooling than it delivered.

Yet here in his corner office, Karl felt a chill.

A *Cathode* script need not rise to the level of *Macbeth*. It was not necessary to have the conceptual wonder of H. G. Wells. It didn't need to be as exciting as *Hellcats of the Navy*.

But the old masked villain gag? What was Willy Ley thinking?

Karl rose from his chair and stretched, not only to relieve the growing tension, but simply to change the geometry of his surroundings. His office was as spare and precise as, he hoped, the inner landscape of his mind: a simple desk and chair, a typewriter on which he wrote first draft memos, a credenza filled with six weeks of *Captain Cathode* scripts, no more, no less.

Karl was a small man with whitish blond hair and blue eyes; a perfect Aryan specimen, if not for the rounded shoulders – he had never been remotely athletic – or, more notably, a limp, the legacy of a wound received in a bombing raid at Peenemunde during the War.

He was relieved to hear the phone ring. His assistant, Abigail. 'The set called,' she said, and Karl knew the message before hearing the words. 'Brant is late again.' Brant Brewer. Captain Cathode himself.

Plucking one of his many sets of dark glasses from the drawer, Karl was out of his office and looming over Abigail before she had replaced the receiver in its cradle. 'Contact Saul Greene and tell him Mr. von Kampen is unhappy.' Greene was Brewer's agent. Karl knew the call would be a pointless exercise; you rarely saw agent without client. But Brewer might be motivated by a warning.

'Mr. von Kampen will be even less happy to know that Harold Dann of Kellogg's will be on set at nine.' Dann was the chief buyer for Kellogg's, the breakfast cereal company that was trying to gain full sponsorship of *Cathode*, a move that would double the series' budget ... and would make Karl rich.

'Stall him,' Karl said. Angered to the point of violence, he picked the morning *Herald* off Abigail's desk. He immediately fokused on the lead article about a body turned to stone near the Griffith Park Observatory.

'Ah, the Medusa Killer has struck again.' The series of awful deaths went back three months. All jokers, turned to stone. 'And the sun rose this morning, too.'

'Karl, you are evil.'

'The word is "cynical."' It amused him to pretend that he knew English better than Abigail did. She actually had a degree from some Eastern college.

'Evil, I said, and I'm sticking to it.' Abigail was twenty-five, slim, dark-haired, easy to imagine as the only gal reporter in a newsroom filled with wisecracking men. Karl loved her voice as well as her refreshing disregard of the conventions of a business relationship, such as those forbidding a secretary to address her boss by his first name. 'The only thing that makes this new set different from the usual joker murders is that the victims aren't young women, but men.'

'Actors, I bet,' Karl said bitterly, 'killed by producers.' He gave Abigail a farewell smile, then placed dark glasses on his face. 'As you said ... evil!'

♥

Karl was being unfair to himself. Though he had a rough German sense of humor sharpened by brutal experiences in the war, he empathized with anyone who had a weakness, who was vulnerable.

Anyone who hid a wild card. Karl even had a name for his own: *fokus*, complete with German spelling. Fokus gave him the gift of enhanced vision, the ability to zoom in and often through any object in line of sight. It was not just a physical ability; it was, in fact, a state of mind – a moment when time stretched.

One he was still struggling to control.

As Karl crossed the hot asphalt, a simple glance toward the mountains at the north end of the Valley triggered fokus. Suddenly, distant Mount Wilson, with its observatory and collection of radio and television transmission towers, appeared close-up.

Another blink, and Karl saw the white dome of the huge hundred-inch reflector ... its paint peeling. Another blink, the tower belonging to KNX Radio ... one of its red safety lights burned out.

There was an almost sexual satisfaction in exercising fokus. It had to be private, of course, an easy concession, since fokus also required special circumstances, such as an inviting target, near or far.

It was not a wild card power that made Karl stand out, except for one thing: his eyes blazed red instead of blue. Hence the dark glasses, never out of reach, no matter how often he was teased for being pretentious.

The glasses marked Karl von Kampen just as thoroughly as his German accent. At times he wondered which was the more prominent handicap in 1956 Hollywood – being an ace, or having worked for Hitler?

Entering the soundstage was like stepping into a dark, inviting cave. For a moment Karl could forget the constant concern about money, the pressure from his boss, Frederick Ziv.

He could remove his glasses.

The first to notice Karl's presence on stage was Eugene Olkewitz, the rotund, frequently drunken nat actor who played dog-faced joker Turk, Captain Cathode's sidekick. 'Here comes the Fuhrer! *Wie geht's?*' he added, slapping Karl on the back.

'That's what I came to find out.' Karl did not like Olkewitz. Compared to Brewer, Eugene was a consummate professional, always on time, never missing his mark or forgetting his lines, but he took his minor role far too seriously, and the costume girl said he often took his rubber dog mask home with him. He claimed he liked to stay in character when he rehearsed, but ...

'We've been working around Brant for the first scene,' Olkewitz said. 'Shot our sides, right, baby?'

'Baby' was addressed to 'Nora,' actress Dotty Doyle, the statuesque, blue-eyed marvel whose magnificent legs were constantly on display in her *Cathode* Strato-Jet uniform. Karl reminded himself to compliment the costume designer, who obviously understood that a kiddie show could get away with hemlines that would have been judged scandalous on a series aimed at adults.

'I'm not your baby, Gene.' Dotty didn't even address him directly, planting herself directly in front of Karl. 'And we can't get anything done like this.'

Typical Dotty – informed, cool, business-like, the type of Nordic princess Karl's parents would have welcomed as a mate for their son.

Karl walked around the flats to the front of the set. The lights had been turned off while the grips removed the control panel of Cathode's Strato-jet. 'She's right, Karl,' said Marshall Korshak, the beleaguered director. 'The rest of the day is all Cathode.'

Korshak was nervous even when things went smoothly. He had come to *Cathode* from *Hopalong Cassidy*. Karl forced a smile. 'It could be worse, Marshall. We could have horses.'

'Horses are always there when you need them. Or you get a new one and no one knows the difference.'

At that moment a production assistant hurried past them, uttering, 'He's here!' then continuing on, to avoid being collateral damage in the explosion to come. The same self-protective impulse caused Korshak to announce that he had to take a piss.

Karl steeled himself for the encounter. But once his eyes adjusted to the sharp change of light, he realized it wasn't Brant Brewer, Captain Cathode. It was Harold Dann from Kellogg's.

Dann was pushing forty, dark, heavyset, and balding. And he had the whitest teeth Karl had seen on any human not an actor. Dann, in fact, smiled with every sentence he uttered ... as if he were getting paid per second of dazzle.

Introductions were made to Olkewitz and Dotty. Dann's eyes widened at his first sight of Cathode's female companion. 'I'm thinking we should put *you* on the cereal box,'

'If legs and knockers sell cornflakes, why not?'

Before the banter could escalate, Karl heard: 'What's wrong with you people? Can't you see we have immortal television to make?'

Brant Brewer, known to millions of American youth as Captain Cathode, scourge of the Takisians and their rogue joker allies, strode from the shadows and planted himself in the center of the set, hands on his hips, a poster child for strength, justice, and American values. He was wearing his skintight navy blue flight suit emblazoned with the letter *C* and a lightning bolt. Every time Karl saw his Captain, no matter how angry he might be, he wished for the ability to broadcast in color.

Either that, or the ability to shoot explosive rays from his fokused eyes. 'Brant, you're two hours late.'

'The hair and makeup girl just won't let me out of the trailer.' Brewer's smile was as dazzling as Dann's, but completely natural. Karl didn't doubt that the hair and makeup girl had a crush on the star – most women in the crew did, and no doubt some of the men.

'You're hours late every other day, and it's killing us.'

'We're getting the scenes, Karl.'

'We're working *around you* to get the scenes! And they are never as good as they could be.'

Brewer brandished a script. 'How can this be good? I'm a man in a suit playing tricks on masked idiots. I can't shoot them. I can't throw them out the hatch. All I can do is speak sharply to them and tell them to eat their spinach.' In argument, Brewer reverted to his original Cajun accent, just as Karl grew more Teutonic. It was a wonder they understood each other all.

'Our audience is young children. They see enough violence in their real lives.'

'Children aren't served by horseshit. Are *you* actually reading the scripts, Karl?' Brant's expression changed from defiance to compassion. 'Forget the dramatic ... simplifications. Are the children of America served by this portrayal of aces and jokers? Is putting Gene Olkewitz in a dog mask better than casting a true—'

'Stop it!' Karl could see that Brewer was, as always, shifting the argument away from his own errors to Hollywood's cowardice about the wild card. 'You know we cannot use real jokers. How many times must we discuss that? The series is properly designed. You are part of it, or not. Keep being late to the set and you will be dismissed.'

'Do you want to go down in history as the man who fired Captain Cathode?'

Karl flicked the front of Cathode's costume with his fingers. 'Captain Cathode is whoever wears the suit!'

Then Brewer's visage changed again, radiating warmth and eternal friendship. 'You're the boss.' He looked around, as if searching for allies, and spotted Korshak. 'Are we making television here or what?'

Karl was still so shaken from the encounter that it took him a moment to realize someone behind him was clapping – Dann. 'You are sitting on a gold mine here, Mr. von Kampen.'

'The series does well.'

'And should continue to do well, but the big bucks won't come from the young eyeballs tuning in every afternoon. It will come from what those young people force their parents to buy. The Captain Cathode comic books and toys, the ... the pajamas, the helmets, the models of the Strato-jet, the figurines.'

'And the breakfast cereal.'

'You'd better get control of your actor.' He was not smiling.

Before he could take any steps, Karl had to suffer through a scoring session for next week's five episodes of *Cathode*.

To call it a scoring session was a stretch, of course. Every music cue was stock, already recorded. The spotting was mechanical … every villainous appearance or fake climax received the same melodramatic sting. To Karl, the repetitions were like insect bites: small, but frequent and annoying.

As he left the dub stage, he saw the man he needed. 'Jack!'

Jack Braun, the famed Judas Ace, more recently the star of Ziv's *Tarzan of the Apes*, looked impossibly tan, and bizarrely young in khakis and white shirt. His wild card, of course. 'Hello, Karl. How's your Captain?' Braun's smirk told him he knew all about Brant's absences. Well, Braun still had friends all over the Republic lot.

'He's just what I want to talk to you about, Jack.'

Braun's eyes narrowed. 'You'd be crazy to cast me, Karl. That ace is still a scarlet letter, to mix a few metaphors.'

'I know that. It would be too expensive and risky to recast right now. I want to know why Brant Brewer can't make it to the set on time.'

'I'm too busy with *Tarzan* to keep up with him.'

'You're wired into everything that happens here.'

'Because it's the only way to survive! Take it from a man who had to learn that the hard way.'

'So teach me.'

'You're doing all right on your own.'

Karl merely crossed his arms. He had enough experience with actors to recognize a performance. Today's was 'Jack Braun, Reluctant Hollywood Operator.'

It didn't last. Braun took out one of his cards. 'Okay, the guy you want is named Edison Hill. You can find him here every afternoon after two.'

Karl read the name on the back of the card. 'The Menagerie, Santa Monica Pier. Is this Hill a drunkard or a fag?' The pier was a notorious homosexual stroll, and a favorite haunt for the city's small joker population.

'Neither one, so far as I know. He won't punch you in the nose if you buy him a cocktail, but mostly he's just a guy who knows things, or knows how to find them out. The Menagerie is basically his office.'

Karl never met Braun without wanting to tell him he was a fellow ace – and without instantly realizing the futility of such a gesture. 'You know, Jack, one of these days, all this ... insanity will be over. We should work together.'

Braun smiled with genuine warmth and knowing scepticism. 'It would be great to think so, wouldn't it?'

He almost missed the Menagerie. It was partway down, snuggled up next to the Santa Monica Pier's infamous merry-go-round and surrounded by carny games, food stalls, and freak shows, almost all of them joker owned and operated. Inside, the club was dim and cramped, smelling of stale beer and old sawdust. A female joker was grinding away on the club's tiny stage, twirling the tassels on her sequined brassiere and bumping her posterior to the music.

'I've been coming here for years,' Hill said. 'I have a weakness for beauty unadorned.' He was slim, tallish, good-looking in a B-movie second-banana way, complete with the Dick Powell mustache. He sounded as though he'd grown up far to the east of Los Angeles.

'There are some ... amazing people here,' Karl said.

'They can be an acquired taste,' Hill said. It was mid-afternoon, hardly prime time for any club, and the Menagerie was largely empty. Nevertheless, the dancer on stage was a true beauty by any standards, though when she dropped her bra Karl saw that she had mouths where her nipples should have been. He didn't want to think about what might be under her G-string. 'What do you when you're not doing this?' he asked Hill, out of due diligence more than polite curiosity.

'You could call me a spook,' Hill said, then added, 'Ghost writer. As-told-to projects, speeches. This and that. A few detective stories for the pulps.'

'A good living?'

'Some of the pulp stories pay well enough. But I was in the Navy, pre-war. Caught a spot on my lung and was sent ashore.'

'You didn't go back on active duty during the war?'

'Tried and tried. They wouldn't take me.' Hill set down his drink and laced his fingers together. 'Now, how may I help you?'

Karl quickly recounted his problems with Brant Brewer. 'You think he's a Red?'

'Doubtful.' Karl knew real Hollywood Communists; Brant Brewer was nothing like them.

'Homo?'

Karl opened his hands. 'Well, he *is* an actor.' Meaning that homosexuality was always a possibility.

'Okay, we'll put a pin in that one.' Hill casually glanced to the right and left. When he spoke, Karl could barely hear him. 'That leaves the wild card factor.'

'There are no signs, but ...'

'My fee is twenty dollars a day, plus expenses. Forty up front. Normally it would be half that, but when the case involves wild cards ...' Hill gestured to the denizens of the Menagerie.

'Fine.' Karl carefully counted out four tens.

'You'll get a full report. Where Brewer lives, how he spends his days, what he does – and with whom. You'll enjoy the style, if not the content.'

They agreed to meet at a coffee shop on Franklin and Western the next morning at eight. If Hill needed to reach Karl immediately, he would call the office and identify himself as 'Mr. Edwards.' If Karl needed Hill, he was to call Hill's answering service.

Hill reached for his hat and slid off the stool, then adjusted cuffs, collar, fedora brim. He actually gave Karl a two-finger salute as he departed.

The production wrapped at 7 P.M., an hour over schedule – double overtime for the crew, thanks to Brewer's lateness. But with Mr. Dann of Kellogg's liable to turn up around any corner, Karl chose to avoid further confrontation, and had Abigail phone for his taxi.

He lived in a duplex in the Hills above Hollywood. His landlady was a silent film actress named Estelle Blair, forcibly retired by the introduction of sound, permanently shelved thanks to the wild card, which had made her an invisible woman – a girly-voiced wraith detectable only as a disembodied overcoat and slippers.

Karl had seen a picture of the silent-era Estelle. She had been blond, leggy, a pouty-lipped flapper goddess. He wondered what she looked like now, in her fifties.

Did *she* even know?

She was notoriously difficult to deal with ... except when it came to Karl. She, or rather, her dressing gown, was there to greet him as he was dropped off. 'You work too hard,' she said. 'Have you had dinner?'

'Yes, at the studio.' He made sure to tell Estelle this, even if he hadn't. He did not want to be forced to accept a dinner invitation, and to answer the lingering question of just where a bite of food went from being visible to invisible as Estelle swallowed it.

He accepted his mail, plucking it out of what appeared to be thin air, and went inside.

The furnishings here were as Spartan as in Karl's office at the studio. A couch, a low table, several chairs. The bedroom beyond was similarly underdone, and so was the kitchen.

Other than his twice-daily use of taxis, Karl's one concession to his status as producer was the biggest television on the market, a 17" Zenith X2552, complete with console. He made sure to watch the final cuts of *Cathode* on a screen the same size or even smaller, that being the way the audience would see the show.

Karl normally turned the Zenith on the moment he entered his place ... not only was the box where he made his living, it had now become company, most nights.

But before Karl could switch on the set, he saw in his mail a letter from Herb Cranston. The former director of operations at White Sands – the first human to come face-to-face with Dr. Tachyon – was in town tonight, suggesting dinner at Musso's at eight.

Karl glanced at his watch. Eight-thirty, but Musso's was just down the road.

He called for a taxi.

'Ach, if it isn't Herr Kampen.'

Karl had entered Musso's through the back entrance, and had been scanning the dining room for Herb Cranston; a tricky process, given the booths. The rocket man was sitting at the counter, the remains of what appeared to have been a hearty meatloaf dinner in front of him. And a cocktail or three. 'I only just got your message.'

'Have you eaten?'

'Yes.'

'Well, then, much as I enjoy the atmosphere here, I've heard so much about the jokers of Santa Monica.'

'They should build a sign. JOKERLAND.' It took Karl several seconds to realize that Cranston was interested in actually visiting the pier and sampling the seedy underside of joker life. Normally Karl would have recoiled, as much from ignorance as from disgust. He had been to the pier a few times, and a few times was enough. Joker prostitutes riding the merry-go-round, calling out to passing men. Horrific faces behind stalls, selling cheap souvenirs and fried foods. Knife fights between joker gang members. Deformity, desperation, and drugs mingled with the smells of salt water, grease, and rotting fish.

But tonight two factors had changed. He really wanted to see Cranston ... and he knew a joker club.

It was odd to be visiting a place like the Menagerie twice in a lifetime, let alone a single day.

Santa Monica Pier seemed more glamorous at night, with its colored lights gleaming and music pouring from the merry-go-round. Crowds of nats mingled with the jokers, eating ice-cream sandwiches and hot dogs as they wandered amongst the games and dives and freak shows.

Inside the Menagerie, the joker dancers were somehow more attractive, or possibly just more varied and numerous. 'This gives new meaning to the term "exotic dancer,"' Cranston said. He loved to pun. In their time at White Sands, Karl's English had been too rudimentary to recognize most of them. He no longer had that excuse.

There was a good-sized crowd, too, for a mid-week night. Or so Karl assumed; the pier and its nightlife were not among his areas of expertise.

As a trio of dancers worked the stage – they called themselves the American Girls, and they were, successively, red, white, and blue beneath their flag-themed costumes – a spectacular femcat, complete with spotted fur and swirling tail, joined Karl and Cranston at their table. 'Interested in some company?'

Cranston waved the girl away, and began talking shop. 'Things are finally starting to happen up at Tomlin.'

'Still trying to make sense of Tachyon's secrets? Reverse engineering a Takisian ship?'

'Hell, no! Wright Field's got nothing better to do ... let them waste their time!' Encouraged by the alcohol, and needing to be heard over the roar, Cranston practically shouted. Then, embarrassed, he said, in a quieter voice, 'Karl, we are back in the business of doing our own designs ... and cutting metal. Watch the skies. Pretty soon you're going to see something flying that was made on Earth.' He took another drink, then smiled. 'Just like your little Strato-jet.'

'Congratulations.'

'Some of our White Sands friends are with us. Even Willy Ley.' Ley had gotten out of Germany before the war, becoming a writer of popular journalism about rocketry – which is why Karl had sought him out for *Cathode*, 'The guy we really need is you. You were the most promising one of the bunch.'

'My friend, you are as inaccurate as you are drunk. That "bunch" included von Braun, Rudolf, Dornberger, so many others—'

'I didn't mean in accomplishments. We know you got to Peenemunde straight out of school. And, hell, none of us got out of the starting blocks at White Sands, not after *Baby* showed up.'

Cranston and von Braun and a handful of former Nazi engineers had been ordered to meet Tachyon and his shell-like Takisian ship when it landed at White Sands. Karl and the rest, however, were kept away, occupied with callisthenics, endless reports, and English lessons.

'Did Willy put you up to this?'

Cranston shrugged. 'He simply said we ought to ask.'

'He should not have done that without telling me.'

'Then I wouldn't have been able to surprise you!' Cranston smirked. He was drunk enough that he was beginning to get sentimental. Karl remembered him as a heavy drinker. 'Both of us, so lucky ... the wild card never got us.'

'Yes.'

The wild card *had* gotten Karl von Kampen, of course. In 1947, he had followed Walter Dornberger to Bell Aircraft in Buffalo, and was mired in the tedium of creating designs for a bomber that would likely never be built when he came down with what he thought – hoped – was the flu. After days of fever and delirium, he recovered to find that his vision had been altered: Previously myopic to the point of blindness, he could now see down to a near microscopic level – or up to the level of the best optical telescopes.

He had fokus.

There was a side effect: For several minutes after fokus, Karl's eyes blazed a demonic red. At first he thought it was a temporary effect ... but within a couple of weeks, as he struggled to master his new 'talent,' he realized it was likely permanent, a sign of his status as an ace. That was when he began wearing dark glasses.

Hating the work at Bell, hating Buffalo even more, Karl decided to fulfil a lifelong dream. He wrote to the famed film director Fritz Lang, the man who had made the world's first rocket movie, *The Lady in the Moon*. Lang was a friend of Dornberger's and had a soft spot for discarded German racketeers like Karl von Kampen. The filmmaker offered to give Karl a recommendation, should he ever find himself in Los Angeles ...

Packing all his possessions, Karl had moved to Hollywood the next week. There his fokus established him as a valuable asset to any camera crew. He had risen from assistant to operator or cinematographer to line producer to *Cathode*.

Before Karl could gauge the effect of his lie on Cranston, the femcat had returned. 'Feeling friendlier now that we've had our icebreaker?' she asked, sliding back into his lap.

Cranston seemed more receptive. 'You're a persistent one, aren't you?'

'I'm not sure what that means. It's an awfully big word.' She nibbled on Cranston's ear, to the engineer's all too obvious enjoyment. 'And I like big things.'

Karl found that he enjoyed femcat's antics too. She noted his interest. 'You're too cute to be alone, handsome. See anyone here you'd like to meet?'

'Not at present, thank you.'

The joker girl purred with laughter. 'Ah, a shy one. What do you two do, anyway?'

'He's a rocket scientist,' Karl said, trying to direct the femcat's attention back to Cranston.

Not to be outdone, Cranston said, 'Karl here is the producer of *Captain Cathode*.'

Karl could have killed him. It was one thing to be trolling through a joker club – it was quite another matter to be recognized in one.

Femcat seemed pleased, however. 'Then you know Brant and Gene!'

'Quite well,' Karl said, trying to hide his surprise. 'Do you?'

'Of course! Gene said he would try to get me on the show! Turk needs a girl, don't you think? Cats and dogs, the kids would love it. And think of all you'd save on makeup!' She gave a throaty laugh. 'I'm only doing this to pay the rent, you know. I'm really an actress.'

Of course she was. He knew what kind of actress, too. There was a growing market for joker smut films, he had heard. 'I didn't know they were regulars here,' said Karl. 'How often do they come here?' He fokused on her pretty feline face ... noted the glistening drops of moisture in her whiskers ... a raised brow ... the mouth slightly open. In a nat, they would have been clear signs of hesitation.

Or fear.

The femcat had said too much, and all at once she had seemed to realize it. 'I wouldn't call them "regulars." They're just ... guys I've met. Excuse me.' She slithered off Cranston.

The rocket man didn't seem all that sorry to see her go. 'It's going to be a long drive back to Mojave.'

'In this condition, you'll be lucky to reach Lankershim.'

Karl helped Cranston down to the end of the pier, where a line of cabs was waiting. He had his former colleague dropped at the Roosevelt Hotel, then told the cabbie to head down Hollywood Boulevard to Gower. From there, he walked. It was less than a mile, straight up Gower to Scenic, then a few blocks east to Beachwood. He needed time to let the booze wear off. Time to think.

He could continue as he was ... grinding out episodes of a children's television series until it died. Then another, then another. Until *he* died. Or worse than death, fell out of fashion. He could sell his share of *Cathode* to Kellogg's and use the money to support himself for life. No more silly stories of treacherous aces outwitted by an idiot in a blue suit.

Or he could take up Cranston's offer and return to his life's work.

But he could do none of it until he resolved the Brant Brewer problem.

His star was hanging out at a joker dive. Which might explain the increasing number of late mornings. But what was Gene Olkewitz doing with him? As far as Karl knew, the two were nothing more than set colleagues. And Olkewitz sure wasn't showing up late ...

At the corner of Gower and Franklin, he stopped to use a pay phone. He left an urgent message for Edison Hill.

◆

At eight-thirty the next morning, Karl was still sitting in the coffee shop at Franklin and Western. Emboldened by last night's stroll – and counting on the sunshine and exercise to mitigate his hangover – Karl had walked, eager to hear what Edison Hill had learned.

But Edison Hill had not shown up.

All he could do was wait, and read the *Herald's* follow-up stories about the Medusa Killer. There had been seven such murders over the past twenty months. All victims male, all jokers between the ages of twenty-five and fifty. None of them the obvious victim: no derelicts, hopheads, rentboys. They were as solid citizens as any joker could ever hope to be: veterans, attorneys, accountants, file clerks, mechanics, a man who ran a gas station in Glendale, even an ex-fireman and a couple of former teachers who had lost their jobs when their cards turned. (No parents wanted jokers near their children.)

None of this was immediately relevant to Karl. He wanted to know about handsome, charming, mysterious Brant Brewer … the man who held the keys to Karl's future.

At nine he gave up the wait, dropping a dollar on the counter and calling for a cab. He had already given forty dollars to a man he had met in a joker bar! He would have to have words with Jack Braun the next time he saw him.

Karl von Kampen hated feeling foolish.

He was dropped, as usual, at the front gate. To his surprise, Abigail met him in the parking lot. He regarded her through his glasses. 'Why aren't you in the office?'

'Because Saul Greene is waiting for you.'

'Let me guess—'

'Brant is late again.'

Karl's head began to hurt, and this time it could not be blamed on the previous night's alcohol intake. 'Tell me better news.'

'They found another dead guy in Silver Lake last night … turned to stone, Karl.'

'If Saul Greene gives me any grief, *he'll* be found petrified in Silver Lake. Have him meet me at the set.'

Karl did not want to face the giant agent in his office – and he needed to reassure the skittish Korshak that he would not be blamed for the delays.

Sure enough, Brant Brewer's parking spot was still empty, but next to it was a shiny black two-door Hudson Hollywood, the type of car Karl would buy ... if he bought one. It belonged to Saul Greene.

Who somehow managed to reach the soundstage at the same time as Karl. 'Going to be a hot one again today,' Greene said.

In the best of times, Karl had little patience for Greene and his brand of chat. 'Why are you here instead of your client?'

'Brant is having personal problems. Medical problems.'

'So he's in the hospital.'

'Not yet. His life is not at risk—'

'—only his career.'

Greene took Karl's elbow and somehow moved him several feet away. 'Karl, you and I have never been good friends.'

'In fact, we're barely past the mortal enemy stage.'

'Yet this is a business that runs on friendships, some of them quite unlikely.'

'Do you want to be my friend, Saul? Is that what this is all about?'

'Not me. But ... how well do you understand actors, Karl?'

'I pay them a lot of money to show up and say their lines. What else do I need to know?'

The big man shook his head, as if correcting a child's errors. 'The best of them are empty inside, easy prey for whatever passion or fashion that comes along. It's what makes them good at what they do – becoming other people.'

'So Brant Brewer has somehow imprinted on someone who is chronically tardy?'

'No. I'm saying he needs ... understanding. Flexibility.'

'We're already rearranging every other shooting day, Saul. Have you tried this theory on Harold Dann? Somehow I don't think our new sponsor is going to be understanding about shows that are late, or don't exist!'

'You don't need to bring Kellogg's into this. They're only interested in money.'

'And you are what? An altruist?'

'I'm Brant Brewer's friend. And I'm asking you, as someone who could be your friend, to back off.' Greene leaned close to Karl. There was no friendliness in his manner. 'Stop having him followed.'

'We're done, Saul.' Karl reached for the soundstage door. Only the red light warning that cameras were rolling kept him from opening it.

'How would you like it, Karl? Wouldn't you agree, this is still a bad time to have your … private life made public? What would that do your career?'

Karl stared at the agent. 'Don't threaten *me*.'

Now Greene smiled and spread his hands. 'I'm just offering some friendly advice.' He started to turn, then, over his shoulder, said, 'Nice touch with the glasses, by the way.'

Karl fled into the dark sanctuary of his set, his hands trembling and his stomach sour.

Saul Greene knew his secret.

By the time Brewer showed up just before lunch, Karl had retreated to his office with orders not to be disturbed. There was smoke in the air, apparently from some fire up in the hills. Distant sirens. Karl found it all unnerving.

Yet he was feeling more kindly toward Edison Hill by now. At least he had retreated from judging him to be a con man. Jack Braun would not have recommended anyone like that.

On impulse, he ordered Abigail to find a home address and telephone for Hill. He didn't like waiting.

Then he tried to lose himself in the next *Cathode* scripts. But his worries about Brewer and Greene – and Kellogg's – combined with the sheer banality of the latest story line, plus the numbing rattle of the air conditioner, left him frustrated and unhappy.

He reflected on his association with Brant Brewer. He had simply seen the actor as a face in an 8" × 11" glossy, along with a short list of credits that ranged from secondary roles on Broadway to live television and a few guest roles on other Ziv television series. Black-haired, blue-eyed ... Brewer just looked like a hero. And in the round of auditions, he had shown he could sound like one, too.

A deal had been made through Saul Greene before Karl and Brewer ever had a conversation. And the rigors of producing over a hundred fifteen-minute low-budget episodes in each of two television seasons had made it impossible to progress beyond that. They had never been friends – never shared a meal or a drink. Their only social encounters had been at occasional holiday parties.

He knew even less about the rest of his cast – Olkewitz was another Greene client who had, Karl recalled, been auditioned in character, already wearing the dog mask.

Karl wouldn't have minded getting to know Dotty Doyle a lot better, but his ace complicated his romantic life; fokus diverted normal sexual urges into his own peculiar form of voyeurism. Besides, Karl recoiled from the role of producer preying on actress.

Realizing that it was now close to five P.M. and that he hadn't eaten, he wandered into the outer office, finding it empty except for a note with Edison Hill's home address and phone, and the words 'Tried this. Number not in service.'

Karl was irritated by Abigail's absence until he remembered two things: He had given her permission to leave for a medical appointment. And it was the Edison Hill situation that was unnerving him.

In the best German tradition, he decided to take action.

Hill's address was 8777 Lookout Mountain, an amusing coincidence: Fritz Lang had lived on Lookout Mountain when Karl had visited, a decade back. The location was less than five miles from the studios of *Captain Cathode*.

But it took over an hour to reach it. The route south on Laurel Canyon was blocked by fire trucks at Mulholland Drive.

Karl's cabbie suggested an alternate route, which took them around three sides of a square, down Woodrow Wilson, then through a side canyon, then back up Laurel from the north.

More fire trucks clogged the intersection of Laurel Canyon and

Lookout Mountain, but it was still possible to drive past them, straight up the narrow road.

However, after several turns, Karl's cab ran into the ultimate roadblock: a trio of Los Angeles Police units. 'This is as far as you go,' an office told Karl.

'I'm a resident.' He hated lying, but he needed to reach Hill's house.

'My friend, if you live up here, you should call your insurance agent … We've had four homes burned and we don't have the fire completely contained.'

Karl removed his sunglasses and peered further up the road. Several of the strange little canyon dwellings – vertical structures that reminded Karl of treehouses – were damaged or gone. Trees on the hills were smoking stumps. Even the street sign was soot-smeared. 'But the fire trucks are down at Laurel.'

The officer stared at Karl. 'You should turn around, sir. The smoke is bad for your eyes.'

Karl had tried to press the matter, but then his driver grew impatient. After a laborious Y-turn under the scrutiny of several cops, the cap headed back down the road. 'Here,' Karl said, once they had turned out of sight.

He paid the driver, then began walking back toward what used to be Edison Hill's house.

One of the weblike side roads allowed Karl to skirt the police barrier and climb parallel to Lookout Mountain. He found himself emerging from unburnt foliage to look down on the scene.

On the blackened slope above what used to be 8777 Lookout Mountain lay a strange object … a block of stone that, through Karl's fokus, appeared to be a statue of a human male cowering in fear … a man with a pencil mustache.

It was a long, choking walk down Laurel Canyon past Hollywood Boulevard (which had nothing but houses this far west) to Sunset. There he headed for Schwab's, phoning for a taxi.

Once it had arrived, and was taking him east toward home,

he considered telling the driver to turn north toward Tomlin Air Force Base.

Karl von Kampen had had enough of Hollywood.

As he walked up the steps to his duplex, he smelled the rich fragrance of jasmine, a considerable improvement over the smoke and ash of Laurel Canyon. The cool air revived him. He paused and looked back. As he did, he fokused again, unbidden, and was rewarded with a cascade of images near and far. A robin on a telephone wire. A ball kicked by a neighbor child in a tiny backyard, stopped in mid-flight. A puff of smoke from an exhaled cigarette further down Beachwood. A cloud of moths around a streetlight. On the hillside, a hunched coyote. All of it linked by ribbons of cracked concrete, foliage, pipes, the blur of autos in motion.

Even if Saul Greene or Brant Brewer turned out to be the Medusa Killer, Karl had faced greater challenges. He had built rockets. He had survived a British bombing raid. He had lived through the wild card. He had turned himself into a Hollywood producer!

Surely he could find a way to control Brant Brewer.

Halfway to his front door, he was grabbed. A hand above his elbow. An *invisible* hand. 'Go back,' Estelle Blair said.

It was a challenge to turn casually while trying to spot a potential assailant. Karl wasn't sure of success until he had descended to the sidewalk without feeling a knife blade or bullet in his back.

'Estelle ...' he said.

'Right behind you.'

'What's going on?'

'Two men, nasty-looking, overdressed for the heat. They started sneaking around about an hour ago. I heard them and made myself scarce, if you know what I mean.'

Karl was still making his way back to Beachwood, toward the corner grocery and witnesses. 'I get the idea.'

'I think they were going to follow you inside. One of them had a gun.'

A car started up. Moments later, a Hudson Hollywood rolled down Karl's street and quickly turned south onto Beachwood.

There were two men inside in hats and overcoats, one of them easily big enough to be Saul Greene.

'Are you in some kind of trouble, Karl?'

'Apparently.' He had felt nausea and apprehension at the charred ruins of Edison Hill's house ... now he felt pure fear. Whoever killed Hill had somehow connected them.

'Maybe you can't see clearly with your sunglasses.'

'That may be.' It was possible that Estelle knew his secret, too. She could have been spying on him for the past three years. Silly of him to have chosen a landlady who was the one person immune to fokus.

'Well, my father back in Iowa, bless his soul, had a method for dealing with bothersome people. "Do unto them before they do unto you."'

'Estelle,' Karl said, 'I couldn't agree more.'

Brent Brewer lived on Drexel Avenue, not far from the Farmer's Market and Gilmore Field, north of the Wiltshire Miracle Mile.

The cab stopped at Gilmore Field, where the Hollywood Stars were playing a minor-league baseball game. Karl could walk the four blocks to Brewer's address. It would give him time to further consider his dwindling options.

The sun was setting, offering the promise of relief from the oppressive heat, though the haze in the air would linger for days. Karl was grateful for the lack of a moon – that awful night at Peenemunde had seen a full moon, the better to aid British bombers.

Although two stories tall, Brewer's house was modest in size, situated on impressive grounds behind a fence, largely hidden from the street.

Karl slipped close to the fence, fokusing through the bars and the bushes beyond. He could see Greene's Hollywood parked in the hemispherical driveway, along with other vehicles. He fokused on the peeling paint on the walls of the house, a cricket making a major effort to get across a pavement crack.

No obvious obstacles. But no obvious weapons.

Karl had his plan, and it was worthy of Captain Cathode. He hoped he lived long enough to share the scheme with Willy Ley.

A last glance at the quiet neighborhood around him, then he opened the gate and walked up to the front door. As he became aware of the laughter and music from inside, Karl stepped back. He could still abort the whole mission … Depending on whether the next half hour went according to script, these people would be in danger.

There was also the temptation to simply let it go. Sign the deal with Kellogg's and wash his hands of him. Let the cereal makers worry about Brewer's ability to hit his mark.

No. Brewer had not just brought chaos to Karl's life – he and Saul Greene had almost certainly killed Edison Hill, and who knew how many others. They were monsters, real life versions of the cartoon joker villains of *Captain Cathode*. They needed to be brought down—

Karl knocked on the door. A moment later, a very surprised Gene Olkewitz opened it. Or rather, Turk did. Olkewitz was wearing the dog-face mask.

Karl had half-expected it, but was still shocked to realize that the good captain's sidekick was not just playing the part on camera. 'Is this where I say "*guten abend*"?' Karl said. 'Or should I bark? What are you doing here? Why are you wearing that mask?'

'Joker pussy,' said Olkewitz, smiling a rubbery grin. 'Joker girls are wild, Fuhrer. And so *grateful*.' The actor turned as if to summon help. An angry-looking Saul Greene was pushing through the crowd.

'Are you insane?' Greene said.

'You wanted to see me, Saul. You even came to my house!' Karl smiled to show that he, like everyone in Hollywood since the pre-silent days, knew the old joke.

Greene could only shout, 'Brant!'

Brewer was slipping through a cluster of guests, all of them jokers. And what a collection! A lizard girl. A squamous thing with feet. A man who looked perfectly nat, except for a pair of antennae rising from his head. He spied the femcat from the Menagerie as well, squirming in the lap of a fat man with a face that looked as if it had been carved from oak.

There were half a dozen more. The party was the opposite of Noah's Ark. No joker ever had a perfect mate. Karl felt as if he were back at the Menagerie. The only things missing were the smell of French fries and the tinny music from the merry-go-round next door. Instead, there were embroidered rugs; fussy, brocaded couches; arty pictures on the walls; a Victrola. 'I don't see a television,' Karl said, as Brewer reached him. 'Where do you watch yourself?'

'Would you believe I've never seen an episode?'

Among the many shocking things Karl had heard lately, this was the capper. What kind of actor passed up a chance to watch himself?

'Well, why watch black and white television when you've got a colorful crowd like this every night?' Brewer was saying. That was when Karl noticed the deliciously real Nora-Dolly in a pink sheath dress, her hair swirled into a golden nest, lips the color of blood, her eyes as blue as a tropic sea. He had never seen her looking so desirable, not even in his most shameful fantasies.

She nodded to Karl, then inclined her head toward the corner of the living room, where Harold Dann smiled back at them, tipping a drink in Karl's direction. Karl had not seen the Kellogg's man for several days. Two of the dancers from the Menagerie were with him, the American girls, blue on his left arm, the red girl on his right.

Karl turned to Brewer and Greene. 'I get the idea you're celebrating something.' Had he mistaken a typical Hollywood backroom deal – agent and actor going behind his back to steal *Cathode* from him – for murder?

Before Brewer could answer, Greene and Olkewitz had caught Karl, each man taking an elbow. 'Why don't we talk somewhere else?'

As he was hustled through the crowd, Karl caught Dotty's eye. 'Get out of here,' he told her. 'Get all of them out of here. Tell them … tell them the police are coming. A raid!'

'Oh,' she said.

They wound up in the den, door closed, the three of them, Olkewitz outside standing guard. 'You're either insane, or the bravest man in the world,' Greene said.

'Could I be both?'

Brewer turned to his agent. 'Saul—'

'Shut up, Brant!' Greene faced Karl. 'You actually are rather stupid, Karl. For a rocket scientist, that is.'

'I didn't realize being stupid meant a death sentence in Hollywood. Why, the streets would be empty—'

Greene backhanded him, a vicious move that surprised Karl as much as it hurt. 'You think this is our choice? You're a lucky one! Your ace *helps* you!'

'That's enough, Saul!'

Brant seemed genuinely upset. He put his hands on Greene and gently moved the burly agent aside.

'What are you two?' Karl asked, tasting blood and feeling a loose tooth with his tongue. 'Some kind of team?'

Brewer was not a good enough actor to hide his reaction. 'We need each other. Saul petrifies them. As he does, I feed.' He turned to his sullen, massive partner. 'It's a good thing we found each other.'

'Brant ...' Greene's face was wet with sweat.

'He deserves to know, Saul!' Brewer seemed relieved at having a chance to confess. 'He's made us a lot of money!'

'What, a kiddie TV star and a fourth-rate agent?' Karl couldn't resist turning to Greene. 'Do you only get ten percent of whatever you suck out of your victims?'

Greene raised an arm for a second backhand, but Brewer stopped him. 'Stop it, Saul!' He got between the agent and Karl. 'You hear about junkies and the monkey on their backs? I'd trade this habit for heroin in a second.' He ran a finger across his forehead, wiping sweat. 'And it gets worse in this heat.'

'But what do you get? Blood, bones ...'

Now Greene laughed harshly. 'Well, go ahead, tell him!'

Amazingly, Brant seemed ashamed … unable to frame the words. 'Saul transforms their bodies, and I take their souls. Their … personalities. I can't actually be a hero – I can't play a real human – until I do.'

If he hadn't been half-paralyzed with fear, Karl would have laughed. So Brant Brewer was the ultimate ace actor – a true empty vessel. For a moment Karl felt pity for the man, even for Greene. Everyone in the world claimed to know the physical price of the wild card … but what about mental changes? What twists and tortures had been inflicted on human brains by the Takisian virus?

Then Saul Greene grabbed Karl from behind, a bear hug that Karl knew he would never break. 'Your buddy Hill turned out to be a hero. And you decided to be one, too.' Karl could feel himself growing heavy, thicker. Turning to stone? 'Like I said, Karl. Stupid.'

Karl jammed a hand into his pocket. 'Smell that!' Karl said, forcing out the words. 'That's gas and it has filled the house. All it takes to blow this to the moon is a light.' He managed to pull a lighter from his pocket.

Brant looked worried. 'Saul, watch him …!'

But Saul Greene smiled, and shouted, 'Gene!'

The door opened and Olkewitz entered, a squirming figure in a sheet under one arm. He dropped the bundle on the floor, then sat on it.

Greene never lost his hold. 'We may not be able to see your invisible friend, Karl, but Gene has a great nose for a nat: he sniffed her out.'

The bundle on the floor squirmed as Brant Brewer gently removed the lighter from Karl's stiffening hand. 'It's all right, Estelle,' Karl said. She'd been caught. It was over …

Brant seemed astonished. 'That was your plan? Walk in here and blow us up?'

'My plan …' Karl said, writhing in Greene's grasp, 'was to walk in here and try to talk sense into you! You can kill me the way you killed all the others … but if I die, it won't be just another joker murder. I'm German! I'm your producer! I'm an *ace*.

'Who replaces me? Someone meaner and stronger. And when that happens, how long do you think you two will survive? Wouldn't it just be better to … have some kind of peace?'

He felt as though he was talking to himself. He was rooted now, feeling heavy, his skin hardening. He tried to fokus, and he failed.

Now all he could do was close his eyes and die—

The door suddenly opened. There was a commotion, a shout from Greene: 'Brant!'

Karl opened his eyes and saw that he and Estelle had been left alone. The blanket had already been thrown aside. 'Can you move?'

'Yes,' Karl said, though it wasn't easy. He felt like a man who had been sitting in one position for hours, as if his feet and legs and even hips had fallen asleep.

'I think we should get out of here!'

Painfully, reaching for Estelle's invisible and not especially substantial support, he stomped down the hallway, into the living room.

Dolly and Dann and the joker partiers had gotten the message. The only people present were Brant Brewer, Saul Greene, and Eugene Olkewitz. Brewer was on the stairs, holding the lighter aloft as Greene tried to reach him. He actually struck a pose that could have been seen, nightly, on *Captain Cathode*. 'Put it down, Brant!'

Olkewitz was between them, still in his dog mask. 'Back off, Saul!'

Karl just hurried toward the front door, stumbling into the hot August night, desperate to put as much distance as he could between himself and Estelle, and the house. As he reached the gate, he heard what sounded like the snap of a piece of rotted wood—

The house erupted in a flash of light. A giant's hand slapped Karl, flattening him against a parked car.

Deafened by the blast, his hands and knees skinned and raw from impact, Karl huddled against the side of a car as the fireball blossomed overhead.

He pulled himself up, forcing himself to look, even though the air itself seemed ablaze. 'Estelle!' he called.

'Here, darling!' The voice came from behind him. 'I don't feel so …'

Karl heard a rustling thump as something hit the lawn. He bent to the challenge of trying to cradle an invisible woman.

Behind him, Brant Brewer's house was entirely engulfed, so violently shaken that the second floor had already collapsed into the first. No fire squad would be able to do anything ... by the time they arrived, there would be nothing but ashes.

Two weeks later, on his way to Tomlin Air Force Base, the bus carrying Karl van Kampen stopped on the north side of Palmdale to gas up.

Stretching his legs – still stiff from Saul Greene's Medusa touch – Karl saw the headline of the newspaper the attendant was reading:

ZIV T.V. Introduces New 'Cathode'
George Reeves starred in *Gone With the Wind*
and *From Here to Eternity*

The Kellogg's offer had died with Brant Brewer. Fine. Harold Dann had left L.A. on the first plane back to Michigan, no doubt eager to escape before anyone asked inconvenient questions about what he had been doing at that party. Karl did not care. He wanted out of Hollywood – he had even given away his new Zenith, to Estelle. He owed her much more, not just for saving his life, but for helping him understand why Brant Brewer had killed himself.

'Being a joker was bad enough,' she had told him. 'The suicide rates are appalling, you know. But actors are the most insecure people imaginable. They never know why they are popular or successful, only that they are – for a while. Brant Brewer must have realized that *Captain Cathode* was the best he could ever be. And that when you discovered the truth about him, it was all over.'

Karl von Kampen replaced his dark glasses, and peered into the future.

POWERS

By David D. Levine

At 9.35 A.M. on Monday, May 2, 1960, an unexpected knock sounded on the door of Franciszek Majewski's office. Frank's desk was closest to the door; he stubbed out his cigarette and prepared to answer it. 'Just a moment,' he said.

Most of Frank's documents were already properly stowed in color-coded folders according to their classification, all tidily aligned with the desk's edges. He put his current working set away in its folder, then glanced at his two officemates to make sure they had done the same. Although it was early on a spring day, the windowless office was already stuffy with Washington heat. Harsh fluorescent lights hummed over battered war-surplus file cabinets, scarred green and white linoleum, battleship gray desks edged with decades of cigarette burns. The four heavy safes along the back wall were properly flagged with green 'open' cards, their doors shut but unlocked during the working day.

Frank was preparing an intelligence estimate of Soviet bomber production capacity. His folders contained documents in Russian, German, Polish, and English: news articles, intercepted telegrams, reports from field officers summarizing the findings of their agents. The latter, although the freshest and most exciting, were also the most suspect ... even if the facts presented weren't deliberate mis-information, they could be mistaken, misinterpreted, or completely fabricated by agents desperate for money or thrills. Nothing was certain in this business – that was why they were called 'estimates'

– but through careful correlation of the available information, a sharp analyst could come up with a highly probable guess at the truth.

The man at the door was Robert Amory, Jr., tall and lean and, unlike Frank, still in possession of all his hair. 'What a pleasant surprise!' Frank said as he shook his hand. Robert, the man who had recruited Frank to the CIA, had been his immediate superior before being promoted to Deputy Director of Intelligence. He held a folder in one hand, a red one with a TOP SECRET label.

'I need to speak with you, Frank,' he said. 'Alone. Come with me.'

Frank swallowed hard. He took off his wire-framed glasses and polished them with his handkerchief to hide his discomfiture.

As they walked down the corridor, footsteps echoing on the travertine, Frank felt sweat trickling down his sides, even more than the already muggy day warranted. Any disturbance of routine was worrisome, and having the attention of his superiors focused on himself was more worrisome still. Would this be the day he'd been dreading for so many years?

Robert led Frank to a vault he'd never even walked past before, closing and locking the heavy soundproof door behind him. As the two of them sat at the small table that filled most of the vault's antechamber, Robert offered a cigarette – he smoked Marlboros, which Frank found too harsh, but he gladly took one to calm his nerves.

Robert tapped his cigarette into a heavy glass ashtray with the CIA seal, then extracted a sheet from the folder. 'Sign this.'

'Wh-what is it?' Frank's pulse throbbed behind his collar button.

'I need to read you into a new compartment.'

'Reading in' was the process of authorizing an officer to access a certain compartment of classified information. The sheet contained a brief description of the compartment – it was a photo reconnaissance project involving high-altitude overflights of the Soviet Union – and the usual statement that Frank understood that unauthorized disclosure of any information from the compartment would subject him to penalties up to and including life in prison. Robert had already filled in Frank's name, date of birth, and social security number at the bottom, and Frank signed it with a sense of relief.

Frank didn't yet know why his security clearance was being raised, but whatever the reason, it implied that his secret was still safe.

After Robert countersigned and filed the form, he pulled another folder from one of the vault's drawers. 'Welcome to AQUATONE.' Each compartment was identified by a cryptonym, or code name, beginning with a two-character prefix called a digraph that designated its geographical or functional area. AQUATONE's 'AQ' prefix indicated it was a type of technical asset.

Robert slipped an eight-by-ten glossy from the folder and slid it across the little table. 'This information doesn't leave this room under any circumstances. AQUATONE is one of the blackest projects we have.' Stamped TOP SECRET AQUATONE, the photo showed an airplane ... an extremely unusual airplane. The wings were freakishly long and thin, the fuselage slim as a cigar; it might have been a glider, except for the jet exhaust at the rear. It was painted entirely black, completely lacking in markings or insignia. 'This is the Lockheed U-2,' Robert said. 'It has a ceiling of seventy thousand feet, a top speed of five hundred ten knots, and can remain aloft for up to eight hours without refueling. We've been flying this plane over Russia for almost five years.'

Frank realized the ash was about to fall from his cigarette and flicked it in the ashtray. 'What kind of photos can you get from that altitude?' Seventy thousand feet was practically outer space.

Robert gave a grim little smile. 'Very good ones. And the Soviets don't have anything that can stop it.' He looked Frank in the eye. 'At least, we didn't think they did. But on Sunday one of our U-2s didn't come home.' He handed the folder to Frank.

Frank set down his cigarette and read the papers inside, all stamped TOP SECRET AQUATONE. The plane had taken off from Peshawar, Pakistan, and was supposed to overfly Stalingrad, Archangel, and Murmansk, looking for evidence of ICBM launch facility construction and maintaining absolute radio silence. But it was now well over twenty-four hours late for its landing in Bodo, Norway, and it had to be considered lost. 'What happened?'

'We don't know. It's a very temperamental airplane; could be equipment failure, or pilot error.' The last sheet in the folder was another photograph, a cocky-looking fellow in a flight suit with laces like an old-fashioned corset. 'That's the pilot, Francis Gary Powers. He's one of ours. All the pilots and support staff are Agency personnel.'

The pilot had a hard jaw and dark eyes. He looked to be a little older than Frank's son, maybe thirty.

'We know that plane went down somewhere in the Soviet Union. I want you to find out what the Soviets know. Did they shoot it down? Do they even know it went down? Have they found the wreckage, and if so, what have they learned from it? The plane is equipped with a destructor unit, of course, but it might have failed.'

'And the pilot?'

A hard, level stare. 'Equipped with a curare needle.' He puffed reflectively, blew smoke from his nose. 'But to make the plane fly that high, that far ... it's basically made of toilet paper, Frank. If it goes down, the odds of survival are one in a million.'

Frank picked his cigarette from the ashtray. Ignored, it had burned almost all the way to the filter. He took one last bitter drag and stubbed it out. 'Why me?' Although Frank's heart had slowed as he realized his personal secrets were not the reason for this visit, he still didn't relish the attention the assignment would focus on him.

'I know you, Frank. You're a native Russian speaker, you've got a good eye, and I trust your judgment. And if you do well on this, it could be a big boost to your career.' He gave Frank a conspiratorial wink.

'Thanks.' He tried to smile.

♦

Frank arrived home at 11.10 P.M. that evening. He slipped his key into the lock and opened the door as quietly as he could. But his wife was awake, in robe and slippers, gnawing her nails as she stared out the living-room window. She turned to him as he entered, her round babushka face illuminated by relief that shaded immediately to anger. 'Where *were* you?' she said, her voice strained.

'I'm sorry I'm so late, *kochanie*,' he said, and bent to kiss her cheek. 'I got a new assignment today. I was so tied up in it that I forgot to call.' In fact, he had spent most of the day in the AQUATONE vault, where no phone line penetrated.

She hugged him tightly. 'I was so worried about you, *serduszko*,' she whispered into his shoulder. 'I was afraid that SCARE had found you.'

'Not today, *kochanie*.' He stroked her hair. 'Not today. Our secret is safe … for now.'

Frank remembered every detail of the day that secret had manifested itself. It had been a fine spring day in 1952. Frank was crossing C Street, obeying the walk signal, when he glanced to his left and saw a green 1950 Packard bearing down on him. Frank was seconds away from becoming a bloody pancake on the street. Suddenly there was a rushing sound in his head and the car seemed to slow to a crawl.

Frank had pushed himself backwards, feeling as though he were wading through glue, unable to breathe. A moment later the car sped past. Frank stood shuddering in the street, wondering what had just happened, and ran a hand over his sweating head. It came back with hair stuck to it. He'd always known that he'd go bald, like his father, but hadn't expected it to come on so quickly.

Another such incident had occurred a few months later, when his wife's favorite vase fell off a table, and another a month after that, when one of his nieces was threatened by a vicious dog. Frank hadn't become a successful analyst by ignoring data, however unexpected or counterintuitive, and he soon became convinced that his experiences were not just subjective. He had developed an extraordinary ability.

An ace.

But Tailgunner Joe McCarthy had just begun his hearings, claiming increasing numbers of secret aces infested the government, and negative feelings were beginning to build. Part of Frank's job was to understand and predict political trends in other countries, and he could tell that the life of an ace in the government would shortly become extremely unpleasant. And though he'd been only eight years old when the Bolsheviks had taken over Russia, forcing his wealthy Polish-born parents to flee to the United States, he knew that being different from the mob in a difficult time could be fatal.

At first he hadn't even told his wife of his abilities. But she was smart and observant, and after she noticed how, in moments of stress, he sometimes appeared to 'flicker,' he'd been forced to confess his secret to her. Ironically, she still didn't know he worked for the CIA.

McCarthy's hearings were over now, but fear and distrust of aces remained. Anyone who discovered they had unusual powers was required by law to report to SCARE, which would assign them to jobs in which their powers could be used for the good of the nation. But SCARE had only ever acknowledged two instances of this: Lawrence Hague, the telepathic stockbroker, and David Harstein, known as The Envoy. Neither of them had ever been seen in public again.

Sophia sniffed and wiped her eyes on the sleeve of her robe. 'I'm sorry I snapped at you,' she said. 'Every time you're late I worry that you've gone to … you know, Nevada.' One of the more outrageous theories as to what happened to aces who vanished into SCARE was that they were transported to a top-secret facility in the Nevada desert, a place which they were never allowed to leave except when required for the performance of their duties.

'You know that's just a rumor,' he said.

But he knew the Russians' forced-labor camps were real, even though the Soviet government tried to keep them secret from its own people. The United States would never do such a thing … would they?

♥

Another car drove past, its headlights through the venetian blinds sweeping an arc of striped light across the bedroom ceiling, and

Frank sighed and sat up. Despite his exhaustion and the lateness of the hour, sleep eluded him.

While Sophia snored gently in the other bed, Frank slipped on his robe and slippers and shuffled to the den. The room, with its warm wood panelling, had been his children's bedroom, and the shade of the lamp he now switched on was still painted with cartoon airplanes. But Jenna, the youngest, had married and moved away three years ago.

He seated himself at the chessboard and opened Botvinnik's *One Hundred Selected Games* to the bookmark: game number eighty-nine, Tolush vs. Botvinnik, 1945. He set up the board with quick efficiency, then proceeded to play out the game from the book, pausing at White's tenth move to consider the alternatives Botvinnik discussed. He'd tried just reading, playing out the games in his mind, but actually handling and moving the pieces made the players' strategies and attacks much more comprehensible to him.

Chess made sense. Even though the players' strategies and plans were hidden, the rules were known to everyone, the moves were made in plain sight, and even check had to be declared. But real life was full of hidden dangers. If SCARE were watching Frank, he might never know it until the hammer came down.

After he'd played the game out, Frank yawned, replaced the pieces in their case and the book on the shelf, and headed for the bedroom. As he passed the hall mirror, the headlights of another passing car briefly illuminated his scrawny limbs and growing paunch, and he paused.

There had been a time, not long after his power had manifested, when he'd considered turning himself in to SCARE. He'd entertained juvenile fantasies of a life as a daring ace secret agent, with exciting adventures and a code name. But even then he'd been too old and settled for adventure, and now the man in the mirror was fifty-one years old and looked sixty.

Frank shook his head at the image as he closed the bedroom door behind himself.

♣

Frank shaved with a straight razor, using a cake of shaving soap and a mug and a badger-hair brush, just as his father had. Even Frank's barber used a Gillette razor and shaving cream in a spray can – he said it was easier, neater, and safer – but Frank liked the close shave and the sense of control he got with a straight razor. The old ways were best, and certainly cheaper.

But at 8.15 A.M. on Thursday, May 5, Frank regretted that habit, when the voice of Nikita Khrushchev burst from his bathroom radio, saying something about a 'bandit flight' being 'shot down.' The premier's voice was immediately overlaid with a translation into English, but Frank had heard enough … too much, in fact.

Dabbing at the cut on his neck with a styptic pencil, Frank cursed under his breath in Russian, Polish, and English. He had worked over fourteen hours on Wednesday, but not a single thing he'd seen in all the sources he'd studied had led him to conclude that the Soviets were even aware of the downed U-2's existence, and he had turned in a report to that effect before leaving the office at nine o'clock the previous night.

He'd failed.

Frank's brain swirled with second-guesses and recriminations as he tightened his tie over a neck still unshaven and damp with soap suds. What had he missed? There had been that one, ambiguous data point – something about an increase in security forces in the city of Vladimir – but, though it had nagged at him, he'd been unable to correlate it with anything else, so he had omitted it from the report. Maybe he should have investigated further.

On the radio, Khrushchev continued to berate the Americans for their 'aggressive invasion,' accusing them of 'playing with fire' and seeking to 'torpedo' the upcoming Paris summit meeting. Frank twisted the knob to another station.

It was that troglodyte Elvis Presley, threatening to 'squeeze you tighter than a grizzly bear.'

Frank wasn't sure whether Presley or Khrushchev was the bigger threat to America. Disgusted, he switched the radio off.

Before Frank could even hang up his hat, his officemate Galen informed him that Robert Amory wanted to see him as soon as he got in. Robert's secretary directed him to a crowded conference room. The air in the room was blue with smoke and Frank didn't know half of the men in it.

One he couldn't fail to recognize was Allen W. Dulles, Director of Central Intelligence. With his white hair and mustache, rimless glasses, and old-fashioned collar, he looked more like a banker than a spy. At the moment his expression was grim, jaw clamped tight on the stem of his pipe.

'I'm glad you're here, Frank,' Robert said after he'd made introductions. 'We're briefing the President in' – he shot his cuff, glanced at his watch – 'twenty-five minutes, and I'd like you to attend.'

Frank's mouth went dry. 'I'm sorry I didn't ...'

Robert cut him off with a wave of his hand. 'We'll talk about what went wrong later. Right now we need to get our feet under us.'

◆

The West Wing conference room used for the briefing, with its Colonial-print wallpaper and oil portraits of Revolutionary War generals, reminded Frank of nothing so much as a dentist's waiting room. But when President Eisenhower entered, Frank felt an electric jolt. This was real. This was history.

Frank had never before been in the same room as a president. The familiar face beneath Eisenhower's bald dome looked tired, and he walked with a slight limp, but the eyes behind the glasses with their thick transparent plastic frames seemed searching and intelligent. 'Well, gentlemen,' he said to the room at large, 'we seem to have a bit of a situation here.'

The question on the table was whether to ''fess up,' as the President put it – to admit that the lost plane had been on an espionage mission – or to stick with the prepared cover story, which was that the U-2 was a NASA research plane that had accidentally strayed into Russian airspace. The CIA men present all argued strenuously for the cover story; as Dulles said, 'Although all nations spy, no one admits it.' But Thomas Gates, the Secretary of Defense, worried that if Khrushchev had physical evidence of espionage, the United States could be caught in a lie. 'We don't want to go to Paris with egg on our faces,' he said.

But the President didn't really seem to be listening. 'What I want to know is, what about the pilot? Could he possibly have survived?' Frank was amazed to hear so much concern about one man from a general who had commanded tens of thousands.

Kelly Johnson from Lockheed, a pale man with a florid complexion, spoke up. 'Well, sir,' the engineer said, dabbing at his brow with a handkerchief, 'the aircraft is equipped with an ejection seat and a survival kit ... but, frankly, sir, those are provided mostly to reassure the pilot.' Eisenhower's face sagged at that revelation. 'For security reasons, the operating protocols call for the aircraft to spend all its time over Russia at or near its ceiling, which as you know is seventy thousand feet. And no one has ever bailed out at anything like that altitude and lived.'

The President's eyes pressed closed and he bowed his head for a moment. When he raised his head he looked ten years older. 'Very well,' he said, his eyes flicking back and forth to take in everyone in the room. 'That being the case, we'll stick with the cover story. Thank you for your time, gentlemen.'

As everyone in the room rose, chairs scraping across the linoleum, Eisenhower shook his head and muttered, 'May God have mercy on us all.' If Frank had been five feet farther away he wouldn't have heard it, and he was touched by the man's humanity.

By Friday, Frank's superiors seemed to have forgiven him for his failure, though he hadn't forgiven himself, and he worked all day on the question of what the Soviets knew about the U-2. Photos of wreckage had been published in *Pravda*, and Grechko, the Russians' First Deputy Minister of Defense, had given a speech at the Supreme Soviet claiming that the 'American air pirate' had

been 'shot down,' but there was no indication the Russians knew of the U-2's mission or capabilities.

But there was one nagging piece of information, or rather lack of information, that worried him. There was a rising KGB officer, an ambitious man designated ICICLE, who seemed to have dropped off the Earth on May 1, the same day the U-2 had gone missing. At this point, though, Frank had nothing to connect the man with the U-2 but a vague intuition. As he locked his papers in the safe for the weekend he resolved to dig deeper on Monday.

On Saturday, May 7, Frank was washing his lovingly maintained '56 Rambler in the alley behind the apartment building when Sophia opened the bedroom window and called out, 'Frank, it's someone named Robert. He says he needs to speak with you right away.'

Frank dropped the sponge in the bucket and ran up the steps two at a time. Puffing, hands still dripping with soapy water, he took the call in the den. 'You need to come to the office *now*, Frank.' Robert didn't sound pleased.

'Yes, sir.' There was no point in asking for more details on a nonsecure line.

When Frank arrived at Robert's office, without a word the Deputy Director handed him a sheaf of flimsy yellow telefax pages. It was a transcript of a speech Khrushchev had given to the Supreme Soviet a few hours earlier.

'Comrades,' the Premier had begun, 'I must let you in on a secret. When I made my report, I deliberately refrained from mentioning that the pilot was alive and healthy, and that we had the remnants of the plane.' Frank looked up, aghast.

'Keep reading,' Robert said.

'We did this deliberately,' Khrushchev's words continued, 'because had we given out the whole story, the Americans would have thought up another version. The pilot is safe and sound. He is now in Moscow. His name is Francis G. Powers. According to his testimony, he is a First Lieutenant of the U.S. Air Force in which he served up to 1956, when he joined the Central Intelligence Agency …'

There was more. Much more. Names, dates, flight plans, all accurate. Photos from the plane's cameras, which Khrushchev described as 'not bad.' Even the curare-tipped needle with which Powers was supposed to kill himself. The cover story of a weather research plane that had gone off course by accident was completely exploded.

Powers would be tried as a spy. If found guilty – and the Soviet courts were not known for the leniency – he would face a firing squad.

Frank dropped the speech on the desk in front of him and massaged his temples. He desperately needed a cigarette but, in his haste, had failed to bring any from home. At that moment the door slammed open and Allen Dulles strode into the room, pipe clamped between his teeth. He seemed about to speak to Robert, but then he noticed Frank. 'What is *he* doing here?'

Frank sat paralyzed, held in check by the director's gaze. 'Frank is one of our finest Soviet analysts,' Robert protested.

Dulles cut him off, pulling the pipe from his mouth and pointing at Frank with its stem. 'He completely failed to spot the fact that Khrushchev had the U-2, never mind Powers! I want him *off* this assignment. Get me someone who can tell me what's really going on over there!' With one last withering glance at Frank, he turned and stalked out.

After a moment of stunned silence, Robert slumped in his chair. 'I've never seen him that angry before,' he said. 'Ever.'

Frank gripped the edge of the desk. 'I did the best I could with the available intelligence, sir,' he said, amazed that his voice didn't tremble.

Robert pulled a pack of Marlboros from his desk drawer. Gratefully, Frank accepted one as well. 'It's not just you, Frank,' Robert puffed as he lit up. 'There's something else going on here, and whatever it is, it's something I'm not privy to,' He blew out a plume of smoke. 'I'm sorry, Frank. You really did do your best. You just happened to be in Allen's line of sight at the wrong moment.

Frank took a deep drag, but it didn't help much. Although his heart was slowing, he knew that he had just severely damaged his career, and maybe Robert's as well. 'I'm sorry, too.'

At least, he told himself, he would no longer be in the spotlight.

◆

Over the next few days, the crisis deepened. The White House released a statement blaming the Russians' 'excessive secrecy' for making the U-2 flights necessary and berating them for attacking on 'unarmed civilian airplane.' Khrushchev shot back that Eisenhower was a stooge of the 'Pentagon militarists' and their 'monopoly associates' who really ran the country.

Meanwhile, in Washington, the Democrats took the opportunity to harass a weakened Republican president, saying that it was 'almost incredibly stupid' to send a spy plane over the Soviet Union immediately before the Paris summit. One senator even accused Powers of being a double agent, which prompted an immediate, personal denial from Eisenhower.

All during this time the State Department negotiated with the Soviets to try to free Powers. But it was clear the Soviets knew they controlled the center of the board – they refused to negotiate, and proceeded rapidly with plans for Powers's espionage trial.

Soviet Defense Minister Malinovsky threatened that air bases provided by United States 'accomplices' for U-2 overflights could easily be 'wiped out.' Secretary of Defense Gates, in a carefully worded statement, emphasized that the United States would 'defend its allies in the event of an attack.'

Finally, blinking in the harsh light of newsreel and television cameras, Eisenhower made a statement. 'With a heavy heart,' he said, 'I must announce that the United States is withdrawing from the planned Four Powers Talks in Paris. Under the current circumstances, the prospects for peace seem remote.'

As he spoke, the Strategic Air Command quietly raised its readiness level to DEFCON 3.

Tuesday night, May 10. Or maybe early Wednesday morning. Frank stared at his chessboard, smoke curling from the cigarette between his fingers as he contemplated the endgame of Botvinnik's game number ninety: Romanovsky vs. Botvinnik, 1945. Frank sympathized with Romanovsky, who'd made a straightforward mistake in move ten but then compounded it, becoming flustered by surprise after surprise from the grandmaster Botvinnik. If he'd only been able to keep his wits about him ... but he hadn't. Romanovsky had lost his concentration and the game, and Botvinnik had gone on to become Soviet Champion, then World Champion three years later.

The creak of the den's door startled Frank from his reverie. It was Sophia, blinking in the light of the airplane-decorated lamp. 'Come to bed, *serduszko*,' she said. 'It's late.'

Frank sighed and stubbed out his cigarette, then began replacing the chess pieces in their box. 'I'm sorry, *kochanie*. I can't stop worrying about that U-2 pilot.' Although he'd been pulled from the U-2 project, Frank had been unable to let go of Powers. Where were the Soviets holding him? What had they learned from him? Were they really going to execute him for espionage? The missing KGB man, ICICLE, nagged at Frank like an extracted tooth – he had no new facts about the man, but his intuition insisted that ICICLE and Powers were somehow connected.

'Maybe you should take a Miltown.'

Frank shook his head. 'The poor kid's only a little older than our son.'

'There's nothing you can do to help.'

'Well.' Frank held the last white pawn in his hand. 'I've been thinking about that ...'

'Frank!' The shock in her voice made his head whip around. Her face was rigid with fear and anger. 'Surely you can't be considering turning yourself in to SCARE!'

'I have a unique ability, *kochanie*. Perhaps now is the time to use it. For the good of the country.' He reached to comfort her.

'Madness!' She avoided his arms and stalked across the room, her arms folded tightly across her chest. 'You're not Golden Boy,

Frank, you're a grandfather! A balding, middle-aged bureaucrat! You don't even put pepper on your eggs!' She turned and he saw tears flowing down the lines on her face. 'And think of the children! What will people think if they learn their father is ... one of *them*?'

Frank looked down at the last pawn, still in his hand, and its matching velvet-lined compartment. Every piece had a place where it belonged, and a pawn could not fill the space designed for a queen. He sighed. 'You're right, of course.'

Sophia's slippers shuffled across the floor and she pressed her soft warmth against his back, embracing him from behind. He set down the pawn and turned to gather her up in his arms. They stood that way for a while, rocking gently side to side as they held each other.

'Now come to bed,' Sophia said at last.

Frank turned out the light, leaving the pawn standing in the dark beside the empty chessboard.

Friday, May 13. Frank sat alone in his office, a greasy street-vendor sausage sitting cold and half-eaten on the corner of his desk. He hadn't had a proper lunch in two weeks, instead spending every spare moment on the Powers matter.

In recent days, the already tense international situation had grown steadily worse, with Soviet bombers probing into Alaska and Canada and increasing activity at intermediate-range missile sites threatening Turkey and Pakistan. But Frank had been focusing his attention on the elusive, missing ICICLE. He was no longer the only KGB man who'd vanished; others had also disappeared from play. Correlating that information with the latest signal intercepts on transportation and security budgets, Frank had deduced the epicenter of this mysterious activity: Vladimirsky Central, a high-security prison in the Russian city of Vladimir.

Powers must be there.

Frank was nearly ready to present his findings to his superiors; he just needed a few more facts to back up his intuition. Dulles would be displeased that he'd continued to work on the Powers case, but if Frank could present a solid enough report he'd have no choice but to accept his conclusions. Whether he'd act on those conclusions was another question, but that was beyond Frank's control.

He shuffled through flimsy papers, pink and tan and yellow spattered with red SECRET and TOP SECRET stamps, looking for definitive evidence. This was the very latest intelligence … Frank had nagged the document control officers to the point that they were shoveling anything they could at him just to get rid of him. It was possible that he was the first to see this data.

So when he read the report from an agent in the sleepy Moscow suburb of Noginsk, claiming that Roman Andreyevich Rudenko, Procurator General of the Soviet Union, had been seen with Generals Borisoglebsky, Vorobyev, and Zakharov on a private car aboard an eastbound train, his mouth went dry.

Rudenko was the Soviet equivalent of the U.S. Attorney General. Borisoglebsky, Vorobyev, and Zakharov made up the military division of the Supreme Court of the USSR. And Noginsk was on the route from Moscow to Vladimir.

Espionage trials in the Soviet Union were conducted in secret. If those four were in Vladimir, they could be trying Powers right now. And Frank might be the only one who knew it.

But the agent in Noginsk had made very few previous reports; Frank couldn't determine how much credence to give this one. He needed more data to be certain. Shuffling through stacks and stacks of paper, scanning and discarding each one as quickly as possible, he soon built up a pile of loose sheets on the floor at his feet.

Then something he'd read snagged at his brain just as his fingers were letting go of the sheet. He scrambled to find it again, crumpling and tearing other papers in his haste, then held it up to the light. It was an intercepted telegram from the Bureau of Prisons to the Commandant of the Red Army Orchestra and Chorus.

REGRET MUST CANCEL YOUR PERFORMANCE 17 MAY 1960 AT VLADIMIR PRISON, read the uppercase Cyrillic letters. EXERCISE YARD UNAVAILABLE THAT DAY.

Vladimir Prison. Supreme Court. Procurator General. Secret trial. Exercise yard.

Execution by firing squad.

It was a slim and twisty thread of evidence, to be sure. But Frank had ignored his intuitions before and the result had been nothing but ignominy and shame. His professional speciality – his whole *life* – was assembling estimates from seemingly unconnected facts, and he'd rarely felt such certainty about a conclusion.

The specified date was four days from now. Three days, given the time difference between Washington and Moscow. To have a chance of saving Powers, his superiors would have to be informed *immediately*.

Frank gathered up the papers he'd need to back up his conclusions and charged out the door. He didn't even stop for his hat.

♠

Robert was on a plane to Geneva for a NATO meeting, so Frank swallowed and went to Dulles.

'The Director is in a meeting at the White House,' his secretary said. 'He won't be back here until tomorrow.'

But Frank's progress was checked by the guard at the West Wing security desk. 'I'm sorry, sir, Director Dulles is meeting with the President. Please wait over there.'

'How long?' Frank clutched the folder full of papers as though it were the steering wheel of his destiny.

'I can't tell you, sir.'

Frank sat in the indicated chair, but only for a moment. He bounced up and began pacing the floor.

He glanced at the clock. 4.15 P.M. Moscow time. In forty-five minutes it would be Saturday there. If Frank was right, Powers's execution was set for Tuesday, probably at dawn. Eighty hours from now, more or less.

If he could only turn back the clock . . .

Frank halted in his tracks. 'I'm sorry,' he told the guard, 'I can't wait. I'll have to find some other way.'

He stepped around the corner. There was another guard here,

but his attention was focused outward and Frank was behind him.

This was madness. If Frank actually did what he was contemplating, his life would be changed forever. He might never see his wife or children again. And Powers was just one man, a man who had known even as he'd boarded the U-2 that he might never return from his mission.

But Frank had sworn an oath to defend the United State from all enemies foreign and domestic. Powers was not just one man … his life was symbolic of much more, and rescuing him might prevent a much greater confrontation. Frank's wife might not understand. But what he did for the country, he did for her, and for the children.

He clutched his folder and concentrated.

A rush of sound like a hard wind in Frank's ears stole away the ticking clock and all other sounds. Outside the window, a flag froze in mid-wave.

Frank pushed through the thick, jellylike air past the West Wing guard, who sat unblinking behind his desk. The door behind him felt heavy as lead, but beyond it lay a long, straight corridor, empty except for two armed Marines at rigid attention beside the third door on the left.

Behind that door, as Frank had surmised, was a small, dark conference room where three unmoving men sat at a table, staring grimly at an overhead projector screen. By the projector's light Frank recognized Dulles and Eisenhower; the third seemed vaguely familiar, though Frank couldn't name him.

Frank stared at the President, who sat frozen with the bright rectangle of the screen reflecting in his glasses. In a moment, Frank would reveal himself to him, and his civilian life would be over.

Or he could back out right now, and no one would ever know.

No one but Frank himself.

Frank gasped in a breath, and the roaring in his ears was replaced by the softer sound of the projector's fan. A moment later came another gasp, this one from Dulles, as he noticed Frank's sudden appearance. 'What the devil!' Immediately he leapt to cover the projector's lens with his hand.

That unexpected action drew Frank's attention to the screen. Before Dulles could block the light he took in the words AQUA-TONE and CAPTURED and RAMPART and PILOT.

AQUATONE was the cryptonym for the U-2, Frank knew. And RA was the digraph for cryptonyms related to the wild card virus. If RAMPART was the code name for the captured U-2 pilot, that meant ...

'We have a problem,' said the third man, as he flicked on the room lights. 'This man knows who and what RAMPART is.'

Suddenly Frank realized who the third man was. Lawrence Hague, the stockbroker who'd been the first person inducted into SCARE – a telepath. He was five years older than the newsreel footage Frank had seen of him, but those sharp eyes and high forehead were unmistakable. It was a good thing Frank had gone into the room intending to reveal himself.

'Yes, I have just deduced from the information on that slide that Francis Gary Powers is an ace,' he said. To his own surprise, his voice was level. 'I came here to tell you that he has already been tried and sentenced to death.'

Eisenhower's expression was grim. 'How did you get in here?'

'I too am an ace.' There, he'd said it. No going back now.

'An ace screwup, maybe ...' Dulles snarled.

Eisenhower stood, interrupting Dulles. 'What was that you said about Powers being sentenced?'

Frank quickly laid out the intelligence and his interpretation.

Dulles was frankly skeptical. 'This man couldn't find his own ass with a map and a flashlight,' he sniffed.

'I know this analysis has a lot of problematic connections,' Frank replied. 'But where I fell down before was in failing to respect my intuition.' He turned and addressed Eisenhower directly. 'Mister President, I was born in Russia before the Revolution. I've been watching these Bolsheviks since their earliest days. I know how they work, I know how they think, and I've made a lifetime study of their politics and government. You must believe that I *know* that Powers has either already been convicted of espionage, or will shortly be, and will be put to death by firing squad in the exercise yard at Vladimirsky Central Prison on Tuesday, May 17.'

'Is this your ace power?' Eisenhower asked. 'Some kind of … super deduction?'

'No, Mr. President. Analysis is my *profession*. My *power* is to bring time to a halt. Everything stops but me; from your perspective I appear to move instantaneously.' This was a speech he'd rehearsed in his head a thousand times. 'If you will permit me to demonstrate?'

Dulles rolled his eyes, but Eisenhower looked to Hague, who nodded.

Frank focused his mind. The world began to roar and the three men froze in place. Pushing through the heavy, resistant air, he walked up to each of them and removed the wallets from their inside jacket pockets. He moved to the far corner of the room before releasing time to its usual flow.

'Over here,' he said. All three men started and whirled to face him, then patted their pockets with increasing agitation. He held up the wallets. Hague gave him a slow, appraising nod.

This was a moment he'd been awaiting for five years. He wanted to savor his triumph … but he just felt tired, weary down to his bones, ten years older. It was all he could do to remain standing. 'Mister President,' he said, his voice hoarse, 'I've seen how much Powers means to you. Please, please believe me … what I know, what I've learned, what I can do. Let me help you in any way I can.'

Dulles was the first to recover. 'Sir, this is an outrage,' he sputtered to Eisenhower.

But the President ignored Dulles, turning instead to Hague. 'Is this man telling the truth?'

'As he understands it, yes.'

'Any black marks on his record?' This was directed to Dulles.

'He failed to determine that the Soviets had Powers.'

'He wasn't the only one. Anything else?'

Dulles glowered at Frank before replying. 'Not to my knowledge.'

Eisenhower looked into Frank's eyes for a long time, considering, and despite his own exhaustion Frank realized that this man really did bear the weight of the world on his shoulders, and had for nearly eight years. 'All right,' he said at last. 'Mr. … Mazursky, was it?'

'Majewski, sir.'

Eisenhower straightened. 'Mr. Majewski, by the authority of the Exotic Powers Control Act and the Special Conscription Act, I place you under the command of the Senate Committee on Ace Resources and Endeavors, effective immediately. Do you understand your rights and responsibilities under the Act?'

'I do, sir.'

'Mr. Hague here is the Director of SCARE, and from now on you will be reporting to him. Larry, please read Mr. Majewski into RAMPART.'

Hague pulled a paper from his briefcase and asked Frank to spell his name and provide his date of birth and social security number. The paper bore a SCARE letterhead and resembled the CIA security clearance form, except that the description of the compartment was just a brief handwritten scrawl – 'Francis Gary Powers, abilities and history,' the ink still wet – and the statement about unauthorized disclosure included the words 'any disclosure whatsoever constitutes treason' and 'subject to immediate execution without trial.' Frank swallowed and signed the form, which was then countersigned by Hague, Dulles, and Eisenhower himself.

Hague then explained that Gary Powers, call sign 'Eagle Eye,' was indeed an ace, and America's most important surveillance asset. 'His ace power is incredible distance vision,' Hague said, 'better than our best telescopic cameras. And he's had years of training in understanding what he sees. Powers is irreplaceable, and he *must* be returned unharmed.'

Eisenhower thanked Hague for his presentation and took the floor. 'This meeting was called,' he said, 'to consider alternatives to Eagle Eye and damage control in the wake of his loss. However, now that you're here, I believe we have a chance to rescue him. The unique combination of your knowledge of Russia, CIA training, and ace power seems heaven-sent for this situation. Do I recall correctly that you are a native speaker of Russian?'

'*Da.*' Frank replied. His heart hammered as he realized what Eisenhower was about to suggest.

But Dulles, who'd been steaming quietly, now burst out, 'Mister President! You cannot possibly be considering sending this man into Russia! He's not an operative, he's an analyst! He has no training in subterfuge, evasion, resistance to interrogation ...'

'Allen,' Eisenhower said, 'shut up.' An indefinable note of command in his tone stopped Dulles cold. 'Eagle Eye is so critical to the security of this nation that to recover him I am prepared to risk the loss of our newest asset' – a chill settled in the pit of Frank's gut as he realized the President was referring to him – 'and any resulting collateral damage. In any case, Mr. Majewski is no longer under your command.' He turned away from Dulles in what Frank interpreted as a deliberate snub.

'Mr. Majewski,' Eisenhower continued, now focusing his attention on Frank, 'I'm sorry to place such a burden on you and to put you in so much danger, but as I'm sure you're aware, your country needs you and your unique abilities. Mr. Hague will give you as much in the way of training and assistance as possible before you leave for your mission.'

Frank opened his mouth, but nothing came out. After a couple of attempts, he simply nodded.

The pawn that reaches the last rank, he told himself, becomes a queen.

◆

Hague took him to an office building on F Street, supposedly a real estate law office but actually the headquarters of SCARE. There he underwent a battery of medical tests, administered with polite but firm efficiency by a staff including Dr. Thatcher, a four-foot-tall hairless man with frog-belly white skin, yellow slit eyes, and fangs, who drew a syringe of Frank's blood and proceeded to *taste* it before writing extensive notes in shorthand. It was the first time Frank had ever been in the same room as a joker, but he tried to remain calm.

Immediately thereafter Frank was subjected to a series of

exercises designed to establish the boundaries of his ace power. He held onto a stopwatch – anything that touched his skin was carried with him outside of time – and kept time stopped for as long as he could, which turned out to be about eleven minutes, though it felt like far more. With time stopped he ran laps, and lugged weights of up to thirty pounds. And he did something he'd never even considered before: He took another human being along with him outside of time, a volunteer who walked slowly as Frank led him by the hand. The volunteer said that the experience was strange and frightening – a delirious, semiconscious rush, without volition, like a waking dream of driving at top speed – but after it was over there seemed to be no ill effects. When a second volunteer was added Frank found it too difficult to take even a single step.

After those tests he repeated the medical exam. No one told him a thing about what they'd learned, if anything. Then he was permitted to call his wife, though only under strict observation and only to tell her that he was on a special assignment and would not be able to come home for at least several days.

By now it was nearly two in the morning. The SCARE offices had a few small sleeping rooms, windowless and spare but otherwise fairly comfortable; the door did not lock, either from the inside or the outside. Frank removed his tie and shoes and stretched out on the bed to rest for a bit, certain that his mind was too full of questions and new experiences for sleep.

The next thing he knew, he was being awakened by a polite male secretary, who told him to was six o'clock. He also gave Frank a large, battered suitcase with the Cyrillic initials Ya. G. It contained several changes of clothing – heavy, badly made, and ill-fitting, with labels in Russian – shoes, handkerchiefs, and other furnishings; and what looked to Frank's eye like a genuine Russian passport with his own photograph and the name Jacek Grabowski.

As he shaved with a dull and pitted Russian-made safety razor and gritty soap, Frank reflected that it was a good thing he wasn't used to the smooth, lubricated aerosol shaving cream his barber kept insisting he should try.

The moment he emerged from the bathroom he was hurried

to a meeting with Hague and several other very serious men, who presented him with a thick folder of papers: a detailed plan for Powers's rescue. In order for the timing to work he would have to leave for Andrews Air Force Base within the hour. Did he have any questions?

Frank read the plan over a cup of horrible coffee and a stale doughnut. It seemed to take into account everything he and SCARE had learned about his abilities in the previous day ... by pushing them to their absolute limits. The plan would work, he thought, as long as nothing unexpected happened and Frank maintained the same level of performance.

But there was one part of the plan that Frank couldn't countenance. He would be accompanied by an experienced field officer to help him with insertion and extraction, but the plan called for the officer to accompany Frank into the prison and then, while Frank took Powers out using his wild card talent, make his way out on his own.

'I'm going into Russia to break a man out of an escape-proof prison,' Frank said, stabbing the prison map with a forefinger. 'I won't leave another man behind in his place.'

Hague's hands gripped each other on the tabletop. 'That's his job, Frank. And it's your job to follow my orders.'

Frank met Hague's hard stare with one of his own. 'I won't do it.'

They glared at each other for a long moment, while sweat trickled down Frank's sides under the heavy Soviet jacket. But it was Hague who blinked first. 'Fine,' he said. He turned to one of the other SCARE planners. 'We'll use the alternate plan where Frank goes in and out of the prison by himself.'

Frank was astonished that Hague had collapsed so suddenly and thoroughly.

'Don't be so surprised,' Hague said – although Frank had not spoken. 'I can see exactly where you will and won't compromise.' He stood and extended his hand. 'I think you're a sentimental fool, but I wish you Godspeed.' The planners stood as well.

Frank's knees were quaking so much he could barely lever

himself upright, but he managed. 'Thank you, sir. I'll give it my best effort.'

The plane that Frank boarded at Andrews was a big C-130 Hercules, and Frank was the only passenger. 'All this for me?' he asked the pilot, a slim and leathery Navy man with pale blue eyes whose name patch read A. DEARBORN.

'I fly where I'm told to.' He shrugged.

Takeoff was rough, with the empty cargo compartment rattling and the four huge engines roaring like tornadoes, but the flight soon settled down to routine. 'It's fifteen hours to Helsinki,' Dearborn said, 'including a refuelling stop in Keflavik.'

Frank slept for a while, but despite his exhaustion, earplugs, and his Soviet wool suit, the noise and cold woke him up after a few hours. He read over the rescue plan until he was sure he'd memorized every detail. He inventoried the contents of his suitcase and counted every button on every shirt. By the time Dearborn turned over the controls to his copilot for a break and came back to offer Frank a sandwich, he'd gone all the way from terror to boredom and out the other side to desperation. 'I don't suppose there's a chess set on this plane?'

'You're in luck.' Dearborn hauled one out from his duffel bag, a tiny travel set, the wooden pieces of which plugged into holes in the board. 'Always glad to have another player on one of these long flights,' Dearborn said as he set up the board. 'What's your rating?'

'I ... I don't know. I don't usually play against other people.'

'Ah. Play by mail, then?' Dearborn, playing white, advanced his queen's pawn.

'No. I, ah, I just ... study the games of champions. Play them out on the board. Analyze them.' It was surprisingly painful to confess his hobby. He knew that chess wasn't just an intellectual pastime; it was also a game, to be played with other people as a form of social interaction. But that aspect just wasn't appealing to him. 'I haven't actually played a real game of chess in ... must be ten years.' He advanced his own queen's pawn to confront Dearborn's.

'No time like the present, then.' Dearborn moved his queen's bishop's pawn forward in the classic Queen's Gambit opening.

At this point Frank could decline the Queen's Gambit by advancing his king's pawn – retaining control of the center – or accept it by taking the pawn Dearborn had just advanced – gaining more freedom to act later.

He found himself unable to decide.

He reached out his hand … then drew it back. And again. He trembled with uncertainty.

After so many years of detailed study and analysis of some of the greatest chess games in history … against a human opponent he couldn't even manage a classic opening in a meaningless, casual game.

Dulles was right. He was an analyst, not a field operative. What in God's name did he think he was doing here?

'Hey,' said Dearborn. 'Hey, are you okay?'

'I'm fine,' Frank lied, and blew his nose to mask the tears. The Russian handkerchief was stiff and rough. He folded it, tucked it back in his pocket, drew in a breath, and captured Dearborn's pawn.

He'd given up so much control of his life already. Why not give up control of the center? It might help in the endgame.

Play continued. Dearborn was a stodgy, conservative player, clearly failing to look more than a few moves ahead, but somehow he always seemed to be in just the right place to counter Frank's attacks. 'Just lucky, I guess,' he said, capturing Frank's knight.

'There is no luck in chess.' Frank advanced his remaining knight. 'Check.'

'Maybe so. But I've always been lucky, somehow. It could be me over there right now, instead of Francis Gary Powers.' He took Frank's knight with his bishop.

'Oh?' Frank nudged his queen one square to threaten that bishop.

'Yeah. I was approached by the U-2 program, passed all the exams and interviews, got the clearances, everything. But then I got the mumps – *mumps*, can you believe it? – and missed the window to enter the training. By the time I was cleared to fly again they didn't have any openings.' He swooped the endangered bishop across the board, but as soon as he let go of the piece his face fell. 'Oh … I didn't mean to put it *there*. Nuts.' He frowned, examining the board, then suddenly sat up straight. 'Hey! Checkmate!'

Frank hoped that wasn't an omen.

Frank was met in Helsinki by a bulky man with a wide, unsmiling face who introduced himself in Russian as Pyotr Andreivich Malinov. He took Frank's suitcase to a stodgy gray Volvo sedan, and Frank thought he was just the driver until the door closed and he provided Frank with the confirmation code. He was Frank's field officer, a trustworthy CIA agent of long standing who had often worked with SCARE. 'What's your alias?' Frank asked him. 'What should I call you?'

'You will address me as Pyotr Andreivich Malinov. If you don't know my real name you can't slip up and call me by it. And you, as far as I am concerned, are nothing but Jacek Grabowski, my wife's slightly simple cousin, whom I am escorting to Moscow for the agricultural exposition as a favor to her. If there are any awkward questions, just act stupid.' It was clear that he didn't think that would be much of a challenge.

A protest began to form behind Frank's lips – he was a CIA analyst, he had advanced degrees in economics and foreign affairs – but he kept silent. He would be depending on this man for his life, and he knew his business. There was no sense in antagonizing him.

'Malinov' barely spoke to Frank as they drove to the Helsinki train station, and as soon as they were settled in their hard second-class seats he pulled his hat over his eyes and went to sleep. Frank seethed in his heavy, damp coat. This was the man who was supposed to protect him? But Frank was bone-tired himself, and despite the uncomfortable seat and his many concerns he, too, soon found his eyes falling shut.

As he drifted off to sleep, Frank thought he heard Malinov wish him good night. Perhaps the other man wasn't really asleep at all.

Frank woke with a start at a hard poke in his ribs. Four Russian border guards in steel helmets with machine guns slung across the backs of their long green coats were making their way down the length of the train car. 'Passport,' Malinov hissed.

But Frank's passport wasn't in his coat pocket. Quickly he searched his other coat pockets, his pants pockets, the seat beneath him. 'I ... I'm sorry.' His pulse hammered in his ears.

'Find it,' Malinov muttered under his breath.

Two of the guards approached. 'Passports,' one said crisply.

Malinov handed over his own passport. 'I'm so sorry,' he said, 'but my cousin seems to have misplaced his.' He tapped his temple in a significant gesture and grinned. 'He's Polish.'

Frank wouldn't have thought that any other emotions could penetrate his terror, but he found that anger at the ethnic slur did manage to make itself felt even as he continued to pat his pockets. Malinov and the guards had a chuckle at Frank's expense, which turned into outright laughter when the wayward document turned up in his shirt pocket.

The guard flipped open Frank's fraudulent passport. 'Please confirm for me your date of birth.'

Frank's heart just about stopped. He couldn't remember what birthdate the counterfeit document bore. Was it his own? If not, what was it? Agonized seconds crawled by ... this time, he was frozen and the rest of the world moved.

'Polish,' Malinov said again, and shrugged. This time even the man in the seat across the aisle joined in the laughter. Still laughing, the guard handed back Frank's passport and moved down the aisle.

'You didn't have to insult me like that,' Frank said once the guards had passed into the next car. His heart rate had dropped to only twice normal.

'Laughter reduces suspicion,' Malinov replied, 'and it got you out of that jam.' He shrugged. 'What else would you have had me do?'

♠

Later he realized that he could have used his power to search for the passport, or to inspect it while the guard held it in his hand. But he hadn't thought of it when it might have done some good. Eight years of hiding his power, of pretending to be someone who was no different from anyone else, had kept him from remembering at the key moment what he could do.

What in God's name did he think he was doing here?

Maybe Dulles had been right after all.

♦

On Tuesday, May 17, at three in the morning Moscow time, Frank stood shivering in the rain outside the gate of Vladimirsky Central Prison, feeling very small.

The prison's walls loomed high above; the rain that spattered down into Frank's face formed glowing halos around the floodlights mounted at intervals along the tops of the walls. Armed guards with dogs patrolled the perimeter; the interior was a warren of remote-controlled doors designed to make escape impossible. It was Russia's most secure prison.

Frank was going to walk in, and walk out again with Powers.

Even with Frank's wild card ability, it was only a mole within the prison that would make the rescue possible. The detailed map the mole had provided gave Frank a few places to rest, out of sight, when his power was exhausted; the list of time points clutched in Frank's hand, thrust deep in his coat pocket, would get him past the locked doors.

The first of those times was 3.05 A.M. – still five more minutes. Frank checked his watch, but not even his power could make that second hand move any faster.

Moscow rain tasted of concrete and sulfur.

Finally 3.05 arrived. Frank took a deep breath and concentrated.

The roar of stopped time assaulted his exhausted ears. Raindrops halted in their downward rush, each one revealing itself as an irregular flattened disc, not raindrop-shaped at all. Frank pushed through the gluey air, suspended drops sliding across his face or absorbing into his coat.

He simply walked past the outer gate, a diagonally striped barrier arm whose two armed guards stood frozen in their raincoats in the unmoving rain. The door of the prison building itself was not locked, nor were the next two doors, and the guards at each were no obstacle. But pushing the doors open and closed again took a substantial effort. Heavier and tighter than domestic doors, each one felt to Frank as though it weighed a hundred pounds. He was literally working against time.

Frank mopped his brow and pressed forward, deeper into the prison.

Now came the first of the serious obstacles: an airlock with heavy steel and glass doors on either side, each locked by a deadbolt that could only be opened by the press of a button at the guard station between the doors. But the mole had promised that he could unlatch both doors for one minute, from 3.05 to 3.06, and no one would notice.

Instinctually Frank glanced at his watch as he approached the first door, and felt a moment of panic: It read 3.13. But of course that reflected his personal time. The clock on the wall was frozen at a few seconds past 3.05. He put his weight against the door and, with heavy reluctance, it swung open. The second door was also unlocked – thank God! – but took even more of an effort to open.

After pushing the second door shut, Frank leaned against the cold concrete wall for the space of several gasping breaths. But outside of time there was no rest; even breathing was work. He had to get to his first hiding place before he grew too tired to continue.

The harsh lights inside the security zone battered at Frank's eyes as he slogged through the thick, resistant air toward the safety of a maintenance closet. By the time he reached it, his vision was beginning to swim, and it was all he could do to work the latch and drag the door open. As soon as he shut it, delivering himself into blessed darkness, he released his power. Trembling, he allowed himself to slide down the door until he sat on the floor, panting as quietly as possible. The filthy, dark closet was chill and smelled of chlorine, but it was still better than the unearthly roar and stillness of the world outside of time.

The mole's next time point was 3.15. Ten minutes to rest was not enough. Ten minutes to wait helplessly in a dark closet, trembling in fear each time someone came clomping and rattling by outside the door, was too much.

He imagined the door opening suddenly, flooding the crowded little space with light and exclamations of surprise. If that happened, he could freeze time again and escape that way, but the plan would be disrupted and an alarm might be raised. And where would he hide until the next exit time point?

Finally, finally, the glowing hands pointed to 3.15. So glad to leave this stinking closet, so afraid to face the roar of frozen time, he concentrated and called up his power.

It took all his might to push the petrified door open.

Never before had Frank spent so much time out of time. Every step was climbing a mountain; every door he opened and closed was Sisyphus's rock.

MAXIMUM SECURITY AREA read the stenciled Cyrillic letters over the next time-point door. This one was a sliding door, electrically operated, and though it was unlatched as the mole had promised, all Frank's remaining strength was not enough to force it open. He found a steel truncheon leaning in a corner and used that to lever the door open just enough to squeeze through. Then he had to put the truncheon back, carefully matching it to its remembered position. Damn it, which end had been up? It was getting harder and harder to think straight.

On the other side, he turned ... and immediately confronted a dark and scowling face. Recoiling in panic, he cracked his head on the metal door behind him before his reason overcame his initial reaction. The broad, muscular man in the uniform of a Soviet Army colonel – his name patch read POLYAKOV – was as frozen as everything else in the prison, petrified in the act of charging angrily toward the door Frank had just emerged from. Frank leaned against the door for a moment, rubbing his head and chiding himself for stupidity.

Wait. Polyakov? That name was familiar.

It was one of the possible names listed for the KGB

officer designated ICICLE by the CIA. And now here he was, in Vladimirsky Central Prison, in the maximum security wing where Powers was imprisoned. Frank had been right all along, and now he even had a name for the man.

Frank allowed himself a moment of smug triumph, snapping his fingers under the KGB man's unmoving nose before ducking past him and pressing down the hall. Powers's cell, number thirty-seven, was the first one on the right, with the name POVRZ – 'Powers' in Cyrillic – chalked above the door.

Now nothing stood between Frank and success.

But the door wouldn't open.

Frank tried again, pressing down on the rust-flecked steel handle with all his might. It didn't budge.

The mole was supposed to have arranged for the door to be unlocked from 3.10 to 3.40. Everything else had gone exactly as planned.

Frank rattled the handle one more time. Nothing.

He cast about for some other way to open the door. But it was heavy, solid steel, the lock mechanism and hinges well protected and reinforced, and there was nothing in this empty concrete hallway he could use against it. To have come so far, overcome so much, only to be thwarted by a simple lock!

No, wait. The key. Polyakov, frozen at the moment of striding away from Powers's cell, must have the key.

Frank waded to the unmoving KGB man through air that seemed even thicker than before. It didn't take long to identify the hard lump of keys in Polyakov's pants pocket, but the position of his petrified leg and arm made it impossible for Frank to extract it. He could move the arm by force, he thought, or cut the pocket open with his penknife, but either action would startle Polyakov and make him raise an alarm. And Frank had another ten-minute time point to get through, with Powers, on the way out.

He *had* to get the key from Polyakov, and in such a way that he would not notice.

He moved to a position behind Polyakov, making sure no other frozen eyes could see him where he stood. The sliding door stood open by nine inches. But Polyakov's eyes were downcast ... he'd have to risk it.

He released time to its normal rate.

'—burn the idiot who left it unlocked—' Polyakov muttered as he stepped forward.

Stopping time again so soon was like trying to stop the flow in the middle of a long, hard piss, but somehow Frank managed. He drew in a gasping breath of the roaring, gluey air, then pushed forward to Polyakov's side.

The pocket was now accessible. Thank God! He fished the keys from it – hoping that Polyakov, in mid-stride, wouldn't notice the intrusion – and dragged himself back to Powers's cell. The key stamped 37 fit the lock, though working the latch and opening the door felt like dragging a railroad car uphill.

Powers lay on his side on the bed. He looked like hell, his eyes sunken and his mouth set in a despairing scowl, but it was definitely him.

Frank's heart pounded and his vision began to blur. The roaring in his ears had grown to an onrushing railroad engine. He desperately needed a rest.

But with two doors open and the keys in his hand, he didn't dare. Somehow he had to keep going.

Frank hauled Powers to his feet by brute force. It would probably leave bruises, but there was no alternative. Walking backwards, leading the insensate pilot by both hands, he guided Powers out the door, past the frozen Polyakov, and through the sliding door. Then he went back to close and lock the cell door, replace the keys in Polyakov's pocket, and slide the cellblock door shut. 'I wish I could see your face,' he gasped to Polyakov as he put all his weight against the sliding door handle, 'when you find Powers mysteriously vanished from a locked cell.'

He was supposed to take Powers back to the maintenance closet where he'd rested on the way in, but he couldn't possibly make it that far. Already he was half-learning on Powers even as he guided him down the hall, his vision dimming and his steps wobbly.

Here was a bathroom. It would have to do.

He led Powers inside, barely remembering to reset his watch to the hall clock before closing and locking the door behind himself.

So, so tired ...

No. He couldn't relax just yet.

He lay Powers down on the floor like a stiff, man-sized puppet. He leaned hard on Powers's chest and placed one hand firmly over his mouth and nose.

He let go of time.

'Mmmrrrph!' Powers spasmed and tried to squirm out of Frank's grasp. From his perspective he had just been whipped from his cell in an instantaneous rush and was now being pinned and suffocated by a stranger. But even weakened by seventeen days in Soviet custody, he was stronger than Frank.

'Be still!' Frank hissed into Powers's ear, in English. 'I'm here to rescue you!'

Powers stopped struggling, though every muscle quivered with tension. 'Mmf?'

'I'm from SCARE,' he whispered. 'Lawrence Hague sent me. I am cleared for AQUATONE and RAMPART. We are still inside the prison and if we are discovered here we will both die. Do you understand?'

Powers nodded slowly, his eyes wide above Frank's trembling hand.

Frank released Powers and slumped against the wall, letting his eyes sag closed. He felt a million years old.

'You're an ace?' Powers whispered. He had a slow Virginia drawl.

'Yes. I can stop time. But only for a little while ...'

'More useful than being Mr. Peepers.' Powers's voice dripped with bitterness. Then he took a deep breath, let it out. 'Um, what's your name?'

'Franciszek Majewski. That's Polish for Francis, actually. Just like you.'

Powers rolled his eyes. 'Please, call me Gary. Only my mam and pap call me Francis.'

'I'm Frank.'

They shook hands.

On Friday, May 20, at 11.00 A.M., Frank entered the Oval Office and the President came out from behind his desk to greet him. Dulles and Hague, also present, stood where they were. Although honored by the gesture, Frank couldn't help but notice that Eisenhower did not shake his hand. 'It's okay, Mr. President,' he said. 'I'm not infectious.'

Frank knew he looked like hell. Even though he'd slept much of the way back, including most of the limousine ride from Andrews Air Force Base, he still felt weak; he'd lost much of his remaining hair, vague pains troubled his joints, and his walk had become an old man's shuffling step.

He hoped that a few days or weeks of rest would bring his vitality back, but he feared it would not. Using his power had always aged him unnaturally, far in excess of the minutes or hours he spent outside of time, and the unprecedented effort he'd spent on the Powers rescue mission had surely cost him dearly. He might have lost five years in that one hellish night.

'Welcome back to America, Frank,' Eisenhower said, and escorted him to one on the wing chairs beside the fireplace. 'We're all proud of the work you've done for your country.' Eisenhower glanced at Dulles and Hague. Hague grinned and gave a satisfied nod. Dulles, glowering, stared at his black wingtips.

Eisenhower cleared his throat. 'Allen?'

It took Dulles a long moment to meet Frank's eyes. 'You did well,' he finally admitted.

'Thank you,' Frank said, accepting a cup of coffee from the President's own hand. 'Has there been any … fallout, from Powers's escape?' It was the one question that had nagged at him all the way home. Would Khrushchev, already angered by the spy plane intrusion in his territory, be even more provoked by the mysterious disappearance of Powers from his most secure prison? Had Frank's mission only succeeded in moving the doomsday clock closer to midnight?

Eisenhower shook his head. 'They've acknowledged that they've lost Powers – they couldn't deny it, after his press conference in Helsinki – but publicly they haven't said a word about *how* he escaped, and even in private they've been a bit less belligerent.'

Hague sat in the wing chair opposite Frank. 'They know it must have been an ace who helped Powers escape,' he said, 'but politically they can't admit our aces are better than theirs. They'll just have to swallow their pride and keep quiet.'

But Dulles was less sanguine. 'They kept quiet for five years of U-2 overflights, too.'

Eisenhower shot Dulles a look. 'None of your pessimism, Allen. This is a celebratory occasion.' From his pocket he pulled a folded paper and handed it to Frank. It was an official commendation, on SCARE stationery, signed by the President and sealed with a red ribbon. 'This will go in your file, Frank. I'd love to give you a ticker-tape parade, but …' He shrugged. 'You know how it is.' He held out his hand.

After a moment, Frank understood what the open hand meant, and returned the paper. Of course he could not keep a copy. As a SCARE agent he no longer existed.

Frank swallowed. 'I know you can't acknowledge my work,' he said, 'but …' His voice started to tremble, and he had to stop and try to regain his composure. Eisenhower waited patiently. 'All I ask,' he started again, 'is that you tell my wife I died heroically in the service of my country.' He hoped the secret facility in the Nevada desert at least had air-conditioning.

Hague blinked. 'You think we're going to send you to Watertown Strip?' He smirked and shook his head, and Frank remembered that Hague knew what Frank was thinking. 'No, Frank, that's just a myth.' He and Dulles exchanged glances. 'Well, the part about aces being held prisoner there is. You won't just vanish. In fact, you'll be going home right after we debrief you.'

'You will continue at the CIA,' Dulles said, though it was plain he didn't like the idea, 'as cover, performing assignments for SCARE only when necessary. You'll probably spend as many nights at home as before. Maybe more.'

'It's like being a spy in your own country,' Hague continued. 'And in your case, we already know you can keep a secret.'

The pawn that reaches the last rank becomes a queen, Frank thought. Though even a queen could be captured ... or could be dead of old age in five years. It all depended on how the piece was played. But for now he could return to his home, removed from the board and placed securely back in the space that fit him. 'Thank you, sir,' he said.

'No, thank *you*,' Eisenhower said, and again he held out his hand, this time to shake Frank's. 'Welcome to SCARE, Special Agent Stopwatch.'

SHELL GAMES

by George R. R. Martin

When he'd moved into the dorm back in September, the first thing that Thomas Tudbury had done was tack up his signed photograph of President Kennedy, and the tattered 1944 *Time* cover with Jetboy as Man of the Year.

By November, the picture of Kennedy was riddled with holes from Rodney's darts. Rod had decorated his side of the room with a Confederate flag and a dozen *Playboy* centerfolds. He hated Jews, niggers, jokers, and Kennedy, and didn't like Tom much either. All through the fall semester, he had fun; covering Tom's bed with shaving cream, short-sheeting him, hiding his eyeglasses, filling his desk drawer with dog turds.

On the day that Kennedy was killed in Dallas, Tom came back to his room fighting to hold the tears. Rod had left him a present. He'd used a red pen. The whole top of Kennedy's head was dripping blood now, and over his eyes Rod had drawn little red *X*'s. His tongue was sticking out of the corner of his mouth.

Thomas Tudbury stared at that for a long, long time. He did not cry; he would not allow himself to cry. He began to pack his suitcases.

The freshman parking lot was halfway across campus. The trunk on his '54 Mercury had a broken lock, so he tossed the bags into the backseat. He let the car warm up for a long time in the November chill. He must have looked funny sitting there; a short, overweight guy with a crewcut and horn-rim glasses, pressing his head against the top of the steering wheel like he was going to be sick.

As he was driving out of the lot, he spied Rodney's shiny new Olds Cutlass.

Tom shifted to neutral and idled for a moment, considering. He looked around. There was no one in sight; everybody was inside watching the news. He licked his lips nervously, then looked back at the Oldsmobile. His knuckles whitened around the wheel. He stared hard, furrowed his brow, and *squeezed.*

The door panels gave first, bending inward slowly under the pressure. The headlights exploded with small pops, one after the other. Chrome trim clattered to the ground, and the rear windshield shattered suddenly, glass flying everywhere. Fenders buckled and collapsed, metal squealing in protest. Both rear tires blew at once, the side panels caved in, then the hood; the windshield disintegrated entirely. The crankcase gave, and then the walls of the gas tank; oil, gasoline, and transmission fluid pooled under the car. By then Tom Tudbury was more confident, and that made it easier. He imagined he had the Olds caught in a huge invisible fist, a *strong* fist, and he squeezed all the harder. The crunch of breaking glass and the scream of tortured metal filled the parking lot, but there was no one to hear. He methodically mashed the Oldsmobile into a ball of crushed metal.

When it was over, he shifted into gear and left college, Rodney, and childhood behind forever.

Somewhere a giant was crying.

Tachyon woke disoriented and sick, his hangover throbbing in time to the mammoth sobs. The shapes in the dark room were strange and unfamiliar. Had the assassins come in the night again, was the family under attack? He had to find his father. He lurched dizzily to his feet, head swimming, and put a hand against the wall to steady himself.

The wall was too close. These weren't his chambers, this was all wrong, the smell ... and then the memories came back. He would have preferred the assassins.

He had dreamed of Takis again, he realized. His head hurt, and his throat was raw and dry. Fumbling in the darkness, he found the chain-pull for the overhead light. The bulb swung wildly when he yanked, making the shadows dance. He closed his eyes to still the lurching in his gut. There was a foul taste at the back of his mouth. His hair was matted and filthy, his clothing rumpled. And worst of all, the bottle was empty. Tachyon looked around help-lessly. A six-by-ten room on the second floor of a lodging house named ROOMS, on a street called the Bowery. Confusingly, the surrounding neighborhood had once been called the Bowery too – Angelface had told him that. But that was before; the area had a different name now. He went to the window, pulling up the shade. The yellow light of a streetlamp filled the room. Across the street, the giant was reaching for the moon, and weeping because he could not grasp it.

Tiny, they called him. Tachyon supposed that was human wit. Tiny would have been fourteen feet tall if only he could stand up. His face was unlined and innocent, crowned with a tangle of soft dark hair. His legs were slender, and perfectly proportioned. And that was the joke: slender, perfectly proportioned legs could not begin to support the weight of a fourteen-foot-tall man. Tiny sat in a wooden wheelchair, a great mechanized thing that rolled through the streets of Jokertown on four bald tires from a wrecked semi. When he saw Tach in the window, he screamed incoherently, almost as though he recognized him. Tachyon turned away from the window, shaking. It was another Jokertown night. He needed a drink.

His room smelled of mildew and vomit, and it was very cold. ROOMS was not as well heated as the hotels he had frequented in the old days. Unbidden, he remembered the Mayflower down in Washington, where he and Blythe ... but no, better not to think of that. What time was it anyway? Late enough. The sun was down, and Jokertown came to life at night.

He plucked his overcoat from the floor and slipped it on. Soiled as it was, it was still a marvelous coat, a lovely rich rose color, with fringed golden epaulets on the shoulders and loops of golden braid to fasten the long row of buttons. A musician's coat, the man at the Goodwill had told him. He sat on the edge of his sagging mattress to pull on his boots.

The washroom was down at the end of the hall. Steam rose from his urine as it splashed against the rim of the toilet; his hands shook so badly that he couldn't even aim right. He slapped cold, rust-colored water on his face, and dried his hands on a filthy towel.

Outside, Tach stood for a moment beneath the creaking ROOMS sign, staring at Tiny. He felt bitter and ashamed. And much too sober. There was nothing to be done about Tiny, but he could deal with his sobriety. He turned his back on the weeping giant, slid his hands deep into the pockets of his coat, and walked off briskly down the Bowery.

In the alleys, jokers and winos passed brown paper bags from hand to hand, and stared with dull eyes at the passersby. Taverns, pawnbrokers, and mask shops were all doing a brisk trade. The Famous Bowery Wild Card Dime Museum (they still called it that, but admission was a quarter now) was closing for the day. Tachyon had gone through it once, two years ago, on a day when he was feeling especially guilt-ridden; along with a half-dozen particularly freakish jokers, twenty jars of 'monstrous joker babies' floating in formaldehyde, and a sensational little newsreel about the Day of the Wild Card, the museum had a waxworks display whose dioramas featured Jetboy, the Four Aces, a Jokertown Orgy ... and him.

A tour bus rolled past, pink faces pressed to the windows. Beneath the neon light of a neighborhood pizza parlor, four youths in black leather jackets and rubber facemasks eyed Tachyon with open hostility. They made him uneasy. He averted his eyes and dipped into the mind of the nearest: *mincing pansy looka that hair dye-job fershure thinks he's inna marching band like to beat his fuckin' drums but no wait shit there's better we'll find us a good one tonight yeah wanna get one that squishes when we hit it.* Tach broke the contact with distaste and hurried on. It was old news, and a new sport: come down to the Bowery, buy some masks, beat up a joker. The police didn't seem to care.

The Chaos Club and its famous All-Joker Revue had the usual

big crowd. As Tachyon approached, a long gray limo pulled up to the curb. The doorman, wearing a black tuxedo over luxuriant white fur, opened the door with his tail and helped out a fat man in a dinner jacket. His date was a buxom teenager in a strapless evening gown and pearls, her blond hair piled high in a bouffant hairdo.

A block farther on, a snake-lady called out a proposition from the top of a nearby stoop. Her scales were rainbow-colored, glistening. 'Don't be scared, Red,' she said, 'it's still soft inside.' He shook his head.

The Funhouse was housed in a long building with giant picture windows fronting the street, but the glass had been replaced with one-way mirrors. Randall stood out front, shivering in tails and domino. He looked perfectly normal – until you noticed that he never took his right hand out of his pocket. 'Hey, Tacky,' he called out. 'Whattaya make of Ruby?'

'Sorry, I don't know her,' Tachyon said.

Randall scowled. 'No, the guy who killed Oswald.'

'Oswald?' Tach said, confused. 'Oswald who?'

'Lee Oswald, the guy who shot Kennedy. He got killed on TV this afternoon.'

'Kennedy's dead?' Tachyon said. It was Kennedy who'd permitted his return to the United States, and Tach admired the Kennedys; they seemed almost Takisian. But assassination was part of leadership. 'His brothers will avenge him,' he said. Then he recalled that they didn't do things that way on earth, and besides, this man Ruby had already avenged him, it seemed. How strange that he had dreamed of assassins.

'They got Ruby in jail,' Randall was saying. 'If it was me, I'd give the fucker a medal.' He paused. 'He shook my hand once,' he added. 'When he was running against Nixon, he came through to give a speech at the Chaos Club. Afterward, when he was leaving, he was shaking hands with everybody.' The doorman took his right hand out of his pocket. It was hard and chitinous, insectile, and in the middle was a cluster of swollen blind eyes. 'He didn't even flinch,' Randall said. 'Smiled and said he hoped I'd remember to vote.'

Tachyon had known Randall for a year, but he had never seen his hand before. He wanted to do what Kennedy had done, to grasp that twisted claw, embrace it, shake it. He tried to slide his hand out of the pocket of his coat, but the bile rose in the back of his throat, and somehow all he could do was look away, and say, 'He was a good man.'

Randall hid his hand again. 'Go on inside, Tacky,' he said, not unkindly. 'Angelface had to go and see a man, but she told Des to keep your table open.'

Tachyon nodded and let Randall open the door for him. Inside, he gave his coat and shoes to the girl in the checkroom, a joker with a trim little body whose feathered owl mask concealed whatever the wild card had done to her face. Then he pushed through the interior doors, his stockinged feet sliding with smooth familiarity over the mirrored floor. When he looked down, another Tachyon was staring back up at him, framed by his feet; a grossly fat Tachyon with a head like a beachball.

Suspended from the mirrored ceiling, a crystal chandelier glittered with a hundred pinpoint lights, its reflections sparkling off the floor tiles and walls and mirrored alcoves, the silvered goblets and mugs, and even the waiters' trays. Some of the mirrors reflected true; the others were distorting mirrors, funhouse mirrors. When you looked over your shoulder in the Funhouse, you could never tell what you'd find looking back. It was the only establishment in Jokertown that attracted jokers and normals in equal numbers. In the Funhouse the normals could see themselves twisted and malformed, and giggle, and play at being jokers; and a joker, if he was very lucky, might glance in the right mirror and see himself as he once had been.

'Your booth is waiting, Doctor Tachyon,' said Desmond, the maître d'. Des was a large, florid man; his thick trunk, pink and wrinkled, curled around a wine list. He lifted it, and beckoned for Tachyon to follow with one of the fingers that dangled from its end. 'Will you be having your usual brand of cognac tonight?'

'Yes,' Tach said, wishing he had some money for a tip.

That night he had his first drink for Blythe, as always, but his second was for John Fitzgerald Kennedy.

The rest were for himself.

♠

At the end of Hook Road, past the abandoned refinery and the import/export warehouses, past the railroad sidings with their forlorn red boxcars, beneath the highway underpass, past the empty lots full of weeds and garbage, past the huge soybean-oil tanks, Tom found his refuge. It was almost dark by the time he arrived, and the engine in the Merc was thumping ominously. But Joey would know what to do about that.

The junkyard stood hard on the oily polluted waters of New York Bay. Behind a ten-foot-high chain-link fence topped with three curly strands of barbed wire, a pack of junkyard dogs kept pace with his car, barking a raucous welcome that would have terrified anyone who knew the dogs less well. The sunset gave a strange bronze cast to the mountains of shattered, twisted, rusted automobiles, the acres of scrap metal, the hills and valleys of junk and trash. Finally Tom came to the wide double gate. On one side a metal sign warned TRESPASSERS KEEP OUT; on the other side another sign told them to BEWARE OF THE DOGS. The gate was chained and locked.

Tom stopped and honked his horn.

Just beyond the fence he could see the four-room shack that Joey called home. A huge sign was mounted on top of the corrugated tin roof, with yellow spotlights stuck up there to illuminate the letters. It said DI ANGELIS SCRAP METAL & AUTO PARTS. The paint was faded and blistered by two decades of sun and rain; the wood itself had cracked, and one of the spots had burned out. Next to the house was parked an ancient yellow dump truck, a tow truck, and Joey's pride and joy, a blood-red 1959 Cadillac coupé with tail fins like a shark and a monster of a hopped-up engine poking right up through its cutaway hood.

Tom honked again. This time he gave it their special signal, tooting out the *Here-he-comes-to-save-the-daaaay!* theme from the *Mighty Mouse* cartoons they'd watched as kids.

A square of yellow light spilled across the junkyard as Joey came out with a beer in either hand.

◆

They were nothing alike, him and Joey. They came from different stock, lived in different worlds, but they'd been best friends since the day of the third-grade pet show. That was the day he'd found out that turtles couldn't fly; the day he realized what he was, and what he could do.

Stevie Bruder and Josh Jones had caught him out in the schoolyard. They played catch with his turtles, tossing them back and forth while Tommy ran between them, red-faced and crying. When they got bored, they bounced them off the punchball square chalked on the wall. Stevie's German shepherd ate one. When Tommy tried to grab the dog, Stevie laid into him and left him on the ground with broken glasses and a split lip.

They would have done worse, except for Junkyard Joey, a scrawny kid with shaggy black hair, two years older than his classmates, but he'd already been left back twice, couldn't hardly read, and they always said he smelled bad on account of his father, Dom, owned the junkyard. Joey wasn't as big as Stevie Bruder, but he didn't care, that day or any day. He just grabbed Stevie by the back of his shirt and yanked him around and kicked him in the balls. Then he kicked the dog too, and he would have kicked Josh Jones, except Josh ran away. As he fled, a dead turtle floated off the ground and flew across the schoolyard to smack him in the back of his fat red neck.

Joey had seen it happen. 'How'd you do that?' he said, astonished. Until that moment, even Tommy hadn't realized that *he* was the reason his turtles could fly.

It became their shared secret, the glue that held their odd friendship together. Tommy helped Joey with his homework and quizzed him for tests. Joey became Tommy's protector against the random brutality of playground and schoolyard. Tommy read comic books to Joey, until Joey's own reading got so much better that he didn't need Tommy. Dom, a grizzled man with salt-and-pepper hair, a beer belly, and a gentle heart, was proud of that; he couldn't read himself, not even Italian. The friendship lasted through grammar school and high school and Joey's dropping out. It survived their discovery of girls, weathered the death of Dom DiAngelis and Tom's family moving off to Perth Amboy. Joey DiAngelis was still the only one who knew what Tom was.

Joey popped the cap on another Rheingold with the church key that hung around his neck. Under his sleeveless white undershirt a beer belly like his father's was growing. 'You're too fucking smart to be doing shitwork in a TV repair shop,' he was saying.

'It's a job,' Tom said. 'I did it last summer, I can do it full time. It's not important what kind of job I have. What's important is what I do with my, uh, talent.'

'Talent?' Joey mocked.

'You know what I mean, you dumb wop.' Tom set his empty bottle down on the top of the orange crate next to the armchair. Most of Joey's furnishings weren't what you'd call lavish; he scavenged them from the junkyard. 'I been thinking about what Jetboy said at the end, trying to think what it meant. I figure he was saying that there were things he hadn't done yet. Well, shit, I haven't done *anything*. All the way back I asked what I could do for the country, y'know? Well, fuck, we both know the answer to that one.'

Joey rocked back in his chair, sucking on his Rheingold and shaking his head. Behind him, the wall was lined with the bookshelves that Dom had built for the kids almost ten years ago. The bottom row was all men's magazines. The rest were comic books. Their comic books. *Supermans* and *Batmans*, *Action Comics* and *Detective*, the *Classics Illustrateds* that Joey had mined for all his book reports, horror comics and crime comics and air-war comics, and best of all, their treasure – an almost complete run of *Jetboy Comics*.

Joey saw what he was looking at. 'Don't even think it,' he said, 'you're no fuckin' Jetboy, Tuds.'

'No,' said Tom, 'I'm more than he was. I'm—'

'A dork,' Joey suggested.

'An ace,' he said gravely. 'Like the Four Aces.'

'They were a colored doo-wop group, weren't they?'

Tom flushed. 'You dumb wop, they weren't singers, they—'

Joey cut him off with a sharp gesture. 'I know who the fuck they were, Tuds. Gimme a break. They were dumb shits, like you. They all went to jail or got shot or something, didn't they? Except for the fuckin' snitch, whatsisname.' He snapped his fingers. 'You know, the guy in *Tarzan*.'

'Jack Braun,' Tom said. He'd done a term paper on the Four Aces once, 'And I bet there are others, hiding out there. Like me. I've been hiding. But no more.'

'So you figure you're going to go to the *Bayonne Times* and give a fucking show? You asshole. You might as well tell 'em you're a commie. They'll make you move to Jokertown and they'll break all the goddamned windows in your dad's house. They might even draft you, asswipe.'

'No,' said Tom. 'I've got it scoped out. The Four Aces were easy targets. I'm not going to let them know who I am or where I live.' He used the beer bottle in his hand to gesture vaguely at the bookshelves. 'I'm going to keep my name secret. Like in the comics.'

Joey laughed out loud. 'Fuckin' A. You gonna wear long johns too, you dumb shit?'

'God damn it,' Tom said. He was getting pissed off. 'Shut the fuck up.' Joey just sat there, rocking and laughing. 'Come on, big mouth,' Tom snapped, rising. 'Get off your fat ass and come outside, and I'll show just how dumb I am. C'mon, you know so damned much.'

Joey DiAngelis got to his feet. 'This I gotta see.'

Outside, Tom waited impatiently, shifting his weight from foot to foot, breath steaming in the cold November air, while Joey went to the big metal box on the side of the house and threw a switch. High atop their poles, the junkyard lights blazed to life. The dogs gathered around, sniffing, and followed them when they began to walk. Joey had a beer bottle poking out of a pocket of his black leather jacket.

It was only a junkyard, full of garbage and scrap metal and wrecked cars, but tonight it seemed as magical as when Tommy was ten. On a rise overlooking the black waters of New York Bay, an ancient white Packard loomed like a ghostly fort. That was just what it had been, when Joey and he had been kids; their sanctum, their stronghold, their cavalry outpost and space station and castle rolled all in one. It shone in the moonlight, and the waters beyond were full of promise as they lapped against the shore. Darkness and shadows lay heavy in the yard, changing the piles of trash and metal into mysterious black hills, with a maze of gray alleys between them. Tom led them into that labyrinth, past the big trash heap where they'd played king-of-the-mountain and dueled with scrap-iron swords, past the treasure troves where they'd found so many busted toys and hunks of colored glass and deposit bottles, and once even a whole cardboard carton full of comic books.

They walked between rows of twisted, rusty cars stacked one on another; Fords and Chevys, Hudsons and DeSotos, a Corvette with a shattered accordion hood, a litter of dead Beetles, a dignified black hearse as dead as the passengers it had carried. Tom looked at them all carefully. Finally he stopped. 'That one,' he said, pointing to the remains of a gutted old Studebaker Hawk. Its engine was gone, as were its tires; the windshield was a spiderweb of broken glass, and even in the darkness they could see where rust had chewed away at the fenders and side panels. 'Not worth anything, right?'

Joey opened his beer. 'Go ahead, it's all yours.'

Tom took a deep breath and faced the car. His hands became fists at his side. He stared hard, concentrating. The car rocked slightly. Its front grill lifted an unsteady couple of inches from the ground.

'Whooo-eeee,' Joey said derisively, punching Tom lightly in the shoulder. The Studebaker dropped with a clang, and a bumper fell off. 'Shit, I'm impressed,' Joey said.

'Damn it, keep quiet and leave me alone,' Tom said. 'I can do it, I'll show you, just shut your fuckin' mouth for a minute. I've been practicing. You don't know the things I can do.'

'Won't say a fuckin' word,' Joey promised, grinning. He took a swig of his beer.

Tom turned back to the Studebaker. He tried to blot out everything, forget about Joey, the dogs, the junkyard; the Studebaker filled his world. His stomach was a hard little ball. He told it to relax, took several deep breaths, let his fists uncurl. *Come on, come on, take it easy, don't get upset, do it, you've done more than this, this is easy, easy.*

The car rose slowly, drifting upward in a shower of rust. Tom turned it around and around, faster and faster. Then, with a triumphant smile, Tom threw it fifty feet across the junkyard. It crashed into a stack of dead Chevys and brought the whole thing down in an avalanche of metal.

Joey finished his Rheingold. 'Not bad. A few years ago, you could barely lift me over a fence.'

'I'm getting stronger all the time,' Tom said.

Joey DiAngelis nodded, and tossed his empty bottle to the side. 'Good' he said, 'then you won't have any problem with me, willya?' He gave Tom a hard push with both hands.

Tom staggered back a step, frowning. 'Cut it out, Joey.'

'Make me,' Joey said. He shoved him again, harder. This time Tom almost lost his footing.

'Damn it, *stop* it,' Tom said. 'It's not funny, Joey.'

'No?' Joey said. He grinned. 'I think it's fuckin' hilarious. But hey, you can stop me, can't you? Use your damn power.' He moved right up in Tom's face and slapped him lightly across the cheek. 'Stop me, ace,' he said. He slapped him harder. 'C'mon, Jetboy, stop me.' The third slap was the hardest yet. 'Let's go, supes, whatcha waitin' for?' The fourth blow had a sharp sting; the fifth snapped Tom's head half around. Joey stopped smiling; Tom could smell the beer on his breath.

Tom tried to grab his hand, but Joey was too strong, too fast; he evaded Tom's grasp and landed another slap. 'You wanna box, ace? I'll turn you into fuckin' dogmeat. Dork. Asshole.' The slap almost tore Tom's head off, and brought stinging tears to his eyes. '*Stop me*, jagoff,' Joey screamed. He closed his hand, and buried his fist in Tom's stomach so hard it doubled him over and took his breath away.

Tom tried to summon his concentration, to grab and push, but it was the schoolyard all over again, Joey was everywhere, fists raining down on him, and it was all he could do to get his hands up and try to block the blows, and it was no good anyway, Joey was much stronger, he pounded him, pushed him, screaming all the while, and Tom couldn't think, couldn't focus, couldn't do anything but hurt, and he was retreating, staggering back, and Joey came after him, fists cocked, and caught him with an uppercut that landed right on his mouth with a crack that made his teeth hurt. All of a sudden Tom was lying on his back on the ground, with a mouth full of blood.

Joey stood over him frowning. 'Fuck,' he said. 'I didn't mean to bust your lip.' He reached down, took Tom by the hand, and yanked him roughly to his feet.

Tom wiped blood from his lip with the back of his hand. There was blood on the front of his shirt too. 'Look at me, I'm all messed up,' he said with disgust. He glared at Joey. 'That wasn't fair. You can't expect me to do anything when you're pounding on me, damn it.'

'Uh-huh,' Joey said, 'And while you're concentrating and squinting your eyes, you figure the fuckin' bad guys are just gonna leave you alone, right?' He clapped Tom across the back. 'They'll knock out all your fuckin' teeth. That's if you're lucky, if they don't just shoot you. You ain't no Jetboy, Tuds.' He shivered. 'C'mon. It's fuckin' cold out here.'

When he woke in warm darkness, Tach remembered only a little of the binge, but that was how he liked it. He struggled to sit up. The sheets he was lying on were satin, smooth and sensual, and beneath the odor of stale vomit he could still smell a faint trace of some flowery perfume.

Unsteady, he tossed off the bedclothes and pulled himself to the edge of the four-poster bed. The floor beneath his bare feet was carpeted. He was naked, the air uncomfortably warm on his bare skin. He reached out a hand, found the light switch, and whimpered a little at the brightness. The room was pink-and-white clutter with Victorian furnishings and thick, soundproofed walls. An oil painting of John F. Kennedy smiled down from above the hearth; in one corner stood a three-foot-tall plaster statue of the Virgin Mary.

Angelface was seated in a pink wingback chair by the cold fireplace, blinking at him sleepily and covering her yawn with the back of her hand.

Tach felt sick and ashamed. 'I put you out of your own bed again, didn't I?' he said.

'It's all right,' she replied. Her feet were resting on a tiny footstool. Her soles were ugly and bruised, black and swollen despite the special padded shoes she wore. Otherwise she was lovely. Unbound, her black hair fell to her waist, and her skin had a flushed, radiant quality to it, a warm glow of life. Her eyes were dark and liquid, but the most amazing thing, the thing that never failed to astonish Tachyon, was the warmth in them, the affection he felt so unworthy of. With all he had done to her, and to all the rest of them, somehow this woman called Angelface forgave, and cared.

Tach raised a hand to his temple. Someone with a buzzsaw was trying to remove the back of his skull. 'My head,' he groaned. 'At your prices, the least you could do is take the resins and poisons out of the drinks you sell. On Takis, we—'

'I know,' Angelface said. 'On Takis you've bred hangovers out of your wines. You told me that one already.'

Tachyon gave her a weary smile. She looked impossibly fresh, wearing nothing but a short satin tunic that left her legs bare to the thigh. It was a deep, wine red, lovely against her skin. But when she rose, he glimpsed the side of her face, where her cheek had rested against the chair as she slept. The bruise was darkening already, a purple blossom on her cheek. 'Angel ...' he began.

'It's nothing,' she said. She pushed her hair forward to cover the blemish. 'Your clothes were filthy. Mal took them out to be cleaned. So you're my prisoner for a while.'

'How long have I slept?' Tachyon asked.

'All day,' Angelface replied. 'Don't worry about it. Once I had a customer get so drunk he slept for five months.' She sat down at her dressing table, lifted a phone, and ordered breakfast: toast and tea for herself, eggs and bacon and strong coffee with brandy for Tachyon. With aspirin on the side.

'No,' he protested. 'All that food. I'll get sick.'

'You have to eat. Even spacemen can't live on cognac alone.'

'Please ...'

'If you want to drink, you'll eat,' she said brusquely. 'That's the deal, remember?'

The deal, yes. He remembered. Angelface provided him with rent money, food, and an unlimited bar tab, as much drink as he'd ever need to wash away his memories. All he had to do was eat and tell her stories. She loved to listen to him talk. He told her family anecdotes, lectured about Takisian customs, filled her with history and legends and romances, with tales of balls and intrigues and beauty far removed from the squalor of Jokertown.

Sometimes, after closing, he would dance for her, tracing the ancient, intricate pavanes of Takis across the nightclub's mirrored floors while she watched and urged him on. Once, when both of them had drunk far too much wine, she talked him into demonstrating the Wedding Pattern, an erotic ballet that most Takisians danced but once, on their wedding night. That was the only time she had ever danced with him, echoing the steps, hesitantly at first, and then faster and faster, swaying and spinning across the floor until her bare feet were raw and cracked and left wet red smears upon the mirror tiles. In the Wedding Pattern, the dancing couple came together at the end, collapsing into a long triumphant embrace. But that was on Takis; here, when the moment came, she broke the pattern and shied away from him, and he was reminded once again that Takis was far away.

Two years before, Desmond had found him unconscious and naked in a Jokertown alley. Someone had stolen his clothing while he slept, and he was fevered and delirious. Des had summoned help to carry him to the Funhouse. When he came to, he was lying on a cot in a back room, surrounded by beer kegs and wine racks. 'Do you know what you were drinking?' Angelface had asked him when they'd brought him to her office. He hadn't known; all he recalled was that he'd needed a drink so badly it was an ache inside him, and the old black man in the alley had generously offered to share. 'It's called Sterno,' Angelface told him. She had Des bring in a bottle of her finest brandy. 'If a man wants to drink, that's his business, but at least you can kill yourself with a little class.' The brandy spread thin tendrils of warmth through his chest and stopped his hands from shaking. When he'd emptied the snifter, Tach had thanked her effusively, but she drew back when he tried to touch her. He asked her why. 'I'll show you,' she had said, offering her hand. 'Lightly,' she told him. His kiss had been the merest brush of his lips, not on the back of her hand but against the inside of her wrist, to feel her pulse, the life current inside her, because she was so very lovely, and kind, and because he wanted her.

A moment later he'd watched with sick dismay as her skin darkened to purple and then black. *Another one of mine*, he'd thought.

Yet somehow they had become friends. Not lovers, of course, except sometimes in his dreams; her capillaries ruptured at the slightest pressure, and to her hypersensitive nervous system even the lightest touch was painful. A gentle caress turned her black and blue; lovemaking would probably kill her. But friends, yes. She never asked him for anything he could not give, and so he could never fail her.

Breakfast was served by a hunchbacked black woman named Ruth who had pale blue feathers instead of hair. 'The man brought this for you this morning,' she told Angelface after she'd set the table, handing across a thick, square packet wrapped in brown paper. Angelface accepted it without comment while Tachyon drank his brandy-laced coffee and lifted knife and fork to stare with sick dismay at the implacable bacon and eggs.

'Don't look so stricken,' Angelface said.

'I don't think I've told you about the time the Network starship came to Takis, and what my great-grandmother Amurath had to say to the Ly'bahr envoy,' he began.

'No,' she said. 'Go on. I like your great-grandmother.'

'That's one of us. She terrifies me,' Tachyon said, and launched into the story.

Tom woke well before dawn, while Joey was snoring in the back room. He brewed a pot of coffee in a battered percolator and popped a Thomas English muffin into the toaster. While the coffee perked, he folded the hide-a-bed back into a couch. He covered his muffin with butter and strawberry preserves, and looked around for something to read. The comics beckoned.

He remembered the day they'd saved them. Most had been his, originally, including the run of *Jetboy* he got from his dad. He'd loved those comics. And then one day in 1954 he'd come home from school and found them gone, a full bookcase and two orange crates of funny books vanished. His mother said some women from the PTA had come by to tell her what awful things comic books were. They'd shown her a copy of a book by a Dr. Wertham about how comics turned kids into juvenile delinquents and homos, and how they glorified aces and jokers, and so his mother had let them take Tom's collection. He screamed and yelled and threw a tantrum, but it did no good.

The PTA had gathered up comic books from every kid in school. They were going to burn them all Saturday, in the schoolyard. It was happening all over the country; there was even talk of a law banning comic books, or at least the kinds about horror and crime and people with strange powers.

Wertham and the PTA turned out to be right: that Friday night, on account of comic books, Tommy Tudbury and Joey DiAngelis became criminals.

Tom was nine; Joey was eleven, but he'd been driving his pop's truck since he was seven. In the middle of the night, he swiped the truck and Tom snuck out to meet him. When they got to the school, Joey jimmied open a window, and Tom climbed on his shoulders and looked into the dark classroom and concentrated and grabbed the carton with his collection in it and lifted it up and floated it out into the bed of the truck. Then he snatched four or five other cartons for good measure. The PTA never noticed; they still had plenty to burn. If Dom DiAngelis wondered where all the comics had come from, he never said a word; he just built the shelves to hold them, proud as punch of his son who could read. From that day on, it was their collection, jointly.

Setting his coffee and muffin on the orange crate, Tom went to the bookcase and took down a couple of issues of *Jetboy Comics*. He reread them as he ate, *Jetboy on Dinosaur Island*, *Jetboy and the Fourth Reich*, and his favorite, the final issue, the true one, *Jetboy and the Aliens*, Inside the cover, the title was 'Thirty Minutes Over Broadway.' Tom read it twice as he sipped his cooling coffee. He lingered over some of the best panels. On the last page, they had a picture of the alien, Tachyon, weeping. Tom didn't know if that had happened or not. He closed the comic book and finished his English muffin. For a long time he sat there thinking.

Jetboy was a hero. And what was he? Nothing. A wimp, a chickenshit. A fuck of a lot of good his wild card power did anybody. It was useless, just like him.

Dispiritedly, he shrugged into his coat and went outside. The junkyard looked raw and ugly in the dawn, and a cold wind was blowing. A few hundred yards to the east, the bay was green and choppy. Tom climbed up to the old Packard on its little hill. The door creaked when he yanked it open. Inside, the seats were cracked and smelled of rot, but at least he was out of that wind. Tom slouched back with his knees up against the dash, staring out at sunrise. He sat unmoving for a long time; across the yard, hubcaps and old tires floated up in the air and went screaming off to splash into the choppy green waters of New York Bay. He could see the Statue of Liberty on her island, and the hazy outlines of the towers of Manhattan off to the northeast.

It was nearly seven-thirty, his limbs were stiff, and he'd lost count of the number of hubcaps he'd flung, when Tom Tudbury sat up with a strange expression on his face. The icebox he'd been juggling forty feet from the ground came down with a crash. He ran his fingers through his hair and lifted the icebox again, moved it over twenty yards or so, and dropped it right on Joey's corrugated tin roof. Then he did the same with a tire, a twisted bicycle, six hubcaps, and a little red wagon.

The door to the house flew open with a bang, and Joey came charging out into the cold wearing nothing but boxer shorts and a sleeveless undershirt. He looked real pissed. Tom snatched his bare feet, pulled them out from under him, and dumped him on his butt, hard. Joey cursed.

Tom grabbed him and yanked him into the air, upside down. 'Where the fuck are you, Tudbury?' Joey screamed. 'Cut it out, you dork. Lemme down.'

Tom imagined two huge invisible hands, and tossed Joey from one to the other. 'When I get down, I'm going to punch you so fuckin' hard you'll eat through a straw for the rest of your life,' Joey promised.

The crank was stiff from years of disuse, but Tom finally managed to roll down the Packard's window. He stuck his head out. 'Hiya kids, hiya, hiya, hiya,' he croaked, chortling.

Suspended twelve feet from the ground, Joey dangled and made a fist. 'I'll pluck your fuckin' magic twanger, shithead,' he shouted. Tom yanked off his boxer shorts and hung them from a telephone pole. 'You're gonna die, Tudbury,' Joey said.

Tom took a big breath and set Joey on the ground, very gently. The moment of truth. Joey came running at him, screaming obscenities. Tom closed his eyes, put his hands on the steering wheel, and *lifted*. The Packard shifted beneath him. Sweat dotted his brow. He shut out the world, concentrated, counted to ten, slowly, backward.

When he finally opened his eyes, half expecting to see Joey's fist smashing into his nose, there was nothing to behold but a seagull perched on the hood of the Packard, its head cocked as it peered through the cracked windshield. He was floating. He was flying.

Tom stuck his head out of the window. Joey stood twenty feet below him, glaring, hands on his hips and a disgusted look on his face. 'Now,' Tom yelled down, smiling, 'what was it you were saying last night?'

'I hope you can stay up there all day, you son of a bitch,' Joey said. He made an ineffectual fist, and waved it. Lank black hair fell across his eyes. 'Ah, shit, what does this prove? If I had a gun, you'd still be dead meat.'

'If you had a gun, I wouldn't be sticking my head out the window,' Tom said. 'In fact, it'd be better if I didn't have a window.' He considered that for a second, but it was hard to think while he was up here. The Packard was heavy. 'I'm coming down,' he said to Joey. 'You, uh, you calmed down?'

Joey grinned. 'Try me and see, Tuds.'

'Move out of the way. I don't want to squash you with this damn thing.'

Joey shuffled to one side, bare-ass and goose-pimpled, and Tom let the Packard settle as gently as an autumn leaf on a still day. He had the door half open when Joey reached in, grabbed him, yanked him up, and pushed him back against the side of the car, his other hand cocked into a fist. 'I oughtta—' he began. Then he shook his head, snorted, and punched Tom lightly in the shoulder. 'Gimme back my fuckin' drawers, ace,' he said.

Back inside the house, Tom reheated the leftover coffee. 'I'll need you to do the work,' he said as he made himself some scrambled eggs and ham and a couple more English muffins. Using his teke always gave him quite an appetite. 'You took auto shop and welding and all that shit. I'll do the wiring.'

'Wiring?' Joey said, warming his hands over his cup. 'What the fuck for?'

'The lights and the TV cameras. I don't want any windows people can shoot through. I know where we can get some cameras cheap, and you got lots of old sets around here, I'll just fix them up.' He sat down and attacked his eggs wolfishly. 'I'll need loudspeakers too. Some kind of PA system. A generator. Wonder if I'll have room for a refrigerator in there?'

'That Packard's a big motherfucker,' Joey said. 'Take out the seats and you'll have room for three of the fuckers.'

'Not the Packard,' Tom said. 'I'll find a lighter car. We can cover up the windows with old body panels or something.'

Joey pushed hair out of his eyes. 'Fuck the body panels. I got armor plate. From the war. They scrapped a bunch of ships at the Navy base in '46 and '47, and Dom put in a bid for the metal, and bought us twenty goddamn tons. Fuckin' waste a money – who the fuck wants to buy battleship armor? I still got it all, sitting way out back rusting. You need a fuckin' sixteen-inch gun to punch through that shit, Tuds. You'll be safe as – fuck, I dunno. Safe, anyhow.'

Tom knew. 'Safe,' he said loudly, 'as a turtle in its shell!'

Only ten shopping days were left until Christmas, and Tach sat in one of the window alcoves, nursing an Irish coffee against the December cold and gazing through the one-way glass at the Bowery. The Funhouse wouldn't open for another hour yet, but the back door was always unlocked for Angelface's friends. Up on stage, a pair of joker jugglers who called themselves Cosmos and Chaos were tossing bowling balls around. Cosmos floated three feet above the stage in the lotus position, his eyeless face serene. He was totally blind, but he never missed a beat or dropped a ball. His partner, six-armed Chaos, capered around like a lunatic, chortling and telling bad jokes and keeping a cascade of flaming clubs going behind his back with two arms while the other four flung bowling balls at Cosmos. Tach spared them only a glance. As talented as they were, their deformities pained him.

Mal slid into his booth. 'How many of those you had?' the bouncer demanded, glaring at the Irish coffee. The tendrils that hung from his lower lip expanded and contracted in a blind worm-like pulsing, and his huge, malformed blue-black jaw gave his face a look of belligerent contempt.

'I don't see that it's any of your business.'

'You're no damn use at all, are you?'

'I never claimed I was.'

Mal grunted. 'You're worth 'bout as much as a sack of shit. I don't see why the hell Angel needs no damn pantywaist spaceman hanging 'round the place sopping up her booze ...'

'She doesn't. I told her that.'

'You can't tell that woman nothin',' Mal agreed. He made a fist. A very large fist. Before the Day of the Wild Card, he'd been the eighth-ranked heavyweight contender. Afterward, he had climbed as high as third ... until they'd banned wild cards from professional sports, and wiped out his dreams in a stroke. The measure was aimed at aces, they said, to keep the games competitive, but there had been no exceptions made for jokers. Mal was older now, sparse hair turned iron gray, but he still looked strong enough to break Floyd Patterson over his knee and mean enough to stare down Sonny Liston. 'Look at that,' he growled in disgust, glaring out the window. Tiny was outside in his chair. 'What the hell is he doing here? I told him not to come by here no more.' Mal started for the door.

'Can't you just leave him alone?' Tachyon called after him. 'He's harmless.'

'Harmless?' Mal rounded on him. 'His screamin' scares off all the fuckin' tourists, and who the hell's gonna pay for all your free booze?'

But then the door pushed open, and Desmond stood there, overcoat folded over one arm, his trunk half-raised. 'Let him be, Mal,' the maître d' said wearily. 'Go on, now.' Muttering, Mal stalked off. Desmond came over and seated himself in Tachyon's booth. 'Good morning, Doctor,' he said.

Tachyon nodded and finished his drink. The whiskey had all gone to the bottom of the cup, and it warmed him on the way down. He found himself staring at the face in the mirrored tabletop: a worn, dissipated, *coarse* face, eyes reddened and puffy, long red hair tangled and greasy, features distorted by alcoholic bloat. That wasn't him, that couldn't be him, he was handsome, clean-featured, distinguished, his face was—

Desmond's trunk snaked out, its fingers locking around his wrist roughly, yanking him forward. 'You haven't heard a word I've said, have you?' Des said, his voice low and urgent with anger. Blearily, Tach realized that Desmond had been talking to him. He began to mutter apologies.

'Never mind about that,' Des said, releasing his grip. 'Listen to me. I was asking for your help, Doctor. I may be a joker, but I'm not an uneducated man. I've read about you. You have certain – abilities, let us say.'

'No,' Tach interrupted. 'Not the way you're thinking.'

'Your powers are quite well documented,' Des said.

'I don't …' Tach began awkwardly. He spread his hands. 'That was then. I've lost – I mean, I can't, not anymore.' He stared down at his own wasted features, wanting to look Des in the eye, to make him understand, but unable to bear the sight of the joker's deformity.

'You mean you won't,' Des said. He stood up. 'I thought that if I spoke to you before we opened, I might actually find you sober. I see I was mistaken. Forget everything I said.'

'I'd help you if I could,' Tach began to say.

'I wasn't asking for me,' Des said sharply.

When he was gone, Tachyon went to the long silver-chrome bar and got down a full bottle of cognac. The first glass made him feel better; the second stopped his hands from shaking. By the third he had begun to weep. Mal came over and looked down at him in disgust. 'Never knew no man cried as much as you do,' he said, thrusting a dirty handkerchief at Tachyon roughly before he left to help them open.

♦

He had been aloft for four and a half hours when the news of the fire came crackling over the police-band radio down by his right foot. Not very *far* aloft, true, only about six feet from the ground, but that was enough – six feet or sixty, it didn't make all that much difference, Tom had found. Four and a half hours, and he didn't feel the least bit tired yet. In fact, he felt *sensational*.

He was strapped securely into a bucket seat Joey had pulled from a mashed-up Triumph TR–3 and mounted on a low pivot right in the center of the VW. The only light was the wan phosphor glow from an array of mismatched television screens that surrounded him on all sides. Between the cameras and their tracking motors, the generator, the ventilation system, the sound equipment, the control panels, the spare box of vacuum tubes, and the little refrigerator, he hardly had space to swing around. But that was okay. Tom was more a claustrophile than a claustrophobe anyway; he liked it in here. Around the exterior of the gutted Beetle, Joey had mounted two overlapping layers of thick battleship armor. It was better than a goddamned tank. Joey had already pinged a few shots off it with the Luger that Dom had taken off a German officer during the war. A lucky shot might be able to take out one of his cameras or lights, but there was no way to get to Tom himself inside the shell. He was better than safe, he was *invulnerable*, and when he felt this secure and sure of himself, there was no limit on what he might be able to do.

The shell was heavier than the Packard by the time they'd gotten finished with it, but it didn't seem to matter. Four and a half hours, never touching ground, sliding around silently and almost effortlessly through the junkyard, and Tom hadn't even worked up a sweat.

When he heard the report over the radio, a jolt of excitement went through him. *This is it!* he thought. He ought to wait for Joey, but Joey had driven to Pompeii Pizza to pick up dinner (pepperoni, onion, and extra cheese) and there was no time to waste, this was his chance.

The ring of lights on the bottom of the shell threw stark shadows over the hills of twisted metal and trash as Tom pushed the shell higher into the air, eight feet up, ten, twelve. His eyes flicked nervously from one screen to the next, watching the ground recede. One set, its picture tube filched from an old Sylvania, began a slow vertical roll. Tom played with a knob and stopped it. His palms were sweaty. Fifteen feet up, he began to creep forward, until the shell reached the shoreline. In front of him was darkness; it was too thick a night to see New York, but he knew it was there, if he could reach it. On his small black-and-white screens, the waters of New York Bay seemed even darker than usual, an endless choppy ocean of ink looming before him. He'd have to grope his way across, until the city lights came into sight, And if he lost it out there, over the water, he'd be joining Jetboy and J.F.K. a lot sooner than he planned; even if he could unscrew the hatch quick enough to avoid drowning, he couldn't swim.

But he *wasn't* going to lose it, Tom thought suddenly. Why the fuck was he hesitating? He wasn't going to lose it ever again, was he? He had to believe that.

He pressed his lips together, pushed off with his mind, and the shell slid smoothly out over the water. The salt waves beneath him rose and fell. He'd never had to push against water before; it felt different. Tom had an instant of panic; the shell rocked and dropped three feet before he caught hold of himself and adjusted. He calmed himself with an effort, shoved upward, and rose. *High*, he thought, he'd come in high, he'd *fly* in, like Jetboy, like Black Eagle, like a fucking *ace*. The shell moved out, faster and faster, gliding across the bay with swift serenity as Tom gained confidence. He'd never felt so incredibly powerful, so good, so goddamned *right*.

The compass worked fine; in less than ten minutes, the lights of the Battery and the Wall Street district loomed up before him. Tom pushed still higher, and floated uptown, hugging the shoreline of the Hudson. Jetboy's Tomb came and went beneath him. He'd stood in front of it a dozen times, gazing up at the face of the big metal statue out front. He wondered what that statue might think if it could look up and see him tonight.

He had a New York street map, but tonight he didn't need it; the flames could be seen almost a mile off. Even inside his armor Tom could feel the heat waves licking up at him when he made a pass overhead. He carefully began a descent. His fans whirred, and his cameras tracked at his command; below was chaos and cacophony, sirens and shouting, the crowd, the hurrying firemen, the police barricades and the ambulances, big hook-and-ladder trucks spraying water into the inferno. At first no one noticed him, hovering fifty feet above the sidewalk – until he came in low enough for his lights to play on the walls of the building. Then he saw them looking up, pointing; he felt giddy with excitement.

But he had only an instant to relish the feeling. Then, from the corner of an eye, he saw her in one of his screens. She appeared suddenly in a fifth-floor window, bent over and coughing, her dress already afire. Before he could act, the flames licked at her; she screamed and jumped.

He caught her in midair, without thinking, without hesitating, without wondering whether he could do it. He just *did* it, caught her and held her and lowered her gently to the ground. The firemen surrounded her, put out her dress, and hustled her into an ambulance. And now, Tom saw, *everyone* was looking up at him, at the strange dark shape floating high in the night, with its ring of shining lights. The police band was crackling; they were reporting him as a flying saucer, he heard. He grinned.

A cop climbed up on top of his police car, holding a bullhorn, and began to hail him. Tom turned off the radio to hear better over the roar of the flames. He was telling Tom to land and identify himself, asking who he was, what he was.

That was easy. Tom turned on his microphone. 'I'm the Turtle,' he said. The VW had no tires; in the wheel wells, Joey had rigged the most humongous speakers they could find, powered by the largest amp on the market. For the first time, the voice of the Turtle was heard in the land, a booming 'I'M THE TURTLE' echoing down the streets and alleys, a rolling thunder crackling with distortion. Except what he said didn't sound quite right. Tom cranked the volume up even higher, injected a little more bass into his voice. '*I AM THE GREAT AND POWERFUL TURTLE,*' he announced to them all.

Then he flew a block west, to the dark polluted waters of the Hudson, and imagined two huge invisible hands forty feet across. He lowered them into the river, cupped them full, and lifted. Rivulets of water dribbled to the street all the way back. When he dropped the first cascade on the flames, a ragged cheering went up from the crowd below.

'Merry Christmas,' Tach declared drunkenly when the clock struck midnight and the record Christmas Eve crowd began to whoop and shout and pound on the tables. On stage, Humphrey Bogart cracked a lame joke in an unfamiliar voice. All the lights in the house dimmed briefly; when they came back up, Bogart had been replaced by a portly, round-faced man with a red nose. 'Who is he now?' Tach asked the twin on his left.

'W. C. Fields,' she whispered. She slid her tongue around the inside of his ear. The twin on the right was doing something even more interesting under the table, where her hand had somehow found a way into his trousers. The twins were his Christmas gift from Angelface. 'You can pretend they're me,' she'd told him, though of course they were nothing like her. Nice kids, both of them, buxom and cheerful and absolutely uninhibited, if a bit simpleminded; they reminded him of Takisian sex toys. The one on the right had drawn the wild card, but she wore her cat mask even in bed, and there was no visible deformity to disturb the sweet pleasure of his erection.

W. C. Fields, whoever he was, offered some cynical observations about Christmas and small children. The crowd hooted him off the stage. The Projectionist had an astonishing array of faces, but he couldn't tell a joke. Tach didn't mind; he had all the diversion he needed.

'Paper, Doc?' The vendor thrust a copy of the *Herald Tribune* across the table with a thick three-fingered hand. His flesh was blue-black and oily looking. 'All the Christmas news,' he said, shifting the clumsy stack of papers under his arm. Two small curving tusks protruded from the corners of his wide, grinning mouth. Beneath a porkpie hat, the great bulge of his skull was covered with tufts of bristly red hair. On the streets they called him the Walrus.

'No thank you, Jube,' Tach said with drunken dignity. 'I have no desire to wallow in human folly tonight.'

'Hey, look,' said the twin on the right. 'The Turtle!'

Tachyon looked around, momentarily befuddled, wondering how that huge armored shell could possibly have gotten inside the Funhouse, but of course she was referring to the newspaper.

'You better buy it for her, Tacky,' the twin on the left said, giggling. 'If you don't she'll pout.'

Tachyon sighed. 'I'll take one. But only if I don't have to listen to any of your jokes, Jube.'

'Heard a new one about a joker, a Polack, and an Irishman stuck on a desert island, but just for that I'm not going to tell it,' the Walrus replied with a rubbery grin.

Tachyon dug for some coins, found nothing in his pockets but a small, feminine hand. Jube winked. 'I'll get it from Des,' he said. Tachyon spread the newspaper out on the table, while the club erupted in applause as Cosmos and Chaos made their entrance.

A grainy photograph of the Turtle was spread across two columns. Tachyon thought it looked like a flying pickle, a big lumpy dill covered with little bumps. The Turtle had apprehended a hit-and-run driver who had killed a nine-year-old boy in Harlem, intercepting his flight and lifting the car twenty feet off the ground, where it floated with its engine roaring and its tires spinning madly until the police finally caught up. In a related sidebar, the rumor that the shell was an experimental robot flying tank had been denied by an Air Force spokesman.

'You'd think they'd have found something more important to write about by now,' Tachyon said. It was the third big story about the Turtle this week. The letter columns, the editorial pages, everything was Turtle, Turtle, Turtle. Even television was rabid with Turtle speculation. Who was he? What was he? How did he do it?

One reporter had even sought out Tach to ask that question. 'Telekinesis,' Tachyon told him. 'It's nothing new. Almost common, in fact.' Teke had been the single ability most frequently manifested by virus victims back in '46. He'd seen a dozen patients who could move paperclips and pencils, and one woman who could lift her own body weight for ten minutes at a time. Even Earl Sanderson's flight had been telekinetic in origin. What he did not tell them was that teke on *this* scale was unprecedented. Of course, when the story ran, they got half of it wrong.

'He's a joker, you know,' whispered the twin on the right, the one in the silver-gray cat mask. She was leaning against his shoulder, reading about the Turtle.

'A joker?' Tach said.

'He hides inside a shell, doesn't he? Why would he do that unless he was really awful to look at?' She had taken her hand out of his trousers. 'Could I have that paper?'

Tach pushed it toward her. 'They're cheering him now,' he said sharply. 'They cheered the Four Aces too.'

'That was a colored group, right?' she said, turning her attention to the headlines.

'She's keeping a scrapbook,' her sister said. 'All the jokers think he's one of them. Stupid, huh? I bet it's just a machine, some kind of Air Force flying saucer.'

'He is not,' her twin said. 'It says so right here.' She pointed to the sidebar with a long, red-painted nail.

'Never mind about her,' the twin on the left said. She moved closer to Tachyon, nibbling on his neck as her hand went under the table. 'Hey, what's wrong? You're all soft.'

'My pardons,' Tachyon said gloomily. Cosmos and Chaos were flinging axes, machetes, and knives across the stage, the glittering cascade multiplied into infinity by the mirrors around them. He had a bottle of fine cognac at hand, and lovely, willing women on either side of him, but suddenly, for some reason he could not have named, it did not feel like such a good night after all. He filled his glass almost to the brim and inhaled the heady alcoholic fumes. 'Merry Christmas,' he muttered to no one in particular.

Consciousness returned with the angry tones of Mal's voice. Tach lifted his head groggily from the mirrored tabletop, blinking down at his puffy red reflection. The jugglers, the twins, and the crowd were long gone. His cheek was sticky from lying in a puddle of spilled liquor. The twins had jollied him and fondled him and one of them had even gone under the table, for all the good it did. Then Angelface had come to the tableside and sent them away. 'Go to sleep, Tacky,' she'd said. Mal had come up to ask if he should lug him back to bed. 'Not today,' she'd said, 'you know what day this is. Let him sleep it off here.' He couldn't recall when he'd gone to sleep.

His head was about to explode, and Mal's shouting wasn't making things any better. 'I don't give a flyin' fuck *what* you were promised, scumbag, you're not seeing her,' the bouncer yelled. A softer voice said something in reply. 'You'll get your fuckin' money, but that's all you'll get,' Mal snapped.

Tach raised his eyes. In the mirrors he saw their reflections darkly: odd twisted shapes outlined in the wan dawn light, reflections of reflections, hundreds of them, beautiful, monstrous, uncountable, his children, his heirs, the offspring of his failures, a living sea of jokers. The soft voice said something else. 'Ah, kiss my joker ass,' Mal said. He had a body like a twisted stick and a head like a pumpkin; it made Tach smile. Mal shoved someone and reached behind his back, groping for his gun.

The reflections and the reflections of the reflections, the gaunt shadows and the bloated ones, the round-faced ones and the knife-thin ones, the black and the white, they moved all at once, filling the club with noise; a hoarse shout from Mal, the crack of gunfire. Instinctively Tach dove for cover, cracking his forehead hard on the edge of the table as he slid down. He blinked back tears of pain and lay curled up on the floor, peering out at the reflections of feet while the world disintegrated into a sharp-edged cacophony. Glass was shattering and falling, mirrors breaking on all sides, silvered knives flying through the air, too many for even Cosmos and Chaos to catch, dark splinters eating into the reflections, taking bites out of all the twisted shadow-shapes, blood spattering against the cracked mirrors.

It ended as suddenly as it had begun. The soft voice said something and there was the sound of footsteps, the crunch of glass underfoot. A moment later, a muffled scream from off behind him. Tach lay under the table, drunk and terrified. His finger hurt: bleeding, he saw, sliced open by a sliver of mirror. All he could think of were the stupid human superstitions about broken mirrors and bad luck. He cradled his head in his arms so the awful nightmare would go away.

When he woke again, a policeman was shaking him roughly.

Mal was dead, one detective told him; they showed him a morgue photo of the bouncer lying in a pool of blood and a welter of broken glass. Ruth was dead too, and one of the janitors, a dim-witted cyclops who had never hurt anyone. They showed him a newspaper. The Santa Claus Slaughter, that was what they called it, and the lead was about three jokers who'd found death waiting under the tree on Christmas morning.

Miss Fascetti was gone, the other detective told him, did he know anything about that? Did he think she was involved? Was she a culprit or a victim? What could he tell them about her? He said he didn't know any such person, until they explained that they were asking about Angela Fascetti and maybe he knew her better as Angelface. She was gone and Mal was shot dead, and the most frightening thing of all was that Tach did not know where his next drink was coming from.

They held him for four days, questioning him relentlessly, going over the same ground again and again, until Tachyon was screaming at them, pleading with them, demanding his rights, demanding a lawyer, demanding a drink. They gave him only the lawyer. The lawyer said they couldn't hold him without charging him, so they charged him with being a material witness, with vagrancy, with resisting arrest, and questioned him again.

By the third day, his hands were shaking and he was having walking hallucinations. One of the detectives, the kindly one, promised him a bottle in return for his cooperation, but somehow his answers never quite satisfied them, and the bottle was not forthcoming. The bad-tempered one threatened to hold him forever unless he told the truth. I thought it was a nightmare, Tach told him, weeping. I was drunk, I'd been asleep. No, I couldn't see them, just the reflections, distorted, multiplied. I don't know how many there were. I don't know what it was about. No, she had no enemies, everyone loved Angelface. No, she didn't kill Mal, that didn't make sense, Mal loved her. One of them had a soft voice. No, I don't know which one. No, I can't remember what they said. No, I don't know if they were jokers or not, they looked like jokers, but the mirrors distort, some of them, not all of them, don't you see? No, I couldn't possibly pick them out of a lineup, I never really saw them. I had to hide under the table, don't you see, the assassins had come, that's what my father always told me, there wasn't anything I could do.

When they realized that he was telling them all he knew, they dropped the charges and released him. To the dark streets of Jokertown and the cold of the night.

♦

He walked down the Bowery alone, shivering. The Walrus was hawking the evening papers from his newsstand on the corner of Hester. 'Read all about it,' he called out. 'Turtle Terror in Jokertown.' Tachyon paused to stare dully at the headlines. POLICE SEEK TURTLE, the *Post* reported. TURTLE CHARGED WITH ASSAULT, announced the *World-Telegram*. So the cheering had stopped already. He glanced at the text. The Turtle had been prowling Jokertown the past two nights, lifting people a hundred feet in the air to question them, threatening to drop them if he didn't like their answers. When police tried to make an arrest last night, the Turtle had deposited two of their black-and- whites on the roof of Freakers at Chatham Square. CURB THE TURTLE, the editorial in the *World-Telegram* said.

'You all right, Doc?' the Walrus asked.

'No,' said Tachyon, putting down the paper. He couldn't afford to pay for it anyway.

Police barriers blocked the entrance to the Funhouse, and a padlock secured the door. CLOSED INDEFINITELY, the sign said. He needed a drink, but the pockets of his bandleader's coat were empty. He thought of Des and Randall, and realized that he had no idea where they lived, or what their last names might be.

Trudging back to ROOMS, Tach climbed wearily up the stairs. When he stepped into the darkness, he had just enough time to notice that the room was frigidly cold; the window was open and a bitter wind was scouring out the old smells of urine, mildew, and drink. Had he done that? Confused, he stepped toward it, and someone came out from behind the door and grabbed him.

It happened so fast he scarcely had time to react. The forearm across his windpipe was an iron bar, choking off his scream, and a hand wrenched his right arm up behind his back, hard. He was choking, his arm close to breaking, and then he was being shoved toward the open window, running at it, and Tachyon could only thrash feebly in a grip much stronger than his own. The windowsill caught him square in the stomach, knocking the last of his breath right out of him and suddenly he was falling, head over heels, locked helplessly in the steel embrace of his attacker, both of them plunging toward the sidewalk below.

They jerked to a stop five feet above the cement, with a wrench that elicited a grunt from the man behind him.

Tach had closed his eyes before the instant of impact. He opened them as they began to float upward. Above the yellow halo of the streetlamp was a ring of much brighter lights, set in a hovering darkness that blotted out the winter stars.

The arm across his throat had loosened enough for Tachyon to groan. 'You,' he said hoarsely, as they curved around the shell and came to rest gently on top of it. The metal was icy cold, its chill biting right through the fabric of Tachyon's pants. As the Turtle began to rise straight up into the night, Tachyon's captor released him. He drew in a shuddering breath of cold air, and rolled over to face a man in a zippered leather jacket, black dungarees, and a rubbery green frog mask. 'Who ... ?' he gasped.

'I'm the Great and Powerful Turtle's mean-ass sidekick,' the man in the frog mask said, rather cheerfully.

'DOCTOR TACHYON, I PRESUME,' boomed the shell's speakers, far above the alleys of Jokertown. 'I'VE ALWAYS WANTED TO MEET YOU. I READ ABOUT YOU WHEN I WAS JUST A KID.'

'Turn it down,' Tach croaked weakly.

'OH. SURE. Is that better?' The volume diminished sharply. 'It's noisy in here, and behind all this armor I can't always tell how loud I sound. I'm sorry if we scared you, but we couldn't take the chance of you saying no. We need you.'

Tach stayed just where he was, shivering, shaken. 'What do you want?' he asked wearily.

'Help,' the Turtle declared. They were still rising; the lights of Manhattan spread out all around them, and the spires of the Empire State Building and the Chrysler Building rose uptown. They were higher than either. The wind was cold and gusting; Tach clung to the shell for dear life.

'Leave me alone,' Tachyon said. 'I have no help to give you. I have no help to give anybody.'

'Fuck, he's crying,' the man in the frog mask said.

'You don't understand,' the Turtle said. The shell began to drift west, its motion silent and steady. There was something awesome and eerie about the flight. 'You have to help. I've tried on my own, but I'm getting nowhere. But you, your powers, they can make the difference.'

Tachyon was lost in his own self-pity, too cold and exhausted and despairing to reply. 'I want a drink,' he said.

'Fuck it,' said frog-face. 'Dumbo was right about this guy, he's nothing but a goddamned wino.'

'He doesn't understand,' said the Turtle. 'Once we explain, he'll come around. Doctor Tachyon, we're talking about your friend Angelface.'

He needed a drink so badly it hurt. 'She was good to me,' he said, remembering the sweet perfume of her satin sheets, and her bloody footprints on the mirror tiles. 'But there's nothing I can do. I told the police everything I know.'

'Chickenshit asshole,' said frog-face.

'When I was a kid, I read about you in *Jetboy Comics*,' the Turtle said. '"Thirty Minutes Over Broadway," remember? You were supposed to be as smart as Einstein. I might be able to save your friend Angelface, but I can't without your powers.'

'I don't do that any longer. I *can't*. There was someone I hurt, someone I cared for, but I seized her mind, just for an instant, for a good reason, or at least I thought it was for a good reason, but it ... destroyed her. I can't do it again.'

'Boo hoo,' said frog-face mockingly. 'Let's toss 'im, Turtle, he's not worth a bucket of warm piss.' He took something out of one of the pockets of his leather jacket; Tach was astonished to see that it was a bottle of beer.

'Please,' Tachyon said, as the man popped off the cap with a bottle-opener hung round his neck. 'A sip,' Tach said. 'Just a sip.' He hated the taste of beer, but he needed something, anything. It had been days. 'Please.'

'Fuck off,' frog-face said.

'Tachyon,' said the Turtle, 'you can make him.'

'No I can't,' Tach said. The man raised the bottle up to green rubber lips. 'I can't,' Tach repeated. Frog-face continued to drink. 'No.' He could hear it gurgling. 'Please, just a little.'

The man lowered the beer bottle, sloshed it thoughtfully. 'Just a swallow left,' he said.

'Please.' He reached out, hands trembling.

'Nah,' said frog-face. He began to turn the bottle upside down. ''Course, if you're really thirsty, you could just grab my mind, right? *Make* me give you the fuckin' bottle.' He tipped the bottle a little more. 'Go on, I dare ya, try it.'

Tach watched the last mouthful of beer dribble down onto the Turtle's shell and run off into empty air.

'Fuck,' said the man in the frog mask. 'You got it bad, don't you?' He pulled another bottle from his pocket, opened it, and handed it across. Tach cradled it with both hands. The beer was cold and sour, but he had never tasted anything half so sweet. He drained it all in one long swallow.

'Got any other smart ideas?' frog-face asked the Turtle.

Ahead of them was the blackness of the Hudson River, the lights of Jersey off to the west. They were descending. Beneath them, overlooking the Hudson, was a sprawling edifice of steel and glass and marble that Tachyon suddenly recognized, though he had never set foot inside it: Jetboy's Tomb. 'Where are we going?' he asked.

'We're going to see a man about a rescue,' the Turtle said.

Jetboy's Tomb filled the entire block, on the site where the pieces of his plane had come raining down. It filled Tom's screens too, as he sat in the warm darkness of his shell, bathed in a phosphor glow. Motors whirred as the cameras moved in their tracks. The huge flanged wings of the tomb curved upward, as if the building itself was about to take flight. Through tall, narrow windows, he could see glimpses of the full-size replica of the JB–1 suspended from the ceiling, its scarlet flanks aglow from hidden lights. Above the doors, the hero's last words had been carved, each letter chiseled into the black Italian marble and filled in stainless steel. The metal flashed as the shell's white-hot spots slid across the legend:

I CAN'T DIE YET,
I HAVEN'T SEEN *THE JOLSON STORY*

Tom brought the shell down in front of the monument, to hover five feet above the broad marble plaza at the top of the stairs. Nearby, a twenty-foot-tall steel Jetboy looked out over the West Side Highway and the Hudson beyond, his fists cocked. The metal used for the sculpture had come from the wreckage of crashed planes, Tom knew. He knew that statue's face better than he knew his father's.

The man they'd come to meet emerged from the shadows at the base of the statue, a chunky dark shape huddled in a thick overcoat, hands shoved deep into his pockets. Tom shone a light on him; a camera tracked to give him a better view. The joker was a portly man, round-shouldered and well-dressed. His coat had a fur collar and his fedora was pulled low. Instead of a nose, he had an elephant's trunk in the middle of his face. The end of it was fringed with fingers, snug in a little leather glove.

Dr. Tachyon slid off the top of the shell, lost his footing and landed on his ass. Tom heard Joey laugh. Then Joey jumped down too, and pulled Tachyon to his feet.

The joker glanced down at the alien. 'So you convinced him to come after all. I'm surprised.'

'We were real fuckin' persuasive,' Joey said.

'Des,' Tachyon said, sounding confused. 'What are you doing here? Do you know these people?'

Elephant-face twitched his trunk. 'Since the day before yesterday, yes, in a manner of speaking. They came to me. The hour was late, but a phone call from the Great and Powerful Turtle does pique one's interest. He offered his help, and I accepted. I even told them where you lived.'

Tachyon ran a hand through his tangled, filthy hair. 'I'm sorry about Mal. Do you know anything about Angelface? You know how much she meant to me.'

'In dollars and cents, I know quite precisely,' Des said.

Tachyon's mouth gaped open. He looked hurt. Tom felt sorry for him. 'I wanted to go to you,' he said. 'I didn't know where to find you.'

Joey laughed. 'He's listed in the fuckin' phone book, dork. Ain't that many guys named Xavier Desmond.' He looked at the shell. 'How the fuck is he gonna find the lady if he couldn't even find his buddy here?'

Desmond nodded. 'An excellent point. This isn't going to work. Just look at him!' His trunk pointed. 'What good is he? We're wasting precious time.'

'We did it your way,' Tom replied. 'We're getting nowhere. No one's talking. He can get the information we need.'

'I don't understand any of this,' Tachyon interrupted.

Joey made a disgusted sound. He had found a beer somewhere and was cracking the cap.

'What's happening?' Tach asked.

'If you had been the least bit interested in anything besides cognac and cheap tarts, you might know,' Des said icily.

'Tell him what you told us,' Tom commanded. When he knew, Tachyon would surely help, he thought. He *had* to.

Des gave a heavy sigh. 'Angelface had a heroin habit. She hurt, you know. Perhaps you noticed that from time to time, Doctor? The drug was the only thing that got her through the day. Without it, the pain would have driven her insane. Nor was hers an ordinary junkie's habit. She used uncut heroin in quantities that would have killed any normal user. You saw how minimally it affected her. The joker metabolism is a curious thing. Do you have any idea how expensive heroin is, Doctor Tachyon? Never mind, I see that you don't. Angelface made quite a bit of money from the Funhouse, but it was never enough. Her source gave her credit until she was in far over her head, then demanded ... call it a promissory note. Or a Christmas present. She had no choice. It was that or be cut off. She hoped to come up with the money, being an eternal optimist. She failed. On Christmas morning her source came by to collect. Mal wasn't about to let them have her. They insisted.'

Tachyon was squinting in the glare of the lights. His image began to roll upward. 'Why didn't she tell me?' he said.

'I suppose she didn't want to burden you, Doctor. It might have taken the fun out of your self-pitying binges.'

'Have you told the police?'

'The police? Ah, yes. New York's finest. The ones who seem so curiously uninterested whenever a joker is beaten or killed, yet ever so diligent if a tourist is robbed. The ones who so regularly arrest, harass, and brutalize any joker who has the poor taste to live anywhere outside of Jokertown. Perhaps we might consult the officer who commented that raping a joker woman is more a lapse in taste than a crime.' Des snorted. 'Doctor Tachyon, where do you think Angelface bought her drugs? Do you think any ordinary street pusher would have access to uncut heroin in the quantities she needed? The police *were* her source. The head of the Jokertown narcotics squad, if you care to be precise. Oh, I'll grant you that it's unlikely the whole department is involved. Homicide may be conducting a legitimate investigation. What do you think they'd say if we told them that Bannister was the murderer? You think they'd arrest one of their own? On the strength of my testimony, or the testimony of any joker?'

'We'll make good her note,' Tachyon blurted. 'We'll give this man his money or the Funhouse or whatever it is he wants.'

'The promissory note,' Desmond said wearily, 'was not for the Funhouse.'

'Whatever it was, give it to him!'

'She promised him the only thing she still had that he wanted,' Desmond said. 'Herself. Her beauty and her pain. The word's out on the street, if you know how to listen. There's going to be a very special New Year's Eve party somewhere in the city. Invitation only. Expensive. A unique thrill. Bannister will have her first. He's wanted that for a long time. But the other guests will have their turn. Jokertown hospitality.'

Tachyon's mouth worked soundlessly for a moment. 'The *police*?' he finally managed. He looked as shocked as Tom had been when Desmond told him and Joey.

'Do you think they love us, Doctor? We're freaks. We're *diseased*. Jokertown is a hell, a dead end, and the Jokertown police are the most brutal, corrupt, and incompetent in the city. I don't think anyone planned what happened at the Funhouse, but it happened, and Angelface knows too much. They can't let her live, so they're going to have some fun with the joker cunt.'

Tom Tudbury leaned toward his microphone. 'I can rescue her,' he said. 'These fuckers haven't seen anything like the Great and Powerful Turtle. But I can't *find* her.'

Des said, 'She has a lot of friends. But none of us can read minds, or make a man do something he doesn't want to.'

'I *can't*,' Tachyon protested. He seemed to shrink into himself, to edge away from them, and for an instant Tom thought the little man was going to run away. 'You don't understand.'

'What a fuckin' candy-ass,' Joey said loudly.

Watching Tachyon crumble on his screens, Tom Tudbury finally ran out of patience. 'If you fail, you fail,' he said. 'And if you don't try, you fail too, so what the fuck difference does it make? Jetboy failed, but at least he *tried*. He wasn't an ace, he wasn't a goddamned *Takisian*, he was just a guy with a jet, but he did what he could.'

'I want to. I ... just ... *can't*.'

Des trumpeted his disgust. Joey shrugged.

Inside his shell, Tom sat in stunned disbelief. He wasn't going to help. He hadn't believed it, not really. Joey had warned him, Desmond too, but Tom had insisted, he'd been sure, this was

Doctor Tachyon, of course he'd help, maybe he was having some problems, but once they explained the situation to him, once they made it clear what was at stake and how much they needed him – he *had* to help. But he was saying no. It was the last goddamned straw.

He twisted the volume knob up all the way. 'YOU SON OF A BITCH,' he boomed, and the sound hammered out over the plaza. Tachyon flinched away. 'YOU NO-GOOD FUCKING LITTLE ALIEN CHICKENSHIT!' Tachyon stumbled backward down the stairs, but the Turtle drifted after him, loudspeakers blaring. 'IT WAS ALL A LIE, WASN'T IT? EVERYTHING IN THE COMIC BOOKS, EVERYTHING IN THE PAPERS, IT WAS ALL A STUPID LIE. ALL MY LIFE THEY BEAT ME UP AND THEY CALLED ME A FUCKING WIMP AND A COWARD BUT *YOU'RE* THE COWARD, YOU ASSHOLE, YOU SHITTY LITTLE WHINER, YOU WON'T EVEN TRY, YOU DON'T GIVE A DAMN ABOUT ANYBODY, ABOUT YOUR FRIEND ANGELFACE OR ABOUT KENNEDY OR JETBOY OR ANYBODY, YOU HAVE ALL THESE FUCKING POWERS AND YOU'RE *NOTHING*, YOU WON'T DO ANYTHING, YOU'RE WORSE THAN OSWALD OR BRAUN OR ANY OF THEM.' Tachyon staggered down the steps, hands over his ears, shouting something unintelligible, but Tom was past listening. His anger had a life of its own now. He lashed out, and the alien's head snapped around and reddened with the force of the slap. '*ASSHOLE!*' Tom was shrieking. '*YOU'RE THE ONE IN A SHELL.*' Invisible blows rained down on Tachyon in a fury. He reeled, fell, rolled a third of the way down the stairs, tried to get back to his feet, was bowled over again, and bounced down to the street head over heels. 'ASSHOLE!' the Turtle thundered. 'RUN, YOU SHITHEAD. GET OUT OF HERE, OR I'LL THROW YOU IN THE DAMNED RIVER! RUN, YOU LITTLE WIMP, BEFORE THE GREAT AND POWERFUL TURTLE REALLY GETS UPSET! RUN, DAMN IT! YOU'RE THE ONE IN THE SHELL! YOU'RE THE ONE IN THE SHELL!'

And he ran, dashing blindly from one streetlight to the next, until he was lost in the shadows. Tom Tudbury watched him vanish on the shell's array of television screens. He felt sick and beaten. His head was throbbing. He needed a beer, or an aspirin, or both. When he heard the sirens coming, he scooped up Joey and Desmond and set them on top of his shell, killed his lights, and rose straight up into the night, high, high up, into darkness and cold and silence.

That night Tach slept the sleep of the damned, thrashing about like a man in a fever dream, crying out, weeping, waking again and again from nightmares, only to drift back into them. He dreamt he was back on Takis, and his hated cousin Zabb was boasting about a new sex toy, but when he brought her out it was Blythe, and he raped her right there in front of him. Tach watched it all, powerless to intervene; her body writhed beneath his and blood flowed from her mouth and ears and vagina. She began to change, into a thousand joker shapes each more horrible than the last, and Zabb went right on, raping them all as they screamed and struggled. But afterward, when Zabb rose from the corpse covered with blood, it wasn't his cousin's face at all, it was his own, worn and dissipated, a *coarse* face, eyes reddened and puffy, long red hair tangled and greasy, features distorted by alcoholic bloat or perhaps by a Funhouse mirror.

He woke around noon, to the terrible sound of Tiny weeping outside his window. It was more than he could stand. It was all more than he could stand. He stumbled to the window and threw it open and screamed at the giant to be quiet, to stop, to leave him alone, to give him peace, please, but Tiny went on and on, so much pain, so much guilt, so much shame, why couldn't they let him be, he couldn't take it anymore, no, shut up, shut up, *please shut up*, and suddenly Tach shrieked and reached out with his mind and plunged into Tiny's head and shut him up.

The silence was thunderous.

The nearest phone booth was in a candy store a block down. Vandals had ripped the phone book to shreds. He dialed information and got the listing for Xavier Desmond on Christie Street, only a short walk away. The apartment was a fourth-floor walk-up above a mask shop. Tachyon was out of breath by the time he got to the top.

Des opened the door on the fifth knock. 'You,' he said.

'The Turtle,' Tach said. His throat was dry. 'Did he get anything last night?'

'No,' Desmond replied. His trunk twitched. 'The same story as before. They're wise to him now, they know he won't really drop them. They call his bluff. Short of actually killing someone, there's nothing to do.'

'Tell me who to ask,' Tach said.

'You?' Des said.

Tach could not look the joker in the eye. He nodded.

'Let me get my coat,' Des said. He emerged from the apartment bundled up for the cold, carrying a fur cap and a frayed beige raincoat. 'Put your hair up in the hat,' he told Tachyon, 'and leave that ridiculous coat here. You don't want to be recognized.' Tach did as he said. On the way out, Des went into the mask shop for the final touch.

'A chicken?' Tach said when Des handed him the mask. It had bright yellow feathers, a prominent orange beak, a floppy red coxcomb on top.

'I saw it and I knew it was you,' said Des. 'Put it on.'

A large crane was moving into position at Chatham Square, to get the police cars off Freakers roof. The club was open. The doorman was a seven-foot-tall hairless joker with fangs. He grabbed Des by the arm as they tried to pass under the neon thighs of the six-breasted dancer who writhed on the marquee. 'No jokers allowed,' he said brusquely. 'Get lost, Tusker.'

Reach out and grab his mind, Tachyon thought. Once, before Blythe, he would have done it instinctively. But now he hesitated, and hesitating, he was lost.

Des reached into his back pocket, pulled out a wallet, extracted a fifty-dollar bill. 'You were watching them lower the police cars,' he said. 'You never saw me pass.'

'Oh, yeah,' the doorman said. The bill vanished in a clawed hand. 'Real interesting, them cranes.'

'Sometimes money is the most potent power of all,' Des said as they walked into the cavernous dimness within. A sparse noontime crowd sat eating the free lunch and watching a stripper gyrate down a long runway behind a barbed-wire barrier. She was covered with silky gray hair, except for her breasts, which had been shaved bare. Desmond scanned the booths along the far wall. He took Tach's elbow and led him to a dark corner, where a man in a peacoat was sitting with a stein of beer. 'They lettin' jokers in here now?' the man asked gruffly as they approached. He was saturnine and pockmarked.

Tack went into his mind. *Fuck what's this now the elephant man's from the Funhouse who's the other one damned jokers anyhow gotta lotta nerve*

'Where's Bannister keeping Angelface?' Des asked.

'Angelface is the slit at the Funhouse, right? Don't know no Bannister. Is this a game? Fuck off, joker, I ain't playing.' In his thoughts, images came tumbling: Tack saw mirrors shattering, silver knives flying through the air, felt Mal's shove and saw him reach back for a gun, watched him shudder and spin as the bullets hit, heard Bannister's soft voice as he told them to kill Ruth, saw the warehouse over on the Hudson where they were keeping her, the livid bruises on her arm when they'd grabbed her, tasted the man's fear, fear of jokers, fear of discovery, fear of Bannister, the fear of *them*. Tach reached out and squeezed Desmond's arm.

Des turned to go. 'Hey, hold it right there,' the man with the pockmarked face said. He flashed a badge as he unfolded from the booth. 'Undercover narcotics,' he said, 'and you been using, mister, asking asshole junkie questions like that.' Des stood still as the man frisked him down. 'Well, looka this,' he said, producing a bag of white powder from one of Desmond's pockets. 'Wonder what this is? You're under arrest, freak-face.'

'That's not mine,' Desmond said calmly.

'The hell it ain't,' the man said, and in his mind the thoughts ran one after another *little accident resisting arrest what could I do huh? jokers'll scream but who listens to a fuckin' joker only whatymi gonna do with the other one?* and he glanced at Tachyon. *Jeez looka the chickenman's shaking maybe the fucker IS using that'd be great.*

Trembling, Tach realized the moment of truth was at hand.

He was not sure he could do it. It was different than with Tiny; that had been blind instinct, but he was awake now, and he knew what he was doing. It had been so easy once, as easy as using his hands. But now those hands trembled, and there was blood on them, and on his mind as well ... he thought of Blythe and the way her mind had shattered under his touch, like the mirrors in the Funhouse, and for a terrible, long second nothing happened, until the fear was rank in his throat, and the familiar taste of failure filled his mouth.

Then the pockfaced man smiled an idiot's smile, sat back down in his booth, laid his head on the table, and went to sleep as sweetly as a child.

Des took it in stride. 'Your doing?'

Tachyon nodded.

'You're shaking,' Des asked. 'Are you all right, Doctor?'

'I think so,' Tachyon said. The policeman had begun to snore loudly. 'I think maybe I am all right, Des. For the first time in years.' He looked at the joker's face, looked past the deformity to the man beneath. 'I know where she is,' he said. They started toward the exit. In the cage, a full-breasted, bearded hermaphrodite had started into a bump-and-grind. 'We have to move quickly.'

'In an hour I can get together twenty men.'

'No,' Tachyon said. 'The place they're holding her isn't in Jokertown.'

Des stopped with his hand on the door. 'I see,' he said. 'And outside of Jokertown, jokers and masked men are rather conspicuous, aren't they?'

'Exactly,' Tach said. He did not voice his other fear, of the retribution that would surely be enacted should jokers dare to confront police, even police as corrupt as Bannister and his cohorts. He would take the risk himself, he had nothing left to lose, but he could not permit them to take it. 'Can you reach the Turtle?' he asked.

'I can take you to him,' Des replied. 'When?'

'Now,' Tach said. In an hour or two, the sleeping policeman would awaken and go straight to Bannister. And say what? That Des and a man in a chicken mask had been asking questions, that he'd been about to arrest them but suddenly he'd gotten very sleepy? Would he dare admit to that? If so, what would Bannister make of it? Enough to move Angelface? Enough to kill her? They could not chance it.

When they emerged from the dimness of Freakers, the crane had just lowered the second police car to the sidewalk. A cold wind was blowing, but behind his chicken feathers, Doctor Tachyon had begun to sweat.

◆

Tom Tudbury woke to the dim, muffled sound of someone pounding on his shell.

He pushed aside the frayed blanket, and bashed his head sitting up. 'Ow, goddamn it,' he cursed, fumbling in the darkness until he found the map light. The pounding continued, a hollow *boom boom boom* against the armor, echoing. Tom felt a stab of panic. The police, he thought, they've found me, they've come to drag me out and haul me up on charges. His head hurt. It was cold and stuffy in here. He turned on the space heater, the fans, the cameras. His screens came to life.

Outside was a bright cold December day, the sunlight painting every grimy brick with stark clarity. Joey had taken the train back to Bayonne, but Tom had remained; they were running out of time, he had no other choice. Des found him a safe place, an interior courtyard in the depths of Jokertown, surrounded by decaying five-story tenements, its cobblestones redolent with the smell of sewage, wholly hidden from the street. When he'd landed, just before dawn, lights had blinked on in a few of the dark windows, and faces had come to peer cautiously around the shades:

wary, frightened, not-quite-human faces, briefly seen and gone as quickly, when they decided that the thing outside was none of their concern.

Yawning, Tom pulled himself into his seat and panned his cameras until he found the source of the commotion. Des was standing by an open cellar door, arms crossed, while Doctor Tachyon hammered on the shell with a length of broom handle.

Astonished, Tom flipped open his microphones. 'YOU.'

Tachyon winced. 'Please.'

He lowered the volume. 'Sorry. You took me by surprise. I never expected to see you again. After last night, I mean. I didn't hurt you, did I? I didn't mean to, I just—'

'I understand,' Tachyon said. 'But we've got no time for recriminations or apologies now.'

Des began to roll upward. Damn that vertical hold. 'We know where they have her,' the joker said as his image flipped. 'That is, if Doctor Tachyon can indeed read minds as advertised.'

'Where?' Tom said. Des continued to flip, flip, flip.

'A warehouse on the Hudson,' Tachyon replied. 'Near the foot of a pier. I can't tell you an address, but I saw it clearly in his thoughts. I'll recognize it.'

'Great!' Tom enthused. He gave up on his efforts to adjust the vertical hold and whapped the screen. The picture steadied. 'Then we've got them. Let's go.' The look on Tachyon's face took him aback. 'You are coming, aren't you?'

Tachyon swallowed. 'Yes,' he said. He had a mask in his hand. He slipped it on.

That was a relief, Tom thought; for a second there, he'd thought he'd have to go it alone. 'Climb on,' he said.

With a deep sigh of resignation, the alien scrambled on top of the shell, his boots scrabbling at the armor. Tom gripped his armrests tightly and pushed up. The shell rose as easily as a soap bubble. He felt elated. This was what he was meant to do, Tom thought; Jetboy must have felt like this.

Joey had installed a monster of a horn in the shell. Tom let it rip as they floated clear of the rooftops, startling a coop of pigeons, a few winos, and Tachyon with the distinctive blare of *Here-I-come-to-save-the-daaaaaay*.

'It might be wise to be a bit more subtle about this,' Tachyon said diplomatically.

Tom laughed. 'I don't believe it, I got a man from outer space who mostly dresses like Pinky Lee riding on my back, and he's telling me I ought to be subtle.' He laughed again as the streets of Jokertown spread out all around them.

They made their final approach through a maze of waterfront alleys. The last was a dead end, terminating in a brick wall scrawled over with the names of gangs and young lovers. The Turtle rose above it, and they emerged in the loading area behind the warehouse. A man in a short leather jacket sat on the edge of the loading dock. He jumped to his feet when they hove into view. His jump took him a lot higher than he'd anticipated, about ten feet higher. He opened his mouth, but before he could shout, Tach had him; he went to sleep in midair. The Turtle stashed him atop a nearby roof.

Four wide loading bays opened onto the dock, all chained and padlocked, their corrugated metal doors marked with wide brown streaks of rust. TRESPASSERS WILL BE PROSECUTED said the lettering on the narrow door to the side.

Tach hopped down, landing easily on the balls of his feet, his nerves tingling. 'I'll go through,' he told the Turtle. 'Give me a minute, and then follow.'

'A minute,' the speakers said. 'You got it.'

Tach pulled off his boots, opened the door just a crack, and slid into the warehouse on purple-stockinged feet, summoning up all the stealth and fluid grace they'd once taught him on Takis. Inside, bales of shredded paper, bound tightly in thin wire, were stacked twenty and thirty feet high. Tachyon crept down a crooked aisle toward the sound of voices. A huge yellow forklift blocked his path. He dropped flat and squirmed underneath it, to peer around one massive tire.

He counted five altogether. Two of them were playing cards,

sitting in folding chairs and using a stack of coverless paperbacks for a table. A grossly fat man was adjusting a gigantic paper-shredding machine against the far wall. The last two stood over a long table, bags of white powder piled in neat rows in front of them. The tall man in the flannel shirt was weighing something on a small set of scales. Next to him, supervising, was a slender balding man in an expensive raincoat. He had a cigarette in his hand, and his voice was smooth and soft. Tachyon couldn't quite make out what he was saying. There was no sign of Angelface.

He dipped into the sewer that was Bannister's mind, and saw her. Between the shredder and the baling machine. He couldn't see it from under the forklift, the machinery blocked the line of sight, but she was there. A filthy mattress had been tossed on the concrete floor, and she lay atop it, her ankles swollen and raw where the handcuffs chafed against her skin.

'… fifty-eight hippopotami, fifty-nine hippopotami, *sixty* hippopotami,' Tom counted.

The loading bays were big enough. He squeezed, and the padlock disintegrated into shards of rust and twisted metal. The chains came clanking down, and the door rattled upward, rusty tracks screeching protest. Tom turned on all his lights as the shell slid forward. Inside, towering stacks of paper blocked his way. There wasn't room to go between them. He shoved them, *hard*, but even as they started to collapse, it occurred to him that he could go above them. He pushed up toward the ceiling.

'What the fuck,' one of the cardplayers said, when they heard the loading gate screech open.

A heartbeat later, they were all moving. Both cardplayers scrambled to their feet; one of them produced a gun. The man in the flannel shirt looked up from his scales. The fat man turned away from the shredder, shouting something, but it was impossible to make out what he was saying. Against the far wall, bales of paper came crashing down, knocking into neighboring stacks and sending them down too, in a chain reaction that spread across the warehouse.

Without an instant's hesitation, Bannister went for Angelface. Tach took his mind and stopped him in mid-stride, with his revolver half-drawn.

And then a dozen bales of shredded paper slammed down against the rear of the forklift. The vehicle shifted, just a little, crushing Tachyon's left hand under a huge black tire. He cried out in shock and pain, and lost Bannister.

Down below, two little men were shooting at him. The first shot startled him so badly that Tom lost his concentration for a split second, and the shell dropped four feet before he got it back. Then the bullets were *pinging* harmlessly off his armor and ricocheting around the warehouse. Tom smiled. 'I AM THE GREAT AND POWERFUL TURTLE,' he announced at full volume, as stacks of paper crashed down all around. 'YOU ASSHOLES ARE UP SHIT CREEK. SURRENDER NOW.'

The nearest asshole didn't surrender. He fired again, and one of Tom's screens went black. 'OH, FUCK,' Tom said, forgetting to kill his mike. He grabbed the guy's arm and pulled the gun away, and from the way the jerk screamed he'd probably dislocated his shoulder too, goddammit. He'd have to watch that. The other guy started running, jumping over a collapsed pile of paper. Tom caught him in mid-jump, took him straight up to the ceiling, and hung him from a rafter. His eyes flicked from screen to screen, but one screen was dark now and the damned vertical hold had gone again on the one next to it, so he couldn't make out a fucking thing to that side. He didn't have time to fix it. Some guy in a flannel shirt was loading bags into a suitcase, he saw on the big screen, and from the corner of his eye, he spied a fat guy climbing into a forklift ...

His hand crushed beneath the tire, Tachyon writhed in excruciating pain and tried not to scream. Bannister – had to stop Bannister before he got to Angelface. He ground his teeth together and tried to will away the pain, to gather it into a ball and push it from him the way he'd been taught, but it was hard, he'd lost the discipline, he could feel the shattered bones in his hand, his eyes were blurry with tears, and then he heard the forklift's motor turn over, and suddenly it was surging forward, rolling right up his arm, coming straight at his head, the tread of the massive tire a black wall of death rushing toward him ... and passing an inch over the top of his skull, as it took to the air.

The forklift flew nicely across the warehouse and embedded itself in the far wall, with a little push from the Great and Powerful Turtle. The fat man dove off in midair and landed on a pile of coverless paperbacks. It wasn't until then that Tom happened to notice Tachyon lying on the floor under the place the forklift had been. He was holding his hand funny and his chicken mask was all smashed up and dirty, Tom saw, and as he staggered to his feet he was shouting something. He went running across the floor, reeling, unsteady. Where the fuck was he going in such a hurry?

Frowning, Tom smacked the malfunctioning screen with the back of his hand, and the vertical roll stopped suddenly. For an instant, the image on the television was clear and sharp. A man in a raincoat stood over a woman on a mattress. She was real pretty, and there was a funny smile on her face, sad but almost accepting, as he pressed the revolver right up to her forehead.

Tach came reeling around the shredding machine, his ankles all rubber, the world a red blur, his shattered bones jabbing against each other with every step, and found them there, Bannister touching her lightly with his pistol, her skin already darkening where the bullet would go in, and through his tears and his fears and a haze of pain, he reached out for Bannister's mind and seized it ... just in time to feel him squeeze the trigger, and wince as the gun kicked back in his mind. He heard the explosion from two sets of ears.

'*Nooooooooooooooooooo!*' he shrieked. He closed his eyes, sunk to his knees. He made Bannister fling the gun away, for what good it would do, none at all, too late, again he'd come too late, failed, *failed*, again, Angelface, Blythe, his sister, everyone he loved, all of them gone. He doubled over on the floor, and his mind filled with images of broken mirrors, of the Wedding Pattern danced in blood and pain, and that was the last thing he knew before the darkness took him.

♦

He woke to the astringent smell of a hospital room and the feel of a pillow under his head, the pillowcase crisp with starch. He opened his eyes. 'Des,' he said weakly. He tried to sit, but he was bound up somehow. The world was blurry and unfocused.

'You're in traction, Doctor,' Des said. 'Your right arm was broken in two places, and your hand is worse than that.'

'I'm sorry,' Tach said. He would have wept, but he had run out of tears. 'I'm so sorry. We tried, I … I'm so sorry, I—'

'*Tacky*,' she said in that soft, husky voice.

And she was there, standing over him, dressed in a hospital gown, black hair framing a wry smile. She had combed it forward to cover her forehead; beneath her bangs was a hideous purple-green bruise, and the skin around her eyes was red and raw. For a moment he thought he was dead, or mad, or dreaming. 'It's all right, Tacky. I'm okay. I'm here.'

He stared up at her numbly. 'You're dead,' he said dully. 'I was too late. I heard the shot, I had him by then but it was too late, I felt the gun recoil in his hand.'

'Did you feel it jerk?' she asked him.

'Jerk?'

'A couple of inches, no more. Just as he fired. Just enough. I got some nasty powder burns, but the bullet went into the mattress a foot from my head.'

'The Turtle,' Tach said hoarsely.

She nodded. 'He pushed aside the gun just as Bannister squeezed the trigger. And you made the son of a bitch throw away the revolver before he could get off a second shot.'

'You got them,' Des said. 'A couple of men escaped in the confusion, but the Turtle delivered three of them, including Bannister. Plus a suitcase packed with twenty pounds of pure heroin. And it turns out that warehouse is owned by the Mafia.'

'The Mafia?' Tachyon said.

'The mob,' Des explained. 'Criminals, Doctor Tachyon.'

'One of the men captured in the warehouse has already turned state's evidence,' Angelface said. 'He'll testify to everything – the bribes, the drug operation, the murders at the Funhouse.'

'Maybe we'll even get some decent police in Jokertown,' Des added.

The feelings that rushed through Tachyon went far beyond relief. He wanted to thank them, wanted to cry for them, but neither the tears nor the words would come. He was weak and happy. 'I didn't fail,' he managed at last.

'No,' Angelface said. She looked at Des. 'Would you wait outside?' When they were alone, she sat on the edge of the bed. 'I want to show you something. Something I wish I'd shown you a long time ago.' She held it up in front of him. It was a gold locket. 'Open it.'

It was hard to do with only one hand, but he managed. Inside was a small round photograph of an elderly woman in bed. Her limbs were skeletal and withered, sticks draped in mottled flesh, and her face was horribly twisted. 'What's wrong with her?' Tach asked, afraid of the answer. Another joker, he thought, another victim of his failures.

Angelface looked down at the twisted old woman, sighed, and closed the locket with a snap. 'When she was four, in Little Italy, she was run over while playing in the street. A horse stepped on her face, and the wagon wheel crushed her spine. That was in, oh, 1886. She was completely paralyzed, but she lived. If you could call it living. That little girl spent the next sixty years in a bed, being fed, washed, and read to, with no company except the holy sisters.

Sometimes all she wanted was to die. She dreamed about what it would be like to be beautiful, to be loved and desired, to be able to dance, to be able to *feel* things. Oh, how she wanted to *feel* things.' She smiled. 'I should have said thank you long ago, Tacky, but it's hard for me to show that picture to anyone. But I am grateful, and now I owe you doubly. You'll never pay for a drink at the Funhouse.'

He stared at her. 'I don't want a drink,' he said. 'No more. That's done.' And it was, he knew; if she could live with her pain, what excuse could he possibly have to waste his life and talents? 'Angelface,' he said suddenly, 'I can make you something better than heroin. I was … I *am* a biochemist, there are drugs on Takis, I can synthesize them, painkillers, nerve blocks. If you'll let me run some tests on you, maybe I can tailor something to your metabolism. I'll need a lab, of course. Setting things up will be expensive, but the drug could be made for pennies.'

'I'll have some money,' she said. 'I'm selling the Funhouse to Des. But what you're talking about is illegal.'

'To hell with their stupid laws,' Tach blazed. 'I won't tell if you won't.' Then words came tumbling out one after the other, a torrent: plans, dreams, hopes, all of the things he'd lost or drowned in cognac and Sterno, and Angelface was looking at him, astonished, smiling, and when the drugs they had given him finally began to wear off, and his arm began to throb again, Dr. Tachyon remembered the old disciplines and sent the pain away, and somehow it seemed as though part of his guilt and his grief went with it, and he was whole again, and alive.

The headline said TURTLE, TACHYON SMASH HEROIN RING. Tom was gluing the article into the scrapbook when Joey returned with the beers. 'They left out the Great and Powerful part,' Joey observed, setting down a bottle by Tom's elbow.

'At least I got first billing,' Tom said. He wiped thick white paste off his fingers with a napkin, and shoved the scrapbook aside.

Underneath were some crude drawings he'd made of the shell. 'Now,' he said, 'where the fuck are we going to put the record player, huh?'

INTERLUDE TWO

From The New York Times,
September 1, 1966.

JOKERTOWN CLINIC TO
OPEN ON WILD CARD DAY

The opening of a privately funded research hospital specializing in the treatment of the Takisian wild card virus was announced yesterday by Dr. Tachyon, the alien scientist who helped to develop the virus. Dr. Tachyon will serve as chief of staff at the new institution, to be located on South Street, overlooking the East River.

The facility will be known as the Blythe van Renssaeler Memorial Clinic in honor of the late Mrs. Blythe Stanhope van Renssaeler. Mrs. van Renssaeler, a member of the Exotics for Democracy from 1947 to 1950, died in 1953 in Wittier Sanatorium. She was better known as 'Brain Trust.'

The Van Renssaeler Clinic will open its doors to the public on September 15th, the twentieth anniversary of the release of the wild card virus over Manhattan. Emergency room service and outpatient psychological care will be provided by the 196-bed hospital. 'We're here to serve the neighborhood and the city,' Dr. Tachyon said in an afternoon press conference on the steps of Jetboy's Tomb, 'but our first priority is going to be the treatment of those who have too long gone untreated, the jokers whose unique and often desperate medical needs have been largely ignored by existing hospitals. The wild card was played twenty years ago, and this continued willful ignorance about the virus is criminal and inexcusable.' Dr. Tachyon said that he hoped the Van Renssaeler Clinic might become the world's leading center for wild card research, and spearhead efforts to perfect the cure for wild card, the so-called 'trump' virus.

The clinic will be housed in a historic waterfront building originally constructed in 1874. The building was a hotel, known as the Seaman's Haven, from 1888 through 1913. From 1913 through 1942 it was the Sacred Heart Home for Wayward Girls, after which it served as an inexpensive lodging house.

Dr. Tachyon announced that the purchase of the building and a complete interior renovation had been funded by a grant from the Stanhope Foundation of Boston, headed by Mr. George C. Stanhope. Mr. Stanhope is the father of Mrs. van Renssaeler. 'If Blythe were alive today, I know she'd want nothing more than to work at Dr. Tachyon's side,' Mr. Stanhope said.

Initially the work at the clinic will be funded by fees and private donations, but Dr. Tachyon admitted that he had recently returned from Washington, where he conferred with Vice President Hubert H. Humphrey. Sources close to the Vice President indicate that the administration is considering partial funding of the Jokertown clinic through the offices of the Senate Committee on Ace Resources and Endeavors (SCARE).

A crowd of approximately five hundred, many of them obvious victims of the wild card virus, greeted Dr. Tachyon's announcement with enthusiastic applause.

THE LONG, DARK NIGHT OF FORTUNATO

by Lewis Shiner

All he could think about was how beautiful she'd been when she was alive.

'I got to ask you can you identify the remains,' the coroner's man said.

'It's her,' Fortunato said.

'Name?'

'Erika Naylor. Erika with a *K*.'

'Address?'

'Sixteen Park Avenue.'

The man whistled. 'High class. Next of kin?'

'I don't know. She was from Minneapolis.'

'Right. That's where they all come from. You'd think they had a hooker academy there or something.'

Fortunato looked up from the long, horrible wound in the girl's throat and let the coroner's man see his eyes. 'She wasn't a hooker,' he said.

'Sure,' the man said, but he took a step backward and looked down at his clipboard. 'I'll put down "model".'

Geisha, Fortunato thought. She had been one of his geishas. Bright, funny, beautiful, a chef and a masseuse and an unlicensed psychologist, imaginative and sensual in bed.

She was the third of his girls in the last year to be neatly sliced to pieces.

He stepped out onto the street, knowing how bad he looked. He was six foot four and methedrine thin, and when he slumped his chest seemed to disappear into his spine. Lenore had been waiting for him, huddled in her black fake-fur jacket, even though the sun had finally come out. When she saw him she put him straight into a cab and gave the driver her address on West 19th.

Fortunato stared out the window at the long-haired girls in embroidered denim, at the black-light posters in the store windows, at the bright chalk scrawled over all the sidewalks. It was nearly Easter, two winters past the Summer of Love, but the idea of spring left him as cold as the morgue's tile floor.

Lenore took his hand and squeezed it, and Fortunato leaned back in the seat and closed his eyes.

She was new. One of his girls had rescued her from a Brooklyn pimp named Ballpeen Willie, and Fortunato had paid five thousand dollars for her 'contract.' It was well known on the street that if Willie had objected, Fortunato would have spent the five thousand to have Willie hit, that being the current market value of a human life.

Willie worked for the Gambione Family and Fortunato had knocked heads with them more than once. Being black – half black, anyway – and independent gave Fortunato a feature part in Don Carlo's paranoid fantasies. The only thing Don Carlo hated worse were the jokers.

Fortunato wouldn't have put the killings past the old man except for one thing: he coveted Fortunato's operation too much to tamper with the women themselves.

Lenore came from a hick town in the mountains of Virginia where the old people still talked Elizabethan. Willie had been running her less than a month, not long enough to grind off the edges of her beauty. She had dark red hair to her waist, neon-green eyes, and a small, almost dainty mouth. She never wore anything but black and she believed she was a witch.

When Fortunato had auditioned her he'd been moved by her abandon, her complete absorption in carnality, so much at odds with her cool, sophisticated looks. He'd accepted her for training and she'd been at it now for three weeks, turning only an occasional trick, making the transition from gifted call girl to apprentice geisha that would take at least two years.

She led him up to her apartment and stopped with the key in the lock. 'Uh, I hope it's not too weird for you.'

He stood in the doorway while she walked through the room, lighting candles. The windows were heavily draped and he didn't see any appliances except a telephone – no TV, no clocks, not even a toaster. In the barren center of the room she'd painted a huge, five-pointed star surrounded by a circle, right onto the hardwood floor. Behind the sensual smells of incense and musk was the faint sulfurous tang of a chemistry lab.

He locked the front door and followed her into the bedroom. The apartment was thick with sexuality. He could barely move his feet through the heavy, wine-colored carpet; the bed was canopied, with red velvet curtains, and so high off the floor it had stairs leading up to it.

She found a joint in the nightstand, lit it, and handed it to Fortunato. 'I'll be back in a second,' she said.

He took his clothes off and lay down with his hands behind his head, the joint hanging out of his mouth. He took a lungful of smoke and watched his toes uncurl. The ceiling overhead was deep blue, with constellations dabbed on in phosphorescent yellow-green. Signs of the zodiac, as far as he could tell. Magic and astrology and gurus were very hip right now. People at trendy Village parties were always asking each other what sign they were and talking about karma. For himself, he thought the Aquarian Age was just so much wishful thinking. Nixon was in the White House, kids were getting their asses shot off in Southeast Asia, and he still heard the word 'nigger' every day. But he had clients who would love this place.

If the psycho with the knife didn't put him out of business.

Lenore knelt beside him on the bed, naked. 'You have such beautiful skin.' She ran fingertips over his chest, raising gooseflesh. 'I've never seen a color like this before.' When he didn't answer she said, 'Your mother is Japanese, they told me.'

'And my father was a Harlem pimp.'

'You're really fucked up about this, aren't you.'

'I loved those girls. I love all of you. You're more important to me than money or family or ... or anything.'

'And?'

He didn't think he had anything else to say until the words started coming out. 'I feel so ... so goddamned helpless. Some twisted son of a bitch is killing my girls and there's nothing I can do about it.'

'Maybe,' she said. 'Maybe not.' Her fingers tangled in his pubic hair. 'Sex is power, Fortunato. It's the most powerful thing in the universe. Don't ever forget that.'

She took his penis in her mouth, working it gently with her tongue like a piece of candy. It stiffened instantly and Fortunato felt sweat break on his forehead. He put out the joint with a wet fingertip and dropped it over the edge of the bed. His heels skidded on the icy slickness of the sheets and his nose filled with Lenore's perfume. He thought of Erika, dead, and it made him want to fuck Lenore hard and long.

'No,' she said, taking his hand from her breast. 'You brought me in off the streets, you're teaching me what *you* know. Now it's my turn.'

She pushed him down flat on his back, his arms over his head, and ran her black-polished fingernails down the tender skin over his ribs. Then she began to move over his body, touching him with her lips, her breasts, the ends of her hair, until his skin felt hot enough to glow in the dark. Then, finally, she straddled him and took him into her.

Being inside her gave him a rush like a junkie's. He pumped his hips and she leaned into it, taking her weight on her arms, her hair waterfalling around her head. Then, slowly, she lifted her eyes and stared at him.

'I am *Shakti*,' she said. 'I am the goddess. I am the power.' She smiled when she said it, and instead of sounding crazy it just made him want her even more. Then her voice broke into short, rattling breaths as she came, shuddering, throwing her head back and rocking hard against him. Fortunato tried to turn her over and finish it but she was stronger than he would have believed possible, digging her fingers into his shoulders until he relaxed, then caressing him again with aching slowness.

She came twice more before everything turned red and he knew he couldn't hold back any longer. But she sensed it too, and before he knew what was happening she had pulled away and reached down between his legs, pushing one finger hard into the root of his penis. It was too late to stop and the orgasm took him so hard that it lifted his buttocks completely off the bed. She pushed his chest down with her left hand and held on with her right, cutting off the sperm before it could shoot out, forcing it back inside him.

She's killed me, he thought as he felt liquid fire roar back into his groin, burning all the way through to his spinal cord and then lighting it like a fuse.

'*Kundalini*,' she whispered, her face sweating and intent. 'Feel the power.'

The spark rocketed up his backbone and exploded in his brain.

Eventually he opened his eyes again. Time had come out of the sprockets of the projector and he saw everything in single, unrelated frames. Lenore had both arms around him. Tears ran out of her eyes and down his chest.

'I was floating,' he said, when he finally thought to use his voice. 'Up around the ceiling.'

'I thought you were dead,' Lenore said.

'I could see the two of us. Everything looked like it was made out of light. The room was white, and it seemed like it went on forever. There were lines and ripples everywhere.' He felt a little like he'd had too much cocaine, a little like he had his fingers in a socket. 'What did you do to me?'

'Tantric yoga. It's supposed to … I don't know. Give you a charge. I never heard of it taking anybody so hard before.' She turned her face up to him. 'Did you really get out? Out of your body?'

'I guess.' He could smell the peppermint shampoo she used on her hair. He took her face in both his hands and kissed her. Her mouth was soft and wet and her tongue flickered against his teeth. He was still diamond-hard and he started to shake with wanting her.

He rolled onto her and she guided him inside where he could feel her burning for him. 'Fortunato,' she whispered, her lips still so close that they brushed his when they moved, 'if you finish, you'll lose it. You'll be so weak you can barely move.'

'Baby, I don't give a shit. I never wanted anybody this much.' He pushed himself up on his forearms so he could see her, his hips thrusting frantically. Every nerve in his body was alive, and he could feel the power surging through them, then slowly drawing back, massing somewhere at the center of his body, ready to roar out of him, to pump him dry, leave him weak, helpless, drained ...

He pulled away from her, rolled to the end of the bed, and bent double, clutching his knees. 'Jesus!' he screamed. 'What the fuck is happening to me?'

She wanted to stay with him, but he sent her to geisha class anyway. He would be here, he promised, when she got home.

The apartment seemed vast and empty without her, and he had a sudden, chilling vision of Lenore alone on the street, with Erika's killer still loose.

No, he told himself. It wouldn't happen again, not this soon.

He found a gaudy oriental robe in her closet and put it on, and then he walked back and forth through the apartment, pacing out the inaudible hum in his nervous system. Finally he stopped in front of the bookcase in the living room.

Kundalini, she'd said. He'd heard the name before and when he saw a book called *The Rising Serpent* he made the connection. He took it down and started to read.

He read about the Great White Brotherhood of Ultima Thule, located somewhere in Tartary. The lost *Book of Dyzan* and the *vama chara*, the lefthand path. The *kali yuga*, the final, most corrupt of ages, now upon us. 'Do whatever you desire, for in this way you please the goddess.' *Shakti*. Semen as the *rasa*, the juice, of power: the *yod*. Sodomy that revived the dead. Shape shifters, astral bodies, implanted obsessions leading to suicide. Paracelsus, Aleister Crowley, Mehmet Karagoz, L. Ron Hubbard.

Fortunato's concentration was absolute. He absorbed every word, every diagram, flipped back and forth to make comparisons, to study the illustrations. When he finished he saw that twenty-three minutes had passed since Lenore walked out the door.

The trembling in his chest was fear.

In the middle of the night he reached out to touch Lenore's cheek and his fingers came away wet. 'Are you awake?' he said.

She rolled over and huddled tight against him. The warmth of her naked skin electrified and soothed him at the same time, like the taste of expensive whiskey. He combed through her hair with his fingers and kissed her fragrant neck. 'What are you crying for?' he said.

'It's stupid,' she said.

'What?'

'I really believe in that stuff. Magick. The Great Work, Crowley calls it.' She pronounced magic with a long *a* and Crowley with a long *o* like the bird. 'I did the Yoga and learned the Qabalah and the Tarot and the Enochian system. I fasted and did the Bornless Ritual and studied Abramelin. But nothing ever happened.'

'What were you trying for?'

'I don't know. A vision. *Samadhi*. I wanted to see something besides a goddamned Greyhound stop in Virginia where they try to lynch kids for growing out their hair. I wanted out of myself. I wanted what happened to you this afternoon. And it happened to you and you don't even want it.'

'I read some of your books tonight,' he said. In fact he'd read two dozen of them, nearly half of her collection. 'I don't know what's going on, but I don't think it's magic. Not like that guy Crowley's magic. What you did to me set it off, but I think it was something already inside me.'

'You mean that spore thing, don't you? That wild card virus?' She had tensed up involuntarily, just at the mention of it.

'I can't think of anything else it could be.'

'There's that Doctor Whatsisname. He could check you out. He could probably even fix you back, if that was what you wanted.'

'No,' he said. 'You don't understand. When I read those books I could feel all those powers they talked about. Like if you were a high diver and you read about some complicated dive you'd never done, but you knew you could do it if you practiced on it. You said I didn't want this, and maybe I didn't, not right at first. But now I do.' There was one picture, among the giant sex organs and impossible contortions of a Japanese pillow book: the Tantric magician, forehead swollen with the power of his retained sperm, fingers twisted in *mudras* of power. He had stared at it until his eyes burned. 'Now I want it,' he said.

'You've definitely drawn a wild card,' the little man said. 'An ace, I'd say.'

Fortunato had nothing in particular against white people, but he couldn't stand their slang. 'Could you put that in plain English?'

'Your genetics have been rewritten by the Takisian virus. Apparently it was dormant in your central nervous system, probably in the spine. The intromission apparently gave you quite a jolt, enough to activate the virus.'

'So now what happens?'

'The way I see it, you've got two choices.' The little man hopped up onto the examining table across from Fortunato and brushed long red hair back over his ears. He looked like he should be in a rock band or working in a record store. He didn't make a convincing doctor. 'I can try to reverse the effects of the virus. No guarantees there – I've got about a thirty-percent success rate. Every once in a while people end up worse than before.'

'Or?'

'Or you can learn to live with your power. You wouldn't be alone. I can put you in touch with other people in your situation.'

'Yeah? Like the "Great and Powerful Turtle"? So I can fly around and pull people out of wrecked cars? I don't think so.'

'What you did with your abilities would be up to you.'

'What kind of "abilities" are we talking about?'

'I can't say for sure. It looks like they're still coming on. The EEG shows strong telekinesis. The Kirilian chromatograph shows a very powerful astral body that I expect you can manipulate.'

'Magic, is what you're saying.'

'No, not really. But it's a funny thing about the wild card. Sometimes it requires a very specific mechanism to bring it under conscious control. I wouldn't be surprised if you need this Tantric ritual to make it work for you.'

Fortunato stood up and peeled a hundred from the roll in his front pocket. 'For the clinic,' he said.

The little man looked at the money for a long time, and then he stuffed it in his Sgt. Pepper jacket. 'Thank you,' he said, like it hurt him to get the words out. 'Remember what I said. You can call me anytime.'

Fortunato nodded and walked out to look at the freaks of Jokertown.

He'd been six years old when Jetboy exploded over Manhattan, had grown up with the fear of the virus, the memory of the ten thousand who'd died on the first day of the new world. His father had been one of them, lying in bed while his skin split open and healed itself over and over again, the whole cycle not taking more than a minute or two. Until one of the cracks opened through his heart, spewing blood all over their Harlem apartment. And even while the old man lay in his coffin, waiting his turn for a two-minute funeral and a mass grave, he kept splitting open and healing, splitting and healing.

The memory never faded, but in time it got pushed aside by newer ones. Gradually Fortunato came to believe that nothing was going to happen to him. For those the virus didn't touch, life went on the way it always had.

He realized early on that he was going to have to make his own way. From listening to his mother complain about American women he came up with the idea of the prostitute as geisha; at age fourteen he brought home a stunning Puerto Rican girl from his high school for his mother to train. That had been the beginning.

He looked up and saw that night had fallen while he'd been walking aimlessly through Jokertown. The grays and pastels had turned to neon, street clothes to paisley and leopard prints. Just ahead of him demonstrators had blocked off the street with a flatbed truck. There were drums and amps and guitars up there and a couple of heavy-duty extension cords running in through the open door of the Chaos Club.

At the moment the stage was empty except for a woman with long red curly hair and an acoustic guitar. A banner behind her read S.N.C.C. Fortunato had no idea what the letters stood for. She had the audience singing along with some folk song or other. They all went through the chorus a couple of times without the guitar, and then she took a bow and they clapped and she got down off the back of the truck.

She wasn't beautiful in the way Lenore was; her nose was a little large, her skin was not that good. She was in the radical uniform of blue jeans and work shirt that didn't do anything for her. But she had an aura of energy he could see without even wanting to.

Women were Fortunato's weakness. He was like a deer in their headlights. Even as low as he felt he couldn't help but stop and look at her, and before he knew it she was standing next to him, shaking a coffee can with a few coins in the bottom.

'Hey, man, how about a donation?'

'Not today,' Fortunato said. 'I don't have a lot of politics.'

'You're black, Nixon's president, and you don't have any politics? Brother, have I got news for you.'

'Is all this about being black?' Fortunato didn't see another black face in the crowd.

'No, man, it's about jokers. Whoa, did I strike a nerve or

something?' When Fortunato didn't answer she went on anyway. 'You know how long the average life expectancy of a joker in 'Nam is? Less than two months. If you take the percentage of jokers in the U.S. population and divide it by the percentage of jokers in 'Nam, you know what you get? You get about a hundred times too many jokers over there. A hundred *times*, man!'

'Yeah, okay, so what do you want me to do about it?'

'Make a donation. We're going to get lawyers on this and stop it. It's the FBI, man. The FBI and SCARE. It's like McCarthy all over again. They've got lists of all the jokers and they're drafting them on purpose. If they can walk and hold a gun, they're not even getting a real physical, it's off to Saigon. It's genocide, pure and simple.'

'Yeah, okay.' He dug out a twenty and dropped it in the can.

'You know what I wish?' She hadn't even noticed the size of the bill. 'I wish those fucking aces would do something about their own, you know? What would it take for Cyclone, or one of those other assholes, to wipe out those files? Nothing, man, nothing at all, but they're too busy getting headlines.'

She started to walk away and then she looked in the can. 'Hey, thanks, man. You're okay. Listen, here's a flyer. If you want to do some more, call us.'

'Sure,' Fortunato said. 'What's your name?'

'They call me C.C.,' she said. 'C.C. Ryder.'

'Is it the same C.C. as up there?' He pointed to the S.N.C.C. banner.

C.C. shook her head. 'You're funny, man,' she said, and smiled once and faded into the crowd.

He folded up the flyer and stuck it in his pocket and turned off the Bowery. All the talk about jokers had left him feeling disconnected. Just down the street was a mirror-walled club called the Funhouse, owned by a guy named Desmond who had a trunk instead of a nose. He was one of Fortunato's customers, always wanting a geisha with finer skin or darker hair or a sweeter face than Fortunato could find for him. Fortunato could not stand the thought of seeing him just then.

On the side streets hardly anyone wore masks anymore, and eyes stared back defiantly at him from upside-down faces or heads the size of cantaloupes. Your new brothers and sisters, he told himself. For every ace there were ten of these, lurking in alleys while the lucky ones put on capes and talked their lame jargon and jetted around fighting each other. The aces had the headlines and the talk shows, and the freaks and cripples had Jokertown. Jokertown and the jungles of Vietnam, if C.C.'s story was right.

But the only place Fortunato wanted to be was back in Lenore's apartment, making love to her. And this time he would let go, and if it made him weak it wouldn't matter, and things would go back to the way they always had been.

Except that sooner or later the killer was going to move again. Vietnam was halfway around the world, but the killer was right here, maybe in this very block.

He stopped walking, looked up, and saw that his subconscious had brought him right to the alley where they told him they'd found Erika.

He thought about what C.C. had said. Using power to take care of your own.

When Lenore had jolted him out of his body he'd seen things he'd never seen before, swirls and patterns of energy that he had no name for. If he could get out again he might see something the cops had missed.

A wino in a long, filthy overcoat started at him. It took Fortunato a second to realize the man had long, floppy, basset ears and a moist, black nose. Fortunato ignored him, shutting his eyes and trying to remember the feeling.

He might as well have been trying to think himself to the moon. He needed Lenore but he was afraid to bring her here. Could he do it at her place, then fly back here? Would he be able to keep it going that long? What would happen to his physical body if he did?

Too many questions. He called her from a pay phone and told her where to meet him.

'Do you have a gun?' he asked.

'Yes. Ever since ... you know.'

'Bring it.'

'Fortunato? Are you in trouble?'

'Not yet,' he said.

◆

By the time he got back to the alley with Lenore he'd drawn a crowd. They all wore Salvation Army leftovers: baggy pants, ripped and stained flannel shirts, jackets the color of dried grease. One short old woman looked like a wax museum statue that had started to melt. Off to her right was a teenaged boy, standing next to a rack of garbage cans, vibrating. When the vibrations got to a certain pitch the cans would bang together like a spastic cymbal section and the woman would turn on them in a fury and kick at them. The others were less obviously deformed: a man with suckers on the ends of his fingers, a girl whose features had been squared off with ridges of hardened skin.

Lenore held onto Fortunato's arm. 'What now?' she whispered.

Fortunato kissed her. She tried to pull away when the audience of freaks started to snicker, but Fortunato was insistent, opening her lips with his tongue, moving his hands over the small of her back, and finally she began to breathe heavily and he felt the power stirring at the base of his spine. He moved his lips down Lenore's shoulder, her long fingernails digging into his neck, and then he raised his eyes until he was looking at the dog-man. He felt the power flow into his eyes and voice and said, quietly, 'Go away.'

The dog-man turned and walked out of the alley. One at a time he ordered the others away and then he said, 'Now,' and guided her hand into his trousers. 'Do it to me, what you did before.' He slid his hands up under her sweater and moved them slowly over her breasts. Her right hand closed over him and her left went around his waist, comforting him with the weight of her S&W .32. He closed his eyes as the heat began to build, letting the brick wall behind him take his weight. In seconds he was ready to come, his astral body bobbing like a loosely held balloon.

And then, like stepping sideways out of a moving car, he slipped free.

Every brick and candy wrapper glistened with clarity. As he concentrated, the rumble of traffic slowed and deepened until it was barely audible.

They'd found Erika in a doorway deep in the alley, severed arms and legs stacked like firewood in her lap, head attached by less than half the thickness of her neck. Fortunato could see the stains of her blood deep within the molecules of the concrete, still glowing faintly with her life essence. The wood of the doorframe still held a trace of her perfume and a single thread of ash-blond hair.

The baritone murmur of the street dropped to a vibration so low that Fortunato could feel the individual wave peaks pass through him. Now he could see the indentation Erika's body had made in the concrete stoop, the infinitesimal trace her shoes had pressed into the asphalt. And beside them the footprints of her killer.

They led from the street to Erika's body and back again, and at the curb they met the imprint of a car. He had no idea what kind of a car it had been, but he could see the tracks it had left, thick and black and fibrous, as if it had been burning rubber the entire way.

He stopped for an instant and looked back at his material body frozen in Lenore's arms. Then he let the tracks of the car pull him out into the street, across to Second Avenue, then south to Delancey. He felt himself gradually weakening, his vision clouding up and the background noises of the city starting to shake the edge of his hearing. He concentrated harder, pulling the last reserves of strength out of his physical body.

The car turned north on the Bowery and paused in front of a shabby gray warehouse. Fortunato bore down on the sidewalk, saw the footprints as they crossed from the car to the building's front door.

He followed them upstairs. He felt as if he'd been tied to a giant elastic band and run to its limit. Each stair took more out of him than the last. Finally the footprints disappeared at the entrance to a loft, and he knew he was finished.

The traffic noise spun up to speed around him and he shot backward the way he'd come, drawn irresistibly home to his body. Blissful, exhausted, as if he'd drained himself in sex, he fell into it like a diver into a pool. Lenore staggered under his sudden dead weight and then he slid down into unconsciousness.

'No,' she said, and rolled away from him. 'I can't.'

She had purple circles under her eyes and her body was limp with exhaustion. Fortunato wondered how she'd been able to get him into a taxi and help him up the stairs to her apartment.

'I don't understand,' he said.

'You build up a charge, and then sex burns it off. You see? The power, the *shakti*. Except with tantric magick you absorb the energy back into you. Not just yours, but whatever energy I give up to you.'

'So when you come, you give up this *shakti*.'

'Right.'

'And you've given me all you have.'

'That's right, big guy. I'm all fucked out.'

Fortunato reached for the phone.

'What are you doing?'

'I know where the killer is,' he said, dialing. 'If you can't give me the strength to take him, I'll have to get it somewhere else.' He didn't like the way it came out but he was too tired right then to care. Tired and something else. His brain hummed with the knowledge of his power, and he felt it changing him, taking control.

The phone rang at the other end and then he heard Miranda answer it. He covered the mouthpiece with his hand and turned back to Lenore. 'Will you help?'

She closed her eyes and did something with her mouth that was almost a smile. 'I guess a hooker should know better than to be jealous.'

'Geisha,' Fortunato said.

'All right,' Lenore said. 'I'll show her what to do.'

They had a line each of cocaine and some intense Vietnamese pot. Lenore swore it would only help tune them into each other. Miranda, tall, black-haired, lush, the most physically adept of his women, stripped slowly to garter belt, stockings, and a black brassiere so thin he could see the dark ovals of her nipples.

Forty minutes later Lenore had passed out across the foot of the bed. Miranda, her head hanging down over the edge, arms spread in a mock crucifix, shut her eyes. 'That's it,' she whispered. 'I can't come any more. I may never come again.'

Fortunato pushed himself up onto his knees. He was covered with an even sheen of sweat and he thought he could see a golden light radiating from underneath his skin. He saw himself in the mirror over Lenore's dresser and wasn't alarmed or even surprised when he saw that his forehead had begun to swell with power.

He was ready.

The cab let him off two blocks away on Delancey. He had Lenore's .32 shoved in the back of his pants for insurance, hidden by his black linen jacket. But if he could, he would do the job with his own hands. Either way, the cops were not going to get a chance to put the killer back on the streets.

His eyes wouldn't quite focus and he had to keep his hands in his pockets because he didn't trust them. For some reason he was not afraid at all. He felt fifteen again, like he'd felt when he started making it with the girls his mother trained. For months he'd been afraid to try because of what his mother might say or do; once he gave in he no longer cared.

It was the same now. He was reckless, charged with the dark scent and hot, moist pressure of sex, barely functioning in the real world at all. I'm going to face a killer, he told himself, but they were only words. In his guts he knew he was going to protect his women, and that was all that mattered.

He climbed the stairs to the loft. It was after midnight, but he could hear the stereo blasting the Rolling Stones' 'Street-Fighting Man' through the steel door. He pounded on it with the bottoms of his fists.

He swallowed hard and his throat turned cold.

The door opened.

On the other side was a boy of seventeen or eighteen, pale, thin, but well-muscled. He had long blond hair and a face that might have been beautiful except for an eruption of pimples around the chin, clumsily hidden with makeup. He wore a yellow shirt with black polka dots and faded denim bell-bottoms.

'You want something?' he finally asked.

'To talk to you,' Fortunato said. His mouth was dry and his eyes were still not focusing right.

'What about?'

'Erika Naylor.'

The boy had no reaction. 'Never heard of her.'

'I think you do.'

'You a cop?' Fortunato didn't answer. 'Then fuck off.'

He started to close the door. Fortunato remembered the alley, ordering the jokers away. 'No,' he said, staring hard into the boy's colorless eyes. 'Let me in.'

The boy hesitated, looking stunned, but not giving in. Fortunato hit the door with his shoulder, knocking the boy all the way back into the loft and onto the floor.

The room was dark and the music deafening. Fortunato found an overhead light switch and flipped it on, then took an involuntary step back as his brain registered what he saw.

It was Lenore's apartment twisted into perversion, the hip, sexy fashion of occultism taken all the way into torture and murder and rape. As in Lenore's apartment there was a five-pointed star on the floor, but this one was hasty, uneven, scratched into the boards with something sharp and then splattered with blood. Instead of velvet and candles and exotic wood, there was a gray-striped mattress in one corner, a pile of dirty clothes, and a dozen or more Polaroid pictures tacked to the wall with a staplegun.

He knew what he was going to find, but he walked over to the wall anyway. Of the fourteen nude, dismembered women he recognized three. The latest, in the lower righthand corner, was Erika.

He couldn't think with the music blaring at him. He looked around for the record player and saw the blond boy get up onto shaky legs and stumble toward the door. 'Stop!' Fortunato shouted, but without eye contact it didn't mean anything.

Enraged and panicking, Fortunato charged. He caught the boy around the waist and drove him into the bare plasterboard wall.

And then suddenly he was trying to hold on to a raging animal, all knees and fingernails and teeth. Fortunato pulled away instinctively and watched the razor edge of an enormous switchblade flash between them, slicing through his jacket and his shirt and his skin, coming away outlined in red.

I'm going to die, Fortunato thought. The gun was stuck in the back of his pants, too far away to reach before the blade came around again, cutting deeper, sliding all the way in. Killing him.

He looked at the blade. Before he knew what he was doing he was staring hard at it, concentrating, the way he had when he read the books in Lenore's apartment, the way he had in the Jokertown alley.

And time slowed.

He could see not only his own blood on the knife, but the blood of the others, of Erika and all the other women in the photographs, washed away, but still held in the memory of the metal.

He backed away from the insane blond boy, moving with dream slowness through thickened air, but still moving faster than the boy or his knife. He reached behind him, felt the slick grips of the gun under his fingers. The Rolling Stones had slowed to a dirge as he brought the gun around, pointed it at the boy, saw the pale eyes go wide.

Don't kill him, he thought suddenly. Not until you know why. He shifted the barrel until it pointed at the boy's right shoulder, and pulled the trigger.

The noise started as a vibration in Fortunato's hand, accelerated like a rocket, became a roar, a short bang of thunder, and then time was rolling again, the boy rocking back with the impact of the bullet but his eyes not showing it, scooping the knife out of his useless right hand with his left and lurching forward again.

Possessed, Fortunato thought with horror, and shot him through the heart.

Staggering back, Fortunato pulled his shirt open and saw that the long, shallow cut across his chest had already stopped bleeding, would not even need stitches. He slammed the door to the hallway and walked across the room to kick out the plug of the phonograph. And then, in the strangled silence, he turned to face the dead boy.

The power rippled and surged inside him. He could see the blood of the women on the dead boy's hands, see the trail of blood that led from the crude pentagram on the floor, see the tracks where the boy had stood, the shadows where the women had died, and there, faintly, as if it had been somehow erased, the marks left by something else.

Lines of power still lingered inside the pentagram, like heat waves shimmering off a highway in the desert. Fortunato ground his hands into fists, felt cool sweat trickle down his chest. What had *really* happened here? Had the boy somehow conjured a demon? Or had the boy's madness just been a tool in something vastly larger, something infinitely worse than a few random killings?

The boy could have told him, but the boy was dead.

Fortunato went to the door, put his hand on the knob. He closed his eyes and rested his forehead against the cold metal. Think, he told himself.

He wiped his fingerprints off the pistol and threw it next to the body. Let the cops draw their own conclusions. The Polaroids should give them plenty to think about.

He turned to go again, and again he couldn't leave the room.

You have the power, he told himself. Can you walk away from here, knowing you have the power, refusing to use it?

Sweat ran down his face and arms.

The power was in the *yod*, the *rasa*, the sperm. Incredible power, more than he knew how to control yet. Enough to bring the dead back to life.

No, he thought. I can't do it. Not just because the thought made him sick to his stomach, but because he knew it would change him. It would be the point of no return, the point where he gave up being completely human.

But the power had already changed him. He had already seen things that those without it would never understand. Power corrupts, he'd been told, but now he saw how naive that was. Power enlightens. Power transforms.

He unfastened the dead boy's belt, unzipped the bell-bottomed jeans, and pulled them off. The boy had crapped and pissed in them when he died, and the smell made Fortunato wince. He threw the jeans in a corner and rolled the dead boy onto his stomach.

I can't do this, Fortunato thought. But he was already hard, and the tears rolled down his face as he knelt between the dead boy's legs.

He came almost immediately. It left him weak, weaker than he'd thought possible. He crawled away, pulling his pants back up, sick and disgusted and exhausted.

The dead boy began to twitch.

Fortunato got to the wall, pulled himself onto his feet. He was dizzy and his head throbbed with pain. He saw something on the floor, something that had fallen out of the dead boy's pants. It was a coin, an eighteenth-century penny, so fresh that it looked reddish in the harsh light of the loft. He put the penny in his pocket in case it meant something later.

'Look at me,' he said to the dead boy.

The dead boy's hands clawed at the floor, gouging out bloody splinters. Slowly he pulled himself onto his hands and knees, and then lurched clumsily onto his feet. He turned and looked at Fortunato with empty eyes.

The eyes were horrible. They said that death was nothingness, that even a few seconds of it had been too much.

'Talk to me,' Fortunato said. Not anger anymore, but the memory of anger, kept him going. 'Goddamn your white ass, talk to me. Tell me what this means. Tell me why.'

The dead boy stared at Fortunato. For an instant something flickered there, and the dead boy said, 'TIAMAT.' The word was whispered, but perfectly clear. Then the dead boy smiled. With both hands he reached up to his own throat and ripped it bloodily out through the skin of his neck and then, while Fortunato watched, tore it in half.

Lenore was asleep. Fortunato threw his clothes into the garbage and stood in the shower for thirty minutes, until the hot water ran out. Then he sat by candlelight in Lenore's living room and read.

He found the name TIAMAT in a text on the Sumerian elements of Crowley's magick. The serpent, Leviathan, KUTULU. Monstrous, evil.

He knew beyond question that he had found only a single tentacle of something that defied his comprehension.

Eventually he slept.

He woke up to the sound of Lenore closing the latches on her suitcase.

'Don't you see?' she tried to explain. 'I'm just like a – a wall outlet that you come home to plug into to recharge. How can I live like that? You got what I always wanted, real power to do real magick. And you lucked into it, without even wanting it. And all the study and practice and work I did all my life doesn't mean shit because I didn't catch some fucking alien virus.'

'I love you,' Fortunato said. 'Don't go.'

She told him to keep the books, to keep the apartment too if he wanted. She told him she would write, but he didn't need magick to know she was lying.

And then she was gone.

He slept for two days, and on the third Miranda found him and they made love until he was strong enough to tell her what happened.

'As long as he's dead,' Miranda said. 'The rest I don't care about.'

When she left him that night for her client, he sat in the living room for over an hour, unable to move. Soon, he knew, he would have to start looking for the other being whose traces he'd seen in the dead boy's loft. Even the thought of it paralyzed him with loathing.

Finally he reached for Crowley's *Magick* and opened it to Chapter V. 'Sooner or later,' Crowley said, 'the gentle, natural growth is succeeded by depression – the Dark Night of the Soul, an infinite weariness and detestation of the work.' But eventually would come a 'new and superior condition, a condition only rendered possible by the process of death.'

Fortunato closed the book. Crowley knew, but Crowley was dead. He felt like the last human on a barren rock of a planet.

But he wasn't the last human. He was one of the first of something new, something that had the potential to be better than human.

That woman at the demonstration, C.C. She'd said you should take care of your own. What would it cost him to save hundreds of jokers from dying in the heat and rotting dampness of Vietnam? Not very much. Not very much at all.

He found the flyer in the pocket of his jacket. Slowly, with growing conviction, he dialed the numbers.

TRANSFIGURATIONS

by Victor Milán

November night wind whipped his trousers, stinging skinny legs like triffid tendrils as he shoehorned himself into a small club not far from campus. The murk throbbed like a wound, pulsing red and blue and noise. He stopped, hovering there in the door with the lumpy orange-and-green plaid coat in which his mother had packed him off to MIT three years before hanging on his narrow shoulders like a dead dwarf. *Don't be such a coward, Mark*, he told himself. *This is for science.*

The band lunged at 'Crown of Creation' and wrestled it to the floor as he instinctively sought the darkest corner, teacup in hand – he'd learned how unhip it was to order Coke or coffee, at least.

Other than that he'd learned none of the moves in weeks of research. The way he was dressed, in his high-water pants and pastel polyester shirt of the sort that always pooched out at the sides like a sail in the wind, he might've been in danger of being taken for a narc – this was the fall that followed Woodstock, the year Gordon Liddy invented the DEA to give Nixon an issue to distract attention from the war – but Berkeley and San Francisco were hip towns, university towns; *they* knew a science student when they saw one.

The Glass Onion had no dance floor as such; bodies swayed in crepuscular crimson and indigo glow between tables or crowded into a clear space before the tiny stage, with a whisper of beads and buckskin fringe and the occasional dull glint of Indian jewelry. He kept as far from the action's center as he could, but being Mark he inevitably bumped into everyone he passed, leaving a wake of glares and thin embarrassed 'excuse me's' behind him. His prominent ears burning, he had almost reached his goal, the little rickety table made out of a Ma Bell cable spool with a single dented green auditorium chair beside it and an unlit candle in an empty peanut butter jar plunked down on it, when he ran smack into somebody.

The first thing that happened was that his massive horn-rim glasses slid down the ramp of his nose and disappeared in the dark. Next he grabbed the person he'd bumped with both hands as his balance went. The teacup hit the floor with a crash and a clatter. 'Oh, dear, oh, please excuse me, I'm sorry ...' tumbled from his mouth like gumballs from a broken machine.

He realized there was a certain softness of the person his skinny hands were clinging to so fervently, and a smell of musk and patchouli detached itself from the general miasma and drilled its way right up into his sensorium. He cursed himself: *You had to go and run over a beautiful woman.* At least she *smelled* beautiful.

Then she was patting him on the arm, murmuring that she was sorry, and they both bent down to the floor together in search of teacup and glasses while the bodies went round and round around them, and they bumped heads and recoiled amid apologies, and Mark's fevered fingers found his glasses, miraculously intact, and fit them back in front of his eyes, and he blinked and found himself staring from a distance of five inches into the face of Kimberly Ann Cordayne.

Kimberly Ann Cordayne: the girl, yes, of his dreams. Childhood sweetheart, unrequited, from the moment he'd first beheld her, pinafored and five, riding her trike down the modest suburban SoCal street where they both lived. He'd been so entranced by her Hallmark Card perfection that the raspberry scoop fell off his ice cream cone to hot doom on the sidewalk and he never noticed. She pedaled over his bare toes and cruised on with her pert nose in the air, never acknowledging his existence. From that day his heart had been lost.

Hope and despair surged up like surf within him. He straightened, his tongue too tied to produce words. And she yelled, 'Mark!

Mark Meadows! Fuck, but it's good to see you.' And hugged him.

He stood there blinking like an idiot. No female who wasn't a relative had ever hugged him before. He swallowed spastically. *What if I get an erection?* Belatedly, he made feeble patting gestures at the small of her back.

She pushed away, held him at arm's length. 'Let me look at you, brother. Why, you haven't changed a bit.'

He winced. The taunting would begin now, for his skinniness, his clumsiness, his crew cut, the pimples still sprinkled across scrawny, allegedly postadolescent features – and his most recent, most aggravating deficit, his utter and complete inability to be anywhere near With It. In high school, Kimberly Ann had evolved from indifference into his foremost tormentor – or, rather, a succession of jocks on whose overelaborated biceps she hung, cooing encouragements, had assumed the role.

But here she was tugging him toward that corner table. 'Come on, man. Let's talk about the bad old days.'

It was an opportunity for which he'd hopelessly hoped three quarters of his life. Face-to-face with his paragon of love and beauty while the band on stage assaulted the Beatles' 'Blackbird' – and he couldn't think of one damned thing to say.

But Kimberly Ann was more than happy to do the talking. About the changes she'd been through since good old Rexford Tugwell High. About the far-out people she'd met at Whittier College, how they turned her on and opened her eyes. How she'd dropped out midway through her senior year and come here, the Bay Area, the bright mecca of Movement. How she'd been finding herself ever since.

Perhaps he hadn't changed, but she most definitely had. Gone was the straight black ponytail, pleated skirts, pastel lipstick and nail polish, the prim stewardess perfection of an up-and-coming Bank of America executive's one daughter. Kimberly's hair had grown long, hanging down well past her shoulders in a great kinky cloudy Yoko Ono mane. She wore a frilly peasant blouse embroidered with mushrooms and planets, a voluminous skirt tie-dyed into what reminded Mark of nothing so much as fireworks displays in Disneyland. He knew her feet were bare, from having stepped on one. She looked more beautiful than he ever could have imagined.

And those pale eyes, winter-sky eyes, that had so often frozen him in the past, were glowing at him with such warmth he could barely stand to look at them. It was heaven, but somehow he couldn't buy it. Being Mark, he had to question.

'Kimberly—' he began.

She held up two fingers. 'Hold it right there, dude. I left that name behind me with my bourgeois ways. I'm Sunflower now.'

He bobbed his head and his Adam's apple. 'Okay – Sunflower.'

'So what brings you here, man?'

'It's an experiment.'

She eyed him across the rim of her jelly-jar wineglass, suddenly wary.

'I just finished my undergrad work at MIT,' he explained in a rush. 'Now I'm here to get my doctorate in biochemistry from the University of California at Berkeley.'

'So what's that got to do with this scene?'

'Well, what I've been working on is figuring out just how DNA encodes genetic information. I published some papers, stuff like that.' At MIT they'd compared him to Einstein, as a matter of fact, but you'd never catch him saying that. 'But this summer I found something that interests me a lot more. The chemistry of mind.'

Blue blankness, her eyes.

'Psychedelics. Psychoactive drugs. I read all the material – Leary, Alpert, the Solomon collection. It really – what's the expression? Really turned me on.' He leaned forward, fingers plucking unconsciously at the felt-tip pens nestled in their plastic protector in his breast pocket. In his excitement he sprinkled the spool tabletop with unconscious spittle. 'It's a really vital area of research. I think it might lead to answering the really important questions – who we are, and how, and why.'

She looked at him with half a frown and half a smile. 'I still don't get it.'

'I'm doing fieldwork to establish a context for my research. On the drug culture – the, uh, the counterculture. Trying to get an angle on how hallucinogen use affects people's outlook.'

He moistened his lips. 'It's really exciting. There's a whole world I never knew existed – *here*.' A nervous tic encompassed the Onion's smoky confines. 'But somehow I can't really, well, make contact. I've bought all the Grateful Dead records, but I still feel like an outsider. I – I almost feel I'd like to be part of this whole hippie thing.'

'Hippie?' she said with a patrician snort. 'Mark, where've you been? It's 1969. The hippie movement's been dead for two years.' She shook her head. 'Have you actually done any of these drugs you're trying to study?'

He flushed. 'No. I … uh – I'm not ready to get to that stage.'

'Poor Mark. You're so uptight. Looks as if I'm going to have my work cut out for me, trying to show you what it is that's happening, Mr. Jones.'

The reference skimmed his flattop, but suddenly his face brightened and his nose and cheekbones and whatnot went in happy directions, and he showed his horsy teeth. 'You mean you'll help me?' He grabbed her hand, snatched his fingers away as if afraid they'd leave marks. 'You'll show me around?'

She nodded.

'Great!' He picked up the teacup, clinked it against an upper tooth, realized it was empty and clacked it down again. 'I've been wondering why – that is, I – well, you've never, ah, *talked* to me like this before.'

She took one of his hands in both of hers and he thought his heart would stop. 'Oh, Mark,' she said, tenderly, even. 'Always the analytical one. It's just that since my eyes have been opened, I've realized that everyone's beautiful in his own way, except the pigs who oppress the people. And I see you – still straight. But you haven't sold out, man. I can tell; I can read it in your aura. You're still the same old Mark.'

His head whirled like a carousel out of control. Cynical, his left brain tossed up the hypothesis that she was homesick, that he was part of a childhood and past she had cut herself off from, perhaps, too completely. He brushed it aside. She was Kimberly Ann, invulnerable, unapproachable. Any minute now she'd recognize him for the impostor he was.

She didn't. They talked on into the night – or rather, she talked and he listened, wanting to believe but still unable to. When the band took a long-overdue break, somebody cued up side one of Destiny's new album on the sound system. The *gestalt* burned itself irrevocably in: darkness and colored lights playing in the hair and face of the most beautiful woman in his world, and behind it the husky baritone of Tom Marion Douglas singing of love and death and dislocation, of elder gods and destinies best not hinted at. It changed him, that night. But he didn't know yet.

He was almost too surfeited with wonder to be elated or even surprised when, halfway through the band's exiguous second set, Kimberly stood up suddenly, clutching his hand. 'This is getting to be a drag. These guys don't know where it's at. Why don't you come over to my pad, drink a little wine, get a little high?' Her eyes challenged, and there was a bit of that old haughtiness, the old ice, as she pulled on waffle-stomper boots with red laces. 'Or are you too straight for that?'

He felt as if he had a cotton ball sitting in the middle of his tongue. 'Ah, I – no. I'd be more than happy to.'

'Far out. There's hope for you yet.'

In a daze Mark followed her out of the club, to a liquor store with a massive sliding San Quentin grating over the windows, where a balding pasty-faced proprietor sold them a bottle of Ripple under a gaze of fish-eyed distaste. Mark was a virgin. He had his fantasies, the *Playboy* magazines with their pages stuck together stacked among the scientific papers under the tumbledown bed in his apartment on the fringes of Chinatown. But not even in fantasy did he ever dare to imagine himself coupled with the resplendent Kimberly Ann. And now – he drifted the streets as if weightless, barely noticing the freaks and street people who exchanged greetings with Sunflower as they passed.

And he barely noticed on the rickety backstairs when Sunflower said, '... meet my old man. You'll love him; he's a really heavy dude.'

Then the words crunched into his brain like a lead mallet. He stumbled. Kimberly caught him by the arm, laughing. 'Poor Mark. Always so uptight. Come on, we're almost there.'

So he wound up in this little one-lung apartment with a hot plate and a leaky faucet in the bathroom. By one wall a salvaged mattress with a madras-print coverlet rested on a door propped on cinder blocks. Crosslegged on the spread beneath a giant poster of the beatified Che sat Philip, Sunflower's Old Man. He was dark-eyed and intense, a black tee shirt stretched over his brawny chest with a blood-red fist and the word *Huelga* lettered under it. He was watching clips of a demonstration on a little rumpsprung portable TV with a coat-hanger aerial.

'Right on,' he was saying as they came in. 'The Lizard King has his head together. These clean-for-Gene work-within-the-system aces like Turtle don't know what it's all about: confrontation with fascist Amerika. Who the fuck are you?'

After Sunflower took him off to one corner and explained to him in a fierce whisper that Mark was not a police spy but an old, old friend, and don't embarrass me, asshole, he consented to shake Mark's hand. Mark craned past him at the TV; the bearded face of the man now being interviewed looked familiar somehow.

'Who's that?' he asked.

Philip lifted a lip corner. 'Tom Douglas, of course. Lead singer for Destiny. The Lizard King.' He scanned Mark from flattop to penny loafers. 'Or maybe you've never heard of him.'

Mark blinked, said nothing. He knew of Destiny and Douglas – as research he'd just bought their new album, *Black Sunday*, plain maroon cover dominated by a huge black sun. He was too embarrassed to say so.

Sunflower's eyes went faraway. 'You should have seen him today at the demonstration. Facing down the pigs as the Lizard King. Truly far out.'

Amenities out of the way, the two of them broke out a contrivance of glass and rubber tubing, tamped its bowl full of dope, and lit up. Had Sunflower by herself offered Mark the grass, he would have accepted. But now he was feeling strange and alien again, as if his skin didn't fit him right, and he refused. He slouched in the corner next to a pile of *Daily Workers* while his host and hostess sat on the bed and smoked dope and stocky intense Philip lectured him about the Necessity for Armed Struggle until he thought his head was going to fall off, and he drank the whole bottle of sickly sweet wine by himself – he didn't drink, either – and finally Kimberly began to snuggle up close to her Old Man and fondle him in a way that made Mark distinctly uneasy, and he mumbled excuses and stumbled out and somehow found his way home. As the first light of dawn drooled in the windows of his own dingy flat, he regurgitated the contents of the Ripple bottle into his cracked porcelain toilet, and it took him fifteen flushes to get it clear again.

So began Mark's courtship of Sunflower, née Kimberly Ann Cordayne.

'*I want you* …' The words spilled across the wind, insolent, suggestive, the voice like molten amber with a whiskey edge for all the New Year's-noisemaker quality of the little Jap transistor. Wojtek Grabowski pulled his windbreaker tighter over his wide chest and tried not to hear.

The crane reared back like a zombie dinosaur, swayed a girder toward him. He gestured to the operator with exaggerated underwater moves. '*I want you* …' the voice insisted. He felt a flash of irritation. '*A blast from the past – 1966, and Destiny's first hit song,*' the announcer had warbled in his professional-adolescent voice. These Americans, Wojtek thought, they think 1966 is ancient history.

'Turn off that boogie-woogie shit,' somebody growled.

'Fuck you,' the radio's owner said. He was twenty years old, two meters tall, and six months out of 'Nam. Marine. Khe Sanh. The argument ended.

Grabowski wished the boy would turn the radio off, but he didn't like to push himself forward. He was tolerated – a solid worker, who could drink the strongest man on-site under the table of a Friday night. But he kept to himself.

As the girder came down and the crew swarmed up to fix it in place and the cold wind off the bay drilled through thin nylon and aging skin, he thought how strange it was to find himself here – him, the middle child of a prosperous Warsaw household, the small sickly one, the studious. He was going to be a doctor, a professor. His brother Kliment – half envied, wholly admired, big, bold, dashing, with a cavalryman's black mustache – was going into the Officers' Academy, was going to be a hero.

Then the Germans came. Kliment was shot in the back of the head by the Red Army in Katyn Wood. Sister Katja disappeared into the field-brothels of the Wehrmacht. Mother died in the last bombardment of Warsaw, while the Soviets squatted on the Vistula and let the Nazis do their dirty work for them. Father, a minor government functionary, outlived the war a few months before collecting his own bullet in the back of the neck, purged by the puppet Lublin regime.

Young Wojtek, dreams of university forever shattered, spent six and a half years as a partisan in the woods, ended them a fugitive, exiled to a foreign land with only a single hope to keep his blood beating.

'*I* want *you*.' The repetition was beginning to grate on him. He'd grown up with Mozart and Mendelssohn. And the message ... This was no love song, it was a lust song – an invitation to rut.

Love meant more to him – a moment of cool moisture, sluicing across his vision, wiped away by the wind's chill hand. He remembered marrying Anna, his partisan girl, in what the Stukas had left of a village church, and afterward the priest himself had hitched up his threadbare cassock and played Bach's *Toccata and Fugue* on the organ, miraculously intact, while a starveling girl crouched to work the bellows. Next day they'd lie in ambush for the facists, but that night, that night ...

Another girder rose. Anna had left before him, smuggled out by helpful British operatives in June of 1945, bound for America with their child in her womb. He fought as long as he could, then followed.

Now he dwelt in a land he loved almost as a lover. He had nothing else. In twenty-three years he had found no sign of the woman he loved and the child she must have borne. Though, sweet Mary, how he'd searched.

'*I waaaaaant you ...*'

He shut his eyes. If I must endure that banal lyric one more time ...

'*... to die with me.*'

The music diminuendoed in an eerie wail. For a moment he stood very still, as if the wind had turned the sweat to ice within his shirt. What had seemed a mere syrup confection was infinitely more – more evil. Here was a man, anointed spokesman of youth, for whom the blandishments of love – or even lust – were degraded into a *totentanz*, a ritual of death.

The girder clipped an upright and rang like a cracked bell. Grabowski shook himself, gestured the crane man to stop. At the same time, he strained, heard the announcer say the name Tom Douglas.

It was a name he would remember.

Mark hoped it was a courtship. Two days later Sunflower caught him coming out of a meeting with his sponsor and took him for a walk in the park. She let him tag along to the night spots and late-night rap sessions, to protest rallies in People's Park, to concerts. Always as her friend, her protégé, the childhood friend she had made it her personal crusade to redeem from straightness. But not, unfortunately, in the exalted role of her Old Man.

He found reason to hope, however. He never saw the studly Philip again. In fact, he never saw one of Sunflower's boyfriends more than once. They were all intense, passionate, brilliant (and at pains to tell you so). Committed. And muscular; *that* much of Kimberly's taste hadn't changed. That gave Mark many choice moments of despair, but deep inside his skinny bosom he nursed the notion that someday she would feel the need of a rock of stability, and would come to him as a seabird to land.

But still, he never, never made it across the gap that yawned between him and the world he yearned for – the world Sunflower inhabited and personified.

He survived that winter on hope and the chocolate-chip-oatmeal cookies his mother sent.

And music. He came from a household where they sang along with Mitch, and Lawrence Welk occupied the same pinnacle as J.F.K. Rock 'n' roll was never permitted to sully the air of his parents' house. He himself had been as oblivious to it as to everything outside of his lab and his private fantasies. He hadn't been aware of the Beatles' invasion, Mick Jagger's arrest for lycanthropy at the Isle of Wight concert, of the Summer of Love and the acid-rock explosion.

Now it all came rushing in on him. The Stones. The Beatles. The Airplane. The Grateful Dead. Spirit and Cream and the Animals, and the Holy Trinity: Janis, Jimi, and Thomas Marion Douglas.

Tom Douglas most of all. His music brooded like an ancient ruin, dark, foreboding, hooded. Though his real affinity was to the gentler Mamas & Papas sound of an era already history, Mark was drawn to the Douglas touch – dark humor, darker twists – even as the Nietzschean fury implicit in the music repelled him. Perhaps it was that Douglas was everything Mark Meadows wasn't. Famous and vibrant and courageous and With It and irresistible to women. And an ace.

Aces and the Movement: in many ways they blasted into the mainstream of public consciousness flying formation like the heavy-metal warbirds Mark's father had led into battle over North Vietnam. There were more rock 'n' roll aces than among any other segment of the population. Their powers tended not to be subtle. Some had the ability to project dazzling displays of lights, others made extravagant music without the need of instruments. Most, though, played mind games with the audience by means of illusion or straight emotional manipulation. Tom Douglas – the Lizard King – was the head-trip master of them all.

◆

Spring arrived. Mark's faculty adviser pressured him for results. Mark began to despair, hating himself for his lack of resolution, or whatever defect of manhood kept him from precipitating himself into the drug scene, unable to continue his research until he did. He felt like the fly preserved in a lucite ice cube his parents had inexplicably possessed when he was a child.

April saw him withdraw from the world into microcosm, to the paper reality inside his peeling walls. He had all Destiny's records, but he couldn't play them now, or the Dead, or the Stones, or martyred Jimi. They were a taunt, a challenge he could not meet.

He ate his chocolate cookies and drank his soda pop and emerged from his room only to indulge a nostalgic childhood vice: love of comic books. Not only the old classics, fables of Superman and Batman from the days of innocence before humanity drew the wild card, but also their modern successors, which featured the fictionalized exploits of real aces, like the penny dreadfuls of the Old West. He devoured them with addict's fervor. They fulfilled by proxy the longing that had begun to eat him up from inside.

Not for metahuman powers; nothing so exotic. Not his craving for acceptance into the mysterious world of Counterculture, nor the desire for the lithe braless body of the former Kimberly Ann Cordayne that kept him awake night after sweaty night. What Mark Meadows desired more than anything in the world was *effective personality*. The ability to do, to achieve, to make a mark; good or bad, it scarcely mattered.

An evening toward April's end, Mark's retreat was shattered by a knock on his apartment door. He just lay there on his thin mattress on sheets unchanged in living memory, burying his long nose farther in the pages of Cosh Comics' *Turtle* number 92. His first reaction was fear, then anger at the intrusion. The world, he'd decided, was too much for him; he'd resolved to let it alone. Why couldn't it do as much for him?

Again the knock, imperative, threatening the thin veneer of wood over emptiness. He sighed.

'What do you want?' He edged the words with a whine.

'Are you going to let me in, or am I going to have to smash through this papier-mâché thing your pig landlord calls a door?'

For a moment Mark just lay there. Then he laid the comic on the mottled hardwood floor by the bed, and in his dingy tired socks padded to the door.

She stood there with hands on hips. She had on another Fourth of July skirt and a faded pink blouse, and against the spring Bay chill she'd pulled on a Levi's denim jacket with a black United Farm Workers eagle stenciled on the back and a peace symbol sewn on the left breast. She pushed into the room and slammed the door behind her.

'Look at this shit,' she said with a gesture that bisected the walls at breastbone level. 'How can a human being live like this? Living on processed sugar' – a nod at a plate of half-devoured cookies and a glass of brown soda that had been flat last week – 'and wadding your mind with that pig-authoritarian bullshit' – another knife-edge gesture toward *Turtle*, lying in a crumpled heap on the floor. She shook her head. 'You're eating yourself alive, Mark. You've cut yourself off from your friends, the people who love you. This has got to stop.'

Mark just stood there. He'd never seen her look so beautiful, though she was berating him, talking like his mother – or more correctly, his father. And then his skinny body began to vibrate like a tuning fork, because it struck him that she had said she loved him. It wasn't the sort of love he'd yearned and burned for from her. But emotionally he couldn't be a chooser.

'It's time you came out of your shell, Mark. Out of this womb-room of yours. Before you turn into something from *Night of the Living Dead*.'

'I've got work to do.'

She cocked an eyebrow and nudged *Turtle* 92 with a booted toe. 'You're coming with us.'

'Where?' He blinked. 'Who?'

'Haven't you heard?' A shake of the head. 'Of course not. You've been locked here in your room like some kind of monk. Destiny's back in town. They're playing a concert at the Fillmore tonight. My dad sent money. I have tickets for us – you, me, and Peter. So get your clothes on; we've got to leave now so we don't have to stand in line forever. And for god's sake try not to dress like such a straight.'

Peter looked like a surfer and thought he was Karl Marx. His looks reminded Mark uncomfortably of an earlier boyfriend of Kimberly Ann's, the football team captain who'd busted his nose in high school for staring at her too avidly. Standing outside in a threadbare tweed jacket and his one pair of jeans, breathing humid air and used smoke, he listened while Peter delivered the same lecture on the Historical Process all Sunflower's boyfriends gave him. When Mark didn't agree avidly enough – he could never make enough sense out of all these manifestos to form much of an opinion – Peter fixed him with an ice-blue Nordic glare and growled, 'I will destroy you.'

Later Mark found the line was a direct steal from the old man with the beard himself. Right now it made him want to melt through the tired pavement outside the auditorium. It didn't help that Sunflower was standing there beaming at the two of them as if they'd just won her a prize.

Fortunately Peter got into a screaming argument with the cops who frisked them for booze at the door, diverting his wrath from Mark. Guiltily, Mark hoped the cops would slam Peter over his blond head with a nightstick and haul him off to the slammer.

But Destiny was concluding its most tumultuous tour ever. Tom Douglas, whose consumption of booze and mind-altering chemicals was as legendary as his ace powers, had been getting mean drunk before every show. The Lizard King was on a rampage; last week's New Haven concert had culminated in a riot that trashed Yale's Old Campus and half the town. In their own clumsy way the cops were trying to avoid confrontation tonight. Frisking wasn't the shrewdest way to go about it, but the cops – and the Fillmore management – weren't eager to have the kids getting any wilder than Tom Douglas was going to make them anyway. So the audience got shaken down as they came in, but gingerly. Peter and his golden head went unbusted.

Mark's first Destiny concert was everything he might have imagined, raised to the tenth power. Douglas, characteristically, was two hours late onstage – equally characteristically, so fucked up he could barely stay standing, much less keep from pitching off into the mob of adoring fans. But the three musicians who made up the rest of Destiny were among the tightest performers in rock. Their expertise covered a multitude of sins. And gradually, around the solid skeleton of their playing, Douglas's ramblings and inchoate gestures resolved into something magical. The music was a blast of acid, dissolving Mark's lucite prison around him, until it reached his skin, and stung.

At the end of the set the lights went out like the shutting of a great door. Somewhere a drum began a slow, thick beating. From darkness broke a tormented guitar wail. A single blue spot spiked down to illuminate Douglas, alone with the mike in the center of the stage, his leather pants glittering like snakeskin. He began to sing, a soft low moan, increasing in urgency and volume, the intro to his masterpiece, 'Serpent Time.' His voice soared in a sudden shriek, and the lights and the band boomed suddenly about him like storm surf breaking against rocks, and they were launched on an odyssey to the furthest reaches of the night.

At last he took upon him the aspect of the Lizard King. A black aura beat from him like furnace heat and washed across the audience. Its effect was elusive, illusive, like some strange new drug: some onlookers it lifted to pinnacles of ecstasy, others it crammed down deep into hard-packed despair; some saw what they most desired, others stared straight down the gullet of Hell.

And in the center of that midnight radiance Tom Douglas seemed to grow larger than life, and now and again there flickered in place of his broad half-handsome features the head and flaring hood of a giant king cobra, black and menacing, darting left and right as he sang.

As the song climaxed in a howl of voice and organ and guitar,

Mark found himself standing with tears streaming unabashed down his thin cheeks, one hand holding Sunflower's, the other a stranger's, and Peter sitting glumly on the floor with his face in his hands, mumbling about decadence.

The next day was the last of April. Nixon invaded Cambodia. Reaction rolled across the nation's campuses like napalm.

Mark found Sunflower across the Bay, listening to speeches in the midst of an angry crowd in Golden Gate Park. 'I can't do it,' he shouted over the oratory din. 'I can't cross over – can't get outside myself.'

'Oh, *Mark!*' Sunflower exclaimed with an angry, tearful shake of her head. 'You're so selfish. So – so *bourgeois*.' She whirled away and lost herself in the forest of chanting bodies.

That was the last he saw of her for three days.

He searched for her, wandering the angry crowds, the thickets of placards denouncing Nixon and the war, through marijuana smoke that hung like scent around a honeysuckle hedge. His superstraight attire drew hostile looks; he shied away from a dozen potentially ugly encounters that first day alone, despairing ever more of his inability to become one with the pulsating mass of humanity around him.

The air was charged with revolution. He could feel it building like a static charge, could almost smell the ozone. He wasn't the only one.

He found her at an all-night vigil a few minutes before midnight of May third. She was crosslegged on a small patch of etiolated grass that had survived the onslaught of thousands of protesting feet, idly strumming a guitar as she listened to speeches shouted through a bullhorn. 'Where have you been?' Mark asked, sinking to the ankles in mud left by a passing shower.

She just looked at him and shook her head. Frantic, he plopped himself down beside her with a small squelching splash. 'Sunflower, where have you been? I've been looking all over for you.'

She looked at him at last, shook her head sadly. 'I've been with the people, Mark,' she said. 'Where I belong.'

Suddenly she leaned forward, caught him by the forearm with surprising strength. 'It's where you belong too, Mark. It's just that you're so – so selfish. It's as if you're armored in it. And you have so much to offer – now, when we need all the help we can get, to fight the oppressors before it's too late. Break out, Mark. Free yourself.'

Surprised, he saw a tear glimmering off in one corner of her eye. 'I've been trying to,' he said honestly. 'I ... I just can't seem to do it.'

A breeze was blowing in off the sea, cool and slightly sticky, occasionally shouldering aside the words garbling out of the megaphone. Mark shivered. 'Poor Mark. You're so uptight. Your parents, the schools, they've locked you into a straitjacket. You've got to break out.' She moistened her lips. 'I think I can help.'

Eagerly he leaned forward. 'How?'

'You need to tear down the walls, just like the song says. You need to open up your mind.'

She fumbled for a moment in a pocket of her embroidered denim jacket, held out her closed hand, palm up. 'Sunshine.' She opened her hand. A nondescript white tablet rested on the palm. 'Acid.'

He stared at it. Here it was, the object of his long vicarious study: quest and quest's goal alike. The difficulty of obtaining LSD legally – and his deeply engrained reluctance to attempt to attain it on the black market, along with his instinctive fear that his first attempt to purchase any would land him in San Quentin – had helped him put off the day of reckoning. Acid had been offered him before in hip camaraderie; always he refused it, telling himself it was because you never could be sure what was in a street drug, secretly because he'd always been afraid to step beyond the multi-plex door it presented. But now the world he yearned to join was surging about him like the sea, the woman he loved was offering him both challenge and temptation, and there it sat slowly melting in the rain.

He grabbed it from her, quickly and gingerly, as if suspecting it would burn his fingers. He poked it well down into a hip pocket of his black pipestem trousers, now so thoroughly imbued with mud they resembled an inept experiment in tie-dyeing. 'I've got to think about it, Sunflower. I can't rush something like this.' Not knowing what more to say or do, he started to untangle his lanky legs and stand.

She caught him by the arm again. 'No. Stay here with me. If you go home now you'll flush it down the john.' She drew him down beside her, closer than he'd ever actually been to her before, and he was suddenly acutely aware that her usual blond vanguard fighter was nowhere in evidence.

'Stay here, among the people. Right beside me,' she husked beside next to his ear. Her breath fluttered like an eyelash on his lobe. 'See what you have to gain. You're special, Mark. You could do so much that really *matters*. Stay with me tonight.'

Although the invitation wasn't as comprehensive as he might have wished, he settled himself back into the mud, and so the night passed in cold communion, the two of them huddling inside the dubious shelter of her jacket, shoulder to shoulder, while orators thundered revolution – the final confrontation with Amerika.

By early-morning gray the demonstration began to autolyze. They drifted together to a little all-night coffeehouse near the campus, ate an organic breakfast Mark couldn't taste, while Sunflower spoke urgently of the destiny lying in his reach: 'If only you could break *out* of yourself, Mark.' She reached out and took one of his long, pale hands in a tan compact one. 'When I ran into you at that club last fall, I was glad to see you because I guess I was homesick for the old days, bad as they were. You were a friendly face.'

He dropped his eyes, blinking rapidly, startled by her open admission that she sought him out because of what he was rather than who he was. 'That's changed, Mark.' He looked up again, tentative as a deer surprised in an early morning garden, ready to flee at the slightest hint of danger. 'I've come to appreciate you for what you are. And what you could be. There's a real person hiding beneath that crew cut and those horn-rimmed glasses and uptight

Establishment clothes you wear. A person crying to be let out.'

She put her other hand on top of his, stroked it lightly. 'I hope you let him out, Mark. I very much want to meet him. But the time's come for you to make the decision. I can't wait any longer. The time has come to choose, Mark.'

'You mean—' His tongue tripped. To his fatigue-fogged mind she seemed to be promising much more than friendship – and at the same time threatening to withdraw even that, if he could not bring himself to act.

He walked her home to the backstairs apartment. On the landing outside she grabbed him suddenly behind the neck, kissed him with surprising ferocity. Then she vanished inside, leaving him blinking.

'They finally taught them little Commie fuckers a lesson. Right on, I say; right fuckin' *on.*'

Standing to one side of the base of the skyscraper-in-progress, sipping hot tea from a thermos, Wojtek Grabowski listened to his coworkers discussing the news they'd just heard on the omnipresent transistor: the National Guard had fired into a rally on Ohio's Kent State University campus, several students known dead. They seemed to think it was high time.

He did too, but the news filled him with sadness, not elation.

Later, walking the beams up above the world so high, he reflected on the tragedy of it all. American soldiers were fighting to defend American values and rescue a brother nation from Communist aggression – and here were fellow Americans spitting on them, reviling them. Ho Chi Minh was portrayed as a hero, a would-be liberator.

Grabowski knew that was a lie. He had bled to learn just what Communists meant by 'liberation.' When he heard them hailed as heroes, his murdered friends and family rose up in a chorus at the back of his mind, crying denunciations.

It just wasn't what the protesters stood for, it was who they were. Children of privilege, overwhelmingly upper-middle-class, lashing out with the petulance of the spoiled against the very system that had given them comfort and security unparalleled in human history. 'Amerika eats its young,' they screamed – but he saw it differently: America was in danger of being devoured by its young.

They were led by false prophets, led horribly astray. By men like Tom Douglas. He'd read up on the singer since his song had so shocked him, last November. He knew now that Douglas was one of the tainted, marked by the alien poison released that afternoon in September of 1946, a child of the evil new dawn whose birth Grabowski himself had witnessed from the deck of a refugee ship moored off Governor's Island. No wonder the children rose like serpents to strike their elders, when they were counseled by men Satan had marked his own.

'Hey,' shouted the huge ex-Marine with the radio. 'Them hippie bastards are filling the streets down at city hall, bustin' windows and burnin' American flags!'

'The fuckers!'

'We gotta do something! It's revolution, right here and now.'

The young vet pulled on his Levi's jacket and settled his steel hat on his crew cut head. 'It's only a few blocks from here. I don't know about you, but I *am* gonna do something about it.' He led a rush toward the lift cage.

Grabowski would have shouted, No, wait, don't go! You must leave this to the authorities – if brother begins fighting brother, the forces of disorder will have won. But speech was denied him.

Because he was as furious as the rest, and fearful, for he alone had seen firsthand the consequences of this *revolution* everyone talked about. And in his emotion he had gripped a girder with all his might.

His fingers had sunk into the steel as if it were the soft sticky paste Americans called ice cream.

He was himself marked with the mark of the Beast.

Mark passed the rest of the day in a strange haze compounded of lust, hope, and fear. He missed the word from Kent State. While the rest of America reacted in horror or approbation, he spent the night locked in his apartment with a plateful of cookies, poring through his papers and well-thumbed books on LSD, taking out the acid tablet, turning it over and over in his fingers like a talisman. When the sun was weakly established in the sky a transient surge of resolution made him pop it in his mouth. A quick slug of flat orange soda pop washed it down before nerve could fail him again.

From his reading he knew acid generally took between an hour and an hour and a half to kick in. He tried to slide past the time by flipping from the Solomon anthology to Marvel comics to the *Zap* comix he'd accrued in his pursuit of understanding. After an hour, too nervous to await the drug's effects by himself any longer, he left his apartment. He had to find Sunflower, tell her he'd found his manhood, had taken the fateful step. Also, he was afraid to be alone when the acid hit.

Finding Sunflower was always like tracking a flower petal kicked about by the breeze, but he knew she gravitated toward UCB, which had long since replaced the moribund Haight as the locus of hip Bay Area culture, and she worked spasmodically at a head shop near People's Park. So, at about nine-thirty on the morning of May 5, 1970, he wandered into the park – and straight up against the most spectacular confrontation between aces of the entire Vietnam epoch.

For one brief shining moment, everyone – Establishment and enemies alike – *knew* the time had come for fighting in the streets. If the revolution was coming, it was coming *now*, in the first hot flush of fury following the Kent State massacre. Bay Area radical leaders had called a mammoth rally that morning in People's Park – and not just the police forces of the Bay Area but Ronald Reagan's own contingent of the National Guard had turned out to take them on.

By a quarter to ten the police had withdrawn from the park, establishing a *cordon sanitaire* around the campus area to prevent conflagration from spreading. It was just the kids and several deuce-and-a-half trucks spilling National Guardsmen in battle dress and gas masks from under their canvas covers forty meters away. With a loose clattering squeal and diesel chug, an M113 armored personnel carrier pulled to a halt behind the line of fixed bayonets, treads chewing at the sod like mouths. A man in captain's bars sat stiff and resolute in the cupola behind a fifty-caliber machine gun, wearing what looked like a Knute Rockne football helmet on his head.

Students ebbed from the green line like mercury from a fingertip. They'd been shouting to bring the war home; like their brothers in Ohio, it seemed they'd succeeded in doing just that. The Guard was regularly called in to break up demonstrations – but the boxy, ugly shape of the APC represented something new, a note of menace even the most sheltered couldn't miss. The crowd faltered, buzzing alarm.

Into the space between the lines a single figure stepped, slim in black leather. 'We came to be heard,' said Thomas Marion Douglas, his voice pitched to carry, 'and we're damned well going to *be* heard.'

Behind him the crowd began to solidify. Here was a superstar – an ace – taking his stand with them. Across the bayonet hedge the eyes of National Guard troopers flickered nervously behind the thick lenses of their masks. They were mostly young men who'd joined the Guard to avoid being drafted and sent to 'Nam; *they* knew who was facing them. Many owned Destiny records, had Douglas's haughty features staring down from posters on their bedroom walls. It was harder, somehow, to use bayonet or rifle-butt against someone you *knew*, even if it was only as a face on a record jacket or in a photo spread in *Life* magazine.

Their captain was of sterner stuff. He barked an order from the cupola. Tear-gas guns coughed, a half-dozen small comets arched down around Douglas and among the crowd surging up to join him. Billows of thick white smoke, CS gas, hid the singer from view.

Taking a shortcut through an alley, Mark had managed to miss the police lines. At this moment he emerged to a perfect sideline view of his very own idol standing with smoke swirling around him like a medieval martyr at the stake. He stopped and stared openmouthed at the confrontation shaping up before him.

The acid kicked in.

He felt reality's collagens dissolve, but the scene before him was too intense for hallucination. As the stiff morning breeze tattered the curtains of gas, a man standing with legs braced and fists raised appeared, auburn hair streaming back from a broad face that somehow flickered, interspersed with the head of a giant cobra, scales gleaming black, hood extended. The Guardsmen drew back; the Lizard King was in their midst.

The King moved forward in a sinuous glide. Uniforms gave way. Someone jabbed at him with a bayonet, or maybe just didn't back off quickly enough. A flick of the wrist, seeming lazy and disdainful but delivered with superhuman speed, and the rifle went spinning away as its owner stumbled backward to the grass with a yelp of terror. The captain in his iron box shouted hoarsely, trying to pull together the fraying strands of his men's determination.

But as he assumed his Lizard King aspect, Douglas loosed his mind games upon them; their eyes began to wander, seeking visions of desperate beauty or mind-numbing horror, each affected in his own way by the Lizard King's black aura.

The crowd was advancing now, chanting, shouting, menacing. The Guard captain did the only thing he could – his thumb pulsed once against the fifty-caliber's butterfly trigger. The gun vomited noise to bust glass and a Volkswagen flame, streaming tracers over the protesters' heads.

Triumphant an eyeblink before, the crowd came apart in screaming panic. The noise of the shots struck Mark like a giant pillow and spun him backward along endless, twisting corridors. But the scene stayed before him, light at the end of a tunnel, terrible and insistent. No one had been hit by the burst, but the protesters, like Mark himself, had come up for the first time against the reality their prophet Mao had tried to impress on them: where power comes from.

Tom Douglas was standing so close that muzzle-flash singed his eyebrows. He didn't flinch, though the noise struck him with a force a truckload of speakers couldn't match. Instead he met it with a roar of his own that sent Guardsmen tumbling like frightened puppies.

A prodigious leap and he stood on the upper deck of the APC. He bent, grasped the gun's barrel, heaved. The heavy Browning came away from its mounting like a sapling torn up by the roots. He held the weapon above his head, both-handed, then with a single convulsion of shoulders and biceps bent the barrel almost double. Having displayed his contempt for the Establishment and its war machines, he tossed the ruined machine gun after the troopers, now in full rout, and bent forward to pluck the now-terror-stricken captain from the cupola by the front of his blouse. He held the man up before him, legs kicking feebly.

And was struck down from behind by a blow driven with the full awesome strength of an unknown ace.

Mark snapped. With a shriek his soul vanished into swirling dark. His body turned and blindly ran.

Wojtek Grabowski saw the sinister serpent figure in black leap onto the APC and tear the weapon from its mountings and knew it had been the right choice to live.

Only devout Catholicism had stopped him from throwing himself to his death. He'd hurried from the site – already deserted as the workers rushed to attack the demonstrators – and home to his cramped apartment to a nightlong vigil of misery and silent prayer.

With dawn had indeed come Light; and he knew with a warm rush that his ace affliction was divinely sent, a blessing not a curse. Revolution threatened his adopted home, led by those who'd sworn allegiance to the forces of darkness. He had washed, dressed, made his own way to the park with peace in his heart.

Now he was confronted with a beast that seemed to have many heads, knew that he was face-to-face with the hated Tom Douglas himself.

Fury blasted into him. The ace transformation overtook him, bulking his muscles hugely to fill his baggy clothes to the bursting point. The steel hat of his profession was on his head, a yard-long pipefitter's wrench in his hand. Lingering doubts about using his strength against normal humans vanished; here was an enemy worthy of him, an ace, a traitor – a servitor of Hell.

He raced forward, vaulted onto the vehicle even as the snake-headed creature in black plucked its commander from the hatch. Students cried warnings Douglas didn't hear. Hardhat raised his wrench and struck at the back of a head now bushy-haired, now black and glabrous and obscene.

The blow would have pulped the skull of a normal human, or torn his head from his shoulders. But the constant shifting of Douglas's appearance confused Grabowski's aim. The blow glanced off. Douglas dropped the squirming officer and slumped bonelessly off the vehicle as momentum carried the wrench downward to buckle the aluminum top-armor like tinfoil.

Thinking he had killed him, Grabowski felt strength ebb. He needed rage to stay in the meta state, but all he felt was shame. Desperate, he turned to face the crowd. 'Go home,' he shouted in his hoarse, harsh English. 'Go home now. Is over. You must not fight no more. Obey your leaders and live in peace.'

They stood and stared at him with sheep's faces. Morning dew had sucked the tear gas down into it and poisoned the grass. A few white CS tendrils writhed on the ground like dying snakes. Tears streamed down Grabowski's face. *Wouldn't they listen?*

From the rear of the crowd a young man shouted, 'Fuck you! *Fuck you, you mother fuckin' fascist!*'

To have that epithet thrown at him, a man who still carried fascist bullets in his flesh, by some spoiled, insolent, ignorant puppy – anger filled him in abundance, and with it that inhuman strength.

Fortunately for him, because about then Tom Douglas got his wits back, jumped to his feet, grabbed the Hardhat by the ankles, and yanked his boots out from under him. Grabowski's helmet struck the deck like a giant cymbal. Every bit as furious as the man who'd taken him down, Douglas caught him as he fell, slammed him against the side of the vehicle, and began to piledrive blows into him with his own ace strength.

But Grabowski too had more than human durability. He dragged his wrench up between their bodies, thrust Douglas violently away. Douglas's feet slipped once on the wet grass, he caught himself with serpent agility and lunged forward to the attack – only to check himself and go up on tiptoe like a ballet dancer while a savage two-handed swipe of the wrench whined within an inch of his abdomen.

Douglas dove inside the wrench's deadly arc. He grappled his opponent, slamming punches in under the short ribs. Grabowski took a quick step backward, put a hand on Douglas's sternum, and pushed. Douglas fell back a step. The wrench lashed out, and this time only Douglas's metahuman reflexes saved him from catching it square in the front of his skull.

The tool-steel beak raked his forehead. Blood cascaded. He backpedaled furiously, wiping his eyes with one hand while the other thrashed about in an attempt to ward the following blow.

Hardhat swung his wrench like a baseball bat and took Douglas under the right arm with a sound that echoed through the park like a grenade explosion. Douglas went down. Hardhat stood over him with legs spread wide, raising the wrench slowly above his head like a headsman preparing the stroke. Blood drooled from the corner of his mouth. He was berserk, beyond compunction, beyond compassion, devoid of anything but the need to smash his opponent's skull like a snail on a rock.

But even as the gleaming blood-dripping wrench started down, a golden chain wrapped around it from behind and stopped the blow before it was launched.

With a fighter's reflex Hardhat instantly relaxed his arms, allowing his wrench to travel in the direction the sudden restraint pulled. Then he snapped the weapon forward and down, spinning as he did so to throw the entire augmented weight of his body against the slack. But as he moved, a houlihan rippled down the chain and it loosened, so that the wrench slithered free with a musical sound. Motion unchecked by expected impact, Hardhat spun around completely, staggering forward, continued through another half-turn so that he faced his opponent across five meters of muddy, trampled earth.

A youth stood there, slender and tall, golden hair falling to his shoulders, dangling a saucer-sized peace medallion of gold on a long chain. Despite Bay-morning chill he wore only a pair of jeans. To the short, dark Grabowski, he looked like nothing so much as a figure stepped from a Nazi recruiting poster.

'Who are you?' Hardhat snarled. Then, realizing he had spoken in his own tongue, repeated it in English.

The youth frowned briefly, as if perplexed. 'Call me Radical,' he said then with a grin. 'I'm here to protect the people.'

'*Traitor!*' Hardhat launched himself, swinging the wrench. Radical danced aside. No matter how savagely Hardhat attacked, no matter how he feinted, his opponent eluded him with apparent ease. Frustrated at his attempts to strike the golden youth, Hardhat turned once again to Douglas, still moaning on the ground. And Radical was there, peace symbol weaving a golden figure of eight in the air before him, warding Hardhat's most ferocious blows with sparks of coruscance while soldiers and students alike stood transfixed by the spectacle.

But if Hardhat couldn't strike past the amulet, Radical seemed unwilling or unable to counterattack. Noting this, Hardhat backed away, waving his wrench menacingly. After a moment Radical followed, flowing like mist. Hardhat circled widdershins. Radical kept pace. Slowly the Pole drew his long-haired opponent away from the recumbent Douglas.

Lightning fast, he wheeled left and hurled himself at the onlookers. Though his speed wasn't as great as Radical's it was greater than a norm's, and he was among the crowd of protesters before any could react, wrench upraised to smash. Caught by surprise, Radical was unable to react in time.

The wrench stayed up, frozen like a fly in lucite. Radical sprang forward, driven to attack by desperation, swinging his peace medallion at the back of the tree-trunk neck below the helmet's sweep. It connected with the chunk of an ax striking wood; not as mighty a blow as the Lizard King could have delivered, not to be compared in the least with the terrible force of Grabowski's wrench, but sufficient to scramble Hardhat's senses, send him pitching face first into the grass and mud and crumpled signs.

Radical poised above him, swinging his medallion in a slow circle at his side. A moment later Douglas joined him, rubbing his side and grimacing. 'Think he cracked a few ribs, there,' he rasped in his familiar dirt-road baritone. 'What the hell?'

Even as they watched, the inhumanly squat form of Hardhat dwindled into a stocky, balding man in baggy clothes, lying with his face in the mud, sobbing as if his heart were broken. Shaking his shaggy mane, Douglas turned to his benefactor. 'I'm Tom Douglas. Thanks for saving my ass.'

'The pleasure's mine, man.'

And then Douglas stepped forward and embraced the taller blond man, and a cheer went up from the crowd. The National Guard soldiers were already in retreat, leaving their APC behind. The revolution would not come today, or ever, perhaps, but the kids had been saved.

As the television cameras churned, Tom Douglas proclaimed Radical his comrade in arms and called into being a celebration as wild as any the Bay Area had known. While the police kept their uneasy perimeter and the National Guard licked its wounds, thousands of kids poured into the park to hail the conquering heroes. The abandoned M113 provided an impromptu stage. Tents dotted the park like colorful mushrooms. Music and drugs and booze flowed freely, all that day and all that night.

At the center of it all glowed Tom Douglas and his mysterious benefactor, surrounded by beautiful, compliant women – none more so than the willowy brunette with eyes like impacted ice everybody called Sunflower, who appeared to have sprouted from Radical's hip like a postnatal Siamese twin. The newcomer would give no other name than Radical, and he turned away all questions as to his origin, and how he happened to be at that place at that time, with a grin and a shy 'I was here because I was needed here, man.' At dawn the next day, he slipped quietly away from the dwindling festivities and vanished.

He was never seen again.

In the spring of 1971, charges against Tom Douglas stemming from the People's Park confrontation were dropped – at the recommendation of Dr. Tachyon, who'd been called in by SCARE to help investigate the incident – just as Destiny's album City of Night *hit the stands. Shortly thereafter, Douglas electrified the rock world by announcing he was retiring – not just as a musician, but as an ace.*

So he took Doc Tachyon's experimental trump cure, and was one of the fortunate thirty percent on whom it worked. The Lizard King disappeared forever, leaving behind Thomas Marion Douglas, norm.

Who was dead in six months. His overuse of drugs and alcohol had achieved such heroic proportions that only ace endurance kept him alive. Once that was gone his health deteriorated rapidly. He died of pneumonia in a seedy hotel in Paris in the fall of 1971.

As for Hardhat – interviewed by Dr. Tachyon the day after the confrontation, hospitalized for observation with a mild concussion, Wojtek Grabowski insisted his foes had not defeated him. 'All you need is love' ran the received wisdom of the day – and love had brought him down. Or so he claimed. Because when he hurled himself against the crowd, he found himself staring into the face of Anna, his wife, lost to him for two decades and a half.

Not quite Anna, he said tearfully; there were differences, in the color of hair, the shape of nose. And, of course, Anna would not now be a woman in her early twenties.

But their daughter would be. Grabowski was convinced he had seen, at last, the child he had never known. The horrible knowledge that his anger had almost led him to destroy that which he cherished most in all the world bled the strength from him in an instant, so that what Radical's medallion struck was a being in transition from full ace strength to a normal human state.

Touched, Dr. Tachyon helped Grabowski search the Bay Area for his daughter. Privately he never expected to find her; at the moment Grabowski believed he saw her, Tom Douglas had been recovering, his Lizard King aspect still active. And that black aura could make you see what you most wished to see. As far as Tachyon was concerned, it had.

To none of his surprise, the search turned up nothing. In any event, he was able to devote little time to Grabowski, no matter how much the man's plight affected him. He returned East after three weeks of assisting Grabowski and SCARE investigators. A couple of months later he learned that Grabowski had vanished, no doubt to pursue the search for his family. Since then, no more had been heard of Wojtek Grabowski, or Hardhat.

And as for Radical ...

In the early morning hours of May 6th, 1970, Mark Meadows staggered out of an alley opening into People's Park with his head full of white noise, clad only in his one pair of jeans. He had no memory of what had happened to him, scarcely realized where he was. He found himself amongst the remnants of last night's celebrants, heavy-eyed with fatigue but still chattering like speed freaks about the fantastic events of the last twenty-four hours. 'You should have *been* there, man,' they told him. And as they described the events of yesterday morning, strange fragments of memory, surreal and disjointed, began to bubble to the surface of Mark's mind: perhaps he *had*.

Was he remembering his own experiences? Or was the last of the acid casting up images to match the breathless, vivid descriptions a dozen eyewitnesses pressed on him at once? He didn't know. All that he knew was that the Radical represented the realization of his wildest dream: Mark Meadows as Hero.

And when he saw Sunflower standing nearby, hair disarrayed, eyes dreamy, and she said to him, 'Oh, Mark, I just met the most *fantastic* dude,' he knew that whatever hopes he'd had of being more than Sunflower's friend had just gone *poof*. Unless he were, in fact, the Radical.

He knew what to do, of course. He'd learned more than he consciously realized during his street apprenticeship with Sunflower;

by nightfall he was crosslegged on his own mattress among his cookies and comic books, clutching two weeks' living-expenses worth of LSD. He was so exalted when he popped the first tab that he barely needed the drug to get off.

Which was all he did. No Radical transformation. Nothing. He just ... *tripped out*.

For a week he didn't leave the apartment, living on moldy crumbs, slamming down increasing doses of acid as fast as the effects of the last charge faded. *Nothing.* When at last he staggered forth for more drugs he'd already taken on a blur around the edges.

So began the quest.

INTERLUDE THREE

From 'Wild Card Chic,'
by Tom Wolfe, *New York*, June 1971.

Mmmmmmmmmmmmmmmm. These are nice. Little egg rolls, filled with crabmeat and shrimp. Very tasty. A bit greasy, though. Wonder what the aces do to get the grease spots off the fingers of their gloves? Maybe they prefer the stuffed mushrooms, or the little Roquefort cheese morsels rolled in crushed nuts, all of which are at this very moment being offered them on silver platters by tall, smiling waiters in Aces High livery ... These are the questions to ponder on these Wild Card Chic evenings. For example, that black man there by the window, the one shaking hands with Hiram Worchester himself, the one with the black silk shirt and the black leather coat and that absolutely unbelievable swollen forehead, that *dangerous*-looking black man with the cocoa-colored skin and almond-shaped eyes, who came off the elevator with three of the most ravishing women any of them have ever seen, even here in this room full of beautiful people – is he, an ace, a palpable ace, going to pick up a little egg roll stuffed with shrimp and crabmeat when the waiter drifts by, and just pop it down the gullet without so much as missing a syllable of Hiram's cultured geniality, or is he more of a stuffed mushroom man at that ...

Hiram is splendid. A large man, a *formidable* man, six foot two and broad all over, in a bad light he might pass for Orson Welles. His black, spade-shaped beard is immaculately groomed, and when he smiles his teeth are very white. He smiles often. He is a warm man, a gracious man, and he greets the aces with the same quick firm handshake, the same pat on the shoulder, the same familiar exhortation with which he greets Lillian, and Felicia and Lenny, and Mayor Hartmann, and Jason, John, and D.D.

How much do you think I weigh? he asks them jovially, and presses them for a guess, three hundred pounds, three fifty, four hundred. He chuckles at their guesses, a deep chuckle, a resonant chuckle, because this huge man weighs only thirty pounds and he's set up a scale right here in the middle of Aces High, his lavish new restaurant high atop the Empire State Building, amid the crystal and silver and crisp white tablecloths, a scale like you might find in a gym, just so he can prove his point. He hops on and off nimbly whenever he's challenged. Thirty pounds, and Hiram does enjoy his little joke. But don't call him Fatman anymore. This ace has come out of the deck now, he's a new kind of ace, who knows all the right people and all the right wines, who looks absolutely correct in his tuxedo, and owns the highest, *chic*-est restaurant in town.

What an evening! The tables are set all around, the silver gleaming, the tremulous little flames of the candles reflected in the encircling windows, a bottomless blackness with a thousand stars, and it is that moment Hiram loves. There seem to be a thousand stars inside and a thousand stars outside, a Manhattan tower full of stars, the highest grandest tower of all, with marvelous people drifting through the heavens, Jason Robards, John and D.D. Ryan, Mike Nichols, Willie Joe Namath, John Lindsay, Richard Avedon, Woody Allen, Aaron Copland, Lillian Hellman, Steve Sondheim, Josh Davidson, Leonard Bernstein, Otto Preminger, Julie Belafonte, Barbara Walters, the Penns, the Greens, the O'Neals ... and now, in this season of Wild Card Chic, the aces.

That knot of people there, that cluster of enthralled, adoring, *excited* people with the tall, thin champagne glasses in their hands and the rapt expressions on their faces, in their midst, the object of all their attention, is a little man in a crushed-velvet tuxedo, an *orange* crushed-velvet tuxedo, with tails, and a ruffled lemon-yellow shirt, and long shiny red hair. Tisianne brant Ts'ara sek Halima sek Ragnar sek Omian is holding court again, the way he must have done once on Takis, and some of the marvelous people about him are even calling him 'Prince' and 'Prince Tisianne,' though they don't often pronounce it right, and to most of them, now and forever, he will remain Dr. Tachyon. He's *real*, this prince from another planet, and the very *idea* of him – an exile, a hero, imprisoned by the Army and persecuted by HUAC, a man who has lived two human lifetimes and seen things none of them can imagine, who labors selflessly among the wretched of Jokertown, well, the excitement runs through Aces High like a rogue hormone, and Tachyon seems excited too, you can tell by the way his lilac-colored eyes keep slipping over to linger on the slender Oriental woman who arrived with that other ace, that dangerous-looking Fortunato fellow.

'I've never met an ace before,' the refrain goes. 'This is a first for me.' The thrill vibrates through the air of Aces High, until the whole eighty-sixth floor is *thrumming* to it, a first for me, never known anyone like you, a first for me, always wanted to meet you, a first for me, and somewhere in the damp soil of Wisconsin, Joseph McCarthy spins in his coffin with a high, thin whirring sound, and all his worms have come home to roost now. These are no Hollywood poseurs, no dreary politicians, no faded literary flowers, no pathetic jokers begging for help, these are *real nobility*, these aces, these enchanting electric aces.

So beautiful. Aurora, sitting on Hiram's bar, showing the long, long legs that have made her the toast of Broadway, the men clustered around her, laughing at her every joke. Remarkable, that red-gold hair of hers, curled and perfumed, tumbling down across her bare shoulders, and those bruised, pouting lips, and when she laughs, the northern lights flicker around her and the men burst into applause. She's signed to make her first feature film next year, playing opposite Redford, and Mike Nichols will direct. The first ace to star in a major motion picture since – no, we wouldn't want to mention *him*, would we? Not when we're having so much fun.

So astonishing. The things they can *do*, these aces. A dapper little man dressed all in green produces an acorn and a pocketful of potting soil, borrows a brandy snifter from the bartender, and grows a small oak tree right there in the center of Aces High. A dark woman with sharply sculpted features arrives in jeans and a denim shirt, but when Hiram threatens to turn her away, she claps her hands together and suddenly she is armored head to toe in black metal that gleams like ebony. Another clap, and she's wearing an evening gown, green velvet, off the shoulder, perfect for her, and even Fortunato looks twice. When the ice for the champagne buckets runs low, a burly rock-hard black man steps forward, takes the Dom Perignon in hand, and grins boyishly as frost rimes the outside of the bottle. 'Just right,' he says when he gives the bottle to Hiram. 'Any longer and I'd freeze it solid.' Hiram laughs and congratulates him, though he doesn't believe he has the honor. The black man smiles enigmatically. 'Croyd,' is all he says.

So romantic, so tragic. Down there by the end of the bar, in gray leather, that's Tom Douglas, isn't it? It is, it *is*, the Lizard King himself, I hear they just dropped the charges, but what *courage* that took, what commitment, and say, whatever happened to that Radical fellow who helped him out? Douglas looks terrible, though. Wasted, haunted. They crowd close around him, and his eyes snap up and briefly the specter of a great black cobra looms above him, dark counterpoint to Aurora's shimmering colors, and silence ripples across Aces High until they leave the Lizard King alone again.

So dashing, so flamboyant. Cyclone knows how to make an entrance, doesn't he? But that's why Hiram insisted on the Sunset Balcony, after all, not just for drinks out under the summer stars and the glorious view of the sun going down across the Hudson, but to give his aces a place to land, and it's only natural that Cyclone would be the first. Why ride the elevator when you can ride the winds? And the way he dresses – all in blue and white, the jumpsuit makes him look so *lithe* and *rakish*, and that cape, the way it hangs from his wrists and ankles, and then balloons out in flight when he whips up his winds. Once he's inside, shaking Hiram's hand, he takes off his aviator's helmet. He's a fashion leader, Cyclone, the first ace to wear an honest-to-god *costume*, and he started back in '65, long before these other aces-come-lately, wore his colors even through those two dreary years in 'Nam, but just because a man wears a mask doesn't mean he has to make a fetish of hiding his identity, does it? Those days are past, Cyclone is Vernon Henry Carlysle of San Francisco, the whole world knows, the fear is dead, this is the age of Wild Card Chic when *everyone* wants to be an ace. Cyclone came a long way for this party, but the gathering wouldn't be complete without the West Coast's premier ace, would it?

Although – taboo thought that it is, with stars and aces glittering all around on a night when you can see fifty miles in every direction – really, the gathering isn't *quite* complete, is it? Earl Sanderson is still in France, though he did send a brief, but sincere, note of apology in reply to Hiram's invitation. A great man, that one, a great man greatly wronged. And David Harstein, the lost Envoy, Hiram even ran an ad in the *Times*, DAVID WON'T YOU PLEASE COME HOME? but he's not here either. And the Turtle, where is the Great and Powerful Turtle? There were rumors that on this special magical night, this halcyon time for Wild Card Chic, the Turtle would come out of his shell and shake Hiram's hand and announce his name to the world, but no, he doesn't seem to be here, you don't think … god, no … you don't think those old stories are *true* and the Turtle is a joker after all?

Cyclone is telling Hiram that he thinks his three-year-old daughter has inherited his wind powers, and Hiram beams and shakes his hand and congratulates the doting daddy and proposes a toast. Even his powerful, cultivated voice cannot cut through the din of the moment, so Hiram makes a small fist and does that thing he does to the gravity waves and makes himself even lighter than thirty pounds, until he drifts up toward the ceiling. Aces High goes silent as Hiram floats beside his huge art-deco chandelier, raises his Pimm's Cup, and proposes his toast. Lenny Bernstein and John Lindsay drink to little Mistral Helen Carlysle, second generation ace-to-be. The O'Neals and the Ryans lift their glasses to Black Eagle, the Envoy, and the memory of Blythe Stanhope van Renssaeler. Lillian Hellman, Jason Robards, and Broadway Joe toast the Turtle and Tachyon, and everyone drinks to Jetboy, father of us all.

And after the toasting come the causes. The Wild Card Acts are still on the books, and in this day and age that's a disgrace, something must be done. Dr. Tachyon needs help, help for his Jokertown Clinic, help with his lawsuit, how long has *that* been dragging on now, his suit to win custody of his spaceship back from the government that wrongly impounded it in 1946 – the shame of it, to take his *ship* after he came all that way to help, it makes them angry, all of them, and *of course* they pledge their help, their money, their lawyers, their influence. A beautiful woman on either side of him, Tachyon speaks of his ship. It's alive, he tells them, and by now it's certainly lonely, and as he talks he begins to weep, and when he tells them that the ship's name is *Baby*, there's a tear behind many a contact lens, threatening the artfully applied mascara below. And of course something must be done about the Joker Brigade, that's little better than genocide, and …

But that's when dinner is served. The guests drift to their assigned seats, Hiram's seating chart is a masterpiece, measured and spiced as precisely as his gourmet food, everywhere just the right balance of wealth and wisdom and wit and beauty and bravura and celebrity, with an ace at every table of course, of *course*, otherwise someone might go away feeling cheated, in this year and month and hour of Wild Card Chic …

DOWN DEEP

by Edward Bryant
and Leanne C. Harper

As she dodged cabs, crossing Central Park West and entering the park, Rosemary Muldoon knew she was in for a difficult afternoon. She distractedly maneuvered through a late-afternoon mob of dog-walkers gathered on the sidewalk and looked for Bagabond.

As an intern with New York's Social Services Department, Rosemary got all the interesting cases, the ones no one else would handle. Bagabond, the enigmatic transient she had drawn this afternoon, was about the worst. Bagabond had to be at least sixty, and smelled as if she hadn't bathed in half that time. That was something Rosemary had never gotten used to. Her family was not what one could call nice, but each person bathed daily. Her father insisted on it. And nobody refused her father.

She had been drawn to the detritus of society precisely because of their alienation. Few had any connection with their pasts or their families. Rosemary recognized this but told herself that it did not matter what the reason was; the result was the important thing. She could help them.

Bagabond was standing beneath a grove of oaks. As Rosemary approached her, she thought she saw Bagabond gesturing and talking to a tree. Shaking her head, Rosemary pulled out Bagabond's file. It was slim. Real name unknown, age unknown, place of origin unknown, history unknown. According to the sparse information, the woman lived on the streets. The best guess of the previous social worker was that Bagabond had been released from a state institution to provide space. The bag lady was paranoid but probably not dangerous. Because Bagabond had refused to give any information, there had been no way to help her. Rosemary put away the paperwork and marched toward the old woman dressed in layers of ragged clothing.

'Hello, Bagabond. My name is Rosemary and I'm here to help you.' Her gambit failed. Bagabond turned her head and stared at two kids throwing a Frisbee.

'Don't you want a nice, safe, warm place to sleep? With hot meals and people to talk to?' The only response she received was from the biggest cat she had ever seen outside a zoo. It had walked over to Bagabond and was now staring at Rosemary.

'You could take a bath.' The bag lady's hair was filthy. 'But I need to know your name.' The huge black cat looked at Bagabond and then glared at Rosemary.

'Why don't you come with me and we'll talk?' The cat began to growl.

'Come on …' As Rosemary reached toward Bagabond, the cat sprang. Rosemary jumped back, tripping over the handbag she'd set on the ground. Lying on her back, she could see eye to eye with the very angry feline.

'Nice kitty. Stay right there.' As she started to get up, the black cat was joined by a slightly smaller calico cat.

'Okay. I'll see you another time.' Rosemary grabbed her bag and the file and retreated.

Her father never understood why she wanted to deal with the poor of the city, the 'filth,' as he called them. Tonight she was going to have to suffer through another chaperoned evening with her parents and her fiancé. An arranged marriage, in this day and age. She wished it was easier to stand up to her father and say no. Her family was a creature of tradition. She just did not fit in.

Rosemary had her own apartment which, until recently, she had shared with C.C. Ryder. C.C. was a vocal hippie. Rosemary had made sure that her father and C.C. never met. The consequences were too horrible to consider. Keeping her two lives separate was essential.

It was a line of thought that took her too close to the pain. C.C. was gone. She had disappeared into the city. Rosemary was frightened for C.C. and for herself, for what it meant about the city.

Rosemary looked up from the park bench where she had collapsed. It was time to get the file back to the office and head for Columbia and class.

'What a terrific night.' Lombardo 'Lucky Lummy' Lucchese was feeling great, just great. After two whole years of working numbers and small-time protection, he had at last made it into the foremost of the Five Families. They knew talent and he had plenty. Walking down 81st toward the park with his three friends, he was on top of the world.

He had to go pay his respects to his fiancée, Maria. What a mouse! But a mouse who was the only child of Don Carlo Gambione could be very valuable in the years to come. Later he would celebrate with his buddies. Now he had to get some cash so he could buy mousy Maria some nice flowers to show his devotion. Maybe carnations.

'I'm gonna go downstairs. Pick up some money,' Lummy said.

'Want some company?' Joey 'No-Nose' Manzone asked.

'Nah. You kiddin'? After next week, I'll be in the big money. I just wanna do one more job. For old time's sake. See ya later.'

Splashing through oil-iridescent puddles, Lummy whistled as he swung along toward the illuminated globe marking the stairs to the 81st Street subway station. Nothing could bring him down tonight.

What a perfectly dreadful evening, Sarah Jarvis thought. The sixty-eight-year-old woman had never in her life expected to be invited to an Amway party. The very thought. It had taken hours for her friend and her to leave. Of course, it was raining by that time and, of course, there was not an on-duty cab to be found. Her friend lived in the next building. Sarah had to go all the way uptown to Washington Heights.

Sarah hated the subway. That stale smell always nauseated her. She disliked the noisy parts of the city anyway, and the subway was among the loudest. Tonight, though, everything was quiet. Alone on the platform, Sarah shivered under her tweed jacket.

Peering over the edge of the platform and along the tunnel, she thought she saw the light of the uptown AA local. Something was there, but it seemed to move so slowly. Sarah turned away and looked at the advertising placards. She examined the poster calling for the re-election of that nice Mr. Nixon. In the adjacent newspaper vending machines, the headlines told of burglars breaking into a Washington hotel and apartment house. Watergate? What a funny name for a building, she thought. The *Daily News* led with a story about the so-called Subway Vigilante. The police were attributing five slayings over the past week to the mysterious killer. The victims had all been drug dealers and other criminals. The murders had all taken place in the subways. Sarah shuddered. The city was quite different than it had been in her childhood.

First she heard the steps, clattering down the stairs and past the deserted token booth. Then whistling, a peculiar tuneless drone, as the person entered the station. Despite herself, she was caught between apprehension and relief. Somewhat ashamed of her reaction, she decided she wouldn't mind a little human company.

As soon as she saw him, she was not so sure. Sarah had never been all that fond of black leather jackets, particularly those worn by slightly greasy, smirking young men. She turned her back firmly and focused on the wall across the tracks.

As the old woman turned her back, Lucky Lummy grinned broadly and touched the tip of his tongue to his upper lip.

'Hey, lady, got a light?'

'No.'

One corner of Lummy's mouth twitched as he moved toward her back. 'Come on, lady, be nice.'

He missed the tension gathering in her shoulders as Sarah remembered that self-defense class she had attended last winter.

'Just give me the purse, lad— *aiee!*' He screamed as Sarah turned and crushed his instep with her sensible but sophisticated beige pump. Lummy jerked back and aimed a punch at her face. Sarah evaded him by stepping backward and slipping on something slimy. Lummy grinned and started toward her.

Wind rushed past them from the tunnel as the AA train approached the station.

Neither noticed that a dozen people had all managed to get to the subway entrance simultaneously. Most of the crowd had attended a late showing of *The Godfather* and were continuing an animated discussion of whether or not Coppola had exaggerated the Mafia's role in modern crime.

Someone who *hadn't* been at the screening was a transit worker who had had a long and trying day. He just wanted to go home and get dinner, not necessarily in that order. The newspapers had been pushing again; even that Joker Rights stuff couldn't keep them occupied all the time. The transit man had been pulled off his regular track-checking duties to spend eighteen hours searching vainly for alligators in sewers and subway tunnels, conduit shafts, and deep utility holes. He mentally cursed his employers for kowtowing to the sensationalist press, and especially cursed the bird-dogging reporters he'd finally ditched.

The transit worker hung back a little, trying to stay out of the melee as the group fumbled for tokens and started through the gates. The moviegoers chattered as they went.

With a roar and braking screech of metal on metal, the AA local burst out of the tunnel.

On the platform, all manner of people confronted each other. Swearing in Italian, Lummy let go of his victim and looked around for a bolt-hole.

The first two couples had entered and were staring at the scene in front of them. One of the men moved toward Lucky Lummy as the other man grabbed his date and tried to retreat.

The doors of the local hissed open. At this time of night, there were few passengers on the train and no one got off.

'There's never a transit cop when you need one,' said the

wouldbe rescuer. Momentarily, Lummy considered leaping for the punk and punching out his lights. Instead he feinted at the man, then half-limped, half-ran into the last car. The doors snapped closed and the train began to move. It might have been the light, but the bright grafitti on the sides seemed to change.

From inside the car, Lucky Lummy laughed and gestured obscenely at Sarah, who was feeling for bruises and trying to re-arrange her soiled clothing. Lummy aimed a second gesture at the woman's inadvertent rescuers as the entire group converged on Sarah.

Abruptly Lummy's face contorted with fear and then outright terror as he began beating on the doors. The man who had tried to stop Lummy caught one last glimpse of him clawing at the rear door of the car as the train sped into darkness.

'What a creep!' said the date of the would-be rescuer. 'Was he one of those jokers?'

'Naw,' said his friend. 'Just a garden-variety asshole.'

Everyone froze as they heard the screams from the uptown tunnel. Over the diminishing roar of the local, they could hear Lummy's hopeless, agonized cries. The train vanished. But the screams lasted until at least 83rd Street.

The transit worker moved toward the downtown tunnel as the hero of the hour was congratulated by the mostly unharmed Sarah, as well as by the rest of the onlookers. Another transit employee came down the steps at the other end of the platform.

'Hey!' he yelled. 'Sewer Jack! Jack Robicheaux. Don't you ever sleep?'

The exhausted man ignored him and let himself through a metal access door. As he walked down the tunnel, he began shedding his clothes. A watcher might have thought she had seen a man squat-ting down and crawling along the damp floor of the tunnel, a man who had grown a long snout filled with sharp, misshapen teeth and a muscular tail capable of smashing the watcher into jam. But no one saw the flash of greenish-gray scales as the erstwhile transit worker joined the darkness and was gone.

Back on the 81st Street platform, the spectators were still so transfixed by the echoes of Lummy's dying screams that few noted the rumbling, bass roar from the other direction.

Her last class over, Rosemary walked wearily toward the 116th Street subway entrance. One more task completed for today. Now she was on her way to her father's apartment to see her fiancé. She had never had much enthusiasm for that, but these days she had little enthusiasm for anything at all. Rosemary moved through the days wishing that something in her life would be resolved.

She shifted her armload of books to her right arm as, one-handed, she sifted through her purse for a token. Walking through the gate, she paused, standing to one side to stay out of the path of the other students. Judging from the placards carried by a number of the people, the latest antiwar rally must have just ended. Rosemary noted some apparently normal kids carrying signs lettered with the Joker Brigade's informal slogan: LAST TO GO – FIRST TO DIE.

C.C. had always been into that. She had even sung her songs at a few of the less-rowdy gatherings. One day she had even brought home a fellow activist, a guy named Fortunato. While it was nice that the man was involved with the Joker Rights movement, Rosemary didn't like pimps, geishas or no geishas, in her apartment. It had caused one of the few fights she had ever had with C.C. In the end C.C. had agreed to check with Rosemary more closely about future dinner guests.

C.C. Ryder had tried and tried to convince Rosemary to become active, but Rosemary believed that helping a few people directly could do as much good as standing around shouting condemnations of the 'Establishment.' Probably a lot more good. Rosemary knew she came from a conservative family. Her room-mate rarely let her forget it.

Rosemary took a deep breath and launched herself into the flood of people. All the late classes had evidently gotten out at the same time.

As Rosemary walked onto the platform, she moved around the rear of the crowd so she could end up at the far side of the waiting area. She didn't feel like being that close to people right now. Moments later she felt the flood of dank tunnel air and shivered inside her damp sweater.

Deafening, depressing, the local swept by her. All the cars had been defaced, but the last car was even more peculiarly decorated. Rosemary was reminded of the tattooed woman in the Ringling Brothers show she had seen in the old Garden. She had often wondered at the psychology of the kids who wrote on the sides of the trains. Sometimes she didn't like what their words revealed. New York was not always a nice place to live.

I won't think about it. She thought about it. The image of C.C. lying comatose in the I.C. ward of St. Jude's glittered in her mind. She saw the shiny life-support machines. Because C.C. had had no relatives to notify, Rosemary had even been there when the nurses changed the dressings. She remembered the bruises, the black and poisonously blue patches that covered most of C.C.'s body. The doctors were unsure exactly how many times the young woman had been raped. Rosemary had wanted to empathize. She couldn't. She wasn't even sure how to begin. All she could do was to wait and hope. And then C.C. had vanished from the hospital.

The last car looked to be empty. As Rosemary started toward it, she glanced at the graffito. She stopped dead, her eyes tracking the words written on the dark side of the car:

Parsley, sage, Rosemary?
Time …
Time is for others, not for me.

'C.C.! What?' Disregarding the other people who had spotted the unoccupied car, she pushed her way to the doors. They were closed. Rosemary dropped her books and tried to claw the doors open. She felt a nail break. Failing, she beat on the doors until the train began to pull slowly out of the station.

'No!'

Rosemary's eyes filled with tears at the final sight of her name and another of C.C.'s lyrics:

You can't fight the end,
But you can take revenge.

Rosemary said nothing else, only stared after the train. She looked down at her fists. The apparently steel door had been soft and yielding, warm. Had someone given her acid? Was it a coincidence? Was C.C. living underground? Was C.C. alive at all?

It was a long time before the next train came.

He hunted in the near-darkness.

The hunger was upon him; the hunger that seemed never to be fully satisfied. And so he hunted.

Dimly, ever so faintly, he recalled a time and a place when it had been different. He had been someone – what was that? – something else.

He looked, but saw little. In this gloom and especially in the foul water choked with debris, his eyes served little use. More important were the tastes and smells, the tiny particles that told him both what lay in the distance – meals to seek patiently – and of the immediate satisfactions that hovered, unsuspecting, just beyond the length of his snout.

He could hear the vibrations: the powerful, slow movements from side to side as his tail muscled through the water; the crushing, but distant waves beating down from the city above; the myriad tiny actions of food scurrying about in the darkness.

The filthy water broke around his wide, flat snout, the current streaming to either side of the raised nostrils. Occasionally the transparent membranes would slide down across the protruding eyes, then slip up again.

As large as he was – barely able to fit through some of the tunnels he had traversed during this time of feeding – he made very little noise. Tonight most of the sounds that accompanied him came from the prey, were cried out during the devouring.

His nostrils gave him the first inkling of the feast to come, but was shortly followed by messages from his ears. Although he hated to leave this sanctuary that covered nearly all of his body, he knew he must go where the food was. The mouth of another tunnel loomed to one side. There was barely enough room in the passageway for even so flexible a body as his to turn and enter the new watercourse. The water became shallower and ended altogether within two body-lengths of the entrance.

It didn't matter. His legs worked well enough, and he could move almost as silently as before. He could still smell the prey waiting for him somewhere ahead. Nearer. Near. Very close. He could hear sounds: squeaks, squeals, the scurrying of feet, the brush of furry bodies against stone.

They wouldn't expect him; there were few predators in these tunnels deep down. He was upon them in an instant, the first one crushed between his jaws, its death-cry warning the others. The prey scattered in panic. Except for those without escape routes, there was no attempt to fight back. They ran.

Most who lived longest scurried away from the monster in their midst – and encountered the bricked-up end of the tunnel. Others tried to sprint around him – one even daring to leap across his scaly back – but the lashing tail smashed them against the unyielding walls. Still others ran directly into his mouth, cowering only in the split second before the great teeth came together.

The agonized squeals peaked and subsided. The blood flowed deliciously. The meat and hair and bones lay satisfyingly in his stomach. A few among the prey still lived. They crawled away from the slaughter as best they could. The hunter started to follow, but his meal sat heavily. For now he was too sated to follow, or to care. He made it as far as the edge of the water and then stopped. Now he wanted to sleep.

First he would break the silence. It was allowed. This was his territory. It was *all* his territory. The great jaws opened and he issued a penetrating, rumbling roar that echoed for many seconds through the seemingly endless labyrinth of tunnels and ducts, passageways and stone corridors.

When the echoes finally died, the predator slept. But he was the only one.

Rosemary said hello to Alfredo, who was on security duty tonight. He smiled at her as she signed in, and shook his head when he saw the stack of books she carried.

'I can get you help with that, Miss Maria.'

'No thanks, Alfredo. I can manage just fine.'

'I remember carrying your books for you when you were just a *bambina*, Miss Maria. You used to say you wanted to marry me when you grew up. No more, eh?'

'Sorry, Alfredo, I'm just fickle.' Rosemary smiled and batted her eyes. It wasn't easy to joke or even be pleasant. She wanted this evening, this day, to end.

She was alone in the elevator and took the opportunity to rest her head against the side of the car for a moment. She indeed remembered Alfredo carrying her books to school. It had been during one of the wars in her childhood. What a family.

When the elevator doors opened, the two men in front of the entry to the penthouse came to attention. They relaxed as she approached, but each looked unusually solemn.

'Max. What's happened?' Rosemary looked questioningly at the taller of the two identically black-suited men.

Max shook his head and opened the door for her.

Rosemary walked between the oppressive, dark oak-paneled walls toward the library. The ancient oil paintings did nothing to relieve the gloom.

At the door of the library, she started to knock, but the heavy, carved doors swung inward before she struck them. Her father stood in the doorway, his silhouette illuminated by the lamp on his desk.

He took both her hands and held them tightly. 'Maria, it's Lombardo. He's no longer with us.'

'What happened?' She stared at her father's face. The areas beneath his eyes were dark. His jowls sagged even more than she remembered.

Her father gestured. 'These young men brought the news.'

Frankie, Joey, and Little Renaldo stood clumped together. Joey literally held his hat in his hands.

'We told Don Carlos, Maria. Lucky Lum – er, Lombardo was coming right over here but he stopped for a minute in the subway.'

'He wanted to get some gum, I think.' Frankie volunteered the information as if it had some significance.

'Yeah, anyway. He didn't come out. We were just hanging around,' said Joey, 'so we decided to find out what was going on when we heard about a ... disturbance in the station. When we got there, we found out what happened.'

'Yeah, they found him in about two dozen—'

'Frankie!'

'Yes, Don Carlo.'

'That will be all for tonight, boys. I will see you in the morning.'

The three young men nodded and touched their foreheads in Rosemary's direction as they left.

'I'm sorry, Maria,' said her father.

'I don't understand. Who would have done this?'

'Maria, you know Lombardo worked with our family business. Others knew that. And they knew he was about to become my son. We think it may have been someone trying to hurt me.' Don Carlo's voice sounded sad. 'There have been other incidents lately. There are those who want to take away what we have worked for a lifetime to achieve.' His voice hardened again. 'We won't let them get away with this. I promise, Maria!'

'Maria, I have some nice lasagna. Your favorite. Please, try to eat.' Rosemary's mother spoke from out of the shadows. She rose to take Rosemary to the kitchen, escorting her with an arm around her shoulders.

'Mama, you shouldn't have held supper for me.'

'I didn't. I knew you would be late and so I saved some for you.'

Rosemary said to her mother, 'Mama, I didn't love him.'

'Ssh. I know.' She touched her daughter's lips. 'But you would have grown to care for him. I could see how well you got along.'

'Mama, you don't—' Rosemary was interrupted by her father's voice following them from the library.

'It has to be *melanzanes*, blacks! Who else would be attacking us now? They have to be coming down from Harlem through the tunnels. They've wanted our territories for years. Especially they want a *susina* like Jokertown. No, jokers would never dare do this on their own, but the blacks could be using them as a distraction.'

Rosemary heard silence, followed by tinny squeaks from the telephone. Her mother tugged at her arm.

Don Carlo said, 'They must be stopped now or they will threaten all the Families. They're savages.'

Another pause.

'I do *not* exaggerate.'

'Maria ...' said her mother.

'Tomorrow morning, then,' said Don Carlo. 'Early. Good.'

'See, Maria. Your father will take care of it.' Her mother led Rosemary into the harvest-gold kitchen with all its bright appliances, the walls lined with framed samplers of old-country homilies. She thought of telling her mother about C.C. and the subway, but it seemed impossible now. It had to have been her imagination. She just wanted to sleep. She didn't want to eat. She couldn't take anything else tonight.

The bag lady stirred in her sleep and one of the pair of large cats beside her moved out of the way. He raised his head and sniffed at his companion. Leaving the woman with an opossum curled against her stomach, the two cats silently stalked out into the darkness of the abandoned subway tunnel. The neglected 86th Street cutoff took them toward food.

Both cats were hungry themselves, but now they hunted for their woman's breakfast. Using a drainage tunnel, they exited into the park and out beneath the maples to the street. When a *New York Times* delivery truck paused at a light, the black cat looked at the calico and pointed his muzzle at the truck. As the truck pulled away, they leaped aboard. Settled on the back of the truck, the black created the image of mounds of fish and shared it with the calico. Watching the city blocks pass, they waited for the telltale scent of fish. Finally, as the truck slowed, the calico smelled fish and impatiently jumped down from the vehicle. Yowling angrily, the black followed her down an alley. Both stopped when the scent of strange humans overwhelmed the food. Farther down the alley was a crowd of jokers, crude parodies of normal humans. Dressed in rags, they searched through the garbage for food.

A wedge of light spilled into the alley as a door opened. The cats smelled fresh food as a well-dressed man, larger than any of the scavengers, carried boxes into the alley.

'Please.' The fat man spoke to the paralyzed jokers in a soft voice filled with pain. 'I have food for you here.'

The frozen scene ended as the jokers rushed together toward the cartons and began ripping them open. They jostled each other and fought for position to get at the rich food.

'Stop!' A tall joker cried out in the midst of the chaos. 'Are we not men?'

The jokers paused and withdrew from the boxes, allowing the fat man to dole out the food to each of them. The tall joker was the last to be served. As the host handed him food, he spoke again. 'Sir, we thank Aces High.'

In the darkness of the alley, the cats observed the jokers' meal. Turning to the calico, the black formed the image of a fish's skeleton and they moved back toward the street. On 6th Avenue, the black sent a picture of Bagabond to the calico. They loped uptown until a slow-moving produce truck provided a ride. Many blocks later, the truck neared a Chinese market and the black recognized the familiar scent. As the truck began to brake, both cats leaped out. They kept to the dark beyond the range of the streetlights until they reached the open-air grocery.

It was still long before dawn and the truckers were unloading the day's fresh produce. The black cat smelled freshly slaughtered chicken; his tongue extended to touch his upper lip. Then he uttered a short growl to his companion. The calico leapt onto a display of tomatoes and began to claw them to pieces.

The proprietor yelled in Chinese and hurled his clipboard at the marauding cat. He missed. The men unloading the truck stopped and stared at the apparently insane feline.

'Worse'n Jokertown,' one muttered.

'That's one big sumbitchin' kitty,' said the other.

As soon as their attention was fixed on the calico cat destroying the tomatoes, the waiting black cat sprang to the back of the truck and seized a chicken in his mouth. The black was a very large cat, at least forty pounds, and he lifted the chicken with ease. Leaping off the tailgate, he ran into the darkness of the alley. At the same time, the calico dodged a broom handle and bounded after.

The black cat waited for the calico halfway down the next block. When the calico reached him, both cats howled in unison. It had been a good hunt. With the calico occasionally aiding the black in lifting the chicken onto curbs, they loped back to the park and the bag lady.

A fellow street dweller had once called her Bagabond in one of his more sober moments and the name had stuck. Her people, the wild creatures of the city, called her by no name, only by their images of her. Those were enough. And she only remembered her name once in a while.

Bagabond pulled around herself the fine green coat that she had found in an apartment-house dumpster. She sat up, careful not to displace the opossum. With the opossum settled in her lap and a squirrel on each shoulder, she greeted the proud black and calico cats with their prize. Moving with an ease that would have amazed the few street denizens who had anything to do with her, the woman reached out and patted the heads of the two feral cats. As she did, she formed the image in her mind of a particularly scrawny chicken, already half-eaten, being dragged out of a restaurant garbage can by the pair.

The black stuck his nose into the air and snorted gently as he obliterated the image in both his head and Bagabond's. The calico merged a meow with a growl in mock anger and stretched her head toward the woman's. Catching Bagabond's eye, the calico replayed the hunt as she had perceived it: the calico at least the size of a lion, surrounded by human legs much like mobile tree trunks. Brave calico spotting the prey, a chicken the size of a house. Fierce calico leaping toward a human throat, fangs bared ...

The scene went blank as Bagabond abruptly focused elsewhere. The calico began to protest until a heavy black paw rolled her over on her back and held her down. The calico stilled her protest, head twisted to the side to watch the woman's face. The black was stiff with anticipation.

The picture formed in all three minds: dead rats. The image was obliterated by Bagabond's anger. She rose, shaking off the squirrels and setting the opossum to one side. Without hesitation, she turned and started into one of the tangential, descending tunnels. The black cat bounded silently past and moved ahead to act as a scout. The calico paced the woman.

'*Something's eating my rats.*'

The tunnels were black; sometimes a little bioluminescence shed the only light. Bagabond couldn't see as well as the cats, but she could use their eyes.

The black picked up a strange scent when the three of them were deep beneath the park. The only connection he could make was with a shifting creature that was equal parts snake and lizard.

A hundred yards farther, they came upon a devastated rats' nest. None of the rats lived. Some were half-eaten. All the bodies had been mangled.

Bagabond and her companions stumbled on in the wet tunnel. The woman slid off a ledge and found herself hip-deep in disgusting water. Unidentifiable chunks batted against her legs in the moderate current. Her temper was not improved.

The black cat bristled and projected the same image as a few minutes before, but now the creature was even larger. The cat suggested they all three back out of this passageway now. Quickly. Quietly.

Bagabond blocked out the suggestion as she sidled along a slimy wall to another ravaged nest. Some of these rats were still alive. Their simple picture of their destroyer was the shadowy image of an impossibly large and ugly snake. She shut off the brains of the mortally injured and moved on.

Five yards down the passage was an alcove that provided drainage for a section of the park above. The entrance was three feet above the floor of the tunnel. The black crouched there, muscles taut, ears laid back, yowling softly. He was scared. The calico disdainfully started for the opening, but the black knocked her aside. The larger cat looked back at Bagabond and sent every negative image he could.

Carried by her anger, Bagabond indicated she would go in first. She took a breath, gasped, and crawled into the alcove.

It was lit by a grating in the roof, some twenty feet above. The gray light fell on the naked body of a man. He looked to Bagabond to be in his thirties, muscled but not overly so. No flab. Bagabond noted vaguely that he didn't look as wasted as most of the derelicts she had seen. For a moment, she thought he was dead, yet another victim of the mysterious killer. But as her mind focused on the man, she realized he was just asleep.

The cats had followed her into the chamber. The black growled in confusion. His senses told him the trail of the lizard-snake thing ended here – it ceased where the man lay. Bagabond felt something strange about the man. She didn't usually try to read humans; it was too difficult. Their minds were complex. They plotted, schemed. Slowly she knelt beside him and extended her hand.

The man woke up, caught sight of the dirty street person about to touch him, and jerked away.

'Wha' you want?'

She stared at him.

He realized he was naked and hauled himself to the entry of the cave passage— He heard a deep growl, recoiled, barely evaded a swipe from the claws of the biggest cat he'd ever seen. For a moment, he felt himself sliding into the darkness inside his mind. Then he was into the main tunnel and gone.

The cats were crying with questions, but Bagabond had no answers. Almost, she thought. Inside his mind. I almost felt … what? Gone.

Bagabond, the calico, and the black searched for another hour, but they found no more trace of the strange scent. There was no monster in the tunnel.

The transients, derelicts, bag ladies, and other street people began their day early, when the best cans and bottles were to be found. Rosemary had slipped out of the penthouse early as well. She had barely slept, and that morning, knowing what was almost certainly happening behind the closed doors of the library, she wanted to get out quickly. The dons were declaring war.

Central Park with its trees, bushes, and benches was heaven for a certain portion of the street people. This sunny morning, Rosemary was looking for a few she had undertaken to help. As she reached the second park bench beyond the stone bridge, a man in tattered clothing hid a bottle in a bush beside the bench and jumped to his feet. He wore an olive-drab fatigue jacket with a less-faded place on one shoulder where the Joker Brigade 'cannon fodder' patch had once been sewn. Rosemary had suggested it was not prudent to wear the patch this far uptown.

'Hello, Crawler,' said the social worker. Somewhere in his late twenties – Rosemary couldn't tell from the vet's sunburned face – he had taken his nickname from his Army job in Vietnam: tunnel crawler. He'd re-upped twice. Then Crawler had seen enough.

'Hey, Rosemary. You got my new goggles yet?' Crawler wore a makeshift pair – cheap 14th Street sunglasses, the eyepieces built up with dirty white adhesive tape. Underneath, Rosemary knew his eyes were dark and overlarge, extraordinarily sensitive.

'I've requested the funding. It will be a while before we can get them. You know red tape – just like in the service.'

'Shoot.' But the derelict still smiled as he fell in step beside her.

Rosemary hesitated, then said. 'You can still check in with the V.A., you know. They'll fix you up.'

'Fuck no,' said Crawler, sounding alarmed. 'Guys like me, they go in a V.A. and they never come back out.'

Rosemary started to say, 'That's nonsense,' but thought better of it. 'Crawler, do you know anything about the underground? You know, the subway tunnels and all that?'

'Some. I mean, I need the shelter. I just don't like *bein*' down there. 'Sides, there's creepy stuff goin' on down there. I hear things about alligators, stuff like that. Maybe it's all from winos with the d.t.'s, but I don't wanna find out.'

'I'm looking for someone,' said Rosemary.

Crawler wasn't listening. 'Only the really weird people *live* down there.' He mumbled something. '... even stranger than down on the East Side – you know, the Town. *She* lives down deep.' Crawler pointed at the crone sitting on the ground under a maple tree. She was a hundred yards away, but Rosemary could have sworn there were pigeons sitting on the woman's head and a squirrel perched on her shoulder. Rosemary cocked her head and looked back at the little man.

'That's just Bagabond,' she said. 'No need to worry about her ...' Rosemary realized that Crawler was no longer with her. He was panhandling a well-dressed businessman getting exercise by walking to work. She shook her head in mixed disapproval and resignation.

By the time Rosemary turned back toward Bagabond, the pigeons and squirrel were gone. Rosemary shook her head to clear it. My imagination really is working overtime, she thought, walking toward the bag lady. Just another lost soul.

'Hello, Bagabond.'

The old woman with stringy hair turned her head away and stared across the park.

'My name is Rosemary. I talked to you before. I tried to find you a nice place to live. Do you remember?' Rosemary squatted down on the ground to speak at Bagabond's level.

The black cat she had seen before came up to Bagabond and began rubbing against her. She stroked its head and murmured incomprehensible sounds.

'Please talk to me. I want to get you food. I want to get you a good place to live.' Rosemary held out her hand. The ring on her third finger glittered in the sun.

The woman on the ground drew her legs up against herself and clutched the plastic trashbag filled with her treasures. She began rocking back and forth and crooning. The black cat turned to look at Rosemary and she flinched against its glare.

'I'll talk to you later. I'll come back and see you.' Rosemary rose stiffly. Her face tightened, and for just a moment, she felt like crying to ease the frustration. She only wanted to help. Someone. Anyone. To feel good about something.

She walked away from Bagabond and back toward Central Park West and the subway entrance. Her father's war council had frightened her. She had never liked what he did, and her entire life seemed to be a search for escape and redemption, atonement. The sins of the fathers. Rosemary wanted peace, but whenever she thought she could get it, it retreated beyond her grasp. C.C. had been a last chance. So was each one of the derelicts she failed to help. There was a key to reaching Bagabond. There had to be.

Rosemary descended the steps, waited, dropped in her token, walked down the second stairway onto the platform in a daze. The blast of cool air entered the station followed by the AA train. Rosemary barely glanced up from the floor and moved stiffly toward the nearest car.

As she was about to step onto the train, her eyes widened and she stepped back into the crowd, drawing glares and a few curses for breaking the flow. That last car. It had more of C.C.'s lyrics painted on the side in a shade of red that reminded her of blood. C.C. had always been something of a manic-depressive and Rosemary had always known her mood by what she wrote or sang. The C.C. who had written these words was depressed beyond even Rosemary's experience:

Blood and bones
Take me home
People there I owe
People there gonna go
Down with me to
Hell Down with me to Hell

Approaching the car, Rosemary saw words she *knew* had not been there seconds ago.

> *Rosie, Rosie, pretty Rosie*
> *Leave this place*
> *Forget my face*
> *Don't cry*
> *Rosie, Rosie, pretty Rosie*

'I'm going to find you, C.C. I'm going to save you.' Rosemary again fought to get into the car she now realized was covered with fragments of C.C.'s songs, some that she recognized, others that had to be new. Once more the car rejected her. Breathing hard, eyes wide, Rosemary watched the car move into the tunnel. She gasped as the side of the car was suddenly covered with tears of blood.

'Holy Mary, Mother of God ...' Rosemary absurdly remembered the stories of saints from her childhood. For just a moment, she wondered if the world was ending, if the wars and the deaths, the jokers and the hate, truly prefigured the Apocalypse.

It was noon.

American B–52s were bombing Hanoi and Haiphong. Quang Tri was shaky, as the North Vietnamese were on the march. In Washington, D.C., politicians exchanged increasingly frantic phone calls about a recent burglary. The question in some quarters was, is Donald Segretti an ace?

The midtown Manhattan rush was ferocious. At Grand Central Station, Rosemary Muldoon looked for raggedy shadows she could follow into the darkness of the underground. A dozen blocks north, Jack Robicheaux plied his regular trade, clattering through the permanent darkness on his small electric cart, checking track integrity in tunnel after tunnel. And somewhere under the abandoned 86th Street cutoff, just beneath the floor of the south edge of Central Park Lake, Bagabond drifted on the edge of sleep, warmed by the cats and other beasts of her life.

Noon. The war beneath Manhattan was starting.

'Let me quote to you from a speech given once by Don Carlo Gambione himself,' said Frederico 'the Butcher' Macellaio. He grimly surveyed the groups of capos and their soldiers gathered around him in the chamber. In the '30s, the huge room had been an underground repair facility for midtown transit. Before the Big War, it had been closed and sealed off when the T.A. decided to consolidate all maintenance yards across the river. The Gambione Family had soon taken the space over for storage of guns and other contraband, freight transfer, and occasional burials.

The Butcher raised his voice and the words echoed. 'What will make the difference for us in battle will be two things: discipline and loyalty.'

Little Renaldo was standing off to one side with Frankie and Joey. 'Not to mention automatic weapons and H.E.,' he said, smirking.

Joey and Frankie exchanged glances. Frankie shrugged. Joey said, 'God, guns, and glory.'

Little Renaldo commented, 'I'm bored. I wanna go shoot somethin'.'

Joey said a little louder, so the Butcher could hear, 'Hey, are we goin' to roust some rummies, or what? Who's fair game? Just the blacks? Jokers too?'

'We don't know who their allies are,' said the Butcher. 'We know they wouldn't act alone. There are traitors from among our own race helping them for money.'

Little Renaldo's manic grin widened. 'Free-fire zone,' he said. '*Hoo*-boy.' He tugged his boonie hat down snug.

'Shit,' said Joey, 'you weren't even there.'

Little Renaldo gave him a thumbs-up. 'I saw that John Wayne movie.'

'That's the word from the Man, huh?' said Joey.

The Butcher's smile was thin and cold. 'Anybody gives you problems, just waste 'em.'

The groups began to move out, scouts, squads, and platoons. The men had their M-16s, pump scatterguns, a few M-60 machine guns, grenades and launchers, rockets, riot gas, sidearms, knives, and enough blocks of C-4 to handle any kind of heavy demolition.

'Hey, Joey,' said Little Renaldo. 'What you gonna shoot?'

Joey slapped a magazine into the AK-47. This weapon wasn't from the Gambione armory. It was his own souvenir. He touched the polished wooden stock. 'Maybe a 'gator.'

'Huh?'

'Don't you read any of them rags that's been talking about the giant alligators down here?'

Little Renaldo looked at him doubtfully and shivered. 'The jungle-jokers are one thing. I don't want to go up against no big lizards with teeth.'

It was Joey's turn to grin.

'No such things, right?' said Little Renaldo. 'You're just shittin' me, right?'

Joey shot him a jaunty thumbs-up.

Jack had lost all track of time. He knew it had been a long while since he'd shunted his track maintenance vehicle off the main line onto a spur. Something was wrong. He decided to check out some of the more obscure routes. It was as though a piece of ice pressed against a spot just north of his tailbone.

He'd heard trains, but they had passed at a distance. The tunnels he now traveled were seldom used except for diverted routes during high congestion, track fires, or other problems on the main line. He also heard far-off reports that sounded like gunfire.

Jack sang. He filled the darkness with zydeco, the bluesy Cajun-Black mixture he remembered from his childhood. He started with the Big Bopper's 'Chantilly Lace' and Clifton Chenier's 'Ay-Tete-Fee,' segued into a Jimmy Newman medley and Slim Harpo's 'Rainin' in My Heart.' He'd just pulled the switch and slid the car onto a spur he knew he hadn't checked in at least a year, when the world blew apart in a flash of red and yellow flame. He'd had time to sing one line of 'L'Haricots sont pas sales' when the darkness fragmented, the pressure waves slammed against his ears, and the car and he took different, spinning, twisting directions through the air.

All he really had time to say was, 'Wha' de hail—' as he fetched up against the stone of the tunnel's far wall and crumpled to the floor. For the moment, he was stunned by concussion and flash. He blinked and realized he could see smoke swirling, and the hand-held lights that illuminated the smoke.

He heard a voice say, 'Jesus Christ, Renaldo! We weren't going up against a tank.'

Another voice said, 'Sorta sorry to do this one. Hate to kill anybody sounded that much like Chuck Berry.'

'Well,' said a third, 'at least he had to be a spook.'

'Check it out, Renaldo. Guy probably looks like an open can of Spam, but you better find out for sure.'

'Yo, Joey.'

The lights came closer, bobbing in the dissipating smoke.

They're gon' kill me, Jack thought, reverting to the dialect of his childhood. There was at first no emotion to the realization. Then the anger started. He let the feeling sweep over him. The anger escalated to rage. Adrenaline pricklings agonized his nerves. Jack felt the first brush of what he had used to think was the onset of *loup-garou* madness.

'Hey, I think I see something! Off to your left, Renaldo.'

The one called Renaldo approached. 'Yeah, I got him. Now I'll make sure.' He raised his weapon, taking aim with the light held tight along the stock.

That pushed Jack over the edge. *You chill son of a bitch!*

Pain, welcome pain, wracked him. He ... *changed*.

His brain seemed to spin, his mind folding in on itself endlessly down into the primal reptile level. His body was elongating, thickening; his jaw thrust forward, the teeth springing up in profusion. He felt the length of perfectly toned muscles, the balance of his tail. The utter power of his body ... he felt it completely.

Then he saw the prey in front of him, the menace.

'Oh, my God!' Little Renaldo cried. His finger tightened on the trigger of the M-16. The first burst of tracers went wild. He never had the chance for a second.

The creature that had been Jack lunged forward, the jaws closing around Renaldo's waist, twisting and tearing at his flesh. The man's light spun, smashed, and went out.

The other men started firing wildly.

The alligator registered the cries, the screams. The smell of terror. Good. The prey was easier when it located itself. He dropped Renaldo's corpse and moved toward the lights, the bull roar of his challenge filling the tunnel.

'For the love of God, Joey! Help me!'

'Hold on. I can't see where you went!'

The corridor was narrow, the materials old and decaying. Caught between two equally tempting morsels, the alligator twisted around in the confined space. He saw flashes of light, felt a few stinging impacts, mainly in his tail. He heard the prey screaming.

'Joey, it busted my leg!'

More flashes. An explosion. Acrid smoke choked his nostrils. Irregular chunks of stone fell from the ceiling. Rotten beams splintered. Deteriorated cement collapsed. Part of the floor beneath him gave way and his twelve-foot length tumbled heavily down an incline. Smoke, dust, and solid debris rained from above.

The alligator smashed into a thin metal hatch that had never been engineered for this kind of force. The aluminum tore like ripping canvas and he toppled into an open shaft. He fell for another twenty feet before crashing into a spider's nest of wooden beams. Bits of debris followed for a little while. Then there was silence, both above and below. The alligator rested in darkness. When he tried to flex his body, nothing much happened. He was thoroughly jammed into a wooden cat's cradle. A beam was wedged securely across his snout. He couldn't even open his jaws.

He attempted to roar, but the sound came out more as a muffled growl. He blinked his eyes, seeing nothing. His strength was dwindling, shock taking its toll.

He didn't want to die here. He wished to end in the water.

Worse, the alligator didn't want to die hungry.

He was starved.

Bagabond felt something she hadn't experienced for a long time, sympathy, for Rosemary Muldoon. She knew the social worker wanted to help, but how could Bagabond tell her that she didn't need help? Puzzled by that emotion, Bagabond discovered another one. She could be happy with the caring and companionship of her friends, however nonhuman they might be.

She did have a warm place to sleep. Her home beneath Central Park was close to the steam tunnels. Bagabond had slowly furnished it with the best the street had to offer. A broken red director's chair was the only furniture, but there were rags and blankets deeply covering the floor. A velvet painting of lions on the veld leaned against one wall and a wooden carving of a leopard stood in one corner. One of the leopard's legs was missing but it occupied a place of honor.

Drowsing there in the abandoned 86th Street cutoff tunnel, Bagabond even remembered the person she had once been, Suzanne Melot— The surge of pain that crashed across her mind interrupted her thoughts. The strength of the cry caused the black cat to moan in pain. As the wave receded, the black sent to Bagabond the same image he had taken from the creature that had attacked the rats. Bagabond agreed mentally. Neither could *she* quite nail down the image. The creature seemed to be a huge lizard, but it somehow wasn't entirely animal. And it *was* hurt.

Bagabond sighed and rose. 'We have to find it if we are going to have peace and quiet.' The black was not in favor of this solution until another wave of anguish came. He snarled and ran into the tunnel to Bagabond's left. The calico felt only the edge of the pain as it passed through Bagabond and the black. Bagabond replayed a little of the cry of pain and the calico flattened to the ground, ears back. The image of the black appeared in Bagabond's mind and the calico dashed down the tunnel in pursuit. Bagabond told the calico to wait for her, and they began to track both the black and the injured creature.

It took time to find them. The creature really *did* resemble nothing so much as a giant lizard. It was trapped beneath a fall of timbers in an unfinished tunnel. The black crouched a few feet away, staring at this apparition.

Bagabond looked at the trapped creature and laughed. 'So there really are alligators in the sewers.' The alligator twitched its tail, knocking a few bricks across the tunnel. 'But that's not all you are, is it?'

There was no way she and the cats could free the alligator. Bagabond knelt and examined the timbers trapping the beast as she called her friends to help her. She reached out and stroked the alligator's head, calming him with the images she sent. She sensed the creature drifting in and out of consciousness.

The animals arrived at different times. An uneasy peace held as Bagabond directed each according to its abilities. Rats gnawed, a pair of wild dogs provided muscle, the opossums and raccoons carried off small stones. The black and the calico aided Bagabond in controlling the volatile mix of animals.

When the smaller debris had been cleared away and timbers and boards shifted or gnawed through, Bagabond began hauling on the alligator. Between her tugging and his struggles, Jack fought his way free. Bagabond ended up with a very tired and bruised alligator across her lap. The black and the calico told the creatures who had helped to leave.

The two cats watched as Bagabond rubbed the underside of the alligator's jaw, calming the creature. As she stroked it, the snout and tail began to shorten. The scaly hide became smooth, pale skin. The stubby limbs elongated into arms and legs. In a few minutes, Bagabond was holding the naked, bruised body of the man they had found before. As the change took place, Bagabond realized that at some indefinable point, she could no longer control this creature or read his thoughts. Somehow she had missed the critical division between man and beast.

She got up, lifting the man off her, and walked toward the end of the tunnel. The calico accompanied her. The black stayed beside the man.

Why? Bagabond thought.

Why? the black countered. The work they had just done, as seen through the cat's eyes, played across her mind.

The calico looked from one to the other. She had not been invited into this conversation.

Alligator, Bagabond explained, *not human.*

In her mind the alligator became a man.

'Curiosity ...' Bagabond spoke aloud for the first time since the rescue operation had commenced.

The black sent a picture of a black cat on its back with paws in the air.

Bagabond sat down beside the man. In a few minutes he began to move. Painfully he sat up. In the dim light filtering from above, he recognized Bagabond as the old woman he had seen the day before.

'Wha' happen? I remember running into a bunch of crazies with guns, and then things get fuzzy.' He tried to focus on the crone, who kept splitting into two images. 'I think maybe I've got a concussion.'

Bagabond shrugged and pointed at the beams from the roof-collapse behind him. By straining his eyes, he could see what looked like hundreds of pawprints on the floor and the walls around the cave-in. In the center of the devastation, Jack also saw the imprint of a monstrous tail.

'Christ, not again.' Jack turned back to Bagabond. 'When you got here, what did you see?'

She turned partly away from him, still silent. He saw her mouth quirk in a partial smile beneath the stringy hair. Was she mad?

'*Merde.* What am I going to do?' Jack was almost bowled over by the pair of black paws that struck his chest. 'Easy, boy. You're the biggest kitty I've seen since I left the swamps.' The black cat's eyes stared into his with an odd intensity. 'What is it?'

'He wants to know how you do it.' The old woman's voice did not match her appearance. It was young and held a touch of humor. 'Be careful. You're spaced, just like you were coming out of Thorazine.' She took his arm as he tried to stand.

When he was upright, she said, 'You're not going to make it far like that.' She began to take off her coat.

'*Mon Dieu*. Thanks.' Feeling his skin flush, Jack shrugged into her green cloth coat and wrapped it around himself. It covered him from neck to knees, but left his arms bare from the elbows down.

'Where do you live?' Bagabond gazed at him without expression. Jack appreciated the kindness.

'Downtown. Down on Broadway near the City Hall station. Are we anywhere close to a train?' Jack was not used to being lost, and found that he disliked the feeling intensely.

In answer, Bagabond picked her way to the tunnel entrance. She didn't look back to see if he was following when she turned to the right.

'Your mistress, she is a little strange. No offense,' Jack said to the black cat. It paced him as he trailed the bag lady. The cat looked up at him, sniffed, and twitched his tail.

'Who am I to talk, eh?'

Although Jack attempted to keep up with Bagabond, he quickly fell behind. Eventually, at the black's appeal, she returned and helped support the man, pulling his arm across her shoulders.

Jack finally recognized the tunnels as they came into the 57th Street station. He was amazed at the change in Bagabond as they made their way onto the platform. Even though she was still holding him up, the woman seemed to hang off him. She shuffled now instead of striding, and kept her eyes on the ground. Those waiting on the platform gave them plenty of room.

The subway pulled in, the last car covered with unusually bright graffiti. Bagabond hauled Jack toward the vividly decorated car. Jack had time to read some of the more coherent phrases covering the side.

Are you unusual?
Did you feel the fire?
Are you burning inside?
The flames devour us all,
But never let us die.
It never ends, forever in flame.

Jack thought some of the phrases changed as he watched, but that had to be an effect of his concussed brain. Bagabond pulled him inside. The doors closed, leaving some very angry transit customers outside.

'Stop?' Bagabond was nothing if not economical with her words, Jack thought.

'City Hall.' Jack slumped and rested his head against the back of the seat, closing his eyes as the train rolled downtown. He did not notice that the seat molded itself around his body to support it while he slept. He failed to realize that the doors never again opened until they reached his stop.

The cats were not entirely happy with this subway ride. The calico was flatly terrified. Ears laid back, tail straight and fluffed out, she leaned into Bagabond's side. The black gingerly kneaded the floor of the car. The texture was only partially familiar. He wondered at the heat and the confusing scent all around him.

Bagabond tried to focus on the interior of the dark car. There were no sharp angles here. Dim shapes seemed to change form subtly in her peripheral vision. I've felt nothing like this, she thought, since the acid trip. She extended her consciousness beyond the cats and Jack. She couldn't define the *who* that she briefly contacted. But she felt the overwhelming comfort, the warmth, and the protectiveness that surrounded them here.

Cautiously she settled back in her seat and stroked the calico.

'This is it,' said Jack.

He had recovered sufficiently to lead their small party through the City Hall station, beyond a bewildering succession of maintenance closets, and into another labyrinth of unused tunnels. He'd rigged sections of the passages with lights which he turned on and off as needed as they proceeded toward his home. When he opened the last door, he stood aside and waved Bagabond and the cats inside. He smiled proudly as they stared around the long room.

'Wow, man.' Bagabond flinched as she took in the opulent

furnishings and decor. The immediate impression was of red velvet and claw-footed divans.

'You *are* younger than you look. That was my reaction too. Reminded me of Captain Nemo's stateroom ...'

'*20,000 Leagues Under the Sea.*'

'Yeah, right. You saw it too. One of the first movies I ever saw over to the parish theater.' They walked down the crimson-carpeted stairs flanked by gold stanchions and plush velvet ropes. Both cats ran ahead of them, the calico using the Victorian armchairs as hurdles. The electric light was augmented by flickering gas flames that gave the room an atmosphere out of the last century. The black cat trotted over the Persian carpets to the edge of the platform and looked back at the two humans.

'He wants to know what this is and what's behind that door.' Bagabond steadied Jack as they moved slowly down the staircase. 'You need to lie down.'

'Soon enough. This is my home and behind the door is my bedroom. If we could head in that direction ...' They started across the room. 'This was the first subway in New York, built by a man named Alfred Beach back after the War Between the States. It only ran for two blocks. The Boss Tweed didn't want it so he shut it down, then they forgot about it. I found it a while after I started working for the Transit Authority – one of the benefits of the job. Don't know why it held up so well, but it's a good place for me. Just took a little cleaning up, is all.' They had walked to the other end of the room and Jack reached out to turn the handles on the ornate cast-bronze door. The center circle swung open. 'This used to be the entrance to the pneumatic tube.'

'I didn't expect this.' Bagabond was surprised to find that the interior of the tunnel was sparsely furnished. There was a home-made bed constructed out of pine boards, an equally homemade bookcase, and a plank chest.

'All the comforts of home. Even my complete collection of Pogo books.' Jack looked innocently at Bagabond and she laughed, then seemed surprised at it.

'Where's your iodine?' Bagabond looked around for a first aid kit.

'Don't use that stuff. Can you get me some of those?' Jack pointed up at the spiderwebs.

'You're kidding.'

'Best poultice in the world. My grandma taught me that.'

When Bagabond turned back to him, he had pulled on a pair of shorts and had a shirt in his hand. She handed over the spiderwebs and helped him bandage the worst abrasions.

'So how did *you* end up down here?' Jack lay back on the bed, wincing slightly, while Bagabond perched gingerly on the edge.

'You're sure not like those social workers.' Bagabond watched the cats outside the door as they chased each other around the room. She turned back to him with an appraising look. 'And *they* like you.

'They let me out a while ago and I ended up back in the city. No place else to go. Met the black, started talking to him, and he talked back. So did a lot of the other animals, the ones that aren't human, anyway. I get along. I don't need people, don't want people around. People always mean bad luck for me. I can talk to you, too, when you're that other one, you know? Out there they call me Bagabond. I had another name once but I don't remember it much.'

'They call me Sewer Jack.' Jack said it bitterly, in contrast to Bagabond's flat recitation. The burst of emotion she caught held screams, bright lights, and fear, and the haven of the swamp.

'It was here – the creature. What *are* you?' Bagabond was confused; she had never before met this mixture of man and animal, with whom she could only sometimes communicate.

'Both. You saw.'

'Do you control it? Can you make yourself change?'

'Did you ever see Lawrence Talbot as the wolfman? I change when I lose control or when I allow the beast to take over. I'm not cursed by the full moon; I'm cursed all the time. The *loup-garou* is a legend where I come from. The Cajuns all believe in it. When I was young, I did too. I was afraid I would hurt someone, so I went as far away as I could go. New York was a foreign country; no one would know me or bother me here.'

His eyes focused on her now instead of the past. 'Why the act? You can't be over forty-five.'

'Twenty-six.' She looked down at Jack, wondering why it mattered. 'It keeps them from bothering me so much.'

Jack glanced through the open door at the railway clock on the opposite wall. 'I'm getting hungry. How about you?'

Rescuing C.C. What had seemed to be a wonderful idea had turned into a nightmare. Rosemary had followed some derelicts into the steam tunnels beneath Grand Central Station. At first she tried asking anyone she met about C.C. But as she moved farther into the dank passages, those living there scuttled away. There was only occasional light from gratings in the street above, or from the derelicts' smoky fires. Her fatigue and fear began taking their toll; she fell again and again into the muck on the tunnel floors.

One horrible moment, she was attacked by a filthy creature who clawed at her, cackling. She fought him off but her purse was gone now. Rosemary was hopelessly lost. She heard occasional sounds that seemed to be gunshots and explosions. *I'm in hell.*

Ahead were two glowing spots that glared at her through the darkness. They receded as she came nearer. The iridescent green lights mesmerized her.

The spots came into focus and Rosemary saw the cat crouched in the darkness. Retreating a few feet and growling, it watched as Rosemary approached a wounded cat, the comrade it guarded. Chest crushed, one leg nearly severed from its body, the injured cat was dying. The guardian would allow no more pain to be inflicted. When she heard the low crying, she ignored the eyes and knelt beside the injured cat. Rosemary realized there was nothing she could do, but she held it. The cat began to purr before it choked and died.

The guardian lifted its head and howled a eulogy before pivoting and running into the gloom.

Rosemary laid the body on the ground in front of her and placed its head and legs in comfortable positions, sat back, and began sobbing. It seemed as if she cried forever before she started walking toward the sounds of the guns, gasping from her sobs.

After raiding the refrigerator – Bagabond could understand why Con Ed never noticed the power tap, but how did he ever get the refrigerator down here? – Jack went back into his bedroom to get some sleep. Bagabond and the cats explored Jack's domain, which included making sure they could get out the door he had locked behind them.

They quickly discovered the limits. Bagabond sat down on an overstuffed horsehair sofa. The black joined her while the calico continued her game of crossing the room without touching the floor. Bagabond pondered and, for the first time in years, the black was not invited to join her. Bagabond was amazed at the way Jack lived. It made her life of moving from one temporary home, a pile of rags, to another, suddenly seem wrong and filled with discomforts she had previously ignored.

She and Jack had discussed the probability that they were both aces. What luck. The virus had ruined both their lives. She would never again be the innocent child she was before the acid and the virus flooded her mind with the alien perceptions of the animal world. She thought *she* had had a miserable childhood. It was why she left home. But to grow up thinking you were something like a werewolf, a creature cursed by God.

Why had she been so open with him? There was no one still alive in the city who knew as much about her as Jack now did. It was because they were alike; they knew what it was like to be different and to have stopped looking for ways to be like everybody else.

The claws across the back of her hand drew blood before her attention came back to the real world. Her eyes met those of the black cat, and horrifying images filtered through others' eyes began pouring into her mind: rat nests destroyed by machine-gun fire; yelling men frightening an opossum, her children clinging to her back as she ran, one falling, dying; cats fleeing, being shot, murdered; a cat fighting to protect her kittens before a grenade destroyed the litter, leaving the mother with a leg nearly blown off; a woman who looked like that damn social worker cradling a dying cat. The blood – more and more of it – of those who were her only friends.

'The kittens. They can't!' Bagabond stood up and found herself shaking.

'What's goin' on?' Jack, awakened by Bagabond's cry, emerged from his room still half-asleep.

'They're killing them! I've got to stop them.' Bagabond clenched her fists, turning away from him. Flanked by the cats, she headed for the stairs.

'Not without me.' Jack ducked back into his room, grabbed Bagabond's green coat, flashlights, and a pair of sneakers, and followed them up the staircase.

Slowed by tying on the sneakers as he ran, he caught up with them at the first tunnel junction.

'Not that way.' Jack stopped the trio as they entered the right-hand tunnel. He thrust Bagabond's coat at her. He aimed one of the flashlights at the other passage.

'It's how we came in.' In her panic, Bagabond had lost much of her trust in Jack.

'It'll just take you to the subway. There's a faster way to get back to the park. I've got a track-car. Follow me?' Jack waited for Bagabond's nod and plunged into the lefthand tunnel at a trot.

The scenes of carnage in Bagabond's mind grew sharper as they approached Central Park and abandoned the car. As they came up on the next branching of the tunnels, Jack lifted his head and sniffed. 'Whoever they are, they're using up an army's worth of gunpowder. What's the plan?'

'We need to find out who they are so we know how to stop them. Right?' Bagabond wasn't at all sure what to do.

'I bet they're *mes amis* with the guns, but I have no idea who's the boss.'

An image appeared of the calico walking with Jack, the black with Bagabond.

'Far out.' Bagabond patted the head of the immense black cat. 'Good idea.'

'What idea?'

'The black thinks we should split up until we find out what is going on. If one of the cats is with each of us, we can stay, um ...'

'In communication. Yeah. You can at least see what's going on.' Jack nodded thoughtfully. 'I used to love war movies, but I get lousy reception at my place. Let's go, Sarge.' He spoke to the calico, who leaped ahead of him. '*Bon chance.*'

Bagabond nodded and moved in the other direction.

In a profound darkness barely relieved by darting beams from the caving helmets worn by armed men, Don Carlo Gambione surveyed the desolation that was his kingdom.

His lieutenant sounded almost apologetic. 'Don Carlo, I fear our troops became too enthusiastic about their task.'

Don Carlo looked down at the bodies illuminated in the light from the Butcher's flash. 'Zeal in a matter such as this,' he said, 'is no vice.'

'We've found their headquarters,' said the Butcher. 'Our men discovered it less than an hour ago.' He stabbed a finger at the map. 'About 86th Street. Under the park. Close to Central Park Lake. It looked inhabited. That's when I called you.'

'I am grateful,' said his leader. 'I want to be present when the flame of our enemies' ill-conceived brushfire rebellion is extinguished. I knew there must be a reason why they should rise up now.' Don Carlo's voice rose as well. The Butcher stared at him.

'I want their heads,' said Don Carlo. 'We shall set them on spikes at Amsterdam and 110th Street.' Wide, his eyes shone ferally in the electric lamplight.

The Butcher gently put a hand on the Don's wrist. 'We'd better go uptown now, *Padrone.* I told the men to wait in place, but they are so – enthusiastic.'

For a moment, Don Carlo's gaze swung around wildly at the bodies littering the dirty concrete. Rags soaked with blood. 'Such tragedy! The pain, the pain …' He stared directly down at the corpse at his feet. It was a white man, the gangling arms and legs sprawled out like the limbs of a broken marionette. There was no peace in the lined, sun-scorched face. Only agony reflected in the too-wide dark eyes. Smashed makeshift goggles lay in the blood pooled from the man's head. The don unconsciously nudged the shoulder of the faded fatigue jacket with the toe of one polished boot. 'This one was a true jungle-joker …' His voice trailed off.

Don Carlo looked away. He drew himself straight, taking strength from the almost-holy knowledge of what he must do. He leaned closer to the Butcher's sober face. 'These things we do …' he said. 'It is sad, very sad. But sometimes we must attack and even destroy the way of life we love in order to preserve it.'

Despite his bravado – *why am I trying to impress that raggedy woman?* – Jack took his time moving into the tunnels. The long ride back up to the park had returned to him his limp and considerable pain. Whenever he heard a noise, he froze. The calico showed remarkable patience. She ranged fifty feet or so ahead and then returned if it was clear. Jack wished desperately he could talk to her.

The sounds now were not imaginary. They grew louder. Jack began to hear unintelligible shouts. He jumped at every gunshot or explosion. He stopped using the flashlight because he was afraid someone would see it. The calico stayed a few feet away now. Jack had rubbed dirt on his face to cut down reflection.

Boots scuffed against the concrete floor just ahead of him. He started to back up and ran into one of the hunters, who was as surprised as he was.

'What the hell! Joey! Joey, I got one!'

The man in the hardhat with the attached light swung the butt of his gun at Jack's head.

'Where is he, Sly?'

The rifle-butt had just grazed Jack's skull. He managed to sprint out of the light and up an apparent dead-end passage. Jack tried to mold himself to the wall and wished he could change into something useful, like concrete or dirt. As the thought crossed his mind, he recognized the itching that meant he was getting scaly. Jack fought it off by slowing his breathing and exerting control. That's all he needed now. Where's the calico? he thought. Bagabond'll *kill* me if that cat's hurt.

'He has to be down here, Joey. There's nowhere else to go.' The voice sounded as if it were an inch away.

'Toss in a grenade and keep movin'. We're supposed to be sealing off their base.'

'Aw, Joey, come on.'

'Sly, you're crazy, man. Move it.'

There was the sound of metal bouncing on rock. Jack caught a glint of light from the grenade before the adrenaline wiped his brain clean. *Merde* was his last conscious thought.

The blast roar was accompanied by some rockfalls, but there hadn't been as much graft in this section. The roof held.

'Check it out, Sly.'

'All right, Joey. Thanks.' Sly was known for being almost as crazy as Little Renaldo.

Why me, Joey wondered.

'*Nothing's* left. Just a few rags and a sneaker. The right one.'

'Come on, then. We've got a lot of ground to cover.'

Neither man noticed the calico crouched on a rock projecting from the wall near the ceiling. The calico leaped down and nosed through the torn and bloody clothing. She sent the scene to Bagabond and set out to meet her.

Bagabond stood quietly against the far wall of the 86th Street cutoff. She petted the calico gently and did her best imitation of a harmless old woman. The black had warned her the mafiosi were coming, but they were behind her by the time she tried to retreat. Too many to fight, so she came passively. Now she silently gazed at the shambles they had made of her place. Her single guard had his attention fixed on Don Carlo.

'Somehow they must have escaped,' said the Butcher apologetic-ally.

'I want them,' said Don Carlo. He stared around at the large vel-vet painting in its cheap wooden frame, one corner torn: a pride of lions stalked zebras on the veld. 'They *were* here,' he said. 'Savages.'

'Don Carlo, sir, I …' It was Joey.

'What?'

'It is Maria, Don Carlo. I found her wandering down here.' Joey escorted Rosemary up to her father. She did not appear to see him or register anything else. Her face was vacant, almost peaceful. Rosemary was a docile rag doll, lost somewhere back in the tunnels.

Don Carlo looked at her with astonishment and then concern. 'Maria, what is wrong, *mia*? Joey, what happened to her?'

'I don't know, Don Carlo. She was like this when I found her.'

Bagabond looked up from under her stringy hair. 'Rosemary, couldn't you stay out of *this* either? Social workers … Too nosy.' Bagabond spoke under her breath. The guard turned around at her muttering, but shook his head and returned his attention to the excitement.

'Take care of her for me, Joey, until I finish with this.' Turning to the Butcher, Don Carlo said, 'Does the old woman know any-thing?'

'That's what we're going to find out.' Light caught the blade of the Butcher's stiletto as he started toward Bagabond. Then he stopped and listened attentively.

Everyone in the tunnel was listening. The rumbling that had at first seemed to be just another train in the distance got too loud, too quickly. There were yells from the west tunnel, even a scream of pain as the subway car appeared out of the darkness, traveling where no car could possibly be, with no third rail, on ruined tracks. The car glowed with a white phosphorescence, wraithlike. The route sign read CC LOCAL. It came to a stop in the middle of the gathering. The garish designs on its sides changed so rapidly it was impossible to focus on them.

'C.C.!' Rosemary, who had been standing to one side with Joey, eluded his grasp and ran to the phantom car. She stretched out her arms as if to embrace the thing, but as she touched the side, she recoiled. Then Rosemary extended one hand to touch what was not metal. 'C.C.?'

Colors radiated from the spot she touched and then vanished. The car became black and almost vanished from the sight of the watchers. Words appeared as they had before: lyrics of songs C.C. had written and only her best friend, Rosemary, had ever heard. The watchers stood, too stunned to move.

You can sing about pain
You can sing about sorrow
But nothing will bring a new tomorrow
Or take away yesterday

Images appeared on the side of the car as if projected there. The first scene was an attack, a rape in a subway station. A hospital bed with the figure of Rosemary recognizable beside it. Someone in a hospital gown walked down fire escapes.

'That's how you got out of the hospital, C.C. Why did you run away?' Rosemary looked up and spoke to the car as if it were a friend.

The next scene showed another subway station, another attack, but the person in the hospital gown was a witness this time. She tried to stop the attack and was flung aside, hurled onto the tracks. The colors of pain and rage. The trash and just about anything else unsecured on the unoccupied platform – vending machines, discarded newspapers, a dead rat, *everything* – was sucked down onto the tracks as if pulled into the voracious heart of a black hole. A train with six cars shrieked into the station. Suddenly another car joined it. The attacker, escaping, entered the new car and – the scene turned to crimson, as though blood were washing across the phantom car. More subway stations, more crimson. Another attacker in a leather jacket, an old woman.

'Lummy?' Rosemary stepped back from the sight of her fiancé caught in mid-mugging. '*Lummy?*'

'Lombardo!' Don Carlo was livid at seeing his son-to-be enter the car and be slaughtered. 'Joey, get Maria away from that ... thing. Ricardo, where is the rocket launcher? You'll get your chance now. Frederico, move that old woman over by the car. I want them all destroyed. Now!'

Rosemary fought Joey as he hauled her out of range. 'Christ,' he said, not to her, not to anyone in particular. 'It's just like it used to be in the villages. Jesus.' Bagabond went quietly, holding the calico cat tightly to her.

Ricardo sighted the rocket launcher carefully. Bagabond straightened.

Forty pounds of angry, wild black cat hit Ricardo squarely in the back. He fell forward as the tube tilted up and the rocket he had just fired headed for the roof. It exploded in a shower of red and gold sparks.

Rosemary pulled away from Joey and ran for the car.

Water began spraying into the tunnel. Jagged concrete blocks started to separate along their sealed junctures and then more water poured in.

'Ricardo, you idiot, you blew a hole in Central Park Lake!' Frederico the Butcher yelled at someone who was no longer an interested party. The mafiosi scattered down the tunnels in disarray.

'Get into the car. Come on!' Rosemary grabbed Bagabond.

'Maria, I'm coming for you. Hold on.' Don Carlo struggled against the rising flood to save his only daughter.

'Papa, I'm going with C.C.'

'No! You must not. It's cursed.' Don Carlo tried to move farther and realized his leg was trapped. He thrust both hands into the chilly water in an effort to free it and grasped scaly skin. He looked down and saw rows of ivory teeth. Implacable reptilian eyes looked back at his.

Rosemary had gotten everyone on board, even the black cat. The car began to move back up the west tunnel.

'Wait. Jack's back there. Don't leave him.' Bagabond tried to open the doors. Rosemary grabbed her shoulders.

'Who's Jack?'

'My friend.'

'We can't go back,' said Rosemary. 'I'm sorry.'

Bagabond sat in the rear seat, once more flanked by her two cats, and stared back at the water rushing into the tunnel behind them as they moved toward higher ground.

As the subway car climbed the 86th Street incline, the skirt of dark water followed, lapping at C.C.'s flanged wheels. She eventually reached a rise in the tunnel where the tide behind ceased to follow. C.C. stopped, started to roll back, locked her brakes.

Her passengers crowded against the rear connecting door, straining to see anything of what they had left in the darkness.

'Let us out, C.C.,' said Rosemary. 'Please.'

The subway car obligingly opened her side doors with a hiss. The four of them, two human and two feline, clambered down to the road-bed and stood at this new beach. The calico sniffed at the water's edge and turned away. She whined and looked up at Bagabond.

'Wait,' said the bag lady. An unaccustomed smile played for just a moment.

Rosemary strained, concentrating, attempting to peer through the darkness. The last thing she remembered seeing was her father trying to reach her, then just his face, his eyes. Finally nothing.

'There,' said Bagabond flatly.

They all tried to make something out. 'I don't see anything,' said Rosemary.

'There.'

Now they all saw something: a vee of ripples trailing from a wide, shovel-blade of a snout. They saw the pair of armor-protected eyes protruding from the water, inspecting the group on shore.

The cats began to yowl with excitement, the calico leaping back and forth, the black switching his tail like a blacksnake whip.

'That's Jack,' said Bagabond.

After a time, the dust literally settled, the water receded, wounds were bandaged, bodies buried, and the long-suffering city crews did their best to clean up the mess at union scale. Manhattan returned to normal.

The bottom of Central Park Lake was resealed and the basin refilled. Reports of sea monsters (more properly, lake monsters) were persistent but unverified.

Sixty-eight-year-old Sarah Jarvis finally realized what hidden identity surely must lurk beneath the surface of the President. In November 1972, she voted for George McGovern.

The fortunes of Joey Manzone rose – or at least they changed. He moved to Connecticut and wrote a novel about Vietnam that didn't sell, and a book about organized crime that did.

Rosa-Maria Gambione legally changed her name to Rosemary Muldoon. She completed her Columbia degree in social work and aids Dr. Tachyon with C.C. Ryder's therapy. She has entered law school and is contemplating a takeover of the family business.

C.C. Ryder is still one of the doctor's toughest cases, but there is apparently some progress in bringing both her mind and body back to human form. C.C. continues to create fine, sharp-edged lyrics. Her songs have been recorded by Patti Smith, Bruce Springsteen, and others.

From time to time – especially during bad weather – Bagabond and the black and calico cats move into the Alfred Beach pneumatic subway tube with Sewer Jack Robicheaux. It is a comfortable arrangement, but has necessitated a few changes. Jack no longer hunts rats. A common lament around the Victorian dining room is, 'Wha' dis now, chicken *again*?'

INTERLUDE FOUR

From 'Fear and Loathing in Jokertown,'
by Dr. Hunter S. Thompson, *Rolling Stone*, August 23, 1974.

Dawn is coming up in Jokertown now. I can hear the rumble of the garbage trucks under my window at the South Street Inn, out here by the docks. This is the end of the line, for garbage and everything else, the asshole of America, and I'm feeling close to the end of my line too, after a week of cruising the most vile and poisonous streets in New York ... when I look up, a clawed hand heaves itself over the sill, and a minute later it's followed by a face. I'm six stories above the street and this speed-crazed shithead comes climbing in the window like it's nothing. Maybe he's right; this is Jokertown, and life runs fast & mean here. It's like wandering through a Nazi death camp during a bad trip; you don't understand half of what you see, but it scares the piss out of you just the same.

The thing coming in my window is seven fucking feet tall, with triple-jointed daddy-long-legs arms that dangle so low his claws cut gouges in the hardwood floor, a complexion like Count Dracula, and a snout on him like the Big Bad Wolf. When he grins, the whole damn thing opens on a foot of pointed green teeth. The fucker even spits venom, which is a good talent to have if you're going to wander around Jokertown at night. 'Got any speed?' he asks as he climbs down from the window. He spies the bottle of tequila on the nightstand, snares it with one of those ridiculous arms of his, and helps himself to a big swallow.

'Do I look like the kind of man who'd do crank?' I say.

'Guess we'll have to do mine then,' Croyd says, and pulls a fistful of blacks from his pocket. He takes four of them and washes them down with more of my Cuervo Gold ...

... imagine if Hubert Humphrey had drawn a joker, picture the Hube with a trunk stuck in the middle of his face, like a flaccid pink worm where his nose ought to be, and you've got a good fix on Xavier Desmond. His hair is thin or gone, and his eyes are gray and baggy as his suit. He's been at it for ten years now, and you can tell it's wearing him out. The local columnists call him the mayor of Jokertown and the voice of the jokers; that's about as much as he's accomplished in ten years, him and his sorry hack Jokers' Anti-Defamation League – a couple of bogus titles, a certain status as Tammany's best-loved joker pet, invitations to a few nice Village parties when the hostess can't get an ace on such short notice.

He stands on the platform in his three-piece suit, holding his fucking hat in his trunk for Christ's sake, talking about joker solidarity, and voting drives, and joker cops for Jokertown, doing the old soft-shoe like it really meant something. Behind him, under a sagging JADL banner, is the sorriest lineup of pathetic losers you'd ever want to see. If they were blacks they'd be Uncle Toms, but the jokers haven't come up with a name for them yet ... but they will, you can bet your mask on that. The JADL faithful are heavy into masks, like good jokers everywhere. Not just ski masks and dominoes either. Walk down the Bowery or Chrystie Street, or linger for a while in front of Tachyon's clinic, and you see facial wear out of some acidhead's nightmare: feathered birdmasks & deathsheads & leather ratfaces & monks cowls & shiny sequined individualized 'fashion masks' that go for a hundred bucks a throw. The masks are part of the color of Jokertown, and the tourists from Boise and Duluth and Muskogee all make sure and buy a plastic mask or two to take home as souvenirs, and every half-blind-drunk hack reporter who decides to do another brainless write-up on the poor fucked-up jokers notices the masks right off. They stare so hard at the masks that they don't notice the shiny-thin Salvation Army suits and faded-print housedresses the masked jokers are wearing, they don't notice how *old* some of those masks are getting, and they sure as shit don't pick up on the younger jokers, the ones in leather & Levi's, who aren't wearing any masks at all. 'This is what I look like,' a girl with a face like a jar of smashed assholes told me that afternoon outside a rancid Jokertown porn house. 'I could give a shit if the nats like it or not. I'm supposed to wear a mask so some nat bitch from Queens won't get sick to her stomach when she looks at me? Fuck that.'

Maybe a third of the crowd listening to Xavier Desmond are wearing masks. Maybe less. Whenever he stops for applause, the people in the masks slap their hands together, but you can tell it's an effort, even for them. The rest of them are just listening, waiting, and they've got eyes as ugly as their deformities. It's a mean young bunch out there, and a lot of them are wearing gang colors, with names like DEMON PRINCES & KILLER GEEKS & WEREWOLVES. I'm standing off to the side, wondering if the Tack is going to show up as advertised, and I don't see who starts it, but suddenly Desmond just shuts up, right in the middle of a boring declaration about how aces & jokers & nats is all god's chillums under the skin, and when I look back over they're booing him and throwing peanuts, they're pelting him with salted peanuts still in the shell, bouncing them right off his head and his chest and his fucking trunk, tossing them into his hat, and Desmond is just standing there gaping. He's supposed to be the voice of these people, he read it in the *Daily News* and the *Jokertown Cry*, and the sorry old fucker doesn't have the least little turd of an idea of what's going down ...

... just past midnight when I walk outside of Freakers to piss casually into the gutter, figuring it's a safer bet than the men's room, and the odds against a cop cruising through Jokertown at this time of night are so remote that they're laughable. The streetlight is busted, and for a moment I think it's Wilt Chamberlain standing there, but then he comes closer and I notice the arms & claws & snout. Skin like old ivory. I ask him what the fuck his problem is, and he asks me if I'm not the guy wrote the book about the Angels, and a half-hour later we're sitting in a booth in the back of an all-night place on Broome Street, while the waitress pours gallons of black coffee for him. She has long blond hair and nice legs, and on the breast of her pink uniform it says *Sally*, and she's good to look at until you notice her face. I discover that I'm looking down at my plate whenever she comes near, which makes me sick & sad & pissed off. The Snout is saying something about how he never learned algebra, and there's nothing wrong with me that about four fingers of king-hell crank wouldn't cure, and after I mention that the Snout shows me his teeth and mentions that while there's a definite scarcity of real high-voltage crank around these days, it just so happens that he knows where he can put his hands on some ...

... 'We're talking *wounds* here, we're talking real deep-bleeding poisonous *wounds*, the kind that can't be treated with a fucking Band-Aid, and that's all Desmond's got up his trunk, just a fucking lot of Band-Aids,' the dwarf told me, after he gave me his Revolutionary Drug Brothers handshake, or whatever the fuck the goddamned thing is supposed to be. As jokers go, he got a pretty decent draw – there were dwarfs long before the wild card – but he's still damned pissed-off about it.

'He's been holding that hat in his trunk for ten years now, and all that ever happens is the nats shit in it. Well, that's *over*. We're not asking anymore, we're telling them, the JJS is *telling* them, and we'll stick it right in their pretty pearl-like ears if we have to.' The JJS is the Jokers for a Just Society, and it's got about as much in common with the JADL as a piranha has with one of those giant pop-eyed white goldfish you see waddling around in decorative pools outside of dentists' offices. The JJS doesn't have Captain Tacky or Jimmy Roosevelt or Rev. Ralph Abernathy helping out on its board of directors – in fact it doesn't have a board of directors, and it doesn't sell memberships to concerned citizens and sympathetic aces either. The Hube would feel damned uncomfortable at a JJS meeting, whether he had a trunk on his face or not ...

... even at four in the morning, the Village isn't Jokertown, and that's part of the problem, but mostly it's just that Croyd is hotwired & crazy on meanass crank, and as far as I can tell he hasn't slept for a week. Somewhere in the Village is the guy we set out to find, a half-black all-ace pimp who's supposed to have the sweetest girls in the city, but we can't find him, and Croyd keeps insisting that the streets are all changing around, like they're alive & treacherous & out to get him. Cars slow down when they see Croyd swinging down the pavement with those long triple-jointed daddy-long-legs strides of his, and speed up fast again when he looks over at them and snarls. We're in front of a deli when he forgets all about the pimp we're supposed to find and decides he's thirsty instead. He wraps his claws around the steel shutters, gives a little grunt, and just *yanks* the whole thing out of the brick storefront and uses it to smash in the window glass … halfway through the case of Mexican beer we hear the sirens. Croyd opens his snout and spits at the door, and the poison shit hits the glass and starts burning right through it. 'They're after me again,' he says in a voice full of doom & hate & speedfreak rage & paranoia. 'They're all after me.' And then he looks at me and that's all it takes, I know I'm in deep shit. 'You led them here,' he says, and I tell him no, I like him, some of my best fucking friends are jokers, and the red & blue flashers are out front as he jumps to his feet, grabs me, and *screams*, 'I'm not a joker, you *fuck*, I'm a goddamned *ace*,' and throws me right through the window, the *other* window, the one where the plate glass was still intact. But not for long … while I'm lying in the gutter, bleeding, he makes his own exit, right out the front door with a six-pack of Dos Equis under his arm, and the cops pump a couple rounds into him, but he just laughs at them, and starts to climb … His claws leave deep holes in the brick. When he reaches the roof, he howls at the moon, unzips his pants, and pisses down on all of us before he vanishes …

STRINGS

by Stephen Leigh

The death of Andrea Whitman was entirely Puppetman's doing. Without his powers, the sullen lust that a retarded boy of fourteen felt for a younger neighbor girl would never have been fired into a molten white fury. By himself, Roger Pellman would never have lured Andrea into the woods behind Sacred Heart School in the suburbs of Cincinnati, and there ripped the clothing from the terrified girl. He would never have thrust that strange hardness into Andrea until he felt a sagging, powerful release. He would never have looked down at the child and the trickle of dark blood between her thighs and felt a compelling disgust that made him grasp the large flat rock alongside them. He would never have used that stone to bludgeon Andrea's blond head into an unrecognizable pulp of torn flesh and splintered bone. He would never have gone home with her gore splattered over his naked body.

Roger Pellman would have done none of that if Puppetman had not been hiding in the recesses of poor Roger's damaged mind, feeding on the emotions he found there, manipulating the boy and amplifying the adolescent fever that wracked the body. Roger's mind was weak and malleable and open; Puppetman's rape of it was no less brutal than what Roger did to Andrea.

Puppetman was eleven. He hated Andrea, hated her with the horrible anger of a spoiled child, hated her for having betrayed and humiliated him. Puppetman was the revenge fantasy of a boy infected with the wild card virus, a boy who'd made the mistake of confessing to Andrea his affection for her. Perhaps, he'd told the older girl, they might one day marry. Andrea's eyes had gone wide at that and she'd run away from him giggling. He'd begun to hear the mocking whispers the very next day at school, and he knew even as the flush burned in his cheeks that she'd told all her friends. Told everyone.

When Roger Pellman tore away Andrea's virginity, Puppetman had felt the faint stirring of that heat himself. He'd shuddered with Roger's orgasm; when the boy slammed the rock into the girl's weeping face, when he'd heard the dull crack of bone, Puppetman had gasped. He staggered with the pleasure that coursed through him.

Safe in his own room, a quarter-mile away.

His overwhelming response to that first murder frightened him at the same time that it drew him. For months afterwards, he was slow to utilize that power, afraid to be so rapturously out of control again. But like all forbidden things, the urge coerced him. In the next five years, for various reasons, Puppetman would emerge and kill seven times more.

He thought of that power as an entity apart from himself. Hidden, he was Puppetman – a lacing of strings dangling from his invisible fingers, his collection of grotesque dolls capering at the ends.

TEDDY, JIMMY STILL SCRAMBLING
HARTMANN, JACKSON, UDALL WAIT FOR COMPROMISE
New York Daily News, July 14, 1976

HARTMANN PROMISES FLOOR FIGHT
JOKERS' RIGHTS ISSUE ON PLATFORM
The New York Times, July 14, 1976

Senator Gregg Hartmann stepped from the elevator cage into the foyer of the Aces High. His entourage filed into the restaurant behind him: two secret service men; his aides John Werthen and Amy Sorenson; and four reporters whose names he'd managed to forget on the way up. It had been a crowded elevator ride. The two men in the dark glasses had grumbled when Gregg had insisted that they could all make the trip together.

Hiram Worchester was there to meet the group. Hiram was an impressive sight himself, a man of remarkable girth who moved with a surprising lightness and agility. He strode easily across the carpeted reception area, his hand extended and a smile lurking in his full beard. Light from the falling sun poured through the large windows of the restaurant and gleamed from his bald head. 'Senator,' he said jovially. 'Good to see you again.'

'And you, Hiram.' Then Gregg smiled ruefully, nodding at the crowd behind him. 'You know John and Amy, I think. The rest of this zoo will have to introduce themselves. They seem to be permanent retainers anyway.' The reporters chuckled; the bodyguards allowed themselves thin, fleeting smiles.

Hiram grinned. 'I'm afraid that's the price you pay for being a candidate, Senator. But you're looking well, as usual. The cut of that jacket is perfect.' The huge man took a step back from Gregg and looked him up and down appraisingly. Then he leaned closer and lowered his voice conspiratorially. 'You should give Tachyon a few hints concerning his attire. Really, what the good doctor wore here this evening ...' Chestnut eyes rolled heavenward in mock horror, and then Hiram laughed. 'But you don't need to hear me prattling on; your table's ready.'

'I understand that my guests have already arrived.'

That sent the corners of Hiram's mouth down in a frown. 'Yes. The woman is fine, even though she drinks too much for my taste, but if the dwarf were not here under your aegis, I'd have him thrown out. It isn't so much that he's created a *scene*, but he's dreadfully rude to the help.'

'I'll make sure that he behaves, Hiram.' Gregg shook his head, running fingers through ash-blond hair. Gregg Hartmann was a man of plain and undistinguished appearance. He was neither one of the well-groomed and handsome politicians that seemed to be the new breed of the 70s, nor was he of the other type, the pudgy and self-satisfied Old Boys. Hiram knew Gregg as a friendly, natural person, one who genuinely cared for his constituents and their problems. As chairman of SCARE, Gregg had demonstrated a compassion for all those affected by the wild card virus. Under the senator's leadership, various restrictive laws concerning those infected by the virus had been relaxed, stricken from the books, or judiciously ignored. The Exotic Powers Control Act and the Special Conscription were still legally in effect, but Senator Hartmann forbade any of his agents to enforce them. Hiram often marveled at Gregg's deft handling of sensitive relations between the public and the jokers. 'Friend of Jokertown' was what *Time* had dubbed him in one article (accompanied by a photograph of Gregg shaking the hand of Randall, the doorman at the Funhouse – Randall's hand was an insect's claw, and at the center of the palm was a grouping of wet, ugly eyes). For Hiram, the senator was that rare Good Man, an anomaly among the politicians.

Gregg sighed, and Hiram saw a deep weariness behind the senator's good-natured facade. 'How's the convention going, Senator?' he asked. 'What chance does the Jokers' Rights plank have?'

'I'm fighting for it as hard as I can,' Gregg answered, and he glanced back at the reporters; they watched the exchange with unfeigned interest. 'We'll find out in a few days when we have the floor vote.'

Hiram saw the resignation in Hartmann's eyes; that gave him all the information he needed – it would fail, like all the rest. 'Senator,' he said, 'when this convention's over, I expect you to stop by here again. I'll prepare something special just for you; to let you know that your work's appreciated.'

Gregg clapped Hiram lightly on the back. 'On one condition,' he replied. 'You have to make sure that I can get a corner booth. By myself. Alone.' The senator chuckled. Hiram grinned in return.

'It's yours. Now, tonight, I'd recommend the beef in red wine – it's very delicate. The asparagus is extremely fresh and I made the sauce myself. As for dessert, you must taste the white chocolate mousse.'

Elevator doors opened behind them. The secret service men glanced warily back as two women stepped out. Gregg nodded to them and shook Hiram's hand again. 'You need to take care of your other guests, my friend. Give me a call when this madness is over.'

'You'll be needing a White House chef, too.'

Gregg laughed heartily at that. 'You'll need to speak to Carter or Kennedy about that, Hiram. I'm just one of the dark horses in this one.'

'Then they're passing by the best man,' Hiram retorted. He strode off.

The Aces High occupied the observation tower of the Empire State Building. From the expansive windows, the diners could gaze out to a view of Manhattan Island. The sun touched the horizon beyond the city harbor; the golden dome of the Empire State Building tossed reflections into the dining room. In the gold-green sunset, Dr. Tachyon was not difficult to spot, seated at his customary table with a woman Gregg did not recognize. Hiram had been right, Gregg saw immediately – Tachyon wore a dinner jacket of blazing scarlet trimmed with a collar of emerald-green satin. Purple sequins traced bold patterns on the sleeves and shoulders; mercifully, his pants were hidden, though a band of iridescent orange could be glimpsed under the jacket. Gregg waved, Tachyon nodded. 'John, please take our guests over to the table and make introductions for me. I'll be over in a second. Amy, would you come with me?' Gregg threaded his way through the tables.

Tachyon's shoulder-length hair was the same improbable red as his jacket. He ran a dainty hand through the tangled locks as he rose to greet Gregg. 'Senator Hartmann,' he said. 'May I present Angela Fascetti? Angela, this is Senator Gregg Hartmann and his aide Amy Sorenson; the senator's the man responsible for much of the funding of my clinic.'

After a few pleasantries, Amy excused herself. Gregg was pleased when Tachyon's companion took the hint without any prompting from Amy and left the table with her. Gregg waited until the two women were a few tables away and then turned to Tachyon. 'I thought you'd like to know that we've confirmed the plant in your clinic, Doctor. Your suspicions were right.'

Tachyon frowned, deep lines creasing his forehead. 'KGB?'

'Probably,' Gregg answered. 'But as long as we know who he is, he's relatively harmless.'

'I still want him out of there, Senator,' Tachyon insisted politely. He steepled his hands before his face, and when he glanced at Gregg, his lilac eyes were full of an old hurt. 'I've had enough difficulty with your government and their previous witch-hunts. I want nothing to do with another. I mean no offense by that, Senator; you've been a good man with whom to work and very helpful to me, but I'd rather keep the clinic entirely away from politics. My desire is to help the jokers, nothing more.'

Gregg could only nod at that. He resisted an impulse to remind the doctor that the politics he claimed he wished to avoid also paid some of the clinic's bills. His voice was laden with sympathy. 'That's *my* interest as well, Doctor. But if we simply fire the man, the KGB will have a new plant in place within a few months. There's a new ace working with us; I'll talk with him.'

'Do whatever you wish, Senator. I'm not interested in your methods so long as the clinic remains unaffected.'

'I'll see that it is.' Across the room, Gregg saw Amy and Angela making their way toward them.

'You're here to meet with Tom Miller?' Tachyon inquired, one eyebrow arching. He nodded his head slightly in the direction of Gregg's table, where John was still making introductions.

'The dwarf? Yes. He's—'

'I know him, Senator. I suspect he's responsible for quite a lot of death and violence in Jokertown in recent months. He's a bitter and dangerous man, Senator.'

'That's exactly why I want to forestall him.'

'I wish you luck,' Tachyon commented dryly.

JJS PROMISES VIOLENCE IF PLANK DEFEATED
The New York Times, July 14, 1976

Sondra Falin felt mixed emotions as Gregg Hartmann approached the table. She'd known that she was going to face this difficulty

444

tonight and perhaps had drunk more than she should have. The liquor burned in her stomach. Tom Miller – 'Gimli,' as he preferred to be called in the JJS – fidgeted next to her, and she laid an unsteady hand on the thick muscles of his forearm.

'Keep your fucking paws off me,' the dwarf growled. 'You ain't my goddamn grandmother, Sondra.'

The remark stung her more than it otherwise might have; she could only look down at her hand; at the dry, liverspotted skin hanging loose over thin bones; at the swollen and arthritic knuckles. *He'll look at me and smile like a stranger and I can't tell him.* Tears stung her eyes; she wiped at them savagely with the back of her hand, then drained the glass that sat before her. Glenlivet: it seared her throat all the way down.

The senator beamed at them. His grin was more than just the professional tool of a politician – Hartmann's face was natural and open, inviting confidence. 'Excuse my rudeness in not coming right over,' he said. 'I'd like to say that I'm very glad that the two of you agreed to meet with me tonight. You're Tom Miller?' Gregg said, turning to the bearded visage of the dwarf, his hand extended.

'No, I'm Warren Beatty and this here's Cinderella,' Miller replied sourly. His voice had the twang of the Midwest. 'Show him your slipper, Sondra.' The dwarf cocked his head belligerently at Hartmann, pointedly ignoring the hand.

Most people would have ignored the insult, Sondra knew. They would have drawn back their hand and pretended that it had never been offered. 'I met Mr. Beatty last night at the *Rolling Stone* party,' the senator said. He smiled, his hand the focus of attention around the table. 'I even managed to shake *his* hand.'

Hartmann waited. In the silence, Miller grumbled. At last the dwarf took Hartmann's fingers in his own ham-fisted grip. With the touch, Sondra seemed to see Hartmann's smile go cold for a moment, as if the contact had pained him slightly. He quickly let go of Miller's hand. Then his composure returned. 'Good to meet you,' Hartmann said. There was no trace of sarcasm in his voice, only a genuine warmth, a relief.

Sondra understood how she had come to love this man. *It's not*

*you who loves him; it's only Succubus. She's the one Gregg knows.
To him, you're just an old, shriveled woman whose politics are in
question. He'll never know that Succubus is the same person, not
if you want to keep him. All he'll ever see is the fantasy Succubus
makes for him. That's what Miller said we have to do, and you'll
obey him, won't you?*

No matter how much it hurts you.

Now it was her turn to shake Gregg's hand. She felt her fingers
trembling as they touched; Gregg noticed it as well, for a faint sympathy seemed to tug at the corners of his mouth. Still, there was
only curiosity and interest in his gray-blue eyes; no recognition
beyond that. Sondra's mood darkened again. *He's wondering what
horrible things afflict this old woman. He wonders what ugliness is
sitting inside me, what horrors I might reveal if he knew me.*

She reached for another glass of scotch.

Her mood continued to deepen throughout the meal. The
pattern of conversation seemed set. Hartmann would introduce
a topic, and Miller would respond with unjustified sarcasm and
scorn, which in turn the senator smoothed over. Sondra listened
to the interplay without joining in. The others around the table
evidently felt the same tension, for the stage remained open for the
two chief players, with the others inserting their lines as if on cue.
The dinner, despite the hovering solicitude of Hiram, tasted like
ashes in her mouth. Sondra drank more, watching Gregg. When
the mousse was set aside and the conversation turned serious,
Sondra was quite well drunk. She had to shake her head to clear
the fog.

'... need you to promise that there will be no public displays,'
Hartmann was saying.

'Shit,' Miller replied. For a moment, Sondra thought that he
might actually spit. The sallow, pitted cheeks under Gimli's ruddy
beard swelled and his maniacal eyes narrowed. Then he banged a
fist on the table, rattling dishes. The bodyguards tensed in their
seats, the others around the table jumped at the sound. 'That's the
same crap *all* you politicians hand out,' the dwarf growled. 'The JJS
has heard it for years now. Be good and roll over like a good dog

and we'll throw you a few table scraps. It's time we were let in on the feast, Hartmann. The jokers are *tired* of leftovers.'

Hartmann's voice, in contrast to Miller's, was soft and reasonable. 'That's something I agree with, Mr. Miller, Ms. Falin.' Gregg nodded to Sondra, and she could only frown in return, feeling the drag of the wrinkles around her mouth. 'That's exactly why I've proposed that the Democratic party add the Jokers' Rights plank to our presidential platform. That's why I've been out trying to collar every last vote I can get for it.' Gregg spread his hands wide. In another person his speech might have had a hollow sound, a falseness. But Gregg's words were full of the long, tired hours he'd spent at the convention, and that lent them truth. 'That's why I'm asking you to try to keep your organization calm. Demonstrations, especially anything of a violent nature, are going to prejudice the middle-of-the-road delegates against you. I'm asking you to give me a chance, to give *yourselves* a chance. Abandon your plan to march to Jetboy's Tomb. You don't have a permit; the police are already on edge from the crowds in the city, and they'll move in on you if you try.'

'Then, stop them,' Sondra said. The scotch slurred her words, and she shook her head. 'No one questions the fact that you care. So stop 'em.'

Hartmann grimaced. 'I can't. I've already advised the mayor against such actions, but he's adamant. March, and you invite confrontation. I can't condone your breaking the law.'

'Roll over, doggie,' Miller drawled, and then he howled loudly, throwing his head back. Around the dining room, patrons began to glance toward them. Tachyon peered at them with frank anger and Hiram's worried face emerged from the kitchen doors. One of the secret service men began to rise but Gregg waved him down. 'Mr. Miller, please. I'm trying to talk realities with you. There's only so much money and help available, and if you persist in antagonizing those who control them, you'll only hurt yourselves.'

'And I'm telling *you* that fucking "reality" is in the streets of Jokertown. C'mon down and rub your nose in the shit, Senator. Take a look at the poor creatures wandering the streets, the ones the virus wasn't kind enough to kill, the ones that drag themselves down the sidewalk on stumps, the blind ones, or the ones with two heads or four arms. The ones who drool as they talk, the ones who hide in darkness because the sun burns them, the ones for whom the slightest touch is agony.' Miller's voice rose, the tone vibrant and deep. Around the table, jaws had dropped; the reporters scribbled notes. Sondra could feel it as well, the throbbing power in that voice, compelling. She'd seen Miller stand before a jeering crowd in Jokertown and in fifteen minutes have them listening quietly, nodding to his words. Even Gregg was leaning forward, caught.

Listen to him, but be careful. His voice is that of the snake, mesmerizing, and when he's snared you, he'll pounce.

'That's your "reality,"' Miller purred. 'Your goddamn convention's just an act. And I tell you now, Senator' – his voice was suddenly a shout – 'the JJS *will* take our protests into the streets.'

'Mr. Miller—' Gregg began.

'*Gimli!*' Miller shouted, and his voice went strident, all its power gone, as if Miller had used up some inner store. '*My fucking name's Gimli!*' He was on his feet, standing on his chair. In another, the posture would have seemed ludicrous, but none of them could laugh at him. 'I'm a fucking *dwarf*, not one of your "*misters*"!'

Sondra tugged at Miller's arm; he shrugged her away. 'Let me alone. I want them to see how much I *hate* them.'

'Hate's useless,' Gregg insisted. 'None of us here hate you. If you knew the hours I've put in for the jokers, all the drudge work that Amy and John have gone through ...'

'*You don't fucking live it!*' Miller screamed it. Spittle flew from his mouth, dappling the front of Gregg's jacket. Everyone in the room stared now, and the bodyguards lurched from their seats. Only Gregg's hand held them back.

'Can't you see that we're your allies, not enemies?'

'No ally of mine would have a face like yours, Senator. You're too damn normal. You want to feel like one of the jokers? Then let me help you learn what it's like to be pitied.'

Before any of them could react, Miller crouched. His thick,

powerful legs hurled him toward the senator. His fingers curled like claws as he reached for Gregg's face. Gregg recoiled, his hands coming up. Sondra's mouth was open in the beginning of a useless protest.

And the dwarf suddenly collapsed onto the table as if a gigantic hand had struck him out of the air. The table bowed and splintered under him, glasses and china cascading to the floor. Miller gave a high, pitiful squeal like a wounded animal as Hiram, a molten fury on his red face, half-ran across the dining room toward them, as the secret service men vainly tugged at Miller's arms to get him off the floor. 'Damn, the little shit's *heavy*,' one of them muttered.

'*Out of my restaurant!*' Hiram thundered. He bulled his way between the bodyguards and bent over the dwarf. He plucked up the man as if he were a feather – Gimli seemed to bob in the air, buoyant, his mouth working soundlessly, his face bleeding from several small scratches. 'You are *never* to set foot in here again!' Hiram roared, a plump finger wagging before the dwarf's startled eyes. Hiram began to march toward the exit, towing the dwarf as if pulling a balloon and scolding him the entire time. 'You insult my people, you behave abominably, you even threaten the senator, who's only trying to help ...' Hiram's voice trailed off as the foyer doors swung shut behind him, as Hartmann brushed china shards from his suit and shook his head to the bodyguards. 'Let him go. The man has a right to be upset – you'd be too if you had to live in Jokertown.'

Gregg sighed and shook his head at Sondra, who gaped after the dwarf. 'Ms. Falin, I beg you – if you've any control over the JJS and Miller, please hold him back. I meant what I said. You only endanger your own cause. Truly.' He seemed more sad than angry. He looked at the destruction around his feet and sighed. 'Poor Hiram,' he said. 'And I promised him.'

The alcohol she'd consumed made Sondra dizzy and slow. She nodded to Gregg and realized that they were all looking at her, waiting for her to say something. She shook her gray, wizened head to them. 'I'll try,' was all she could mutter. Then: 'Excuse me, please.' Sondra turned and fled the room, her arthritic knees protesting.

She could feel Gregg's stare on her hunched back.

FLOOR VOTE ON JOKERS' RIGHTS TONIGHT
The New York Times, July 15, 1976

JJS VOWS MARCH ON TOMB
New York Daily News, July 15, 1976

The high-pressure cell had squatted over New York for the past two days like an enormous tired beast, turning the city unseasonably hot and muggy. The heat was thick and foul with fumes; it moved in the lungs like the Jack Daniel's Sondra poured down her throat – a burning, sour glow. She stood in front of a small electric fan perched on her dresser, staring into the mirror. Her face sagged in a cross-hatching of wrinkles; dry, gray hair was matted with sweat against a brown-spotted scalp; the breasts were empty sacks hanging flat against the bony rib cage. Her frayed housecoat gaped open, and perspiration trickled down the slopes of her ribs. She hated the sight. Despairing, she turned back into the room.

Outside, on Pitt Street, Jokertown was coming fully awake in the darkness. From her window, Sondra could see them, the ones that Gimli always ranted about. There was Lambent, far too visible with the eternal glow of his skin; Marigold, a cluster of bright pustules bursting on her skin like slow blossoms; Flicker, sliding from sight in the darkness as if illuminated by a slow strobe light. All of them seeking their small comforts. The sight made Sondra melancholy. As she leaned against the wall, her shoulder bumped a photograph in a cheap frame. The picture was that of a young girl perhaps twelve years old, dressed only in a lacy camisole that slipped over one shoulder to reveal the upper swell of pubescent breasts. The shot was overtly sexual – there was a haunting wistfulness in the child's expression and a certain affinity to the eroded features of the old woman. Sondra reached over to straighten the frame, sighing. The paint covered by the photograph was darker than that on the walls, testifying to how long it had been in place.

Sondra took another pull on the Jack Daniel's.

Twenty years. In that time, Sonya's body had aged two-and-a-half times as much. The child in the photo was Sondra, the picture taken by her father in 1956. He'd raped her a year before, her body already showing the signs of puberty though she'd been born five years earlier in '51.

Careful footsteps sounded on the stairway outside her apartment and halted. Sondra frowned. *Time to whore again. Damn you, Sondra, for ever letting Miller talk you into this. Damn you for ever coming to care for the man you're supposed to be using.* Even through the door she could feel the faint prickling of the man's pheromonal anticipation, amplified by her own feelings for him. She felt her body yearning to respond sympathetically and she relaxed her control. She closed her eyes.

At least enjoy the feel of it. At least be glad that for a little while you'll be young again. She could feel the quick changes moving in her body, straining at the muscles and tendons, pulling her into a new shape. The spine straightened, oils lathed the skin so that it lost its dry brittleness. Her breasts rose as a sexual heat began to throb in her loins. She stroked her neck and found the sagging folds gone. Sondra let the housecoat fall from her shoulders.

Already. So fast tonight. They'd been lovers for six months now; she knew what she'd find when she opened her eyes. Yes – her body was sleek and young with a fleecing of blond hair at the joining of her legs, her breasts small as they had been in her photo. This apparition, this mind-image of her lover: it was childlike, but not innocent. *Always the same. Always young, always fair; some vision of his past, perhaps. A waif, a virgin-whore.* Her fingertip brushed a nipple. It lengthened, thickening as she gasped at the touch, aroused. There was a wetness between her thighs already.

He knocked. She could hear his breath, a little too fast after the climb up the three flights, and found that his rhythm matched her own. Already she was lost in him. She unlocked the door, slid the deadbolt over. When she saw that there was no one in the hallway with him, she opened the door fully and let him stare at her naked-ness. He wore a mask – blue satin over the eyes and nose, the thin mouth below it lifted in a smile. She knew him – she needed only the response of her body. 'Gregg,' she said, and the voice was that of the child she had become. 'I was afraid that you weren't going to be able to be here tonight.'

He slid into the room, shutting the door behind him. Without saying anything, he kissed her long and deep, his tongue finding hers, his hands stroking the flank of her body. When he finally sighed and pulled away, she laid her head against his chest.

'I had a difficult time getting away,' Gregg whispered. 'Sneaking down the back stairs of my hotel like some thief ... wearing this mask ...' He laughed, a sad sound. 'The voting took forever. God, woman, did you think I'd desert you?'

She smiled at that and took a mincing step away from him. Taking his hand in her own, she guided him between her legs, sighing as his finger entered her warmth. 'I've been waiting for you, love.'

'Succubus,' he breathed. She chuckled softly, a child's giggle.

'Come to bed,' she whispered.

Standing beside the rumpled mattress, she loosened his tie and unbuttoned his shirt, biting gently at his nipples. Then she knelt before him, unlacing his shoes, taking off his socks before unfastening his belt and slipping his pants down. She smiled up at him as she stroked the rising curve of his penis. Gregg's eyes were closed. She licked him once, and he groaned. He started to remove the mask and she stopped him. 'No, leave it on,' she told him, knowing that it was what he wanted her to say. 'Be myste-rious.' Her tongue ran along his length again and she took him in her mouth until he gasped. Pushing him back on the mattress and cupping him gently, she teased him into heat, following the path of his needs, his lust amplifying her own until she was lost in the spiraling, bright feedback. He growled deep in his throat and pulled her away, rolling her over and spreading her legs roughly. He thrust into her; pounding, moving, his eyes bright behind the mask; his fingers digging into her buttocks until she cried out. He was not gentle; his excitement was a maelstrom in her mind, a swirling storm of color, a gasping heat that flailed both of them. She could feel his climax building; instinctively, she went with that welling of scarlet, her teeth clenched as his nails cratered her flesh and he slammed himself into her again and again and again …

He groaned.

She could feel him voiding inside her, and she continued to move under him, finding her own climax a moment later. The whirling began to subside, the colors faded. Sondra clung to the memory of it, hoarding the energy so that she could keep this shape for a time.

He was staring down at her behind the mask. His gaze traveled her body – the marks on her breasts, the red, inflamed gouges of his nails. 'I'm sorry,' he said. 'Succubus, I'm very sorry.'

She pulled him down beside her on the bed, smiling as she knew he wanted her to smile, forgiving him as she knew he needed to be forgiven. She kept the thread of arousal in him so that she could remain Succubus. 'It's all right,' she soothed him. She bent to kiss his shoulder, his neck, his ear. 'You didn't mean to hurt me.'

She glanced at his face, reached behind his head, and loosed the strings of his mask. His mouth sagged in a frown, his eyes were bright with his apology. *Touch him, feel the fire in him. Comfort him.*

Whore.

This was the part of it that Sondra despised, the part that reminded her of the years when her parents had sold her body to the rich of New York. She'd been Succubus, the best-known and most expensive prostitute in the city from '56 to '64. Nobody had known that she was only five when it started, that a joker had been attached to the ace she'd drawn from the wild card deck. No, they'd only cared that as Succubus she would become the object of their fantasies – male or female, young or old, submissive or dominant. Any body or any shape: a Pygmalion of masturbatory dreams. A vessel. No one knew or cared that Succubus would inevitably collapse into Sondra, that her body aged far too rapidly, that Sondra hated Succubus.

She'd sworn when she fled her parental captivity twelve years before that she'd never let Succubus be used again – Succubus would only give pleasure to those who had little chance for pleasure otherwise.

Damn Miller. Damn the dwarf for talking me into this. Damn him for sending me to this man. Damn me for finding that I like Gregg too much. And most of all damn the virus for forcing me to remain hidden from him. God, that dinner at the Aces High yesterday ...

Sondra knew that the affection Hartmann claimed to have for her was genuine, and she hated the realization. Yet her concern for the jokers was genuine as well, and her involvement with the JJS was a deep commitment. Knowing the government and, especially, SCARE was crucial. Hartmann influenced the aces that were beginning to side with the authorities after long, hidden years: Black Shadow, the Shaker, Oddity, the Howler. Through Hartmann, the JJS had been able to channel government monies to the jokers – Sondra had discovered the lowest bids on several government contracts; they'd been able to leak the information to joker-owned companies. Most importantly, it was because she controlled Hartmann that she was able to keep Miller from finally turning the JJS into the violent radical group that the dwarf wanted. While she could dangle the senator from Succubus's hands, she could limit Gimli's ambition. At least, that was her hope – after the Aces High fiasco, she was no longer certain. Gimli had been grim and sullen at their meeting this evening.

'You're tired, love,' she said to Gregg, tracing the line where his light hair dipped into a widow's peak.

'You wear me out,' he replied. The smile returned, tentative, and she brushed his lips with her own.

'You seem distracted, that's all. The convention?' Her hand slid down his body, over the stomach that age was beginning to soften. She caressed his inner thighs, using Succubus's energies to relax him, to put him at ease. Gregg was always tense, and there was also that wall in his mind that he would never open, a weak mindblock that would be useless against most of the aces she knew. She doubted that Gregg even realized that the block was there, that he too had been touched, however mildly, by the virus.

She felt the first resurgence of his passion.

'It wasn't very good there,' he admitted, cuddling her to him. 'The vote didn't have a chance, not with all the moderates against it – they're all afraid of a conservative groundswell. If Reagan can knock Ford out of the nomination, then the whole show's up in the air. Carter and Kennedy were both dead set against the plank – neither one of them wanted to be stuck supporting causes they weren't sure about. As the front-runners, their nonsupport was too much.' Gregg sighed. 'It wasn't even close, Succubus.'

The words seemed to coat her mind with ice and she had to fight to hold her form as Succubus. By now the word would be spreading through Jokertown. By now Gimli would know; he'd be organizing the march for tomorrow. 'You can't reintroduce the plank?'

'Not now.' He stroked her breasts, circling her aureola with a forefinger. 'Succubus, you don't know how I looked forward to seeing you after all this. It's been a very long and frustrating night.' Gregg turned to her and she snuggled against him comfortably, though her mind raced.

Musing, she nearly missed his words. '... if the JJS insists, it's going to be very bad.'

Her hand stopped moving on him.

'Yes?' she prompted.

But it was already too late. Already, she could feel the tug of his lust. His hand closed on hers. 'Feel,' he said. His hardness throbbed on her thigh. Again, she began to sink into him, helpless. Her concentration left her. He kissed her and her mouth burned; she straddled his body, guiding him into her once more. Inside, trapped, Sondra railed at Succubus. *Damn you, he was talking about the JJS.*

Afterward, exhausted, Gregg would say very little. It was all she could do to convince him to leave the apartment before her form collapsed and she became an old woman again.

SENATOR WARNS OF CONSEQUENCES AS MAYOR
VOWS ACTION

The New York Times, July 16, 1976

CONVENTION MAY TURN TO DARK HORSE
New York Daily News, July 16, 1976

'OKAY, DAMMIT! MOVE IT OVER *THERE*. IF YOU CAN'T MANAGE TO WALK, GO OVER TO GARGANTUA'S CART. LOOK, I KNOW HE'S STUPID, BUT HE CAN PULL A FUCKING *CART*, FOR CRISSAKES.'

Gimli exhorted the milling jokers from the tailgate of a rusty Chevy pickup truck, waving his short arms frantically, his face flushed with the effort of screaming, sweat dripping from his beard. They were gathered in Roosevelt Park near Grand, the sun baking New York from a cloudless sky, the early morning temperature already in the high eighties and heading for a possible three figures. The shade of the few trees did nothing to ease the sweltering – Sondra could barely manage to breathe. She felt her age with every step as she approached the pickup and Gimli, dark circles of perspiration under the arms of her calico sundress.

'Gimli?' she said, and her voice was a cracked and broken thing.

'NO, ASSHOLE! MOVE IT OVER THERE BY MARIGOLD! Hello, Sondra. You ready to walk? – I could use you to keep the back of the group organized. I'll give you Gargantua's cart and the cripples – that'll give you a place to ride that's away from the crowds and you can keep the ones in front moving. I need someone to make sure Gargantua doesn't do anything too fucking dumb. You got the route? We'll go down Grand to Broadway, then across to the Tomb at Fulton—'

'Gimli,' Sondra said insistently.

'*What*, goddammit?' Miller put his hand on his hip. He wore only a pair of paisley shorts, exposing the massive barrel chest and the stubby, powerful legs and arms, all liberally covered with reddish-brown curly hair. His bass voice was a growl.

'They say the police are gathering around the park gates and putting up barricades.' Sondra glared at Miller accusingly. 'I told you that we were going to have trouble getting out of here.'

'Yeah. Piss. Fuck 'em, we'll go anyway.'

'They won't let us. Remember what Hartmann said at the Aces

High? Remember what I told you he mentioned last night?' The old woman folded her bony arms over the tattered front of the sundress. 'You'll destroy the JJS if you get into a fight here ...'

'What's the matter, Sondra? You suck the guy's cock and take in all his political crap as well?' Miller laughed and hopped down from the pickup to the parched grass. Around them, two hundred to three hundred jokers milled about near the Grand Street entrance to the park. Miller frowned into Sondra's glare and dug bare toes into the dirt. 'All right,' he said. 'I'll go fucking look at this, since it bothers you so much.'

At the wrought-iron gate, they could see the police putting up wooden barricades across their intended path. Several of the jokers came up to Sondra and Miller as they approached. 'You gonna go ahead, Gimli?' one of them asked. The joker wore no clothes – his body was hard, chitinous, and he moved with a lurching, rolling gait, his limbs stiff.

'I'll tell you in a minute, huh, Peanut?' Gimli answered. He squinted into the distance, their bodies throwing long shadows down the street. 'Clubs, riot gear, tear gas, water cannon. The whole fucking works.'

'Exactly what we wanted, Gimli,' Peanut answered.

'We'll lose people. They'll get hurt, maybe killed. Some of them can't take clubs, you know. Some of them might react to the tear gas,' Sondra commented.

'Some of them might trip over their own goddamn feet, too.' Gimli's voice boomed. Down the street, several of the cops looked toward them, pointing. 'Since when did you decide that the revolution was too dangerous, Sondra?'

'When did you decide that we had to hurt our own people to get what you want?'

Gimli stared back at her, one hand shielding his eyes from the sun. 'It ain't what *I* want,' he said slowly. 'It's what fair. It's what's just. Even you said that.'

Sondra set her mouth, wrinkles folding around her chin. She brushed back a wisp of gray hair. 'I never wanted us to do it this way.'

'But we are.' Gimli took a deep breath and then bellowed toward the waiting jokers. 'ALL RIGHT. YOU KNOW THE ORDER – JUST KEEP GOING NO MATTER WHAT. SOAK YOUR HANDKERCHIEFS. STAY IN THE RANKS UNTIL WE REACH THE TOMB. HELP YOUR NEIGHBOR IF HE NEEDS IT. OKAY, LET'S GO!' The power was in his voice again. Sondra heard it and saw the reaction of the others; the sudden eagerness, the shouted responses. Even her own breath quickened to hear him. Gimli cocked his head toward Sondra, a mocking gleam in his eyes. 'You coming or are you going to go fuck someone?'

'It's a mistake,' Sondra insisted. She sighed, pulling at the collar of the dress and looking at the others, who stared at her. There was no support from them, not from Peanut, not from Tinhorn, not from Zona or Calvin or File – none of those who sometimes backed her during the meetings. She knew that if she stayed behind now, any hope she had of holding Miller in check would be gone. She glanced back at the park, at the groups of jokers huddling together and forming a rough line; the faces were apprehensive, but nonetheless resolute. Sondra shrugged her shoulders. 'I'm going,' she said.

'I'm *so* happy,' Gimli drawled. He snorted his derision.

THREE DEAD, SCORES INJURED IN JOKER RIOT
The New York Times, July 17, 1976

It was not pretty, it was not easy. The planning commission of the NYPD had made copious notes that supposedly covered most of the eventualities if the jokers *did* decide to march. Those who were in charge of the operation quickly found that such advance planning was useless.

The jokers spilled out of Roosevelt Park and onto the wide pavement of Grand Street. That in itself was not a problem – the police had blocked traffic on all through-streets near the park as soon as the reports of the gathering had come in. The barricades were across the street not fifty yards from the entrance. It was hoped that the march organizers would simply fail to get the protest together or, coming upon the ranks of uniformed cops in riot gear, they would turn back into the park where officers on horseback could disperse them. The police held their clubs in ready hands, but most expected not to use them – these were jokers, after all, not aces. These were the crippled, the infirm, the ones who'd been twisted and deformed: the useless dregs of the virus.

They came down the street toward the barricades, and a few of the men in the front ranks of the police openly shook their heads. A dwarf led them – that would be Tom Miller, the JJS activist. The others would have been laughable if they were not so piteous. The garbage heap of Jokertown had opened up and emptied itself into the streets. These were not the better-known denizens of Jokertown: Tachyon, Chrysalis, or others like them. These were the sad ones who moved in darkness, who hid their faces and never emerged from the dirty streets of that district. They'd come out at the urging of Miller, with the hope that they could, in their very hideousness, cause the Democratic Convention to support their cause.

It was a parade that would have been the joy of a carnival freak show.

Later, the officers indicated that none of them had actually wanted the confrontation to turn violent. They were prepared to use the least amount of force possible while still keeping the marchers off the downtown Manhattan streets. When the front ranks of the jokers reached the barricades, they were to quickly arrest Miller and then turn the others back. No one thought that would be difficult.

In retrospect, they wondered how they could have been so damned stupid.

As the marchers approached the barrier of wooden sawhorses behind which the police waited, they slowed. For long seconds, nothing happened at all, the jokers coming to a ragged, silent halt in the middle of the street. The heat reflecting off the pavement sheened the faces with sweat; the uniforms of the police were damp. Miller glowered in indecision, then motioned forward those behind him. Miller pushed aside the first sawhorse himself; the rest followed.

The riot squad formed a phalanx, linking their plastic shields, braced. The marchers hit the shields; the officers shoved back, and the line of marchers began to bow, buckling in on itself. Those behind pushed, crushing the front ranks of jokers against the police. Even then the situation might have been manageable – a tear-gas shell might have been able to confuse the jokers enough to send them running back to the relative safety of the park. The captain in charge nodded; one of the cops knelt to fire the canister.

Someone screamed in the crush. Then, like tenpins scattering, the first row of the riot squad went down as if some miniature tornado had blown them away. '*Jesus!*' one of the police screamed. 'Who the fuck …' The police clubs were out now; as the jokers hit the lines, they began to use them. A low roar dinned between the high buildings lining Grand Street, the sound of chaos let loose. The cops swung the clubs in earnest as frightened jokers began to fight back, striking out with fists or whatever was at hand. The joker with the wild TK power was throwing it everywhere with no control whatsoever: jokers and police and bystanders all were flung at random to roll in the streets or crash up against buildings. Tear-gas pellets dropped and exploded like a growing fog, adding to the confusion. Gargantua, a monstrous joker with a comically small head set on his massive body, moaned as the stinging gas blinded him. Hauling a wooden cart with several of the less ambulatory jokers set in it, the childlike giant went berserk, the cart careering after him with his riders clinging to the sides desperately. Gargantua had no idea which way to run; he ran because he could think of nothing else to do. When he encountered the re-formed police line, he pummeled wildly at the clubs that struck him. A blow from that clumsy, huge fist was responsible for one of the deaths.

For an hour the formless battle swirled within a few blocks of the park entrance. The injured lay in the streets, and the sound of sirens wailed, echoing. It was not until midafternoon that any semblance of normalcy could be restored. The march had been broken, but at a great cost to all involved.

That long and hot night, the police patrolling Jokertown found their cruisers pelted with rocks and garbage, and the ghostly shades of jokers moved in the back streets and alleys with them: glimpses of rage-distorted faces and raised fists; futile, frustrated curses. In the humid darkness, the residents of Jokertown leaned down from fire escapes and open windows in the tenements to throw empty bottles, flowerpots, trash: they thudded against the roofs of the police vehicles or starred the windshields. The cops stayed judiciously inside their cruisers, the windows up and the doors locked. Fires were set in a few of the deserted buildings, and the fire-fighting crews that came to the calls were assaulted from the shadows of nearby houses.

Morning came in a pall of smoke, a veil of heat.

In 1962, Puppetman had come to New York City and there found his nirvana in the streets of Jokertown. There was all the hatred and anger and sorrow that he could ever wish to see, there were minds twisted and sickened by the virus, there were emotions already ripened and waiting to be shaped by his intrusions. The narrow streets, the shadowed alleys, the decaying buildings swarming with the deformed, the innumerable bars and clubs catering to all manner of warped, vile tastes: Jokertown was thick with potential for him, and he began to feast, slowly at first, and then more often. Jokertown was his. Puppetman perceived of himself as the sinister, hidden lord of the district. Puppetman could not force any of his puppets to do anything that went against their will; his power was not that strong. No, he needed a seed already planted in the mind: a tendency toward violence, a hatred, a lust— then he could place his mental hand on that emotion and nurture it, until the passion shattered all controls and surged out. They were bright and red-hued, those feelings. Puppetman could see them; even as he fed on them; even as he took them into his own head and felt the slow building of a heat that was sexual in intensity; as the pounding, shimmering flare of orgasm came while the puppet raped or killed or maimed.

Pain was pleasure. Power was pleasure.

Jokertown was where pleasure could always be found.

HARTMANN PLEADS FOR CALM
MAYOR SAYS RIOTERS WILL BE PUNISHED
New York Daily News, July 17, 1976

John Werthen came into Hartmann's hotel room from the connecting door of the suite. 'You're not going to like this, Gregg,' he said.

Gregg had been lying on his bed, his suit jacket thrown carelessly over the headboard, his hands behind his head as he watched Cronkite talk about the deadlocked convention. Gregg turned his head toward his aide. 'What now, John?'

'Amy called from the Washington office. As you suggested, we gave the problem of Tachyon's Soviet plant to Black Shadow. We just heard that the plant was found in Jokertown. He'd been strung up to a streetlamp with a note pinned to his chest – pinned *through* his chest, Gregg; he wasn't wearing any clothes. The note outlined the Soviet program, how they're infecting "volunteers" with the virus in an effort to get their own aces, and how they're simply killing the resulting jokers. The note went on to identify the poor schmuck as an agent. That's all: the coroner doesn't think that he was conscious through most of what the jokers did to him, but they found parts of the guy up to three blocks away.'

'Christ,' Gregg muttered. He let out a long breath. For a long minute, he lay there as Cronkite's cultured voice droned on about the final vote on the platform and the obvious deadlock between Carter and Kennedy for the nomination. 'Has anyone talked to Black Shadow since?'

John shrugged. He loosened his tie and opened the collar of his Brooks Brothers shirt. 'Not yet. He'll say that *he* didn't do anything, you know, and in his own way, he's right.'

'Come on, John,' Gregg replied. 'He knew damn well what would happen if he tied the guy up with that note on him. He's one of those aces who think they can do things their way without worrying about the laws. Call him in; I need to talk with him. If he can't work our way, then he can't work for us at all – he's too dangerous.' Gregg sighed and swung his legs over the side of the bed, rubbing at his neck. 'Anything else? What about the JJS? Have you managed to reach Miller for me?'

John shook his head. 'Nothing yet. There's talk that the jokers will march again today – same route and all, right past city hall. I hope he's not that stupid.'

'He'll march,' Gregg predicted. 'The man's hungry to be in the limelight. He thinks he's powerful. He'll march.'

The senator stood and bent over the television set. Cronkite went silent in midsentence. Gregg stared out the windows. From his vantage point in the Marriott's Essex House, he could look down at the green swath of Central Park caught between the towers of the city. The air was stagnant, unmoving, and the blue haze of pollution hid the further reaches of the park. Gregg could feel the heat even with the air-conditioning in the room. Outside, it would be sweltering once more. In the warrens of Jokertown, the day would be unbearable, rendering already quick-fused tempers even shorter.

'Yes, he'll march,' Gregg said again, softly enough that John did not hear it. 'Let's go to Jokertown,' he said, turning back into the room.

'The convention?' John inquired.

'They won't settle anything for days yet. That doesn't matter at the moment. Let's collect my shadows and get going.'

JOKERS! YOU'RE BEING DEALT A BAD HAND!
– from a pamphlet handed out by JJS workers at the July 18th rally

Gimli exhorted the crowds under the brilliant noon sun. After the night of chaos in Jokertown, the mayor had put the city's police force on double shifts and canceled all leaves. The governor had placed the National Guard on standby. Patrols stalked the borders of the Jokertown district, and a curfew was imposed for the following night. The word that the JJS would attempt another march to Jetboy's Tomb had spread quickly through Jokertown the previous evening, and by morning, Roosevelt Park was swirling with activity. The police stayed away after two unsuccessful attempts to sweep the jokers out of the park resulted in broken heads and five injured officers. There were simply more of the jokers willing to march with the JJS than the authorities had predicted. The barricades were set in place on Grand Street once more, and the mayor harangued the assembled jokers via bullhorn. He was roundly jeered by those at the gates.

From the rickety dais they'd erected, Sondra listened to Gimli as the dwarf's strong voice swept the jokers up in its ferocity. 'YOU'VE BEEN TRAMPLED, SPAT UPON, REVILED LIKE NO OTHER PEOPLE IN HISTORY!' he exclaimed, and they screamed their agreement. Gimli's face was rapt, shiny with sweat, the coarse strands of his beard dark with the heat. 'YOU'RE THE NEW NIGGERS, JOKERS. YOU'RE THE NEW SLAVES, THE ONES BEGGING FOR RELEASE FROM A CAPTIVITY NO WORSE THAN THAT OF THE BLACKS. NIGGERS. JEWS. COMMUNISTS. YOU'RE ALL THOSE THINGS TO THIS CITY, THIS COUNTRY!' Gimli flung an arm toward the ramparts of New York. 'THEY WOULD HAVE YOU STAY IN YOUR GHETTO; THEY WOULD HAVE YOU STARVE. THEY WANT YOU TO BE KEPT IN YOUR PLACE SO THEY CAN PITY YOU, SO THEY CAN DRIVE DOWN THE STREETS OF JOKERTOWN IN THEIR CADILLACS AND THEIR LIMOUSINES AND LOOK OUT THE WINDOWS, SAYING "GOD, HOW CAN PEOPLE LIKE THAT STAND TO *LIVE!*"' The last word was a roar and it echoed through the park, all of the jokers rising to shout with Gimli. Sondra looked out on the mass of people, speckling the lawn under the glaring sun.

They'd all come out, the jokers, pouring from the streets of Jokertown. Gargantua was there, his immense body bandaged; Marigold, Flicker, Carmen, five thousand or more like them all behind. Sondra could feel the excitement pulsing as Gimli lectured them, his own bitterness snaking out like a poison into the air, infecting them all. *No*, she wanted to say. *No, you can't listen to him.*

Please. Yes, his words are full of energy and brilliance; yes, he makes you want to raise your fists and pump them skyward as you march with him. Still, can't you see that this is not the way? This is not the revolution. This is only the madness of a man. The words echoed in her mind, but she could not speak them. Gimli had caught her in his spell with the others. She could feel the arc of a smile on her chapped lips, and around her the other members of the cadre were yelling. Gimli stood at the front of the dais, his arms wide as the shouts became louder and louder, as a chant began to rise from the massed throat of the crowd.

'*Jokers' Rights! Jokers' Rights!*'

The beat hammered at the waiting ranks of police, at the inevitable crowd of bystanders and reporters.

'*Jokers' Rights! Jokers' Rights!*'

Sondra heard herself saying it along with the others.

Gimli jumped down from the dais, and the burly dwarf began to lead them toward the gates. The crowd began to move, a mob with no pretense of order. They spilled out of Roosevelt Park from the gates into the side streets. Taunts were shouted toward the waiting line of police. Sondra could see the flashing lights of the cruisers, could hear the drone of the trucks with the water cannon. That strange, undefinable roar she'd heard the day before was rising again, louder even than the continuing chant. Sondra hesitated, not knowing what to do. Then she ran toward Gimli, her legs aching. 'Gimli,' she began, but she knew the complaint was hopeless. His face was a leer of satisfaction as the protesters spilled from the park into the street. Sondra looked down toward the barricade, toward the line where the police waited.

Gregg was there.

He stood in front of the barricades, several officers and the secret service men with him. His shirtsleeves rolled up, his collar open and his tie loosened, he looked weary. For a moment, Sondra thought that Miller would march past the senator, but the dwarf stopped a few yards from the man – the marchers came to a ragged, uneasy halt behind him. 'Get the fuck out of the way, Senator,' Gimli insisted. 'Get out of the way or we'll just trample you underneath with all your goddamn guards and reporters.'

'Miller, this isn't the way.'

'There *is* no other way, and I'm tired of talking about it.'

'Please, let me talk just a few minutes more.' Gregg waited, glancing from Gimli to Sondra, to the others of the JJS in the crowd. 'I know you're bitter about what happened to the Jokers' Rights plank. I know that the way the jokers have been treated in the past is disgraceful. But dammit, things are changing. I hate to counsel you to have patience, but that's what this needs.'

'Time has run out, Senator,' Miller said. His mouth gaped open with a grin; the crowns of his teeth were dark and pitted.

'If you go forward, you'll guarantee a riot. If you'll go back to the park, I can keep the police from interfering any further.'

'And just what the hell good does that do us, Senator? We'd like to rally at Jetboy's Tomb. That's our right. We'd like to stand on the steps and talk about thirty years of pain and torment for our people. We'd like to pray for the ones who died and let everyone see by looking at us just how goddamn lucky the ones who died were. That's all – we ask for the rights that any other normal person has.'

'You can do all of that in Roosevelt Park. Every one of the national papers, all the networks will cover it – that's a guarantee, as well.'

'That's all you have to bargain with, Senator? It ain't much.'

Gregg nodded. 'I know it, and I apologize for it. All I can say is that if you'll turn your people back into the park, I'll do what I can for you, for all of you.' Gregg spread his hands wide. 'That's all I can offer. Please, tell me that it's enough.'

Sondra watched Miller's face. The shouting, the chanting continued behind their backs. She thought that the dwarf would laugh, would jeer at Gregg and push his way on past to the barricades. The dwarf shuffled bare feet on the concrete, scratched at the thatch of hair on his wide chest. He stared at Gregg with a scowl, rage in his deepset eyes.

And then, somehow, he took a step back. Miller's gaze dropped, and the tension in the street seemed to dissolve.

'All right,' he said. Sondra almost laughed. There were amazed protests from the others, but Gimli swung around to them like an angry bear. 'Dammit, you fucking heard me. Let's give the man a chance – one day, no more. It ain't gonna hurt us to wait one more day.'

With a curse, Gimli pushed his way back into the crowd, heading toward the park gates once more. Slowly, the others turned to follow. The chant began again, halfheartedly, and then died.

Sondra stared at Gregg for a long time, and he smiled at her. 'Thank you,' Gregg said in a quiet, tired voice. 'Thank you for giving me a chance.'

Sondra nodded. She could not speak to him; she was afraid that she would try to hug him, to kiss him. *You're just an old crone to the man, Sondra. A joker like the rest.*

How did you do it? she wanted to ask him. *How did you make him listen when he'd never listen to me?*

She could not frame the questions – not with that old woman's mouth, not with that old woman's voice.

Sighing, limping on swollen knees, she made her way back.

HARTMANN DEFUSES RIOT
TALK WITH JJS LEADER GAINS REPRIEVE
The New York Times, July 18, 1976, special edition.

JOKERTOWN IN CHAOS
New York Daily News, July 19, 1976

The JJS rally returned to Roosevelt Park. Through the rest of the sultry day, Gimli, Sondra, and the others gave speeches. Tachyon himself appeared to address the crowd in the afternoon, and there was a strange festival atmosphere to the gathering. The jokers sat on the grassy knolls of the park, singing or talking. Picnic lunches were shared with those nearest; drinks were poured and offered. Joints could be seen making the rounds. In a sense, the rally became a spontaneous celebration of jokerhood. Even the most deformed jokers walked about openly. The celebrated masks of Jokertown, the anonymous facades behind which many of the Jokertown residents were accustomed to hide, were dropped for the time.

For most, it was a good afternoon, something to take their minds off the heat, off the paucity of their existence – you shared life with your fellows, and if your troubles seemed overwhelming, there was always someone else to look at or talk to who might make you feel that things were not quite so awful after all.

After a morning that had seemed doomed to violence and destruction, the day had turned gentle and optimistic. The mood was one of hilarity, as if some corner had been turned and the darkness was left behind. The sun no longer seemed quite so oppressive. Sondra found that her own mood was elevated. She smiled, she joked with Gimli, she hugged and sang and laughed with the rest.

Evening brought reality.

The deep shadows of Manhattan's skyscrapers slid over the park and merged. The sky went ultramarine and then stabilized as the skyglow of the city's lights held back full darkness, leaving the park in a hazy murk. The city radiated the day's heat back into twilight; there was no relief from the heat, and the air was deathly still. If anything, night seemed more oppressive than day.

Later, the police chief would point to the mayor. The mayor in turn would point to the governor, whose office would claim that no orders originated there. No one seemed certain just who had ordered the action. And later, it simply didn't matter – the night of the 18th exploded into violence.

With a shout and a blare of bullhorns, the insanity began.

Mounted police, followed by club-wielding lines, began to sweep the park from south to north, intending to drive the jokers onto Delancey and then back into Jokertown. The jokers, disoriented and confused at the unexpected attack and urged on by the frantic Gimli, resisted. A club-swinging melee ensued, hampered by the darkness of the park. For the police, anyone without a uniform was fair game. They ranged through the park striking anyone they could touch. Screams and cries punctuated the night. Gimli's attempt at organizing the resistance broke down quickly, and small groups of the jokers were herded toward the streets, any who turned beaten or maced. Those who fell were trampled. Sondra found herself in one of those crowds. Panting, trying to keep her balance in the jostling flight, her hands over her head to protect herself from the clubs, she managed to find temporary safety in an alley off Stanton. There, she watched as the violence spread out of the park and into the streets.

Small scenes drifted past her.

A CBS cameraman was filming as a dozen policemen on motorcycles pushed a group of jokers toward a railing that shielded the ramp of an underground parking garage across the street from Sondra. The jokers were running; some of them jumped over the railing. Lambent was among them, illuminating the scene with the phosphorescent glow of his skin, a pitiful target unable to hide from the oncoming police. He vaulted the railing in desperation, plunging into the eight-foot drop beyond it. The police saw the cameraman then – one of them yelled 'Get the fucking camera!' – and the cycles wheeled around with a throaty rumble, the headlights arcing across the buildings. The cameraman began to run backward away from them, still filming. A club lashed out as the police went past; the man rolled in the street, moaning as the camera tumbled to the pavement, its lens shattered.

A joker stumbled by the mouth of the alley, obviously dazed, holding a blood-soaked handkerchief to his temple though the cut gaped open down past his ear, soaking the collar of his shirt. It was obvious how he had been caught – his legs and arms were canted at all the wrong angles, as if they'd been pasted on his trunk by a drunken sculptor. The man hobbled and lurched, the joints bending backward and sideways. Three cops came walking quickly alongside him. 'I need a doctor,' the joker said to one of them. When the officer ignored him, he tugged at the sleeve of the uniform. 'Hey,' he said. The cop pulled a can of mace from its holster on his belt and sprayed the contents directly into the joker's face.

Sondra gasped and sank deeper into the alley. When the police kept walking, she fled the other way.

Through the night, the violence spread out in the Jokertown streets. A running battle raged between the authorities and the jokers. It was a spree of destruction, a celebration of hate. No one slept that night. Masked jokers confronted the lurking cruisers, overturning some of them; burning cars illuminated intersections. Near the waterfront, Tachyon's clinic looked like a castle under siege, ringed by armed guards with the distinctive figure of the doctor himself running about trying to keep some semblance of sanity in the night. Tachyon, along with a few trusted aides, made forays into the streets to pick up the injured, both jokers and policemen.

Jokertown began to come apart, dying in fire and blood. Teargas fumes drifted through the streets, acrid. By midnight, the National Guard had been called in and issued live ammunition. The SCARE offices of Senator Hartmann issued a call for those aces working for the government to aid in calming the situation.

The Great and Powerful Turtle hovered over the streets like one of the war machines in George Pal's *War of the Worlds*, sweeping the combatants away from each other. Like many of the other aces, he seemed to take no side in the confrontation, using his abilities to break up the running battles without subduing either jokers or police. Outside Tachyon's clinic (where by one A.M. the wards were nearly full and the doctor was beginning to bed down the injured in the corridors) the Turtle picked up a wrecked, burning Mustang and hurled the car into the East River like a flaming meteorite, trailing sparks and smoke. He prowled South Street, shoving rioters and Guardsmen in front of him as if he wielded an invisible, giant plow.

On Third Street, the Guardsmen had rigged jeeps with wiremesh covers and attached large frames of barbed wire to the fronts of the vehicles. They used these to move crowds of jokers out of the main avenue and into the side streets. Spontaneous fires triggered by a hidden joker exploded the gas tanks of the jeeps, and Guardsmen ran screaming, their uniforms aflame. Rifle fire began to chatter.

Near Chatham Square, the sound of the rioting began to swell to immense, ear-shattering proportions as the Howler, dressed all in yellow, stalked the chaotic streets, his mouth open in a wail that contained all he had heard, amplified and redoubled. Where

Howler walked, jokers flung hands over ears, fleeing from this torrent of noise. Windows shattered when Howler raised the frequencies, walls shivered as he sobbed in the bass range. 'STOP THIS!' he raged. 'GO INSIDE, ALL OF YOU!'

Black Shadow, who had revealed himself as an ace only a few months before, indicated his sympathies quickly. He watched the conflicts silently for a time. On Pitt Street, where a band of beleaguered jokers fought with taunts, thrown bottles, and the garbage at hand against a water cannon and a squad of Guardsmen with bayonets fixed to their rifles, Black Shadow stepped into the fray. The street went instantly black for perhaps twenty feet around the ace with the navy-blue uniform and orange-red domino mask. The impenetrable night persisted for ten minutes or more. Screams came from inside the well of dark, and jokers fled. When the darkness moved off and the lights of the city again reflected from the wet pavement, the Guardsmen lay in the street unconscious, the water cannon pouring a harsh stream into the gutters, unattended.

Sondra saw that last confrontation from the window of her apartment. The violence of the night frightened her. To escape the fright, she twisted the cap from the bottle of Jack Daniel's on her dresser, pouring a long, harsh slug down her throat. She gasped, wiping at the back of her mouth with her hand. Every muscle in her body protested. Her arthritic legs and hands shot agony when she moved. She went to bed and lay down. She could not sleep – the sounds of rioting drifted in from the open window, she could smell smoke from nearby fires and see the shuddering flames dancing on her walls. She was afraid that she would have to leave the building; she wondered what she would try to save if it came to that.

There was a soft knock at her apartment door. At first, she was not certain that she heard it. It was repeated, quiet and persistent, and she groaned to her feet.

As she approached the door, she knew who it was. Her body felt it. Succubus felt it. 'No,' Sondra whispered to herself. *No, not now.* He rapped on the door again.

'Go away, please, Gregg,' she said, leaning against the door, keeping her voice quiet so he could not hear the old woman's tones in it.

'Succubus?' His voice was insistent. His arousal tugged at her, and she wondered at it. *Why now? Why here? God, I can't let him see me like this, and he won't go away.* 'Just a minute,' she said, and she let down the barriers that caged Succubus. Her body began its change, and she felt the swirling of his passion inciting her own. She stripped away Sondra's clothes, flinging them away into a corner. She opened the door.

Gregg was masked, his entire head covered with a grotesque smiling clown's face. It leered at her as he pushed his way inside. He said nothing; his hands were already unzipping his pants, pulling out his stiffening cock. He did not bother to undress, engaged in no foreplay at all. He pushed her down onto the hardwood floor and jammed himself into her, thrusting with gasping breaths as Succubus moved under him, matching his ferocity and cooperating with this loveless rape. He was brutal: his fingers dug into her small, firm breasts, the nails tearing small, bleeding crescents of skin. He crushed her nipples between thumb and forefinger until she cried out – he desired pain from her tonight; he needed her to cringe and cry and yet to be the willing victim. He slapped her face; when she brought her hands up to stop him from doing it again, her nostrils drooling blood, he twisted her wrist viciously.

And when he was done with her, he stood over her looking down, the clown's head laughing at her, his own face unreadable behind the mask. She could see only his eyes, glistening as he stared at her.

'It had to be that way,' he said. There was no apology in his voice. Succubus nodded; she had known that and accepted it. Sondra wailed inside her.

Hartmann zipped up his pants. The front of his shirt was soiled with blood and their fluids. 'Do you understand at all?' he asked her. His voice was gentle, calm; it begged her to listen, to sympathize. 'You're one person who accepts me without my having to do anything. You don't care that I'm a senator. I don't have to—' He stopped and brushed at his suit. 'You love me. I can feel that.

You care for me, and I don't have to *make* you care. I wish ...' He shrugged. 'I need you.'

Perhaps it was because she could not see his face. Perhaps it was because his roughness, when before he had always been so tender, had driven Succubus's empathy deeper into him than in the past. But she could feel his thoughts for a moment as he left her sprawled on the floor, and what she sensed made her shiver despite the awful heat. He was thinking of the rioting outside, and in the senator's mind was no loathing, no distaste; there was only a glow of pleasure, a sense of proprietorial accomplishment. She glanced at him in astonishment.

It's been him. All along, it's been him using us, not the other way around.

At the door, Gregg turned and spoke to her. 'Succubus, I do love you. I don't think you can understand that, but it's true. Please, believe that. I need you more than I need all the rest.'

Behind the mask, she could see the brightness of his pupils. She was astonished to see that he was crying.

Somehow, with all the strangeness Sondra had witnessed during this night, that did not seem so strange at all.

Puppetman found that his safety lay in anonymity, in the appearance of innocence. After all, none of the puppets ever knew that he had touched them, none of them could tell anyone what had happened inside their minds. They had simply ... *snapped.* Puppetman had only let them act out their own feelings; there was always ample motivation for whatever crimes his puppets might commit. If they were caught, no matter.

In 1961, graduating from Harvard Law School, he had joined a prestigious New York law firm. In five years, after a successful career as a criminal lawyer, he moved into politics. In 1965, he was elected New York city councilman. He was mayor from '68 to '72, when he became New York senator.

In 1976, he saw his chance to become President. In the past, he'd always thought in terms of '80, of '84. But the Democratic

National Convention went to New York in the Bicentennial year, and Puppetman knew that here was his moment.

The groundwork had all been laid.

He had fed many times from the deep cup of bitterness inside Tom Miller.

Now he would drink fully.

FIFTEEN DEAD AS JOKERTOWN BURNS
The New York Times, July 19, 1976

The morning sun was misted by dark smoke. The city broiled under the renewed heat, worse than the days before. The violence had not ended with the morning. The streets of Jokertown were awash in destruction, littered with the detritus of the night's turmoil. The rioters fought guerilla battles with the police and Guardsmen, hampering their movements through the streets, overturning cars to block intersections, setting fires, taunting the authorities from balconies and windows. Jokertown itself was ringed with squad cars, jeeps, and fire equipment. Guardsmen in full gear were stationed every few yards on Second Avenue. Along Chrystie, the guards massed around Roosevelt Park, where once again the jokers were gathering. Gimli's voice could be heard deep in the crowd, haranguing them, telling them that today they would march no matter what the consequences. All of the Democratic candidates made an appearance near the stricken area, to be photographed with concerned, stern expressions as they gazed at the burnt-out shell of a building or spoke with a not-too-misshapen joker. Kennedy, Carter, Udall, Jackson – they all made certain they were seen and then took their limos back to the Garden, where the delegates had cast two inconclusive rounds of votes for the candidacy. Only Hartmann came and stayed near Jokertown, chatting with the newsmen and trying unsuccessfully to coax Miller out from the depths of the crowd to negotiate.

At noon, with the temperature touching three figures and a breeze from the East River bringing the smell of burning to the city, the jokers came out of the park.

Gregg had never handled so many puppets before. Gimli was still the key, and he could feel the dwarf's raging presence maybe a hundred yards back into the crowd of jokers that filled Grand. In this swirling mess, Miller alone would not be enough to turn the jokers back at the right time. Gregg had made certain that he'd been able to shake the hands of the JJS leaders over the past few weeks; every time, he'd used that contact to plunge into the mind before him and open the pathways that would allow him access from a distance. A mob was like any herd of animals – turn enough of the leaders and the rest would inevitably follow. Gregg had most of them: Gargantua, Peanut, Tinhorn, File, perhaps twenty others. A few of them such as Sondra Falin he'd ignored – the old woman reminded him of someone's decrepit grandmother and he doubted her ability to sway the mob. Most of the puppets already had a fear in them – it would be easy to use that, to expand that fright until they turned and fled. Most of them were reasonable people; they wanted confrontation no more than anyone else. They had been goaded into it – Hartmann's doing. Now he would undo it, and in the process make himself the candidate of choice. Already the tide of the convention had turned away from Kennedy and Carter. With the delegates now absolved of their first vote commitment, they were free to elect the candidate of their choice – in the last ballot, Hartmann had placed a rising third. Gregg smiled despite the cameras aimed toward him: the rioting of the night before had given him a pleasure that he had not thought he would ever feel – so much passion had nearly overwhelmed him, a strange melding of lusts.

The line of Guardsmen began to shift as the jokers approached. They spilled out all along the length of Chrystie, shouting slogans and brandishing signs. Bullhorns blared orders and curses back and forth; Gregg could hear the taunts of the jokers as the Guardsmen formed a line of bayonets. At the intersection of Delancey Street, Gregg saw the hovering shell of the Turtle above the Guardsmen; there, at least, the protesters were kept back without harm. Farther south toward the main gates, where Hartmann stood in a circle of guards, it was not so easy.

The jokers came on, pushing and shoving, the mass of those behind propelling those who might have otherwise turned back into the park. The Guardsmen were forced to make a decision – use the bayonets or try to push the jokers back with linked arms. They chose the latter. For a moment, it looked as if some balance had been reached, then the ranks of Guardsmen began to slowly bend. With a cry, a knot of jokers broke through the line and reached the street. Shouting, the rest poured through. Once again, a running battle ensued, disorganized and confused. Hartmann, well back from the fighting for the moment, sighed. He closed his eyes as the impressions of his puppets began to reach him. If he wished, he could have lost himself then, could have plunged into that roiling sea of emotion and fed until satiated.

But he could not wait that long. He had to move while there was still some form to the conflict. Gesturing to the guards, he began to move forward toward the gates, toward the presence of Gimli.

Sondra was with the rest of the main cadre of the JJS. As they marched through the main gate, she tried again to tell Gimli about that strangeness she'd sensed in Hartmann last night. 'He thought he was controlling all of this. I swear it, Gimli.'

'Just like any other fucking politician, old woman. Besides, I thought you liked him.'

'I do, but—'

'Look, why the hell are you here?'

'Because I'm a joker. Because the JJS is my group too, whether I agree with what you're doing or not.'

'Then shut up, dammit. I've got a lot to handle here.'

The dwarf glared at her and moved away. They were walking at a slow, funeral pace toward the waiting Guardsmen. Sondra could see them through those in front of her. Then the vision was gone as the jokers crowded into the constriction of the gates; hobbling, limping, making their way as best they could. Many of them bore signs of the struggle of the day before; heads wrapped in bandages, slings – they proffered them to the Guardsmen like badges of honor. The bodies in front of Sondra suddenly halted as they hit the line of Guardsmen; someone shoved her from behind and she almost fell. She hugged the person before her, feeling leathery skin under her hands, seeing lizard-like scales covering a massive back. Sondra cried out as she was crushed, pushing away with feeble arms, muscles wobbling inside loose bags of skin. She thought she would fall, when suddenly the pressure was released. She staggered. Her eyes caught the sun then; she was momentarily blinded. In the confusion, she could see fists swinging in front of her, accompanied by shouts and cries. Sondra began to retreat, trying to find a way past the conflict. She was shoved, and when she struck back, a club slammed against the side of her head.

Sondra screamed. Succubus screamed.

Her vision was lost in swirls of color. She could not think. She held her hands over the cut and the hands felt odd. Blinking away blood from the cut on her temple, she tried to look at them. They were young, those hands, and even as she gaped at them in confusion, she felt the sudden intrusion of other passions.

No! Go back inside, damn you! Not here, not in the streets, not with all these people around! Desperately, Sondra tried to place the controls back on Succubus, but her head rang with the concussion and she could not think. Her body was in torment, shifting fluidly in response to everyone about her. Succubus touched each of the minds and took the shape of its sexual desires. She was first female, then male; young and old, thin and fat. Succubus wailed in confusion. Sondra ran, her shape altering with each step, pushing against the hands that reached out for her in sudden odd lust. Succubus responded as she had to; she took the thread of desire and wove it into passion. In an ever-widening circle, the rioting ended as jokers and Guardsmen alike turned to pursue the quick tug of desire. Succubus could feel *him* as well, and she tried to make her way toward Gregg. She didn't know what else to do. He controlled this; she knew that from last night. He could save her. He loved her – he had said so.

♥

The cameras followed Senator Hartmann's progress toward the gate where a few scuffles were just beginning. When his bodyguards tried to hold the senator back, he shrugged their hands aside. 'Dammit, someone has to try,' he was heard to say.

'Oh, *good* stuff,' one of the reporters muttered.

Hartmann pushed forward. The bodyguards looked at one another, shrugged, and followed.

Gregg could feel the presence of most of his puppets in the area near the gate. With the Turtle holding back the jokers at the other end of the park, Gregg realized that this would be his best opportunity. Getting Gimli and the others to retreat now would turn everyone back. If the rioting continued into the night again, no matter – Gregg would have quite amply demonstrated his calm sureheadedness in a crisis. The papers would be full of the account the next morning and all the networks would feature his face and name prominently. That would be enough to ensure the nomination with a grand momentum into the campaign itself. Ford or Reagan; it wouldn't matter who the Republicans chose.

Keeping his face grim, Gregg strode toward the center of the conflict. 'Miller!' he shouted, knowing the dwarf was close enough to hear him. 'Miller, this is Hartmann!' As he shouted, he gave a tug at Miller's mind and closed down that molten heat of rage, laving it with cool azure. He felt the sudden release, felt the beginning of the dwarf's disgust at the vision around him. Hartmann twisted the mind again, touching the core of fright in the man and willing it to grow, a cold whiteness.

It's out of control, Gregg whispered to the man. *You've lost it now and you can't get it back unless you go to the senator. Listen: he's calling for you. Be reasonable.*

'Miller!' Gregg called again. He felt the dwarf begin to turn, and Gregg pushed the Guardsmen in front of him aside so that he could see.

Gimli was to his left. But even as Hartmann began to call to him, he saw the joker's attention shift away toward the gate. There, pursued by a crowd of jokers and Guardsmen, Gregg saw her.

Succubus.

Her form was erratic, a hundred faces and bodies flickering on her as she ran. She saw Gregg in that same instant. She cried out to him, her arms outstretched. 'Succubus!' he shouted back. He began to shoulder his way toward her.

Someone caught her from behind. Succubus twisted away, but other hands had her now. With a shrill scream, she fell. Gregg could see nothing of her then. There were bodies all around her; shoving, striking each other in their fury to be near her. Gregg heard the grotesque, dry crack of bones snapping. '*No!*' Gregg began to run. Gimli was forgotten, the riot was forgotten. As he came nearer to her, he could sense her presence, could feel the pull of her attraction.

They piled on top of her, the swarming, snarling mob pummeling her, tearing at Succubus and each other in an attempt to find release. They were like maggots wriggling over a piece of meat, their faces strained and fierce, their hands clawed as they pawed at Succubus, thrusting. Blood fountained suddenly from somewhere below the writhing pack. Succubus screamed; a wordless, shrill agony that was suddenly, eerily, cut off.

He felt her die.

Those around her began to pull back, a horror on their faces. Gregg could see the body huddled on the ground. A thick smear of blood spilled around it. One of the arms had been ripped completely from its socket, her legs were twisted at strange angles. Gregg saw none of that. He stared only at her face: he saw the reflection of Andrea Whitman lying there.

A rage grew in him. The intensity of it swept everything else aside. He could see nothing around him – not the cameras, not his bodyguards, not the reporters. Gregg could only see *her*.

She had been his. She had been his without having to be a puppet, and they had taken her from him. They had mocked him; as Andrea had mocked him years ago, as others had mocked him who had also died. He had loved her as much as he could love anyone. Gregg grasped the shoulder of a Guardsman who stood over the body, his cock hanging down from unzipped pants. Gregg jerked him around. 'You *asshole!*' As he shouted, he struck the man in the face repeatedly. 'You goddamn *asshole!*'

His fury spilled out from his mind unrestricted. It flowed to his puppets. Gimli bellowed, his voice as compelling as ever. 'You see! See how they kill?' The jokers took up the cry and attacked. Hartmann's bodyguards, suddenly fearful as the violence was renewed, dragged the senator away from the combat. He cursed them, resisting, fighting to be loose, but this time they were adamant. They pulled him back to the car and his hotel room.

HARTMANN ENRAGED AT KILLING, ATTACKS DEMONSTRATORS CARTER APPEARS TO BE WINNER

The New York Times, July 20, 1976

HARTMANN 'LOSES HEAD' MUST SOMETIMES FIGHT BACK, HE SAYS

New York Daily News, July 20, 1976

He salvaged what he could from the fiasco. He told the waiting reporters that he'd simply been appalled by what he'd witnessed, by the unnecessary violence done to the poor Succubus. He'd shrugged his shoulders, smiled sadly, and asked them if they, too, might not have been moved by such a scene.

When they finally left him, Puppetman retired to his room. There, in the solitude of his room, he watched the proceedings on television as the convention elected Carter as his party's next presidential candidate. He told himself that he didn't care. He told himself that next time it would be his. After all, Puppetman was still safe, still hidden. No one knew his secret.

In his mind, Puppetman lifted a hand and spread his fingers. The strings pulled; his puppets' heads jerked up. Puppetman felt their emotions, tasting the spice of their lives.

For that night, at least, the feast was bitter and galling.

INTERLUDE FIVE

From 'Thirty-Five Years of Wild Cards, a Retrospective,'
Aces! magazine, September 15, 1981.

'I can't die yet, I haven't seen *The Jolson Story.*'
— Robert Tomlin

'They are an abomination unto the Lord, and on their
faces they bear the mark of the beast, and their number
in the land is six hundred and sixty-six.'
— anonymous anti-joker leaflet, 1946

'They call it quarantine, not discrimination. We are
not a race, they tell us, we are not a religion, we are
diseased and so it is right that they set us apart, though
they know full well that the wild card is not contagious.
Ours is a sickness of the body, theirs a contagion of the
soul.'
— Xavier Desmond

'Let them say what they will. I can still fly.'
— Earl Sanderson, Jr.

'Is it my fault that everyone likes me, and no one likes you?'

             – David Harstein (to Richard Nixon)

'I like the taste of joker blood.'

             – graffiti, NYC subway

'I don't care what they look like, they bleed red just like anybody else … most of them, anyway.'

             – Lt. Col. John Garrick, Joker Brigade

'If I'm an ace, I'd hate to see a deuce.'

             – Timothy Wiggins

'You want to know if I'm an ace or a joker? The answer is yes.'

             – The Turtle

I'm a joker, I'm insane,
And you cannot say my name
Coiled in the streets
Waiting only for night
I am the serpent who gnaws
the roots of the world

             – 'Serpent Time,' Thomas Marion Douglas

'I'm delighted to have Baby returned to me, but I have no intention of leaving earth. This planet is my home now, and those touched by the wild card are my children.'

             – Dr. Tachyon, on the occasion of the return of his spaceship

'They are the demon children of the Great Satan, America.'

— Ayatollah Khomeini

'In hindsight, the decision to use aces to secure the safe return of the hostages was probably a mistake, and I take full responsibility for the failure of the mission.'

— President Jimmy Carter

'Think like an ace, and you can win like an ace. Think like a joker, and the joke's on you.'

— *Think Like An Ace!* (Ballantine, 1981)

'The parents of America are deeply concerned about the excessive coverage of aces and their exploits in the media. They are bad role models for our children, and thousands are injured or killed each year while attempting to imitate their freak powers.'

— Naomi Weathers, American Parents League

'Even their kids want to be like us. These are the '80s. A new decade, man, and we're the new people. We can fly, and we don't need no bogus airplane like that nat Jetboy. The nats don't know it yet, but they're obsolete. This is a time for aces.'

— anonymous letter in *Jokertown Cry,* January 1, 1981

GHOST GIRL TAKES MANHATTAN

By Carrie Vaughn

Jennifer didn't know where Tricia was taking her until her friend dragged her out of the subway car onto the 2nd Avenue-Lower East Side platform. She'd spent the last four stops getting more and more worried – past Midtown, past Washington Square Park, past any place that they had any business being, and Tricia kept saying, 'No, that's where we always go, I want to try someplace new, it'll be *fun!*'

'Trish, are you *crazy*? What are we *doing* here?' Jennifer clung to her friend with both hands and tried to slow her progress to the tiled hallway and stairs up to Houston Street. She looked around, drawing even closer to Tricia. She'd never seen so many jokers in one place. Half the people standing on the platform were jokers. She'd seen jokers before; you didn't live in New York – even if you never got all that far from Columbia's campus – without seeing jokers. Most of the time you only saw one or two, and their jokers were mild – they had feathers for hair or maybe rabbit ears. But here whole bodies had been wracked, transformed, made monstrous. A man passed by her and left a trail of slime on the concrete. Jennifer tried not to stare.

Tricia pulled her up the stairs and onto the street, where the chaos increased. 'Come on, the Fads are playing CBGB and I really really want to go, and if I'd told you beforehand you never would have come. Right? You'd have gotten all huffy and snobby like you're doing right now.'

'I'm not snobby,' Jennifer said, trying not to pout. She'd never even heard of the Fads.

'Come on, live a little. Nothing's going to happen.'

Meekly now, Jennifer walked with her friend – still keeping close enough that their arms touched. 'My parents would flip out if they knew I was anywhere near Jokertown.'

Tricia said, 'So don't tell them. You don't tell them everything, do you?'

'No.' In fact, Jennifer didn't. She had the one big secret she was keeping from absolutely everybody. Even Tricia. She couldn't tell Tricia that a lot of the reason she didn't want to go out was because she was sure that one of these days, someone would find out. Someone would look at her and *know*.

Especially someone in Jokertown. Some of them didn't just have deformities, the physical scars of the wild card virus. Some of them had powers. Some of them would be able to read her mind and they'd *know*. After that, Jennifer didn't know what would happen. She'd never really gotten that far thinking about it. Best just to pretend nothing was wrong at all.

If it weren't for Tricia, Jennifer would never get out to explore the city at all. And they usually had a good time, in the end.

At Tricia's urging, and trusting her friend not to lead her *too* far astray, Jennifer had dressed for a night out: a black off-the-shoulder minidress, high-heeled sandals, her blond hair feathered and sprayed into place. Tricia was wearing leopard-print hot pants and an oversized shirt with a gold belt, and her heels were even higher.

'Here it is, here it is!' Tricia said, tugging Jennifer's arm to make her hurry.

Maybe she expected something glitzy, the way Tricia was carrying on. Like Studio 54. But on any other day Jennifer would have walked right by this place without noticing it. It was hardly anything at all, just a tiny graffitied storefront with a white awning next to a restaurant supply warehouse. It didn't even have a marquee. But it did have a crowd standing out front, sharing the sidewalk with a couple of homeless jokers propped against the brick wall.

With Tricia in the lead, they plowed through people on the way to the front door. Both nats and jokers made up the crowd. Maybe even an ace or two, but who could tell? Jennifer wasn't going to tell anyone.

A guy at the door was charging cover, and Jennifer was digging in her bag for a five when Tricia tugged on her arm. 'Do you have an extra five? I can't find mine.' She wore a pleading look.

Jennifer sighed and handed her an extra five. So much for cab fare home. But they'd come up with something; they always did.

Inside, the lights were stark; the walls were black and covered with stickers and spray paint. A bar ran along one wall, a door opened to the back, and a stage was tucked in a corner. A band was playing. A handwritten poster taped to the wall above them read SONIC YOUTH. They were really young – one of the guitarists was a woman with wild blond hair. They were wearing masks and might have been punks or jokers or both. Unless she got closer, Jennifer probably wouldn't be able to tell.

The music was loud, not really danceable, and no one was really dancing. But people were moving. A crowd of them, up close to the stage, jumping, crashing into each other, reaching toward the stage. The woman guitarist was singing, sort of, shouting lyrics that were barely audible over the instruments: roaring guitars and crashing drums. Sweat was flying off her hair. The place was roasting under all the lights.

Tricia squealed and bounced in place. 'Isn't this—' – and inaudible.

'What?' Jennifer shouted back.

'Hey!' said a tall guy – skinny, dark hair, black T-shirt that said THE RAMONES on it in faded letters – shifting to stand in front of them. 'Can I get you two drinks?'

Tricia squealed again and twined her arm around his. Jennifer rolled her eyes.

After seeing a couple of guys in mohawks out front, Jennifer had expected scary punks with spiked hair and army jackets, combat boots and spray-painted T-shirts. She'd expected chains and fights breaking out. This wasn't like that. While some actual real live punks were part of the crowd, a lot of the guys looked somewhere between punk and normal, with torn jeans and black T-shirts and surly expressions, but they didn't have the weird hair and all the metal and slogans. A lot of the women didn't dress much different than the guys, but others were decked out, like Jennifer and Tricia. Hair full of color and teased and sprayed in halos around their heads, short skirts and colored tights, high heels and big earrings, pink lip gloss and glaring eye shadow. An absolutely gorgeous couple stood in the corner near the stage. They had impeccable hair, cut and styled like models in a magazine. He wore an expensive-looking white suit and she wore a clinging black cocktail dress, silver jewelry, and smoked from a cigarette holder. Totally affected, but intriguing all the same. Then there was a bunch of regular partiers – young, normal college kids, maybe a little glassy-eyed, looking for the next high. Jennifer had been worried she'd stand out, that people would know she didn't belong and give her a hard time. But she didn't stand out, and no one gave her a hard time.

About a third of the crowd were jokers, and Jennifer hardly noticed at first. Because they didn't stand out, either. Some of them wore masks. Or they might have been nats wearing masks. She simply couldn't tell. And it didn't seem to matter.

Jennifer caught a glimpse of another couple at the other end of the bar. They looked like the rest of the crowd on the surface, jeans and T-shirts, unpretentious, except they were maybe ten years older than most of the people here.

Then Jennifer gasped. She shook Tricia. 'Is that Mick Jagger and Jeri Hall?'

Tricia had been in the middle of a drink and spilled part of what smelled like a gin and tonic down her chin, but she managed to look anyway. Her eyes went big. 'Oh my God, and he's talking to *David Byrne*!'

Jennifer didn't know who David Byrne was.

Another band played right before the Fads came on stage. By then, Tricia was completely drunk, and Jennifer was propping her up because she kept falling into other people. No one seemed to mind, and Jennifer tried not to be embarrassed, but she hadn't come along to be Tricia's babysitter.

No, on second thought, she probably had. Tricia had probably only asked her because Jennifer was the responsible one and would get them both home in one piece. Jennifer had been nursing the same rum and Coke for an hour. She was sure Tricia had been popping pills. Everyone seemed to be popping pills.

The place was hot like a greenhouse, full of sweat, cigarette smoke, and alcoholic breath.

It seemed to take forever for one band to leave the stage and the other to take it, and when Tricia realized the Fads were up, she squealed and ran to the front, shoving to get past people, laughing when they shoved back. Jennifer shouted after her, but couldn't even hear herself.

The Fads were three guys. Two of them were jokers – the intriguing kind. The lead singer had glowing hair, thin white strands, neck length, that lit up at the end like one of those fiber-optic lamps in kitsch shops. The guitarist had too many fingers on each hand. Too many to count, because they moved too quickly over the strings of his instrument, creating a bizarre pattern of sounds. The drummer seemed to be normal, a shirtless punk with spiky bleached hair and a safety pin in his left ear.

The so-called music consisted of manic drumming and not much of a melody. The singer shouted. Jennifer couldn't make out too many of the lyrics. Stuff about hating your parents, setting things on fire, and wondering when the bombs were going to fall.

Finally, the band finished. There was a lot of screaming.

'I have to pee,' Tricia announced, grabbing Jennifer's hand and pulling her to the back of the club. Jennifer caught her as she was falling over.

'Are there even bathrooms here?' Jennifer asked, dubious. She wasn't sure she wanted to see them, based on what the rest of the place looked like. Tricia just rolled her eyes – the 'could you be any less cool?' expression.

The place was a cave, black walls closing in, graffiti adding to the sensory overload. A staircase off to the side did indeed lead down to the bathrooms. Jennifer smelled them before they reached them. The sweaty, musty smell of the rest of the club gave way to an undertone of sewer. She wrinkled her nose.

Tricia kept her balance by holding onto Jennifer as she shoved through the door and into the women's restroom. Here, the sewer smell poured out, unadulterated. The floor was sticky, and Jennifer was afraid to look in the stalls at the toilets and what was no doubt overflowing out of them.

The mess – at the level of serious health hazard – didn't keep a mob of women from crowding in front of a graffiti-trimmed mirror, spraying their hair and touching up their eyeliner.

Tricia seemed to have forgotten her need to actually use the facilities. She fell against a wall, plastered with stickers and posters, and beamed up at some heavenly vision. 'That was amazing, that was *so* amazing!'

Next to them, a woman in fishnets, a plaid skirt, and leather bustier was holding a mirror flat, a couple of lines of white powder neatly laid out on top of it. A similarly dressed friend bent close and inhaled the cocaine.

The first caught Jennifer staring. 'Want some?' she said. 'I've got plenty.'

Jennifer quickly shook her head and thought about how uncool she really was.

'Sure, yeah, thanks!' Tricia said, leaning forward while the woman held the mirror steady.

'Tricia—' Jennifer said, but the second line of coke was already gone up Trish's nose. And could this night get any worse?

Tricia straightened, her face flush, rubbing her nose and giggling. 'Oh my God, I have a great idea.'

'No, not another one,' Jennifer muttered. She was breathing through her mouth because the smell seemed to be getting worse.

Water gurgled from the one of the stalls, and some of the other girls shouted, 'Geez, you didn't actually flush that, did you? God!'

Tricia grabbed Jennifer's hand again and headed back for the door. 'I want to follow them.'

'Follow who?'

'The Fads! Tony! I want to try to meet them!'

'Tony?'

'The lead singer! Isn't he so cool?'

'Trish, do you know how late it is? It's time to go!'

'Just a minute, it'll only take a minute.'

Somehow, Tricia steered them back up the stairs and down a hallway to an unguarded doorway. The walls were covered with old posters and flyers advertising shows here, some of them going back years. She even recognized some of the bands. Wow, the Police played here? And Blondie? Really? But Tricia was on a mission, unhesitating. She'd broken away, and Jennifer hurried to catch up.

They had seemed to emerge from the crowd, but people closed around them again at the end of the hallway, which opened into back rooms, dressing rooms, and storage. Jennifer recognized the lead singer – he was signing autographs on the backs of flyers and tickets while what seemed like a dozen or so women pressed around him. His glowing hair made a halo, reflecting light onto his face. The other two band members stood in the corner, entertaining those who couldn't get close to Tony. Shouldn't there be bouncers here?

'Hey there.'

Tricia turned to see a guy standing behind her, grinning. He seemed a little old for the crowd, thirties instead of twenties, his face rugged and weatherworn, clean-shaven, with crew-cut black hair. He wore a tight white T-shirt and jeans that managed to look expensive despite being faded.

She blinked at him, uncertain that he'd even been speaking to her.

'You must be new around here,' he said.

'Who, me?' she said, then immediately felt stupid. 'No, I'm here with a friend.' She pointed over her shoulder. Tricia had pulled down her top to expose half a breast, which the lead singer was now signing with a marker.

The guy smiled wider. 'Want one?' He showed her a round metallic case cupped in his hands, full of little white pills.

Not again. She tried her best to smile while gesturing his hand away. 'No, no thanks, I'm fine.'

'I love these parties, these bands get the best drugs.'

'Oh,' she said.

'That's my terrible secret. I don't care much for the music. Don't tell anyone.' He leaned close and winked.

Was he hitting on her? Was he trying to pick her up? She wasn't sure she even knew how to respond. She was simultaneously appalled and flattered. She blushed hot enough that she might have felt steam coming off her head.

'Oh, I won't, trust me. I really ought to get back to my friend—'
But when she looked, the band was gone. So was Tricia. 'Tricia?' Jennifer called. She ran out the back door into the alley behind the club. A beat-up, rusted Cadillac was parked there. The band was climbing inside, making a quick getaway.

The lead singer with the glowing hair had his arms around Tricia's middle, had nearly lifted her off her feet while she squirmed and pushed at his arms. She was saying something, screaming maybe, though Jennifer couldn't hear her over the shouting crowd and the noise still thundering in the club behind her.

'*Tricia!*' Jennifer held her hands to her mouth and called.

She'd already been pulled into the car, despite her struggles.

Jennifer shouted again, '*Tricia!*' and clattered down the stage-door steps, nearly stumbling in her high heels, intending to chase after the ratty Cadillac. Instead, she ran into a crowd that wouldn't let her pass. Jennifer was tall; she could see over most of their heads. But she couldn't seem to push her way through.

A hulking man – a joker, fangs jutting up from his lower jaw and glittering black scales standing in for hair – purposefully blocked her way after she ran up against him. Jennifer tried to dodge around him but he side-stepped to block her.

'Hey, baby, what's your hurry?'

'My friend,' she insisted, desperate. 'They've taken my friend. Did you see her? She didn't want to go, they just took her!'

He smiled. His fangs made him look like a bulldog. 'Darlin', that chick is having the time of her life.'

Jennifer stared, horrified. 'Did you *see* her?' She pointed at the car, now rolling away with her friend inside. 'She was fighting them! She's almost passed out drunk—'

The joker laughed. 'Jealous they didn't pick you? Maybe you can have some fun with me.'

'She needs help!'

The guy grabbed for her, but she slipped away, batting at his hands. He only laughed. The car turned a corner.

Tricia had been kidnapped. Right under her nose. Right under *everyone's* nose.

Jennifer remembered seeing a pay phone by the bathrooms. She ran back inside and down the stairs. It would have been just her luck to reach the phone and find that it was broken, but it wasn't. She did put her hand in something sticky smeared on the receiver, though. Grimacing, she wiped it and her hand on the wall to clean it off as well as she could. Hunching over to give herself a bubble of private space, blocking the noise by covering her ear, she dialed the operator.

'Operator.'

'Hello! I need the police!' The line clicked and crackled static. She gnawed her lip, sure she'd lost the connection, until a voice came on.

'Police dispatch.'

'Hello, yes? It's my friend! My friend's been kidnapped!'

'Excuse me?'

Jennifer could barely hear. She was shouting. 'My friend! She's been kidnapped!'

'Ma'am, can you tell me what happened?'

'We were at a club. Some men, some guys from the band, they pulled her into their car. She was struggling, she's not in her right mind, and they took advantage—'

'Wait a minute.' Now the guy on the line sounded amused. 'So you're out partying and she ditched you to run off with the band—'

'No, I'm telling you, they dragged her off! She was almost passed out and they *took* her!'

'Ma'am, where are you?'

She hesitated. This wasn't going well, and it was about to get worse. 'I'm at this club on the Bowery—'

The dispatcher hung up.

Jennifer growled and slammed the receiver on its hook. Why hadn't Tricia waited for her? Why didn't she fight back? What if she never saw Tricia again? Her friend would end up raped and dead in a gutter and it would be all Jennifer's fault.

She tried again; maybe going through a main desk instead of the operator would help. Trouble was, she didn't have any extra change in her little bag. Just a few bills for drinks. She sighed. Then she looked around, to make sure nobody was watching.

Quickly, she rested her hand against the metal front of the pay phone – then slipped it inside. Her hand went insubstantial, passing through the casing as if it were air. She felt around a moment and found the change bin, grabbed some coins, and pulled her hand back out. The coins ghosted along with her. Now, she had change.

No matter what, her ace meant she could always use a pay phone.

Five years ago, when she was fourteen, it had happened for the first time. She had poured herself a glass of orange juice, picked it up – and it fell. The glass slipped out of her hand. Except she'd been watching it – it had slipped *through* her hand. She'd stood for a long time, the broken glass and puddle of spilled orange juice at her feet, staring at the translucent outline of her hand and the kitchen floor, visible through her no-longer-solid flesh. Her mother came in then, saw the mess, and asked if she was all right, assuming it was just a normal accident. Jennifer had quickly put her hand behind her back. When she looked at it again, it was solid. Normal.

Months of fear and experimentation followed. Her first thought was that she was fading, that she would eventually vanish. She developed insomnia, afraid of disappearing in her sleep. But eventually, she learned she could control the power. She could reach through solid objects. She practiced reaching into drawers, lockers at school, her father's strongbox. It was a heck of an ace. She didn't dare tell anyone about it.

She shoved a couple of dimes into the coin slot, dialed information, and asked for the main desk at the nearest police precinct. She talked to someone who must have been a desk sergeant, telling the story all over again, trying to sound calm and desperate at the same time so the officer would take her seriously.

This guy hung up on her, too.

Wiping tears from her eyes, Jennifer stomped up the stairs.

Yet another band was playing. Back in the main part of the club, she elbowed down a mobbed hallway and fell into the wall of rough, screeching music rocking from the stage, not stopping when anyone called, brushing away groping hands. It might have been her imagination, it might have been that the world had turned suddenly dark and ominous, but the crowd seemed to have grown rowdier. The slamming in front of the stage had grown more violent. Jennifer kept to the fringes and focused on the front of the club and the open door, ignoring the mass of people around her and the acid gnawing at her gut.

What was the good of being an ace if you couldn't actually do anything useful? If you couldn't actually help anyone? Why couldn't she be psychic so she could know where they were taking her? Or fly, so she could follow the car?

She made it out the front door and into the – relatively – fresh air. A crowd still gathered there, people coming and going, lingering. Not knowing what to do, she leaned against the brick storefront and rested, rubbing sweat and hair from her face. Maybe if she went to a police station in person. Maybe if she could find someone who knew the band. They had to have a manager or someone who knew where they might have gone.

'Hey kid. What's wrong?'

It was the guy in the white T-shirt with the pills. He might have been outside the whole time, or he might have just come from the front door. Maybe he was following her.

He slouched against the wall, far enough away that he couldn't reach out and grab her. It made her slightly less suspicious of him. 'Why do you care?' She glared, then looked away, not wanting him to think she was flirting with him. Not that he really looked like he was flirting. In spite of herself, she sniffed a deep breath and tears fell down her cheeks. She said, 'My friend, Tricia? She's gone, and no one cares, no one will do anything.'

'Ditched you, did she?' he said, wearing a wry smile.

'No, that's just it, she's been kidnapped! The band, they took her, she was drunk and they pulled her into the car, I saw the whole thing!'

'You're sure she didn't just decide to go party with the band?'

'Without me? She wouldn't do that.' Jennifer shook her head to emphasize. Though to be fair, she wouldn't put anything past Tricia, who had been *really* drunk. She sniffed back another round of tears.

'Hey,' the guy said. 'I know where the after-party is. I can take you, if you want.'

'Really?' she said, wary. She imagined *herself* being pulled into a ratty car ...

'Yeah, it's just a couple of blocks from here. I know the guy who runs it, and if you show him a little leg you'll get in just fine.'

She looked away, blushing.

'It's like I said, these guys have the best parties with the best drugs. Let's go check it out, all right?'

'You're sure Tricia will be there?'

'If she went with the band, yeah, I am.' He stepped out on the sidewalk and offered her the crook of his arm, an oddly sweet, archaic gesture. She followed him, but didn't take the arm; he seemed amused rather than offended by this.

They walked for a block or so. The noise of CBGB faded, replaced by the noise of other bars, slightly different, the shades of music and flavor of the crowd shifting from the punk atmosphere. Her gaze was drawn by the jokers she saw lingering in doorways and walking on the street. They stared at her, and she made a point to not stare back. She hunkered in on herself, trying to be inconspicuous.

The man from the club didn't seem bothered by any of it. He walked with an easy stride, comfortable, like walking through Central Park on a sunny day.

'What's your name?' he asked after a stretch of silence.

'Jennifer,' she said. Then wondered if she should have told him something else. Then decided it was a common enough name, it didn't matter, it wasn't like he could look her up. Then realized she was walking down Bowery with a total stranger.

'Jennifer. Nice to meet you. I'm Croyd.'

'Hi,' she said, smiling nervously.

'I take it you don't spent much time in this part of town.'

'Not really. I go to Columbia.' She winced. Why had she told him that?

'Yeah? That's great. School, you know. It's great. And here we are. It should be just up these stairs.'

Sure enough, the noise of a party drifted down from a rooftop patio. Jennifer felt hopeful. The band would be here, Tricia would be here, and Jennifer would yell at her for running off like that. Then maybe they could finally go home, and the ringing in her ears would stop.

Croyd politely stepped aside to let her go first, and she ran up the stairs and into a warehouselike room. Not much had been done with the low-rent loft: the floors were concrete, the bar was set up on folding tables, and the walls needed a coat of paint. But there was a stereo, a turntable, and immense speakers pouring forth more of the same kind of rough music from the club. Nobody was dancing – there wasn't enough room. Groups of people seemed to be talking – shouting – but Jennifer didn't know how anybody heard each other. French doors along one wall opened onto a patio, and the party continued there.

How was she ever going to find Tricia in this mess?

The guy who seemed to be in charge of the bar was a joker. He was of average height and build, but was covered with thick blue fur; she couldn't see his features. His mouth and eyes were only shadows. He seemed to glance at her.

'You can have anything you want, but put something in the jar, right?' He pointed to a large pickle jar, stuffed with cash, on the corner of the table.

'I'm looking for my friend. She's with the band, I think. The Fads? Are they here? Have you seen her?'

'The Fads?' he said, shouting, leaning close. The fur around his mouth rippled.

'Yeah! My friend, she's shorter than me, with brown hair, have you seen her?'

'Haven't seen 'em. They haven't been by.'

She stared. Now what? 'Are you sure? They just played a club up the street, CBGB—'

'Babe, I know the band, I know where they play, they haven't been here, I haven't seen your friend. Now, do you want something or not?'

Without answering, she let the crowd push her away from the table. Glancing around, she realized she'd lost track of Croyd as well, and didn't know if that made her nervous or relieved. Fine, then. This left her no worse off than she was before. She just had to find someone who knew the band and knew where they'd gone. This wasn't totally hopeless. Resolved, she turned around and elbowed her way back to the makeshift bar. If the bartender knew the band, maybe he'd tell her where they were.

She was thrown off course when a woman ran into her. Jennifer stumbled on her heels, but stayed upright by splaying her legs. She even managed to catch the woman, preventing them both from crashing to the floor.

The woman was in her twenties, with beautiful, delicate features, but a tired, haunted expression. She'd chewed all the lipstick off her lips. She wore a wide-necked knit dress.

Jennifer tried to catch the woman's gaze, but she kept glancing over her shoulder. 'Are you okay?' Jennifer asked.

When Jennifer spoke, the woman's attention focused on her. Her lips pursed, determined. 'Will you hold this for me?' she said, and pressed a key on a ring with a plastic tag into Jennifer's hand.

Her fingers instinctively closed around it. The woman shoved away from Jennifer and disappeared. 'Hey!' Jennifer followed her progress for a little while, watching her straight black hair bobbing in a sea of people, then she was gone, another anonymous partyer. Jennifer tried to follow but couldn't seem to elbow her way through.

When the gunshot blasted through the space, Jennifer thought it was a bottle from the bar smashing. Only when everyone started screaming and ducking did she realize the noise wasn't so harmless. But with everyone else scrambling and panicking before she even realized what was happening, she was left standing, looking around like an idiot.

A group of men had paused at the top of the stairs and fanned out. Four of them, obviously part of some gang, bulky and tough. They wore masks, the cheap Halloween kind that they might have bought in any Jokertown dime store. They all carried handguns; one had fired into the ceiling, and still held the gun up. He might have been a joker, he was so big – dense, almost, thick arms and legs, muscles like cables, barely any neck to speak of it. One of the others was obviously a joker, with furred arms and claws for hands. The other two may have been normal, or may have been jokers – the masks hid any deformities they might have had. Once again, it didn't seem to matter. Joker or nat, they were big, mean, and angry.

Jennifer just knew something like this was going to happen in this part of town. She'd kill Tricia for dragging her here. If she wasn't already dead.

'We know you're up here!' said the big one with the gun. He stalked forward, scanning faces. 'Hand it over and no one gets hurt!'

Panic had carried most of the crowd onto the patio. The woman who'd crashed into Jennifer was gone. *Hand it over* ... Jennifer unconsciously looked at the key in her hand. And that was a mistake.

The thug caught sight of her, standing there cupping a small object in her hand, no doubt looking vapid and confused. His expression turned determined, satisfied, and he marched toward her.

Her heart raced, her skin turned clammy, she took a step back – and she fell.

Kept falling.

She thought for a moment she was blacking out, fainting, her mind scattering to pieces. Her vision turned to shadows and her body turned to helium, weightless and scattered, dizzy. Every pore was dizzy, turned upside down. She couldn't breathe.

Then the world came back, she gasped a breath, and walls sped past – she really was falling, but only for a second, then she hit the floor. Everything had changed – the rooftop bar was gone, the room was dark and empty of people. The man with the gun marching forward had vanished, which was a huge relief.

But no, none of that had disappeared. She looked up at a bare ceiling, girders and vents showing. She'd fallen from there. And she was naked.Goose bumps covered her arms, back, legs. She hugged her knees close, curling up to hide herself. Her entire body had ghosted through the floor. Through her *clothing*. She was sitting naked on the linoleum floor of what looked like the back room of a liquor store. Stacked cardboard boxes labeled Coors and Pabst and Hamm's surrounded her. By luck she had fallen in the walkway leading from a back door to the front of the store. What would have happened if she had fallen in the middle of a stack of boxes? If her body had turned solid there? She couldn't even imagine. She shivered.

She kept staring at the ceiling, unsure of what had really happened, even though she knew, she just *knew*. Like the glass of orange juice through her hand. Her whole body through the floor.

I can walk through walls, she thought. And she wanted to try it, then and there. Except she was naked. What good was walking through walls if you had to be naked?

But she was still holding the key in her tightly closed fists; its teeth dug into her skin. She'd been so focused on holding on it, she'd brought it with her through the floor.

When the back door slammed open, she scrambled behind a tower of boxes. She listened for heavy boot steps, for the sound of growling, even. The gang had busted open the door, they'd found her, and now they were going to do unspeakable things to her. She hoped she could fall through the floor again, though she wasn't sure how she'd done it the first time.

'Hey kid. Jennifer. You in here? Don't tell me you went all the way through to the sewers.'

It was Croyd.

'I'm here. I'm kind of … I mean, my clothes didn't exactly come with me.'

'I know, I have them. Why didn't you say you were an ace?'

'Because I haven't told *anybody*. Nobody knows. At least, nobody used to know.'

'Probably smart,' he said, matter-of-fact, and not at all shocked. 'But do you have any idea how useful a power like that is? I remember this time back in '53, the feds tried to lock me up but I got lucky and walked right out again.'

'What are you talking about?'

'Never mind. Here.' He held out her dress in her general direction. When she crept out to reach for it, he was politely looking the other way.

She hurried to pull the dress on. He'd managed to grab her bra and panties as well, for which she was grateful. Even the shoes. Her jewelry was missing, though. She was really going to have to figure out how she did that, and how she could do it again without losing everything. While slipping on her dress she asked, 'What's going on? Who were those guys?'

'I was going to ask you that – why were they so interested in you? What did you do?'

'Nothing! I just had this run-in, and, well, this woman gave me this.' She showed him the key. The tag on it showed a number: 51337.

'You have a knack for being in the wrong place at the wrong time, don't you?'

'I just want to find Tricia and go home.' She hopped while slipping the strap of her sandal over her heel.

'Come on,' Croyd said. 'We'd better get out of here.'

'What? Why—'

She followed his nervous gaze out the door and into the alley and got her answer – the gang had followed them. The leader's massive body blocked their way out, and he seemed all too ready to just shoot her and Croyd.

Jennifer didn't know if she could sink through the floor again. And if she did it here, where would she end up? Maybe if she ran through the wall …

'Freeze!' Croyd shouted at them. And they did. The lead thug's mouth was open to speak, but he remained silent. Croyd let out a sigh.

Jennifer looked at him. Wonderingly, she said, 'You're an ace, too.'

He winced. 'Yeah, well, the thing is, I'm really not. It's more of a deuce.'

'A what?'

'It only lasts five minutes. We gotta run now.'

He shoved her past the frozen thugs. They ran.

They took a twisting path, turning every corner they came to in an effort to make following them more difficult. Jennifer didn't know if it would help. Then again, she was becoming thoroughly lost. Maybe now if she called the police, they'd help.

Not that she could call anyone for help. Not that she was alone on a dark street with a strange man she didn't know at all. How could she be so stupid …

Croyd took an extra turn into an alley next to a condemned brownstone, a tucked-away entrance that she would have missed on her own. It gave them an opportunity to catch their breaths.

'Let me see that,' Croyd said, indicating the key she still held in her hand.

Reluctant to hand it over, she held it up where he could see it. After a moment, he said, 'It looks like it's for a post-office box.'

'So?' Jennifer said, still trying to catch her breath. She rubbed her foot where a blister was developing.

'I'm guessing this is part of a drop gone wrong. Probably drugs or stolen goods or something. That woman was supposed to hand over the key. Those guys are supposed to either pick up the goods or the cash. We're in the middle of a doublecross.'

'That doesn't make me feel any better,' she said.

'I know someone who might be able to tell us where this goes to.' He reached for it; she pulled it out of his way.

'What about Tricia?'

'Who?'

'My friend, the one who was kidnapped.'

'I'm sure she's fine.'

'I need to find her!'

'I'll tell you what: You let me find out what that key goes to, and I'll help you find your friend.'

'Because you've already been such a big help with that.'

'Hey, gimme a break,' he said, arms spread in a weak apology. 'This girl I know, she isn't far. Let's just check it out, then I'll help you find Tricia. I know a couple more places we could go look for her. Okay?'

She pouted, and because she didn't know what else to do, she said, 'Okay.'

Croyd popped a pill from his case and said, 'Good. Let's go.'

They walked on. The neighborhood didn't get any better. She hadn't seen a cab in blocks. She hugged herself and wondered what kind of mess she'd gotten herself into. Tried to reassure herself that she could get out of anything. If anyone tried to tie her up, she'd just ghost through the ropes. She could walk through walls, dammit.

Croyd had been trying to make conversation, and Jennifer was trying to ignore him. He finally said, 'Look, I'm only trying to help. I ought to just freeze you and take that key.'

'Except you won't, because I'm sure you're cooking up some scheme to talk me into helping you rob a bank or something.' When he didn't say anything, she huffed. 'You really were, weren't you?' She started walking faster.

'Yeah, fine, maybe I was,' he said, hurrying to keep up. If she could have walked any faster in her heels, she would have. 'But you really ought to think about it. A power like yours doesn't come along every day.'

'Don't you get it? I don't want this power, I wish I didn't have it!'

'Come on, I thought every kid wanted to be an ace. Get your picture in the papers, go to fancy dinners at Aces High—'

'And do what? Be a freak? I'm a nice girl from a nice Long Island family and I just want to be left alone.'

'You could call yourself Ghost Girl,' he suggested.

'Ghost Girl?'

'You know, an ace name. Something for the papers to call you. I can see it: "Ghost Girl, Famous Ace Jewel Thief, Strikes Again."' He spread his arms in imitation of the headline.

'I am *not* calling myself Ghost Girl.' Surely she could come up with something more interesting than that. Something more mysterious, more *alluring* … 'Do you have an ace name?'

'The Sleeper.' His smile slipped, like he wasn't happy about it.

'That's kind of weird. I thought it would be something like The Freezer.'

He shrugged. 'That's just the way it goes.'

She stopped at a corner, uncertain which way to turn. The streetlights in this neighborhood all seemed to be broken. All the storefronts had heavy steel grilles over them. That didn't make her feel any better. If she got into trouble – more trouble, anyway – she hoped she could just sink out of sight again.

They were in Jokertown proper, now, not just the boundaries. People stared at them. Jennifer was dressed, but she might as well have been naked, the way she shivered when they looked at her.

'This isn't exactly safe, is it?' she said, hugging herself.

'Seriously? Look, if we keep moving, we'll be fine.'

The skeleton of a burned building, blackened steel frame sprouting from a bed of debris, stood on the next corner. A casualty of the Jokertown riots that hadn't been rebuilt. This was a whole other world, one she hadn't really paid attention to before. And there but for the grace of God … She didn't know how she'd gotten the wild card virus. She didn't know how she'd gotten an ace and not a joker. She didn't want to think about it.

They made their way back to Bowery, but farther south. Here, the street was almost crowded, and Jennifer hadn't expected that, not in the middle of the night. All-night bars and diners were open, groups loitered at a couple of corners, there even seemed to be a group of women on one block – then Jennifer figured out who they were and what they were doing there. Music from a boom box rattled down one alley. No cops in sight, of course.

A neon glow shone up ahead, and Croyd said, 'There it is. My friend is one of the bartenders.'

A block away, Jennifer stopped and stared.

The giant neon sign in front of the building showed a six-breasted woman in lurid red and golds. The lights flashed in sequence; it almost looked like the breasts were jiggling, with cut-rate fireworks igniting around her. Another length of flashing red neon declared, FREAKERS. Tame print signs announced JOKER GIRLS! And XXX HOT XXX! The doorway was through the neon stripper's spread legs.

'Oh my God,' Jennifer said.

'Just about everyone has that reaction,' Croyd said, grinning.

'I don't think I can go in there.'

'Sure you can.' He took hold of her elbow and pulled her into the street.

They had to dodge traffic – there was actually traffic, even at this hour. Croyd walked with confidence to the front door, right between the neon dancer's legs, which cast a weird pink glow over the sidewalk. Everyone looked sunburned.

A joker with what looked like Texas longhorn horns swooping from his temples and polished black hooves instead of hands crossed his arms and stepped in front of the door to block their way. 'Hey, Bruce, let us in, will ya?' Croyd said.

The bouncer narrowed his gaze. 'And you are …?'

'I'm Croyd.'

'Prove it.'

'Remember that time last year with the blue twins and the bottle of tequila?'

The bouncer's eyes went wide and he gave a soft smile of reminiscence. 'Oh, yeah. You're looking good this time.' He stepped aside, and Croyd steered Jennifer through the door.

'You know him? Why didn't he recognize you?' Jennifer said.

'Long story.' Let's take care of this key business.'

Jennifer needed a moment to let her eyes adjust to the cavelike darkness, until they emerged into the main room, which was scattered with flashing lights and a glittering mirror ball. The Hall and Oates blasting way too loudly on the sound system was almost a comfort. At least it was more familiar than what she'd heard at the club earlier. She could at least dance to this. And so could the stripper on the revolving stage in the center of the room. The woman was unreal – tall, slinky, with an absolute mane of brick-red hair teased away from her face and flowing down her back. And that was before you got to the slender green lizard tail curling behind her, swaying back and forth, then seductively wrapping around a brass pole while she leaned forward and removed the scrap of black fabric standing in for a bra.

Jennifer looked everywhere but the stage and saw a lot of male nats nursing drinks, leaning forward, studying the dancer with what seemed to be obsessive intensity. Croyd had sidled up to the bar where he was talking to ... it took Jennifer a second look to see that it was a woman. She didn't have a head. Or rather, her head seemed to grow from the middle of her chest, so that her chin rested between her breasts, nestled in the cleavage created by a black push-up bra. Long black hair fell over the straight line between her shoulders. She was wiping down the bar with a cloth and smiling at Croyd, who leaned on an elbow and put on a flirting smile. 'How you doing, Sheila?'

'Just fine, hon. Haven't seen you in a while.'

'You know how it is. Been out of it.'

'Well, you're looking good this time around. I hope you're planning on enjoying it.' She cocked a hip and winked, a move that would have been seductive if she didn't look so ... *weird*. Jennifer crossed her arms and tried not to fidget. Sheila the bartender looked her up and down. 'Who's your new friend?'

'Just someone I'm helping out,' Croyd said. 'Jennifer, can you show her the key? It's okay, I promise.'

Reluctantly, Jennifer held out the key.

'May I?' Sheila said and took it from her hand when Jennifer nodded.

The joker closed her eyes – and you couldn't actually look at her eyes without staring at her breasts – and pressed the key to her forehead. The Hall and Oates ended and the lizard-tailed joker sashayed offstage, replaced by one who had the scaled and clawed feet of a bird. The next song: 'Superfreak.'

After a moment, Sheila said, 'It's from the post office over on Doyers. I can't tell any more than that, I'm afraid.' She shrugged – her shoulders lifted above her hair – and started to hand the key to Croyd. Jennifer intercepted and took custody of it. The joker grinned.

'Thanks, babe,' Croyd said. 'I owe you one.'

'Anytime, hon.'

'What was that all about?' Jennifer asked as they moved away from the bar.

'Sheila's a psychometric. She can sense things about an object – where it came from, who it belongs to, that sort of thing.'

'That's useful,' she said.

'About as useful as walking through walls. If you'd actually *use* it.'

In her effort to keep from looking at the stage, Jennifer caught a glimpse through a doorway into a private side room. And she swore she saw the Fad's spike-haired drummer sitting there. She broke away from Croyd and ran.

The room was a small lounge with a smaller, private stage, decorated in black shag carpet and red plush chairs. Flickering black light brought out glowing decorations on the walls and the sparkling white bikinis worn by a pair of girls dancing for the drummer's sole benefit. Neither girl was Tricia, which was something of a relief.

As she approached, the guy reached up to stuff a bill in the waistband of one of the girl's panties. The girl had glowing, mood-ring-like skin that swirled colors, blue to red to orange. And the guy really was the drummer.

Jennifer shoved him away from the stage so she could face him down. He dropped the bill.

'What have you done with Tricia?'

'Hey!' the dancer said, crossing her arms in protest.

'Who are you?' said the drummer.

'Where's the rest of the band? Where's Tricia?'

'Um ...' the drummer said.

Jennifer wasn't finished. 'And what are you doing *here*? You had groupies hanging all over you back at the club, and now you're here *paying* for it?'

'It feels dirtier when you pay for it,' Croyd said. He stood to the side, watching like this was a show. The drummer shrugged and winced in agreement.

Jennifer was about ready to scream. 'Where's Tricia?'

'Look, babe, I don't know who you're talking about.'

'The band,' Croyd said. 'Where did the rest of the band go to party? They took her friend along.'

'Oh, yeah. The real wild chick? Totally high?'

Yeah, that was Tricia. Jennifer sighed.

'Oh. Um. They probably went to Tony's place.'

'Where?'

'I'm not going to tell *you*, you're probably some crazy stalker.'

'No, my friend Tricia's the crazy one. I just need to find her—'

'Uh, Jennifer?' Croyd touched her shoulder and turned her to face the doorway.

The beefy thug from the gang filled the doorway. She could see the murder in his eyes through the mask.

'There's a back door,' Croyd whispered. 'We'll make a break—'

Enough. Jennifer held the key up where the big guy could see it, then reached over and dropped it down the drummer's shirt.

'Now we make a break for it,' she said, and ran ahead of Croyd for the back door.

The noise of chaos – overturning furniture, screeching women, the works – erupted behind her, and as entertaining as the scene probably was, Jennifer didn't dare turn to look.

They went through a hallway with dressing rooms and out a back door into yet another dank alley.

'What did you do that for?' Croyd said.

'Because the key's not important, now that we know what it opens,' Jennifer said. 'But we have to get to the post office before they do.'

'What? *Oh.* Here we go, then.'

They jogged in silence. Jennifer kept waiting for the sound of shouting and pounding footsteps behind her. She kept glancing over her shoulder, but they seemed to have delayed the gang, at least for the moment.

'Stop looking so nervous,' Croyd said at one point. 'You look suspicious.'

Easy for him to say. She tried not to pay attention to what was waiting to pounce on her.

She had to distract herself. 'So, how do you rob a bank?'

He looked at her sidelong. 'Seriously?'

'Yeah.' Her tone made the request a dare.

'You don't. I mean, not anymore. With all the security and surveillance they've got now it's not worth it. Instead you go after private safes. Cat burglary. Or you go after armored cars when they're moving the money. You case the area, look for the weaknesses. Don't ever try to take too much. Be picky, you know? Take the good bits of a stash rather than all of it. And once you have it, don't hang on to it, thinking you can get a better price. Turns out that's the tricky part – fencing stolen goods, or laundering the money. But there's people around. It helps to have the contacts.'

She nodded thoughtfully. It all made sense.

'It also helps to have a really powerful ace,' Croyd added, winking. 'Super strength, walking through walls.'

Ahead of them along the narrow street, voices shouted, and Jennifer stalled. Whoever it was sounded angry, and they were running closer. The gang had found them somehow, got ahead of them, cut them off—

Croyd grabbed her arm, pulled her toward the wall, pressed his body to hers, and kissed her. Full-on make-out, arms wrapped around her, trapping her against the brick. In the meantime, a gang of teenagers ran by, shouting taunts at each other and at the pair of them. Not the gang at all. Just a bunch of kids.

Croyd was still kissing her. Distracting her. She finally pushed him away. 'What do you think you're doing?'

'I figured we'd look less suspicious that way,' he said, his grin cockier than ever.

Huffing in frustration, she shoved him again, slapped him for good measure, and marched away. He only chuckled.

Turned out they didn't have far to go to reach the post office in question. Just a couple of blocks. The place was a modern concrete block tucked in between brick tenements at the edge of Chinatown. A small lobby giving access to the mailboxes was still open, lit by a weak, yellowish light on the far wall. If they were going to get jumped by an angry gang, this was the place it would happen, Jennifer thought.

They found the box with the number from the tag. Croyd stood aside. 'Care to do the honors?'

Jennifer stared at the brass-colored door a moment, not sure she wanted to know what was inside. Not sure she wanted to reach in, sight unseen. Like maybe it could be filled with poisonous snakes or mousetraps. Most likely it was just filled with someone's junk mail.

She took a deep breath and reached through the door. Her hand brushed against something rectangular, papery – an envelope, stuffed full, which seemed encouraging. She took hold of it, ghosted it with the rest of her hand, and she drew it through the door.

She and Croyd studied a business-sized envelope full of cash. Hundred dollar bills, dozens of them. 'Christ, there's gotta be thirty grand there,' Croyd said.

Jennifer had never seen so much cash in one place, except in the movies. On the other hand, Croyd could just eyeball it and know what it was worth. What was all this about? Who was the woman who'd given her the key in the first place? What kind of deal was going on? Was it drugs, smuggling, ransom money, something else entirely? Her imagination failed her. The money seemed to burn in her hand.

Frowning, she closed up the envelope, hugged it close, and left the post office. Croyd was right with her. 'You're not doing too badly on your first night as a criminal.'

'I'm not a criminal. I'm taking this to the police.'

'What? Oh, no you're not.'

'I am.' The Jokertown precinct house had to be around here somewhere. If anyone tried to mug her on the way, she'd just ghost into the nearest building.

Croyd said. 'These are the same police who listened to you all sympathetic-like when you told them about your friend, right?'

'It's the right thing to do.'

'Hon, there's right and then there's right. The police around here – they ain't right. You take it to them, they're going to ask you all kinds of questions about where it came from and they're not going to listen to any of your answers. You'll end up in a cell – not that it's a problem for you. But they'll get you in their records and that's never good. They'll drive on up to Columbia to haul your ass back to jail and you can kiss your shiny education good-bye. On the other hand, we're keeping this cash out of the hands of some *really* bad people – Mr. Brick Wall and his friends. I say we take the money, buy ourselves a couple bottles of something nice, head back to my place, and have a nice little party of our own.'

She almost said yes. Tricia would have said yes. A tiny part of her thought about what a great adventure that would be. Even if she knew next to nothing about Croyd and wasn't sure she liked what she did know.

The sensible Long Island girl won out. She quickened her stride, marched away from him, and said, with an indignant huff, 'No.'

'Jennifer, I like you. I really don't want to do this.'

'Do what?' she said, glancing over her shoulder at the same time Croyd said, 'Freeze!'

And then he was gone. She shook her head, clearing a residue of dizziness. She was just looking over her shoulder and then – that bastard. That despicable rat bastard. He was gone, of course. He'd only had a five-minute head start, but that was enough to turn a corner and lose himself in the night-time streets. Not that she planned on chasing after him. What could she do if she caught him?

He'd even left the envelope sticking out of the top of her dress. Tucked it right in after he'd taken out the money, like she was some kind of trash bin. Probably felt her up as well. Like it was a big joke.

But no – she pulled out the envelope, and it still had money in it. Croyd had only taken what looked like half the cash. She giggled. A rat bastard gentleman. What a strange man.

'Hey! You!'

The now-familiar silhouette of Mr. Brick Wall and his henchmen turned the corner and set off toward her.

'We're gonna mess you up!' the leader shouted.

She ran. She was getting good at running in the sandals. Not that she'd be able to keep the sandals. She couldn't outrun these guys. She wouldn't survive if they caught her. That didn't leave much choice. She veered into the wall to her right and thought, *hold on, hold on, hold on …*

Her bra, her panties, money. She could get by with that much. Bra, panties, money, bra, panties, money. She hit the wall and kept going.

Kicked in gear by the adrenaline, the power came almost easily. Her whole body ghosted. She could feel herself go insubstantial, feel the solid walls moving around her like a stiff breeze. She could even feel the money in her hand, like holding a shadow. And when she emerged – she was in a room full of people. Jennifer stopped cold on the red plush carpet and stared back at two dozen well-dressed men and women seated at various tables staring back at her. It looked like an after-hours party at a restaurant. Nearby, a waiter paused in the middle of lifting a plate of cheesecake from his tray. Several people had forks raised to open mouths. A cup clattered on a tabletop – someone dropped their coffee.

She'd left her dress and sandals behind, but still wore her bra and panties. Definitely didn't meet the dress code. She wondered if they'd been expecting any entertainment. More important, though, she still carried the envelope of money. Squeezing it, she let it anchor her. Ignoring the flush burning through her skin, she smiled wide and gave the gathering a little wave. 'Have a great night, folks!' Then she ran straight through the wall on the other side of the room.

'Well, that's Manhattan for you,' someone muttered as she slipped away.

She discovered that the power wasn't just a matter of passing through barriers, but of traveling through them. She didn't have to fall through the sidewalk in order to end up at the Grand Street subway platform; she could sink through the sidewalk, the walls, and emerge where she wished. Not that it helped, because when she stepped out to the platform and rematerialized, two of the big thug's henchmen were right there, masks and all. They'd broken through the closed subway gate somehow. As they raced toward her, she simply backed up and into the wall again, ghosting, hiding in solid matter.

Maybe she could stay there, part of the concrete wall, until they vanished. But no, she had to keep moving. If she stayed still, she could feel herself start to scatter, rootless. As if her cells were drifting apart. The feeling made her dizzy and ill, so she kept going. Out of the subway and back to the street, but instead of keeping to the sidewalk, where the gang was no doubt looking for her, she moved obliquely, as the crow flies, cutting through buildings and alleys. Her feet became cut and bruised, running barefoot through the worst the city's streets had to offer. She shivered, every part of her exposed to the cold.

She wasn't sure how far she'd gone. Mostly, she was concerned with putting as much distance between her and the gang as she could. Maybe half an hour had passed, the way her lungs burned. She felt like half the night had gone by.

Emerging from a condemned tenement, she came into view of the East River, which gave her an idea of just how far she'd gone. Maybe she was safe now.

Dizziness shook her eyesight and made her stomach turn over. She slumped against the wall, and instead of falling through it, just fell against it, scraping her shoulder. She'd done too much, she had to rest. Obviously. What would happen if she kept ghosting? Kept turning insubstantial, walking through walls until she forgot how to be solid anymore, until her molecules started fluttering away on vagrant breezes? She could see it happen, and that terrified her. That she could imagine it so clearly seemed to be a message. Her ace was trying to tell her something.

She ran, and instead of going through the walls this time, she took the long way around the corner, then followed the river north.

The pervasive darkness and shadows on the streets were broken up ahead by a doorway guarded by lions. Stone lions. Around the corner from this grand entryway was another, wider door with a bright white light shining within. The word EMERGENCY shone in red letters on a lit-up sign above it. Above the stone lions, another sign was lit by an overhead lamp: BLYTHE VAN RENSSAELER MEMORIAL CLINIC.

If she wasn't safe in a hospital, she wasn't safe anywhere.

She approached the emergency entrance, but hesitated when she spotted an incredibly tall green-skinned joker standing in front of it. He wore a uniform – and where did a nine-foot-tall man go to find security uniforms? Night guard, then.

She decided to avoid the entrance and instead went around the block to ghost in through a back wall. Dizziness followed her. She really didn't want to have to do that again anytime soon. Fortunately, the lights were dim and the hallways empty. She found an unlocked supply closet where, as she hoped she would, she found medical scrubs. She even found a pair of spare shoes – surgical booties, really, but they'd do. The greenish shirt and pants weren't high fashion, but they covered her up. She put a white lab coat over the scrubs for good measure.

She made her way to the emergency room waiting area and sat in the first chair she came to.

The place wasn't quiet. A voice scratched over a loudspeaker down a tile corridor, a drunk man was complaining to a nurse at a desk, and across the room a woman – with skin like sandpaper and hair like wires – was soothing a crying baby. The baby was swathed in a blanket, and Jennifer couldn't tell if it was a joker, too. Oddly enough, despite all this, the scene was peaceful. No music was blaring, no one was chasing her, no one harassing her. She sighed out a breath and with it some of her anxiety, sank back into the chair, and dozed.

She started awake when a siren outside blared – an ambulance pulling up. A moment later a pair of EMTs rushed through the main door pushing a stretcher. The person lying on it barely fit, his immense limbs hanging over the edges. His cabled muscles tensed as he clawed weakly at the people trying to help him. Jennifer recognized the patient's shape – the big thug, Mr. Brick Wall. He was bleeding through his shirt as though from a stab wound. The stretcher disappeared behind a curtained-off section as a doctor and nurse rushed to attend him.

Jennifer cringed in her seat, hugging herself, trying to hide, fearful at who else would come through the door and what would happen if they found her. But no one did. She didn't have to ghost through yet another wall. But she didn't relax again. She kept staring at that curtain, waiting for the gang leader to climb off his bed and come after her.

'My dear, do you need help?'

The voice came from behind, and she flinched away from it.

He was a small man, slim, and rather startling: He had metallic red hair tied back in a ponytail, fine features, and under his white lab coat he had on a lemon yellow shirt with poetic flounces and tight green pants. She blinked at him.

'My apologies, I didn't mean to frighten you,' he said, his hands making a comforting gesture. His accent was odd, exotic, and rather alluring.

'No, it's okay, it's just … I'm just tired.'

'I thought at first you were a nurse, but I don't know you, do I?'

'No.' She looked away, chuckling.

'You seem to be in some distress. Can I do anything to help?'

He had a kind face and a gentle smile. She liked him, and resisted an urge to fall into his arms, sobbing, telling him absolutely everything. 'No, I – I'm fine. I just need to rest, I think,' she said.

He studied her – he had the strangest violet eyes. For a moment he seemed about to say something, to argue with her. Then he pursed his lips and the moment passed. 'All right, then. But don't hesitate to ask if you need anything.'

'Thanks.'

He moved away, managing elegance even in a white lab coat, even though he seemed as exhausted as she.

The drunk man had come to rest about ten seats away. 'He probably just read your mind, you know.'

'What?' Jennifer said.

'That's what he does. He reads minds. That's Doctor Tachyon.'

Of course he was. Then he knew. He'd looked at her, read her mind – and he knew she was an ace. He knew all about her. And he hadn't said anything. Nothing had happened. She almost laughed.

When the sky outside the emergency room door started turning pale, Jennifer decided it was time to leave. She still hadn't found Tricia.

But according to the drummer, Tricia was with Tony. Maybe he was in the phone book. Maybe she could just look him up, call him, ask to speak to Tricia … Surely someone at CBGB knew where he lived. Or his phone number. She could still find Tricia, she wasn't at the end of the line yet.

She walked west, back toward the Bowery. The streetlights had dimmed without Jennifer noticing, and a news truck rumbled by. Morning, already. She'd been running around all night. What an adventure. She had to smile.

Morning traffic increased, pedestrians emerging onto the sidewalk, shopkeepers opening the grates in front of the windows. People glanced at her – wild-haired, in flimsy booties, medical scrubs, and a lab coat – but they didn't stare. She didn't look normal, but for this part of town, what was? She decided feeling self-conscious about it was pointless.

Ahead, she saw a sign for a diner that seemed to be popular, and her stomach growled at her. She was starving, and a big plate of eggs and pancakes sounded like the perfect remedy. And she even had ten grand or so tucked in the pocket of the lab coat to pay for a good breakfast. Maybe she'd treat everyone in the diner.

She walked past the window to the front door. Stopped. Backed up a couple of steps, and looked. There, in the center booth right next to the window, was Tricia. Sitting next to her were the other two guys from the band, the singer and guitarist and another groupie. The guitarist was tapping twenty fingers on the tabletop; the singer's glowing hair seemed dull and limp in the daylight. They were drinking coffee and laughing about something like nothing was wrong. Empty plates and a coffeepot sat on the cluttered table. They might have been sitting there all night.

Jennifer tapped gently on the glass. The alternative was smashing in the window with her fist.

Tricia looked up, her mouth fell open, and she blinked her surprise. Jennifer marched to the front door and inside, and then to the table. Tricia was still staring, dumbfounded. Jennifer crossed her arms. The other three people in the booth cringed at her frown.

Finally, Tricia spat out words. 'Omigod, Jennifer, where've you been? You totally missed the best party *ever*!'

Like it was all her fault she'd missed the party and not been ditched in the seediest neighborhood in town. So many things she could say right now.

Jennifer thought about it a minute. 'Actually, I think my party was probably better than yours.' She flapped the edges of the white lab coat, showing off her new outfit. 'Why didn't you wait for me, Trish? Why didn't you at least tell me where you were going? I've been running all over looking for you.'

Tricia squirmed in the booth, gave a lopsided shrug, and batted her eyes. 'I thought you were right behind us. Honest.'

Jennifer had nothing to say to that. It was way past time to go home. She turned and walked out. She didn't expect Tricia to run after her, and Tricia once again entirely met expectation. But she did call, 'Jennifer, wait! God, you don't have to be so *square*.'

Shoulder against the wall, Jennifer lingered outside the diner, too tired to be angry, too numb to think, not knowing what to do next. Running around all night, and what did she have to show for it? Blistered feet. A newfound appreciation for her ace. And an envelope full of cash.

She couldn't hand the money over to the police. She didn't feel right spending it. What else could she do but drop it down the sewer for some bum to find and spend on booze?

Or maybe …

♦

She went back to the Jokertown Clinic. She remembered seeing a sign hanging on the wall inside the door, next to a lockbox with a slot cut into it. DONATIONS, the sign read, with smaller text underneath that said, EVERY PENNY HELPS!

Jennifer slipped in through the door and crept along the wall, hoping to avoid notice. The place was quiet; the nurse she'd seen last night was at the desk, head resting on her arms. Her shift had to be nearly up.

Quickly, Jennifer stuffed the envelope through the slot. It took some doing – the slot was made for coins and bills, not annual salaries. But she succeeded, and the envelope fell in with a satisfying thud.

For a moment, she stared at the box. She could change her mind. She could pull it right back out again. Then again, no she couldn't. Like Croyd said, there was right and there was right, and this felt more right than anything had all night.

On the other hand, she needed subway fare to get home. She ghosted her hand into the donation box, pulled out a single wrinkled bill. Then she retrieved a second one, to replace the clothes and jewelry she'd lost. It was only fair, right? She had her fingers halfway through the box for a third bill when she stopped herself. This was already more than even.

She nearly skipped out of the emergency room. Hands in the pockets of the lab coat, she walked up the street, chin up, smiling.

COMES A HUNTER

by John J. Miller

'If you wish to find the unclouded truth, do not concern yourself
with right and wrong.'

— Seng-ts'an: *Hsin-hsin Ming*

I.

Brennan watched all the color fade from the landscape as the
bus came down from the quiet coolness of the mountains to the
sweltering stickiness of a summer city day. Endless asphalt parking
lots replaced meadows and grassy fields. Buildings grew taller and
crowded closer to the roadway. Leaden light-poles supplanted the
trees on the median and along the road. Even the sky turned sullen
and gray, threatening rain.

He disembarked at the Port Authority with the other passengers. They scattered to their myriad destinations, their eyes averted
in the habitual manner of the big-city dweller, without giving him
a second glance. Not that there was anything about him to cause
someone to glance twice.

He was tall, but not excessively so. His build was more lithe
than bulky. His hands were large. Suntanned and scarred, veins
and cords stood out on their backs like thick wires. His face was
dark and lean and unremarkable. He wore a denim jacket, frayed
and sunbleached, a dark cotton tee shirt, a fresh pair of blue jeans,
and dark running shoes. He carried a small soft-sided bag in his
left hand and a flat leather case in his right.

Forty-second Street outside the Port Authority building was
crowded. He merged into the flow of the foot traffic, allowing it
to take him into an area of Manhattan that was only slightly less

seedy than some of the more polite parts of Jokertown. He extricated himself from the swarm of pedestrians after a few blocks and went up the decaying stone steps of the Ipswhich Arms, a blowsy hotel that apparently catered to the local hooker trade. It looked as if business was bad. People were apparently going to Jokertown for their kicks. They were cheaper there and, even if only a fraction of what he had read was true, a lot kickier.

The desk clerk looked dubious when he came in alone and with luggage, but took his money and gave him directions to a room that was as small and dirty as he had thought it would be. He closed the door, put his bag on the floor, and carefully set his leather case on the sagging bed.

The room was sweltering, but Brennan had been in hotter places. He felt confined by the filthy bare walls around him, but opening a window wouldn't have helped. He laid down on the bed and stared at the peeling ceiling without seeing the roaches racing above his head. The words of a letter he had received the day before kept running through his mind.

'*Captain Brennan, he is here. I have seen him, but I am afraid that he saw and recognized me as well. Come to the restaurant. Be cautious, but open.*'

There was no signature, but he recognized Minh's elegant, precise hand. There was no address, but he didn't need one. Minh had hidden him in his restaurant for several days when he had surreptitiously returned to the States three years before. And Brennan had no doubt to whom his old friend referred in the letter. It was Kien.

He closed his eyes and saw a face: masculine, lean, predatory. He tried to make it vanish. He tried to blank it from his mind by conjuring from the depths of his consciousness the sound of one hand clapping. He tried, but failed. The face smiled, mocking him. It began to laugh.

He sat on the bed, waiting for the darkness and what it would bring.

II.

The air was flat and unmoving and clogged Brennan's nostrils with the miasma of seven million people crammed too closely together. After three years in the mountains he was unused to the city, but he was still able to take advantage of it. One man among thousands, he was seen but not noticed, heard but not remembered, as he walked to Minh's restaurant on Elizabeth, carrying his flat leather case.

It was early evening and the street was still crowded with potential customers, but the restaurant was closed. That was strange.

The vestibule, the only part of the restaurant's interior visible from the street, was dark. The sign hanging on the inside of the outer glass door said 'Closed. Please call again.' in English and Vietnamese. Three men, city punks, lounged on the street in front of the building, joking among themselves.

Brennan walked to the corner, trying to drape his sudden apprehension with a cloak of calmness. He ran through a series of breathing exercises that had been Ishida's first lesson to him when he had decided to give direction to his life by studying the Way. Apprehension, fear, nervousness, hatred – these would do him no good. He needed the ineffable calmness of an unbroken, unclouded mountain pool.

Kien was still alive. Of that he never had a doubt. Kien was a cunning and ruthless survivor to whom the fall of Saigon was merely an inconvenience. It would have taken him some time, but Brennan knew that he must have built a network of agents as potent and relentless as his network in Vietnam. These agents, given the few days that it took the letter to be written, delivered, and acted upon, could have tracked Minh down.

He turned the corner and, unnoticed by the other pedestrians on the street, slipped into a side alley bordering Minh's restaurant. It was dark there, and as quiet and rank as death. He crouched next to a pile of uncollected garbage, listening and watching. He saw nothing, as his eyes adjusted to the deeper gloom of the alley, besides scavenging cats. He heard nothing but the rustling sounds they made as they searched through the garbage.

He set his case down and flicked open its latches. He could barely see in the gloom, but he needed no light at all to assemble what lay inside. He snapped on and dogged down the limbs, upper and lower, to the central grip, and with sure, practiced strength slipped the string over the lower tip, stepped through, set the tip of the lower limb against his foot, bent the upper limb against the back of his thigh, and slipped the string over its tip. He brushed the taut string with his fingers and smiled at the low thrumming sound it produced.

He held a recurved bow, forty-two inches long, made of layers of fiberglass laminated around a yew core. Brennan knew it was a good bow. He had made it himself. It pulled at sixty pounds, powerful enough to bring down a deer, bear, or man.

The case also held a three-fingered leather glove which Brennan slipped on his right hand and a small quiver of arrows which he attached to his belt by Velcro tabs. He pulled one free. It was tipped by a hunting broadhead with four razor-sharp vanes. He nocked it loosely to the taut string and, more silent than the cats scrabbling through the uncollected garbage, crept to the restaurant's back door.

He listened, but could hear nothing. He tried the door, found it unlocked, and cracked it open half an inch. An arc of light spilled out and he found himself looking into a swatch of the kitchen. It, too, was empty and quiet.

He slid inside, a silent blot of darkness in the stainless steel and white porcelain room. Keeping low, moving fast, he went to the double swinging doors that led out into the dining area and cautiously peeked through the oval window set into the door. He saw what he had been afraid he would see.

The waiters, cooks, and customers were huddled together in one corner of the room under the watchful eyes of a man armed with an automatic pistol. Two others held Minh spread-eagled against a wall while a third worked him over. Minh's face was bruised and bloody, his eyes were swollen shut. The man who was beating him methodically with a leather sap was also questioning him.

Brennan slipped down below the window, his teeth clenched, rage swelling the veins in his neck and reddening his face.

Kien had recognized Minh and ordered him hunted down. Minh was one of the few people in America who could identify Kien, who knew that he had methodically and ruthlessly used his position as an ARVN general to betray his country, his men, and his American allies. Brennan, of course, also knew Kien for what he was. He also knew that whatever place Kien had made for himself in America, those in authority would respect, listen to, and probably even fear him. Brennan, on the other hand, since he had walked away from the Army in disgust during the debacle of the Fall of Saigon, was an outlaw. No one in authority knew that he was back in the States, and he wanted to keep it that way.

He reached into his back pocket, withdrew a hood, and slipped it on, covering his features from his upper lip to the top of his head.

He took a moment to breathe deep, to drown his emotions in a void of nothingness, to forget his rage, his fear, his friend, his need for revenge, to forget even himself. He became nothing so that he would be all. He was not angry, not calm. He rose silently to his feet and stepped through the door, sank down on one knee behind a table and drew his first shaft.

The quiet, assured words of Ishida, his roshi, filled his mind like the somnolent tolling of a great bell.

'*Be simultaneously the aimer and the aimed, the hitter and hit. Be a full vessel waiting to be emptied. Loose your burden when the moment is right, without thinking or direction, and in that manner know the Way.*'

He stared without seeing, forgetting whether his targets were men or bales of hay, loosed his first shaft, dropped his hand to the quiver at his belt, took out his next arrow, nocked, lifted the bow, and drew the string while the first shaft was still on its way.

The first arrow hit while he was shifting his aim to take in the third target. They realized they were being attacked by the time the second arrow had struck and the fourth was released. By then it was too late.

He had chosen the order of his targets before becoming

submerged in the void. The first was the man guarding the hostages with the drawn gun. The shaft struck him in the back, high on the left side. It skewered his heart, sliced through one lung, and burst out half a foot from his chest. The impact hurled him forward, astonished, into the arms of a waiter. They both stared at the bloody aluminum shaft protruding from his chest. The gunman opened his mouth to swear or pray, but blood gushed forth, drowning his words. He slumped forward, his legs gone rubbery, and the waiter dropped him.

The two who held Minh released him. He slumped to the floor as they reached for the weapons at their belts. One had his hand pinned to his stomach before he could draw; the other was nailed to the wall. He dropped his pistol and clutched at the shaft pinning him like an insect staked to a drying-board. The last, the one who had been questioning Minh, whirled around and was struck in the side. The arrow angled upward, slipped between his ribs, pierced his heart, and punched upward through his right shoulder.

Nine seconds had elapsed. The sudden silence was broken only by the pained weeping of the man nailed to the wall.

Brennan crossed the room in a dozen strides. The hostages were still too stunned to move. Two of the thugs were dead. Brennan took no pleasure in their deaths, as he took no pleasure in killing deer to provide meat for his table. It was just something that had to be done. Neither did he waste his pity on them.

The one who was gutshot was curled up on the floor, unconscious and in shock. The other, pinned to the wall by the shaft that had pierced his chest, was still alert. Fear twisted his face and when he looked into Brennan's eyes his sobbing grew to a wail.

Brennan stared at him without remorse. He drew a shaft from his quiver. The man started to babble. Brennan slashed out. The broadhead cut the man's throat as easily as if it were a razor. Brennan dispassionately stepped aside from the sudden spurt of blood, slipped the arrow back into the quiver, and knelt down by Minh.

He was badly hurt. All his limbs were broken – it must have been agonizing to have been held up the way he was – and internal damage must have been massive. His breathing was shallow and shuddering. His eyes were swollen shut. They probably wouldn't have focused even if he could have opened them.

'*Ông là ai?*' he breathed at Brennan's gentle, probing touch. Who are you?

'Brennan.'

Minh smiled a ghastly smile. Blood bubbled on his lips and gleamed on his teeth.

'I knew you would come, Captain.'

'Don't speak. We have to get help—'

Minh shook his head. The effort cost him. He coughed and grimaced in pain.

'No. I am dying. I must tell you. It is Kien. This proves it. They wanted to know if I told anyone, but I would say nothing. They don't know of you.'

'They will,' Brennan promised.

Minh coughed again.

'I had hoped to help. Like the old days. Like the old days.' His mind wandered for a moment and Brennan looked up.

'Call an ambulance,' he ordered. 'And the police. Tell them there's three more on the street in front. Move.'

One of the waiters leaped to follow his orders while the others watched in mute incomprehension.

'Help you,' Minh repeated, 'help you.' He fell silent for a moment and then seemed to make a supreme effort to speak rationally and clearly. 'You must listen. Scar has kidnapped Mai. I was following him, trying to get a lead to where he had taken Mai, when I saw him and Kien together in the back of a limousine. Go to Chrysalis, Crystal Palace. She might know where he's taken her. I couldn't … find … out.' His last sentence was interrupted by bloody fits of coughing.

'Why did they take her?' Brennan asked gently.

'For her hands. Her bloody hands.'

Brennan wiped the beads of sweat from Minh's forehead.

'Rest easy now,' he said.

But Minh didn't listen. He rose up, clutching Brennan's arm.

'Find Mai. Help. Her.'

He settled back, sighed. Blood bubbled on his lips.

'*Tôi met*,' he said. I am tired.

Brennan clenched his jaw against the ache and answered softly in Vietnamese.

'Rest, then.'

Minh nodded and died.

Brennan let him down gently and sat back on his heels, blinking rapidly. Not another one, he said to himself. Not another death. It was another thing Kien had to answer for.

He stood, looked around, and saw nothing but fear on the faces of the people he had rescued. There was no sense in waiting. The police would only ask awkward questions. Like his name. There were plenty of people who would like to know that Daniel Brennan was still alive and back in the United States, Kien only one among them.

He had to leave before the police arrived. He had to follow the slim lead that Minh had left him. Chrysalis. Crystal Palace.

But he stopped, turned to the freed hostages.

'I need a pen,' he said.

One of the waiters had a felt-tip marker that he wordlessly handed to Brennan. He paused for a moment. He wanted Kien to wake up at night in a cold sweat, thinking, wondering. It wouldn't get to him right away, but, with enough messages, enough dead agents, it eventually would.

He scrawled a message next to the man nailed to the wall by his arrow. It said: '*I'm coming for you, Kien.*' He stopped before signing it. His name wouldn't do. It would take the fear of the unknown from his attacks and give Kien, his agents, and his government contacts too concrete a clue to follow. He smiled as sudden inspiration struck him.

The code name of his last mission in Vietnam, when Kien had betrayed him and his unit into the hands of the North Vietnamese, had been Operation Yeoman. That name would make Kien think. He might suspect that it was Brennan who stood behind the name, but he wouldn't know for sure. It would gnaw at him in the night and salt his dreams with memories of deeds he'd thought long buried. It was also an appropriate name in a grimly ironic way. It suited him well.

He signed the short message *Yeoman* and then, in a burst of final inspiration, drew a small ace of spades, the Vietnamese symbol of death and ill-fortune, and colored it in. The Vietnamese waiters and kitchen help muttered to themselves at the sight of the mark, and the waiter from whom Brennan had borrowed the pen refused to take it back with quick, birdlike shakes of his head.

'Suit yourself,' Brennan said. 'How do I get to the Crystal Palace?'

One of them stammered directions and Brennan went back out through the kitchen, into the dark alley. He disassembled his bow, slipped it back into its case, and was gone before the police arrived. Still wearing his mask, he kept to the alleys and dark streets, passing other phantom figures in the darkness. Some watched him, some were absorbed in their own doings. None tried to stop him.

The Crystal Palace, on Henry, was part of a block-long three-story rowhouse. About half the row had been destroyed in the Great Jokertown Riot of 1976 and had never been rebuilt. Some of the debris had been cleared away, some remained in great piles sitting next to tottering walls. As Brennan passed he saw eyes, whether human or animal he couldn't tell, gleaming out from cracks and crevices within the piles of wreckage. He wasn't tempted to investigate. He went farther down the street to where the rowhouse was still intact, up the short stone staircase under a canopied entrance, through a small antechamber, and found himself in the main taproom of the Crystal Palace.

It was dark, crowded, and smoky. There was an occasional obvious joker, like the short, blubbery, tusked fellow peddling newspapers by the door and the bicephalic singer on the small stage managing some nice harmony on a Cole Porter tune. Some were normal enough until one looked close. Brennan noticed one man, normal, handsome even, except that he lacked a nose and mouth and had instead a long, curled proboscis that he extended like a straw into his drink as Brennan watched. Some wore costumes that called attention to their strangeness, as if to proclaim their infection in a defiant manner. Some wore masks to hide their deformities, although some who wore masks were naturals, or nats, in joker slang.

'You a salesman?'

It took Brennan a moment to realize that the question was directed at him. He looked over to the end of the long wooden bar where a man sat on a high stool, swinging his short, stubby legs well clear of the floor. He was a dwarf, about four feet tall and four feet wide. His neck was as tall as a can of tuna fish and as thick as a man's thigh. He looked as solid and expressionless as a slab of marble.

'Those your samples?' he asked, gesturing at Brennan's case with a hand that was twice the size of Brennan's.

'Just the tools of my trade.'

'Sascha.'

One of the bartenders, a tall, thin man with a pencil mustache and an oily curl of hair falling limply over his forehead, turned toward the dwarf. Brennan had noticed him out of the corner of his eye, mixing and dispensing drinks with incredible speed and surety. When he turned at the dwarf's call Brennan saw that he had no eyes, only a blank, unbroken expanse of skin covering his sockets. The bartender looked in his direction and nodded rapidly.

'He's okay, Elmo, he's okay.' The dwarf nodded and took his eyes off Brennan for the first time since he had spoken. Brennan frowned, was about to speak, but the bartender beat him to it. He pointed down to the other end of the bar and said, 'She's over there.'

Brennan pursed his lips. The eyeless man smiled briefly and turned away to mix another drink. Brennan looked in the direction the bartender had indicated and caught his breath.

A woman sat at a corner table with a slim, light-skinned black man who was wearing a red kimono splashed with yellow dragons and embroidered with what Brennan took to be mystical formulae. He was handsome, but for the bulging forehead that marred his profile. The chair he sat in was ordinary. The woman's chair was throne-sized, with a black walnut frame and red velvet cushions.

She set down the thimble-sized crystal glass from which she was sipping a honey-colored liqueur, looked directly at Brennan, and smiled.

She wore pants that clung to her lithe figure and a sheathlike wrap that gathered over her right shoulder, leaving half her chest naked. Her skin was completely invisible, exposing vague, shadowy muscles and the organs that labored underneath them. Brennan could see blood pulsing in the network of veins and arteries that ran through her flesh, could see her ghostly, semi-transparent muscles shift and glide at her slightest movement, could even see, faintly, the beating of her heart within the cage of her ribs and the fluttering of her lungs as they labored evenly and unceasingly.

She smiled at him. Brennan knew that he stared, but he couldn't help himself. She looked too bizarre to be beautiful, but she was fascinating. Her exposed breast was totally invisible, save for its fine network of interlacing blood vessels and its large, dark nipple. Her face – well, who could tell? Her eyes were blue; her cheek-bones, under the sheath of jaw muscle, high; her nose a cavity in her skull. Her lips, like the nipple of her breast, were visible. They were full and inviting and curved in a sardonic smile. She had no hair to hide her white skull. He threaded his way through the crowd toward her table and she watched him with what seemed to be, if he could read her bizarre expression, detached amusement. He watched the mechanism of her throat work as she sipped her drink.

'Forgive me,' he began, and ran down to silence.

She laughed. It was good-humored, with no bitterness, reproach, or anger. 'Forgiveness granted, masked man,' she said. 'I'm a sight to behold. No one seeing me for the first time can act casual about it. I'm Chrysalis, owner and proprietress of the Crystal Palace, as I guess you know. This is Fortunato.'

The black looked at Brennan and he could see the man's eastern blood in the shape of his eyes. They nodded at each other word-lessly. There was, Brennan realized, an aura of power about this man. He was an ace, of that Brennan was suddenly sure.

'What's your name?' Chrysalis asked him.

She spoke in a cultured British accent, which would have surprised Brennan if he hadn't already exceeded his surprise quotient for the evening. Her voice had grown thoughtful, her expression seemed calculating.

'Yeoman,' Brennan said, wondering how open he could afford to be.

'Interesting. It's not your real name, of course.'

Brennan looked at her silently.

'Would you like to know it?' her companion asked. Fortunato smiled lazily and she shrugged and smiled back noncommittally.

Fortunato looked at Brennan. His eyes grew deeper, darker. Brennan sensed a swirling vortex of power growing in them, power he suddenly realized was directed toward him. He flashed with anger, his fists clenching, and he knew that he couldn't keep the spore-given ability of Fortunato from penetrating into the core of his brain. There was only one thing he could do.

He took a deep breath, held it, and let all thought drain from his mind. He was back in Japan again, facing Ishida, trying to answer the riddle the roshi has posed him when he had first sought entry to the monastery.

'A sound is heard when both hands are clapped. What is the sound of one hand clapping?'

Wordlessly Brennan had thrust forth one hand, clasped into a fist. Ishida had nodded, and Brennan's training began in earnest. He called upon that training now. He entered deeply into zazen, the state of meditation where he emptied himself of all thought, feeling, emotion, and expression. A timeless time passed and, as if from a long distance away, he heard Fortunato mutter, 'Extraordinary,' and he brought himself back.

Fortunato looked at him with a modicum of respect in his eyes. Chrysalis watched them both carefully.

'You're into Zen?' Fortunato asked.

'A humble student,' Brennan murmured, his voice sounding even to him as if coming from a distant mountain peak.

'Maybe I'd better speak to Yeoman alone,' Chrysalis said.

'If you want.' Fortunato stood.

'A moment.' Brennan shook himself like a dog shedding water and returned entirely to the room. He looked at Fortunato. 'Don't do that again.'

Fortunato pursed his lips, nodded. 'I'm sure we'll meet again.'

He left the table, threading his way through the crowded room.

Brennan took his chair as Chrysalis gazed at him with what seemed to be a calculating expression.

'Strange that I haven't heard of you before,' she said.

'I've just come to town.'

Her gaze had become penetrating, captivating. It was with some effort that Brennan pulled his gaze away from her eyes floating naked in their hollow sockets.

'On business?' she asked. Brennan nodded and she sipped her drink, sighed, put her glass down. 'I can see that you're not in the mood for small talk. What do you want of me?'

'Your bartender,' he began. 'How does he get along so well without eyes?'

'That's an easy one,' Chrysalis said with a smile. 'I'll give it to you for free. Sascha's a telepath, among other things. Don't worry. Whatever secrets you're hiding behind your mask are safe. He's a skimmer. He can only read surface thoughts. Makes his job easier, makes the Crystal Palace safer. He tells Elmo who the dangerous, the sick, the twisted, are. And Elmo gets rid of them.'

Brennan nodded, feeling a little safer. He was glad to learn that the bartender's ability was limited. He didn't like the thought of anyone poking about in his brain.

'What else?' Chrysalis asked.

'I need to know about two men. A man named Scar and his boss, Kien.'

Chrysalis looked at him and frowned. At least, the muscles of her face bunched up. Like her bodily musculature, they looked wispy, insubstantial, as if that which made her flesh and skin totally invisible affected them to the point of translucency.

'You know that they're connected? That's something maybe only three people outside their own circle know. Are they friends of yours?' Sudden anger blazed across Brennan's face and she flinched. 'No. I guess not.'

Her words brought to life memories of treachery and violence. Sascha turned his blind gaze to their corner. Elmo stood on tiptoes, craning his thick neck. Around the room half a dozen people fell silent. One man clutched his temples and fainted dead away. He whimpered like a whipped dog as the others at his table tried to bring him out of his trance. Chrysalis broke her gaze from Brennan's, waved Elmo off, and the tension began, slowly, to dissipate.

'They're dangerous, both of them,' she said calmly. 'Kien's Vietnamese, an ex-general. He showed up about, oh, eight years ago. He quickly insinuated himself into the drug trade and now owns a large share of it. In fact, he has his fingers in most other illegal activities in the city, while maintaining a facade of solid respectability. Owns a string of dry-cleaning establishments and restaurants. Donates to the proper charities and political parties. Gets invited to all the big social events. Scar's one of his lieutenants. He doesn't report directly to Kien. The general keeps himself well insulated.'

'Tell me more about Scar.'

'Local boy. I don't know his real name. He's called Scar because of the strange tattoos he's had smeared all over his face. They're supposed to be Maori tribal markings.'

Brennan must have looked incredulous because Chrysalis shrugged. He watched muscles shift and bones rotate in their sockets. The nipple of her exposed breast bobbed up and down on its pad of invisible flesh.

'He supposedly got the idea from an anthropologist from NYU who was studying his street gang. Something about urban tribalism. Anyway, he's one mean dude. He's Kien's chief muscle. Unbeatable in a fight.' She gazed at him shrewdly. 'You're going up against him.'

It was a statement, not a question.

'What makes him unbeatable?'

'He's an instantaneous teleport. He can vanish quicker than

anyone can move and reappear anywhere he wants to. Usually behind his opponent. He's also mean as hell. He could be big stuff, but he likes to kill too much. He's content with being one of Kien's lieutenants. Not that he does badly for himself.' She toyed with her glass for a moment, then looked directly at Brennan. 'Are you an ace?'

Brennan said nothing. Their eyes locked for a long moment and then Chrysalis sighed.

'You have nothing. You're just a man. A nat. What makes you think you can take Scar?' she repeated.

'As you said, I'm a man. He's kidnapped the daughter of a friend of mine. I'm the only one left to go after her.'

'The police?' Chrysalis began reflexively, then laughed at her own suggestion. 'No. Scar, through Kien, has enough police protection. I take it you have no solid evidence that Scar has the girl? No. What about one of the other aces? Black Shadow, Fortunato perhaps …'

'There's no time. I don't know what he's doing to her. Besides' – he stopped for a moment and looked back ten years – 'this is personal.'

'So I suspected.'

Brennan drew his gaze back into the room. He stared hard at Chrysalis.

'Where can I find Scar?'

'I'm in the business of selling information and I've already given you plenty for free. That tidbit will cost you.'

'I have no money.'

'I don't need money from you. I do you a favor, you do me one.'

Brennan scowled. 'I don't like being in anyone's debt.'

'Then find your information elsewhere.'

The need to be doing something was burning in Brennan. 'Very well.'

She took a sip of her liqueur and regarded the crystal goblet, held in a hand whose flesh was as clear as the goblet itself.

'He has a big place on Castleton Avenue, Staten Island. It's isolated and fenced in and sits on extensive grounds. He likes to hunt. Men.'

'He does?' Brennan asked, his gaze thoughtful, considering.

'Why did Scar kidnap this girl? Is she special in any way?'

'I don't know,' Brennan said, shaking his head. 'I thought it was to keep her father quiet because he had seen Scar and Kien together, but the sequence of events is all wrong. Minh saw them together when he was following Scar, trying to pick up clues about the kidnapping. He told me that they took her for her "bloody hands." That mean anything to you?'

Chrysalis shook her head.

'Can't you get him to be less cryptic?'

'He's dead.'

She reached out, put one of her hands on his and something passed between them. 'You probably won't heed my warnings, but I'll give them anyway. Be careful.' Brennan nodded. Her hand, invisible on his, was warm and soft. He watched blood pulse rhythmically through it. 'Possibly,' she continued, 'you'd like to discharge some of your debt?'

'How?' Brennan asked, meeting the subtle challenge of her tone and expression.

'If you survive your encounter with Scar, come back to the Palace, tonight. Don't worry about the time. I'll be waiting for you.'

There was no mistaking her meaning. She offered entanglements that he had avoided for a long time, relationships that he had wanted no part of for years.

'Or do you find me repulsive?' she asked matter-of-factly in the lengthy silence that stretched between them.

'No,' he said more curtly than he had intended. 'It's not that, not that at all.'

His voice sounded harsh in his own ears. He had isolated himself so long from human contact that the thought of entering into any kind of intimate relationship was frightening.

'Your secrets will be safe from me, Yeoman,' Chrysalis said.

He took a deep breath, nodded.

'Good.' Her smile returned. 'I'll expect you.'

He turned without a word, and her smile slipped from her face. 'If,' she said so softly that only she heard the words, 'you can do the impossible. If you can beat Scar.'

III.

There were, Brennan thought, two ways to go about this. He could be surreptitious. He could sneak into Scar's mansion, not knowing what security system he might have, and flit from room to room, not knowing what was in each room, not even knowing if Mai was in the building. Or he could just walk in, putting his trust in luck, nerve, and his ability to think on his feet.

He unmasked after he left the Crystal Palace and found a cab. The cabbie was reluctant to take him out to Staten Island, but he flashed a couple of twenties and the hack became all smiles. It was a long ride, by cab and ferry, and Brennan spent it in unhappy reminiscence. Ishida would have disapproved, but then, Brennan knew, he had never been the best of the roshi's students.

He had the cabbie drop him off a block or so from the Castleton address that Chrysalis had given him, paid the fare, and gave the hack a tip that wiped out most of his cash reserves. As the cab pulled away he moved quietly in the shadows until he stood across the street from Scar's place. It was as Chrysalis had described.

The house itself was a hulking stone mansion set a couple hundred yards off the street. A few lights shone through scattered windows on each of the three floors, but there was no illumination on the outside. The wall that encircled the grounds was stone, about seven feet high, surmounted by strands of electrical wire. The small glass-sided guardbox that stood by the wrought-iron gate held a single sentinel. It didn't look as if the security would be very difficult to breach, but the mansion was definitely too big to search room by room.

It would have to be boldness, nerve, and luck. A lot of luck, Brennan thought as he walked briskly from the shadows.

The man in the guardbooth was watching a small television set, a talk show hosted by a beautiful woman with wings. Brennan, who hadn't watched television since his return to the States, never-theless recognized her as Peregrine, one of the most visible aces, the hostess of *Peregrine's Perch*. She was watching an immense bearded man in a chef's hat doing something culinary. They chat-ted amiably as his large hands moved with surprising grace and Brennan realized that he was Hiram Worchester, alias Fatman, another of the more-public aces.

The guard was engrossed in Peregrine, who wore an undeniably attractive costume that was slit down nearly to her navel. Brennan had to rap on the glass door of the booth to get his attention, though he had made no effort to conceal his approach.

The guard opened the door.

'Where did you come from?'

'A cab.' Brennan gestured vaguely over his shoulder. 'I sent it away.'

'Oh, oh sure,' the guard said. 'I heard it. What do you want?'

Brennan was about to say that Kien sent him about the girl, but he bit the words back at the last instant. Chrysalis had told him that only very few people knew that Kien and Scar were connected. This flunky certainly wasn't one of them.

'The boss sent me. About the girl,' he said, keeping as vague as possible while making his voice assured and knowing.

'The boss?'

'Call Scar. He knows.'

The guard turned, picked up a phone. He hung up after a few seconds of muffled conversation and touched a panel in front of him. The wrought-iron gate swung open silently.

'Go on in,' he said, turning back to the television, where Hiram and Peregrine were eating sugar-coated chocolate crepes with delighted looks on their faces. Brennan hesitated briefly.

'One more thing,' he said.

The guard sighed, turned slowly, more than half-watching the television set.

Brennan rammed his palm, hard, in an upward motion against the guard's nose. He felt bone buckle and shatter at the force of his blow. The man convulsed once as splinters of bone knifed through his brain, and then went utterly slack. Brennan snapped off the television as Fatman and Peregrine were finishing the crepes, and dragged the body into the yard and dumped it behind some concealing shrubbery. Regretfully, he left his bowcase stashed there as well, but, so as not to go totally unarmed, extracted a spare bowstring and looped it loosely around his hips, under the waistband of his jeans.

He walked briskly up the drive to the mansion.

Scar needed a gardener. The yard had turned feral. The grass hadn't been cut all summer; the shrubberies had gone crazy. Untended, they had spilled over their original boundaries and provided a fairly dense undergrowth beneath the thick, untrimmed trees. It was more of an acre or two of forest than a front yard and for a moment it made Brennan long for the quiet peacefulness of the Catskills. Then he was at the front door and he remembered what had brought him here. He rang the bell.

The man who answered the front door had the insolence of a city punk and the gun that he carried under his armpit in a shoulder rig looked big enough to bring down an elephant.

'Come on in. Scar's got a client. They're with the girl.'

Brennan frowned at the man's back as he led him into the mansion. What was going on? Prostitution? Weird sex? He wanted to question the man who was leading him to the rear of the mansion, but knew that it was best to keep his mouth shut. He'd find answers soon enough.

Scar kept a little better care of the interior of his mansion than he did of the yard, but not much. The marble parquet floor was filthy, and there were stale odors clogging the air that made Brennan sick. He was afraid to breathe too deeply, lest he find himself able to identify some of the odors. A stairway swept upward into the upper stories of the mansion, but they stayed on the first floor, heading toward the rear of the building.

His guide turned to the left, passed through a metal detector which beeped once, and looked back at Brennan. Brennan followed him. The detector was silent. The thug nodded and led Brennan into a well-lit room that had four other people in it. One was a tough, identical for all practical purposes to the one who had met Brennan at the door. Another was a woman with long blond hair. She wore a mask that covered her entire face.

Another was Mai. She looked up at him dully as he entered the room and quick stifled the look of recognition that came to her face when she saw him. It had been three years since he had seen her. She had grown into a beautiful young woman, small, delicate, fine-featured, with thick, glossy hair and dark, dark eyes. She looked unharmed, if terribly tired. There were circles under her eyes and Brennan could read the weariness in her every muscle by the way she held herself.

The last was Scar. He was tall and lean, dressed in tee shirt and black chinos. His face was a nightmare. The patterns tattooed on it in black and scarlet turned it into the leering, bestial face of a demon. His eyes were sunk in black pits, his teeth inset in a scarlet cave. Brennan was surprised to see, when Scar smiled at him, that his teeth weren't filed.

'What's your name, man?' he asked in the thick argot of the inner city. 'I ain't never seen you before.'

'Archer,' Brennan lied automatically. 'What's going on here?'

Scar flashed his smile again. It twisted his face into odd contortions that showed nothing of humor.

'You just in time, man. The sister here is going to demonstrate her power, aren't you?'

Everyone looked at Mai, who bowed her head in silent, wearied resignation.

'She *can* do it?' the masked woman asked, her voice oddly eager and sibilant.

Scar only nodded and gestured at Mai. The two thugs watched with disinterest. Scar kept shifting his gaze back and forth to Brennan, Mai, and the woman.

'Tell the man,' he said, watching Brennan closely as Mai approached the woman, 'that I was going to tell him all about her. I was just checking things out.'

Brennan nodded impatiently, aloof and hard-eyed outside, indecisive inside. Mai walked to the woman without glancing in his direction. Whatever was going to happen, he thought, couldn't be too bad. She seemed to be taking things calmly enough. He decided to wait.

'You have to take the mask off,' Mai told the woman quietly. She drew back a little and glanced at the men watching her, but obeyed. Brennan watched impassively as she unmasked, Scar watched with a slight, sly smile. She was obviously ashamed of her face. Brennan had seen worse, but it was enough to evoke leering whispers from Scar's men. She had no chin and only a slight lower jaw. Her nose consisted of flat nostrils set above her lipless mouth. Her forehead was tiny. Her whole face was thrust forward in a reptilian manner that was enhanced by the colorfully beaded texture of her skin. She looked all the world like a Gila monster with long blond hair.

'I used to be beautiful,' she said, looking down.

Scar's men snickered aloud, but Mai took her rough-skinned cheeks between her palms and said quietly, 'You will be again.'

The woman looked up at her, a world of pain in her eyes. Mai gazed calmly at her, her face blank with the serenity of a madonna. For a moment nothing happened. Brennan glanced from her to Scar, who was watching him carefully, then back again. Then, where her palms touched the leathery skin of the woman's cheeks, blood began to run in little trickles. It seemed to be welling from the woman's cheeks, Mai's palms, or both. Tiny rivulets ran from between Mai's fingers, down the backs of her hands to her wrists. Mai moaned and Brennan stared at her as her face changed. Her chin receded, her jaw shrank. Her forehead narrowed and her skin became thick and pebbly and banded in orange and black and scarlet. It took some minutes. Brennan watched with pursed lips. Scar watched him watch. He smiled malevolently, his tattooed face a demonic mask.

Two lizard-women faced each other, one blond, one dark-haired. The woman looked at Mai wide-eyed, Mai looked back reassuringly. She sighed, longly, like a lover after release, and she began to change. Her skin lost its roughness, its bright color. The bone beneath it shifted back to normal configurations. Her lips twitched slightly, perhaps at the pain of the metamorphosis, but she said nothing. It took a moment longer, but the blond woman, too, began to change. Skin softened, bleached itself. Bone flowed like soft wax. Tears ran down her high, fine cheeks, whether from pain or joy, Brennan couldn't tell. The transformation took some minutes. When the tiny rivulets of blood ceased to flow, Mai took her hands from the woman's face. The woman was right. She had been beautiful, and was again. Weeping silently, she took Mai's hand and pressed a kiss into her palm. Mai smiled at her and swayed tiredly. Brennan could see that willpower alone kept her on her feet. Every line and muscle of her body cried out in weariness.

The woman reached down to a purse on a small table near where she stood and took out a thick envelope. Scar gestured. One of his smirking thugs took it, put it in his back pants pocket, and escorted the woman from the room.

'Well, man, what you think?'

'Fantastic,' Brennan said, still looking at Mai. 'What is it, genetic manipulation of some sort?'

'I don't know about that shit,' Scar said. 'I just heard that she was healing jokers in the neighborhood, and I figured why should she fix up those poor jokers when she can fix up jokers who'll pay plenty. So I snatched her.'

Brennan turned away from Mai and met Scar's eyes.

'She's worth a lot. You should have told Kien about her. I'll have to take her to him.'

Scar puckered his tattooed lips in mock consternation.

'You will? You seem to know a lot, man. How come you don't know that I told the man about her when that gook saw us together in the back of the man's limo?' He turned, looked at Mai, and added maliciously, 'And then the man had the old gook hit so he wouldn't tell no one about it.'

'My father?' Mai asked.

Scar nodded, grinning like a devil. Mai gasped, swayed, and would have fallen if Scar's man hadn't grabbed her roughly by the arm. Brennan moved.

He launched himself across the room, ripped the gun from the man's shoulder rig, jammed the barrel against his chest, and pulled the trigger. There was an immense roar as the blast lifted the man off his feet and threw him against the wall. He left a red smear as he slumped to the floor, his eyes open and unbelieving.

Brennan whirled, but Scar was gone. He saw a flicker at the edge of his vision and felt sharp pain as Scar chopped down on his wrist, knocking the gun from his grasp. Scar ducked Brennan's sweeping arm, kicked the gun across the room, and vanished silently and utterly.

He reappeared between Brennan and the gun, smiling crazily.

'You need a gun to go up against Scar? You some kind of crazy nat,' he said. 'What name you want on your tombstone?' He reached into the pocket of his chinos and with a practiced flick of his wrist opened a six-inch-long straight razor.

He vanished again and Brennan felt a sudden biting pain in his side. He heard Mai's cry, threw himself away, rolled, and stood. Blood ran down his side where Scar had slashed a long, shallow cut across his ribs. He barely had time to stand before Scar appeared again, slashed his cheek open, and popped away. It was as Chrysalis had said. He was fast and precise in his teleporting. And he did enjoy his work.

'I cut you slowly, man,' he said, appearing with killing lust in his eyes, 'I cut you till you beg me to finish you.' He twitched his wrist, flicking Brennan's blood off the edge of his blade. It was bright in the room, bright and closed in. Brennan was trapped, confined, and he knew he didn't have a chance in hell. Scar would cut him to ribbons, laughing, as he tried to reach the gun. He breathed deeply, calming his racing mind, drawing, as Ishida had taught him, into a state of serene tranquility, and he knew what he had to do. Scar slashed his back as he turned, ran, and hurled himself through the French windows in the rear of the room. He burst out of the light onto a dark patio.

Scar smiled a genuinely happy smile and stepped out onto the patio after him. He whistled tunelessly and watched Brennan run into the yard and blunder into a thick patch of trees.

'Hey, nat!' he called out. 'Where are you, man? I tell you what. You give me a good hunt, I'll cut you a few times then finish you fast. You disappoint me, I'll cut your balls off. Even the gook chick won't be able to grow you a new pair.'

Scar laughed at his joke, then followed Brennan into the dark. He stopped after a moment and listened. He heard nothing but the sounds of the wind in the trees and, distantly, occasional cars moving in the far streets. His prey was gone, vanished into the night. Scar frowned. Something was wrong. He walked deeper into the trees.

And from nowhere, a ghost silent among shadows, Brennan rose from his hiding place, his waxed nylon bowstring wrapped around his fists. He looped the string around Scar's throat from behind, yanked, and twisted. Flesh and gristle crumpled and Scar vanished. He reappeared a few feet away, clutching at his crushed windpipe. He tried to suck in air, but nothing reached his laboring lungs. He opened his mouth to say something at Brennan, to curse him or plead with him, but no words came. He vanished again, but reappeared a microsecond later in the same place, his tattooed face screwed up in pain and fear, his concentration shattered, his control gone. Brennan watched him flicker crazily among the trees, desperation on his face, teleporting madly, nonsensically. Finally he appeared, spewing blood from his mouth, staggered against a tree, dropped his razor, and fell face up. Brennan approached cautiously, but he was dead. He hunkered over him, and took out the felt-tip pen that the waiter had given him in Minh's restaurant. He drew an ace of spades on the back of Scar's right hand, and, to be sure that Kien wouldn't miss it, placed the hand over Scar's marked face.

He made his way back through the trees silently, like the ghost of a forest animal. Mai was waiting for him on the patio. She didn't seem surprised when it was he who emerged from the trees. She knew him, and what he could do.

'Captain Brennan, is Father really dead?'

He nodded, unable to say the words. She seemed to shrink, to look frailer, more tired, if that were possible. She closed her eyes and tears welled silently from beneath their lids.

'Let's go home.'

He led her into the welcome darkness of the night.

IV.

He left after she bandaged his wounds, promising to drop by when he could, sadness for her welling inside him, merging with the grief he himself felt at Minh's death. Another comrade, another friend, gone.

Kien had to be brought down. It was up to him, one man, alone, with nothing but the strength of his hands and the cunning of his mind. It would take a long time. He needed a base to operate from, and equipment. Special bows, special arrows. He needed money.

He drew back into the shadows of the Jokertown night, waiting for a certain type of man to come by, a street merchant who exchanged packets of white powder for green bills crumpled in sweaty desperation.

He breathed deeply. The night stank with the countless scents of seven million people and their myriad hopes, fears, and desperations. He was one of them now. He had left the mountains and returned to humanity and he knew that this return would bring with it disappointment and grief and lost hopes. And comfort, some part of him said, wondering at the warm touch of invisible flesh and the sight of a visible heart beating faster and faster with growing passion.

A sudden noise, a softly scraping step, caught his attention. A man passed him. He was dressed richly for a poor neighborhood, and he walked with jaunty arrogance. This was the one for whom he waited.

Brennan slipped quietly among the shadows, following him. The hunter had come to the city.

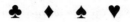

EPILOGUE:
THIRD GENERATION

By Lewis Shiner

Jetboy dove out of the sky in his rocket-sleek plane, speed lines roaring off the swept-back wings. Twenty-millimeter cannons barked ragged calligraphy and the tyrannosaur staggered as the shells tore into him.

'Arnie? Arnie, turn out that light!'

'Yes, Mother,' Arnie said. He slid the fifty-four-page special *Jetboy on Dinosaur Island* back into its plastic bag. He switched off his reading light and carried the comic across the familiar darkness of his bedroom and put it away in the closet.

He had a complete run of *Jetboy Comics* in one of the waxed cardboard boxes they used to ship chickens to grocery stores. On the shelf above it were stacked scrapbooks full of clippings about the Great and Powerful Turtle and the Howler and Jumpin' Jack Flash. And next to them stood the dinosaur books, not just the kid stuff with the crude drawings, but textbooks on paleontology and botany and zoology.

Hidden in the back of another box of comics was the *Playboy* that had Peregrine in it. Lately, looking at those pictures had made Arnie feel strange, kind of nervous and excited and guilty all at the same time.

His parents knew about his obsessions, all but the *Playboy*, anyway. It was only the wild card business that bothered them. Arnie's grandfather had been on the street that day, had seen it with his own eyes when Jetboy exploded into history. A year later Arnie's

543

mother had been born with low-grade telekinesis, just enough to move a coin a few inches across a plastic tablecloth. Sometimes Arnie wished she'd just been normal. Better that than to get a power that wasn't good for anything.

He'd made his grandfather tell him about it over and over. 'He wanted to die,' the old man would say. 'He saw the future, and he wasn't in it. Just wasn't any place for him anymore.'

'Hush, Grandpa,' Arnie's mother would say. 'Don't talk that way in front of Arnie.'

'I know what I saw,' the old man would say, and shake his head. 'I was there.'

Arnie crept quietly back to bed and lay on his stomach, pleasantly aware of the pressure on his groin. He thought about Dinosaur Island. There was no question in his mind that it was real. Aces were real. Aliens were real– they had brought the wild card to earth.

He turned on his side and pulled his knees up toward his chest. What would it be like? When he was eight he'd driven through Utah with his parents and he'd made them stop at Vernal. They'd gone on the Prehistoric Nature Trail, and Arnie had run ahead to be by himself with the life-sized dinosaur models. Dinosaur Island would look like that, he thought, the rugged brush-covered hills in the background, the diplodocus big enough that he could walk under its belly, the struthiomimus like a huge, scaly ostrich, the pteranodon crouched like it had just glided in for a landing.

His eyes closed and he could see them moving now, not just the crummy dinosaurs you could see on TV but the special ones: the tiny, vicious deinonychus, the 'terrible claw.' Or the hideous, lumpy ankylosaur, a thirty-five-foot horned toad with a club on its tail that could dent steel plate.

And deep in his brain, inflamed by the rich, yeasty endocrine soup in which it floated, the wild card virus hovered over a cell, paused, then pumped out its alien message and died. And so, on and on it went, spiraling down through the years in a double helix of fear and ecstasy, mutilation and miraculous change ...

APPENDIX

THE SCIENCE OF
THE WILD CARD VIRUS:

Excerpts from the Literature

... Fearful beyond imagining, worse in many ways than what we saw in Belsen. Nine out of ten affected by this unknown pathogen die horribly. No treatment helps. The survivors aren't a lot more lucky. Nine out of ten of *them* are somehow transformed, by a process I can't even begin to understand, into *something else*– sometimes not even remotely human. I've seen men turn into effigies of galvanized rubber, children sprouting extra heads ... I can't go on. And what's worst is, they're still alive. Still alive, Mac.

Strangest of all, maybe, are the ten percent of survivors, the one in a hundred of those who actually contract the sickness. They don't show any outward signs of change, mostly. But they have— I have to call them powers. They can do things a normal human can't. I've seen a man soaring into the sky like a V-2, looping the loop and returning to land lightly on his feet. A berserk patient tearing a heavy steel gurney apart as if it were tissue paper. Not ten minutes ago a woman walked through the wall of the little office for this onetime warehouse where I've shut myself away for a few minutes' respite. A naked woman, gorgeous, a real pinup type, glowing with a rosy light that seemed to come from inside her body, smiling a fixed glassy smile.

I'm not cracking up, Mac. I haven't gone round the bend into madness or morphine. Not yet. Even if I'm lucky to get an hour or two of sleep a night– and then the horror fills my dreams, so I'm almost glad to crawl out of my cot and face the reality of what's happened here. These things are happening, they're real. You may read about it yourself someday, if the brass don't succeed in clamping the lid down. I don't see how they can– this is *Manhattan*, for Christ's sake, and the victims number tens of thousands.

Thank God it's not catching. Thank God for that. As far as we can see, it only develops in those directly exposed to the dust or whatever it was– and not in all of them, or we'd have a million more. As it is, quarantine is impossible, even adequate sanitation. We've had an outbreak of influenza in our wards, expecting typhus any hour ...

They say some kind of aliens are behind it all, men from outer space. Given what we've all seen, that doesn't sound far-fetched. I've heard it noised around at the highest levels that they've even caught one. I hope it's true. Then they can stick the bastard in the docket with the Nazi bosses at Nuremberg, and hang him like the animal he is ...

> —personal letter from Captain Kevin McCarthy,
> United States Army Medical Corps,
> September 21, 1946

Accounts of the incident make it clear that the vessel containing xenovirus Takis-A exploded at an altitude of 30,000 feet, well within the so-called jet stream. In its dormant state the virus is encased in a durable protein sheath, the 'spores' so often and incorrectly referred to in the lay press, which experiment has shown to be resistant to extremes of temperature and pressure such as to permit its survival under natural conditions from several hundred feet beneath the ocean to the upper limits of the stratosphere. Viral particles were borne eastward across the Atlantic on the jet stream, washing out at random intervals by droplets of rain, or settling naturally; the precise mechanisms still await demonstration or observation. This accounts for the mid-Atlantic *Queen Mary* tragedy (September 17, 1946), as well as the subsequent outbreaks in England and on the Continent. (Note: Rumors persist of a large-scale outbreak in the USSR, but Premier Khrushchev's regime continues to maintain a silence as absolute as its predecessors on the matter).

Wind and ocean currents provided short-term dispersal of the virus over a substantial area of the eastern United States (map 1). More alarming by far have been subsequent irruptions of the virus, in spite of the fact that it does not appear to be infectious, widely distributed across both time and geographic distance. In 1946 alone there were over a score of outbreaks reported, and almost a hundred isolated cases, extending clear across the United States and southern Canada (map 2).

The location of the majority of major international outbreaks provides a clue as to a possible pattern: Rio de Janeiro (1947), Mombasa (1948), Port Said (1948), Hong Kong (1949), Auckland (1950), to name a few of the most notorious – all major seaports. The problem was how to account for appearances of the virus, generally in isolated incidents, in locations as far from the sea as the Peruvian Andes and the remote uplands of Nepal.

As our investigation reveals, the answer clearly lies in the durability of the protein coat. The virus can be carried by any means, human, mechanical, animal, or natural, and survives indefinitely unless exposed to destructive agents such as fire or corrosive chemicals. The majority of North American outbreaks, and the relatively large occurrences in seaports have been per-suasively traced (McCarthy, *Report to the Surgeon General*, 1951) to items awaiting shipment in the docks and warehouses of the affected district of Manhattan. Others have been attributed to the precipitation of viral particles onto vessels and vehicles in transit. Individuals, even birds and animals (who are never affected), can carry the particles on their person without knowing it. The Nepalese outbreak, referred to above, for example, was traced to a *naik* of the Gurung clan, whose regiment, the King's Gurkha Rifles, was involved in attempting to contain the ghastly communal violence of August 10-13 in Calcutta, India, in which the Hindu and Muslim communities blamed one another for an outbreak of the virus, with a resulting loss of life estimated at twenty-five thousand; the Gurkha corporal himself never developed the disease.

... how many deposits of dormant virus remain, dusted across rooftops, gathered in sediment in rivers and sewers, lying in deposits in the soil, still borne aloft on the jet stream, cannot be determined. How serious a threat it still poses to the public health is still equally inascertainable. In this context the inability of the virus to affect the vast majority of the populace should be borne in mind ...

—Goldberg and Hoyne, 'The Wild Card Virus: Persistence and Dispersal,' *Problems in Modern Biochemistry*, Schinner, Pack, and Ozawa, eds.

The ability of the wild card virus to alter its host's genetic programming resembles that of terrestrial herpes viruses. It is, however, much more comprehensive, altering DNA throughout the host's body, rather than affecting and being expressed in a certain location– e.g., the lips or genitalia – as are the herpes family.

We know that xenovirus Takis-A affects a larger percentage of an exposed population than originally assumed – perhaps as much as one-half of one percent. In many cases the virus merely appends its own code to the host DNA; this is the dormant form, in which the virus has no objective existence, but exists only in the form of information – another trait it shares with the herpesform viruses. It may remain passive and undetected indefinitely, or some trauma or stress to the host may cause it to express itself, generally with shattering results. Amounting as it does to 'reprogramming' of the host's genetic code, the virus (in either active or passive form) is truly inheritable, like blue eyes or curly hair

Apparently anticipating its predominantly lethal effects, the Takisian scientists who created the virus designed it to perpetuate itself as, in effect, a recessive 'wild card gene.' Recessive, because a dominant gene that produced lethal mutations in ninety percent of offspring and rendered another nine percent either unable or unlikely to reproduce would survive only a few generations, even if, as is estimated, thirty percent of all those with xenovirus-modified DNA carry the dormant form.

The wild card therefore follows the conventional rules of inheritance for recessive traits. Only in cases where both parents carry the viral code does any possibility of producing an affected off-spring exist; even then the chance is only one in four, versus a fifty percent chance of producing a carrier with no chance of expressing the virus, and another one-in-four chance of an offspring who does not carry the code ...

—Marcus A. Meadow, *Genetics*, January 1974, pp. 231-244

Despite the Red-baiting paranoia of the late 1940s and early 1950s and the 'findings' of the House Committee on Un-American Activities, aces fared no better behind the Iron Curtain than in this country, and in fact considerably worse. The party line was laid down by Trofim D. Lysenko, semiliterate maven of Stalinist science, that the supposedly alien 'wild card' was merely a mask for diabolical bourgeois capitalist-imperialist experimentation. In Korea, captured Americans were made to sign confessions of germ warfare in an apparent attempt to account for the outbreak of the virus that swept that nation, North and South, in 1951. Meanwhile, anyone showing signs of metahuman talents within the Soviet sphere simply disappeared, some to forced-labor camps, others to labs– and no few to shallow graves.

With Stalin's death in 1953 came a minor relaxation. Khrushchev acknowledged the existence of aces, and they began to 'enjoy' the status they had in the United States – i.e., they had the privilege of serving in the military or GPU (later KGB), or vanishing into the Gulag Archipelago. As the 1960s passed, strictures against them relaxed, if not to the extent that they did in the United States, and state-sponsored superheroes were permitted to become media personalities, like cosmonauts and Olympic stars.

Why the initial rejection of blatant reality? The Brezhnev/Kosygin regime admitted in 1971 that Lysenko was a joker, in whom the virus was expressed as hideous disfigurement; the existence of aces was a personal affront to the former farmer. As to why Stalin went along with the anti-ace campaign, the rampant paranoia of the dictator's later years in particular is generally considered sufficient explanation. However, several highly placed defectors of the late 1960s and early 1970s repeated the rumor that Comrade

Nikita sometimes, late at night in his cups with boon companions, boasted that he himself had slain the former dictator with his own hand in the cellar of the Lubyanka Prison – *driving a stake through his heart* ...

—J. Neil Wilson, 'Back in the USSR,' *Reason*, March 1977

Xenovirus Takis-A, colloquially called wild card, was an experimental organic device developed by the Ilkazam, a leading family among the Psi Lords of Takis. Written into its DNA is a program that reads the genetic code of the host organism and modifies that code in order to enhance the host's innate propensities and characteristics. Such an optimization gratifies as never before the great Takisian drive to cultivate personal (and by extension familial) *virtú*. Takisians already possess potent mental powers; by means of wild card the Ilkazam sought to bring forth a multiplicity of wild talents in its members, ensuring its preeminence for many years to come.

The challenge the Ilkazam researchers faced was to produce a program that would identify and enhance *desirable* characteristics; no one wants to be a better hemophiliac. Biochemical individuality among Takisians, however, is even more marked than in humans, who are one of the most biochemically diverse species on Terra. To develop software capable of discerning favorable characteristics – an 'intelligent' program – and enhancing them, and which could be implemented in the viral DNA, required experimentation on an extravagant scale. Given the nature of Takisian society there were always plenty of subjects available for even the most drastic experimentations, Takisians as a whole not having many hang-ups about insisting the subjects volunteer. However, even Takis lacked a sufficiently large supply of criminals and vanquished political enemies – not a distinction commonly drawn in that culture – to provide the sort of experimental base needed to fully develop such a complex tool. Fortunately, from the Takisian point of view, a pool of creatures of astonishingly similar genetic makeup presented itself ... Earth.

... Most wild card enhancements aren't favorable to survival, or are survival traits taken to lethal lengths, such as keying the adrenaline fight-or-flight system so high that the slightest stress forces the victim into overdrive, burning him out in a single burst of terminal speed-trip frenzy. Nine out of ten survivors had undesirable characteristics enhanced, or desirable ones enhanced in undesirable ways. The 'joker' takes forms ranging from the hideous through the painful to the pathetic or merely inconvenient. A victim might be reduced to a formless blob of mucus like the familiar Jokertown resident Snotman, or might be transformed into a partial animal likeness like tavern-keeper Ernie the Lizard. He might acquire a power that in other circumstances would make him an ace, such as the limited but uncontrollable levitation of the Floater. The manifestation may be quite minor, like the mass of tentacles that form the right hand of Dorian Wilde, Jokertown's decadent poet laureate.

In certain cases the distinction between classifications is blurred, as in the aforementioned Ernie, whose slightly-greater-than-human strength and the protection offered by his scaly hide are insufficient to make him a true ace. Another, more horrific example is the tragic Burning Woman incident of the late 1970s, in which the virus affected a young woman by causing her body to burn with an inextinguishable flame, but to regenerate itself even as her flesh was consumed. The victim begged passersby to kill her, and finally died in Jokertown's Blythe van Renssaeler Memorial Clinic, apparently as a result of euthanasia– a resulting indictment against Dr. Tachyon was quashed. Whether her card qualified as joker or black queen cannot be determined.

Because it is designed to interact with its host's individual code, no two expressions of wild card are alike. Moreover, its behavior differs from subject to subject …

… That as many as ten percent of those who contracted the virus survived its effects is a tribute to the skill of Takisian genetic software and hardware artistes. For a first large-scale test, among a subject population different from that for which it was originally designed, the relase of the virus on Terra was a tremendous success which would greatly have pleased its creators, had they learned of its outcome.

Earth, on the other hand, had a different point of view.

—Sara Morgenstern, 'Blues for Jokertown: Forty Years of Wild Cards,' *Rolling Stone*, September 16, 1986

EXCERPTS FROM THE MINUTES OF THE AMERICAN METABIOLOGICAL SOCIETY CONFERENCE ON METAHUMAN ABILITIES

(Clarion Hotel, Albuquerque, New Mexico, March 14-17, 1987)

Talk presented March 16, 1987, by Dr. Sharon Pao K'ang'sh'i of the Harvard University Department of Metabiophysics.

Gentlepersons of the Society, I thank you. I shall come directly to the point. Research by our team at Harvard indicates that metahuman abilities, the colloquially called 'superpowers' engendered by the Takisian wild card virus, are exclusively of psychic origin, and in all but rare cases are exercised through the instrumentality of *psi.*

(Session called to order by Chairperson Ozawa.)

I understand that my preceding statement might be considered a rhetorical excess of the kind perpetrated by certain of my predecessors, which caused the still-fledgling field of metabiophysics to be considered a pseudoscience of the caliber of numerology and astrology by a number of serious scientists. Yet honesty, and the press of empirical evidence, compel me to reiterate: metahuman abilities are specialized forms of psychic power.

We now have a better idea of just what wild card did to its victims. In so-called ace cases, the virus appears to have acted first by enhancing innate psychic ability, which gave direction to the overall progress of the gene-code rewrite. This explains the high degrees of correspondence between the personalities and proclivities of known aces and their metahuman abilities – why, for example, devoted pilots such as Black Eagle acquired powers including that of flight, why the obsessed 'avenger of the night' Black Shadow has such control over darkness, why the reclusive Aquarius presents a half-human, half-delfin appearance and can in fact transform himself into a sort of super-*Tursiops*. A microscale telekinesis appears to be one of the mechanisms by which wild card effects its changes, enabling the subject subconsciously to choose, or at least influence, the nature of the transformation she or he undergoes.

I understand the enormity of the implication that people might, in some sense, have 'chosen' to draw a joker or black queen. Speculation in that direction is, however, beyond the scope of our present researches.

One of the great puzzles of the post-wild-card epoch has been precisely how the alien virus, however advanced the technology that produced it, was able to give certain individuals the ability to violate well-established natural laws, such as conservation of mass and energy, the square-cube law, the inviolability of the speed of light itself. At the time the virus was unleashed, science was inalterably hostile to the existence even of psychic powers – justifiably, given the lack of compelling experimental corroboration for such phenomena. It has now been compelled to accept people being able to project fire and lightning, to transform themselves into animals, to fly, or to contrive mechanical appliances that enabled them to do these and similar things in flagrant disregard for principles of mechanics and engineering.

Of course, even by 1946 clues were available in the theoretical reaches of quantum physics. In fact, then-modern technology, up to and including nuclear weapons and the fusion devices in the process of development, was largely based upon quantum mechanics, much of the work being done on the basis of 'we know it works, but we don't know *how*.' Given the impetus of the reality of wild card, psi powers were quickly given a quantum mechanical rationale; 'action over distance' without apparent recourse to the strong, electroweak, or gravitic forces being a feature, for example, of the curious interconnectedness of particles that have interacted, postulated by Einstein, Podolsky, and Rosen in their famous 'paradox,' and established with some finality by the Aspect experiment in France in 1982 ...

... A fairly obvious instance of TK-based power is shape changing. The subject – in almost all cases subconsciously – rearranges her or his component atoms to produce a gross structure that differs considerably from the original: for example, Elephant Girl's rather unsettling transformation into a flying *Elephas maximus* in apparent violation of the mass-energy conservation principle. At least in the case of Elephant Girl, this is explained by subconscious TK on the subatmomic level; Ms. O'Reilly can apparently summon into being a cloud of virtual particles and maintain them in existence immensely longer than they would normally exist. (A discussion of virtual particles is, of course, likewise beyond the scope of this presentation. I refer the interested to articles concerning, for example, the particles that 'carry' the strong interaction, and that for an infinitestimal instant violate the conservation principle.) As part of restoring herself to her original appearance, Ms. O'Reilly permits the virtual particles that made up the 'phantom' mass to lapse into nonexistence.

It was Elephant Girl's ability to fly in defiance of all known aeronautical principles that sparked the line of inquiry leading to the conclusions expressed in this paper. Simply put, Elephant Girl's, Peregrine's, and *all* known aces' flight or levitation is simply a variation on TK. In this sense, the Great and Powerful Turtle is the archetypal flying ace, in that he acknowledgedly flies by means of his telekinetic ability. But no trick of physics would permit Elephant Girl's ears or even Peregrine's magnificent wings to uphold even a small human in flight, to say nothing of a full-grown Asiatic elephant. They, like the Turtle, fly through use of mind power alone ...

... Energy projections provide another thorny problem simply explained by – again – TK. Jumpin' Jack Flash appears to project blasts of flame from the palms of his hands, and moreover can manipulate the fire he produces in remarkable ways. But this individual does not actually project the flame, in the sense that it is not emitted from his own body; in point of fact, it isn't strictly speaking flame. His TK enables him to regulate the Brownian motion of the circumambient air. He creates a 'hot spot' of highly excited particles approximately one micron from the flesh of his palm, and then uses TK to direct the resultant stream of incandescent gas.

... Superluminal-flight powers present a special case. In most cases (and it's beneficial to keep in mind that each wild card transformation is unique) the individual with the capacity for light-speed or faster-than-light travel has the ability to emulate a single photon, or tachyon in the latter instance, becoming a 'macrophoton' or 'macrotachyon' in a manner similar to the 'macroatom' devices University of Sussex researchers under Terry Clark, which can emulate the behavior of a single boson. The spaceships that conveyed the wild card virus to this planet, as well as the humanoid alien known as Dr. Tachyon, employed the same principle for their superluminal drive – which led to the coining of the word by which the only earth resident not born on this planet is known to this day.

Faster-than-light travel has proven of only limited utility to aces to date, owing to limits of duration and the problems of navigation over long distances, so far insuperable to our technology. Or so we infer from the fact that no ace has ever journeyed beyond the limits of the solar system (present orbit of Neptune) and returned ...

...A salient feature of the so-called 'gadgets'– antigravity belts, dimensional portals, armored suits– is the fact that none of them can be replicated. On disassembly and examination they're often found to make no mechanical or electrical sense. Each is a nonreproducible result. This explains why some enterprising gadget-master hasn't marketed, say, a personal light-speed flying belt, or an antigravity forklift. *Only the creator could make one that would work.* In some cases, the components consist of ludicrous assemblages of debris, up to and including apple cores, hairpins, and the torsos of Barbie dolls. Others consist only of a *diagram* of a circuit, which, like the chimerical Hieronymus machine, work as an actual circuit 'should.'

The explanation is, once again, a manifestation of psychic

ability. The creator has, in effect, impressed himself upon his work in a metaphysical (in the current scientific meaning) sense. This explanation makes sense of the frequently observed phenomenon that there seems to be a limit to certain 'gadget-masters' creativity, that they will sometimes have to disassemble an old device to get a new one to work. This explanation also makes it simple to predict that attempts by governments all over the world to replicate the astounding Modular Man android are doomed to failure, unless one or more contract the services of 'wild talents' of their own ...

... A feature of almost all aces is a higher-energy metabolism than 'normal' humans possess. Some seem able to summon up the energy to fuel their abilities from within themselves, or (for want of a better way of putting it) from the Cosmos. Others either need external sources of energy to power their talents, or find themselves aided by the availability of such sources. The black strongman known as the Harlem Hammer, for example, finds it necessary to consume a substantial amount of heavy-metal salts in his diet to maintain the high-level reactions of his metabolism, as well as a number of 'bone-seekers' such as strontium-90 and barium-140, which seem to be replacing the calcium in his bones, giving them greater-than-normal durability and strength. Jumpin' Jack Flash draws strength and sustenance from exposure to fire and heat. Others derive their extrahuman energy from 'batteries,' which generally prove to be of the same genus as the Hieronymus-type devices. Whatever the source of this energy, no ace has yet been discovered who could not exhaust her or his supply, in a reasonably short time, by intensive exertion of metahuman abilities. Some can 'recharge' simply by resting for a time, others actually require an external power supply. Again, each case is unique ...

Further confirmation of the 'psychic' hypothesis comes from the case of the so-called Sleeper, who possesses a different set of meta-abilities every time he awakens from sleep. Any other model for the function of ace powers would have difficulty accounting for this phenomenon ...

My colleagues and I are willing, in sum, to go so far as to say that psi can account for all observed ace-abilities – and that no other explanation can …

THE FIRST WILD CARDS DAY
or,
THE GAME THAT ATE MY LIFE

by George R.R. Martin

In the books, Wild Cards Day is celebrated every September 15, in memory of September 15, 1946, the day that Jetboy spoke his immortal last words while Dr. Tod loosed an alien virus over Manhattan.

In real life, September 15, 1946 happens to be the day that Howard Waldrop was born … and Howard, coincidentally, wrote 'Thirty Minutes Over Broadway,' the opening story of the first *Wild Cards* book, wherein all these events take place.

In the books, September 20 is a day of no special note. In real life, however, it marks the day of *my* birth, two years and five days after Howard. September 20 is the true Wild Cards Day. It was on that day in 1983 that Vic Milán gave me a role-playing game called *Superworld* as a birthday present, thereby unknowingly planting the first seed of the Wild Cards universe.

As I unwrapped that gift, I was still a relative innocent where role-playing games were concerned. Mind you, I had played plenty of games over the years. I had paid my bills directing chess tournaments in the early '80s, while trying to establish myself as an SF writer. Before that I had been captain of my college chess team, and of my high school chess team before *that*. Role-playing had not yet been invented when I was a kid, but we had checkers and Sorry and Parcheesi for rainy days, and Hide and Seek and Ringoleavio and Oh O'Clock for warm summer evenings. Although my parents never owned a house, that did not stop me from building vast real

561

estate empires across a Monopoly board. There was Broadside and Stratego as well, and all through childhood I never lost a game of Risk (I always commanded the red armies, and refused to play if denied 'my' color). After a while none of my friends dared to face me, so I'd set up the board in the bedroom and fight wars against myself, playing all six armies, inventing kings and generals to command them, merrily invading, attacking, and betraying myself for hours. And maybe that was role-playing of sorts, now that I come to think of it.

But it was not until I arrived in New Mexico in 1980 that I began to game regularly. Some of the Albuquerque writers had a small gaming group, and they invited me to come sit in on a session. I was pretty dubious at the time. I had seen kids playing D&D at cons, pretending to be Thongor the Barbarian and Pipsqueak the Hobbit while killing monsters and looking for treasure. I had read too much bad sword and sorcery in my youth for that to have much appeal. And there were all these weirdly shaped dice you had to roll to determine whether you lived or died. I would sooner have joined a weekly poker game or an on-going game of Diplomacy. I was much too old and sophisticated for this role-playing stuff, after all. Still, if this was what the local writers were into, I figured I might as well give it a try.

Famous last words, those.

This Albuquerque gaming group included Walter Jon Williams, Victor Milán, John J. Miller, his wife Gail Gerstner Miller, and Melinda M. Snodgrass, all of whom would eventually become important contributors to the Wild Cards anthologies. Royce Wideman and Jim Moore were also part of the group, and my own sweet lady Parris joined in with me. At the time we got involved, the gang was mostly playing a *Call of Cthulhu* campaign run by Walter, and less frequently Vic's *Morrow Project* scenario, so those were the first two games I sampled.

They were great fun ... and nothing like I had imagined roleplaying to be. I had fallen in with writers, and these games were *stories*. Playing Walter's game was like stepping into the pages of an H.P. Lovecraft story, except that the characters were more fully realized than Lovecraft's ever were. There was triumph and tragedy, heroism and cowardice, love affairs and betrayals, and every now and again a shuggoth, too. Our weekly sessions were part communal storytelling and part Improv Theater, part group therapy and part mass psychosis, part adventure and part soap opera. We created some wonderful characters and lived inside them, and many a night never rolled those funny twenty-sided dice at all.

After a few months, I began to make noises about wanting to try and run a game myself. As much fun as the players were having, it seemed to me that the GM was having even more. He was the creator, the conductor leading the orchestra, the team captain and the opposing team rolled up in one omnipotent package. 'God,' the group called our GMs. Who doesn't want to play god? I finally succumbed to the temptations and designed my own *Cthulhu* adventure for the gang. Once I had tasted the joys of godhood there was no turning back ... even though this particular lot of players were so damned sharp that they unraveled the central mystery of my game about sixteen minutes into the action.

That was more or less where things stood when my birthday rolled around, and Vic gave me that fatal copy of *Superworld*. The gang had tried another superhero game before my time and hadn't liked it much ... but this was a new system, and Vic knew that I was a comic book fan from way back. I had cut my teeth on funny books while growing up in Bayonne, New Jersey. Superman and Batman had more to do with me learning to read than Dick and Jane ever did, and the first stories I ever published were amateur superhero 'text stories' in the dittoed comic fanzines. *Superworld* seemed made for me, and me for *Superworld*.

What happened next was almost scary. I came up with a campaign and my friends came up with characters, and we began to play, and before any of us knew what was happening *Superworld* had swallowed us all. At first we were playing once a week, alternating *Superworld* with sessions of Walter's game or Vic's. But soon we stopped playing *Morrow Project* entirely, and then *Call of Cthulhu* as well. It was all *Superworld*. We would assemble at suppertime, play until two or sometimes three in the morning, then post-mortem the game we had just played for another hour or so. Many a time dawn caught me while I was driving home from Albuquerque to Santa Fe. Within half a year we were playing twice a week, with one campaign running in Albuquerque and a second in Santa Fe, and the same players participating in both. Once, at an especially dull SF con, we adjourned to my room and played *Superworld* all weekend, leaving the game to do our panels and readings and then rushing back.

A number of characters who would later grace the *Wild Cards* books made their first appearances in those games, albeit in early 'rough draft' versions significantly different from their later selves. Melinda's first character was Topper, but a Topper who had only her costume in common with the bit player who would appear in *Ace in the Hole*. Walter's firstborn was Black Shadow, with powers and personality both rather different from his later Wild Cards incarnation. In the game, Shad was the brother of Vic's character, who would become the Harlem Hammer of the anthologies. Chip Wideman played a succession of surly antiheroes and the sweet-natured Toad Man before devising Crypt Kicker, toxic shit-kicker from hell. John J. Miller had Nightmare, who never did make it into the books. And Jim Moore … well, I could tell you about Jim Moore's characters, but if I did the PC police would have to kill you. The first incarnation of Hiram Worchester was pure comic relief: a well-meaning oaf who fought crime from a blimp and called himself Fatman. And the primordial Turtle might have had Tom Tudbury's name, power, and shell, but he shared none of his history or personality.

Many of these early creations were retired when the players got a better feel for the campaign, and for the nuances of the *Superworld* rules. Topper hung up her top hat, Black Shadow faded back into the shadows, the Harlem Hammer went back to repairing motor-cycles. In place of Shad, Walter introduced Modular Man and his mad creator. Vic Milán unveiled Cap'n Trips and all of his friends, and John Miller brought in Yeoman to displace Nightmare. Some of the gang had gotten it right on the first try, though; Gail never played anyone but Peregrine, and Parris was Elephant Girl from the start; the book version of Radha O'Reilly was pretty much a clone of the earlier game version.

The game was deeply and seriously addictive for all of us ... but for me most of all. I was god, which meant I had lots of planning and preparation to do before the players even arrived. The game ate their nights and their weekends, but it ate my life. For more than a year, *Superworld* consumed me, and during that time I wrote almost nothing. Instead I spent my days coming up with ingenious new plot twists to frustrate and delight my players, and rolling up still more villains to bedevil them. Parris used to listen at my office door, hoping to hear the clicking of my keyboard from within, only to shudder at the ominous rattle of dice.

I told myself it was writer's block. My last book, an ambitious rock and roll fantasy called *The Armageddon Rag*, had failed dismally despite great reviews, and my career was in the dumps, enough to block anyone. Looking back now, though, it's plain to see that I wasn't blocked at all. I was creating characters and devising plots every day, like a man possessed. It was the opposite of being blocked. I was in a creative frenzy, of the sort I sometimes experienced on the home stretch of a novel, when the real world seems to fade away and nothing matters but the book you are living by day and dreaming of by night. That was *exactly* what was happening here, only there was no book ... yet. There was only the game.

I don't know just when my fever broke, or why. Maybe my steadily diminishing bank account and rapidly increasing debt had something to do with it. I loved the game, I loved all these wonderful characters that my friends and I had created, I loved the egoboost I got from my players after an especially exciting session ... but I loved having a house to live in, too, which meant I had to keep making those pesky mortgage payments. And godhood, intoxicating as it was, did not pay.

Thus it was that one day, while rolling up yet another batch of really nifty villains, I said the magic words:

'There's got to be some way to make some money from this.'

It turned out there was ... but for that story, you'll need to come back next month.

George R.R. Martin
May 15, 2001